THE

OR, THE

THOUSAND AND ONE NIGHTS.

ACCURATELY DESCRIBING THE

MANNERS, CUSTOMS, LAWS, AND RELIGION, OF THE EASTERN NATIONS.

LONDON:

PUBLISHED BY E. LLOYD, 12, SALISBURY-SQUARE, FLEET-ST
AND SOLD BY ALL BOOKSELLERS.

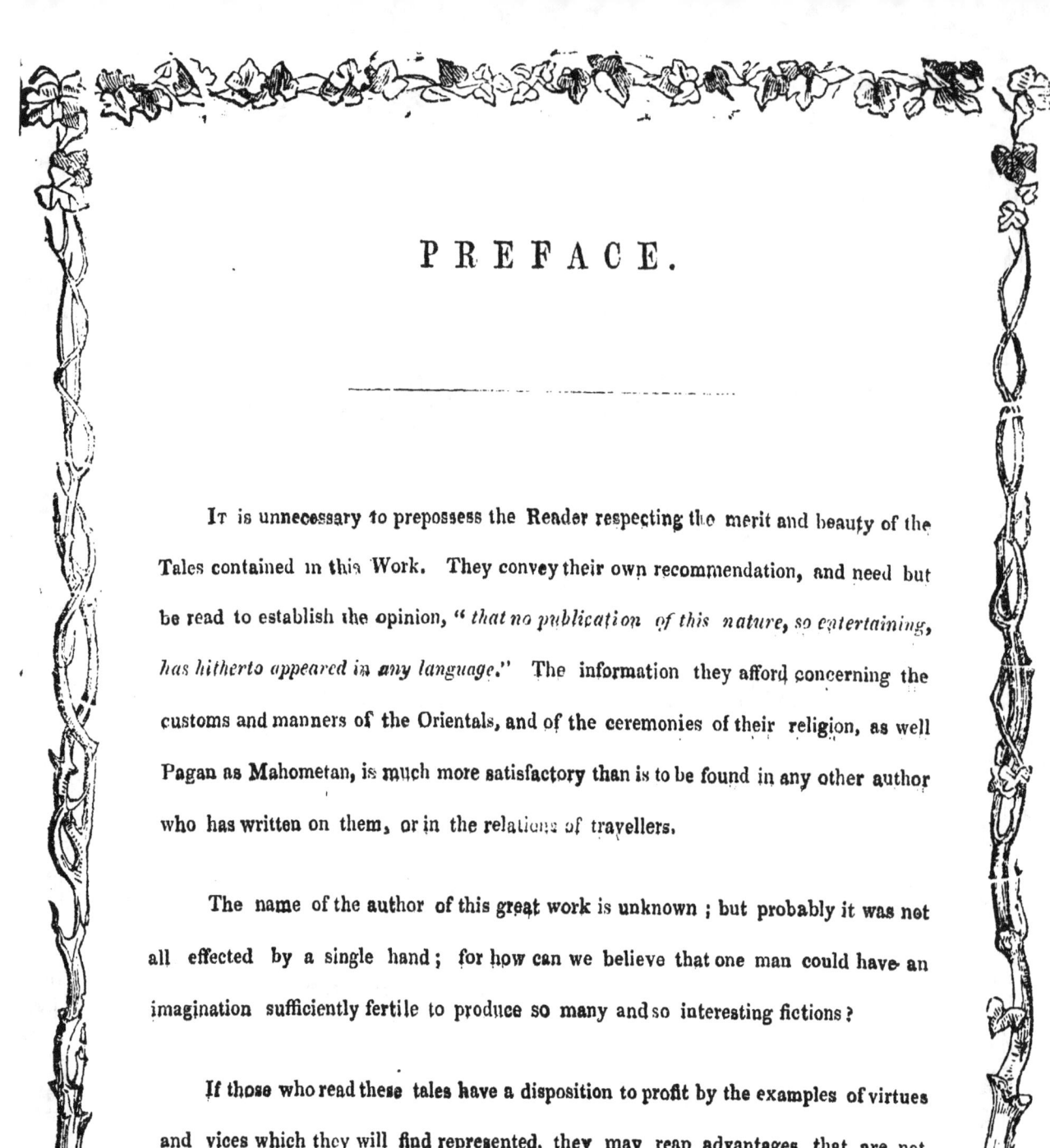

PREFACE.

It is unnecessary to prepossess the Reader respecting the merit and beauty of the Tales contained in this Work. They convey their own recommendation, and need but be read to establish the opinion, "*that no publication of this nature, so entertaining, has hitherto appeared in any language.*" The information they afford concerning the customs and manners of the Orientals, and of the ceremonies of their religion, as well Pagan as Mahometan, is much more satisfactory than is to be found in any other author who has written on them, or in the relations of travellers.

The name of the author of this great work is unknown; but probably it was not all effected by a single hand; for how can we believe that one man could have an imagination sufficiently fertile to produce so many and so interesting fictions?

If those who read these tales have a disposition to profit by the examples of virtues and vices which they will find represented, they may reap advantages that are not to be gained from other stories, which are more adapted to corrupt than to reform the manners of mankind.

London,
August, 1847.

The Arabian Nights' Entertainments.

THE chronicles of the Susanians, the ancient kings of Persia, who extended their empire into the Indies, over all the dependent islands, to a considerable distance beyond the Ganges, and as far as China, acquaint us, that there was formerly a king of that potent family, the most excellent prince of his time; he was equally beloved by his subjects for his wisdom and prudence, and dreaded by his neighbours on account of his valour and his warlike and well-disciplined troops. He had two sons, the eldest named Schahriar, the worthy heir of his father, and endowed with all his virtues; the youngest, Schahzenan, a prince of not less merit than his brother.

After a long and glorious reign, the king died; and Schahriar ascended the throne. Schahzenan, though excluded from all share of the government by the laws of the empire, and obliged to live a private life, was so far from envying the happiness of his brother, that he made it his study to please him, which he effected without much difficulty. Schahriar, who had naturally a great affection for that prince, was so charmed with his complaisance, that, from an excess of friendship, he determined to divide his dominions with him, and gave him the kingdom of Great Tartary. Schahzenan went immediately and took possession of it, and fixed the seat of his government at Samarcande, the metropolis of the country.

When they had been separated ten years, Schahriar, having a passionate desire to see his brother, resolved to send an embassador to invite him to his court. He made choice of his prime vizier for the embassy, sent him to Tartary with a retinue answerable to his dignity, and he made all possible haste to Samarcande. When he came near the city, Schahzenan had notice of it, and went to meet him with the principal lords of his court, who, to put the more honour on the sultan's minister, appeared in magnificent apparel. The king of Tartary received the embassador with the greatest demonstrations of joy; and immediately asked him concerning the welfare of the sultan, his brother.

The vizier, having acquainted him that he was in health, gave him an account of his embassy. Schahzenan was so much affected with it that he answered thus :—

"Sage vizier, the sultan, my brother, does me too much honour; he could propose nothing in the world so acceptable: I long as passionately to see him as he does to see me. Time has been no more able to diminish my friendship than his. My kingdom is in peace, and I desire no more than ten days to get myself ready to go with you; so that there is no necessity for your entering the city for so short a time. I pray you pitch your tents here, and I will order provisions in abundance for yourself and your company."

The vizier did accordingly; and as soon as the king returned, he sent him a prodigious quantity of provisions of all sorts, with presents of great value.

In the mean while, Schahzenan made ready for his journey, took order about his most important affairs, appointed a council to govern in his absence, and named a minister, of whose wisdom he had sufficient experience, and in whom he had an entire confidence, to be their president. At the end of ten days, his equipage being ready, he took his leave of the queen his wife, and went out of town in the evening with his retinue, pitched his royal pavilion near the vizier's tent, and discoursed with that embassador till midnight. But willing once more to embrace the queen, whom he loved entirely, he returned alone to his palace, and went straight to her majesty's apartment, who, not expecting his return, had taken one of the meanest officers of her household to her bed, where they lay both fast asleep, having been in bed a considerable while.

The king entered without any noise, and pleased himself to think how he should surprise his wife, who, he thought, loved him as entirely as he did her; but how great was his surprise, when, by the light of the flambeaux, which burn all night in the apartments of those eastern princes, he saw a man in her arms! He stood immoveable for a time, not knowing how to believe his own eyes; but, finding that it was not to be doubted,

"How!" says he to himself: "I am scarce out of my palace, and but just under the walls of Samarcande, and dare they put such an outrage upon me? Ah, perfidious wretches! your crime shall not go unpunished. As king, I am to punish wickedness committed in my dominions; and as an injured husband, I must sacrifice you to my just resentment."

In a word, this unfortunate prince, giving way to his rage, drew his scimitar, and, approaching the bed, killed them both with one blow, turning their sleep into death; and afterwards taking them up, threw them out of window into the ditch that surrounded the palace.

Having avenged himself thus, he went out of town privately, as he came into it; and, returning to his pavilion, without saying one word of what had happened, he ordered the tents to be struck, and to make ready for his journey. This was speedily done; and before day he began his march, with kettle-drums and other instruments of music, that filled every one with joy, except the king, who was so much troubled at the disloyalty of his wife, that he was seized with extreme melancholy, which preyed upon him during his whole journey.

When he drew near the capital of the Indies, the Sultan Schahriar and all his court came out to meet him. The princes were overjoyed to see one another, and alighted: after mutual embraces, and other marks of affection and respect, they mounted again, and entered the city, with the acclamations of vast multitudes of people. The sultan conducted his brother to the palace he had provided for him, which had a communication with his own by means of a garden; and was so much the more magnificent that it was set apart as a banqueting-house for public entertainment, and other diversions of the court, while the splendour of it had been lately augmented by new furniture.

Schahriar immediately left the king of Tartary, that he might give him time to bathe himself, and to change his apparel; and as soon as he had done he came to him again, and they sat down together upon a sofa or alcove. The courtier kept at a distance, out of respect, and those two princes entertained one another suitably to their friendship, their nearness of blood, and the long separation that had passed betwixt them. The time of supper being come, they ate together, after which they renewed their conversation, which continued till Schahriar, perceiving that it was very late, left his brother to his rest.

The unfortunate Schahzenan went to bed; and though the conversation of his brother had suspended his grief for some time, it returned upon him with more violence, so that, instead of taking his necessary rest, he tormented himself with cruel reflections. All the circumstances of his wife's disloyalty presented themselves afresh to his imagination in so lively a manner that he was like one beside himself. In a word, not being able to sleep, he got up, and, giving himself over to afflicting thoughts, they made such an impression upon his countenance that the sultan could not but take notice of it, and said thus to himself:—

"What can be the matter with the king of Tartary that he is so melancholy? Has he any cause to complain of his reception? No, surely; I have received him as a brother whom I love, so that I can charge myself with no omission in that respect. Perhaps it grieves him to be at such a distance from his dominions, or from the queen his wife. Alas! if that be the matter, I must forthwith give him the presents I designed for him, that he may return to Samarcande when he pleases."

Accordingly, next day, Schahriar sent him part of those presents, being the greatest rarities and the richest things that the Indies could afford. At the same time he endeavoured to divert his brother every day by new objects of pleasure, and the finest treats; which, instead of giving the king of Tartary any ease, did only increase his sorrow.

One day, Schahriar, having appointed a great hunting-match, about two days' journey from his capital, in a place that abounded with deer, Schahzenan prayed him to excuse him, for his health would not allow him to bear him company. The sultan, unwilling to put any constraint upon him, left him at his liberty, and went a-hunting with his nobles. The king of Tartary, being thus left alone, shut himself up in his apartment, and sat down at a window that looked into the garden. That delicious place, and the sweet harmony of an infinite number of birds which chose it for a place of retreat, must certainly have diverted him, had he been capable of taking pleasure in anything: but being perpetually tormented with the fatal remembrance of his queen's infamous conduct, his eyes were not so often fixed upon the garden as lifted up to heaven to bewail his misfortune.

While thus a prey to grief, an object was presented to his view which quickly engaged all his thoughts. A secret gate of the sultan's palace suddenly opening, there came out at it twenty women, in the midst of whom marched the sultaness, who was easily distinguishable from the rest by her majestic air. This princess, thinking that the king of Tartary was gone to the chace with his brother the sultan, came up with her retinue near the windows of his apartment; for the prince, curious to observe them, had placed himself so that he could see all that passed in the garden, without being perceived himself. He observed that the persons who accompanied the sultaness threw off their veils and long robes, that they might be at more freedom; but his astonishment was extreme when he saw ten of them were blacks, and that each of them took his mistress. The sultaness, on her part, was not long without her gallant. She clapped her hands, calling out "Masoud! Masoud!" and immediately a black came down from a tree, and hastily ran to her.

Modesty will not allow, nor is it necessary, to relate what passed between the blacks and the ladies. It is sufficient to say, that Schahzenan saw enough to convince him that his brother had as much cause to complain as himself. This amorous company continued together till midnight, when, having bathed all together in a large piece of water, which was one of the chief ornaments of the garden, they dressed themselves, and all re-entered the palace by the secret door, except Masoud, who climbed up his tree, and got over the garden-wall the same way as he came.

These proceedings, having passed in the king of Tartary's sight, gave him occasion to make a multitude of reflections.

"How little reason had I," said he, "to think that no one was so unfortunate as myself! It is certainly the unavoidable fate of all husbands, since the sultan my brother, who is sovereign of so many dominions, and the greatest prince of the earth, could not escape it. Such being the case, what a fool am I to kill myself with grief! I will throw it off; and the remembrance of a misfortune so common shall never after this disturb my quiet."

From that moment Schahzenan forbore to afflict himself. He had been unwilling to sup till he had witnessed the whole scene that was acting under his window: he now called for his supper, ate with a better appetite than at any time since his leaving Samarcande, and listened with pleasure to the agreeable concert of vocal and instrumental music that was appointed to entertain him while at table.

After this he continued in very good humour; and when he knew that the sultan was returning, he went to meet him, and paid him his compliments with an air of gaiety. Schahriar at first took no notice of this great alteration, but expostulated with him modestly, why he would not bear him company at hunting the stag; and, without giving him time to reply, entertained him with an account of the great number of deer and other game they had killed, and the pleasure he had received in the sport. Schahzenan heard him with attention, gave pertinent answers, and, being divested of that melancholy which formerly overclouded his wit, he said a thousand agreeable and pleasant things to the sultan.

Schahriar, who expected to have found him still a prey to grief, was overjoyed to see him so cheerful, and spoke to him thus:—

"Dear brother, I return thanks to Heaven for the happy change it has made on you during my absence; I am extremely rejoiced at it: but I have a request to make of you, and conjure you not to deny me."

"I can refuse you nothing," replied the king of Tartary; "you may command Schahzenan as you please: pray speak; I am impatient to know what it is you desire of me."

"Ever since you came to my court," replied Schahriar, "I have found you swallowed up by a deep melancholy, and I in vain attempted to remove it by every sort of diversion. I imagined it might be occasioned by reflecting on the distance you are from your dominions; or that love might have a great share in it; and that the queen of Samarcande, who, no doubt, is an accomplished beauty, might be the cause of it. I do not know if I am mistaken in my conjecture; but I must own that this was the particular reason why I did not importune you upon the subject, for fear of making you uneasy. But, without my having been able to contribute in any manner, I find now, on my return, that you are in the best humour possible, and that your mind is entirely delivered from that black vapour which disturbed it. Pray do me the favour to tell me why you were so melancholy, and how you came to be so no longer?"

At this discourse, the king of Tartary continued for some time in a reverie, contriving what he should answer; but at last he thus replied:—

"You are my sultan and master, but excuse me, I beseech you, from answering your question."

"No, dear brother," said the sultan, "you must answer: I will take no denial."

Schahzenan, being unable to withstand these pressing entreaties, replied,—

"Well, then, brother, I will satisfy you, since you command me;" and, having told him of the queen of Samarcande's treachery, "this," said he, "was the cause of my grief: pray judge whether I had not sufficient reason to give myself up to it."

"Oh, my brother!" said the sultan (in a tone which showed that he entertained the same sentiments of the offence as the king of Tartary), "what a horrible story do you tell me! How impatient was I till I heard it out! I commend you for punishing the traitors who put upon you so violent an outrage. Nobody can blame you for that action: it was just; and, for my part, had the case been mine, I could scarcely have been so moderate as you were. I should not have been satisfied with the life of one woman; I verily think I should have sacrificed a thousand to my fury. I cease now to wonder at your melancholy. The cause of it was too sensible, and too mortifying, not to make you yield. O Heaven! what a strange adventure! Nor do I believe the like ever befel any man but yourself. But, in short, I must praise God, who has comforted you: and since I doubt not that your consolation is well grounded, be so good as to let me know what it is, and conceal nothing from me."

Schahzenan was not so easily persuaded to be explicit on this point as he had been on the other, because of his brother's immediate concern in it. Being, however, obliged to yield to his pressing entreaties, he answered,—

"I must then obey you, since your command is absolute; yet am afraid that my obedience will occasion your trouble to be greater than even mine was. But you must blame yourself for it, since you force me to reveal a circumstance which I should otherwise have buried in eternal oblivion."

"What you say," answered Schahriar, "only increases my curiosity. Hasten to discover the secret, whatever it be."

The king of Tartary, no longer able to refuse, related to him the particulars of all that he had seen: of the blacks in disguise; of the lewd passion of the sultaness and her ladies; and, of course, he did not forget Masoud.

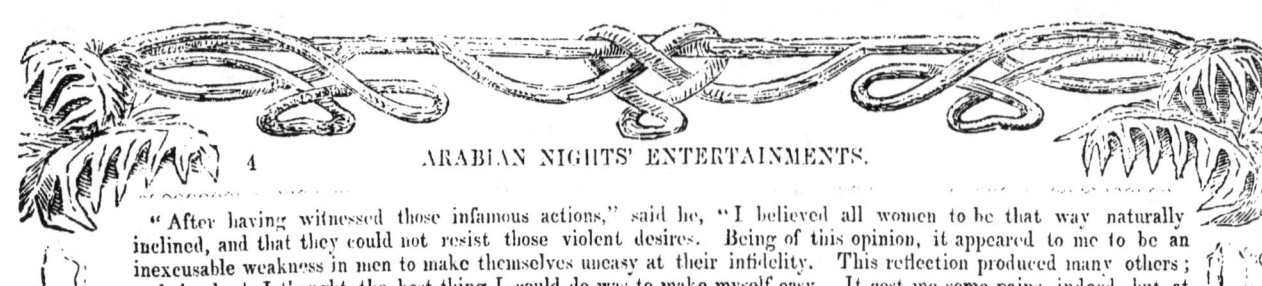

"After having witnessed those infamous actions," said he, "I believed all women to be that way naturally inclined, and that they could not resist those violent desires. Being of this opinion, it appeared to me to be an inexcusable weakness in men to make themselves uneasy at their infidelity. This reflection produced many others; and, in short, I thought the best thing I could do was to make myself easy. It cost me some pains, indeed, but at last I conquered; and if you take my advice, you will follow the same example."

Though the counsel was judicious, the sultan could not submit to it, but fell into a rage.

"What!" said he, "is the sultaness of the Indies capable of prostituting herself in so base a manner? No, brother, I cannot believe what you say, except I had seen it with my own eyes—yours must certainly have deceived you: the matter is so important, that I must have ocular proof to be satisfied."

"Dear brother," answered Schahzenan, "that you may, without much difficulty. Appoint another hunting-match, and when we are out of town, with your court and mine, we will stop under our pavilions; at night, let you and I return without attendants to my apartment, and I have no doubt that the next day you will see what I saw."

The sultan, approving the stratagem, immediately appointed a new hunting-match; and that same day the pavilions were erected at the place appointed.

On the morrow the two princes set out with all their retinue: they arrived at the place of encampment, and stayed there till night. Then Schahriar summoned his grand vizier, and, without acquainting him with his design, commanded him to stay in his place during his absence, and to suffer no person to go out of the camp upon any occasion whatever. Having given this order, the king of Tartary and he took horse, and passing through the camp *incog.* returned to the city, and went to the palace occupied by Schahzenan. Here they reposed till an early hour next morning, when they went to place themselves at the window from which the king of Tartary had witnessed the scene with the blacks. They enjoyed the fresh air for some time, as the sun had not yet risen; and, conversing together, often cast their eyes toward the secret door. It at length opened; and, in few words, the sultaness appeared, with her ladies and the ten disguised blacks, and, calling upon Masoud, the sultan saw more than enough to convince him of his dishonour and misfortune.

"O Heavens!" cried he, "what indignity! what horror! Can the wife of a sovereign, such as I am, be capable of so infamous an action? After this, let no prince boast of his being perfectly happy. Alas! my brother," continued he, embracing the king of Tartary, "let us renounce the world; honesty is banished from it; if it flatter us one day it betrays us the next. Let us abandon our dominions and grandeur: let us go into foreign countries, where we may lead an obscure life, and conceal our misfortune."

Though Schahzenan disapproved of such a resolution, he did not think proper to contradict Schahriar in the heat of his passion.

"Dear brother," said he, "your will shall be mine: I am ready to follow whither you please; but promise that you will return if you meet with any one who is more unhappy than ourselves."

"I agree to it," replied the sultan, "but I much doubt whether we shall."

"I am of a different opinion," continued the king of Tartary; "I fancy our journey will be but short."

Having said this, they went secretly out of the palace, going by another way than that by which they entered. They travelled as long as it was day, and lay the first night under the trees. Getting up about break of day, they went on till they reached a fine meadow upon the banks of the sea, in which meadow there were thickets of great trees at some distance from each other. Sitting down under those trees to rest and refresh themselves, the chief subject of their conversation was the lewdness of their wives.

They had not sat long before they heard a horrible noise from the sea, and a terrible cry, which filled them with fear; then the sea opening, there rose up a figure like a great black column, which reached almost to the clouds. This redoubled their alarm; and, rising immediately, they climbed into a tree to hide themselves. They had scarcely got up, when, looking to the place whence the noise came, and where the sea opened, they observed that the black column advanced, winding about towards the shore, cleaving the water before it. At first they could not think what it might be; but they soon found that it was one of those malignant genii that are mortal enemies to mankind, and always doing them mischief. He was black, hideous, had the appearance of a giant of prodigious stature, and carried on his head a large glass box, shut with four locks of fine steel. He entered the meadow with his burthen, and laid it down just at the foot of the tree in which the two princes were, who looked upon themselves as dead men. Meanwhile the geni sat down by his box, and, opening it with four keys that he had at his girdle, there came out a lady magnificently apparelled, of a majestic stature, and a perfect beauty. The monster made her sit down by him; and eyeing her with an amorous look,—

"Lady," said he, "the most accomplished of all ladies who are admired for their beauty, my charming mistress, whom I carried off on your wedding-day, and have loved so constantly ever since, let me sleep a few moments by you: I found myself so very sleepy that I came to this place to take a little rest."

Having thus spoken, he laid down his huge head on the lady's knees, and, stretching out his legs, which reached as far as the sea, he fell asleep, and made the banks echo with his snoring.

The lady, happening at the same time to look up, saw the two princes at the top of the tree, and made a sign to them with her hand to come down without noise. Their fear was excessive when they found themselves discovered; and they supplicated the lady, by other signs, to excuse them; but she, after having gently removed the head of the monster from her knees, and laid it softly on the earth, rose up, and desired them, in a low but quick voice, to come down to her immediately. They in vain signified to her by gestures that they were afraid of the geni.

"Descend!" said she, in the same tone; "if you do not hasten to obey me, I will awaken him, and myself demand your death."

The princes were so intimidated by this threat, that they began to come down with all possible precaution, lest they should disturb the geni. When they had descended the lady took them by the hand, and, going a little farther with them under the trees, made a very urgent proposal to them. At first they rejected it; but she obliged them to comply by fresh menaces. Having obtained what she desired, she perceived that each of them had a ring on his finger, which she demanded. As soon as she received them, she went and took a box from the packet that contained her toilet, and pulled out a string of other rings of all sorts, which she showed them, asking them if they knew what those jewels signified?

"No," said they; "but we hope you will be pleased to tell us."

"These are," replied she, "the rings of all the men to whom I have granted my favours. There are full fourscore and eighteen of them, which I keep as tokens of remembrance: and I asked yours, for the same reason, to make up my hundred. So that," continued she, "I have had a hundred gallants already, notwithstanding the vigilance of this wicked geni, who never leaves me. He gains no advantage by locking me up in this glass box, and hiding me in the bottom of the sea: I cheat him for all his cares. You may see by this, that, when a woman has formed a project, no husband or gallant can hinder her from carrying it into execution. Men had better not put their wives under restraint, if they wish to preserve them chaste."

The lady, having thus spoken to them, put their rings upon the same string with the rest, and sitting down by the monster, as before, laid his head again upon her lap, and made a sign for the princes to retire.

They returned immediately by the same road they came; and when they were out of sight of the lady and the geni, Schahriar said to Schahzenan,—

"Well, brother, what do you think of this adventure? Has not the geni a very faithful mistress? and do not you agree that there is no wickedness equal to the malice of women?"

"Yes, brother," answered the King of Tartary; "and you must also agree that the monster is more unfortunate, and has more reason to complain, than ourselves. Therefore, since we have found what we sought for, let us return to our dominions, and let not what has happened hinder us from again marrying. For my part, I know a method by which I think I shall keep inviolable the faith that any woman may plight to me. I will say no more of it at present, but you will hear of it in a little time, and I am sure you will follow my example."

The sultan agreed with his brother; and, continuing their journey, they arrived in the camp the third night after they had left it.

News of the sultan's return being spread, the courtiers presented themselves early in the morning before his pavilion. He gave orders for them to enter, received them with a more agreeable air than formerly, and made each of them some gratification. After which, declaring he would go no farther, he commanded them to take horse, and returned speedily to his palace.

He had no sooner arrived than he ran to the apartment of the sultaness, whom he ordered to be bound before him, and delivered her to his grand vizier, with an injunction to strangle her; which was accordingly executed by that minister without inquiring into her crime. The enraged prince did not stop here; he cut off the heads of all the sultaness's ladies with his own hand. After this rigorous punishment, being persuaded that no woman was chaste, he resolved, in order to prevent the dislovalty of such as he should afterwards marry, to wed one every night, and have her strangled next morning. Having imposed this cruel law upon himself, he swore that he would observe it immediately after the departure of the king of Tartary, who very soon took leave of him, and, being loaded with magnificent presents, set forward on his journey.

Schahzenan being gone, Schahriar ordered his grand vizier to bring him the daughter of one of his generals. The vizier obeyed: the sultan lay with her, and, delivering her the next morning into the hands of his minister to be put to death, he commanded him to get another for the next night. Whatever reluctance the vizier felt in executing such orders, as he owed a blind obedience to the sultan his master, he was forced to submit. He brought him then the daughter of a subaltern officer, whose head also he cut off the next day. After her he brought a citizen's daughter, and, in a word, there was every day a maid married and a wife murdered.

The rumour of this unparalleled inhumanity occasioned a general consternation in the city; nothing was heard but cries and lamentations. Here a father in tears, and inconsolable for the loss of his daughter; and there, tender mothers, dreading lest theirs should share the same fate, making the air resound beforehand with their groans: so that, instead of the commendations and blessings which the sultan had hitherto received, all his subjects united in imprecations against him.

The grand vizier, who, as has been already said, was unwillingly the executioner of this horrid injustice, had two daughters, the eldest named Scheherazade, and the youngest Dinarzade. The latter was a lady of great merit; but the elder had courage, wit, and penetration, infinitely above her sex: she had studied very many books, and had such an extraordinary memory, that she never forgot what she read. She had successfully applied herself to philosophy, physic, history, and the liberal arts; and in verse exceeded the best poets of her time: besides which, she was a perfect beauty; and all her fine qualifications were crowned by solid virtue.

The vizier passionately loved a daughter so worthy of his tender affection. One day, as they were discoursing together, she said to him,—

"Father, I have a favour to beg of you, and most humbly pray you to grant it me."

"I will not refuse it," answered he, "provided it be just and reasonable."

"In regard to the justice of it," said she, "there can be no question; and you may judge of it by the motive which obliges me to demand it of you. I have a design to arrest the course of that barbarity which the sultan exercises upon the families of this city. I would dispel those just fears which so many mothers entertain of losing their daughters in so fatal a manner."

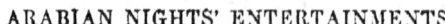

"Your design, daughter," replied the vizier, "is very commendable; but the disease you will remedy seems to me incurable: how do you pretend to effect what you propose?"

"Father," said Scheherazade, "since by your means the sultan celebrates every day a new marriage, I conjure you, by the tender affection you bear me, to procure me the honour of his bed."

The vizier could not hear this solicitation without horror.

"O Heavens!" replied he, in a passion, "have you lost your senses, daughter, that you make so dangerous a request to me? You know the sultan has sworn by his soul that he will never lie more than one night with the same woman, and to order her to be killed the next morning; and would you wish that I should propose you to him? Do you consider well to what your indiscreet zeal will expose you?"

"Yes, dear father," replied the virtuous daughter, "I know the peril I encounter, but it does not frighten me. If I perish, my death will be glorious; and, if I succeed in my enterprise, I shall render my country an important service."

"No, no," said the vizier; "whatever you can represent to induce me to let you throw yourself into that horrible danger, do not imagine that I will ever agree to it. When the sultan shall order me to strike my poniard into your heart, alas! I must obey him; and what a dreadful employment is that for a father! Ah! if you do not fear death, yet at least avoid occasioning me the mortal grief of seeing my hand stained with your blood."

"Once more, father," said Scheherazade, "grant me the favour I desire."

"Your stubbornness," replied the vizier, "will make me angry; why will you run headlong to your ruin? They who do not foresee the end of a dangerous enterprise can never bring it to a happy issue. I am afraid the same fate will befal you that happened to the ass, which was well, but he could not keep himself so."

"What misfortune befel the ass?" asked Scheherazade.

"I will tell you," replied the vizier, "if you will attend to me."

FABLE.

THE ASS, THE OX, AND THE LABOURER.

VERY rich merchant had several country-houses, where he had abundance of cattle of all kinds. He went, with his wife and family, to one of those estates, in order to improve it himself. He had the gift of understanding the language of beasts; but with this condition, that he should interpret it to nobody, on pain of death; and he was thus prevented communicating to others what he had learned by means of this gift.

He had in the same stall an ox and an ass. One day, as he sat near them, and diverted himself with seeing his children play about him, he heard the ox say to the ass,—

"Sprightly, oh, how happy I think you, when I consider the ease you enjoy, and the little labour that is required of you! You are carefully rubbed down and washed, you have well-dressed corn and fresh clean water. Your greatest business is to carry the merchant, our master, when he has any little journey to make; were it not for that, you would be perfectly idle. I am treated in quite a different manner, and my condition is as unfortunate as yours is pleasant. Midnight has scarcely passed when I am fastened to a plough, and made to work all the day in tilling the ground; which fatigues me so much, that sometimes my strength fails me. Besides, the labourer, who is always behind me, beats me continually. By drawing the plough, my tail is all flayed: in short, after having worked from morning till night, when I am brought in, I receive only sorry dry beans, not so much as cleansed from the sand, to eat, or other things equally bad: and, to heighten my misery, when I have filled my belly with such ordinary food, I am forced to lie all night in my own dirt; so that you see I have reason to envy your lot."

The ass did not interrupt the ox till he had ended what he had a mind to say; but, when he had ceased speaking, answered,—

"They who call you a foolish beast are right: you are too simple. You let them carry you whither they please without showing any resolution. In the meantime, what advantage do you gain by all the indignities you suffer? You kill yourself for the ease, pleasure, and profit of those who give you no thanks for so doing. But they would not treat you in this manner, if you had as much courage as strength. When they come to fasten you to the stall, why do you not make resistance? why do you not oppose them with your horns, and show that you are angry, by striking your foot against the ground? in short, why do you not frighten them by bellowing aloud? Nature has furnished you with means to procure you respect, but you do not make use of them. They bring you sorry beans and bad straw: eat none of them; only smell them, and leave them. If you follow the counsel I give you, you will quickly find a change, for which you will thank me."

The ox took the ass's advice in very good part, and owned he was very much obliged to him for it.

"Dear Sprightly," added he, "I will not fail to do all that you have recommended, and you shall see how I can acquit myself." They held their peace after this discourse, of which the merchant heard every word.

Early the next morning the labourer came to take the ox: he fastened him to the plough, and drove him to his ordinary work. The ox, who had not forgotten the ass's counsel, was very troublesome and untoward all that day; and in the evening, when the labourer brought him back to the stall, and began to fasten him to it, the malicious beast, instead of presenting his horns willingly as usual, was restive, and went backward bellowing, and then lowered his horns, as if he would have pushed at the labourer; in a word, he acted precisely as the ass had advised him. The day following the labourer came, as before, to take the ox to his labour; but, finding the manger full of beans, the straw that he had put in the night before not touched, and the ox lying on the ground with his legs stretched out, and panting in a strange manner, he, believing him to be sick, pitied him; and, thinking that it would be useless to take him to work, went immediately and acquainted the merchant with the circumstance.

The merchant, finding that the ox had followed the mischievous advice he had received, thought fit to punish the ass for it.

"Go," said he to the labourer, "and put the ass in the ox's place, and be sure to work him hard."

The labourer obeyed. The ass was forced to draw the plough all that day, which fatigued him so much the more, as he was not accustomed to that sort of labour: besides which, he had been so soundly beaten that he could scarcely stand when he returned.

Meanwhile the ox was very contented: he ate up all that was in his stall, and rested himself the whole day. He rejoiced in having followed the ass's advice, blessed him a thousand times for it, and did not fail to compliment him upon it when he saw him come back. The ass answered not a word, so vexed was he with the treatment he had received.

"But," said he to himself, "I have brought this misfortune upon myself by my own imprudence; I lived happily—everything smiled upon me. I had all that I could wish for. It is by my own fault that I am reduced to this miserable condition; and, if I cannot contrive some way to get out of it, I am certainly undone!"

As he spoke thus, his strength was so much exhausted that he fell down, apparently half dead, at the foot of his manger.

*　　　*　　　*　　　*　　　*

Here the grand vizier addressed himself to Scheherazade,—

"Daughter," said he, "you act like the ass: you will expose yourself to destruction by your false prudence. Be advised by me; remain easy, and seek not so hasten your death!"

"Father," replied Scheherazade, "the example you bring will not make me change my resolution: I shall never cease importuning you until you present me to the sultan as his bride."

The vizier, perceiving that she was determined in her demand, replied,—

"Alas! then, since you will continue obstinate, I shall be obliged to treat you in the same manner as the merchant I named just now treated his wife in a short time afterwards."

*　　　*　　　*　　　*　　　*

The merchant, understanding that the ass was in a pitiable condition, was curious to hear what passed between him and the ox; therefore, after supper, he went out by moonlight, his wife bearing him company, and sat down by them. When he arrived, he heard the ass say to the ox,—

"Comrade, tell me, I pray you, what you intend to do to-morrow, when the labourer brings you meat."

"What will I do?" said the ox: "why, continue to act as you taught me. I will get from him, and threaten him with my horns, as I did yesterday: I will feign myself sick, and just ready to die."

"Beware of that," interrupted the ass, "it will ruin you; for, as I came home this evening, I heard the merchant, our master, say something that makes me tremble for you."

"Alas! what did you hear?" said the ox; "as you love me, hide nothing from me, my dear Sprightly."

"Our master," replied the ass, "spoke these sad words to the labourer,—' Since the ox does not eat, and is unable to work, I would have him killed early to-morrow. We will give his flesh as an alms to the poor, for God's sake: as for his skin, that will be of use to us, and I would have you take it to the currier to dress: therefore do not fail to send for the butcher.' This is what I had to tell you," continued the ass. "The anxiety I feel for your preservation, and my friendship for you, obliged me to let you know it, and to give you new advice. As soon as they bring you your bran and straw, rise up and eat heartily. Our master will, by this, think that you are cured, and no doubt will recal his orders for killing you; whereas, if you behave otherwise, you are certainly lost."

This discourse had the effect which the ass intended. The ox was strangely troubled at it, and bellowed out for fear. The merchant, who had listened very attentively, now fell into such a fit of laughter, that his wife was surprised at it.

"Pray, husband," said she, "tell me what you laugh at so heartily, that I may laugh with you."

"Wife," replied he, "you must content yourself with hearing me laugh."

"No," said she, "I will know the reason."

"I cannot give you that satisfaction," answered he; "only that I laugh at what our ass just now said to our ox. The rest is a secret, which I am not at liberty to reveal."

"And what hinders you from revealing the secret?" said she.

"If I tell it you," replied he, "it will cost me my life."

"You only jeer me!" cried his wife; "what you tell me now cannot be true. If you do not satisfy me presently with what you laugh at, and tell me what the ox and ass said to each other, I swear by Heaven that you and I shall no longer bed together."

Saying these words, she went into the house, and, seating herself in a corner, cried there all night. Her husband lay alone, and finding next morning that she continued to lament,—

"You are a very foolish woman," said he, "to afflict yourself in this manner: the occasion is not worth the trouble; and it is of as little importance for you to know, as I am much interested in keeping the secret. Then think no more of it, I conjure you."

"I shall think so much of it," said she, "as never to cease weeping till you have satisfied my curiosity."

"But I tell you very seriously," replied he, "that it will cost me my life, if I yield to your indiscretion."

"Let what may happen," answered she, "I will not recede."

"I perceive," said the merchant, "that it is impossible to bring you to reason; and since I foresee that you will occasion your own death by your obstinacy, I will call in your children, that they may see you before you die."

Accordingly he called for them; and sent for her father and mother, and other relations. When they were assembled, and had heard the cause of their being summoned, they employed all their eloquence to convince her that he was in the wrong, but to no purpose: she told them she would rather die than yield that point to her husband. Her father and mother spoke to her alone, and represented to her that what she desired to know could be of no importance to her; but neither authority nor entreaties had any effect. When her children saw that nothing would prevail to bring her out of her sullen temper, they wept bitterly. The merchant himself was like a man delirious, and had almost determined to risk his own life to save that of his wife, whom he tenderly loved.

Now, my daughter, said the vizier to Scheherazade, this merchant had fifty hens and a cock, with a dog that

attended vigilantly to all that passed. While the merchant was sitting down, as I said, and considering what he had best do, he saw his dog run towards the cock, as he was treading a hen, and heard him speak to him thus :—

"Cock, Heaven will certainly not let you live long ! are you not ashamed to do that act to-day?"

The cock, standing up on tip-toe, answered the dog fiercely,—

"And why should I not do it to-day, as well as other days ?"

"If you do not know," replied the dog, "then I tell you, that this day our master is in great perplexity. His wife would have him reveal a secret, which is of such a nature, that the discovery would cost him his life. Things are come to such a state, that it is to be feared he will scarcely have resolution enough to resist his wife's obstinacy ; for he loves her, and is affected with the tears that she continually sheds. Perhaps it may cost him his life : we are all alarmed ; and you only insult our melancholy, and have the imprudence to divert yourself with your hens."

The cock answered the dog's reproof thus :—

"What ! is our master possessed of so little sense ? He has but one wife, and cannot govern her ; while I, who have fifty, make them all do what I please. Let him recal his reason, and he will soon find a way to relieve himself from his trouble."

"How ?" said the dog ; "what would you have him do ?"

"Let him go into the room where his wife is," replied the cock, "and, looking the door, take a good stick, and thrash her well : and I will answer for it, the discipline will bring her to her right wits, and make her forbear to ask him any more to tell her what he ought to conceal."

The merchant had no sooner heard what the cock said, than he arose, took up a thick stick, went to his wife, whom he found still crying ; when, shutting the door, he belaboured her so soundly, that she cried out,—

"It is enough, husband, it is enough ! let me alone, and I will never ask the question more."

At these words, and perceiving that she repented of her impertinent curiosity, he ceased beating her ; and opening the door, her friends entered : they were glad to find her cured of her obstinacy, and complimented her husband upon this happy expedient to bring his wife to reason."

———

"Daughter," added the grand vizier, "you deserve to be treated in the same manner as the wife of the merchant."

"Father," replied Scheherazade, "I beg you will not take it ill that I persist in my opinion. I am not at all moved by the story of that woman. I could relate to you numbers of tales to persuade you that you ought not to hinder my design. Besides, pardon me for declaring to you, that your opposing me would be in vain ; for if your paternal affection should induce you to refuse granting my request, I would go and offer myself to the sultan."

In short, the father, overcome by the resolution of his daughter, yielded to her importunity ; and, though very much grieved that he could not divert her from such a fatal resolution, he went that minute to acquaint the sultan, that next night he should bring him Scheherazade.

The sultan was much surprised at the sacrifice which the grand vizier made to him. "How could you resolve," said he, "to bring me your own daughter ?"

"Sir," answered the vizier, "it is her own offer ; the sad destiny that attends it would not frighten her ; she prefers, before her life, the honour of being for one night wife to your majesty."

"But do not deceive yourself, vizier," said the sultan ; "to-morrow, when I put Scheherazade into your hands, I expect you will take away her life ; and, if you fail, I swear that you yourself shall die."

"Sir," replied the vizier, "my heart, without doubt, will be full of grief in executing your commands ; but it is to no purpose for nature to murmur ; though I am her father, I will answer for the fidelity of my hand to execute your order."

Schahriar accepted his minister's offer, and told him he might bring his daughter when he pleased.

The grand vizier went with the answer to Scheherazade, who received it with as much joy as if it had been the most agreeable event possible : she thanked her father for having obliged her in so sensible a manner ; and perceiving that he was overwhelmed with grief, she said, to console him, that she hoped he would never repent his having married her to the sultan ; but that, on the contrary, it would afford him cause to rejoice all the rest of his life.

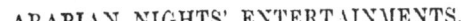
Her whole employment now was to put herself in a condition to appear before the sultan; but, before she went, taking her sister Dinarzade apart, she said to her,—

"My dear sister, I have need of your help in a concern of very great importance, and must request you not to deny me. My father is going to conduct me to the sultan, to be his wife. Do not let this frighten you, but hear me with patience. As soon as I am before the sultan, I will pray him to permit you to lie in the bride-chamber, that I may enjoy your company this one night more. If I obtain that favour, agreeably to my hopes, remember to awaken me to-morrow morning, an hour before day, and to address me in words to this effect:—*My sister, if you be not asleep, I pray you, while waiting the return of day, which will soon appear, tell me one of the pleasant stories of which you have read so many.* Immediately I will comply; and I hope by this means to deliver the city from the present consternation. Dinarzade answered, that she would obey with pleasure what her sister required of her.

The hour of going to bed being arrived, the grand vizier conducted Scheherazade to the palace, and, after having introduced her to the sultan's apartment, retired. As soon as the sultan was left alone with her, he ordered her to uncover her face, and found it so beautiful, that he was perfectly charmed with her; but perceiving her to be in tears, asked her the reason.

"Sir," answered Scheherazade, "I have a sister, who loves me tenderly as I love her, and I could wish that she might be allowed to be all night in this chamber, that I may see her and bid her once more adieu. Will you be pleased to allow me the comfort of giving her this last testimony of my friendship?"

Schahriar having consented to it, Dinarzade was sent for, who came with all possible expedition. The sultan went to bed with Scheherazade, upon an alcove raised very high, according to the custom of the monarchs of the East; and Dinarzade lay in a bed that was prepared for her, near the foot of the alcove.

An hour before day, Dinarzade, being awake, failed not to remember her sister's order: "*My dear sister,*" cried she, "*if you be not asleep I pray you, while waiting the return of day, which will soon appear, tell me one of those pleasant stories of which you have read so many.—*Alas, this may perhaps be the last time that ever I shall have that pleasure!"

Scheherazade, instead of answering her sister, addressed herself to the sultan.

"Sir," said she, "will your majesty be pleased to allow me to give my sister this satisfaction?"

"With all my heart," answered the sultan.

Then Scheherazade bade her sister listen; and, addressing herself to Schahriar, began with the following tale:—

THE MERCHANT AND THE GENI.

IR.—There was formerly a merchant, who had a large estate in lands, goods, and money. He employed many deputies, factors, and slaves. Being obliged, occasionally, to take journeys, for the purpose of consulting with his correspondents, one day an affair of importance summoned him to a considerable distance from his residence. Mounting on horseback, he took a portmanteau behind him, in which he had put some biscuits and dates, having a desert country to pass over, where he could obtain no kind of provisions. He arrived without any accident at the end of his journey; and, having despatched his business, took horse again, in order to return home.

The fourth day of his journey he was so much incommoded by the heat of the sun, and the reflection of that heat from the earth, that he turned out of the road to refresh himself under some trees which he saw in the country. He there found, at the foot of a great walnut-tree, a fountain of very clear running water : and, alighting, he fastened his horse to a branch of the tree, and seating himself by the fountain, took some biscuits and dates out of his portmanteau, and, as he ate his dates, threw the shells about on each side of him. When he had finished his frugal repast, being a good Mussulman, he washed his hands, his face, and his feet, and said his prayers.

He had not made an end, but was still on his knees, when he saw a geni, all white with age, and of an enormous bulk, appear. The geni advancing towards him, with a scimitar in his hand, thus addressed him, in a terrible voice :—

"Rise up! that I may kill thee with this scimitar, as thou hast killed my son !" accompanying these words with a frightful cry.

The merchant, as much terrified at the hideous shape of the monster as at the words he had spoken, answered him, trembling,—

"Alas! my good lord, of what crime can I have been guilty towards you, that you should take away my life ?"

"I will," replied the geni, " kill thee as thou hast killed my son."

"O Heaven !" cried the merchant, "how should I kill your son ? I did not know him, nor ever saw him."

"Didst thou not sit down when thou camest hither ?" replied the geni. " Didst thou not take dates out of thy portmanteau, and, as thou atest them, didst thou not throw the shells about on both sides of thee ?"

"I did all that you say," answered the merchant : " I cannot deny it."

"If it be so," replied the geni, "I tell thee that thou hast killed my son; and in this way—when thou threwest thy nut-shells about, my son was passing, and one of them fell into his eye, which killed him; therefore I must kill thee."

"Ah! my lord, pardon me !" cried the merchant.

"No pardon," answered the geni ; "no mercy. Is it not just to kill him who has killed another?"

"I agree to it," said the merchant ; "but surely I have not killed your son ; and if I had, I should have done it innocently ; therefore I beg of you to pardon me, and to suffer me to live."

"No, no," said the geni, persisting in his resolution ; "I must kill thee, since thou hast killed my son ;" when, taking the merchant by the arm, he threw him with his face upon the ground, and lifted up his scimitar to cut off his head.

In the meanwhile the merchant, all in tears, protested he was innocent, bewailed his wife and children, and supplicated the geni in the most moving expressions that could be uttered. The geni, with his scimitar still lifted up, had sufficient patience to hear the unhappy man finish his lamentations, but would not relent.

"All this whining," said the monster, " is to no purpose ; though thou shouldst shed tears of blood, they would not hinder me from killing thee, as thou killedst my son."

"Why !" replied the merchant, "can nothing move you ? Will you absolutely take away the life of a poor innocent?"

"Yes," replied the geni, " I am resolved."

When the merchant saw that the geni was going to cut off his head, he cried out aloud, and said to him,—

"For Heaven's sake, hold your hand ! and allow me one word : be so good as to grant me a short respite. Give me but time to bid my wife and children adieu, and to divide my estate among them by will, that they may not go to law with each other after my death ; and, when I have so done, I will return to this place, and submit to whatever you shall please to order concerning me."

"But," said the geni, " if I should grant you the time you demand, I doubt you will never come back."

"If you will believe my oath," answered the merchant, " I swear by all that is sacred that I will not fail to return, and meet you here."

"What time do you require ?" said the geni.

"I ask a year," replied the merchant ; " less time would not suffice to regulate my affairs, and to prepare myself to die without regret. But I promise you that this day twelvemonths I will return under these trees, to put myself into your hands."

"Do you take Heaven to witness this promise ?" said the geni.

"I do," answered the merchant, " I repeat it, and you may rely on my oath."

At these words, the geni left him near the fountain, and disappeared.

The merchant, being recovered from his fright, mounted his horse, and set forward on his journey ; but if he were glad, on the one hand, that he had escaped a danger so imminent, he was infinitely distressed on the other, when he thought of his fatal oath. When he reached home, his wife and children received him with all the demonstrations of perfect joy ; but he, instead of making them suitable returns, wept bitterly : whence they rightly conjectured that something extraordinary had befallen him.

His wife inquired the reason of his excessive grief and tears.

"We are all overjoyed," said she, " at your return ; but you alarm us to see you in this condition. Pray tell us the cause of your sorrow."

"Alas !" replied the husband, " how should I be otherwise? I have but a year to live !"

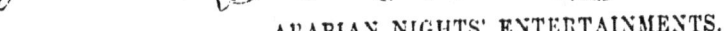

He then told them what had passed between him and the geni, and that he had given his oath to return at the end of the year, to receive death from his hands.

When they heard this sad news, they began to lament bitterly. His wife made a pitiful outcry, beat her face, and tore her hair, while the children, being all in tears, made the house resound with their sobs ; and the father, unable to overcome nature, mixed his tears with theirs : in a word, it was the most affecting spectacle ever beheld.

Next morning, the merchant applied himself to put his affairs in order ; and first of all to pay his debts. He made presents to all his friends, distributed considerable alms to the poor, gave his slaves of both sexes their liberty, divided his estate among his children, appointed guardians for such of them as were not yet of age, and, after restoring to his wife what belonged to her by contract of marriage, he added, over and above, all that he was by law permitted.

At length the year expired, and he was compelled to set out. He put his burial clothes in the portmanteau ; but never was there such grief seen, as when he bade adieu to his wife and children. They could not resolve to part, determining to go and die with him ; but knowing that he must quit these objects of his tenderest affection, he thus addressed them :—

" My dear wife and children," said he, " I obey the order of Heaven in leaving you ; follow my example, submit courageously to this necessity, and remember that it is the destiny of man to die."

Having said these words, he tore himself out of hearing the regrets and cries of his family ; and, setting off on his journey, arrived, on the day appointed, at the place where he had seen the geni. He alighted, and seating himself by the fountain, waited the coming of the geni with all the sorrow imaginable. While he languished in this cruel expectation, a good old man, leading a bitch, appeared, and drew near him : they saluted each other, after which the old man said to him,—

" Brother, may I ask why you are come into this desert place, where there are only evil spirits, and consequently you cannot be safe ? Looking upon these fine trees, indeed, one would think the place inhabited ; but it is truly a wilderness, where it is dangerous to stay long."

The merchant satisfied his curiosity, and related to him the adventure which obliged him to be there. The old man listened to him in astonishment, and when he had ended, cried out,—

" This is the most surprising thing in the world ! and you are bound by an oath which must be inviolable. However," continued he, " as I feel interested in the event, I will be witness of your interview with the geni ;" and sitting down by the merchant, they entered into serious conversation together.

While the merchant and the old man that led the bitch were talking, there came another old man, followed by two black dogs. Advancing, he saluted them, and inquired what they did in that place. The old man who conducted the bitch told him the adventure of the merchant and geni, with all that had passed between them, particularly the merchant's oath. He added, that this was the day agreed on, and that he had determined to stay and see the issue.

The second old man, thinking it was also worthy his curiosity, resolved to remain likewise ; he accordingly sat down by them ; and they had scarcely began to talk together, before there came a third old man, who, addressing himself to the two former, asked why the merchant that sat with them looked so melancholy. They told him the subject of his distress, which appeared so extraordinary to him, that he also wished to witness the result, and for that end seated himself beside them.

Shortly, they perceived in the field a thick vapour, like a cloud of dust raised by a whirlwind, advancing towards them, which suddenly vanished, and disclosed the geni, who, without saluting them, approached the merchant with his drawn scimitar, and taking him by the arm, " Get thee up," said he, " that I may kill thee as thou didst kill my son !" The merchant and the three old men, being terrified, began to lament, and to fill the air with their cries.

When the old man that led the bitch saw the geni seize the merchant, and was proceeding to kill him without pity, he threw himself at the feet of the monster, and kissing them,—

" Prince of genii," said he, " I most humbly request you will suspend your anger, and do me the favour to hear me. I will recount to you the history of my life, and of the bitch you see ; and if you think it more wonderful and surprising than the adventure of the merchant you are about to kill, I hope you will pardon the poor unfortunate man a third of his crime."

The geni took some time to consider, but at last answered, " Well, then, I agree to it."

THE HISTORY OF THE FIRST OLD MAN AND THE BITCH.

I SHALL begin, then : listen to me, I pray you, with attention. This bitch you see is my cousin, nay, more, my wife : she was only twelve years of age when I married her ; so that I may justly say she ought as much to regard me as her father, as her kinsman, and husband.

We lived together thirty years without having children ; yet her barrenness did not hinder me treating her with a great deal of complaisance and friendship. The desire of having children only, made me buy a slave, by whom I had a son, who was extremely promising. My wife, being jealous, conceived a hatred both for mother and child, but disguised her sentiments so well, that I did not know them till it was too late.

Meantime my son grew up, and was already ten years old, when I was obliged to undertake a journey. Before my departure, I recommended to my wife, of whom I had no mistrust, the slave and her son, and prayed her to take care of them during my absence, which lasted a whole year. Making use of that time to gratify her hatred, she applied herself to magic ; and when she had acquired enough of that diabolical art to enable her to execute her horrible contrivance, the wretch carried my son to a desolate place, where, by her enchantments, she changed him into a calf, and gave him to my farmer to fatten, pretending she had bought him. Her fury did not stop at this abominable action ; she likewise changed the slave into a cow, and gave her also to my farmer.

At my return, I asked for the mother and child.

" Your slave," said she, " is dead ; and as for your son, I know not what is become of him ; I have not seen him these two months."

I was grieved at the death of my slave; but as my son had only disappeared, as she told me, I flattered myself I should soon see him return. However, eight months passed, and I had not heard of him, when the festival of the great Bairam happened; to celebrate which, I sent to my farmer for one of the fattest cows to sacrifice, and he complied accordingly. The cow that he brought me was the slave herself, the unfortunate mother of my son. I tied her; but, as I was preparing to sacrifice her, she bellowed pitifully, and I could perceive streams of tears run from her eyes. This seemed to me very extraordinary; and finding myself, in spite of all exertion, seized with pity, I could not resolve to give her the blow, but ordered my farmer to get me another. My wife, who was present, became enraged at my compassion; and, opposing herself to an order which disappointed her malice, cried out,—

"What are you doing, husband? Sacrifice that cow; your farmer has not a finer, nor one more fit for the purpose.

Out of complaisance to my wife, I again approached the cow, and, combating my pity which suspended the sacrifice, was going to give her the fatal blow, when the victim, redoubling her tears and bellowing, disarmed me a second time. I then put the mall into the farmer's hands, saying,—

"Take and sacrifice her yourself, for her tears and bellowing pierce my heart."

The farmer, less compassionate than myself, sacrificed her; but, when he flayed her, he found her entirely bones, though to us she had appeared very fat.

"Take her to yourself," said I to the farmer; "I quit her to you: give her in treats or alms to whom you choose; and if you have a very fat calf, bring it to me in her stead."

I did not inquire how he disposed of the cow; but he soon after took her away, and returned with a very fat calf. Though I knew not that the calf was my son, yet I could not avoid being moved at the sight of him. On his part, as soon as he saw me, he made so great an effort to come to me, that he broke his cord; he threw himself at my feet, with his head against the ground, as if he would excite my compassion, and conjure me not to be so cruel as to take his life; signifying, as much as it was possible for him to do, that he was my son.

I was more surprised and affected with his action than I had been with the tears of the cow: I felt a tender pity which made me concern myself for him, or, rather, nature did its duty.

"Go," said I to the farmer, "carry home that calf, take great care of him, and bring me another in his stead immediately."

As soon as my wife heard me say this, she again cried out,—

"What are you doing, husband? Take my advice; sacrifice no other calf but that."

"Wife," said I, "I will not sacrifice him; I will spare him; and pray do not you oppose it."

The wicked woman disregarded my desire: she hated my son too much to consent that I should save him; and demanded the sacrifice with such obstinacy, that I was obliged to comply. I tied the poor creature, and taking up the fatal knife, I was going to strike it into my son's throat, when, turning his eyes, bathed in tears, towards me in a languishing manner, he so much affected me, that I had not strength to kill him, but let the knife

fall, telling my wife positively that I would have another calf to sacrifice and not that. She used all her endeavours to make me change my resolution; but I continued firm, and, to pacify her, promised that I would sacrifice him at the Bairam next year.

The following morning, my farmer desired to speak with me alone.

"I come," said he, "to tell you a piece of news, for which I hope you will return me thanks. I have a daughter, who has some skill in magic. Yesterday, as I carried back the calf, which you would not sacrifice, I perceived her laugh when she saw him, and the moment afterwards begin to weep. I asked her why she acted so contrarily at the same time."

"Father," replied she, "the calf that you bring back is our landlord's son: I laughed for joy at seeing him still alive; and I wept at the remembrance of the sacrifice that was yesterday made of his mother, who was changed into a cow. These two metamorphoses were made by the enchantments of our master's wife, who hated the mother and son."

"This is what my daughter told me," said the farmer, "and I came to acquaint you with it."

At these words, O geni! I leave you to think how much I was surprised. I went immediately with my farmer, to speak to his daughter myself. As soon as I arrived, I went first to the stall where my son was: he could not answer my embraces, but received them in such a manner, as fully satisfied me he was my son.

The farmer's daughter came.

"My good maid," said I, "can you restore my son to his former shape?"

"Yes," replied she, "I can."

"Ah!" returned I; "do but effect it, and I will make you mistress of all my fortune."

She replied to me, smiling,—

"You are our master, and I know very well what I owe to you; but, understand, I will restore your son into his former shape, only on two conditions; the first is, that you give him to me for my husband; and the second is, that you allow me to punish the person who changed him into a calf."

"For the first," said I, "I agree to it with all my heart, nay, I promise you more, a considerable estate for yourself, independent of what I design for my son. In a word, you shall see how I will reward the great service I expect of you. As to what relates to my wife, I agree to it also: a person who has been capable of committing so criminal an action deserves very well to be punished. I leave her to you: do what you please with her; only I must pray you not to take her life."

"I am going, then," answered she, "to treat her as she has treated your son."

"I consent to it," said I, "provided you first restore my son to me."

The maid then took a vessel of water, pronounced words over it that I did not understand, and, addressing herself to the calf,—

"O calf!" said she, "if thou wast created, by the Almighty and Sovereign Master of the world, such as thou appearest at this moment, continue in that form; but if thou be a man, and art changed into a calf by enchantment, return to thy natural figure, with the permission of the Sovereign Creator."

As she spoke these words, she threw water upon him, and in an instant he recovered his proper form.

"My son! my dear son!" cried I, immediately embracing him, in such a transport of joy that I knew not what I was doing—"Heaven has sent us this young maid to destroy the horrible charm by which you were environed, and to avenge the injury done to you and your mother. I doubt not that, in acknowledgment, you will take your deliverer to wife, as I have promised."

He consented with joy; but before they were married, the maiden changed my wife into a bitch; and this is her that you see. I wished she might have this form rather than another less agreeable, that we might keep her in the family without horror.

Since that time my son has become a widower, and is gone to travel: several years having elapsed since I heard of him, I am come abroad to inquire after his welfare; and not being willing to trust any person with my wife until

I return, I thought fit to carry her everywhere with me. Such is the account of myself and this bitch: is it not one of the most marvellous and surprising histories?

"I agree," said the geni; "and, for that reason, I forgive the merchant the third of his crime."

When the first old man, sir, continued the sultaness, had finished his relation, the second, who led the two black dogs, addressed himself to the geni.

"I am going to tell you," said he, "what happened to me and these two black dogs you see by me; and I am certain you will find my history yet more surprising than that which you have just now heard; but when I have told it you, I hope you will be pleased to pardon the merchant the second third of his crime."

"Yes," replied the geni, "provided your history surpasses that of the bitch."

Then the second old man began in this manner :—

THE HISTORY OF THE SECOND OLD MAN AND THE TWO BLACK DOGS.

 REAT Prince of Geni, you must know that we are three brothers, I and the two black dogs you see. Our father left each of us, when he died, one thousand sequins: with that sum we all entered into the same profession; we became merchants. In a little time after we had opened shop, my eldest brother, one of these two dogs, resolved to travel and trade in foreign countries. With this design, he sold his estate, and purchased goods proper for the trade he intended.

He went away, and was absent a whole year: at the end of which time, a poor man, whom I thought had come to ask alms, presented himself in my shop. I said to him,— "God help you!"

"God help you also!" answered he; "is it possible you do not remember me?"

Upon this, I looked at him attentively, and knew him.

"Ah, brother!" cried I, embracing him, "how could I know you in this state?"

I made him enter my house, and inquired concerning his health, and the success of his travels.

"Do not ask me that question," said he; "when you see me, you see all. It would only renew my grief to tell you all the particulars of the misfortunes that have befallen me during my absence, and reduced me to this deplorable condition."

I immediately shut up my shop, and taking him to a bath, gave him the best clothes in my wardrobe. I examined my books, and finding that I had doubled my stock, that is to say, that I was worth two thousand sequins, I gave him half. "With that, brother," said I, "you may forget your loss."

He joyfully accepted the offer, re-established his affairs, and we lived together as before.

Some time after, my second brother, who is the other of these two dogs, would also sell his estate. His other brother and myself did all we could to divert him from it, but to no purpose; he sold it, and with the money bought such goods as were suitable to the trade he designed. He joined a caravan, and took a journey. He returned at the end of the year in the same condition as his elder brother; and I, having gained another thousand sequins, gave him them, with which he furnished his shop, and continued to follow his profession.

One day my brothers came to seek me, to propose a trading voyage with them; I immediately rejected their proposal. "You have travelled," said I, "and what have you gained by it? Who can assure me that I shall be more successful than you have been?"

In vain they represented to me all which seemed likely to dazzle and encourage me to tempt my fortune; I constantly refused. However, they importuned me so much, that, after having resisted their solicitations five whole years they overcame me at last; but when we were to make preparations for our voyage, and to buy goods necessary for the undertaking, I found they had spent all, and that not one farthing remained of the thousand sequins I had given to each of them. I did not reproach them in the least for it. On the contrary, my stock being six thousand sequins, I shared the half of it with them; at the same time saying—

"My brothers, we will venture these three thousand sequins, and hide the rest in some sure place, that, in case our voyage be not more successful than those you have already made, we may have wherewith to console ourselves, and enable us to follow our former way of living."

I gave to each of them a thousand sequins; and, keeping as much for myself, I buried the other three thousand in a corner of my house. We purchased our merchandise; and after having embarked it on board a vessel which we freighted among us three, we put to sea with a favourable wind. After two months' sail, we happily arrived at a port, where we landed, and had a very great sale for our goods. I, especially, sold mine so well, that I gained ten for one, and we brought commodities of that country, to transport and sell in our own.

We were nearly ready to embark, in order to return, when I met, upon the banks of the sea, a lady, handsome enough, but poorly clad. She came directly up to me, kissed my hand, and prayed me, with the greatest earnestness imaginable, to marry her, and take her along with me. I made some difficulty to agree to what she demanded; but she said so many things to persuade me—that I ought to make no objections to her poverty, that I should have all the reasons in the world to be satisfied with her conduct—that I yielded. I ordered suitable apparel to be made for her; and after having married her, according to the proper form, I took her on board, and we set sail.

During the voyage, I found the wife I had taken possessed so many good qualities, that I loved her every day more and more. In the meantime, my two brothers, who had not managed their affairs so well as I did mine, envied my prosperity; and their malice carried them so far as to conspire against my life; so that one night, when my wife and I were asleep, they threw us both into the sea.

My wife was a fairy, and consequently, geni, you know very well she could not be drowned; but as for me, I should have been lost without her help. I had scarcely fallen into the water, before she took me up, and carried me to an island. When it was day, the fairy said to me,—

"You see, husband, that, by saving your life, I have not ill-rewarded your kindness to me. You must know that I am a fairy, and that, being upon the bank of the sea when you were going to embark, I entertained a strong inclination for you: I had a mind to try your goodness, and presented myself before you under the disguise in which you saw me. You have dealt very generously with me, and I am excessively glad in having found an opportunity of testifying my acknowledgment to you; but I am incensed against your brothers, and nothing will satisfy me but their lives."

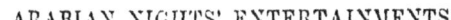

I listened to this discourse of the fairy with admiration. I returned thanks in the best manner I could, for the great kindness she had afforded me.

"But, madam," said I, "respecting my brothers, I beg you to pardon them: whatever cause they have given me, I am not cruel enough to desire their death."

I related to her the particulars of what I had done for them, which so much increased her indignation, that she cried out,—

"I must immediately fly after those ungrateful traitors, and take speedy vengeance on them! I will sink their vessel, and throw them to the bottom of the sea!"

"No, my good lady," replied I, "in the name of Heaven, act not so; moderate your anger, consider that they are my brothers, and that we should return good for evil."

I pacified the fairy by these words, and, as soon as I had spoken them, she transported me in an instant from the island where we were to the roof of my own house, which was terraced, and I disappeared in a moment. I descended, opened the doors, and dug up the three thousand sequins that I had hid. I afterwards went to the place where my shop was, which I opened, and was complimented by the merchants, my neighbours, upon my return. When I re-entered my house, I perceived these two black dogs, which came to me in a very submissive manner: I knew not what it meant, and was much astonished at it. But the fairy, who appeared immediately, said to me,—

"Husband, do not be surprised to see these two black dogs in your house; they are your two brothers."

I shuddered at these words; and asked her by what power they were so transformed.

"It was my doing," said she; "at least I gave the commission to one of my sisters to do it, who, at the same time, sunk their ship. You have lost the goods you had on board, but I will make you a compensation. As to your two brothers, I have condemned them to remain five years in that form. Their perfidiousness too well deserves such a penance."

In short, after having told me where I might hear of her, she disappeared.

Now the five years being expired, I am travelling in quest of her; and as I passed this way, I met this merchant and the good old man who leads the bitch, and sat down by them. This is my history, O prince of genii! do not you think it most extraordinary?

"I own it," said the the geni; "and therefore remit the merchant the second third of the crime which he had committed against me."

As soon as the second old man had finished his story, the third began, after making the same demand of the geni as the two former: that is to say, to pardon the merchant the other third of his crime, provided the story he had to tell him exceeded, in singular events, the two he had already heard. The geni made him the same promise as he had done the others.

"Hearken then," said the old man to him.

—— Sir, continued the sultaness, the third old man related his history to the geni: I cannot tell it you, because it is not come to my knowledge; but I know that it so much exceeded the two preceding stories in the variety of wonderful adventures, that the geni was astonished; and had no sooner heard the end, than he said to the third old man,—

"I remit the remaining third part of the merchant's crime. He ought to be very much obliged to all three of you, for having delivered him of his peril by your stories, without which he had not now been in the world."

Having thus spoken, he disappeared, to the great joy of the company.

The merchant failed not to give his three deliverers the thanks he owed them. They rejoiced to see him out of danger; after which he bade them adieu, and each of them went on his way. The merchant returned to his wife and children, and passed the remainder of his days in peace.

* * * * *

But, sir, continued Scheherazade, how pleasant soever the stories I have recited may have been to your majesty, they do not approach that of the fisherman. Shahriar desiring her to relate it, Scheherazade, resuming her discourse, proceeded as follows:—

THE STORY OF THE FISHERMAN.

IR,—There was one time a fisherman, so very old and poor, that he could scarcely earn enough to maintain himself, his wife, and three children. He went every morning early to fish; and imposed as a law upon himself, not to cast his nets above four times a day. He set out one morning by moonlight, and coming to the sea-bank, undressed himself, and cast in his nets. As he drew them toward the shore, finding them very heavy, he thought he had got a good draught of fish, and rejoiced within himself: but, in a moment after, perceiving that instead of fish, there was nothing in his nets but the carcase of an ass, he was very much chagrined.

When the fisherman, vexed at having made such a sorry draught, had mended his nets, which the carcase of the ass had broken in several places, he threw them in a second time. As he drew them out, he again experienced great resistance, which made him suppose they were full of fish: but he found only a pannier filled with gravel and slime, which grieved him extremely.

"O Fortune!" cried he, in a lamentable tone, "be not angry with me, nor persecute a wretch who prays thee to spare him! I came hither from my house to seek for a livelihood, and thou pronouncest death against me. I have no other trade by which to gain a subsistence, and, notwithstanding all my care, I can scarcely provide what is absolutely necessary for my family. But I am in the wrong to complain of thee; thou takest pleasure in persecuting honest people, and leaving great men in obscurity, whilst thou showest favour to the wicked, and advancest those who have no virtue to recommend them."

Having uttered this complaint, he threw away the pannier in a fret; and, washing his nets from the slime, cast them the third time: but he brought up nothing more than stones, shells, and mud. It is impossible to express his

despair; his senses had nearly forsaken him. However, when day began to appear, he did not forget to say his prayers, like a good Mussulman, and afterwards added this petition :—

"Lord! thou knowest that I cast my nets only four times a day; I have already drawn them three times without the least reward for my labour: I am to cast them but once more: I pray you to render the sea favourable to me, as you did to Moses."

The fisherman, having finished his prayer, cast his nets the fourth time. When he thought it right, he drew them as formerly, with great difficulty; but, instead of fish, found in them only a vessel of yellow, copper, which, by its weight, seemed to be full of something; and he observed that it was closely shut, and secured with lead, having the impression of a seal upon it. This rejoiced him.

"I will sell it," said he, "to the founder, and, with the money which it produces, buy a measure of corn."

He examined all sides of the vessel, and shook it, to discover if what was within would make any noise; but he heard nothing. This circumstance, with the impression of the seal upon the leaden cover, made him think it contained something precious: to ascertain which, he took a knife, and opened it with very little labour. He presently turned the mouth downward, but nothing appeared, which surprised him extremely. He placed it before him, and while he looked upon it attentively, there came out a very thick smoke, which obliged him to retire two or three paces backwards.

This smoke mounted as high as the clouds, and, extending itself upon the sea, and along the shore, formed a great mist, which, we may well imagine, very much astonished the fisherman. When the smoke was all out of the vessel it reunited itself, and became a solid body, of which there was formed a geni twice as high as the greatest of giants. At the sight of a monster of such unsizable bulk, the fisherman would willingly have fled; but was so troubled and frightened, that he could not move a step.

"Solomon," cried the geni immediately, "Solomon, great prophet of Heaven! pardon, pardon! I will never more oppose thy will: I will obey all thy commands."

When the fisherman heard these words of the geni, he recovered his courage, and said to him,

"Thou proud spirit, what is this that you talk? It is about eighteen hundred years since the prophet Solomon died, and we are now at the end of time. Tell me your history, and how you happened to be shut up in this vessel."

The geni, turning to the fisherman with a fierce look, answered,—

"Speak to me with more civility; thou art too bold to call me a proud spirit."

"Well, then," replied the fisherman, "shall I speak to you with more civility, and call you the owl of good luck."

"I say," answered the geni, "speak to me more civilly before I kill thee."

"Why will you kill me?" said the fisherman: "I have given you your liberty; have you already forgotten it?"

"No; I have not forgotten it," replied the geni; "but that will not prevent me killing thee; and I have only one favour to grant."

"And what is that?" said the fisherman.

"It is," answered the geni, "to give thee thy choice of the manner in which thou wouldst have me take thy life."

"But wherein have I offended you?" asked the fisherman; "am I thus to be rewarded for the service I have done you?"

"'I cannot treat you otherwise," said the geni; "and to convince you, hearken to my story :—

"I am one of the rebellious spirits that opposed themselves to the will of Heaven: all the other genii acknowledged Solomon, the great prophet, and submitted to him. Sacar and I were the only genii that would not submit to such degradation. To avenge himself, that great monarch sent Asaph, the son of Barakhia, his chief minister, to apprehend me. Asaph accordingly seized my person, and carried me by force before his master's throne.

"'Solomon, the son of David, commanded me to quit my accustomed mode of living, to acknowledge his power and to submit myself to his commands: I boldly refused to obey, telling him, I would rather expose myself to his utmost resentment, than swear fealty and submission to him as he required. To punish me, he enclosed me in this copper vessel; and to be certain that I might not break prison, he himself stamped his seal upon this leaden cover on which the great name of God was engraven. He then gave the vessel to one of the genii who had submitted to him, with orders to cast it into the sea; which, to my great sorrow, were immediately executed.

"'During the first hundred years' imprisonment, I swore that if any one should deliver me before the century had expired, I would make him rich even after his death: but that period elapsed, and nobody rendered me that good office. In the second century, I made an oath, that I would open all the treasures of the earth to any one who should set me at liberty; but with no better success. During the third, I promised to make my deliverer a potent monarch, to be always near him as a spirit, and to grant him every day three demands, of what nature soever they might be; but this century ran out as well as the two former, and I still remained in confinement. At last, being angry, or rather mad, at finding myself a prisoner so long, I swore, that if afterwards any one should release me, I would kill him without pity, and grant him no other favour, but to choose what kind of death he would die; and therefore, since thou hast delivered me to-day, I give thee that choice.'"

This discourse extremely afflicted the poor fisherman.

"I was most unfortunate," cried he, "to come hither, to do an act of good service to one who is so ungrateful! Pray, consider your injustice, and revoke such an unreasonable oath: be merciful to me, and Heaven will pardon you. If you generously grant me my life, Heaven will protect you from all attempts against your safety."

"No, thy death is certain," said the geni; "only choose how thou wilt die."

The fisherman, perceiving the geni to be determined, was excessively grieved, not so much for himself as for his three children, and bewailed the misery they must be reduced to by his death. He still endeavoured to appease the geni. "Alas!" said he, "deign to take pity on me, in consideration of the good office I have done you." "I have told thee already," replied the geni, "it is for that very reason I must kill thee." "That is strange!" said the fisherman; "are you resolved to return evil for good? The proverb says, 'He that renders good to one who deserves it not, is always ill rewarded.' I confess I thought it false; for, in effect, there can be nothing more contrary to reason, or the laws of society. Nevertheless, I now find, by cruel experience, that it is but too true." "Let us not lose time," replied the geni, "all thy reasonings shall not divert me from my purpose; make haste, and tell me how thou desirest to be killed."

Necessity is the mother of invention. The fisherman bethought himself of a stratagem. "Since I must die, then," said he to the geni, "I submit to the will of Heaven! but, before I choose the manner of death, I conjure you, by the great name which was engraven upon the seal of the prophet Solomon, the son of David, to answer me truly one question I have to ask you."

The geni, finding himself constrained by this adjuration to a positive answer, trembled; and replied to the fisherman, "Ask what thou wilt, but do not delay."

The geni having promised to speak the truth, the fisherman said to him,—" I would know if you were actually in this vessel—dare you swear it by the great name of God ?" " Yes," replied the geni ; " I swear by that great name that I was, and it is a certain truth." " In good faith," answered the fisherman, " I cannot believe you : the vessel would not hold one of your feet only, and how could it possibly contain your whole body ?" " I swear to thee, notwithstanding," replied the geni, " that I was there just as thou now seest me. Is it possible that thou believest me not after the great oath which I have taken ?" " Not I, truly," said the fisherman ; " nor will I believe you, unless you convince me."

On which the body of the geni was dissolved and changed into smoke, extending itself, as before, upon the sea and upon the banks ; and then, being gathered together, it began to re-enter the vessel, which it continued successively, by a slow and equal motion, till nothing was left out. As soon as it had disappeared, a voice came forth, saying to the fisherman, " Well, incredulous fellow ! I am entirely in the vessel : dost thou not believe me now ?"

The fisherman, instead of answering the geni, took the cover of lead, and having speedily shut the vessel, " Geni," cried he, " it is now your turn to beg favour, and choose which way you will die. But no, it will be better that I should throw you into the sea, whence I took you ; and then I will build a house upon the bank, where I will dwell to give notice to all fishermen who come to throw in their nets, to beware of such a wicked geni as thou art, that hath made an oath to kill him who shall set thee at liberty."

The geni, enraged at these insulting expressions, used all his efforts to get out of the vessel again, but it was not possible, for the impression of Solomon's seal prevented him ; so, perceiving that the fisherman had got the advantage of him, he thought fit to dissemble his anger. " Fisherman," said he, in a pleasant tone, " take heed how you do what you say. What I spoke to you before was only in jest, and you should not consider it seriously." " O geni !" replied the fisherman, " thou who wast but a moment ago the greatest of all genii, art now the least of them, thy crafty discourse will avail thee nothing, but to the sea thou shalt return. If thou hast been in the sea so long as thou hast told me, thou mayst very well stay there till the day of judgment. I begged thee, in God's name, not to take away my life, and thou didst reject my prayers ; I am obliged to treat thee in the same manner."

The geni omitted nothing, to prevail upon the fisherman. " Open the vessel," said he, " give me my liberty, I pray thee, and I promise to satisfy thee to thy utmost wish." " Thou art a mere traitor," replied the fisherman : " I should deserve to lose my life, if I were such a fool as to trust thee : thou wouldst not fail to treat me in the same manner as a certain Grecian king treated the physician Douban. It is a story I have a mind to tell thee ; listen to it."

THE STORY OF THE GRECIAN KING AND THE PHYSICIAN DOUBAN.

IN the country of Zouman, in Persia, there was a king whose subjects were originally Greeks. The king was covered with the leprosy, and his physicians, having in vain employed all their remedies to effect a cure, knew not how to act, when a very able physician, called Douban, arrived at his court.

The physician had studied his science in Greek, Persian, Turkish, Arabian, Latin, Syriac, and Hebrew books ; besides which, he was an expert philosopher, and knew perfectly the good and bad qualities of all sorts of plants and drugs. As soon as he was informed of the king's distemper, and understood that his physicians had given him over, he clad himself in the best apparel he could, and found means to present himself to the king. " Sir," said he, " I know that all your majesty's physicians have been unable to cure you of the leprosy ; but, if you will do me the honour to accept my services, I will myself engage to cure you, without either drenches or external applications."

The king listened to his proposition. " If you are able," answered he, " to perform what you say, I promise to enrich you and your posterity ; and, without considering the presents I may make you, you shall be my chief favourite. Do you assure me, then, that you will cure me of my leprosy, without making me take any draught or applying any external remedy ?" " Yes, sir," replied the physician, " I flatter myself I shall be successful, through God's assistance ; and to-morrow I will attempt the proof."

In fine, the physician Douban returned to his residence, and made a mallet, the handle of which he hollowed, wherein he put the drug that was to effect the cure. He prepared also a ball, in such a manner as suited his purpose ; with which, next morning, he went to present himself before the king, and, falling down at his feet, kissed the ground. After a profound reverence, the physician Douban, rising up, told the king he judged it proper that his majesty should take horse, and go to the place where he used to play at the mell. The king complied ; and, when he arrived there, the physician approached him with the mell that he had prepared. " Sir," said he to him, " exercise yourself with this mell, and strike the ball with it, until you find yourself very warm. When the remedy I have put in the handle of the mell is heated with your hand, it will penetrate your whole body ; and as soon as you sweat you may discontinue the exercise, for the medicine will then have had its effect. As soon as you are returned to your palace, go into the bath, and cause yourself to be well washed and rubbed ; then retire to bed, and, when you rise to-morrow, you will find yourself cured."

The king took the mell, and, urging his horse after the ball which he had thrown, he struck it. The ball was driven back by the officers who played with him ; he struck it again ; and in fine, played so long that his hand and his whole body were in a perspiration, when the medicine enclosed in the handle of the mell operated as the physician said. Then the king left off play, returned to his palace, entered the bath, and attended very exactly to what his physician had prescribed.

Next morning, when the king arose, he perceived, with as much astonishment as joy, that his leprosy was cured, and his body as clean as if he had never been attacked by that distemper. As soon as he was dressed, he entered the hall of public audience, where he mounted his throne, and showed himself to his courtiers, who, solicitous to know the success of the new remedy, were there early. When they saw the king perfectly cured, all of them expressed an extreme joy.

The physician Douban, entering the hall, bowed himself before the throne, with his face to the ground. The king, perceiving him, called him, made him sit by his side, showed him to the assembly, and bestowed on him all the praise that he merited. The prince did not stop here; but as he treated all his court that day, he made him eat at his table alone with him : and, towards night, when he was about dismissing the company, he caused him to be clad in a long rich robe, like those that his favourites usually wore in his presence; besides which he ordered him two thousand sequins. The next day, and the day following, he ceased not to caress him : in short, this prince, thinking he could never enough acknowledge his obligations to that able physician, bestowed new favours upon him every day.

But this king had a grand vizier, who was avaricious, envious, and naturally capable of all sorts of mischief. He could not see, without envy, the presents that were given to the physician, whose other merits had begun to make him jealous; and he therefore resolved to lessen him in the king's esteem. To effect his purpose, he went to the king, and told him privately that he had some advice to give him, which was of the greatest importance. The king having asked what it was, "Sir," said he, "it is very dangerous for a monarch to put confidence in a man whose fidelity he never tried. Though you heap favours upon the physician Douban, and show him the utmost kindness, your majesty does not know but he may be a traitor, who has introduced himself into this court merely to assassinate you." "From whom have you this," asked the king, "that you dare tell it me? Do you consider to whom you speak, and that you advance a thing which I shall not easily believe?" "Sir," replied the vizier, "I am very well informed of what I have had the honour to represent to your majesty; therefore do not let your dangerous confidence lull you to repose. If your majesty be asleep, be pleased to awake; for I once more repeat it, the physician Douban did not leave the heart of Greece, his country, he is not come hither to settle himself at your court, but to execute that horrible design of which I have just now spoken."

"No, no, vizier," replied the king, "I am certain that this man, whom you treat as a villain and a traitor, is one of the best and most virtuous of men ; and there is nobody in the world I love so much. You know by what remedy, or rather miracle, he cured me of my leprosy : if he had had a design upon my life, why did he save me? he needed only to have left me to my disease, and I could not have escaped : my life was already half gone. Cease, then, to inspire me with unjust suspicions. Instead of listening to you, I tell you that, from this day forward, I will give that great man a pension of a thousand sequins a month for his life : though I should share with him my riches and dominions, I could never sufficiently recompense him for the good he has done me. I perceive it is a virtue that raises your envy ; do not think that I will be unjustly prejudiced against him. I remember too well what a vizier said to King Sinbad, his master, to prevent his putting to death the prince, his son."

The vizier's curiosity being excited, he said to the king, "Sir, I pray your majesty to pardon me, if I have the boldness to demand of you what the vizier of King Sinbad said to his master, to divert him from cutting off the prince, his son." The Grecian king had the complaisance to satisfy him. "That vizier," answered he, "after having represented to King Sinbad that he ought to beware, lest, on the accusation of a mother-in-law, he should commit an action of which he might afterwards repent, told him his story."

THE STORY OF THE HUSBAND AND THE PARROT.

GOOD man had a handsome wife, whom he so tenderly loved, that he could scarcely allow her to be out of his sight. One day, urgent affairs obliging him to tear himself from her, he went into a place where all kinds of birds were sold, and bought a parrot, which not only spoke very well but could also give an account of everything that was done before it. He carried it in a cage to his house, prayed his wife to put it in her chamber, and to be careful of it during a journey he was compelled to undertake, and then set off.

At his return he did not forget to ask the parrot concerning what had passed in his absence : and the bird told him things that gave him occasion to upbraid his wife. She thought some of her slaves had betrayed her, but all of them swore they had been faithful to her; and they were convinced it must have been the parrot that had told tales.

Prepossessed of this opinion, the wife herself thought of a way to remove her husband's jealousy, and at the same time revenge herself on the parrot, which she had thus effected :—Her husband being gone another journey, she commanded a slave, in the night-time, to turn a hand-mill under the parrot's cage ; she desired another to throw water, in form of rain, over the cage : and a third she ordered to take a glass and turn it to the right and to the left before the parrot, so that the reflections of the candle might shine on its face. The slaves spent great **part** of the night in performing what their mistress commanded, and acquitted themselves very dexterously.

Next day the husband returned, and again examined the parrot concerning what had passed during his absence. The bird answered, "Good master, the lightning, thunder, and rain so much disturbed me all night, that I cannot tell you how much I have suffered by it." The husband, who knew that there had been neither thunder, lightning, nor rain that night, fancied that the parrot, not having told him the truth in this, might also have deceived him in regard to his wife ; on which he took it out of the cage, and threw it with so much force to the ground that he killed it. Yet he afterwards understood, through his neighbours, that the poor parrot had told the truth, when it gave him an account of his wife's base conduct, which made him repent having killed it.

* * * *

When the Grecian king, said the fisherman to the geni, had finished the story of the parrot—"And you, vizier," added he, "in consequence of the envy you have conceived against the physician Douban, who never injured you, would have cut him off; but I will be careful, for fear I should have cause to repent as the husband did the killing of his parrot."

The mischievous vizier was too much interested in effecting the ruin of the physician Douban to stop here. "Sir," said he, "the death of the parrot was of little importance, and I do not believe his master long regretted him. But why should your fear of wronging an innocent man hinder you from putting this physician to death? Is it not enough that he is accused of a design against your life, to authorise you to take away his? When the subject of consideration is to secure the life of a king, bare suspicion ought to pass for certainty ; and it is better to sacrifice the innocent than spare the guilty. But, sir, what I have hinted to you is not merely suspicion; the physician

Douban has, unquestionably, a mind to assassinate you. It is not envy which makes me his enemy; it is solely the concern I take in preserving your majesty's life, my zeal for your safety, that compels me to give you advice of such importance. If it be false, I deserve the same punishment as a vizier formerly received." "What had that vizier done," said the Grecian king, "to deserve punishment?" "I will inform your majesty," replied the vizier "if you will be pleased to hear me."

THE STORY OF THE VIZIER WHO WAS PUNISHED.

HERE was a king, who had a son passionately fond of the chase. He frequently allowed him to take that diversion, but ordered his grand vizier to attend him constantly, and never to lose sight of him.

One hunting-day, the huntsmen having roused a deer, the prince thinking the vizier followed him, pursued the game so far, and with so much earnestness, that he was quite alone. He stopped, and, finding himself bewildered, endeavoured to return by the same track he came, to rejoin the vizier, who had not been sufficiently careful to follow him, but wandered still farther.

Whilst he rode about, not keeping any regular course, he encountered, by the way-side, a handsome lady, who wept bitterly. Stopping his horse, he asked who she was, how she happened to be alone in that place, and if she wanted assistance. "I am," replied she, "daughter to an Indian king: as I was taking the air on horseback in the country, I became sleepy, and fell from my horse, which is got away, and I know not what is become of him." The young prince, taking compassion on her, asked her to get up behind him, to which she willingly agreed.

As they passed by the ruins of a house, the lady expressed a desire to alight. The prince accordingly stopped his horse, and suffered her to descend: he also dismounted himself, and approached the ruins, leading his horse by the bridle; but judge what was his surprise, when he heard the lady within pronounce these words:—" Rejoice, my children! I bring you a handsome young man, and very fat;" and other voices answer immediately, "Mamma, where is he, that we may eat him presently? for we are very hungry."

The prince had heard enough to convince him of his danger. He found that the lady who called herself daughter to an Indian king, was wife to one of those savage demons called ogres, who remain in desert places, and make use of a thousand wiles to surprise and devour passengers. Being thus terrified, the prince remounted his horse immediately.

The pretended princess that moment appeared, and, perceiving that she had missed her prey, cried, "Fear nothing, prince. Who are you? Whom do you seek?" "I am lost," replied he, "and am seeking my road." "If you have lost your way," said she, "recommend yourself to God: he will deliver you out of your perplexity." Then the prince, as he could not believe she spoke sincerely, but thought she was sure of him, lifted up his hands to heaven, saying, "Almighty Lord, cast thine eyes upon me, and deliver me from this enemy!"—After this prayer, the ogress re-entered the ruins, and the prince rode off with all possible haste. He happily found the right track, and arrived safely at his father's court, to whom he gave a particular account of the danger he had encountered through the vizier's neglect; on which the king, incensed against that minister, ordered him to be strangled immediately.

*　　　　*　　　　*　　　　*　　　　*　　　　*

"Sir," continued the Grecian king's vizier, "to return to the physician Douban if you do not take care, the confidence you put in him will be fatal to you: I am very well assured that he is a spy sent by your enemies to attempt your majesty's life. He has cured you, you will say; but, alas! who can convince you of that? He has, perhaps, cured you only in appearance, and not radically: who knows but that the remedy he has applied may, in time, have pernicious effects?"

The Grecian king, who had naturally very little sense, had not sufficient penetration to discover the wicked design of his vizier, nor firmness enough to persist in his first opinion. This discourse staggered him. "Vizier," said he, "thou art in the right: he may be come on purpose to take away my life, which he may easily effect by the mere smell of some one of his drugs. We must consider how we should act in this case."

When the vizier found the king in such a temper as he wished, "Sir," said he, "the surest and most speedy method you can adopt to secure your life is, to send immediately for the physician Douban, and order his head to be cut off as soon as he arrives." "Truly," replied the king, "I think that is the way I ought to prevent his design." When he had thus spoken, he called for one of his officers, and desired him to go for the physician, who, not being aware of the king's intention, came to the palace in haste.

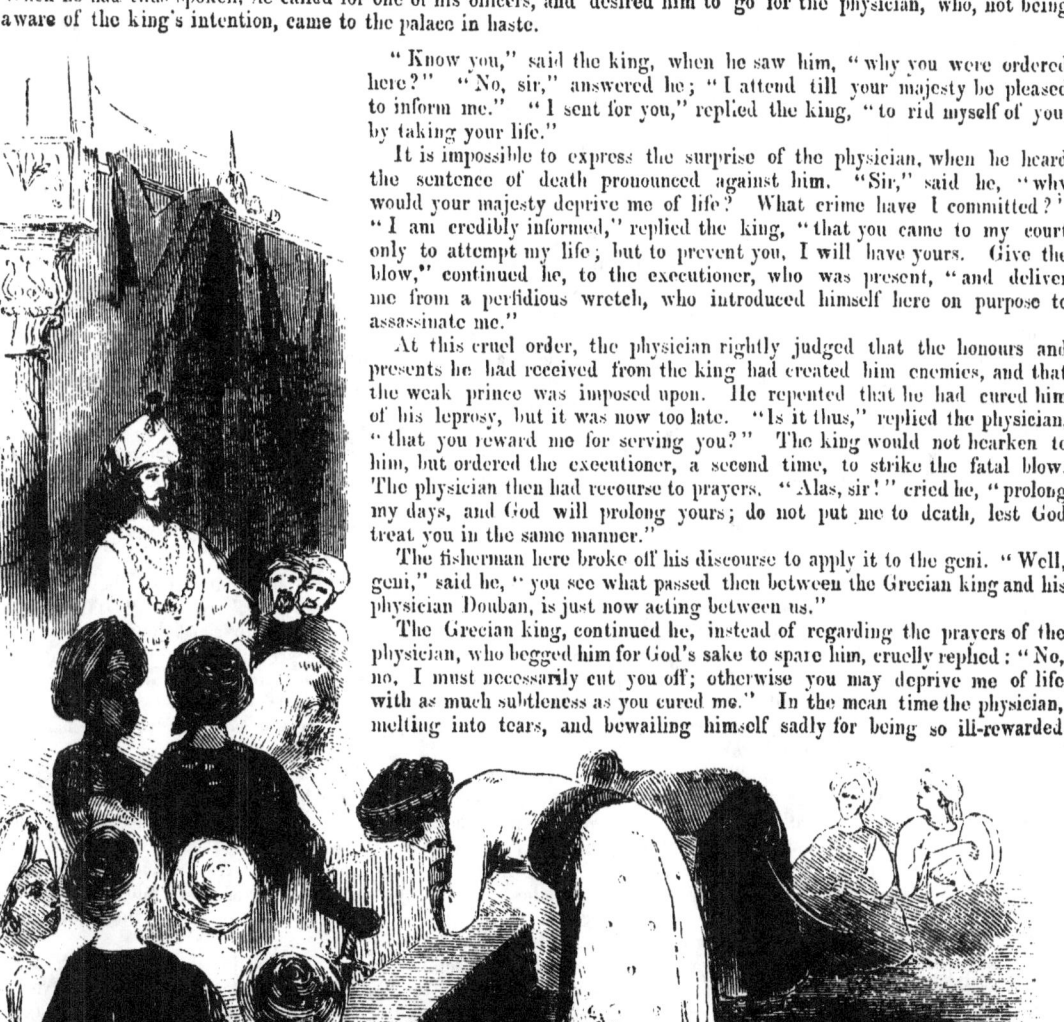

"Know you," said the king, when he saw him, "why you were ordered here?" "No, sir," answered he; "I attend till your majesty be pleased to inform me." "I sent for you," replied the king, "to rid myself of you, by taking your life."

It is impossible to express the surprise of the physician, when he heard the sentence of death pronounced against him. "Sir," said he, "why would your majesty deprive me of life? What crime have I committed?" "I am credibly informed," replied the king, "that you came to my court only to attempt my life; but to prevent you, I will have yours. Give the blow," continued he, to the executioner, who was present, "and deliver me from a perfidious wretch, who introduced himself here on purpose to assassinate me."

At this cruel order, the physician rightly judged that the honours and presents he had received from the king had created him enemies, and that the weak prince was imposed upon. He repented that he had cured him of his leprosy, but it was now too late. "Is it thus," replied the physician, "that you reward me for serving you?" The king would not hearken to him, but ordered the executioner, a second time, to strike the fatal blow. The physician then had recourse to prayers. "Alas, sir!" cried he, "prolong my days, and God will prolong yours; do not put me to death, lest God treat you in the same manner."

The fisherman here broke off his discourse to apply it to the geni. "Well, geni," said he, "you see what passed then between the Grecian king and his physician Douban, is just now acting between us."

The Grecian king, continued he, instead of regarding the prayers of the physician, who begged him for God's sake to spare him, cruelly replied: "No, no, I must necessarily cut you off; otherwise you may deprive me of life with as much subtleness as you cured me." In the mean time the physician, melting into tears, and bewailing himself sadly for being so ill-rewarded by the king, prepared for death. The executioner bound up his eyes, tied his hands, and proceeded to draw his scimitar.

Then the courtiers who were present, moved with compassion, begged the king to pardon him, assuring his majesty that he was not culpable, and that they would be answerable for his innocence, but the king was inflexible, and answered them in such a manner, that they dared not make any reply.

The physician being on his knees, his eyes bandaged, and ready to receive the fatal blow, addressed himself once more to the king. "Sir," said he, "since your majesty will not revoke the sentence of death, I beg, at least, that you will permit me to return to my house, to give orders about my burial, to bid farewell to my family, to distribute alms, and to bequeath my books to those who are capable of making good use of them. I have one book in particular, which I would present to your majesty: it is very precious and worthy to be laid up carefully in your treasury." "Why," asked the king, "is that book so precious, as you talk of?" "Sir," said the physician, "because it contains an infinite number of curious things of which the chief is, that when you have cut off my head, if your majesty will give yourself the trouble to open the book at the sixth leaf, and read the third line of the left page, my head will answer all the questions you ask it." The king, curious to see so wonderful a thing, deferred his death till next day, and sent him home under a strong guard.

During the time, the physician put his affairs in order; and a report being circulated that an extraordinary prodigy was to happen after his death, the viziers, emirs, officers of the guard, and, in a word, the whole court, repaired next day to the hall of audience, that they might be witnesses of it.

The physician Douban, being soon brought in, advanced to the foot of the throne, with a great book in his hand; he there called for a basin, upon which he laid the cover that the book was wrapped in, and presenting the book to the king, "Sir," said he, "take that book, if you please; when my head is cut off, order that it may be put into the basin upon the cover of the book: as soon as it is put there, the blood will stop; then open the book, and my head will answer your questions. But, sir," continued he, "suffer me once more to implore your majesty's clemency; for God's sake grant my request: I protest to you that I am innocent." "Your prayers," answered the king, "are in vain; and if it were only to hear your head speak after your death, it is my will that you should die." As he said this, he took the book out of the physician's hand, and ordered the executioner to do his duty.

The head was so dexterously cut off that it fell into the basin, and was no sooner laid upon the cover of the book than the blood stopped; then, to the great astonishment of the king and all the spectators, it opened its eyes, and said, "Sir, will your majesty be pleased to open the book?" The king opened it; and finding that one leaf was, as it were, glued to another, that he might turn it with more ease, he put his finger to his mouth, and wet it with his spittle. He did the same till he came to the sixth leaf; when, finding no writing on the place where he was desired to look for it, "Physician," said he to the head, "here is nothing written." "Turn over some more leaves," replied the head. The king continued to turn over, always putting his finger to his mouth, until the poison, with which each leaf was imbued, had taken its effect: the prince then found himself suddenly seized with an extraordinary fit, his sight failed, and he fell down at the foot of his throne in strong convulsions.

As soon as the physician Douban, or rather his head, saw that the poison had effectually operated, and that the king had but a few moments to live: "Tyrant!" it cried, "now you see how princes are treated who, abusing their authority, destroy innocent men: God punishes soon or late their injustice and cruelty." Scarcely had the head spoken these words, before the king expired, and the head itself lost what little life remained.

*   *   *   *   *

When the fisherman had concluded the history of the Greek king and his physician Douban, he explained its application to the geni, whom he still kept shut up in the vessel. "If the Grecian king," said he, "had suffered the physician Douban to live, God would have preserved him for it: but he rejected his most humble prayers, and therefore God punished him. It is the same with thee, O geni! Could I have prevailed with you to grant me the favour I demanded, I should now have pitied you; but since, notwithstanding the extreme obligation you were under to me for having set you at liberty, you still persisted in your design to kill me, I am obliged in my turn to be equally hardhearted. I am going, by leaving you in this vase, and throwing you into the sea, to render your life harmless—that is the vengeance I mean to take."

"Fisherman, my good friend!" said the geni, "I conjure thee once more not to be guilty of so cruel an action; consider that it is not good to avenge oneself, while, on the other hand, it is commendable to return good for evil: do not treat me as Imma treated Ateca formerly." "And what did Imma to Ateca?" asked the fisherman. "Oh!" said the geni, "if thou wish to know, open the vessel: dost thou think that I can be in a humour to tell stories in so close a prison? I will tell thee as many as thou desirest, when thou lettest me out." "No," replied the fisherman, "I will not let thee out, do not expect it; I am just going to throw you to the bottom of the sea." "Yet one word more!" cried the geni: "I promise not to injure thee; nay, so far from that, I will show thee how thou mayest become exceedingly rich."

The hope of delivering himself from poverty prevailed with the fisherman. "I could listen to you," said he, "were there any credit to be given to your word: swear to me, by the great name of God, that you will faithfully perform what you promise, and I will open the vessel;—I do not believe you will dare to break such an oath."

The geni swore to him, and the fisherman then took off the covering of the vessel. At that instant the smoke came out; and the geni, having resumed the form he had before, immediately kicked the vessel into the sea. This action frightened the fisherman: "Geni," said he, "what is the meaning of that? will you not keep the oath you just now made? And must I say to you as the physician Douban said to the Grecian King, 'Suffer me to live, and God will prolong your days?'"

The geni laughed at the fisherman's fear: "No, fisherman," answered he, "be not afraid: I did it merely to divert myself, and to see if thou wouldst be alarmed: to persuade thee that I am in earnest, take thy net and follow me." As he spoke these words, he walked before the fisherman, who, having taken up his nets, followed him, but with some mistrust. Passing by the town, they reached the top of a mountain, whence they descended into a vast plain, which conducted them to a great pond that lay between four hills.

When they arrived at the side of the pond, the geni said to the fisherman, "Cast in thy nets and take fish." The fisherman did not doubt he should catch some, because he saw a great quantity in the pond; but he was extremely surprised when he observed they were of four colours, white, red, blue, and yellow. He threw in his nets, and brought out one of each colour: having never seen the like, he could not but admire them; and judging that he might get a considerable sum for them, he was very joyful. "Carry these fish," said the geni to him, "and present them to the sultan: he will give thee more money for them than thou ever hadst in thy life. Thou mayest come every day to fish in this pond; but I give thee warning not to throw in thy nets more than once daily; otherwise you will repent it. Take heed, and remember my advice: if you follow it exactly, you will receive benefit." Having thus spoken, he stamped his foot upon the ground, which opening, it swallowed up the geni, and again closed.

The fisherman, resolved to follow the geni's advice exactly, took care not to cast in his nets a second time; but returned to the town, very well satisfied with his fish, and making a thousand reflections upon his adventure. He went straight to the sultan's palace, according to the geni' directions, to present him the fish.

The sultan was very much surprised when he saw the four fishes which the fisherman had brought him. He took them up one after another, to consider them with attention; and after having long admired them, "Take these fishes," said he to his prime vizier, "and carry them to the skilful cook-maid that the Emperor of the Greeks has sent me. I imagine that they must be as good as they are beautiful."

The vizier carried them himself to the cook, and, delivering them into her hands, "There," said he, "are four fishes just brought to the sultan: he orders you to dress them." Having acquitted himself of his commission, he returned to the sultan, his master, who ordered him to give the fisherman four hundred pieces of gold of the coin of that country, which he did accordingly.

The fisherman, who had never possessed so much cash at one time, could scarcely believe his good fortune, but thought it must be a dream; however, he afterwards found it to be real, when he had, with the money, provided necessaries for his family.

When the sultan's cook-maid had cleaned the fishes, she put them, with oil, in a frying-pan upon the fire, and as soon as she thought them fried enough on one side, she turned them upon the other; but, O monstrous prodigy! scarcely were they turned, before the wall of the kitchen opened, and a young lady of admirable beauty and comely size entered. She was habited in flowered satin, of the Egyptian fashion, with pendants in her ears, a necklace of large pearls, and bracelets of gold, garnished with rubies, and a rod of myrtle in her hand. She approached the frying-pan, to the great consternation of the cook-maid, who stood immoveable at the sight, and striking one of the fishes with the end of the rod—"Fish, fish," said she, "art thou in thy duty?" The fish not answering, she repeated these words, when the four fishes lifted up their heads together, and said to her, "Yes, yes: if you reckon, we reckon; if you pay your debts, we pay ours; if you fly we vanquish, and are content." As soon as they had uttered these words, the lady overturned the frying-pan, and entered again into the open part of the wall, which shut immediately, and became as it was before.

The cook-maid, who had been much terrified, now coming a little to herself, went to take up the fishes which had fallen upon the burning coals, but found them quite black, and not fit to be carried to the sultan. At this misfortune she was grievously troubled, and began to weep most bitterly. "Alas!" said she, "what will become of me! if I tell the sultan what I have seen, I am sure he will not believe me; how much he will be enraged against me!"

While she was thus afflicting herself, the grand vizier entered, and inquired if the fishes were ready. She related to him all that had happened, which, as will readily be imagined, astonished him greatly; but, without mentioning it to the sultan, he invented an excuse that satisfied him. Immediately sending for the fisherman, the vizier bade him bring four more such fish, telling him an accident had happened to the other, that had rendered them unfit to be carried to the sultan. The fisherman, without mentioning what the geni had told him, in order to excuse himself from bringing them that day, said he had a great distance to go for them, but would certainly bring them the next morning.

Accordingly, the fisherman set off during the night, and, reaching the pond, threw in his nets; drawing them out, he found four such fishes as the former, each of a different colour, and carried them to the vizier at the time appointed. The minister took them, carried them to the kitchen, and shutting himself up alone with the cook-maid, she gutted them, and put them on the fire, as she had acted with the four others the day preceding. When they were fried on one side, and she had turned them upon the other, the kitchen wall again opened, and the same lady appeared, with the rod in her hand; she went to the frying-pan, struck one of the fishes, spoke to it as before, and all four, raising their heads, gave her the same answer; on which she overturned the frying-pan with her rod, and retired through the opening in the wall whence she came. The grand vizier having witnessed what had passed, "This is too surprising and extraordinary," said he, "to be concealed from the sultan: I will inform him of this prodigy." Accordingly he found the sultan, and gave him a faithful account of all that had happened.

The sultan, being much surprised, expressed great impatience to convince himself. For this purpose, he sent immediately for the fisherman: "Friend," said he to him, "cannot you bring me four more such fishes?" The fisherman replied, "If your majesty will be pleased to allow me three days to obtain what you desire, I will promise to comply." His request being granted, he went to the pond for the third time, and met with the same success as before, for, at the first throwing-in of his net, he took out four such fishes, which he carried immediately to the sultan, who was so much the more rejoiced, as he did not expect them so soon, and again ordered him four hundred pieces of gold.

As soon as the sultan had got the fish, he commanded them to be carried into his closet, with all that was necessary for frying them. Having shut himself up there with his vizier, that minister gutted them, and put them in the pan upon the fire; and when they were fried on one side, he turned them upon the other. Then the wall of the closet opened, but, instead of the young lady, there came out a black, habited like a slave, and of gigantic stature, with a large green batoon in his hand. He advanced towards the pan, and touching one of the fishes with his batoon, said to it, in a terrible voice, "Fish, fish, art thou in thy duty?" At these words, the fishes raised up their heads, and answered, "Yes, yes, we are: if you reckon, we reckon; if you pay your debts, we pay ours; if you fly, we vanquish, and are content."

The fishes had scarcely uttered these words, when the black threw the pan into the middle of the closet, and reduced the fishes to a coal. Having done this, he retired fiercely, and entering again into the hole of the wall, it shut, and appeared in the same state as it was before.

"After what I have seen," said the sultan to the vizier, "it will not be possible for me to be easy in my mind. These fish, without doubt, signify something extraordinary, of which I wish to be satisfied." He then sent for the fisherman; and when he appeared, "Fisherman," said he to him, "the fishes you brought us have made me very uneasy: where did you catch them?" "Sir," answered he, "I took them in a pond situated between four hills, beyond the mountain that we see from hence." "Know you that pond?" said the sultan to the vizier. "No, sir," replied the vizier, "I never so much as heard of it; and yet sixty years have not elapsed since I hunted beyond that mountain, and in the environs." The sultan asked the fisherman how far the pond might be from the palace. The fisherman answered it was not above three hours' journey. On this assurance, and there being still day enough to reach the pond before night, the sultan commanded all his court to take horse, and the fisherman served them for a guide. They ascended the mountain, and at the foot of it they saw, to their great surprise, a vast plain, that nobody had observed till then. In fine, they came to the pond, which they found actually situated between four hills, as the fisherman had said. The water of it was so transparent, that they observed all the fishes were like those which the fisherman had carried to the palace.

The sultan stopped upon the bank of the pond; and, after some time regarding the fishes with admiration, he demanded of his emirs, and all his courtiers, if it were possible they had never seen this pond, which was within so short a distance of the town? They all answered, that they had never so much as heard of it. "Since you all agree," said he, "that you never heard of this pond, and as I am no less astonished than yourselves at the novelty, I am resolved not to return to my palace till I know how it came hither, and why all the fish in it are of four colours." Having thus spoken, he ordered his court to encamp; and immediately his pavilion and the tents of his household were arranged upon the banks of the pond.

When night approached, the sultan retired under his pavilion, and spoke to the grand vizier by himself, thus:— "Vizier, my mind is very uneasy—this pond transported hither, the black that appeared to us in my closet, and the fishes that we heard speak: all these things so much excite my curiosity, that I cannot resist the impatient desire I feel to be satisfied. For this purpose I am meditating a design, which I shall certainly execute: I intend to withdraw alone from the camp; and I order you to keep my absence secret; stay in my pavilion, and to-morrow morning, when the emirs and courtiers come to attend my levee, send them away, telling them that I am somewhat indisposed, and desire to be alone: the following day, say the same, which continue till I return."

The grand vizier endeavoured to divert the sultan from this design: he represented to him the danger to which he might be exposed, and that all his labour would perhaps be useless; but his eloquence had no effect; the sultan was resolved to prepare himself to set off. He accordingly took a habit fit for walking, and, provided with a scimitar, as soon as he perceived that all was quiet in the camp he departed alone.

He directed his steps towards one of the hills, which he mounted without much difficulty: he found the descent still more easy; and, when he reached the plain, walked on till the sun arose. Perceiving before him at a considerable distance, a great building, he rejoiced at the sight, in hopes of being informed there of what he had a desire to know. When he approached, he found it was a magnificent palace, or rather a very strong castle, of black marble, highly polished, and covered with fine steel, as smooth as a glass mirror. Delighted that he had so speedily met with something worthy his curiosity, he stopped before the front of the castle, and considered it with much attention.

He afterwards advanced to the gate, which was divided in the middle, one half being open. Though he was at liberty to enter, he thought it advisable to knock. He knocked at first softly, and waited for some time; but nobody appearing, and supposing he had not been heard, he knocked louder; still no one answered: he knocked again and to no purpose, which surprised him extremely, for he could not think that a castle, in so good repair, was without inhabitants. "If there be nobody in it," said he to himself, "I have nothing to fear; and if there be, I have wherewith to defend myself."

At length he entered, and, when he had reached the porch, he cried, "Is there nobody here to receive a stranger who required some refreshment as he passed by?" He repeated the same two or three times; but, though he spoke very high, he received no answer. This silence increased his astonishment. Proceeding, he came to a very spacious court, and looked on every side to see if he could discover anybody, but perceived no living being. The sultan then entered the great halls, which were hung with silk tapestry; the alcoves and sofas were covered with stuffs of Mecca, and the porches with the richest stuffs of the Indies, mixed with gold and silver. He passed afterwards into an admirable saloon, in the middle of which was a great fountain, with a lion of massy gold at each corner. Water issued from the mouths of the four lions; and this water, as it fell, formed diamonds and pearls, which was no bad accompaniment to a jet of water, that, springing from the middle of the fountain, rose almost as high as the bottom of a cupola, painted after the Arabian manner.

The castle, on three sides, was encompassed by a garden, with flower-pots, water-works, groves, and a thousand other fine things, concurring to embellish it; and what rendered the place altogether admirable was an infinite number of birds, that filled the air with their harmonious notes, and always remained there; nets being spread over the trees and fastened to the palace, to prevent them straying.

The sultan walked a long time, from apartment to apartment, where all appeared very grand and magnificent. Being tired, he sat down in an open closet, which commanded a view of the garden; and while there, reflecting upon what he had already seen and then saw, he suddenly heard the voice of one complaining, accompanied with

lamentable cries. He listened with attention, and distinctly heard these sad words, "Oh, Fortune! who wouldst not suffer me longer to enjoy a happy fate, and hast rendered me the most unforuunate man in the world, forbear to persecute me, and, by a speedy death, put an end to my sorrows! Alas! is it possible that I still live, after so many torments as I have suffered?"

The sultan, affected with these piteous complaints, rose up, and went towards the place whence the sounds proceeded. Stopping at the gate of a great hall, he opened it, and saw a handsome young man, richly habited, seated upon a throne, raised a little above the ground. Melancholy was painted in his looks. The sultan approached, and saluted him; the young man returned the salute by a low inclination of his head, but not rising, he said to the sultan, "My lord, I am very well satisfied that you deserve I should rise to receive you, and render you all possible honour, but I am hindered from so doing by a very strong reason, and, therefore, hope you will not be offended." "My lord," replied the sultan, "I am very much obliged to you for your good opinion. As to the reason of your not rising, whatever be your apology, I heartily accept of it. Drawn hither by your complaints, and affected by your grief, I come to offer you my help; would to God that it depended on me to ease you of your trouble, I would do my utmost to effect it. I flatter myself that you would willingly relate to me the history of your misfortunes; but pray tell me, first, the signification of the pond near the palace, where the fishes are of four colours—what this castle is—how you happened to be here—and why you are alone?"

Instead of answering the question, the young man began to weep bitterly. "Oh, how inconstant is Fortune!" cried he; "she takes pleasure in pulling down those men whom she had raised up. Where are they who enjoy quietly the happiness which they hold of her, and whose days are always calm and serene?"

The sultan, moved with compassion to see him in that condition, prayed him forthwith to relate the cause of his excessive grief. "Alas! my lord," replied the young man, "how is it possible that I should not be afflicted; and why should not my eyes be inexhaustible fountains of tears?" At these words, lifting up his gown, he showed the sultan that he was a man only from the head to the girdle, and that the other half of his body was black marble.

The sultan was strangely surprised when he saw the deplorable state of the young man. "That which you show me," said he, "while it fills me with horror, excites my curiosity: I am impatient to hear your history, which, no doubt, is extraordinary; and I am persuaded that the pond and the fishes make a part of it; therefore I conjure you to tell it me. You will find some consolation in it, since it is certain that unfortunate people experience a sort of ease in relating their distresses." "I will not refuse you this satisfaction," replied the young man; "though I cannot give it to you without renewing my grief. But I caution you beforehand, to prepare your ears, your mind, and even your eyes, for things which surpass all that imagination can conceive the most extraordinary."

THE HISTORY OF THE YOUNG KING OF THE BLACK ISLES.

YOU must know, my lord, that my father, who was called Mahmoud, was king of this country. This is the kingdom of the Black Isles, which takes its name from the four little neighbouring mountains; for those mountains were formerly isles; and the capital, where the king, my father, had his residence, was in the place now occupied by the pond that you have seen. The sequel of my history will inform you of all these changes.

The king, my father, died when he was seventy years of age. I had no sooner succeeded him, than I married; and the lady whom I chose to share the royal dignity with me was my cousin. I had every reason to be satisfied with the marks of affection she gave me, and, for my part, I had conceived so much tenderness for her, that nothing was comparable to our union, which lasted five years; at the end of which time, I perceived that the queen, my cousin, had no more delight in me.

One day, while she was at the bath, after dinner I found myself sleepy, and threw myself upon a sofa; two of her ladies, who were then in my chamber, came and sat down, one at my head, and the other at my feet, with fans in their hands, to moderate the heat, and to hinder the flies from troubling me during my repose. They thought I was asleep, and spoke very low; but I only shut my eyes, and heard every word of their conversation.

One of the ladies said to the other,—"Is not the queen much in the wrong not to love such an amiable prince as ours?" "Certainly," replied the second, "for my part, I cannot comprehend it; and I know not why she goes out every night, and leaves him alone! Is it possible that he does not perceive it?" "Alas!" answered the first, "how should he perceive it? She mixes every evening in his drink the juice of a certain herb, which makes him sleep so soundly all night, that she has time to go where she pleases; and as day begins to appear, she comes and lies down by him again; then she awakens him by some odour which she puts under his nose."

You may judge, my lord, how much I was surprised at this discourse, and with what sentiments it inspired me; yet whatever emotions it occasioned, I had sufficient command over myself to dissemble, and feigned to awake, without having heard one word of it.

The queen returned from the bath; we supped together; and before we went to bed she herself presented me with a cup of water, such as I was accustomed to drink; but, instead of raising it to my mouth, I approached a window that stood open and threw out the water so privately, that she did not observe it, and put the cup into her hands again to persuade her I had drunk it.

We retired to bed together; and soon after, believing that I was asleep, though I was not, she arose with so little precaution, that she said, loud enough for me to hear it distinctly, "Sleep; and may you never wake again!" She dressed herself speedily, and left the chamber.

As soon as the queen, my wife, went out, I got up, dressed in haste, took my scimitar, and followed her so quickly, that I soon heard the sound of her steps before me, and then walked softly after her, for fear of being heard. She passed through several gates, which opened upon her pronouncing some magical words; and the last she opened was that of the garden, which she entered. I stopped at that gate, that she might not observe me as she crossed a grass-plot; and looking as well as the obscurity of the night would permit, I perceived that she entered a little wood, the walks of which were guarded by thick palisadoes. I went thither by another way, and gliding behind the palisadoes of a long alley, I saw her there walking with a man.

I listened attentively to their discourse, and heard her speak thus to her gallant:—"I do not deserve to be upbraided by you for want of diligence. You know very well what hinders me; but if all the tokens of love that I have already given you be not sufficient, I am ready to give you still greater proofs of my sincerity: you need but command me; you know my power. I will, if you desire it, before sunrising, change this great city and this fine palace into frightful ruins, which shall be inhabited only by wolves, owls, and ravens. Would you have me transport all the stones of these walls, so solidly built, beyond Mount Caucasus, and out of the bounds of the habitable world? Speak but the word, and it shall be done."

As the queen finished speaking, her gallant and she reached the end of the walk, and turning to enter another, passed before me. I had already drawn my scimitar, and her gallant being next to me, I struck him in the neck and felled him to the ground. I thought I had killed him, and therefore retired speedily, without discovering myself to the queen, whom I wished to spare, because she was my kinswoman.

In the meantime, the blow I had given her gallant was mortal; but she preserved his life by the power of her enchantments: in such a manner, however, that he could not be said to be either dead or alive. As I crossed the garden to return to the palace, I heard the queen crying lamentably; and, judging by that how much she was grieved. I was pleased that I had spared her life.

When I entered my apartment I again went to bed, and, satisfied with having punished the villain who had injured me, I fell asleep. Next morning, when I awoke, I found the queen lying near me.

I cannot tell whether she slept or not; but I arose without making any noise, and retired to my closet, where I finished dressing myself. I afterwards went and held my council, and, at my return, the queen, clad in mourning, her hair loose, and part of it torn off, presented herself before me, "Sir," said she, "I come to beg your majesty not to be surprised at seeing me in this condition; three afflicting occurrences, news of all which I have just now received, are the cause of my heavy grief, of which you see but faint resemblances." "Alas! what is the news, madam?" I asked. "The death of the queen, my dear mother," answered she; "that of the king, my father, killed in battle; and that of one of my brothers, who has fallen down a precipice."

I was not ill-pleased that she made use of this pretext to hide the true cause of her sorrow; and I thought she did not suspect me of having killed her gallant. "Madam," said I, "so far am I from blaming your grief, that I assure you I bear all the share of it I ought. I should be very much surprised if you were insensible to so great a loss. Continue to weep: your tears are so many proofs of your excellent disposition! but I hope, nevertheless, that time and reason will moderate your distress."

She retired into her apartment, where, giving herself up wholly to sorrow, she went an entire year in mourning and affliction. At the end of that time, she begged permission of me to build a burying-place for herself within the bounds of the palace, where she would remain, she told me, to the end of her days. I agreed to her request, and she erected a stately edifice, with a cupola, as may be seen here, and she called it the Palace of Tears. When it was finished, she caused her gallant to be brought thither, from the place to which she had him conveyed the same night that I wounded him: she had hindered his dying by the drink that she made him take, and which she continued to carry to him herself every day after he was in the Palace of Tears.

Yet, with all her enchantments, she could not cure the wretch; he was not only unable to walk, and to help himself, but had also lost the faculty of speech, and gave no other signs of life than by his looks. Though the queen had only the consolation of seeing him, and saying to him what her foolish passion inspired, she every day made him two long visits: I was very well informed of all this, but feigned ignorance.

One day I went out of curiosity to the Palace of Tears, to see how the princess employed herself, when entering a place where she could not see me, I heard her thus speak to her gallant:—"I am in the highest degree afflicted to see you in this condition; I am as sensible as you are yourself of the tormenting grief you endure; but, dear soul! I always speak to you, and you do not answer me! How long will you be silent? Speak but one word. Alas! the sweetest moments of my life are those I spend here, in partaking of your distress. I cannot live at a distance from you; and would prefer the pleasure of always seeing you, to the empire of the universe."

At these words, which were several times interrupted by her sighs and sobs, I lost all patience; and, discovering myself, I approached her: "Madam," said I, "you have mourned enough; it is time to put an end to a sorrow which dishonours us both: you have too much forgotten what you owe to me and yourself." "Sir," replied she, "if you have any kindness or rather complaisance left for me, I beseech you not to constrain me: allow me to abandon myself to mortal grief; it is impossible for time to lessen it."

When I saw that my discourse, instead of bringing her to her duty, tended only to increase her rage, I ceased speaking and retired. She afterwards continued every day to visit her gallant; and, for two whole years, gave herself up to despair.

I went a second time to the Palace of Tears, while she was there; I again hid myself, and heard her thus address her gallant: "It is now three years since you spoke one word to me!—you return no answer to the tokens of love I give you by my discourse and my groans! Is it insensibility or contempt? O tomb! have you abated that excessive love he had for me? Have you shut those eyes that showed me so much affection, and were all my joy? No, no, I do not believe it. Tell me, rather, by what miracle you became intrusted with the rarest treasure that ever the world possessed."

I confess, my lord, I was enraged at these words; for, in short, this cherished lover, this adored mortal, was not such an one as you would imagine him to have been. He was a black, a native of the Indies. As I said, I was so enraged at this discourse, that I discovered myself suddenly, and addressing the tomb in my turn, "O tomb!" cried I, "why do you not swallow that monster who disgraces nature? or, rather, why do you not ingulf the gallant and his mistress?"

I had scarcely uttered these words, when the queen, who was seated by the black, rose up like a fury. "Ah, cruel man!" said she, "thou art the cause of my grief—think not that I am ignorant. I have dissembled too long: it was thy barbarous hand that reduced the object of my affection to this lamentable state; and you are so hard-hearted as to come and insult a despairing lover!" "Yes," said I, transported with rage, "it was I who chastised that monster according to his desert: I ought to have treated thee in the same manner. I repent now that I did not do it: thou hast abused my goodness too long!" As I spoke these words, I drew out my scimitar, and lifted up my hand to punish her: but she, tranquilly beholding me, said, with a jeering smile, "Moderate thy anger. At the same time, she pronounced words I did not understand; and afterwards added, "By virtue of my enchantments, I command thee immediately to become half marble and half man." Instantly, my lord, I became such as you see me: already a dead man among the living, and a living man among the dead.

After this cruel sorceress, unworthy the name of queen, had thus metamorphosed me, and conveyed me into this hall by another enchantment, she destroyed my capital, which was very flourishing and populous: she abolished the houses, the public places, and markets, and made the pond and desert country of it that you have seen. The fishes of four colours in the ponds were the four sorts of people, of different religions, who inhabited the place: the white were the Mussulmen; the red, the Persians, worshippers of fire: the blue, the Christians; and the yellow, the Jews. The four little hills were the four islands that gave name to this kingdom. I learned all this from the enchantress, who, to add to my affliction, told me with her own mouth those effects of her rage. But this is not all: her revenge was not satisfied with the destruction of my dominions and the metamorphosis of my person; she comes every day, and gives me, over my naked shoulders, a hundred blows with a cat-o'-nine-tails, which covers me

with blood: after which she puts on me a coarse stuff of goats' hair, and throws over it this robe of brocade that you see, not to honour, but to mock me.

*   *   *   *   *

At this part of the discourse the young king could not restrain his tears; and the sultan's heart was so pierced with the relation that he could not speak one word to comfort him. Shortly after, the young king, lifting up his eyes to Heaven, cried out, "Mighty Creator of all things! I submit myself to thy judgments, and the decrees of thy providence: I endure my calamities with patience, since such is thy will; but I hope thine infinite goodness will reward me for it."

The sultan, much moved by the recital of so strange a history, and animated to revenge this unfortunate prince, said to him, "Tell me whither this perfidious sorceress retires, and where her unworthy gallant may be found, who is buried before his death?" "My lord," replied the prince, "her gallant, as I have already told you, is in the Palace of Tears, in a tomb in the form of a dome; and that palace joins to this castle on the side of the gate. As to the enchantress, I cannot precisely tell whither she retires; but every day, at sun-rising, she goes to see her gallant, after having executed her bloody vengeance upon me, as I have related; and you will perceive I am not in a condition to defend myself against so great cruelty. She carries to him the drink with which she has hitherto prevented his dying, and always complains of the silence he has invariably preserved since he was wounded."

"Oh, unfortunate prince!" said the sultan, "you can never be sufficiently bewailed! No person could be more sensibly touched by your condition than I am: never did such an extraordinary misfortune befal any man! and those who publish your history will have the advantage of relating an occurrence that surpasses all that has ever yet been written. There is but one thing wanting—the revenge which is due to you; and I will omit no exertion to accomplish it."

In fine, the sultan, discoursing upon this subject with the young prince, told him who he was, and for what end he entered the castle: and thinking on a means of revenge, he communicated to him his project. They agreed upon the measures they were to adopt for effecting their design, but deferred the execution of it till the next day. In the meantime, the night being far spent, the sultan took some repose; but the poor young prince passed the night, as usual, without rest, having never slept since he was enchanted; though he now conceived hopes of being speedily delivered from his misery.

Next morning, as soon as daylight appeared, the sultan arose; and, in order to execute his design, he hid in a corner his upper garment, which would have been cumbersome to him, and went to the Palace of Tears. He found it enlightened with an infinite number of flambeaux of white wax; and a delicious odour issued from several boxes of fine gold, of admirable workmanship, ranged in excellent order. As soon as he perceived the bed whereon the black lay, he drew his scimitar, and killed the wretch without resistance: he then dragged his corse into the court of the castle, and threw it into a well. After this exploit, he went and lay down on the black's bed, placing his scimitar near him under the counterpane, and remained there to execute what he had designed.

The sorceress very soon arrived. Her first care was to go into the chamber where her husband, the King of the Black Isles, was confined: having stripped him, she proceeded to give him a hundred stripes on his shoulders with unexampled barbarity. The poor prince, making the palace resound with his lamentations, conjured her in the most affecting manner, to pity him; but the cruel woman would not cease till she had struck him a hundred times: "You had no compassion on my lover," said she, "and you are to expect none from me."

When the enchantress had given the king her husband a hundred stripes, she again put on his covering of goat's hair, and his brocade gown over all. She afterwards went to the Palace of Tears; and, as she entered, renewed her cries and lamentations: then approaching the bed, where she thought her gallant still remained, "What cruelty," exclaimed she, "it was to disturb the happiness of so tender and passionate a lover as I am! O thou who reproachest me that I am too inhuman, when I make thee feel the effects of my resentment—cruel prince!—does not thy barbarity surpass my vengeance! Ah, traitor! in attempting the life of the object whom I adore, hast thou not robbed me of mine?—Alas!" continued she, addressing herself to the sultan, thinking she spoke to the black, "my soul! my life! will you always remain silent? Are you resolved to let me die, without giving me so much comfort as to tell me that you still love me? My soul! speak to me, at least one word, I conjure you!"

Then the sultan, feigning to have awakened out of a deep sleep, and counterfeiting the language of the blacks, answered the queen, in a grave tone, "There is no force or power but in God alone, who is almighty." At these words the enchantress, who did not expect a reply, gave a great shout, to signify her excessive joy. "My dear lord!" said she, "do not I deceive myself? Is it certain that I hear you, and that you speak to me?" "Unhappy wretch!" replied the sultan, "art thou worthy that I should answer thy discourse?" "Alas!" said the sorceress, "why do you reproach me thus?" "The cries," replied he, "the groans, and tears of thy husband, whom thou daily treatest with so much indignity and barbarity, hinder me sleeping night and day. I should have been cured long since, and have recovered the faculty of speech, hadst thou disenchanted him. That is the cause of the silence I have preserved, and of which you complain." "Very well," said the enchantress, "to appease you, I am ready to do whatever you command; would you have me restore him to his primitive form?" "Yes," replied the sultan, "hasten to set him at liberty, that I may be no more isturbed with his cries."

The sorceress immediately went out of the Palace of Tears. She took a cup of water, and pronounced words over it which caused it to boil as if it had been on the fire. She afterwards proceeded to the hall where the young king, her husband, was, and threw the water upon him, saying, "If the Creator of all things did form thee as thou art at present, or if he be angry with thee, do not change; but if thou art in that state merely by virtue of my enchantments, resume thy natural shape, and become what thou wast before." She had scarcely spoken these words, when the prince, finding himself restored to his former condition, rose up freely, with inexpressible joy, and returned thanks to God. The enchantess then said to him, "Instantly leave this castle! and never return here on pain of death."

The young king, yielding to necessity, left the sorceress without reply, and retired to a remote place, where he impatiently waited the event of the project which the sultan had so happily begun. Meanwhile the enchantress returned to the Palace of Tears, and supposing that she still spoke to the black, "Dear love!" said she, "I have done what you ordered; let nothing now hinder you giving me that satisfaction of which I have been so long deprived."

The sultan continued to counterfeit the language of the blacks. "That which you have just now performed," said he, quickly, "has little effect towards my cure; you have only eased me of part of my disease; you must cut it up by the roots." "My lovely black," replied she, "what do you mean by the roots?" "Unfortunate woman," said the sultan, "do you not understand that I mean the town and its inhabitants, and the four islands which you have destroyed by your enchantments! Every midnight the fishes raise their heads out of the pond, and cry for vengeance against thee and me. This is the true cause of the delay of my cure. Go! speedily restore things as they were; and, at your return, I will give you my hand, and you shall help me to rise."

The enchantress, filled with hope from these words, cried out, in a transport of joy, "My heart, my soul! you shall soon be restored to your health; for I will instantly execute what you command." Accordingly she went that moment; and, when she arrived at the brink of the pond, she took a little water in her hand, and sprinkling it, she pronounced some words over the fishes and the pond, and the city was immediately re-established. The fishes became men, women, or children; Mahometans, Christians, Persians, or Jews, freemen or slaves, as they were before; every one having recovered his natural form. The houses and shops were very soon filled with their inhabitants, who found all things in the same situation, and in the same order, as before the enchantment. The sultan's numerous retinue, who were encamped in the largest square, were not a little astonished to see themselves, in an instant, in the middle of a large, fine, and well-peopled city.

To return to the enchantress. As soon as she had made this wonderful change, she returned with all diligence to the Palace of Tears that she might reap the fruits of her solicitude. "My dear lord," cried she, as she entered, "I come to rejoice with you on the recovery of your health: I have done all that you required of me, so pray rise, and give me your hand." "Come near," said the sultan, still counterfeiting the language of the blacks. She approached. "You are yet not near enough," continued he; "come nearer." She obeyed. Then he rose up, and, seizing her by the arm so suddenly that she had not time to perceive his features, with a single blow of his scimetar he cut her asunder, one half of her body falling one way, and the other another. This being achieved, he left the carcase upon the place, and, quitting the Palace of Tears, went in search of the young King of the Black Isles, who waited for him with impatience. When he had found him, "Prince," said he, embracing him, "rejoice! you have no more to fear; your cruel enemy is dead."

The young prince returned thanks to the sultan in a manner that showed he was perfectly sensible of the kindness he had experienced; and, in acknowledgment for the important service, wished him a long life, and all happiness. "You may henceforward," said the sultan, "dwell peaceably in your capital; unless you will go to mine, which is so near. I would receive you there with pleasure, and you should experience as much honour and respect as if you were at home." "Potent monarch, to whom I am so much indebted," replied the king; "you think, then, that you are very near your capital?" "Yes," answered the sultan; "I know it: my capital is not at the distance of above four or five hours' journey." "You cannot reach it in less time than a whole year," said the prince. "I do believe, indeed, that you came hither from your capital in the time you mention, because mine was enchanted; but, since the enchantment is taken off, circumstances are changed. However, this shall not hinder me from following you, were it to the utmost corners of the earth. You are my deliverer; and that I may, during my whole life, give you proofs of my gratitude, I will willingly accompany you, and leave my kingdom without regret."

The sultan was exceedingly surprised to learn that he was so far from his dominions, and could scarcely believe it possible. But the young King of the Black Isles so plainly convinced him, that he could no longer doubt it. "It is no matter," replied the sultan; "the trouble that I shall encounter in returning to my own country is sufficiently compensated by the satisfaction I have had in obliging you, and in acquiring you for a son: for, since you will do me the honour to accompany me, and I have no child, I consider you as such; and, from this moment, I appoint you my heir and successor."

This discourse between the sultan and the King of the Black Isles concluded with the most affectionate embraces; after which the young king was wholly employed in making preparations for his journey, which were finished in three weeks, to the great regret of his court and subjects, who, at his recommendation, agreed to receive one of his nearest kindred for king.

At length the sultan and the young prince began their journey, with a hundred camels laden with inestimable riches, from the treasury of the young king, followed by fifty cavaliers on horseback, perfectly well mounted and equipped. They had a very happy journey; and when the sultan, who had sent couriers to give advice of his delay, and of the adventure which had occasioned it, approached his capital, the principal officers he had left there came out to receive him, and to assure him that his long absence had not occasioned any alteration in his empire. The inhabitants also met him in vast crowds, receiving him with great acclamations, and made public rejoicings for several days.

On the morrow after his arrival, the sultan gave to his courtiers a very ample account of the occurrences, which, contrary to his expectation, had detained him so long. He then acquainted them with his adoption of the King of the four Black Isles, who was willing to leave a great kingdom to accompany him and live with him, and, in short as an acknowledgment of their loyalty, he rewarded each of them according to his rank at the court.

As for the fisherman, he being the primary cause of the deliverance of the young prince, the sultan gave him a plentiful estate, which rendered him and his family happy during the rest of their lives.

THE STORY OF THE THREE CALENDERS, SONS OF KINGS, AND OF THE FIVE LADIES OF BAGDAD.

NDER the reign of the Caliph Haroun Alraschid, there resided at Bagdad a porter, who, notwithstanding his mean and laborious business, was a fellow of wit and good humour. One morning, while at a place where he usually plied, with a great basket, waiting for employment, a young handsome lady, covered with a large muslin veil, came to him, and said with a pleasant air, "Hark you, porter! take your basket, and follow me." The porter, charmed with these few words, which were pronounced in so agreeable a manner, took his basket immediately, put it on his head, and followed the lady, exclaiming, "O happy day! O day of good luck!"

The lady presently stopped before a gate that was shut, and knocked. A Christian, with a venerable, long, white beard, opened the gate, and she put money into his hand without speaking a word; but the Christian, who knew what she wanted, went in, and shortly returned, bringing a large jug of excellent wine. "Take this jug," said the lady to the porter, "and put it in your basket." This being done, she commanded him to follow her; and, as she proceeded, the porter continued exclaiming, "O happy day! O day of agreeable surprise and joy!"

The lady next stopped at a fruiterer's, where she bought several sorts of apples, apricots, peaches, quinces, lemons, citrons, oranges, myrtles, sweet-basil, lilies, jessamines, and some other kinds of sweet-scented flowers and plants: she bade the porter place them all inside his basket and follow her. As she passed a butcher's stall, she made him weigh her twenty-five pounds of his best meat, which she ordered the porter to put also in his basket.

At another shop she took capers, terragon, small cucumbers, sea-fennel, and several other articles, all preserved in vinegar; at another she bought pistachios, walnuts, small nuts, kernels, almonds, and such-like fruits; and at another she purchased all sorts of confections.

While the porter was placing these things in his basket, perceiving that it grew full, "My good lady," said he, "you ought to have given me notice that you were going to buy so many articles, and then I would have got a horse, or rather a camel, to carry them : I shall have a great deal above my load, if you buy ever so little more." The lady, laughing at the fellow's pleasantry, ordered him still to follow her.

Entering the house of a druggist, she furnished herself with all the varieties of sweet-scented waters, cloves, musk pepper, ginger, several other Indian spices, and a large piece of ambergris : having now quite filled the porter's basket, she again ordered him to follow her. They walked on till they came to a magnificent house, the front of which was adorned with fine columns, and it had a gate of ivory ; there they stopped, and the lady knocked softly.

While the young lady and the porter were waiting for the opening of the gate, the porter made a thousand reflections. He was astonished that so fine a lady should go abroad to purchase provisions : he was persuaded she could not be a slave, her air was too noble, and he, therefore, concluded she must be a woman of quality. He would willingly have asked some questions to satisfy himself, but just as he was preparing to speak, another lady, who opened the gate, appeared to him so beautiful that he was perfectly surprised, or rather confounded, with her charms, and had nearly let the basket fall, with all its contents, for he had never seen any beauty comparable to hers.

The lady who had brought the porter perceived his disorder, and the occasion of it : she diverted herself with the discovery, and took so much pleasure in examining his countenance, that she forgot the gate was opened. "Pray, sister, come in," said the beautiful lady to her ; "what do you stay for ? Do not you perceive this poor man is so heavily laden that he is scarcely able to stand ?"

When she had entered with the porter, the lady who opened the gate shut it, and all three, after having passed through a very fine porch, proceeded into a spacious court encompassed with an open gallery, which communicated with several apartments on the same floor, astonishingly magnificent. At the farther end of the court was a sofa, richly ornamented, with a throne of amber in the middle, supported by four columns of ebony, enriched with diamonds and pearls of an extraordinary size, and covered with satin, embroidered with Indian gold of admirable workmanship. In the centre of the court was a large fountain, bordered with white marble, and full of very clear water, which fell abundantly into it from the mouth of a lion of gilt bronze.

The porter, heavily laden as he was, could not but admire the magnificence of this house, and the neatness that everywhere appeared ; but his attention was more particularly captivated by a third lady, who to him seemed yet more beautiful than the second, who was sitting upon the throne just mentioned ; but she descended from it as soon as she saw the two former ladies, and advanced directly towards them. He judged, from the respect which the others showed her, that she was the principal, in which he was not deceived. This lady was named Zobeide ; the lady who opened the gate was called Safie ; and Amine was the name of her who had been to purchase the provisions.

"Sisters," said Zobeide to the two ladies, "do not you see that this honest man is sinking under his burden ? Why do not you ease him of it ?" Amine and Safie then took the basket, the one before and the other behind, and Zobeide also assisted. Having together placed it on the ground, they emptied it ; and when they had so done, the beautiful Amine took money, and paid the porter liberally.

The porter, who was very well satisfied with the recompense he had received, ought to have taken up his basket and retired ; but he could not summon resolution. Do what he would, he still found himself arrested by the pleasure of seeing three such beauties, who appeared to him equally charming ; for Amine had now laid aside her veil, and he found her as handsome as either of them.

But what most surprised him was, he saw no man about the house, although great part of the provisions he brought in, as the dry fruits, and the different cakes and confections, were chiefly for those who could drink and make merry.

Zobeide thought at first that the porter stayed only to take breath ; but, perceiving that he remained too long, "What do you wait for ?" said she. "Are you not paid sufficiently ?" Turning to Amine, "Sister," continued she, "give him something more, that he may depart contented." "Madam," replied the porter, "it is not that which detains me : I am more than paid. I am sensible that I behave unmannerly in staying longer than I ought ; but I hope you will have the goodness to pardon my astonishment that there is no man with three ladies of such extraordinary beauty. A company of women without men is as melancholy an association, as a company of men without women." To this discourse he added several very pleasing things, to prove what he advanced ; and he did not forget the Bagdad adage, that "One is never well at a table, except there be four in company" ... and so concluded, that, since there were but three of them, they wanted a fourth.

The ladies laughed at the porter's reasoning ; after which Zobeide said to him gravely, "Friend, you are a little too bold ; but though you do not deserve I should enter into particulars with you, I will willingly tell you, that we are three sisters, who manage our affairs so secretly, that nobody knows anything about them. We have too much reason to be cautious of acquainting indiscreet persons with them ; and a good author that we have read, says, "Keep your secret, and do not reveal it to any person. He who reveals a secret is no longer master of it. If your own breast do not keep your secret, how can you expect that he in whom you confide should keep it ?"

"Ladies," replied the porter, "by your air solely, I judged at first you were persons of extraordinary merit ; and I perceive that I am not mistaken. Though Fortune has not given me wealth enough to raise me above my mean profession, yet I have not failed to cultivate my mind as much as I could by reading books of science and history. Allow me, if you please, to tell you, that I also have read in another author a maxim, which I have always happily practised : 'We do not conceal our secrets,' says he, 'but from such persons as are known to all the world to want discretion, and would abuse the confidence we might place in them ; but we make no scruple to discover them to prudent persons, because we are persuaded they will keep them.' A secret with me is as secure as if it were in a closet, the key of which is lost, and the door well sealed."

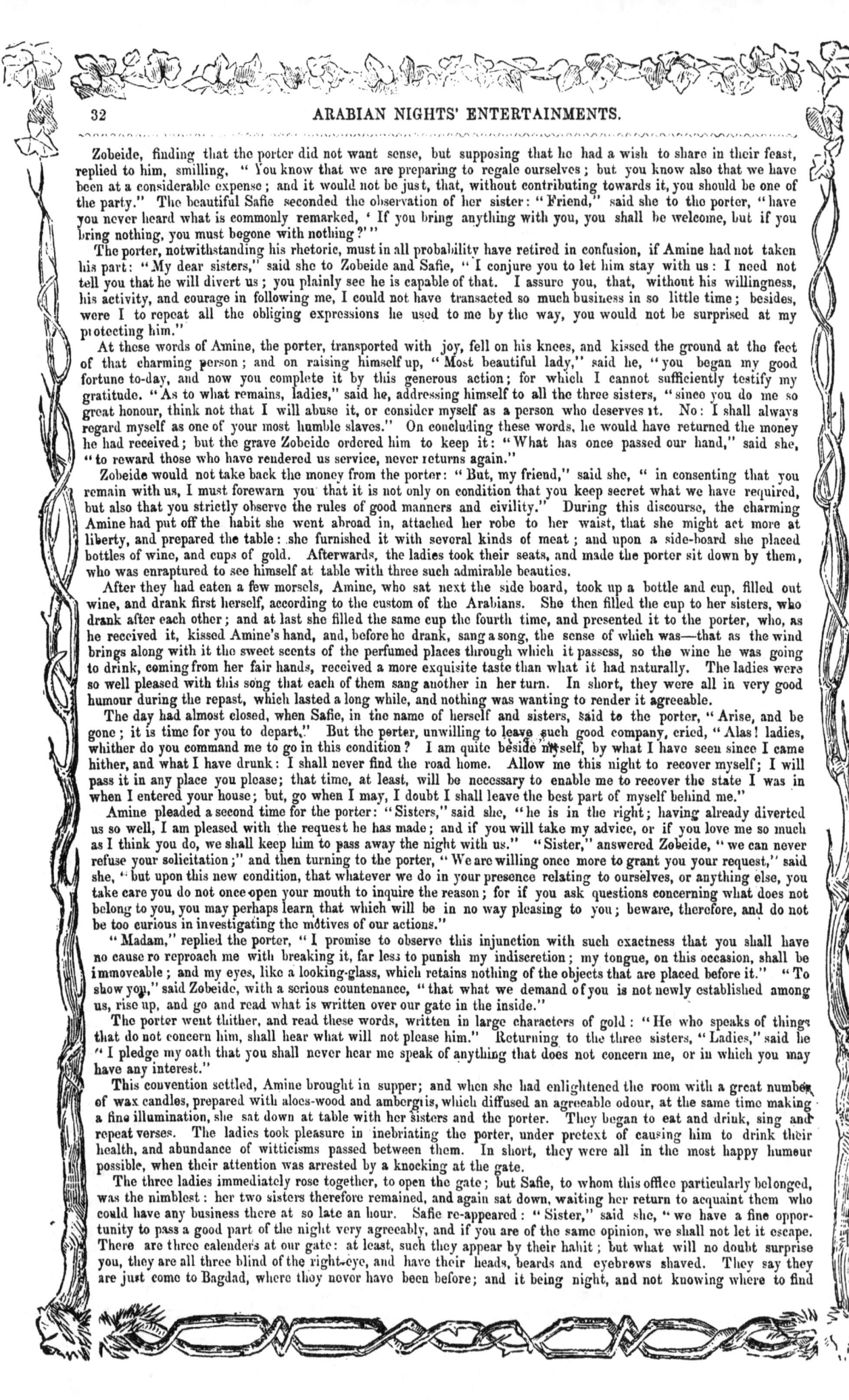

Zobeide, finding that the porter did not want sense, but supposing that he had a wish to share in their feast, replied to him, smiling, " You know that we are preparing to regale ourselves ; but you know also that we have been at a considerable expense ; and it would not be just, that, without contributing towards it, you should be one of the party." The beautiful Safie seconded the observation of her sister : "Friend," said she to the porter, "have you never heard what is commonly remarked, ' If you bring anything with you, you shall be welcome, but if you bring nothing, you must begone with nothing ?' "

The porter, notwithstanding his rhetoric, must in all probability have retired in confusion, if Amine had not taken his part : "My dear sisters," said she to Zobeide and Safie, " I conjure you to let him stay with us : I need not tell you that he will divert us ; you plainly see he is capable of that. I assure you, that, without his willingness, his activity, and courage in following me, I could not have transacted so much business in so little time ; besides, were I to repeat all the obliging expressions he used to me by the way, you would not be surprised at my protecting him."

At these words of Amine, the porter, transported with joy, fell on his knees, and kissed the ground at the feet of that charming person ; and on raising himself up, "Most beautiful lady," said he, "you began my good fortune to-day, and now you complete it by this generous action ; for which I cannot sufficiently testify my gratitude. "As to what remains, ladies," said he, addressing himself to all the three sisters, "since you do me so great honour, think not that I will abuse it, or consider myself as a person who deserves it. No : I shall always regard myself as one of your most humble slaves." On concluding these words, he would have returned the money he had received ; but the grave Zobeide ordered him to keep it : "What has once passed our hand," said she, " to reward those who have rendered us service, never returns again."

Zobeide would not take back the money from the porter : "But, my friend," said she, " in consenting that you remain with us, I must forewarn you that it is not only on condition that you keep secret what we have required, but also that you strictly observe the rules of good manners and civility." During this discourse, the charming Amine had put off the habit she went abroad in, attached her robe to her waist, that she might act more at liberty, and prepared the table : she furnished it with several kinds of meat ; and upon a side-board she placed bottles of wine, and cups of gold. Afterwards, the ladies took their seats, and made the porter sit down by them, who was enraptured to see himself at table with three such admirable beauties.

After they had eaten a few morsels, Amine, who sat next the side board, took up a bottle and cup, filled out wine, and drank first herself, according to the custom of the Arabians. She then filled the cup to her sisters, who drank after each other ; and at last she filled the same cup the fourth time, and presented it to the porter, who, as he received it, kissed Amine's hand, and, before he drank, sang a song, the sense of which was—that as the wind brings along with it the sweet scents of the perfumed places through which it passess, so the wine he was going to drink, coming from her fair hands, received a more exquisite taste than what it had naturally. The ladies were so well pleased with this song that each of them sang another in her turn. In short, they were all in very good humour during the repast, which lasted a long while, and nothing was wanting to render it agreeable.

The day had almost closed, when Safie, in the name of herself and sisters, said to the porter, " Arise, and be gone ; it is time for you to depart." But the porter, unwilling to leave such good company, cried, " Alas! ladies, whither do you command me to go in this condition ? I am quite beside myself, by what I have seen since I came hither, and what I have drunk : I shall never find the road home. Allow me this night to recover myself ; I will pass it in any place you please ; that time, at least, will be necessary to enable me to recover the state I was in when I entered your house ; but, go when I may, I doubt I shall leave the best part of myself behind me."

Amine pleaded a second time for the porter : "Sisters," said she, "he is in the right ; having already diverted us so well, I am pleased with the request he has made ; and if you will take my advice, or if you love me so much as I think you do, we shall keep him to pass away the night with us." "Sister," answered Zobeide, "we can never refuse your solicitation ;" and then turning to the porter, " We are willing once more to grant you your request," said she, " but upon this new condition, that whatever we do in your presence relating to ourselves, or anything else, you take care you do not once open your mouth to inquire the reason ; for if you ask questions concerning what does not belong to you, you may perhaps learn that which will be in no way pleasing to you ; beware, therefore, and do not be too curious in investigating the motives of our actions."

"Madam," replied the porter, " I promise to observe this injunction with such exactness that you shall have no cause ro reproach me with breaking it, far less to punish my indiscretion ; my tongue, on this occasion, shall be immoveable ; and my eyes, like a looking-glass, which retains nothing of the objects that are placed before it." " To show you," said Zobeide, with a serious countenance, "that what we demand of you is not newly established among us, rise up, and go and read what is written over our gate in the inside."

The porter went thither, and read these words, written in large characters of gold : "He who speaks of things that do not concern him, shall hear what will not please him." Returning to the three sisters, "Ladies," said he " I pledge my oath that you shall never hear me speak of anything that does not concern me, or in which you may have any interest."

This convention settled, Amine brought in supper ; and when she had enlightened the room with a great number of wax candles, prepared with aloes-wood and ambergris, which diffused an agreeable odour, at the same time making a fine illumination, she sat down at table with her sisters and the porter. They began to eat and drink, sing and repeat verses. The ladies took pleasure in inebriating the porter, under pretext of causing him to drink their health, and abundance of witticisms passed between them. In short, they were all in the most happy humour possible, when their attention was arrested by a knocking at the gate.

The three ladies immediately rose together, to open the gate ; but Safie, to whom this office particularly belonged, was the nimblest : her two sisters therefore remained, and again sat down, waiting her return to acquaint them who could have any business there at so late an hour. Safie re-appeared : " Sister," said she, " we have a fine oppor-tunity to pass a good part of the night very agreeably, and if you are of the same opinion, we shall not let it escape. There are three calenders at our gate : at least, such they appear by their habit ; but what will no doubt surprise you, they are all three blind of the right-eye, and have their heads, beards and eyebrows shaved. They say they are just come to Bagdad, where they never have been before ; and it being night, and not knowing where to find any lodging, they ventured to knock at our gate; and they pray us, for the love of Heaven, to have the charity to receive them into the house. They care not what place we put them in, provided they be under shelter: they would be satisfied even with a stable. They are young and handsome enough, and seem also to be men of good sense; but I cannot refrain from laughing, when I think of their pleasant and uniform figure." Here Safie, interrupting herself, laughed so heartily, that her two sisters and the porter could not avoid doing the same. " My dear sisters," continued she, " are you willing that they should be received? It is impossible but that, with such persons as I have already described them, we shall finish the day yet better than we began it? They will afford us good diversion, without any expense, for they desire shelter only for this night, and intend to leave us as soon as day appears."

Zobeide and Amine hesitated to grant Safie's request, for a reason with which she herself was well acquainted. But she expressed so great a desire to obtain the favour, that they could no longer refuse. " Go, then," said Zobeide, " and usher them in, but not forget to acquaint them that they must not speak of anything which does not concern them, and to cause them to read what is written over the gate." At these words Safie ran out with joy to admit them; and soon after returned, accompanied by the three calenders.

On entering, they made a profound bow to the ladies who rose up to receive them, telling them, most obligingly, that they were very welcome; that they were glad to have the opportunity of serving them, and of contributing toward their relief from the fatigue of their journey; and, lastly, invited them to be seated.

The magnificence of the place, and the civility they experienced, made the calenders conceive a high idea of their charming landladies; but before they sat down, casting their eyes by chance upon the porter, whom they saw was habited similarly to other calenders with whom they were engaged in controversy, respecting several points of discipline, as they shaved neither their beards nor eye brows, one of them said, " Look here ! I believe we have met one of our revolted Arabian brethren."

The porter, half asleep, and his head being pretty warm with the wine he had drunk, was affronted at these words; and, without stirring from his place, replied fiercely, " Sit you down, and do not interfere with what does not concern you. Have you not read the inscription over the gate? Do not pretend to make people live after your fashion, but follow ours." " Honest man !" said the calender, who had spoken, " do not put yourself in a passion : we should be very sorry to give you the least occasion; on the contrary, we are ready to receive your commands." Upon which, to prevent quarrelling, the ladies interposed, and pacified them.

When the calenders were seated at table, the ladies served them with meat; and Safie, who particularly enjoyed their company, did not let them want for liquor.

After the calenders had eaten and drunk as much as they chose, they signified to the ladies that they should be happy to entertain them with a concert of music, if they had any instruments in the house, and would cause them to be brought. They joyfully accepted the offer; and the fair Safie rose to fetch them : she returned again in a moment, and presented them with a flute of her own country fashion, another of the Persian make, and a tabor. Each man took an instrument, and all the three together began to play an air. The ladies, who knew a merry song suited to the tune, joined the concert with their voices; but the words of the song made them repeatedly stop, and indulge in excessive laughter.

At the height of this diversion, and when the company were in the midst of their jollity, somebody knocked at the gate. Safie left off singing, and went to see who it was——

But, sir, said Scheherazade to the sultan, it is proper your majesty should know what occasioned this knocking so late at the ladies' house; the reason was this :—The caliph Haroun Alraschid was accustomed to walk abroad very often by night, in disguise, that he might himself see that all was tranquil in the city, and that no disorder was committed.

This night the caliph had proceeded rather early on his rambles, accompanied by Giafar, his grand vizier, and Mesrour, the chief of the eunuchs of his palace, all disguised as merchants; and passing through the street where the three ladies dwelt, he heard the sound of music, and great bursts of laughter; on which he said to the vizier, " Go, and knock at the door of that house, where so much noise is made; I will enter, and learn the cause." The vizier in vain represented that it was only some women merry-making; that it appeared their heads were warm with wine; and that he ought not to expose himself to insult from them; besides that, it was not yet an unlawful hour, and therefore, it would not be right to disturb their mirth. " No matter," said the caliph, " I command you to knock them in !"——It was, then, the grand vizier Giafar that knocked at the ladies' door, by the caliph's order, who would not be known.

—— Safie opened the gate, and the vizier perceived by the light of the taper which she held in her hand, that she was an incomparable beauty. He acted his part very well; and with a very low bow, and respectful behaviour, said' " Madam, we are three merchants of Moussol, and arrived about ten days since, with rich merchandise, which we have deposited in a warehouse at a khan [inn], where we have taken lodging. We have been to-day with a merchant of this city, who invited us to a treat at his house; and the wine having put us in humour, he sent for a company of dancers. Night being arrived, and the music and dancers making a great noise, the watch, passing by, caused the gate to be opened, and arrested some of the company; but we had the good fortune to escape, by getting over a wall. Now," continued the vizier, " being strangers, and somewhat overcome with wine, we were afraid of meeting another, and perhaps the same, watch, before we could reach our khan, which is a good way hence. Besides, should we get there, the gates will be shut, and not opened till morning. Therefore, madam, hearing, as we passed, the sound of music, we judged you were not yet going to rest, and took the liberty of knocking at your gate, to beg the favour of a lodging in the house till morning : and, if you think us worthy of your good company, we will endeavour to contribute to your diversion what lies in our power, as some reparation for the disturbance we have occasioned; if not, we only beg permission to stay this night under your porch."

During Giafar's discourse, fair Safie had time to observe the vizier and his two companions, whom he said were merchants, like himself; and she rightly concluded, from their countenances, that they were not common persons : she told them that she was not mistress of the house; but if they would wait a minute's patience, she would return with an answer.

Safie then went to make her report to her sisters, who considered for some time how to determine; but being naturally beneficent, and having already granted the same favour to the three calenders, they at length consented to admit them.

The caliph, his grand vizier, and the chief of the eunuchs, being introduced by the fair Safie, very courteously saluted the ladies and the calenders. The ladies returned their civilities, supposing them to be merchants; and Zobeide, as the principal, said to them, with a grave and serious countenance, which was natural to her, " You are welcome; but, before I proceed farther, I trust you will not be displeased if we desire one favour of you?" " Alas !" exclaimed the vizier, " what favour? we can refuse nothing to such fair ladies." Zobeide replied, " It is that you have only eyes, and no tongue : that you put no questions respecting anything you may happen to see; nor speak of what does not concern you, lest you hear more than will be agreeable." " Madam," answered the vizier, " you shall be obeyed. We are not censorious, nor impertinently curious; it is sufficient for us to notice that which concerns us, without interfering with matters that do not belong to us." At these words they all sat down, and the company uniting, they drank to the health of the new comers.

While Giafar entertained the ladies with discourse, the caliph could not avoid admiring their extraordinary beauty, graceful behaviour, pleasant humour, and ready wit. On the other hand, nothing appeared to him more surprising than the calenders being all three blind of the right eye. He would gladly have been informed of this singularity; but the conditions so lately imposed upon himself and his companions hindered him speaking. This, with the richness and well-judged arrangement of the furniture and neatness of the house, made him suppose it must be some enchanted palace. Their entertainment having fallen upon divertisements and different ways of rejoicing, the calenders arose and danced after their mode, which augmented the good opinion the ladies had conceived of them, and procured them the esteem of the caliph and his companions.

When the three calenders had finished their dance, Zobeide got up, and, taking Amine by the hand, "Pray, sister," said she, "rise, for the company will not be offended at our freedom; their presence need not hinder the performance of our accustomed duty." Amine, who understood her sister's meaning, quitted her seat, and carried away the dishes, the table, the flasks, and cups, together with the instruments on which the calenders had played.

Safie was not idle; she swept the room, arranged everything again in its proper place, snuffed the candles, and put fresh aloe-wood and ambergris to them: she then prayed the three calenders to sit down upon the sofa on one side, and the caliph with his companions, on the other. As to the porter, she said to him, "Get up, and prepare yourself to assist in what we were going to do; a man like you, who is one of the family, ought not to be inactive." The porter, being somewhat recovered from his wine, arose immediately; and having fastened the sleeve of his gown to his belt, answered, "Here am I, ready to obey your commands." "That is very well," replied Safie; "stay till you are spoken to; you shall not be long unemployed." A short time after, Amine entered with a chair, which she placed in the middle of the room; and then went to a closet, which having opened, she beckoned to the porter. "Come hither," said she, "and help me." The porter obeyed: and going into the closet with her, he returned immediately, leading two black bitches: each of them had a collar, to which was attached a chain that he held: they looked as if they had been severely whipped with rods. He advanced with them into the middle of the room.

Then Zobeide rising from her seat between the calenders and the caliph, walked very gravely towards the porter: "Come," said she, with a heavy sigh; "let us perform our duty." After tucking up her sleeves to the elbows, and receiving a rod from Safie, "Porter," said she, "deliver one of the bitches to my sister Amine, and come to me with the other."

The porter did as he was commanded; and as he approached Zobeide, the bitch that he held began to cry, and turning toward Zobeide, held up her head in a suppliant manner; but Zobeide, without regarding the sad countenance of the bitch, which would have excited pity, nor her cries, that resounded through the house, whipped her with the rod till she was out of breath; when, her strength being exhausted, she threw down the rod, and taking the chain from the porter, lifted up the bitch by the paws, and looking upon her with a piteous air, they both wept; after which, Zobeide, with her handkerchief, wiped the tears from the bitch's eyes, kissed her, and returned the chain to the porter, bidding him lead her to the place whence he took her, and bring the other. The porter accordingly led back the whipped bitch to the closet: and receiving the other from Amine, presented her to Zobeide; who, desiring him to hold her as he did the first, took up the rod, and treated her after the same manner: when she had wept over her, dried her eyes, and kissed her, she returned her to the porter; but the lovely Amine spared him the trouble of leading her back to the closet, by doing it herself.

In the meantime, the three calenders, and the caliph with his companions, were extremely surprised at this execution; and could not comprehend why Zobeide, after having so furiously whipped those two bitches, which, by the Mussulman religion, are considered unclean animals, should cry with them, wipe off their tears, and kiss them. They muttered among themselves; and the caliph, who, being more impatient than the rest, was extremely anxious to be informed of the cause of an action that appeared so extraordinary, could not forbear making signs to the vizier to ask the question; but the vizier turned his head another way; till being pressed by repeated signs, he answered by others, that it was not yet time to satisfy the caliph's curiosity.

Zobeide remained some time in the middle of the room, where she had whipped the two bitches, to recover herself from the fatigue. "Dear sister," said the fair Safie to her, "will you be pleased now to return to your place, that I also may perform my part?" "Yes, sister," replied Zobeide; who then went and sat down upon the sofa, having the caliph, Giafar, and Mesrour on her right hand; and the three calenders, with the porter, on her left.

After Zobeide had retaken her place, the whole company preserved silence for some time: at last, Safie, who was seated on a chair in the middle of the room, spoke to her sister Amine: "Dear sister," said she, "rise up, I conjure you; you fully comprehend what I would say." Amine rose, and going into another closet near that whence the bitches were brought, she returned with a case covered with yellow satin, richly embroidered with gold and green silk. Approaching Safie, she opened the case, and took out a lute, which she presented to her. After some time employed in tuning it, Safie began to play, and, accompanying it with her voice, she sang a song on the torments of absence with so much sweetness, that it charmed the caliph and all the company. When she had finished it, as she sang with a great deal of passion and action united, she said to the lovely Amine, "Pray take it, sister; for I can do no more: my voice fails me: oblige the company by playing and singing in my room." "Very willingly," replied Amine, who, taking the lute from her sister Safie, sat down in her place.

Amine, after preluding a short time, to see if the instrument was in tune, played and sang, almost as long, on the same subject, but with such vehemency, and she was so much affected, or rather transported, by the words of the song, that her strength failed her as she concluded it.

Zobeide, wishing to testify her satisfaction, said, "Sister, you have performed wonders; and it is very clear that you feel the grief which you have so naturally expressed." Amine was prevented answering this compliment; her heart was so sensibly touched at the moment, that she thought only of obtaining air, and incautiously exposed a neck and breast, not white, as might have been expected of such a lady as Amine, but, on the contrary, black and full of scars, which induced a kind of horror in the spectators. Nevertheless, what she had done gave her no relief, and she fainted.

While Zobeide and Safie ran to help their sister, one of the calenders could not forbear saying, "We had better have slept in the streets than have come hither, had we been aware of seeing such spectacles." The caliph, who heard this observation, approached him and the other calenders, and asked what might be the meaning of all they saw. "Sir," answered they, "we know no more than you do." "What!" said the caliph, "are not you one of

the family? Cannot you resolve us concerning the two black bitches, and the lady who has fainted away, and has been so basely abused?" "Sir," replied the calenders, "this is the first time that ever we were in the house; and we came in but a few minutes before you."

This augmented the caliph's astonishment. "Perhaps," said he, "that other man who is with you may know something of the matter." One of the calenders made a sign for the porter to approach, and asked him whether he knew why those two black bitches had been whipped, and why Amine's bosom was so scarred. "Sir," said the porter, "I can swear by Heaven, that if you know nothing of all this, we each know as much as the other. It is true I live in the city, but I never was in this house till now; and, if you are surprised to see me here, I am as much so to find myself in your company. What increases my wonder," continued he, "is, that I have not seen any man with these ladies."

The caliph and his company, as well as the calenders, had supposed the porter was one of the family, and doubted not that he could inform them of what they desired to know. Nevertheless, the caliph resolved to satisfy his curiosity cost what it might. "Look ye," said he to the rest, "we are here seven men, and have but three women to deal with; let us oblige them to explain what we wish to know; if they refuse to do so by fair means, we are in a condition to force them."

The grand vizier, Giafar, opposed this advice, and explained to the caliph what might be the consequence of such a proceeding; but, without discovering the prince to the calenders, he still addressed him as if he had been a merchant: "Sir," said he, "consider, I pray you, that our reputation is at stake; you know on what condition only these ladies were willing to receive us, and that we accepted it. What will they say of us, if we infringe it? We shall be still more to blame if any mischief befal us in consequence; for it is not likely that they would demand such a promise, if they did not know themselves capable of making us repent the violation of it."

Here the vizier took the caliph aside, and whispered to him thus:—"Sir, the night will soon be at an end; if your majesty will but be pleased to have so much patience, I will return here to-morrow morning, and take these ladies, and carry them before your throne, when you may learn all that you desire to know." Though this advice was very judicious, the caliph rejected it, and bade the vizier be silent, declaring he was resolved not to wait, but would have satisfaction immediately.

The greatest difficulty was to determine who should carry the message. The caliph endeavoured to prevail on the calenders to speak first; but they excused themselves: at length they all agreed that the porter should be the man. As they were consulting how to word the fatal question, Zobeide, quitting her sister Amine, who had recovered from her swoon, approached them. Having overheard them speaking high, and with some warmth, "Gentlemen," said she, "what is the subject of your discourse? of what are you disputing?"

The porter then spoke: "Madam," said he, "these gentlemen pray you to explain, why you wept over your two bitches after having whipped them so severely; and what caused the bosom of the lady who lately fainted to be so full of scars? This is, madam, what I am ordered to ask in their name."

At these words, Zobeide assumed a stern countenance; and turning toward the caliph and the rest of the company, "Is it true, gentlemen," said she, "that you have ordered him to ask me this question?" All of them, except Giafar, who spoke not a word, answered, "Yes." On which she addressed them in a tone which sufficiently indicated her resentment: "Before we granted you the favour that you demanded," said she, "of being received into our house, and to prevent all occasion of trouble from you, because we are alone, we required a compliance with the condition, that you should not speak of anything which did not concern you, lest you might hear what would not please you; and yet, after we have received and entertained you as well as we possibly could, you make no scruple to break your promise! It is true, our easy temper has occasioned this behaviour, but that shall not excuse you, for your proceedings are not honest." As she spoke these words, she gave three loud knocks with her foot, and clapping her hands as often together, cried, "Come quickly!" Immediately a door flew open, and seven strong robust black slaves, with scimitars in their hands, rushed in; each seized a man, threw him on the ground, dragged him into the middle of the room, and prepared to cut off his head.

The terror of the caliph may be easily conceived: he then too late repented that he had not taken his vizier's advice. In the meantime, this unhappy prince, Giafar, Mesrour, the porter, and the calenders were about losing their lives by their indiscreet curiosity. But before they would strike the fatal blow, one of the slaves said to Zobeide and her sisters, "High, mighty, and adorable mistresses, do you command us to cut their throats?" "Stay," replied Zobeide; "I must first examine them." "Madam!" interrupted the affrighted porter, "in the name of Heaven, do not have me killed for the crime of others! I am innocent; they are to blame. Alas!" continued he, crying, "how pleasantly we passed our time! These blind calenders are the cause of this misfortune; there is no town in the world but what goes to ruin when these inauspicious fellows enter. Madam, I beg you not to destroy the innocent with the guilty; and consider, that it is more glorious to pardon such a wretch as me, deprived of all succour, than to overwhelm him with your power, and sacrifice him to your resentment."

Zobeide, notwithstanding her anger, could not avoid laughing within herself at the porter's lamentation; but, without replying to him, she spoke a second time to the rest:—"Answer me," said she, "and tell me who you are; otherwise you shall not live a moment longer. I cannot believe you to be honest men, nor persons of authority or distinction in your own countries; for, if you were, you would have been more delicate and more respectful to us."

The caliph, who was naturally impetuous, was infinitely more irritated than his companions, to find his life depending upon the command of a lady, justly incensed; but he began to entertain some hopes, when he saw she wished to know who they all were; for he imagined she would not take away his life, if she were informed of his rank and consequence. He, therefore, spoke in a low voice to the vizier, who was near him, to declare speedily who he was; but the vizier, more prudent, willing to save his master's honour, and not to render public the affront he had brought upon himself, answered, "We experience what we deserve." And when, in obedience to the caliph, he would have spoken, Zobeide did not give him time. She had addressed herself to the calenders; and remarking that they were all three blind of one eye, she asked if they were brothers. One of them answered, "No, madam, no otherwise than in quality of calenders; that is to say, in observing the same mode of life." "Were you born blind of the right eye?" said she, speaking to one in particular. "No, madam," replied he, "I lost my eye in so surprising an adventure, that, were it in writing, it would be instructive to everybody. After that misfortune, I shaved my beard and eyebrows, and took the habit of a calender, which I now wear."

Zobeide asked the other two calenders the same question, and received the same answer; but the last who spoke, added, "Madam, to convince you that we are no common persons, and that you may treat us with some consideration, be pleased to understand that we are all three sons of kings. Though we never met together till this evening, yet we have had sufficient time to make that known to each other; and I assure you that the kings from whom we derive our being, made some noise in the world."

At this discourse, Zobeide moderated her anger, and said to the slaves, "Give them their liberty awhile; but remain here. To

those who tell us their history, and the occasion of their coming, do no hurt; let them go where they please; but do not spare those who refuse to afford us that satisfaction."

The three calenders, the caliph, the grand vizier Giafar, the eunuch Mesrour, and the porter were all seated upon a foot-carpet, in the middle of the hall, in the presence of the three ladies, who were upon a sofa, and the slaves stood ready to do whatever their mistresses should command.

＊   ＊   ＊   ＊   ＊

The porter, understanding that he might avert the danger, by telling his history, first spoke. "Madam," said he, "you know my history already, and the occasion of my coming to your house; so that what I have to say will be very short. My lady, your sister there, called me this morning at the place where, as a porter, I plied for employment, that I might earn my bread. I followed her to a vintner's; then to a herb-shop; then to a seller of oranges, lemons, and citrons; then to a dealer in almonds, walnuts, filberts, and other such fruits; next to a confectioner's; and then to a druggist's: from the druggist's, with my basket upon my head, as full as I was able to carry it, I came hither, where you had the goodness to suffer me to continue till now—a favour I shall never forget. This, madam, is my history."

When the porter had concluded, Zobeide said to him, " Save yourself; begone! let us see you no more here." " Madam," returned the porter, "I beg you to let me stay; it would not be just, after the rest have had the pleasure of hearing my history, that I should not also have the satisfaction to hear theirs." Having thus spoken, he seated himself at the end of the sofa, overjoyed in having escaped the peril that so much alarmed him. One of the three calenders, then, directing his discourse to Zobeide, as the principal of the three ladies, and the person who commanded him to speak, began his history, as follows.

THE HISTORY OF THE FIRST CALENDER, A KING'S SON.

MADAM, in order to acquaint you how I lost my right eye, and why I was obliged to assume the habit of a calender, I will first inform you that I was born a king's son. The king my father had a brother, who reigned, as he did, over a neighbouring state. This brother had two children, a prince and a princess; and the prince and I were nearly of an age.

When I had learned all my exercises, and the king my father had granted me a liberty suited to my dignity, I went regularly every year to see the king my uncle, at whose court I remained during a month or eight weeks, and then I returned to my father's. These several journeys were the occasion of a very firm and particular friendship being contracted between the prince my cousin and myself. The last time I saw him, he received me with still greater demonstrations of tenderness than at any former visit; and one day, resolving to give me a treat, he made great great preparations for that purpose. We continued a long while at table; and after we had both supped very well, " Cousin," said he, "you will scarcely be able to guess how I have been engaged since your last journey. It is now a year since your departure hence, during which period I have had a great many workmen employed in perfecting a design that I have conceived. I have caused an edifice to be erected, which is finished, and will soon be inhabited. You will not be displeased to see it. But first you must promise me, upon oath, that you will keep my secret, and be faithful: these two conditions I am obliged to exact."

The love and familiarity that existed between us would not permit me to refuse him anything. I very readily took the oath he required; and then he said to me, " Stay here till I return; I will be with you in a moment." Accordingly, he soon appeared again, leading in a lady of singular beauty, and magnificently apparelled. He did not inform me who she was; neither did I think it would be polite in me to inquire. We reseated ourselves, with the lady, at table; where we continued some time longer, discoursing on indifferent subjects, and drinking bumpers to the health of each other. At length the prince said, " Cousin, we have no time to lose; therefore pray oblige me by taking this lady with you, and conducting her to such a place, where you will see a tomb, newly built, in the form of a dome. You will easily know it: the gate is open; go in there together, and remain till I come. I shall join you directly."

True to my oath, I made no inquiry, but presenting my hand to the lady, agreeably to the directions which the prince my cousin had given me, I conducted her safely to the place, by the light of the moon, without the least difficulty. We had scarcely reached the tomb, when we saw the prince following us, carrying a little pitcher full of water, a hatchet, and a small bag of plaster.

The hatchet served him to break down the empty sepulchre in the middle of the tomb; he then took away the stones one after another, and arranged them in a corner. When these were removed, he dug up the ground, and I saw a trap door below the sepulchre, which he lifted up, and underneath I perceived the head of a staircase, leading into a vault. Then my cousin, speaking to the lady, said, "Madam, it is by this way that we are to go to the place I told you of." The lady, at these words, advanced to the staircase, and descended, and the prince began to follow after; but first turning to me, " My dear cousin," said he, " I am infinitely obliged to you for the trouble you have taken; I thank you: adieu!" " Dear cousin," cried I, "what is the meaning of this?" " Be content," he replied " you can return by the same road you came."

I could get nothing further from my cousin, but was obliged to take leave of him. As I returned to my uncle's palace, the vapours of the wine rose into my head; however, I gained my apartment, and retired to sleep. Next morning, when I awoke, I began to reflect upon what had befallen me the night before; and, after recollecting all the circumstances of so singular an adventure, it appeared to me only a dream. Full of these thoughts, I sent to know if the prince my cousin was prepared to receive a visit, but when information was brought back that he had not slept at home that night, that they knew not what was become of him, and were in much trouble about it, I rightly judged that the strange event of the tomb was but too true. I was sensibly afflicted; and, stealing away privately from my people, went to the public burying-place, where there was a vast number of tombs similar to that which I had seen. I spent the day in considering them, one after another; but could not find that which I sought; and I continued during four days the same fruitless research.

All this time the king my uncle was absent: he had been hunting for several days. I became weary of staying for him; and having prayed his ministers to make my apology to him at his return, I left his palace, and set out towards my father's court, from which I had never before been so long absent. I left the ministers of the king my uncle in great trouble respecting the prince my cousin; but because of the oath I had made to keep his secret, I dared not lessen their inquietude by communicating to the many thing of what I had seen or knew.

I arrived at my father's capital, the usual place of his residence; and, contrary to custom, found a strong guard at the gate of the palace, who surrounded me as I entered. I demanded the reason; when the officer replied, "Prince, the army has proclaimed the grand vizier as successor to your father, who is dead; and I take you prisoner in the name of the new king." At these words, the guards seized me, and carried me before the tyrant. Judge, madam, how much I was surprised and distressed.

This rebel vizier had long entertained a mortal hatred against me; and this was the occasion:—When I was a stripling, I loved to shoot with a cross-bow. Diverting myself one day, upon the terrace of the palace with my bow, a bird happened to pass; I shot, but missed him, and the arrow unfortunately hit the vizier, who was taking the air upon the terrace of his own house, and put out one of his eyes. As soon as I was apprised of this misfortune, I not only sent my excuse to him, but made it in person; yet he always harboured resentment, and, as opportunity offered, made me sensible of it. Now, having me in his power, he expressed his rancour in the most barbarous manner; for he came to me like a madman, the instant he saw me, and thrusting his fingers into my right eye, pulled it out himself. This is the way in which I became blind with one eye.

But this was not the end of the usurper's cruelty: he had me shut up in a box, and commanded the executioner to carry me, in this state, far from the palace, to cut off my head, and leave me to be devoured by the birds of prey. The executioner, with another man, on horseback, carried me, thus confined, into the country, to execute the usurper's barbarous sentence; but, by my prayers and tears, I moved the executioner's compassion. "Go," said he; "speedily quit the kingdom, and be careful never to return; otherwise you will certainly meet with your own ruin, and be the cause of mine." I thanked him for his humanity; and, as soon as I was left alone, comforted myself for the loss of my eye, by considering that I had very narrowly escaped a much greater misfortune.

In the state I was, I could not travel far at a time. I retired to remote places during the day, and proceeded as far by night as my strength would permit. At length I arrived in the dominions of the king my uncle, and reached his capital.

I gave him a long detail of the tragical cause of my return, and of the sad condition he saw me in. "Alas!" cried he, "was it not enough for me to have lost my son, but must I have also news of the death of a brother whom I loved so dearly, and at the same time see you reduced to this deplorable state!" He represented to me his inquietude at not gaining any intelligence of his son, notwithstanding his exertions, and the strict search that had been made. The unhappy father burst into tears as he spoke, and was so much afflicted, that, although I had sworn to the prince to preserve his secret, it was impossible for me to keep it any longer; so I told the king his father all that I knew.

The king listened to me with a degree of comfort; and when I had finished, "Nephew," said he, "what you tell me gives me some hope. I know that my son ordered that tomb to be built; and I can guess nearly at what place: with the idea of it you still retain, I flatter myself we shall find it. But since he ordered it to be built privately, and you took an oath to keep his secret, I am of opinion that, to avoid an alarm, we only ought to go in quest of it."

But he had another reason for wishing to avoid publicity, which he did not then mention, and an important reason it was, as the sequel of my discourse will show.

We disguised ourselves, and went out at a door of the garden which opened into the field; and happily soon discovered what we sought. I remembered the tomb; and was so much the more rejoiced, because I had before searched for it a long time in vain. We entered, and found the iron trap pulled down upon the entrance of the staircase: we had much difficulty to raise it, as the prince had fastened it on the inside with the plaster and water formerly mentioned; but at last we forced it up.

The king my uncle descended first; I followed; and we went down about fifty steps. When we reached the foot of the stairs, we found a sort of ante-chamber full of a thick smoke, of an ill scent, by which the lamp, that gave a very faint light, was obscured. From this ante-chamber we proceeded into another, very large, supported by great columns, and lighted by several branched candlesticks. There was a cistern in the middle, and eatables of several kinds arranged on one side of it; but we were very much surprised at not seeing any person. Before us was a high sofa, which we mounted by several steps; and over this appeared a very large bed, with the curtains drawn close. The king went up, and opening the curtains, perceived the prince his son, and the lady, in bed together, but burnt and changed to a coal, as if they had been thrown into a great fire, and taken out before they were consumed.

But what surprised me most of all, though this spectacle filled me with horror, the king my uncle, instead of testifying sorrow at seeing the prince his son in that dreadful state, spat on his face, and said to him, with an air of indignation, "Such is the punishment of the world; but that of the other will last to eternity;" and not content with having pronounced these words, he took off his sandal, with which he gave his son a violent blow on the cheek.

I cannot express my astonishment, when I saw the king my uncle thus abuse the prince his son, after he was dead. "Sir," said I, "whatever grief this dismal sight may be capable of impressing me with, I am forced to suspend it, to ask your majesty what crime the prince my cousin has committed, that his corse should deserve this treatment?" "Nephew," replied the king, "I must tell you, that my son—unworthy of the name—loved his sister from his infancy, and she had an equal regard for him. I did not oppose their growing affection, because I did not foresee the pernicious consequence; and who could have foreseen it? This tenderness increased with their years, and reached such a point, that I dreaded the result. At last I applied the remedies that were in my power. I not only gave my son a severe reprimand in private, explaining to him the foulness of the passion he was entertaining and the eternal disgrace he would bring upon my family if he persisted in sentiments so criminal. I also made the same representations to my daughter, and besides, shut her up so closely, that she could have no conversation with her brother. But the unfortunate girl had swallowed too deeply of the poison; and all the obstacles which, by my prudence, I could devise, served only the more to inflame their love.

"My son, persuaded of his sister's constancy, on pretence of building a tomb, caused this subterraneous habitation to be made, in the hope of finding an opportunity to possess himself of the culpable object of his flame, and to bring her hither. He chose the time of my absence to enter by force into the place of his sister's confinement;—that is a circumstance which my honour would not suffer me to make public. After so damnable an action, he came and inclosed himself, with her, in this place, which he has supplied, as you see, with all sorts of provisions, that he might for a long time enjoy his detestable pleasures, which ought to be a subject of horror to all the world: but God, who would not suffer such an abomination, has justly punished them both."——At these words he wept, and I joined my tears with his.

After the lapse of some time, he cast his eyes upon me: "Dear nephew," cried he, embracing me, "if I have lost an unworthy son, I shall happily find in you what will better supply the place he occupied." Making some further reflections on the sad end of the prince and the princess his daughter, we again wept.

Returning up the same stairs, we at length departed from this dismal place. We replaced the trap-door, and covered it with earth and the materials with which the tomb had been built, to hide, as much as possible, so terrible an effect of the wrath of God.

We had not been long at the palace, which we reached unperceived, when we heard a confused noise of trumpets, drums, and other warlike instruments. A thick cloud of dust, which almost darkened the air, soon announced the arrival of a formidable army. It proved to be that of the same vizier who had dethroned my father, and usurped his throne; and who, with a vast number of troops, was come to possess himself of that of the king my uncle also.

The king, who then had only his usual guards about him, could not resist so many enemies. They invested the city; and, the gates being opened to them without resistance, they very soon became masters of it, and broke into the palace, where my uncle was, who defended himself till he was killed, after having sold his life at a high rate. For my part, I fought some time; but seeing we must submit to superior force, I considered how to retreat in safety: I had the good fortune to escape through bye-ways, and got to the house of one of the king's servants, on whose fidelity I could depend.

Surrounded with sorrows, and persecuted by Fortune, I had recourse to a stratagem, which was the only means left me to save my life:—I caused my beard and eyebrows to be shaved, and putting on a calender's habit, I passed without being recognised by any person, out of the city: afterwards, by taking the bye-roads, I found it easy to quit my uncle's kingdom.

I avoided passing through towns, until I had entered the empire of the mighty governor of the Mussulmen, the glorious and renowned caliph Haroun Alraschid, when I judged myself out of danger; and, considering what I should do, I resolved to come to Bagdad, intending to throw myself at the feet of this great monarch, whose generosity is everywhere applauded." I shall excite his compassion," said I to myself, "by the relation of my surprising history; without doubt, he will pity an unfortunate prince, and not suffer me vainly to implore his assistance."

In short, after a journey of several months, I arrived yesterday at the gate of this city, into which I entered about the dusk of the evening; and stopping a moment to revive my spirits, and to consider which way I should direct my steps, this calender, you see next to me, came up; he saluted me, and I returned the salute. "You appear," said I "to be a stranger, as I am." "You are not mistaken," he replied. He had no sooner answered, than this third calender, you see, approached. He saluted us, and told us that he also was a stranger, just arrived in Bagdad· As brethren, we then joined together, resolving not to separate.

Meanwhile it was late, and we knew not where to seek a lodging in the city, in which we had no acquaintance, nor had ever been before. But good fortune having conducted us to your gate, we made bold to knock; when you received us with so much charity and goodness, that we are incapable of returning you suitable thanks. This, madam, in obedience to your commands, is the account I had to give respecting the loss of my right eye, why my beard and white eyebrows are shaved, and how I happened to be with you at this time.

"It is enough," said Zobeide; "we are satisfied: you may retire where you please." The calender made his excuse, and begged permission to remain till he had heard the relation of his two comrades, "whom I cannot," he said, 'honourably leave;" and that he might also hear those of the three other persons in company.

The story of the first calender appeared very extraordinary to the whole company, but especially to the caliph; who, notwithstanding the slaves stood by with their scimitars in their hands, could not forbear whispering to the vizier, "I have heard many stories, but never any that approached that of the calender!" Whilst he was thus speaking, the second calender began, addressing himself to Zobeide.

THE STORY OF THE SECOND CALEN-
DER, A KING'S SON.

MADAM, said he, to obey your command, and to show you by what strange accident I became blind of the right eye, it is necessary I should give you the whole account of life.

I was scarcely past my infancy, when the king, my father—for you must know, madam, I am a prince by birth—perceived that I was endowed with a great share of sense, and spared nothing that was proper for improving it. He accordingly selected all the men in his dominions who excelled in sciences and arts to attend to my education.

No sooner could I read and write, than I learned the whole Alcoran by heart—that admirable book, which contains the foundation, the precepts, and the rules of our religion, and that I might be thoroughly instructed in it, I read the works of the most approved authors by whose commentaries it had been explained. To this study I added a knowledge of all the traditions collected from the mouth of our prophet by the great men who were contemporary with him. I was not satisfied in knowing merely all that had any relation to our religion: I made also a particular search into our histories; perfected myself in polite learning, in the works of the poets, and in versification; applied to geography, to chronology, and to speak our language in its purity;

not neglecting, in the meantime, all such exercises as appertain to a prince. But there was one employment to which I became more warmly attached, and in which I succeeded to admiration: it was, the forming of our Arabic characters, wherein I surpassed all the writing-masters of our kingdom, who had acquired the greatest reputation.

Fame conferred on me more honour than I merited; for she had not only spread the renown of my talents through the dominions of the king my father, but had conveyed it as far as the Indian court; the potent monarch of which, desirous to see me, sent an ambassador, with rich presents, to demand me of my father, who was highly gratified with this embassy for several reasons: he was persuaded that nothing could be of greater benefit to a prince of my age, than to travel and see foreign courts; and, besides, he was very glad to gain the friendship of the Indian sultan. I departed with the ambassador, but with only a small retinue, on account of the distance, and difficulty of the roads.

We had been about a month on our journey, when we observed a great cloud of dust approaching, and under it we very soon saw fifty horsemen well armed: they were robbers, coming towards us at full gallop.

As we had ten horses laden with our baggage, and different articles which I was to present to the Indian sultan, from the king my father, and our retinue was small, you will readily believe that the robbers came boldly up to us. Not being prepared to make any opposition, we told them that we were ambassadors belonging to the sultan of the Indies, and hoped they would attempt nothing derogatory from the honour that is due to him. We thought to save our equipage and our lives; but the robbers insolently replied, "For what reason would you have us show respect to the sultan your master? We are not his subjects, nor are we upon his territories." Having thus spoken, they surrounded and attacked us. I defended myself as long as possible; but being wounded and seeing the ambassador, with his servants and mine lying on the ground, I profited by the little strength remaining in my horse, which was also very much wounded, to separate myself from them. I rode away as fast as my horse could carry me; but his strength soon failed him, and, through weariness and the loss of blood, he suddenly fell down dead. I speedily disengaged myself from him; when finding I was not pursued, I concluded that the robbers were not willing to quit the booty they had obtained.

Alone, wounded, destitute of all succour, and in a strange country, I durst not venture into the high road, lest I should again fall into the hands of the robbers. After I had bound up my hurt, which was not dangerous, I walked on during the remainder of the day, and arrived at the foot of a mountain, where I perceived the entrance of a cave: I went in, and, eating some fruits that I had gathered by the way, passed the night with little tranquillity.

I continued my journey the following days without discovering any place where I could remain; but after the lapse of a month, I reached a large town well inhabited, and situated so much the more advantageously, as it was surrounded with several rivers, thereby enjoying a perpetual spring.

The agreeable objects that were then presented to my view afforded me some joy, and suspended for a time the mortal sorrow with which I was overwhelmed, by reflecting on my sad condition. My face, hands, and feet were all become tawny by the heat of the sun; and, through my long journey, my shoes and stockings were entirely worn out, so that I had been forced to walk bare-footed; besides which, my clothes were all in rags.

Entering the town, to learn the language, and to inquire the name of the place, I addressed myself to a tailor who was at work in his shop. Interested by my youth, and by my air, which indicated more than my outward appearance warranted, he made me sit down by him, and asked me who I was, whence I came, and what had brought me thither. I did not conceal any part of my misfortunes, nor make any scruple to discover my quality.

The tailor listened to me with attention; but, when I had ceased speaking, instead of giving me consolation, he augmented my sorrow: "Take heed," said he, "how you discover to any person what you have now declared to me; for the prince of this country is the king your father's greatest enemy, and he will certainly do you some injury, if he should hear of your being in this city." I did not doubt the sincerity of the tailor when he named the prince. But since the enmity which exists between my father and him has no relation to my adventures, you will not be displeased, madam, that I pass it over in silence.

I thanked the tailor for his advice, and signified to him that I should wholly follow his good counsel, assuring him that his favours would never be forgotten by me. As he judged that I must be hungry, he caused food to be brought, and offered me, at the same time, a lodging in his house, which I accepted.

Some days after my arrival, finding I was sufficiently recovered from the fatigue I had endured through my long and tedious journey; and, besides, being sensible that most princes of our religion applied themselves to some art or calling that might be of service to them on a reverse of fortune, he asked me if I had learned any profession whereby I could get a livelihood, so as not to be burdensome to any man. I told him that I understood the laws, both divine and human; that I was a grammarian and a poet; and, above all, that I could write perfectly well. "With all this," said he, "you will not be able, in this country, to purchase yourself one morsel of bread: nothing is of less use here than such knowledge. But be advised by me," he continued; "dress yourself in a labourer's habit; and, since you appear to be strong, and of a good constitution, you shall go into the neighbouring forest and cut down fire-wood, which you may bring to the market to sell; and I can assure you it will produce so good profit, that you may live independent of any person. By this means you will be enabled to wait for the favourable moment when Heaven shall think fit to dispel the clouds of misfortune that thwart your happiness, and oblige me to conceal your birth. I will take care to furnish you with a rope and a hatchet."

The fear of being known, and the necessity I was under of earning a livelihood, induced me to agree to this proposal, notwithstanding the meanness and hardships that attended it.

Early the day following the tailor brought me a rope, a hatchet, and a short coat, and recommended me to some poor people, who obtained their living in the same manner, whom he solicited to take into their company. They conducted me to the forest; and the first day I returned with as much wood upon my head as produced me a half-piece of gold, which is the money of that country; for though the forest was not far distant from the town, yet wood was very scarce there, because few people would be at the trouble of going to cut it. I soon gained a good sum of money, and repaid the tailor what he had advanced for me.

I had continued this mode of living for above a year, when one day, having penetrated farther into the forest than usual, I came to a very pleasant place, where I began to cut down wood. In pulling up the root of a tree, I perceived

an iron ring, fastened to a trap-door of the same metal: I immediately removed the earth that covered it, and having lifted it up, saw a staircase, by which I descended, with my axe in my hand.

When I had reached the bottom of the stairs, I found myself in a large palace, and was much astonished at the light, which appeared as clear in it, as if it had been erected on the earth in the most exposed situation. I proceeded along a gallery, supported by pillars of jasper, the bases and capitals of massy gold, but seeing a lady advance towards me, she appeared of so noble and free an air, and of such extraordinary beauty, that my eyes were prevented beholding any other object than her alone.

To spare the lady the trouble of coming to me, I hastened to meet her; when, as I was saluting her with a low bow, she asked, "What are you—a man or a geni?" "A man, madam," answered I, rising; "I have no correspondence with genii." "By what adventure," said she, with a deep sigh, "are you come hither? I have lived here five-and-twenty years, and have never seen any man but yourself during that time."

Her great beauty, with which I was already smitten, and the sweetness and civility of her manners, gave me the courage to say, "Madam, before I have the honour to satisfy your curiosity, permit me to tell you that I am infinitely gratified with this unexpected rencounter, which offers me an occasion to console myself in the midst of my affliction; and perhaps it may give me an opportunity of adding to your happiness." I faithfully related to her by what strange accident she saw me, the son of a king, in the condition I then appeared in her presence; and how fortune had directed me to discover the entrance into that magnificent, though, judging by appearances, wearisome, prison, in which I had found her.

"Alas, prince!" said she, again sighing, "you are right in believing this rich and pompous prison to be a most wearisome abode; the most charming places in the world cannot delight, when we are detained in them against our will. It is impossible that you have not heard of the great Epitimarus, king of the Isle of Ebony, so called from the precious wood of that name, which it produces in abundance: I am the princess his daughter.

"The king my father had chosen for my husband a prince who was my cousin; but on my wedding-night, in the midst of the rejoicings in the court, and in the capital city of the kingdom of the Isle of Ebony, before I was given to my spouse, a geni took me away. I fainted at the same moment, and entirely lost my senses; and when I recovered I found myself in this palace. I was a long time inconsolable; but time and necessity have accustomed me to see and receive the geni. Twenty-five years, as I before told you, have elapsed since I was brought to this place, where, I must confess, I have all that I can wish for necessary to life, and also everything that could satisfy a princess who only required fine dresses and conveniences.

"Every ten days," continued the princess, "the geni comes hither to sleep with me one night, which he never exceeds; and he excuses himself by saying, that he is married to another wife, who would become jealous if she knew of his infidelity. Meanwhile, if I have any occasion for him by day or night, as soon as I touch a talisman, which is at the entrance of my chamber, the geni appears. It is now the fourth day since he was here, and I do not expect him before the end of six more; so, if you please, you may stay five days, to keep me company, and I will endeavour to entertain you according to your quality and merit."

I esteemed myself too fortunate, in having obtained so great a favour without solicitation, to refuse the obliging offer. The princess made me go into a bagnio, which was the most handsome, the most commodious, and the most sumptuous that could be imagined; and when I came out, instead of my own clothes, I found a very costly suit, which I did not so much esteem for its richness, as that it rendered me more worthy of being in her company.

We sat down on a sofa covered with rich tapestry, with cushions of the rarest Indian brocade to lean upon; and some time after she placed several dishes of delicate meats upon the table. We ate together; and passed the remaining part of the day with very much satisfaction; and at night she received me to her bed.

The next day, as she devised all possible means of pleasing me, she brought in at dinner a bottle of old wine, the most excellent that ever was tasted, and, through complaisance, she drank part of it with me. When my head grew hot with the agreeable liquor, "Fair princess," said I, "you have been too long thus buried alive; follow me, and enjoy the real day, of which you have been deprived so many years: abandon the false light which you have here." "Prince," replied she, with a smile, "leave this discourse. If, out of the ten days, you will grant me nine, and resign the last to the geni, the fairest day in the world would be nothing in my esteem." "Princess," said I, "fear of the geni makes you speak thus. For my part I value him so little, that I will break his talisman, with the conjuration that is written on it, in pieces. Let him come, then; I will expect him; and how brave or redoubtable soever he be, I will make him feel the weight of my arm. I swear to extirpate all the genii in the world, and him first." The princess, who was aware of the consequence, conjured me not to touch the talisman; "for," said she, "it would cause the ruin of us both: I know better than you what belongs to genii." The fumes of the wine did not suffer me to attend to her reasoning; I gave the talisman a kick with my foot, and broke it in several pieces.

The talisman was no sooner broken than the palace began to shake, appearing ready to fall, with a hideous noise, like thunder, accompanied with flashes of lightning, and a great darkness. This terrible concussion in a moment dispelled the fumes of my wine, and made me sensible, but too late, of the folly I had committed. "Princess," cried I, "what means all this?" She answered in a fright, and without any concern for her own misfortune, "Alas! you are undone, if you do not immediately escape!"

I followed her advice; and my fear was so great that I forgot my hatchet and cords. I had scarcely reached the staircase by which I descended, when the enchanted palace suddenly opened, and made a passage for the geni. He asked the princess, in great anger, "What has happened to you, and why did you call me?" "A pain in my stomach," replied the princess, "obliged me to fetch this bottle which you see, out of which I had drank twice or thrice; when, by mischance, I made a false step, and fell upon the talisman, which is broken: and that is all the matter."

At this answer the furious geni said to her, "You are a false woman, and a liar! How came that axe and those ropes there?" "I never saw them till this moment," replied the princess. "Your coming in such an impetuous manner has perhaps forced them up from some place as you passed along, and so you have brought them hither without knowing it."

The geni returned no other answer than reproaches and blows, which I distinctly heard.
Not being able to endure the pitiful cries and
shouts of the princess so cruelly abused, I had
already quitted the habit she made me take, and
resumed my own, which I had laid on the stairs
the day before, when I came out of the bagnio.
I hastened up the staircase, the more penetrated
with sorrow and compassion, as I had been the
cause of so great a misfortune; and as, by sacrificing the fairest princess on earth to the barbarity of a merciless geni, I was become the most
criminal and ungrateful of mankind. "It is true,"
said I, "she has been a prisoner for twenty-five
years; but, setting liberty aside, she wanted
nothing that could render her happy. My madness has put an end to her happiness, and brought
upon her the cruelty of an unmerciful demon!"
I let down the trapdoor, covered it again
with earth, and returned to the city with a burden of wood, which I bound up without knowing what I did, so great was my trouble and
affliction.

My landlord, the tailor, was greatly rejoiced to see me. "Your absence," said he, "has caused me much
inquietude, because of the secret of your birth with which you had entrusted me; and I knew not what to think. I
was afraid that somebody had known you. God be praised for your return!" I thanked him for his zeal and
affection; but I dared not say a word of what had passed, nor mention the reason why I had returned without my
hatchet and cords.

I retired to my chamber, where I reproached myself a thousand times for my excessive imprudence. "Nothing,"
said I, "could have equalled the princess's happiness and mine, had I been contented, and forborne to break
the talisman!"

While I was thus abandoning myself to melancholy thoughts, the tailor entered, saying, "An old man whom I do
not know, has brought your hatchet and cords, which he found in his road, as he tells me. He has learned from your
comrades, who go along with you to the woods, that you lodge here. Come out, and speak to him, for he will deliver
them to nobody but yourself."

At this discourse, I changed colour, and trembled from head to foot. While the tailor was inquiring the cause,
my chamber-door suddenly opened, and the old man not having patience to stay, presented himself to us, with my
hatchet and cords. It was the geni, the ravisher of the fair princess of the Isle of Ebony, who had thus disguised
himself, after having treated her with the utmost barbarity. "I am a geni," said he, "son of the daughter of Eblis,
prince of genii. Is not this your hatchet?" he continued, speaking to me; "and are not these your cords?"

The geni, though he thus questioned me, gave me no time to answer; nor had I the power, so much had his terrible aspect confounded me. He grasped me by the middle of the body, dragged me out of the chamber, and mounting

i

nto the air, carried me up to the skies with such swiftness, that I could only perceive I was so high, without being able to recollect any part of the way I had been carried in a few moments. He decended in like manner to the earth, which, by stamping his foot, he caused to open, and immediately sank down, when I found myself in the enchanted palace, before the fair princess of the Isle of Ebony. But, alas! what a spectacle was there! I saw that which pierced me to the heart. The princess was quite naked, bathed in blood, and laid upon the ground more dead than alive, with her cheeks washed in tears.

"Perfidious wretch!" said the geni to her, pointing at me, "is not this thy gallant?" She cast her languishing eyes upon me, and answered mournfully, "I do not know him: I never saw him till this moment." "What!" said the geni; "he is the cause of thy justly being in that condition, and yet darest thou say thou dost not know him?" "If I do not know him," replied the princess, "would you have me tell a falsehood on purpose to ruin him." "Well, then," said the geni, drawing a scimitar, and presenting it to the princess, "if thou never saw him before, take this scimitar, and cut off his head." "Alas!" replied the princess, "how is it possible I can execute what you require of me? My strength is so far spent, that I cannot raise my arms, and, if I could, how should I have the heart to take away the life of an innocent man, whom I do not know?" "This refusal," said the geni to the princess, "sufficiently proves to me thy crime." Upon which, turning to me, "And thou;" said he; "dost thou not know her?"

I should have been the most ungrateful wretch, and the most perfidious of mankind, if I had not shown myself as faithful to the princess as she was to me, who had been the cause of her misfortunes, Therefore, I answered the geni,

"How should I know her, who never saw her till now?" "If it be so," said he, "take the scimitar, and cut off her head." On this condition, I will set thee at liberty; for then I shall be convinced that thou never didst see her till this moment, as thou sayest." "With all my heart," replied I; taking the scimitar from his hand.

Do not think, madam, that I approached the fair princess of the Isle of Ebony, to be the executioner of the geni's barbarity. I acted in this manner merely to demonstrate by my gestures, as clearly as possible, that, as she had shown her resolution to lose her life for my sake, I would not refuse to sacrifice mine for the love of her. The princess, notwithstanding her pain and suffering, understood my meaning, which she signified by an obliging look, and made me understand her willingness to die, and that she was satisfied I would also willingly die for her. Upon this I stepped back, and threw the scimitar on the ground: "I should for ever," said I to the geni, "be hateful to all mankind, if I were so base as to murder, I do not only say a person of whom I have no knowledge, but a lady like this, who is on the brink of eternity.— Do with me what you please, since I am in your power; but I cannot obey your barbarous commands."

"I see plainly," said the geni, "that you both brave me, and insult my jealousy; but each of you shall know, by the treatment I will give you, of what I am capable." At these words, the monster took up the scimitar, and cut off one of the hands of the princess; which left her only so much life as enabled her to signify to me, with the other, an eternal adieu; for the blood she had before lost, and that which gushed out then, permitted her to live but a moment or two after this last cruelty, the sight of which caused me to faint. When I had recovered, I expostulated with the geni, why he kept me languishing in expectation of death: "Strike!" cried I; "I am ready to receive the mortal blow, and expect it as the greatest favour you can afford me." But instead of complying with my request, "Observe," said he, "how genii treat their wives whom they suspect of infidelity. She has received thee here. If I were certain that she had put a greater affront upon me, I would destroy thee this moment: but I will content myself by transforming thee into a dog, an ape, a lion, or a bird: decide which thou wilt be; I leave the choice to thyself.'

These words gave me some hopes of mollifying him. "O geni!" said I, "moderate your passion; and since you will spare my life, give it me generously. I shall always remember your clemency, if you pardon me, as one of the best men in the world forgave a neighbour, who bore him a mortal hatred." The geni asked me what had passed between those two neighbours, saying he would have patience to hear the story, which I related. And I think, madam, you will not be displeased if I repeat it to you."

THE STORY OF THE ENVIOUS MAN, AND OF HIM WHOM HE ENVIED.

IN a considerable town, two persons dwelt in adjoining houses; one of whom conceived such a violent hatred against the other, that he who was the object of it resolved to remove his dwelling farther off, being persuaded that their near residence was the sole cause of his neighbour's animosity; for though he had rendered him several good offices, he found, nevertheless, that his hatred was not diminished. He accordingly sold his house, with the few goods he had, and retiring to the capital of the country, which was not far distant, he bought a little spot of ground that lay about half a league from the city. There he had a tolerably convenient house, with a fine garden and a sufficiently spacious court, in which was a deep well that was not used.

The honest man having obtained this acquisition, put on the habit of a dervise, or monk, intending to lead a retired life; and he caused several cells to be made in the house, where, in a short time, he established a numerous society of dervises. He very soon became publicly known by his virtue, through which he acquired the esteem of a vast many persons, as well of the commonalty as of the chief men of the city. In short, he was extremely honoured and cherished by all. People came from afar to recommend themselves to his prayers; and all those who resided near him published the blessings which they were persuaded they had received from Heaven through his assistance.

The great reputation of this good man having spread to the town whence he came, the envious man was so much chagrined by the intelligence, that he abandoned his house and his affairs, with a resolution to go and destroy him. With this intent, he presented himself at the new convent of dervises, of which his former neighbour was the superior, who received him with all imaginable tokens of friendship. The envious man told him, he had visited him on purpose to communicate a business of importance, which he could mention only in private: " That nobody may hear us," continued he, "let us, I beg, take a walk in your court; and as night approaches, command your dervises to retire to their cells." The chief of the dervises did as he required.

When the envious man found himself alone with this good man, he pretended to tell him his errand; as they walked side by side in the court, until he had conducted him near the brink of the well: he then gave him a push, and threw him into it, without any body being witness to so wicked an action. Having accomplished his intention, he walked away immediately, got out at the gate of the convent without being seen, and returned to his own house, well satisfied with his journey, being fully persuaded that the object of his hatred was no longer in this world. But he very much deceived himself.

Luckily for the chief of the dervises, this old well was inhabited by fairies and genii, who received and supported him, and carried him to the bottom unhurt. He clearly perceived that there was something extraordinary in his fall; which must otherwise have cost him his life; though he neither saw nor felt anything. But he soon heard a voice, which said, "Do you know what honest man this is, to whom we have rendered this good service?" Other voices answered, "No." The first voice replied, "Then I will tell you:—This man, through the greatest charity that ever was known, left the town he lived in, and has established himself in this place, in the hope of curing one of his neighbours of the envy he had conceived against him. He has acquired here such general esteem, that the envious man, not able to endure it, came hither on purpose to destroy him; in which he would have succeeded, had it not been for the assistance that we have afforded this honest man, whose reputation is so great, that the sultan, who keeps his residence in the neighbouring city, was to pay him a visit to-morrow, and to recommend the princess his daughter to his prayers.

Another voice asked, "What need had the princess of the dervise's prayers?" to which the first answered, "You do not know, it seems, that she is possessed by geni Maimoun, the son of Dimdim, who is fallen in love with her. But I know well how this good chief of the dervises could cure her: the thing is very easy, and I will tell it you. He has a black cat in his convent, with a white spot at the end of her tail, about the size of a small piece of silver coin: let him only pull seven hairs out of this white spot, burn them, and perfume the princess's head with the smoke, and she will not only be instantly cured, but so well delivered from Maimoun, that he will never dare to approach her a second time."

The chief of the dervises lost not a word of the discourse between the fairies and the genii, who maintained a perfect silence all the night after. The next morning, at break of day, when he could discern objects, as the well was broken down in several places, he perceived a hole, by which he got out with ease.

The dervises, who had been seeking for him, were rejoiced to find him safe. He gave them a brief account of the wickedness of that man on whom he had bestowed so kind a reception the day before, and retired into his cell. It was not long before the black cat, of which the fairies and the genii had spoken in their discourses the night preceding, came, as she was accustomed, to caress her master: he took her up, and pulling seven hairs out of the white spot that was upon her tail, laid them aside for his use, when they might be wanted.

The sun had not long risen, when the sultan, who neglected no means that he thought could restore the princess to her perfect health, arrived at the gate of the convent. He commanded his guards to halt, whilst he, with his principal officers, entered. The dervises received him with profound respect.

The sultan took their chief aside: "Good Scheich," said he, "perhaps you already know the cause of my coming hither." "Yes, sir," replied he, gravely; "if I do not mistake, it is the disease of the princess, which procures me this undeserved honour." "It is," said the sultan. "You will afford me new life, if your prayers, as I hope they will, re-establish my daughter's health." "Sir," replied the good man, "if your majesty will be pleased to let her come hither, I flatter myself that, through God's assistance and favour, she shall return perfectly recovered."

The prince, transported with joy, sent immediately to seek his daughter, who very soon appeared, accompanied by a numerous train of ladies and eunuchs; but she was veiled, so that her face could not be seen. The chief of the dervises caused a pall to be held over her head; and he had no sooner thrown the seven hairs upon the burning coals, than the geni Maimoun, the son of Dimdim, gave a loud shriek, without anything being seen, and left the princess at liberty; on which, she removed the veil from her face, and rose up to see where she was. "Where am I?" cried she: "Who brought me hither?" At these words, the sultan, overcome with excess of joy, embraced his daughter, and kissed her eyes: he also kissed the hands of the chief of the dervises, saying to his officers, "Tell me your opinion, what reward does he deserve who has thus cured my daughter?" They all cried, "He deserves her in marriage." "That is precisely my opinion," said the sultan; "and I make him my son-in-law from this moment."

A short time after, the prime vizier died, and the sultan conferred the office on the dervise. The sultan himself dying without male issue, the religious and military orders assembled, and the good man was, by general consent, declared and acknowledged his successor.

The honest dervise being seated on the throne of his father-in-law, as he was one day, in the midst of his courtiers, upon an excursion, he espied the envious man in the crowd of people who stood viewing the procession, as it passed. He called to one of the viziers who attended him, and whispered him in his ear, "Go bring me that man you see there; but be careful not to frighten him." The vizier obeyed. When the envious man was brought into his presence, "Friend," said the sultan, "I am extremely glad to see you," and then, calling to an officer, "Go immediately," continued he, "and cause to be paid to this man, out of my treasury, one thousand pieces of gold: let him also have twenty loads of the richest merchandise in my store-houses, and a sufficient guard to conduct him to his house." After he had given this charge to the officer, he bade the envious man farewell, and proceeded on his route.

* * * * *

HEN I had finished the recital of this story to the geni, the murderer of the princess of the Isle of Ebony, I made the application to himself thus:— 'O geni! you see that this beneficent sultan did not content himself with having forgotten the design of the envious man to take away his life, but treated him kindly, and sent him back with all the presents that I have mentioned." In short, I employed all my eloquence to induce him to imitate so good an example, and to grant me pardon; but I found it impossible to move his compassion.

"All the favour I can grant thee," said he, "is, that I will not take away thy life; but do not flatter thyself that I shall send thee back safe and well. I must let thee feel what I am able to effect by my enchantments. At these words he seized me violently, and carrying me across the vault of the subterranean palace, which opened to afford him a passage, he flew up with me so high, that the earth appeared like a little white cloud; thence he descended like a thunderbolt, and alighted upon the ridge of a mountain.

There he took up a handful of earth, and pronouncing, or rather muttering, some words which I did not understand, threw it upon me: "Quit the shape of a man," said he to me, "and take that of the ape." He immediately vanished, leaving me alone, transformed into an ape, overwhelmed with sorrow, in a strange country, not knowing whether I was near to, or far from, the dominions of my father.

I came down from the top of the mountain, and entered a plain country, which I was a month in travelling through, when I reached the sea-coast. It was then a dead calm, and I espied a vessel at about half a league from the shore. Not to lose this good opportunity, I broke a large branch from a tree, which I dragged into the sea, and placed myself upon it, with a stick in each hand to serve me for oars.

I rowed along in this state, and advanced towards the ship. When I was near enough to be distinctly seen, the seamen and passengers, who were upon the deck, thinking it an extraordinary spectacle, viewed me with great astonishment. In the meantime I got aboard, and seizing a rope, I jumped upon the deck, when, having lost my speech, I found myself in very great perplexity; and, indeed, the danger I then ran was not less than that I had encountered when at the mercy of the geni.

The merchants, being both superstitious and scrupulous, were persuaded that I should occasion some misfortune to their voyage, if they received me; therefore, one exclaimed, "I will knock him down with a handspike!"—another, "I will shoot an arrow through his body!"—a third, "Let us throw him into the sea!" Some one of them would not have failed to execute his design, if I had not taken refuge by the side of the captain; when throwing myself at his feet, and seizing his coat in a supplicating posture, this action, together with the tears which he saw gush from my eyes, moved his compassion: he accordingly took me under his protection, and threatened to make any one repent who should do me the least injury. The captain treated me with much regard; and, on my part, though I had no power to speak, I endeavoured, by my gestures, to show all possible signs of gratitude.

The wind that succeeded the calm was not strong, but favourable; it did not change for five days, and carried us safely to the port of a handsome town, well peopled, and of great trade, where we cast anchor. It was so much the more considerable, as it was the capital city of a powerful state.

Our vessel was very soon surrounded by an infinite number of small boats, full of people, who came either to congratulate their friends upon their safe arrival, to inquire after those whom they had left behind them in the country whence they came, or merely through curiosity to see a ship arrived from a distant land.

Among the rest, some officers came on board, desiring, in the name of the sultan, to speak with the merchants of our vessel. The merchants appearing, one of the officers thus addressed them:—"The sultan, our master, has commanded us to say, that he is very glad of your safe arrival; and he prays you to take the trouble, each of you, to write some lines upon this roll of paper. That you may understand his reason for making this request, you must know, he had a prime vizier, who, besides a great capacity to manage affairs, wrote in the first style of elegance. This minister lately died, at which the sultan is much afflicted; and since he can never behold his writing without admiration, he has made a solemn vow not to give his place to any man unless he can write as well. Numbers of people have presented their writings; but, to this day, nobody in all the empire has been judged worthy to supply the vizier's situation."

Those of the merchants who believed they could write sufficiently well to pretend to this high dignity, wrote, one after another, that they thought fit. After they had finished, I advanced, and took the roll out of the hand of the person who held it. All the people, especially the merchants who had written, expecting I should tear it, or throw it into the sea, were very much alarmed, till they saw how properly I held the roll, making a sign that I would write in my turn, which changed their fears into admiration. Nevertheless, since they had never seen an ape that could write, and could not persuade themselves that I was more ingenious than other apes, they attempted to snatch the roll out of my hand; but the captain took my part once more. "Let him alone," said he; "suffer him to write. If he only scribble the paper, I promise you that I will punish him immediately. If, on the contrary, he write well, as I hope he will, because I never saw an ape so handy and ingenious, and with such ready apprehension, I declare that I will adopt him as my son: I had one who had not by far the wit that he has." Perceiving that no man any longer opposed my design, I took the pen, and wrote, before ceasing, six sorts of hands used among the Arabians; and each specimen contained an extemporary distich or quatrain in praise of the sultan. My writing not merely excelled that of the merchants, but I dare say they had not before seen any so fine in that country. When I had finished, the officers took the roll, and carried it to the sultan.

The sultan scarcely noticed the other writings, but considered mine attentively, with which he was so much pleased, that he said to his officers, "Take the finest horse in my stable, with the richest harness, and a robe of the most sumptuous brocade, to put upon the person who wrote these six hands, and bring him hither to me." At this command, the officers could not refrain from laughing: the sultan became irritated at their boldness, and was ready to punish them; when they said to him, "Sir, we humbly beg your majesty's pardon: these hands were not written by a man, but by an ape." "What do you say!" exclaimed the sultan,—"these admirable characters were not written by the hand of a man?"

"Sir," replied the officers, "we do assure your majesty that it was an ape which wrote them, in our presence." The sultan was too much surprised at this account, not to desire a sight of me, and therefore said, "Do as I directed you, and bring me speedily that wonderful ape."

The officers returned to the vessel, and showed their orders to the captain, who answered, "The sultan' commands must be obeyed." On which they clothed me in a rich brocade robe, and carried me ashore, where they set me on horseback; whilst the sultan waited for me at the palace with a great number of courtiers, whom he had assembled to do me the more honour.

The cavalcade having commenced, the harbour, the streets, the public places, the windows and terraces of the palaces and houses were filled with an infinite number of people of every description, whom curiosity had brought from all parts of the city to see me; for the rumour had spread in a moment, that the sultan had chosen an ape to be his grand vizier. After having been exhibited as a spectacle to the people, who could not forbear expressing their surprise by redoubled shouts and exclamations, I arrived at the palace of the sultan.

I found the prince seated on his throne, in the midst of the grandees of his court. I made three profound reverences; and, at last prostrated myself, and kissed the ground before him, afterwards sitting down on my seat in the

posture of an ape. The whole assembly admired me, and could not comprehend how it was possible that an ape should so well understand how to show the sultan his due respect; and he himself was more astonished than any man. In short, the usual ceremony of the audience would have been complete, could I have added speech to my behaviour, but apes never speak; and the advantage I possessed, of having been a man, did not afford me that privilege.

The sultan having dismissed his courtiers, there only remained by him his chief of the eunuchs, a very young little slave, and myself. He went from the chamber of audience into his private apartment, where he ordered dinner to be brought. As he sat at the table, he gave me a sign to approach, and eat with him. To show my obedience, I kissed the ground; when, rising, I sat down at table, and ate with discretion, and moderately.

Before the table was uncovered, I perceived an ink-horn, which I made a sign should be brought me: having obtained it, I wrote, upon a large peach, some verses, after my own mode, testifying my acknowledgment to the sultan; who having read them, after I had presented him the peach, his astonishment was increased. When the table was uncovered, his attendants brought him a particular liquor, of which he commanded them to give me a glass, I drank, and wrote some verses upon it, that explained the state in which I now found myself, after great sufferings. The sultan read them likewise, and said, a man who was capable of doing so much, ought to be exalted above the greatest of men.

The sultan caused a chess-board to be brought, and inquired, by a sign, if I understood that game, and would play with him. I kissed the ground, and, by placing my hand upon my head, signified that I was ready to receive that honour. He won the first game, but I gained the second and third; when, perceiving he was somewhat displeased, I suffered him to win the fourth: observing, that two potent armies had been fighting very ardently all day, but as they had concluded a peace towards the evening, they would pass the remaining part of the night very quietly together upon the field of battle.

So many things appearing to the sultan, far beyond what any person had either seen or known of the behaviour or knowledge of apes, he would not be the only witness of these prodigies. He had a daughter, called the lady of beauty, to whom the head of the eunuchs, then present, was governor. "Go," said the sultan to him, "and desire your lady to come hither: I am anxious she should enjoy a share of my pleasure."

The chief of the eunuchs went, and immediately returned with the princess. Her face was uncovered; but she no sooner entered the room, than she put on her veil, saying to the sultan, "Sir, your majesty must certainly have forgotten yourself. I am much surprised that you should send for me to appear before men." "How, daughter!" said the sultan; "you know not what you say. Here are only the little slave, the eunuch your governor, and myself, who have the liberty to see your face; and yet you lower your veil, and would make me appear criminal in having sent for you hither." "Sir," replied the princess, "your majesty shall soon understand that I am not in the wrong. The animal you see before you, though it has the form of an ape, is a young prince, son of a great king: he has been thus metamorphosed by enchantment. A geni, the son of the daughter of Eblis, has maliciously done him this injury, after having cruelly taken away the life of the princess of the Isle of Ebony, daughter to king Epitimarus.

The sultan, astonished at this discourse, turned towards me, and no longer speaking by signs, demanded if what his daughter had stated were true. As I could not speak, I put my hand to my head, to signify the affirmative. The sultan then said to his daughter, "How do you know that this is a prince, who has been transformed by enchantment into an ape?" "Sir," replied the lady of beauty, "your majesty may remember that when I was past my infancy, I had an old lady who attended me: she was a most expert enchantress, and taught me seventy rules of magic, by virtue of which I could, in the twinkling of an eye, transport your capital into the midst of the sea, or beyond Mount Caucasus. By this science I know all enchanted persons at first sight. I can tell who they are, and by whom they have been enchanted; therefore, do not be surprised if I relieve this prince from the enchantments which hinder his appearing, in your sight, in his natural form." "Daughter," said the sultan, "I did not suppose you to have understood so much." "Sir," replied the princess, "these things are curious, and worth knowing; but I think I ought not to boast of them." "Since it is so," said the sultan, "you can dispel the enchantment of the prince?" "Yes, sir," answered the princess, "I can restore him to his first shape." "Do so, then," interrupted the sultan; "you cannot afford me a greater pleasure, for I will appoint him my grand vizier, and he shall marry you." "Sir," said the princess, "I am ready to obey you in all that you shall be pleased to command me."

The princess, the lady of beauty, went into her apartment, whence she brought a knife, which had some Hebrew words engraven on the blade. She made us all, the sultan, the master of the eunuchs, the little slave, and myself, go down into a private court adjoining to the palace. Leaving us under a gallery that surrounded it, she went to the middle of the court, where she formed a large circle, and within it she wrote several words in ancient Arabic characters, and others of those which they call the characters of Cleopatra.

When she had finished, and prepared the circle as she judged proper, she placed herself in the centre, while she performed some adjurations, and recited several verses out of the Alcoran. Insensibly the air grew dark, as if it had been night, and the whole world about to be dissolved. We were seized with a violent panic; and his fear increased still more, when we saw the geni, the son of the daughter of Eblis, suddenly appear in the form of a lion of frightful size.

As soon as the princess perceived the monster," "You dog!" said she, "instead of creeping before me, dare you present yourself in this shape, thinking to frighten me? "And thou!" replied the lion; "art thou not afraid of breaking the treaty which we have made, and confirmed by a solemn oath, not to hurt, or do each other any wrong?" "Oh, thou cursed creature!" answered the princess;" thee I can justly reproach with so doing." "Thou shalt quickly have thy reward," returned the lion, fiercely, "for the trouble thou hast given me to return!" Saying this, he opened his terrible mouth, and ran at her to devour her; but she, being on her guard, leaped backward, and had time to pull out one of her hairs; when, by pronouncing three or four words, she changed herself into a sharp sword, with which she cut the lion in two, through the middle of his body.

The two parts of the lion vanished, and the head only remained, which turned itself into a large scorpion. Immediately the princess changed herself into a serpent, and fought the scorpion; which, finding itself worsted, took the form of an eagle, and flew away. But the serpent also, at the same time, assumed the shape of a black eagle, much stronger, and pursued it, so that we lost sight of them both.

Some time after they had disappeared, the ground opened before us, and there came forth a black-and-white cat, with its hair standing erect, and continuing a fearful mewing: a black wolf followed it closely, and gave it no time to rest. The cat, being thus hard pressed, changed itself into a worm; and being near a pomegranate, that had accidentally fallen from a tree which grew on the side of a deep, though not broad canal, the worm pierced the pomegranate in an instant, and hid itself. The pomegranate immediately swelled, and became as large as a

gourd; which, mounting up on the roof of the gallery, rolled there, backward and forward, for some time, and then falling down again into the court, broke into several pieces.

The wolf, which had, in the meanwhile, transformed itself into a cock, immediately began picking up the seeds of the pomegranate one after another; till finding no more, it came towards us with its wings spread, making a great noise, as if it would inquire whether there were any more seed. There was one seed lying on the brink of the canal, which the cock perceived as it returned, and ran speedily thither; but just as the cock was going to pick it up, it rolled into the river, and changed into a little fish.

The cock threw itself into the river, and was transformed into a pike, which pursued the small fish. They both continued under water more than two hours, and we knew not what was become of them; when suddenly, we heard terrible cries, which made us shudder, and, soon after, saw the geni and the princess enveloped in flames. They darted flashes of fire out of their mouths at each other, until they had approached close together; when the flames increased, with a thick burning smoke, which mounted so high, that we had reason to apprehend it would set the palace on fire. But we very soon had a more immediate cause to fear; for the geni, having disengaged himself from the princess, came to the gallery where we stood, and blew flames of fire upon us. We should all have perished, if the princess, running to our assistance, had not forced him, by her efforts, to retire, and defend himself against her; yet, notwithstanding all her diligence, she could not prevent the sultan's beard being burnt, and his face disfigured; the chief of the eunuchs being suffocated, and consumed on the spot; nor a spark entered my right eye, and destroying the sight. The sultan and I expected nothing short of death, when we heard the cry of "Victory! victory!" and suddenly the princess appeared in her natural shape, and the geni reduced to a heap of ashes.

The princess advanced to us; and, that she might not lose time, called for a cup of cold water, which the young slave, who had received no injury from the fire, brought to her. She took it; and, after pronouncing some words over it, threw it upon me, saying, "If thou art an ape by enchantment, change thy form and take that of a man, which thou hadst before." These words were scarcely uttered before I became a man as I was originally, one eye only accepted.

I was preparing to make my acknowledgments to the princess, but she prevented me. Addressing herself to her father, "Sir," said she, "I have gained the victory over the geni, as your majesty has seen: but it is a victory that cost me dear. I have but a few moments to live; and you will not have the satisfaction of concluding the match you intended. The fire has pierced me during the terrible combat, and I find it consumes me by degrees. This would not have happened, had I perceived the last of the pomegranate-seeds, and swallowed it with the others, when I had taken the form of a cock. The geni had fled thither as to his last entrenchment, and upon that the success of the combat depended, which would have been fortunate, and without danger, to me. This oversight obliged me to have recourse to fire, and to fight with these mighty arms I have used, between heaven and earth in your presence. In spite of the power of his redoubtable art and experience, I made the geni know that I understood more than him; I have conquered and reduced him to ashes, but I cannot escape the death which is approaching."

The sultan permitted the princess, the lady of beauty, to conclude the recital of her combat; but when she had finished, he spoke to her in a tone that sufficiently testified his grief:—"My daughter," said he, "you see the condition of your father: alas! I wonder that I am yet alive! Your governor, the eunuch, is dead; and the prince whom you have delivered from his enchantment has lost an eye." He could say no more; for his tears, sighs, and sobs rendered him speechless: his daughter and I were extremely moved with his sorrow, and we wept with him.

While we were vieing with each other in grief, the princess suddenly cried, "I burn! oh, I burn!" She perceived that the fire which was consuming her had seized upon her whole body; and she ceased not to exclaim, "I burn!" until death had ended her intolerable sufferings. The effect of the fire was so extraordinary, that, in a few moments, she was wholly reduced to ashes, like the geni.

I cannot explain to you, madam, how much I was distressed at this dismal spectacle. I had rather, all my life, have continued an ape or a dog, than have seen my benefactress thus miserably perish. The sultan, afflicted beyond all that can be imagined, cried out piteously, beating himself on his head and breast; until, being quite overcome with grief, he fainted away, which made me apprehensive for his life. In the meantime, the sultan's lamentations brought the eunuchs and officers of the court, who, running to him, with difficulty recovered him from the swoon. There was no occasion for that prince or me to give them a long narrative of the occurrence, to convince them of our great misfortune; the two heaps of ashes, into which the princess and the geni had been reduced, were sufficient demonstration. The sultan, who was scarcely able to stand, was obliged to lean on his officers for support, to enable him to reach his apartment.

When the report of this tragical event had spread through the palace and the city, all the people bewailed the fate of the princess, the lady of beauty, and were not insensible to the sultan's affliction. Every person was in deep mourning for seven days, and many ceremonies were performed. The ashes of the geni were thrown into the air, but those of the princess were gathered into a precious urn, to be preserved; and the urn was placed in a stately tomb, which was built for that purpose on the same place where the ashes had been collected.

The grief which the sultan experienced for the loss of his daughter, threw him into a fit of sickness that confined him to his chamber for a whole month. He had not entirely recovered his health, when he sent for me. "Prince," said he, "hearken to the orders that I now give you; your life will be the forfeit if you hesitate to comply." I assured him that I would obey exactly; on which he proceeded thus:—"I have constantly lived in perfect felicity, and was never crossed by any accident; but your arrival has destroyed all my happiness; my daughter is dead, so is the governor, and it is a miracle that I am yet alive. You are the cause of all these misfortunes, with which it is impossible that I should be comforted; therefore, depart hence in peace, but instantly, for I myself must perish

if you remain any longer; I am persuaded that your presence produces mischief. This is all I have to say to you. Go, and take care never to appear again in my dominions; for no consideration whatever should hinder me from making you repent." I endeavoured to speak, but he stopped my mouth by words full of anger, and I was obliged to quit his palace.

Rejected, driven away, abandoned by all the world, and not knowing what would become of me, before I left the city I went into a bagnio, where I caused my beard and eyebrows to be shaved, and took the habit of a calender. I began my journey, not so much deploring my own misery, as the death of the two fair princesses which I had occasioned. I passed through many countries without discovering myself; at last I resolved to come to Bagdad, in the hope of getting myself introduced to the commander of the faithful, and exciting his compassion by giving him an account of my strange adventures. I came hither this evening, and the first man that I met was this calender our brother, who spoke before me. You know the remainder, madam, and how I have the honour to be here.

When the second calender had ended his story, Zobeide, to whom he had addressed himself, said, "It is very well; you may go where you please, I give you permission." But instead of departing, he also petitioned the lady to grant him the same favour she had vouchsafed to the first calender, and sat down by him.

The third calender, perceiving it was his turn to speak, addressed himself, as the others, to Zobeide, and began in this manner:—

THE HISTORY OF THE THIRD CALENDER, A KING'S SON.

OST HONOURABLE LADY,—What I have to relate differs very much from the stories you have already heard. The two princes who spoke before me have each lost an eye by the pure effects of their destiny; but mine I lost through my own fault, and by hastening to seek the misfortune, as you will learn by the sequel of my history.

My name is Agib, and I am the son of a king, who was called Cassib. After his death, I took possession of his dominions, and fixed my residence in the same city where he had before lived. This city is situated on the sea coast; it has one of the finest and safest harbours in the world, with an arsenal large enough for fitting out fifty vessels of war, which are always ready to serve on occasion; to equip fifty merchant-ships, and as many light frigates and pleasure-boats for recreation. My kingdom is composed of several fine provinces upon *terra firma* besides a number of spacious islands, each of which lies almost in view of my capital.

My first proceeding was to visit the provinces. I afterwards fitted out and manned my whole fleet, and went to my islands, to insure the hearts of my subjects by my presence, and to confirm them in their loyalty. Some time after I had returned, I went thither again; and these voyages giving me some taste for navigation, I took so much pleasure in it that I resolved to make discoveries beyond my islands; for which purpose I caused ten ships only to be equipped, embarked on board them, and set sail.

Our voyage was very happy for forty successive days; but on the forty-first night the wind became contrary, and so boisterous, that we were in danger of being lost in the storm. About break of day the wind became calm, the clouds were dispersed, and the sun having brought back fair weather, we approached close to an island, where we remained ten days to take in provisions: this being completed, we again put to sea. After ten days' sail we were in hopes of seeing land; for the tempests we had encountered had so much abated my curiosity that I gave orders to steer back to my own coast, when I perceived that my pilot knew not where we were. In fine, on the tenth day a seaman, who was sent to the mainmast-head to look out for land, reported, that on starboard and larboard he could see only the sky and the sea, which bounded the horizon; but that before him, in the direction of the prow of the vessel, he saw a great blackness.

The pilot changed colour at the relation, and throwing his turban on the deck with one hand, and beating his breast with the other, cried, "Oh, sir! we are all lost—not one of us will escape the danger, which, with all my skill, it is not in my power to avoid!

Having thus spoken, he began to weep like a man who foresaw inevitable destruction; and his distress threw the whole ship's crew into similar terror. I asked him what reason he had thus to despair. "Alas, sir," replied he, " the tempest which we have outlived has carried us so far out of our course, that to-morrow, about noon, we shall be near that blackness, which is nothing less than a black mountain: that mountain is a mine of loadstone, which at this moment attracts your whole fleet towards it, in consequence of the iron and nails that are in your ships. When we approach to-morrow within a certain distance, the power of the magnet will be so violent, that all the nails will be drawn out of the sides and lower part of the ships, and attached to the mountain, so that your vessels will fall to pieces, and sink to the bottom. As loadstone has the virtue to draw all iron to it, whereby its attraction becomes stronger, this mountain, on the side of the sea, is covered with nails drawn out of an infinite number of vessels that have perished by it; and this at the same time preserves and augments its virtue.

"This mountain," continued the pilot, " is very rugged. On the summit of it there is a dome of fine brass, supported by pillars of the same metal; and upon the top of that dome stands a horse, likewise of brass, with a rider on his back, who has a plate of lead fixed to his breast, on which some talismanic characters are engraven. The tradition, sir, is, that this statue is the chief cause of so many ships and men being swallowed up in this place, and that it will ever continue to be fatal to all who have the misfortune to approach it, until such time as it shall be thrown down."

The pilot, having ended his discourse, renewed his lamentations, which infected all the ship's company. I, with the rest, had no other thoughts than that my days were there to be ended. In the meantime, every one took all imaginable precautions to provide for his own safety; and, in the uncertainty of the event, they all made one another their heirs, by a will in favour of those who might happen to be saved.

The next morning we plainly perceived the black mountain, and the idea we had conceived of it made it appear still more frightful than it was. About noon we were near, and we found what the pilot had foretold to be true; for we saw all the nails and iron about the ship fly towards the mountain, where they were fixed, by the violence of the attraction, with a horrible noise: the ships split asunder, and sunk into the sea, which was so deep about that place that we could not sound it. All my people were drowned; but God had mercy on me, and permitted me to save myself by means of a plank, which the wind drove ashore at the foot of the mountain. I did not receive the least injury, my good fortune having conducted me to a landing-place, where there were steps that led to the summit.

At the sight of these steps—for there was no ground either to the right or left whereon a man could set his foot—I gave thanks to God; and, recommending myself to his holy protection, began to ascend. The staircase was so narrow, steep, and difficult, that, had there been ever so little wind, it would have precipitated me into the sea. But at last I reached the top without accident. I entered the dome, and, prostrating myself on the ground, again returned God thanks for his favour and protection.

I passed the night under the dome. While I slept, a venerable old man appeared to me, and said, " Hearken, Agib. When thou art awake, dig up the ground under thy feet. Thou shalt there find a bow of brass, and three arrows of lead, fabricated, under certain constellations, to deliver mankind from the many calamities that threaten them. Shoot the three arrows against the statue, and the rider will fall into the sea; but the horse will fall down by thy side, which thou must bury in the same place whence thou didst take the bow and arrows. This being effected, the sea will swell, and rise up to the foot of the dome that stands on the summit of the mountain. When the

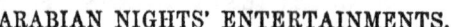

the sea has risen so high, thou will see a boat land with only one man, who will have an oar in each hand. This man will be also of metal, but different from that thou hast thrown down. Step on board to him, without mentioning the name of God, and let him conduct thee. He will in ten days' time convey thee into another sea, where thou wilt find the means of returning home to thy country safe and well—provided, as I have already told thee, thou do not mention the name of God during the whole voyage."

Such was the old man's discourse. As soon as I awoke, I arose, much comforted by this vision, and failed not to observe the directions which the old man had given me. I dug up the bow and arrows from the ground, and shot them at the horseman. With the third arrow, I overthrew him into the sea, and the horse fell by my side, which I buried in the place whence I took the bow and the arrows; and in the meantime the sea swelled, and rose up by degrees. When it had risen to the foot of the dome that stood on the top of the mountain, I saw at a distance on the sea a boat rowing towards me. I praised God, that everything succeeded according to my dream.

At length the boat reached the shore, and I saw the man was of metal, as he had been described.

I stepped aboard, and was very cautious not to pronounce the name of God; indeed, I spoke not one word. I sat down, and the man of metal began to row from the mountain. He continued rowing without ceasing till the ninth day, when I saw some islands, which gave me hopes that I should very soon escape the danger I had encountered. The excess of my joy made me forget the prohibition I had received. "God's name be blessed!" said I, "the Lord be praised!"

I had no sooner uttered these words, than the boat sunk, with the man of metal, leaving me upon the surface. I swam during the remaining part of the day towards the land which appeared nearest. A very dark night succeeded, and not knowing where I was, I swam at a venture. My strength was almost exhausted, and I despaired of being able to save myself, when the wind began to blow hard, and a wave as large as a mountain threw me on a flat, where on retiring it left me. I hastened to get on shore, fearing that another wave might wash me again into the sea. Being safe on land, my first care was to strip, and wring the water out of my clothes; I then laid them down to dry on the sand, which was still pretty warm from the heat of the day.

Next morning the sun soon dried my clothes; I put them on, and went forward to endeavour to learn where fate had thrown me. I had not walked far, before I knew I was upon a little island desert, though very pleasant, where there grew several kinds of trees and wild fruits; but I perceived that it was very far from the continent, which much diminished the joy I experienced on having escaped the danger of the seas. Notwithstanding, I recommended myself to God, and prayed him to dispose of me according to his good-will and pleasure; when I perceived a vessel coming from the main land, with all her sails filled, and her prow directed toward the island.

Not doubting but that they were approaching there, and being uncertain whether they were friends or foes, I thought it not safe for me to be seen: I accordingly got up into a very thick tree, whence I could safely view them. The vessel entered a little creek where ten slaves landed, each carrying a spade and other instruments fit for breaking up the ground. They proceeded towards the middle of the island, where I saw them stop and dig the ground for some time; after which I thought I perceived them lift up a trapdoor. They returned to the vessel, and unloaded several sorts of provisions and furniture, which they carried to the spot where they had been digging, and descended, thereby inducing me to suppose it was a subterraneous place.

I saw them once more go to the ship, and return soon after with an old man, who led a very handsome youth of about fourteen or fifteen years of age. They all descended where the trapdoor had been raised; and when they came up again, having let down the trapdoor and covered it with earth, they returned to the creek where the ship lay, but I remarked that the young man was not in their company, from which I concluded that he remained behind in that place under ground—a circumstance that caused me much astonishment.

The old man and the slaves embarked; and the vessel getting under sail, steered its course towards the main land. When I judged they were at such a distance that they could not see me, I descended from the tree and went directly to the place where I had seen the ground broken. I removed the earth by degrees till I found a stone, two or three feet square. Lifting it up, I saw it covered the head of a staircase, which was also of stone. I went down, and entered a large room where there was a foot carpet, and a couch covered with tapestry, and cushions of rich stuff, upon which the young man sat with a fan in his hand. I was enabled to distinguish all this by the light of two tapers, together with the fruits and flower-pots that were placed about him.

The youth was alarmed at my appearance, but to divest him of his fear, I spoke to him as I approached. "Whoever you are, sir," said I, "be under no apprehension; a king, and the son of a king, as I am, is not capable of doing you the least injury. On the contrary, it is probable that your good destiny has conducted me hither to deliver you out of this tomb, where it seems they have buried you alive for reasons unknown to me. But what embarrasses me, and which I cannot comprehend—for you must know I have been witness to all that has passed since your coming into this island—is, that you suffered yourself to be buried in this place without resistance."

The young man recovering himself at these words, begged me with a smiling countenance, to sit down by him. When I had complied with his request, "Prince," said he, "I have to acquaint you with a matter, that, by its singularity, must very much surprise you.

"My father is a merchant-jeweller, who has acquired, through industry and ingenuity in his profession, considerable wealth. He has a great many slaves and factors, whom he employs in voyages with his own ships, to maintain the correspondence he has established at several courts, which he furnishes with such jewels as they want.

"He had been a long time married without issue, when he dreamed that he should have a son, though his life would not be of very long duration; at which, when he awoke, he was very much concerned. Some days after, my mother acquainted him that she was with child, and the time which she supposed to be that of her conception agreed exactly with the day of his dream. At the end of nine months she was delivered of me, which occasioned great joy in the family.

"My father, who had observed the exact moment of my birth, consulted astrologers respecting my nativity, who told him,—'Your son shall live to the age of fifteen, when he will be in danger of losing his life, and it will be difficult to save it; but if his good destiny should preserve him beyond that time, he will live to be very old. It will be at the same time," they continued, " when the statue of brass, that stands upon the top of the mountain of loadstone, shall be thrown into the sea by Prince Agib, son of King Cassib; and, as the stars prognosticate your son shall be killed fifty days afterwards by that prince."

"As this prediction accorded with my father's dream, it afflicted him very much. In the meantime he took all possible care of my education until the present year, which is the fifteenth of my age. Yesterday he learned, that, about ten days ago, the statue of brass was thrown into the sea by that same prince, whose name I mentioned. This information has cost him so many tears, and has so much alarmed him, that he looks not like himself.

" On the prediction of the astrologers, he has sought by all possible means to falsify my horoscope, and to preserve my life. It is long since he took the precaution to build this subterraneous dwelling, to conceal me till the expiration of fifty days after the demolition of the statue; and therefore, as he has heard that this happened ten days ago, he came hastily hither to hide me, and promised, at the end of forty days, to return and fetch me out. For my part," continued he, " I have good hope; and cannot believe that Prince Agib will come to seek for me in a place under ground, in the midst of a desert island. This, my lord, is what I had to relate."

While the jeweller's son was telling me his story, I laughed to myself at those astrologers who had foretold that I should take away his life; for I thought myself so very unlikely to verify what they had predicted, that he had scarcely finished speaking, when I said to him with great joy, " Dear sir, put your confidence in the goodness of God, and fear nothing; you may consider it as a debt you were to pay, but that you are acquitted of it from this moment. I am heartily glad that, after my shipwreck, I came so fortunately hither, to defend you against all those who would attempt your life. I will not leave you till the forty days are expired, of which the foolish conjectures of the astrologers have made you so apprehensive, and in the meantime I will render you all the service in my power. After which I shall profit by the occasion to get to the main land, by embarking in your vessel, with leave of your father and yourself; and, when I am returned into my kingdom; I shall remember the obligations I owe you, and endeavour to demonstrate my acknowledgments in a suitable manner."

My conversation encouraged the jeweller's son, and gained me his confidence. I was careful, lest I should put him in a fright, not to tell him I was the very Agib whom he dreaded; and I was equally cautious not to give him any cause to suspect it. We discoursed of various matters till night approached, and I found the youth had much good sense. I ate with him of his provisions, of which he had sufficient to have lasted beyond the forty days, though he had more guests than myself. After supper we continued some time in discourse, and then retired to sleep.

The next day, when we arose, I held the basin and water to him to wash; I also provided dinner, and placed it on the table in due time. After this repast I invented a play to divert ourselves, not only then, but the days following. I prepared supper after the same manner as I had prepared dinner; and, having supped, we went to sleep as before.

We had time to contract a friendship for each other. I found he loved me, and for my part I had so great a regard for him, that I have often said to myself, " Those astrologers, who predicted to his father that he should die by my hand, were impostors, for it is not possible that I could commit so base an action." In short, madam, we passed thirty-nine days in our subterraneous residence in the most pleasant manner.

The fortieth day arrived. In the morning, when the young man awoke, he said to me, in a transport of joy, which he could not restrain, " Prince, this is the fortieth day, and I am still living, thanks to God and your good company! My father will soon be here, to give you a testimony of his gratitude, and to furnish you with all that is necessary to enable you to return to your kingdom. But in the meantime," continued he, " I beg you to prepare some water very warm, that I may wash my whole body in the portable bath : I will clean myself, and change my clothes, to receive my father more becomingly."

I placed water on the fire, and, when it was hot, filled the moveable bath. The youth put himself in, and I washed and rubbed him. When he came out, he laid down on his bed, which I had prepared, and I covered him with the clothes. After he had slept some time, he awoke, and said, " Dear prince, pray do me the favour to fetch me a melon and some sugar, that I may eat to refresh myself.."

Of several melons that remained, I selected the best, and laid it on a plate, when, as I could not find a knife to cut it with, I asked the young man if he knew where there was one. " There is a knife," said he, " upon this cornice over my head." I accordingly looked, and saw it there; but in hurrying to reach it, while I had it in my hand, my foot being entangled in the bed-covering, I fell, most unhappily upon the young man, and forced the knife into his heart. He expired the next moment.

At this spectacle, I uttered the most fearful cries : I beat my head, my face, and my breast : I tore my clothes; and threw myself on the ground in unspeakable sorrow and grief. " Alas!" I cried, " only a few hours were wanting to place him out of that danger, from which he sought sanctuary here ! and when I myself thought the danger past, then I became his murderer, and verified the prediction ! But, O Lord !" continued I, lifting up my ace and hands to heaven, " I crave thy pardon ; and, if I am guilty of his death, let me not live any longer."

After this misfortune, I could have embraced death without fear, had it been presented to me. But what we desire, whether good or evil, will not always happen. However, reflecting that all my tears and sorrows would not restore the young man to life, and as the forty days were expired, I might be surprised by his father, I quitted that subterraneous dwelling, and, proceeding up the staircase, laid the great stone upon the entry, and covered it with earth.

I had scarcely finished, when casting my eyes over the sea towards the main land, I perceived the vessel coming to fetch home the young man. Considering how I had best act, I said to myself, " If I am discovered, the old man, when he has seen his son in the state I have left him, will certainly seize me, and perhaps cause me to be massacred by his slaves. All that I can allege to justify myself will be insufficient to persuade him of my innocence. It will be better, then, for me to withdraw, since I have it in my power, than to expose myself to his resentment.

Near the subterraneous habitation there was a large tree with thick leaves, which appeared proper for concealment I ascended it, and was no sooner settled in such a manner that I could not be seen, than I observed the vessel arrive at the same place where she lay the first time.

The old man and his slaves immediately landed, and advanced towards the subterraneous dwelling, with an air that showed they had some hope; but when they saw the earth had been newly removed, they changed countenance, particularly the old man. They raised the stone, and descended. They called the youth by his name; but he answered not, and their fears increased: they searched about, and at length found him, lying upon his bed, with the knife in the middle of his heart, for I had not power to draw it out. At this sight, they cried out lamentably. which renewed my sorrow: the old man fell down in a swoon. The slaves, to give him air, brought him up in their arms, and laid him at the foot of the tree where I was concealed; but notwithstanding all their endeavours to recover him, the unhappy father continued long in that state, and made them more than once despair of his life. At length he revived. Then the slaves brought up his son's corse, dressed in his best apparel; and when they had made a grave, they put him into it. The old man, supported by two slaves, and his face bathed in tears, threw the first earth upon him, after which the slaves filled up the grave.

This being completed, all the furniture was brought out from under ground, and, with the remaining provisions, conveyed on board the vessel. The old man, overcome with sorrow, and being unable to stand, was laid upon a sort of litter, and carried to the ship, which put to sea, and in a short time sailed quite out of sight.

After the old man and his slaves were gone with the vessel, I was left alone upon the island. I passed the night in the subterraneous dwelling, which they had not closed; and when day returned, I walked round the isle, stopping, when I had need of repose, in such places as I thought most suitable.

I led this wearisome life for the space of a month; about which time I perceived that the sea diminished considerably, the island increased in size, and the main land seemed to approach. In effect, the water became so low, that there was but a small stream between me and the *terra firma*. I crossed it, and the water did not reach above the middle of my leg. I travelled so long upon the mud and the sands, that I was very much fatigued. At last I gained more firm ground; and was already at some distance from the sea, when I saw, a good way before me, an appearance like a great fire, which afforded me comfort; " For," said I to myself, " I shall find somebody or other, as it is not possible that this fire should kindle of itself." But, as I advanced, my error was dissipated; and I discovered that what I had supposed to be fire was a castle of red copper, which the rays of the sun made appear, at a distance, as if it had been in flames.

Stopping near the castle, I sat down to admire its beautiful structure, as well as to recover a little from my lassitude. I had not viewed this magnificent building with all the attention it deserved, when I saw ten handsome young men, who appeared to be taking a walk; but what most surprised me was, that they were all blind of the right eye. They accompanied an old man, who was very tall, and of a venerable aspect.

I was strangely astonished to meet so many half-blind men together, and each deprived of the same eye. While I was revolving in my mind, by what adventure all these men could have assembled, they approached, and expressed much joy at seeing me. After the first compliments had passed, they inquired what had brought me thither. I told them my story would be somewhat tedious, but if they would take the trouble to sit down, I would answer their question. They did so; and I related to them all that had happened to me since I left my kingdom, which filled them with amazement.

After I had ended my discourse, the young gentlemen prayed me to go with them into the castle. I accepted the invitation; and we passed through a great many halls, antechambers, bedchambers, and closets, very well furnished, and arrived in a spacious hall, where there were ten small blue sofas placed round, separate from each other, upon which they sat by day, and slept by night. In the middle of this circle there stood an eleventh sofa, not so high as the rest, but of the same colour, upon which the old man before mentioned sat down; and the young gentlemen made use of the other ten. As each sofa would only contain a single person, one of the young men said to me, " Comrade, sit down upon that carpet in the middle of the room; and do not inquire into anything that concerns us, nor the reason why we are all blind of the right eye; be content with what you see, and let not your curiosity carry you further."

The old man had not sat long before he rose up, and went out; he returned in a minute or two, bringing in supper to the ten gentlemen, distributing to each man his proportion by himself: he likewise brought me mine, which I ate by myself, according to the example before me; and, at the end of the repast, he presented to each of us a cup of wine.

My story had appeared to them so extraordinary, that they made me repeat it after supper; and this produced a conversation which lasted a great part of the night. One of the gentlemen, observing that it was late, said to the old man, " You see it is time to sleep, and you do not bring us what is necessary to enable us to acquit ourselves of our duty." At these words, the old man arose, and went into a closet, whence he brought out upon his head, one after another, ten basins all covered with blue stuff: he placed one, with a light, before each gentleman.

They uncovered their basins, in which were ashes, coal-dust, and blacking; and having mixed all together, they rubbed and bedaubed their faces with the composition in such a manner, that they looked very frightful. After having thus disfigured themselves, they began to weep, and lament, beating their heads and breasts, and crying continually, " *This is the fruit of our idleness and our debauches!*"

They passed almost the whole night in this strange occupation. At length they ceased, when the old man brought them water, with which they washed their faces and hands: they also changed their clothes, which were spoiled, and put on others; so that they did not in the least appear as if they had been doing the strange action of which I was a spectator.

You may judge, madam, what constraint I was under all the while: I was a thousand times tempted to break the silence which the gentleman had imposed on me, and ask questions; and it was impossible for me to sleep that night.

The next day, as soon as we arose, we went out to take the air, and I then said to them, " Gentlemen, I declare to you that I must renounce the law which you prescribed to me last night: I cannot observe it. You are men of sense, and all of you have wit in abundance—of which you have convinced me—yet I have seen you do such actions, as none but madmen could be thought capable of. Whatever misfortune befals me, I cannot forbear asking, why you bedaubed your faces with cinders, coal-dust, and blacking; and how it happens that each of you has but

one eye? Some singular circumstance must certainly be the cause, therefore I conjure you to satisfy my curiosity."
To these pressing instances they only answered, that I was not interested in those questions, and should do well to
hold my peace.

We passed that day in conversation upon indifferent subjects; and when night returned, and every person had
supped separately, the old man again brought in the blue basins, and the young gentlemen smeared their faces,
wept, and beat themselves, crying, "*This is the fruit of our idleness and debauches!*" as before. On the morrow,
the same proceeding was repeated, and continued the following nights.

At last, being unable any longer to restrain my curiosity, I earnestly prayed them to satisfy me, or to instruct me
how I might return to my own kingdom; for it was impossible for me to remain in their company, and to see every
night a spectacle so extraordinary, without being permitted to know the reason.

One of the gentlemen answered in behalf of the rest:—" Do not wonder at our conduct in regard to yourself: if
we have not yet granted your request, our hesitation has been an act of kindness, to prevent your experiencing
the sorrow of being reduced to the same condition with us. If you wish to prove our unfortunate destiny, you
need but speak, and we will give you the satisfaction you desire." I told them I was resolved, happen what might.

"Once more," said the same gentleman, "we advise you to restrain your curiosity; it will cost you the loss of your right eye." "No matter," replied I; "I declare to you, that if such a misfortune befal me, I shall not consider you blameable, but impute it solely to myself."

He further represented to me, that when I had lost an eye, I must not hope to remain with them, if I had the inclination, because their number was complete, and no addition could be made to it. I told them that I should feel great satisfaction in continuing with such honest gentlemen, but if there were a necessity for our separation, I was willing even to submit to that; and, let it cost me what it might, I wished them to grant me my request.

The ten gentlemen, perceiving that I was determined in my resolution, then took a sheep, which they killed, and, after they had stripped off the skin, presented me with the knife, telling me it would be useful to me on a certain occasion, which they should explain presently. "We must sew you up in this skin," said they, "with which it is necessary you should be enveloped; and shall then leave you here, and retire. A bird of a monstrous size, called a roc, will soon appear in the air, and, supposing you to be a sheep, will dart down upon you, and carry you up to the skies; but let not that terrify you: he will again direct his flight towards the earth, and lay you upon the top of a mountain. When you find yourself upon the ground, cut the skin with the knife, and throw it off. No sooner will the roc see you, than he will fly away for fear, and leave you at liberty. Do not stay, but walk on till you reach a prodigiously extensive castle, covered with plates of gold, large emeralds, and other precious stones. Proceed to the gate, which always stands open, and walk in. We have been as much in that castle as we have been here. We will tell you nothing of what we saw, or what befel us there; you will learn all yourself: we can only inform you, that it has cost each of us our right eye; and we are doomed to the penance which you have witnessed, because we have been there. The history of each of us in particular is so full of extraordinary adventures, that a large volume would not contain them. But we must explain ourselves no further."

As soon as the gentlemen had ended this discourse, I wrapped myself in the sheepskin, and secured the knife which was given me; and after the young gentleman had taken the trouble to sew the skin round me, they left me on the place, and retired into the hall. The roc they had mentioned soon appeared; he sunk down upon me, seized me between his talons as a sheep, and carried me to the top of the mountain.

When I found myself upon the earth, I did not forget to use the knife; I cut the skin, threw it off, and appeared before the roc, which instantly flew away. This rock is a white bird of monstrous size; his strength is so great, that he can lift up elephants from the plains, and carry them to the summit of mountains, where he feeds upon them.

Anxious to reach the castle, I lost no time, but hastened thither, where I arrived in less than half a day; and I must confess that it surpassed the description I had received.

The gate was open, and I entered a square court, so large that it had round it ninety-nine gates of sanders and aloes wood, and one of gold, without reckoning those of several magnificent staircases, which led to apartments above, besides others that I could not see. The hundred doors I mentioned opened into gardens, store-houses full of riches, or, in fine, into places that contained things wonderful to be seen.

I saw, just before me, a door standing open, through which I entered into a large hall, where were seated forty young ladies of such perfect beauty, that imagination could not exceed it. They were all magnificently apparelled. As soon as they saw me, they rose together; and, without attending to my compliment, said to me, with great demonstrations of joy, "Noble sir, you are very welcome." One of them spoke to me in the name of the others, thus:— "We have been long in expectation of such a gentleman as you. Your mien assures us that you are possessed of all the good qualities we can wish for; and we hope you will not find our company either disagreeable or unworthy of you."

After considerable opposition on my part, they forced me to sit down on a seat raised a little above theirs; and as I signified that it gave me uneasiness, "That is your place." said they: "you are at present our lord, our master, our judge; and we are your slaves, ready to receive your commands."

Nothing in the world, madam, could so much astonish me as the ardour and eagerness of those ladies to render me all the services imaginable. One brought hot water to wash my feet; a second poured sweet-scented water on my hands: some brought me all that was necessary to change my apparel; others served up a magnificent collation; and the rest entered with glasses in their hands, offering to me delicious wine and all was performed without confusion, and in the most charming manner possible. I ate and drank; after which the ladies placed themselves about me, and desired an account of my travels. I gave them a full relation of my adventures, which engaged us till night approached.

When I had ended recounting my story to the forty ladies, some of those who sat nearest me remaining to keep me company, others seeing it was dark, arose to fetch tapers. They brought a very large quantity, which produced a marvellous light, equal to that of the day; but they were so proportionably disposed, that it appeared as if less would have been insufficient.

Other ladies covered a table with dry fruits, sweet meats, and such articles as were proper to make liquor agreeable; and arranged a sideboard with several sorts of wines and other liquors; and others again appeared with musical instruments. When all was ready, they invited me to sit down to supper. The ladies seated themselves with me, and we continued a long while at table. Those who were to play upon the instruments, and to accompany them with their voices, stood up, and made a charming concert. The others began a sort of ball, and danced in couples, one after another, in the most graceful manner.

Midnight had arrived before these amusements ended. Then one of the ladies said to me, "You are fatigued by the journey you have made to-day; it is time you should go to rest. Your apartment is prepared; but, before you retire, select which of us you like best, and take her whom you choose to sleep with you." I answered that I would not be so indiscreet as to offer to make my own choice, since they were all equally beautiful, witty, and worthy of my respects and service, I would not be guilty of so much incivility, as to prefer one before another.

The same lady who had before spoken to me, answered, "We are very well satisfied with your complaisance, and see that fear of creating a jealousy among us occasions your delicacy; but let not that consideration hinder you. We assure you, that the good fortune of her whom you choose will cause no jealousy, for we have agreed that each of us shall receive the same honour, till it go round; and when forty days are past, to recommence.

Choose, then, freely; and lose no time to go and take that repose of which you stand in need." I was obliged to yield to their solicitations, and presented my hand to the lady who spoke. She gave me hers, and we were conducted to a magnificent apartment: the ladies then left us, and each retired to her own chamber.

I had scarcely dressed myself the next morning, when the other thirty-nine ladies entered my chamber, all differently decorated from the day preceding: they bade me good morrow, and inquired concerning my health. Afterwards they conducted me to a bagnio, where they washed me themselves; and, even against my will, rendered me all the services of which I was in want, and when I left the bath, they made me put on another habit yet more magnificent than the former.

We passed nearly the whole day at table; and when the hour of sleep arrived, they prayed me again to make choice of one of them to keep me company. In short, madam, not to weary you with repetitions, I must tell you that I passed a whole year with those ladies, and received them into my bed one after another; and that, during all the time, this voluptuous life was not interrupted by the least unpleasantry. When the year had expired, I was extremely surprised that the forty ladies, instead of appearing with their usual cheerfulness to inquire after my health, entered one morning into my chamber with eyes bathed in tears. They each embraced me with great tenderness, saying, "Adieu, dear prince, adieu! for we must leave you."

Their tears distressed me. I prayed them to tell me the cause of their grief and of the separation they mentioned. "In the name of Heaven, fair ladies," said I, "let me know if it be in my power to comfort you, or if my assistance can be in any way useful to you." Instead of returning a direct answer, "Would to God," cried they, "we had never seen or known you! Several gentlemen, before you, have honoured us with their company; but not one of them had the comeliness, the sweetness, the pleasantness of humour, and the merit which you have: we know not how to live without you!" After they had spoken these words, they again began to weep bitterly. "My dear ladies," said I, "keep me no longer in suspense; tell me the cause of your sorrow." "Alas!" replied they, "what other subject could be capable of grieving us, but the necessity of parting from you? Perhaps, we shall never see you again, though, if you desire it, and have sufficient command over yourself, it is not impossible for us to meet." "Ladies," said I, "I do not understand your meaning; pray, express yourselves more clearly."

"Well, then," said one of them, "to satisfy you, we will acquaint you that we are all princesses, daughters of kings. We live here together in the manner you have seen; but at the end of every year, we are obliged to be absent forty days, upon indispensable duties, which we are not permitted to reveal, and afterwards we return to this castle. Yesterday was the last day of the year; and we must quit you this day, which is the cause of our affliction. Before we depart, we will leave you the keys of everything, especially those belonging to the hundred doors, where you will find enough to satisfy your curiosity, and to sweeten your solitude during our absence. But, for your own welfare, and our interest in particular, we recommend you to forbear opening the golden door. If you should open it, we shall never see you again; and the fear of this arguments our grief. We hope, nevertheless, that you will follow the advice we give you, as you regard your own quiet, and the happiness of your life; so, take heed that you avoid indiscreet curiosity, for thereby you will do yourself a considerable injury. We conjure you, then, not to commit this fault; but to let us have the consolation of finding you here again after forty days. We would willingly carry the key of the golden door with us, but that would be an affront to a prince like you, as doubting his discretion and delicacy."

The discourse of the fair princesses rendered me truly sorrowful. I omitted not to make them sensible how much their absence would afflict me: I thanked them for their good advice, assuring them that I would follow it, and willingly do what was much more difficult, to procure me the happiness of passing the rest of my days with ladies of such rare qualifications. We took leave with the utmost tenderness; I embraced them all: at length they departed, and I remained alone in the castle.

The agreeableness of their company, the good cheer, the concerts, and other pleasures, had so much diverted me during the year, that I had neither time, nor the least desire, to see the wonderful things contained in this enchanted palace. Nay, I did not even notice a thousand rare objects which were every day presented to my view, so much was I charmed with the beauty of those ladies, and with the pleasure of seeing them wholly employed in serving me. I was sensibly afflicted at their departure; and though their absence would be but for forty days, it appeared to me as an age to live without them.

I promised myself to remember the important advice they had given me, not to open the golden door; but as I was permitted to satisfy my curiosity with that exception, I took the first of the keys of the other doors, which were arranged in order.

Opening the first door, I entered an orchard, which I believe the universe could not equal: I even thought that the place which our religion promises us after death could not surpass it: the symmetry, the neatness, the admirable order of the trees, the abundance and diversity of the fruits, of a thousand unknown species, their freshness and beauty, ravished my sight.

I should not forget, madam, to acquaint you, that this delicious orchard was watered in a very particular manner. There were channels formed with art, and so proportionately dug, that they carried water in abundance to the roots of such trees as required it for producing their leaves and flowers: others conveyed it to those that had their fruit formed: some conducted it in lesser quantities to those the fruit of which was growing large; and others carried only a sufficiency to water such trees as had perfect fruit, only requiring to be ripened. Their size very much exceeded the ordinary fruits of our gardens. There were, lastly, channels which watered the trees that bore ripe fruit, and had only occasion for moisture to preserve them from withering.

I could never have been weary of looking at and admiring so charming a place; and I should never have quitted it, had I not conceived a more exalted idea of the other things which I had not seen. I came out at last with my mind filled with those wonders: I shut that door, and opened the next.

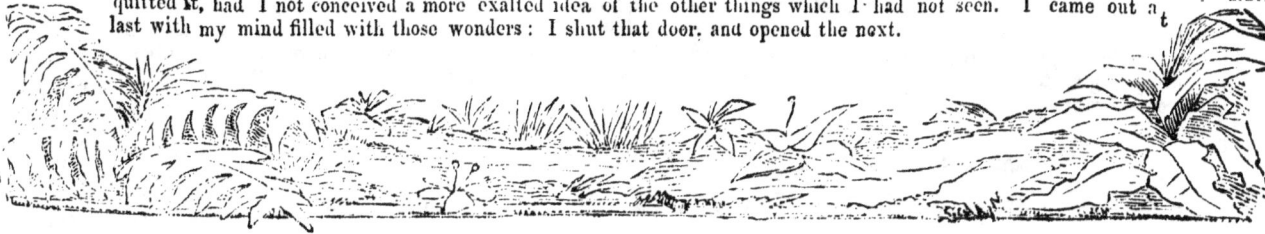

I here found a flower-garden, which was no less extraordinary in its kind. It was spacious, not watered so profusely as the former, but with greater delicacy, no more water being furnished than wha each flower required.

The roses, jessamines, violets, daffodils, hyacinths, anemonies, tulips, narcissuses, pinks, lilies, and an infinite variety of flowers which grew in other places, but at certain times were there flourishing all together; and nothing could be more delicious than the fragrant and exhilarating smell of this garden.

I opened the third door, where I found a large aviary, paved with the finest and most rare marble, of several colours. The cage was composed of sanders and aloes wood: it contained an infinite number of nightingales, goldfinches, canaries, larks, and other singing birds, yet more harmonious, of which I had never heard. The vessels that held their seed and water were of the most precious jasper or agate besides, this aviary was so extremely neat, that, considering its extent, I judged there could not be less than a hundred men employed to keep it in the state it appeared, though I had not seen one person, either here, in the orchard, or in the flower-garden, where I could not perceive a weed, or the least superfluity to offend the sight.

The sun had already set, and I retired, charmed with the warbling of the multitude of birds, which then began to perch upon such places as were convenient for their repose during the night. I went to my chamber, resolving to open all the rest of the doors the days following, except that of gold.

Accordingly, the next day I opened the fourth door, and, if what I had seen before was capable of surprising me, that which then presented threw me into a perfect ecstasy. I entered a large court, surrounded by a building of admirable structure, the description of which I will omit, to avoid prolixity.

This building had forty doors, all open, each of which gave entrance to a treasury; and, of these treasuries, severa were of greater value than the largest kingdoms. The first contained heaps of pearls, and, what is nearly incredible the most precious, which were as large as pigeons' eggs, exceeded in number those of the ordinary size. In the second treasury, were diamonds, carbuncles, and rubies: in the third, emeralds: in the fourth, ingots of gold: in the fifth was money: in the sixth were ingots of silver: in the two following was also money. The rest contained amethysts, chrysolites, topazes, opals, turquoises, hyacinths, and all the other stones that are unknown to us; without mentioning agate, jasper, cornelian, and coral, of which there was a store-house filled, not merely with branches, but even entire trees.

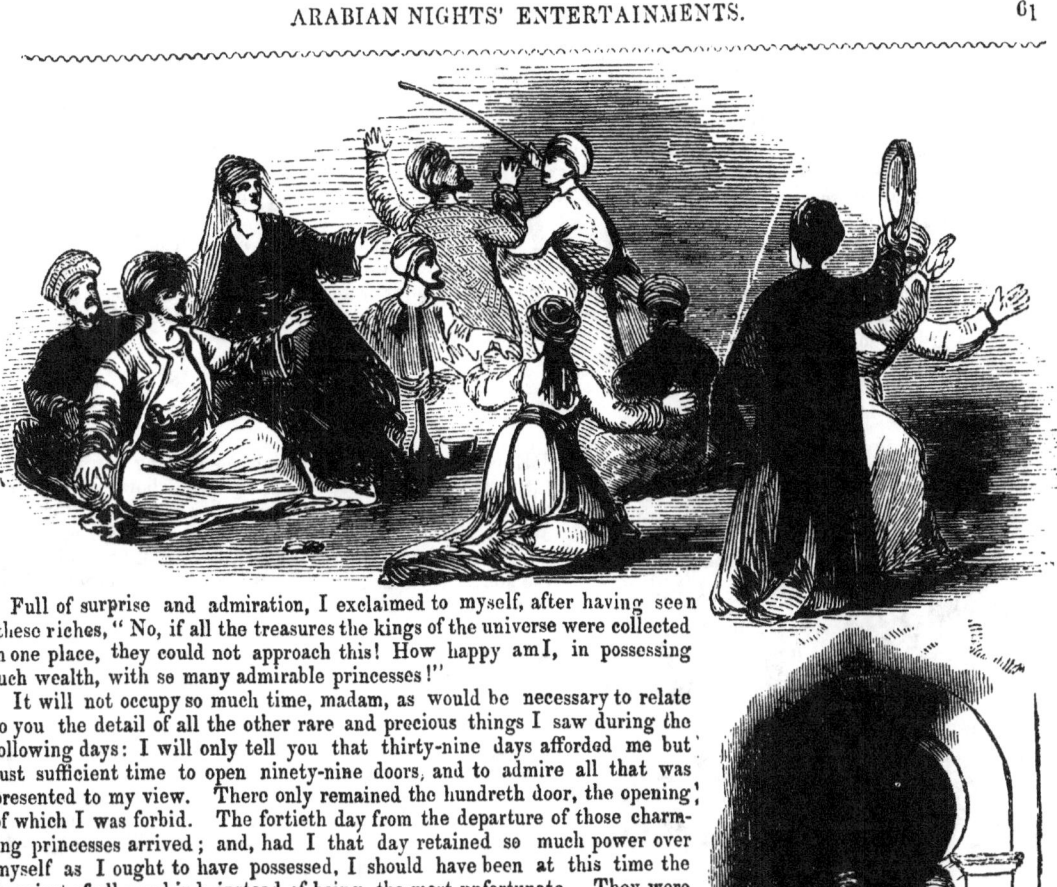

Full of surprise and admiration, I exclaimed to myself, after having seen these riches, " No, if all the treasures the kings of the universe were collected in one place, they could not approach this! How happy am I, in possessing such wealth, with so many admirable princesses!"

It will not occupy so much time, madam, as would be necessary to relate to you the detail of all the other rare and precious things I saw during the following days: I will only tell you that thirty-nine days afforded me but just sufficient time to open ninety-nine doors, and to admire all that was presented to my view. There only remained the hundreth door, the opening of which I was forbid. The fortieth day from the departure of those charming princesses arrived; and, had I that day retained so much power over myself as I ought to have possessed, I should have been at this time the happiest of all mankind, instead of being the most unfortunate. They were to return the next day; and the pleasure of again seeing them ought to have restrained my curiosity; but, through a weakness which I shall ever repent, I yielded to the temptations of the devil, who suffered me to take no repose till I had deliverd myself up to those misfortunes which I have since encountered.

I opened the fatal door, which I had promised not to unclose; and had not advanced a step to enter, when an odour, not unpleasant, but contrary to my constitution, made me swoon. However, I recovered; but, instead of profiting by this warning, to shut the door, and forbear satisfying my curiosity, I went in, after I had stood some time in the air, to lessen the scent, with which I was not again incommoded. I entered an extensive place, very well vaulted, the pavement of which was strewed with saffron; several candlesticks of massy gold, with lighted tapers that smelt of aloes and ambergris, illuminated the place; and the light was augmented by lamps of gold and silver, filled with oil composed of various kinds of odours.

Of a great many objects that arrested my attention, I particularly noticed a black horse, of the handsomest and best shape that ever was seen. I approached to observe him closely, and found he had a saddle and bridle of massy gold curiously wrought. One side of his manger was filled with clean barley sesames, the other with rose-water. I took him by the bridle, and led him forth to view him by the light. I mounted, and wished him to advance; but he did not move. I whipped him with a switch I had picked up in this magnificent stable. He no sooner felt the stroke, than he began to neigh with a horrible noise, and extending his wings, which I had not before perceived, he flew with me into the air quite out of sight. I then thought only of sitting firmly; and, considering the fear that had seized upon me, I kept my seat very well. He afterwards directed his flight towards the earth, and alighting upon the terrace of a castle, without allowing me time to dismount, he shook me out of the saddle with such force, that he made me fall behind him, and with the end of his tail struck out my right eye.

In this manner I lost the sight of one eye, and I then remembered the predictions of the ten young gentleman. The horse again took wing, and disappeared. I arose, very much afflicted at the misfortune I had brought upon myself. I walked upon the terrace, with my hand on my eye, which pained me exceedingly. At length I descended, and proceeded into the hall, which I immediately recognised by the ten sofas placed in a circle, and another, less elevated, in the middle, to be the same castle whence I was taken by the roc.

The ten half-blind gentlemen were not in the hall when I entered, but, with the old man, soon after appeared. They were not surprised to see me again, nor at the loss of my eye. " We are sorry," said they, " that we cannot congratulate you on your return, in the manner we could have desired; but we are not the cause of your misfortune. " I should be in the wrong to accuse you," replied I; " I have drawn it upon myself, and ascribe it solely to my own indiscretion." " If it be a consolation to the unfortunate," said they, " to have fellows, our example ma afford you some comfort. All that has happened to you, we also have experienced. We tasted all kinds of pleasure during an entire year; and we had continued still to enjoy the same happiness, had we not opened the golden door, while the princesses were absent. You have not been wiser than ourselves; and you have met the same punishment. We would gladly receive you among us, to do the penance you have seen us perform, though we know not how long it may continue; but we have already declared the reasons that hindered us. Therefore, depart hence, and go to the court of Bagdad, where you will meet with him who can decide your destiny." They directed the way I should travel, and I took leave of them.

On the road I caused my beard and eyebrows to be shaved, and assumed the habit of a calender. I have had a long journey. In fine, I arrived this evening in this city, at the gate of which I met these my brother calenders, strangers as well as myself. We were much surprised to find that all three were blind of the same eye; but we had not leisure to discourse of our common calamity; we have merely had time to come hither, to implore those favours which you have so generously accorded.

HE third calender having finished relating his adventures, Zobeide addressed him and his fellow calenders thus:—"Go wherever you think fit; you are all three at liberty." But one of them answered, "Madam, we beg you will pardon our curiosity, and permit us to hear the stories of those gentlemen who have not yet spoken." The lady then turning to that side where the caliph, the vizier Giafar, and Mesrour stood, whom she knew not, said to them, "It is now your turn to tell me your adventures; therefore speak."

* * * * * *

The grand vizier Giafar, who had always been the speaker, answered Zobeide thus:—"Madam, in order to obey you, we need only repeat what we have already said before we entered your house. We are merchants of Moussoul, and came to Bagdad to sell our merchandise, which is in the khan where we lodge. We dined to-day with several other persons of our profession, at the house of a merchant of this city; who, after he had regaled us with delicacies and excellent wines, sent for men and women dancers, and musicians. The great noise we made brought in the watch, who arrested some of the company, but we had the good fortune to escape; when, it being already late, and the door of our khan shut, we knew not whither to retire. Chance determined that we should pass along this street, and hear the mirth at your house, which made us resolve to knock at your gate. This, madam, is all the account that we can give you, in obedience to your commands.

After hearing this discourse, Zobeide seemed to hesitate what she should say; which the calenders perceiving, prayed her to grant the same favour to the three Moussoul merchants as she had vouchsafed to them. "Well, then," said she, "I consent; you shall be all equally obliged to me; I pardon you all, on condition that you immediately depart out of this house, and go whither you please."

Zobeide having given this order in a tone that indicated she would be obeyed, the caliph, the vizier, Mesrour, the three calenders, and the porter departed without reply; for the presence of the seven armed slaves kept them in awe. When they were out of the house, and the door shut, the caliph said to the calenders, without discovering himself, "And you, gentlemen, who are strangers, lately arrived in this town, as it is not yet day, which road do you design to take?" "Sir," replied they, "that is what perplexes us." "Follow us then," returned the caliph, "and we will convey you out of danger." After saying these words, he whispered to the vizier, "Take them with you; and to-morrow morning bring them to me: I will have their histories written; for they well deserve a place in the annals of my reign."

The vizier Giafar took the three calenders with him: the porter went to his house; and the caliph, with Mesrour, returned to the palace. The caliph retired to bed; but he could not sleep, his mind was so agitated by the extraordinary things he had seen and heard. Above all, he was anxious to know who Zobeide was, what reason she could have for her severity to the two black bitches, and why Amine's bosom was so disfigured. Day appeared while he was yet occupied with these reflections; he arose, and went to his council-chamber, where he likewise gave audience, and seated himself upon his throne.

The grand vizier entered soon after, and paid his usual respects. "Vizier," said the caliph, "the affairs that we have at present to consider are not very urgent; the mystery of the three ladies and the two black bitches is much more interesting. My mind will not be at ease till I am thoroughly satisfied in all those matters with which I have been so much surprised. Go, fetch those ladies, and bring the calenders at the same time. Make haste, and remember that I impatiently wait your return."

The vizier, who knew his master's impetuous and fiery temper, hastened to the house of the ladies, to whom he communicated the order he had received to carry them before the caliph, without taking any notice of what had passed during the preceding night at their residence.

The ladies put on their veils, and accompanied the vizier; who, as he went by his own house, took the three calenders with him: the calenders in the meantime had learned that they had both seen and spoken to the caliph, without knowing him. The vizier conducted them to the palace; and executed his commission with so much diligence that the caliph was very well satisfied. This prince, that he might preserve a proper decorum before the officers of his court, who were then present, ordered the ladies to be put behind the door-hanging of the room that led to his apartment, and kept the three calenders near him, who, by their respectful behaviour, gave sufficient proof that they were not ignorant before whom they had the honour to appear.

As soon as the ladies were placed the caliph, turning towards them, said,—" When I acquaint you, that, disguised as a merchant, I last night introduced myself at your house, you will doubtless be alarmed. You will be fearful of having offended me; and, perhaps, will suppose that I have sent for you to show some marks of my resentment. But be not afraid; you may rest assured that I have forgiven all that has passed, and am even well satisfied with your conduct. I wish that all the ladies of Bagdad had as much discretion as you have exhibited before me. I shall always remember your moderation, after the incivility we had committed. I was then a merchant of Moussoul; but am now Haroun Alraschid, the seventh caliph of the glorious house of Abbas, that holds the place of our great prophet. I have sent for you merely to know who you are; and to ask for what reason one of you, after severely whipping the two black bitches, wept with them. I am not less curious to learn why another of you has her bosom covered with scars."

The caliph delivered these words very distinctly, and the three ladies heard them perfectly well; nevertheless the vizier Giafar, as an act of ceremony, did not forget to repeat them.

Zobeide, encouraged by the caliph's discourse, immediately proceeded to satisfy his curiosity.

THE STORY OF ZOBEIDE.

OMMANDER of the faithful, (said she,) the relation which I have to recount to your majesty is one of the most surprising that ever was heard. The two black bitches and myself are sisters by the same father and mother; and I shall inform you by what strange accident they were thus metamorphosed. The two ladies who reside with me, and who are now there, are also my sisters by the same father, but by a different mother: she whose breast is covered with scars is called Amine; the name of the other is Safi; and mine is Zobeide.

After the death of our father, his estate was equally divided between us; and when these two sisters had received their portions, they separated from us, and went to live with their mother. My other two sisters and myself stayed with our mother, who was then living: she has since died, and left each of us a thousand sequins.

When we had divided the property which belonged to us, my two elder sisters (for I am the youngest) marrying, they followed their husbands, and left me alone. A short time after their marriage, my eldest sister's husband sold all his goods and lands, and, with the money they produced, and my sister's portion, went with his wife into Africa; where, by riotous living and debauchery, he spent all; when seeing himself reduced to poverty, he found a pretext for divorcing my sister, and put her away.

Returning to Bagdad, not without having suffered incredible hardships in so long a journey, she sought refuge in my house, but in so pitiable a condition, that she would have excited compassion in the hardest heart. I received her with all the affection she could expect, and, inquiring into the cause of her unhappy condition, she told me, with tears, of the inhuman conduct of her husband. I was so much concerned at her misfortune that I wept with her. I afterwards made her enter a bagnio, and clothed her with my own apparel. "Sister," said I, "you are the elder, and I regard you as my mother. During your absence God has blessed the small portion that fell to my share; and the employment I follow is, to feed and rear silkworms. Assure yourself that I have nothing but what is at your service, and as much at your disposal as my own."

We continued very comfortably together for some months. We often discoursed of our third sister, and were surprised that we heard no news of her, when she appeared in as bad a condition as the elder: her husband had treated her in like manner, and I received her with equal friendship.

Some time after, my two sisters, pretending they would not be any longer burdensome to me, expressed a design to marry again. I answered them, that if they had no other reason than to relieve me from their support, they might waive that consideration, and should be very welcome to remain with me; for what I had would suffice to maintain us all, and in a manner answerable to our condition. "But," continued I, "I rather fear you have an inclination to marry: if it be so, I declare I shall be very much astonished. After the experience you have had of the little satisfaction there is in marriage, is it possible you dare to venture a second time? You know how difficult it is to meet with a husband who is a perfectly honest man. Believe what I say, and let us continue to live together as comfortably as we can."

All my persuasion was in vain: they were resolved to marry, and effected their determination. After the lapse of some months, they returned, and made a thousand excuses for not following my advice. "You are our youngest sister," said they, "but you are more wise than we. If you will receive us once more into your house, and account us your slaves, we will never again commit the like fault." "My dear sisters," I replied, "I have not altered my mind with respect to you since our last separation: come again, and share with me what I have." I then embraced them, and we remained together as before.

A whole year thus passed, in perfect tranquillity; when, seeing that God had blessed my little stock, I projected a voyage by sea, to hazard something in commerce. For this purpose I went, with my two sisters, to Balsora, where I bought a ship ready equipped, and loaded her with merchandise that I had conveyed from Bagdad. We set sail with a fair wind, and soon got through the Persian Gulf. When we were in the open sea, we steered our course for the Indies, and on the twentieth day saw land. It was a very high mountain, at the bottom of which we perceived a large town. As we had a fresh gale, we soon reached the harbour, where we cast anchor.

I had not patience to wait for the company of my sisters, but went ashore alone, and proceeded directly to the gate of the town. I there saw a numerous guard of men seated, and others who were standing, each with a staff in his hand; but they made so hideous an appearance, that I was terrified. Perceiving, however, they had not the least motion, even with their eyes, I resumed courage; and approaching nearer, found they were all changed into stone.

I entered the town, and passed through several streets, in which were everywhere men, in various postures, but all petrified and immoveable. At the merchants' quarter, I found most of the shops shut: in such as were open, I likewise observed some people petrified. I looked up to the chimneys, but saw no smoke, which made me conjecture that all within the houses, as well as without, was in the same state of petrifaction.

Being arrived in a vast square, at the centre of the town, I discovered a great gate, covered with plates of gold, the two folds of which were open: a curtain of silk-stuff seemed to be drawn before it; I also saw a lamp suspended over it. After having considered the fabric, I doubted not that it was the palace of the prince who reigned over that country; but, being very much astonished that I had not met with a living creature, I went thither, in the hopes of finding some one. I entered the gate; and my surprise was augmented, when I saw, in the hall, only some porters, or guards, all petrified; some standing, others sitting or leaning.

I crossed a large court, where there were numbers of people: some appeared to be going from me, others as if approaching; though they were all motionless, being in the same state as those I had already seen. I entered another court; and from that I went into a third; but all was a solitude, and there reigned a dreadful silence.

Entering a fourth court, I saw, immediately before me, an elegant building, the windows of which were enclosed with lattices of massy gold. I judged it to be the queen's apartment. I went into a large hall, where were several black eunuchs turned into stone. Thence I proceeded into a room very richly furnished, where I perceived a lady, also petrified; I knew her to be the queen, by the crown of gold that she had on her head. About her neck was a collar of pearls, very round, and larger than hazel-nuts. I advanced close to her, to view them, and thought I had never seen anything finer.

I remained some time, to admire the riches and magnificence of this chamber; but above all, the foot-cloth, the cushions, and the sofa, which was decorated with Indian stuff of gold, with pictures of men and animals in silver, admirably executed.

From the chamber of the petrified queen, I passed through several other apartments and closets richly furnished, which conducted me into a room of extraordinary grandeur, where there was a throne of massy gold, raised several steps above the floor, and enriched with large inchased emeralds: and on the throne was a bed of rich stuff, embroidered with glittering pearls. But what surprised me more than all the rest, was a brilliant light, which proceeded from above the bed. Curious to know whence it arose, I mounted the steps, and lifting up my head, saw, upon a little stool, a diamond, as big as the egg of an ostrich, and of such purity, that I did not perceive the least blemish; it sparkled so bright, that I could not endure the lustre, when viewing it by day.

On each side of the belster of the bed was a lighted flambeau, the use of which I could not comprehend: however, it made me judge that there was some one living in this superb palace; for I could not believe that these torches continued burning of themselves. Several other singularities detained me in this room, which the diamond I have mentioned alone rendered inestimable.

All the doors were open, or merely closed. I surveyed yet other apartments, as handsome as those I had already seen. I went also into the offices and store-rooms, which were full of infinite riches; and I was so entirely occupied with the sight of all these wonders, that I forgot myself. I thought no more of my ship, or of my sisters; my whole object was to gratify my curiosity. Meanwhile night approached, and warned me that it was time to retire. I wished to repass the passage, through the courts by which I had entered; but it was not easy to find. I lost myself among the apartments; and perceiving I had returned into the large room where were the throne, the couch, the large diamond, and the burning torches, I resolved to remain there for the night, and to depart early the next morning, to regain my vessel. I threw myself upon the couch, not without some dread at seeing myself alone in a place so desert; and it was this fear, no doubt, that hindered me from sleeping.

It was midnight, when I heard a voice, like that of a man, reading the Alcoran, after the manner, and in the same tone, as we were accustomed to read it in our mosques. Joyfully I arose, and, taking a torch to guide me, I passed from one chamber to another, on that side whence the voice proceeded: I stopped at the closet door, and was persuaded that the voice came from thence. Setting my torch upon the ground, I looked through a window, and it appeared to me to be an oratory. In short, it had, as we have in our mosques, a niche, that indicates where we must turn to say our prayers; some lamps, suspended and lighted; and two chandeliers, with large tapers of white wax burning.

I saw also a little carpet laid down, like those we have to kneel upon when we say our prayers. A comely young man sat upon this carpet, reciting, with great attention, the Alcoran, which was placed before him upon a desk. At this sight, transported with admiration, I wondered how it happened that he should be the only living creature in a town where all the people were petrified; and I did not doubt that there was something in it very extraordinary.

As the door was a-jar, I opened it and went in; and, standing upright before the niche, said this prayer aloud:— "Praise be to God! who has favoured us with a happy voyage; and may he be graciously pleased to protect us, in the same manner, until we arrive in our own country! Hear me, O Lord, and grant my request."

The young man cast his eyes upon me, and said, "My good lady, pray let me know who you are, and what has brought you to this desolate city? In requital, I will tell you who I am, what has happened to me, why the inhabitants of this city are reduced to the state in which you see them, and why I alone am safe and well in the midst of a terrible disaster."

I related to him, in a few words, whence I came, what had induced me to undertake the voyage, and how I had safely arrived in port, after twenty days' sailing. I then prayed him to acquit himself

of the promise he had made; and represented to him how much I was struck by the frightful desolation that I had seen in all the places through which I had passed.

"My dear lady," said the young man, "have patience for a moment." At these words, he shut the Alcoran, put it into a rich case, and laid it in the niche. I took that opportunity to observe him, and perceived so much grace and beauty in him, that I felt emotions such as I had never before experienced. He made me sit down by him; and, before he began his discourse, I could not forbear saying to him, in a manner that discovered the sentiments with which I was inspired, "Amiable sir, dear object of my soul! I have scarcely patience to wait the explication of all these wonderful things that have been presented to my sight, since I first entered your city; and my curiosity cannot be satisfied too soon. Speak, I conjure you; let me know by what miracle you alone are left alive, surrounded by multitudes of persons who have died in so strange a manner."

"Madam," said the young man, "you have convinced me that you possess a knowledge of the true God, by the prayer you have just now addressed to him. I have to acquaint you with a most remarkable effect of his greatness and power. You must know, that this city was the metropolis of a mighty state, over which the king, my father, reigned. That prince, his whole court, the inhabitants of the city, and all his other subjects, were magi, worshippers of fire, and of Nardoun, the ancient king of the giants, who rebelled against God.

"Though I was born of an idolatrous father and mother, I had the happiness, in my youth, to have a governess, who was a good Mahometan: she knew the Alcoran by heart, and understood the explication of it perfectly well. 'Prince,' would she oftentimes say, 'there is but one true God; take heed that you do not acknowledge any other.' She learned me to read Arabic, and the book she gave me for exercise was the Alcoran. As soon as I was conscious of reason, she explained to me all the principles of this excellent book, and inspired me with all its spirit, unknown to my father, and all the world. She died; but not before she had perfectly instructed me in all that was necessary, to convince me of the truths of the Mussulman religion. Since her death, I have persisted in the .... she enforced, and I abhor the false god, Nardoun, and the adoration of fire.

"Three years and some months ago, a thundering voice was suddenly heard through the whole city, and so distinctly, that no person could avoid hearing every word:—'*Inhabitants, abandon the worship of Nardoun, and of fire, and adore the only God, who shows mercy.*'

"The same voice was heard three years successively; but nobody being converted, the last day of the third year, at three or four o'clock in the morning, all the inhabitants in general were instantaneously changed into stone, each in the same state and posture he then happened to be. The king, my father, shared the same fate; he was metamorphosed into a black stone, as he is to be seen in a part of this palace: and the queen, my mother, experienced a like destiny.

"I am the only person on whom God has not afflicted that terrible chastisement; and ever since I have continued to serve him with more fervency than before. I am persuaded, dear lady, that he has sent you hither for my consolation: I render him infinite thanks; for I confess to you that this solitude is very uncomfortable."

All this relation, and particularly the last words, perfected my love for him. "Prince," said I, "there can be no doubt that Providence has conducted me into your port, to present you with an opportunity of withdrawing from this dismal place. The ship that brought me may persuade you that I am of some consideration at Bagdad, where I have left other property of no trifling amount; and I dare offer you sanctuary there, until the mighty commander of the faithful, the vicegerent of the prophet whom you acknowledge, has rendered you all the honours that are due to your merit. This renowned prince lives at Bagdad; and he will be no sooner informed of your arrival in his capital, than he will convince you that it is not in vain to implore his assistance. It is impossible you can stay any longer in a city where all the objects you see must be insupportable. My vessel is at your service; and you may absolutely dispose of it as you please." He accepted the offer, and we passed the remaining part of the night in discoursing of our embarkation.

Soon as the day appeared, we quitted the palace, and reached the port, where we found my sisters, the captain, and my slaves, all very much alarmed at my absence. After having presented my sisters to the prince, I told them what had hindered my return to the vessel the day preceding; the rencontre with the young prince; his story; and the cause of the desolation of so fine a city.

The seamen were employed during several days in unloading the merchandise I had on board the ship, and embarking, instead, all the most precious things in the palace, as jewels, gold, and silver. We left the furniture, and an infinite number of pieces of plate, because we could not carry them. It would have required several vessels to convey to Bagdad all the riches that were before our eyes.

After we had laden the vessel with such articles as we chose, we took aboard what provisions and water we judged necessary for our voyage; for we had still remaining a great quantity of those provisions that we had shipped at Balsora. In fine, we set sail, with a wind as favourable as we could wish.

The young prince, my sisters, and myself, conversed together very agreeably for some time. But, alas! this good understanding was not of long continuance; for my sisters grew jealous of the friendship they remarked between the prince and me, and maliciously asked me one day, what we should do with him when we arrived at Bagdad. I immediately perceived that they put this question to me, merely to discover my sentiments; and, therefore, resolved to pass it as a jest: I answered I should take him for my husband: and then turning myself to the prince, "Sir," said I, "I beg of you to give your consent. As soon as we reach Bagdad, I design to offer you my person to be your very humble slave, to render you my services, and to acknowledge you as the absolute master of my pleasures."

"Madam," replied the prince, "I know not whether you are in jest or not; but, for my own part, I very seriously declare before these ladies, your sisters, that from this moment I heartily accept your offer;—not to regard you as a slave, but as my lady and my mistress; nor will I assume any power over your actions." My sisters changed colour at this discourse, and I remarked after that time they had no longer the same affection for me as before.

We were in the Persian Gulf, and approached Balsora, where I hoped, if the fair wind continued, we should arrive on the following day; but, in the night, when I was asleep, my sisters watching their time, threw me overboard. They acted in the same manner by the prince, who was drowned. I sustained myself some moments on the water, and by good fortune, or rather miracle, I felt ground. I advanced towards a black place, which, as well as the obscurity permitted me to distinguish, appeared to be land; in effect, I gained a flat shore; and the next morning I found myself on a small desert island, lying at about twenty miles from Balsora. I soon dried my clothes in the sun, and, as I walked, I found several sorts of fruit, and likewise fresh water, which gave me some hope of preserving my life.

I laid myself down in the shade, when I saw a winged serpent, very large and long, coming toward me, wriggling to the right and to the left, and hanging out its tongue, which made me think it had received some hurt. I arose, and perceived another serpent, still larger, following it, holding it by the tail, and endeavouring to devour it. I had compassion on it, and, instead of retracting, had the boldness and courage to take up a stone that chanced to lie by me, and threw it with all my strength at the great serpent, which I struck on the head, and killed. The other finding itself at liberty, took to its wings and flew away. I looked a long while after it in the air, as an extraordinary thing; but having lost sight of it I lay down again in another place in the shade, and fell asleep.

When I awoke, judge what was my surprise at seeing by my side a black woman of somewhat lively and agreeable features, who held two bitches, fastened together, of the same colour. I sat up and asked her who she

was. "I am," replied she, "the serpent which you delivered not long since from my mortal enemy. I thought I could not better acknowledge the important service you rendered me, than by acting as I have done. I knew the treachery of your sisters, and to revenge you on them, as soon as I had gained my liberty by your generous assistance, I summoned several of my companions together, fairies like myself; we have conveyed all the effects that were on board your vessel into your storehouses at Bagdad; and we afterwards sunk the ship. These two black bitches are your sisters, whom I have transformed into this shape. But this punishment is not sufficient, I require you to treat them in such manner as I shall direct."

At these words, the fairy took fast hold of me with one arm, and the two bitches with the other, and transported us to my residence at Bagdad, where I found in my storehouses all the riches with which my vessel had been laden. Before she left me, she delivered to me the two bitches, saying, "Under penalty of the same transformation, I order you, in the name of Him who governs the sea, to give each of your sisters every night a hundred lashes with a rod, as a punishment for the crime they have committed against your person, and the young prince whom they have drowned." I was forced to promise that I would obey her command.

Since that time I have treated them every night, though with regret, in the manner your majesty has witnessed. But I prove to them, by my tears, with how much sorrow and reluctance I acquit myself of this cruel duty; and your majesty will see I am more to be pitied than blamed. If there be anything else, respecting myself, of which you desire to be informed, my sister Amine will fully explain it, by the relation of her story.

Amine, immediately addressing herself to the caliph, began her story in these words:—

THE STORY OF AMINE.

OMMANDER OF THE FAITHFUL, said she, not to repeat what your majesty has already been informed by my sister's story, I shall begin by stating, that my mother having taken a house for herself, to live in during her widowhood, gave me in marriage, with the portion my father left me, to one of the richest heirs in this city.

The first year of our marriage had scarcely passed, when I became a widow, and was left in possession of all my husband's wealth, which amounted to ninety thousand sequins. The interest only of this money was sufficient to support me very honourably. In the mean time, as soon as the first six months of my mourning were elapsed, I caused ten suits of clothes to be made, of such magnificence, that each dress cost a thousand sequins; and when the year was past, I began to wear them.

One day, when I was alone, busy about my private affairs, I was informed that a lady desired to speak with me. I ordered that she should be admitted. She was far advanced in years. Saluting me, by kissing the ground, she said, kneeling, "Dear lady, pray excuse the freedom I take in troubling you; the confidence I have in your charity makes me thus bold. —I must acquaint your ladyship that I have a daughter, an orphan, who is to be married this day; that she and I are strangers, and have not the least acquaintance in this town; this circumstance creates some perplexity, for we wish the numerous family with which we are going to unite ourselves, to think we are not entirely unknown, and without credit. Therefore, most beneficent lady, if agreeable to you to honour the wedding with your presence, we shall feel the greatest obligation, as the ladies of your country will then know that we are not considered here as worthless people, when they shall understand that a lady of your quality has considered us worthy of so great honour. But alas! madam, if you refuse this request, our mortification will be severe; and I know not to whom we can address ourselves."

The poor woman's discourse, accompanied with tears, touched me with compassion. "Good woman," said I, " do not afflict yourself; I will willingly afford you the pleasure you desire; tell me where I am to go, and I will attend you as soon as I have made myself a little decent. The old woman was so transported with joy at this answer, that she kissed my feet, without my being able to hinder her. "Good charitable lady!" said she, rising, "Heaven will reward the kindness you have shown to your servants, and make your heart as joyful as you have made ours. It is not yet necessary you should take that trouble; it will be sufficient if you go with me when I call on you in the evening. Adieu, madam," continued she, "until I have the honour to see you again."

As soon as she had left me, I took the suit I liked best, with a necklace of large pearls, bracelets, rings, and pendants for my ears of the finest and most brilliant diamonds. I had a presentiment of what would befal me.

Night approached, when the old woman arrived at my house, with an air that indicated much joy. She kissed my hand, and said, "My dear lady, the relations of my son-in-law, who are the principal ladies of the town, are now assembled; you may come when you please; I am ready to conduct you." We set off immediately; she walking before me, and I followed with a good number of my female slaves neatly dressed. We stopped in a very broad street recently swept and watered, at a large gate, with a lantern before it, by the light of which I read this inscription over the gate in golden letters—*Here is the everlasting abode of pleasure and delight.* The old woman knocked, and the gate was opened immediately.

They conducted me into a large hall, at the lower end of the court, where I was received by a young lady of incomparable beauty. She came up to me, and, after having embraced me, made me sit down by her upon a sofa, where there was a throne of precious wood, beset with diamonds: "Madam," said she, "you are brought here to assist at a wedding; but I hope this marriage will prove otherwise than you have been led to expect. I have a brother, one of the handsomest and most accomplished men in the world: he is so charmed with the fame of your beauty, that his fate depends upon you; and he will be most unhappy, if you do not pity him. He knows your quality;

and I can assure you he is not unworthy of your alliance. If my prayers, madam, have any effect, I will join them with his, and humbly beg you will not refuse his offer of making you his wife."

Since the death of my husband, I had not yet had any thoughts of marrying again : but I had no power to refuse so charming a lady. As soon as I had given consent by silence, accompanied with a blush that appeared on my face, the young lady clapped her hands; immediately a closet-door opened, and there came out a young man of majestic air, and so graceful behaviour, that I thought myself happy in having made such a conquest. He sat down by me, and I found by the discourse we had together that his merit even exceeded what his sister had stated.

When she saw that we were satisfied with each other, she clapped her hands a second time: and a cadi entered, who drew our contract of marriage, signed it, and caused it to be attested by four witnesses whom he had brought with him. The only thing that my new spouse exacted from me, was, that I should not be seen by, nor speak with, any other man but himself; and he swore to me, upon that condition, that I should have no reason to complain of him. Our marriage was concluded after this manner : so I became the principal actress at a wedding, to which I had been invited as a guest.

About a month after our marriage, having occasion for some stuffs, I asked my husband's leave to go out to purchase them, which he granted ; and I took the old woman of whom I before spoke, she being one of the family, to accompany me, with two of my female slaves.

When we reached the street where the merchants are, the old woman said to me, "My dear mistress, since you want silk stuffs, I must carry you to a young merchant of my acquaintance : he has all sorts ; and, without wearying yourself, by going from one shop to another, I can assure you that you will find at his house what is nowhere else to be met with." I suffered her to conduct me, and we entered the shop of a young merchant, sufficiently well-looking. I sat down, and bade the old woman desire him to show me the finest silk stuffs he had. She wished me to make the demand myself; but I told her, one of the articles of my marriage-contract was not to speak to any man but my husband, and I ought not to break it.

The merchant showed me several stuffs, of which one having pleased me better than the rest, I bade the old woman ask the price. He answered, "I will not sell it for gold or silver, but I will present it to her, if she will permit me to kiss her cheek." I ordered the old woman to tell him he was very rude in making such a preposition. But, instead of obeying me, she said, that what the merchant desired of me was not a matter of such importance; that I had no occasion to speak, but only to present him my cheek; and that it would be an affair very soon settled. Anxious to have the stuff, I was simple enough to take her advice. The old woman and my slaves placed themselves before me, that nobody might see the transaction, and I put up my veil: but, instead of kissing me, the merchant bit my cheek till the blood came.

The pain and surprise was so great, that I fell down in a swoon and continued in this state so long, that the merchant had time to shut his shop, and take to flight. When I recovered, I found my cheek all bloody; but the old woman and my slaves had been careful to cover it with my veil, so that the people who surrounded us could not perceive anything, and supposed my indisposition to be only a fainting fit.

The old woman who accompanied me, extremely troubled at the accident which had happened, endeavoured to afford me comfort :—"My dear mistress," said she, " I beg your pardon : I am the cause of this misfortune. I brought you to this merchant, because he is my country-man ; and I should never have thought him capable of so vile an action. But do not grieve : let us hasten home ; and I will give you a remedy that will cure you in three days so perfectly, that not the least mark shall be visible " The swoon had rendered me so weak, that I was scarcely able to walk. At length I reached home, where, as I entered my chamber, I fainted a second time : meanwhile, the old woman had applied her remedy ; I regained my senses, and went to bed.

Night came, and my husband arrived: he perceived that my head was bound up, and inquired the reason. I answered, that I had the head-ache, and hoped he would be satisfied: but he took a candle, and perceiving my cheek was hurt. " How comes this wound ?" said he. Though I was not very criminal, yet I could not resolve to men-tion the cause : besides, such confession, to a husband, I thought would be somewhat indecent : I therefore told him, that, as I was going for that silk stuff he had given me leave to purchase, a porter, carrying a load of wood, passed so near me in a narrow street, that one of the sticks had scratched my cheek ; but the hurt was trifling.

This statement put my husband in a passion. " The action," said he, " shall not remain unpunished : I will to-morrow give orders to the lieutenant of the police to seize all those brutes of porters, and have them hanged !" Afraid of occasioning the death of so many innocent persons, I said to him, " Sir, I should be sorry that such injustice should be committed. Consider what you do : if I were the cause of so much mischief, I should think myself unpardonable." " Then tell me sincerely," replied he, " what am I to think of your wound ?" I answered, that was occasioned by the inadvertence of a broom-seller, mounted on an ass, who, coming behind me, and looking another way, the ass gave me such a push, that I fell down, and hurt my cheek upon some glass. " Is it so ?" said my husband : " before sun-rising to-morrow, the grand-vizier Giafar shall be informed of this insolence ; and he will have all the broom-sellers put to death." " In the name of God, sir," interrupted I, " let me beg you to spare them ! they are not guilty." " How then, madam !" said he: " what am I to believe ? Speak, for I will absolutely know the truth from your own mouth. " Sir," I replied, " I was seized with a giddiness, and fell down ; that is the whole matter."

My husband now lost all patience. " Ah," cried he, " I have listened to your lies too long." Saying which he clapped his hands, and three slaves entered. " Pull her out of bed," said he, " and lay her in the middle of the chamber. The slaves obeyed his orders ; and, as one held me by the head, and another by the feet, he commanded the third to fetch him a scimitar : when the slave had brought it, " Strike!" said he, " cut her in two ! and then throw her into the Tigris, to feed the fishes. That is the punishment I inflict on those to whom I have given my heart, if they are unfaithful." As he saw that the slave hesitated to obey his orders, " Why do not you strike ?" said he; " who restrains you ? For what are you waiting ?"

" Madam," said the slave, " you approach the last moment of your life ; consider if you have anything you would dispose of before you die." I begged permission to speak one word, which was granted. I lifted up my head, and looking tenderly at my husband, " Alas !" said I, " to what state am I reduced ! Must I, then, die in the prime of my youth ?" I could say no more, for my tears and sighs prevented me. My husband was not in the least moved ; but on the contrary, he uttered reproaches, to which it would have been useless to reply. I had recourse to prayers ; but he regarded them not, and commanded the slave to perform his duty. The old woman, who had been my husband's nurse, entered at that moment, and throwing herself at his feet, endeavoured to appease his wrath :— " My son," said she, " as I have been your nurse, and reared you, let me conjure you to spare her life. Consider that,

he who kills shall be killed; and that you will stain your reputation, and lose the esteem of mankind. What will not the world say of such bloody rage!" She spoke these words with an air so touching, accompanied by so many tears, that they made a strong impression on him.

"Well, then," said he to his nurse, "for your sake, I will grant her life; but she shall carry some marks to make her remember her crime." At these words, one of the slaves, by his order, gave me so many blows, as hard as he could strike, with a little cane, upon my sides and breast, that he fetched off both skin and flesh, and deprived me of sense. After that, he caused the same slaves, the ministers of his fury, to carry me into a house, where the old woman took great care of me. I kept my bed four months: at length I recovered; but the scars you yesterday saw, against my will, have ever since remained.

As soon as I was able to walk and go abroad, I wished to return to the house that I had by my first husband, but I could find only the place. My second husband, in the excess of his wrath, not content with having it demolished, had even caused all the street in which it stood to be rased to the ground. Such violence is, I believe, unparalleled; but against whom could I allege my complaint? The author had taken measures to conceal himself; and I should not, perhaps, have known him. But, supposing I had recognised him, is it not clearly seen that the treatment I received proceeded from absolute power? How, then, should I dare to complain?

Desolate, and totally unprovided. I had recourse to my dear sister Zobeide, who has given your majesty an account of her adventures; to her I made known my misfortune. She received me with her accustomed goodness, and exhorted me to bear with patience. "Such is the way of the world," said she, "which deprives us either of our goods, our friends, or our lovers: and oftentimes of all together." At the same time, in confirmation of what she had said, she gave me an account of the loss of the young prince, occasioned by the jealousy of her two sisters. She told me also in what manner they had been transformed into bitches; and, in the last place, after giving me a thousand testimonials of her friendship, she presented to me my youngest sister, who had likewise taken sanctuary with her after the death of our mother.

Thus, returning thanks to God, for having brought us once more together, we resolved to live a single live, and never again to separate. We have a long time enjoyed this tranquillity; and, as I am charged with the affairs of the house; I always take a pleasure in going myself to buy what provisions are wanted. For this purpose, I went abroad yesterday, and the articles I had purchased I had carried home by a porter, a man of sense and agreeable humour, whom we detained for a little diversion. Three calenders happened to come to our door at the commencement of the night, and prayed us to give them shelter until the next morning; we admitted them on a certain condition, which they accepted, and after we had seated them at our table, they entertained us with a concert after their fashion, when we heard a knocking at our gate. It was by the three merchants of Moussol, men of very good mien, who begged the same favour as the calenders had before obtained; we consented to it, upon the like condition. But neither of the parties observed their engagement; nevertheless, though we had the power, as well as right, to punish them, we contented ourselves with demanding from them their histories, and bounded our revenge, when they had concluded, with dismissing them, and depriving them of the lodging they had demanded.

　　　*　　　　　　*　　　　　　*　　　　　　*　　　　　　*

The Caliph Haround Alraschid was very well satisfied with what he had heard, and publicly declared his astonishment.

Having thus gratified his curiosity, the caliph was willing to afford marks of his grandeur and munificence to the calender princes, and also to give the three ladies some proofs of his bounty. Accordingly, he himself, without the intervention of his minister, the grand-vizier, spoke to Zobeide. "Madam," said he, "this fairy who presented herself to you in the form of a serpent, and imposed so rigorous a law upon you, did she not mention to you her place of abode, or rather did she not promise to see you, and restore those bitches to their natural state?"

"Commander of the faithful," answered Zobeide, "I forgot to tell your majesty that the fairy put into my hand a little packet of hair, saying, that I should one day have occasion for her presence; when, if I burnt only two bits of this hair, she would be with me in a moment, though she were beyond Mount Caucasus." "Madam," said the caliph, "where is the packet of hair?" Zobeide replied, that since that time she had preserved it with so much care, as always to carry it in her possession. In fine, she produced it, and, just opening the case that contained it, showed it to the caliph. "Well," said he, "let us make the fairy come hither: you could not call her in a better time, for I wish to see her."

Zobeide having consented, fire was brought, and she threw the whole packet of hair into it. Instantly the palace began to shake, and the fairy appeared before the caliph, in the figure of a lady, magnificently dressed. "Commander of the faithful," said she to the prince, "you see I am ready to receive your commands. The lady who has called me by your order, rendered me an important service: to prove my gratitude, I avenged her for her sister's perfidy, by changing them into bitches; but, if your majesty desire it, I will restore them to their proper form."

"Charming fairy," replied the caliph, "you cannot afford me greater pleasure; grant me that favour, and I will afterwards find out some means of consoling them for their hard penance. But besides, I have another prayer to make, in behalf of that lady, who has been so cruelly treated by an unknown husband. As you know a great many things, we have reason to believe that you are not ignorant of this; oblige me with the name of this barbarous fellow, who could not be contented with exercising such cruelty upon her person, but has also, most unjustly, taken from her all the property she possessed. I was astonished that a proceeding so unjust, so inhuman, and which has been transacted in defiance of my authority, should have escaped my knowledge."

"To satisfy your majesty," replied the fairy, "I will restore the two bitches to their former state; I will cure the lady of her scars, that it may never appear she was so beaten; and afterwards I will tell you who it was that thus ill-treated her."

The caliph sent to fetch the two bitches from Zobeide's house, and, when they were brought, a glass of water was presented to the fairy, by her desire. She pronounced some words over it, which nobody understood: when, throwing part of it over Amine, and the rest upon the bitches, the latter became two ladies of surprising beauty, and the scars that were on Amine disappeared. Then the fairy said to the caliph, "Commander of the faithful, I must now discover to you the unknown husband whom you wish to find : he is very nearly related to yourself, for it is Prince Amin, your eldest son, brother to the Princess Mamoun. Falling passionately in love with this lady, through the fame he had heard of her beauty, by an intrigue he had her conducted to his house, where he married her. In regard to the blows he caused to be inflicted, he is in some measure excusable ; for the lady, his spouse, had been a little too easy, and her excuses were sufficient to make him believe her more faulty than she was in reality. This is all I can tell to satisfy your curiosity." At these words, she saluted the caliph and vanished.

The prince, filled with admiration, and feeling much satisfaction in the changes which he had effected, performed such actions as will perpetuate his memory to all ages. He first sent for his son Amin, and told him, that he knew of his secret marriage, and informed him on what cause he had wounded Amine. The prince did not wait for his father's commands, to receive her again, but took her immediately.

The caliph then declared that he would give his own heart and hand to Zobeide ; and proposed the other three sisters to the calenders, king's sons, who accepted them for their brides with much gratitude. The caliph had assigned to each of them a magnificent palace in the city of Bagdad, promoted them to the highest dignities of his empire, and admitted them to his councils.

The first cadi of Bagdad being called, with witnesses, executed the contracts of marriage ; and the famous caliph Haroun Alraschid, by establishing the happiness of so many persons who had encountered incredible calamities, drew upon himself a thousand blessings.

THE STORY OF SINDBAD THE SAILOR.

DINARZADE having awakened her sister, the sultaness, as usual, prayed her to tell her another story. Scherazade asked permission of the sultan, and, having obtained it, thus began :—

Sir—Under the reign of the same caliph, Haroun Alraschid, whom I formerly mentioned, there lived at Bagdad a poor porter, named Hindbad. One day, when the heat of the weather was excessive, he was employed to carry a heavy burthen from one extremity of the town to the other. Being very weary, and having still a great distance to go, he arrived in a street, where he found a soft breeze, and the pavement was sprinkled with rose-water. He could not have desired an air more favourable to repose, and to renovate his strength ; he, therefore, placed his burthen on the ground, and sat down on it, near a great house.

He was soon very well pleased he had stopped in this place, for an exquisite odour, arising from wood of aloes and of pastils that issued from the windows of the house mixing with the scent of the rose-water, completely perfumed the air. Besides which, he heard, from within, a concert of various instruments, accompanied by the harmonious warbling of a great number of nightingales, and other birds peculiar to the climate of Bagdad. This delightful melody, and the effluvia of several sorts of victuals, made the porter think there was a feast and great rejoicings within. Having seldom had occasion to pass through that street, he knew not who dwelt in the house ; but, to satisfy his curiosity, he approached some of the domestics, whom he saw standing at the gate in magnificent apparel, and asked the name of their master. "How !" replied one of them ; " you live in Bagdad, and know not that this is the house of Signor Sindbad the Sailor, that famous traveller, who has sailed round the world ?" The porter, who had heard of Sindbad's riches, could not help envying a man whose condition he judged to be as happy as his own was deplorable. His mind being disturbed with these reflections, he lifted up his eyes to heaven, and said, loud enough to be heard, " Almighty Creator of all things, consider the difference there is between Sindbad and me ! I am every day exposed to a thousand fatigues and ills, and can scarcely get coarse barley-bread for myself and my family ; while the happy Sindbad profusely expends immense riches, and leads a life of continual pleasure. What has he performed, to obtain from Thee a lot so agreeable ? and what have I done, to deserve one so miserable ?' Having uttered this complaint, he struck his foot against the ground, like a man entirely devoted to grief and despair.

While the porter was thus indulging his melancholy, a servant came out of the house, and taking him by the arm, " Come follow me" said he ; " Signor Sindbad, my master, wishes to speak with you."

Your majesty may readily imagine that poor Hindbad was not a little surprised at this compliment. After what he had said, he was afraid that Sindbad intended to punish him : he would, therefore, have excused himself, alleging he could not leave his burthen in the middle of the street. But Sindbad's servant assured him that it should be taken care of ; and pressed the porter with so much earnestness, that he was obliged to yield.

The servant conducted him into a large hall, where a number of people sat round a table covered with all sorts of fine dishes. At the upper end was a grave, comely, venerable gentleman, with a long white beard ; and behind him stood a crowd of officers and domestics, all ready to serve him : this gentleman was Sindbad. The porter, whose fear was augmented at the sight of so many people, and of a banquet so sumptuous, saluted the company trembling. Sindbad bade him approach ; and seating him at his right hand, served him himself, and gave him excellent wine, with which the side-board was well furnished.

At the end of the repast, Sindbad, remarking that his guests ate no more, addressed himself to Hindbad, whom he treated as a brother, according to the custom of the Arabians, when they speak familiarly together, and asked him his name and employment. " Signor," replied he, " my name is Hindbad." " I am very glad to see you," returned Sindbad ; " and I dare say the same for all the company ; but I could wish to hear from yourself what you said a while ago in the street." Sindbad, before he sat at table, had heard all his discourse from the window ; and that had occasioned his calling for him.

At this question, Hindbad, very much confused, hung down his head, and replied, " Signor, I confess that my weariness put me in ill humour, and occasioned me to speak some indiscreet words, which I beg you to pardon." " Oh, think not," answered Sindbad, " that I could be so unjust as to harbour resentment : I consider your condition ; and instead of upbraiding you with your complaints, I am sorry for you but: I must rectify an error in which you appear to be, concerning myself. You think, no doubt, that I have

acquired the ease and conveniences which I now enjoy, without labour and trouble. But do not deceive yourself: I did not attain this happy condition without enduring, for several years, all the troubles of body and mind that imagination can conceive. Yes, gentlemen," he continued, addressing himself to the whole company, " I ca assure you, my labours have been so extraordinary, that they were sufficient to discourage the most covetous man from traversing the seas to acquire riches. Perhaps you have only heard indistinct narrations of the wonderful adventures and dangers I encountered in my seven voyages; and, as this opportunity presents, I will willingly give you a faithful recital of them, persuaded that it will be acceptable."

As Sindbad had determined to relate his history more particularly on account of the porter, before he began, he gave orders that his burden, which was left in the street, should be carried to the place were Hindbad wished it to be conveyed. He then proceeded.

THE FIRST VOYAGE OF SINDBAD THE SAILOR.

INHERITED from my ancestors a considerable estate, the greater part of which I dissipated in irregularities during my youth. But I perceived my error; and reflecting, I recalled to mind that riches were perishable, and that those who managed them no better than myself, were soon reduced to indigence.

I thought still more of the lamentable loss of time during a debauched life; time—which of all things is the most precious. Again, I considered that poverty in old age is the last and most deplorable of miseries; and I remembered the words of the great Solomon, which I frequently heard my father repeat, that *death is more tolerable than poverty.* Struck with these reflections, I collected the ruins of my patrimony, and sold all my moveables in the public market, to the highest bidder. I then entered into a contract with some merchants who traded by sea; and consulted those whom I thought most capable of giving me good advice. In fine, I resolved to profit by the little money I had remaining; and when I had taken this resolution, I lost no time in executing it. I went to Balsora, a port in the Persian Gulf, and embarked, with several merchants, on board a vessel that we had fitted out at our joint expense.

We set sail, and steered our course towards the East Indies, through the Persian Gulf, which is formed by the coasts of Arabia Felix on the right, and those of Persia on the left; and is, according to the general opinion, seventy leagues over in the broadest part. Without the gulf, the Levant, or eastern sea, is very spacious. It is bounded on one side by the coasts of Abyssinia, and extends four thousand five hundred leagues, to the isles of Vakvak.

I was at first troubled with what is called the sea-sickness; but I soon regained my health; and have not since been affected with that complaint.

In the course of our voyage, we touched at several islands, where we sold or exchanged our goods. One day while under sail, we were becalmed near a little island, almost even with the surface of the water, which resembled a green meadow. The captain ordered the sails to be furled, and permitted such persons of the crew as chose to land upon the island, of whom I was one.

But during the time we were regaling by eating and drinking, and refreshing ourselves after the fatigue of the sea, the island suddenly trembled, and gave us a violent shock.

Those who remained on board the vessel perceived the agitation of the island, and called to us to re-embark immediately, or we should all be lost, for what we took for land was the back of a whale. The nimblest saved themselves in the boat; others had recourse to swimming; but, for my part, I was still upon the island, or rather the back of the whale, when it dived in the sea; and I had time only to catch old of a piece of wood, that we had brought from the ship to make a fire. Meanwhile, the captain, having received those on board who were in the boat, and picked up some of those who swam, resolved to profit by the favourable gale which had just risen ; and hoisting the sails, deprived me of the hope of regaining the vessel.

I remained thus exposed to the mercy of the waves, driven from side to side, and struggling for my life all the rest of the day and the following night. By the next morning my strength was exhausted, and I despaired of escaping death, when happily a wave threw me against an island. The bank was high and rugged ; and I should scarcely have been able to climb up, had it not been for some roots of trees, which fortune seemed to have preserved in this place for my safety. I stretched myself on the ground where I lay, half dead, until broad day, and the sun appeared. Then, though very weak, in consequence of my great exertion, and of not having taken any kind of nourishment since the day preceding, I crept along to seek for herbs fit to eat. I found some, and had likewise the good fortune to discover a spring of excellent water, which contributed much to my re-establishment. Having recovered my strength, I advanced into the island, walking without following any particular route. I entered a fine plain, where I perceived, at a great distance, a horse feeding. I directed my steps toward it, between hope and fear, uncertain whether I was seeking destruction, or a security for my life. As I approached, I perceived it was a very fine mare, fastened to a stake. Her beauty arrested my attention, but whilst I was looking at her, I heard the voice of a man from under ground. In a moment after, the man appeared, came to me, and demanded who I was. I gave him an account of my adventure; after which, taking me by the hand, he led me into the cave where there were several other people, who were no less amazed to see me, than I was to find them there.

I ate some victuals which they presented to me ; and then, having inquired their business in a place which appeared to me so barren, they told me that they were grooms belonging to King Mihrage, sovereign of the island: that every year, at the same season, they brought thither the king's mares, and fastened them, as I had seen, until they were covered by a horse that came out of the sea; which, after he had so done, endeavoured to devour the mares, but they hindered him by their shouts, and drove him back to the sea : that they then carried home the mares, and that the foals were kept for the king's use, and called sea-horses. They added, that they were to go

home on the morrow; and had I been one day later, I must inevitably have perished, because the inhabited part of the island was at a great distance, and it would have been impossible for me to travel thither without a guide.

They had scarcely ended their discourse, when the horse came from the sea, as they had told me, covered the mare, and afterwards would have devoured her; but at the great noise made by the grooms, he quitted her, and again plunged into the sea.

Next morning, they returned, with their mares, to the capital of the island, and I accompanied them. On our arrival, the King Mihrage, to whom I was presented, asked me who I was, and by what adventure I had entered his dominions. When I had satisfied his curiosity, he told me he was much concerned for my misfortune, at the same time ordering that all my wants should be supplied; which order was executed in such a manner, that I had reason to praise his generosity and the fidelity of his officers.

Being a merchant, I associated with men of my own profession. I particularly inquired for those who were strangers, hoping I might hear news from Bagdad, or find an opportunity to return thither; for King Mihrage's capital is situated on the banks of the sea, and has a fine harbour, where ships arrive daily from different parts of the world. I frequented also the society of the learned Indians, and took delight in hearing them discourse; but that did not hinder me making my court regularly to the king, nor prevent my conversation with the governors, and petty kings, his tributaries, who were about him. They asked me a thousand questions concerning my country; and willing to inform myself of their laws and customs, in return, I made inquiries of them respecting all which appeared to merit my curiosity.

Under the dominion of King Mihrage there is an island named Cassel; in which, they had assured me, every night the sound of kettle-drums was heard, whence the mariners have supposed it to be the residence of Degial. I was very anxious to visit this wonderful place; and in my journey thither, I saw fishes of a hundred and two hundred cubits long; but which occasion more fear than hurt: they are so timorous, that they are put to flight by striking upon boards. I remarked other fishes, about a cubit in length, which had heads like owls.

After my return, while I was one day at the port, a ship arrived. As soon as she had cast anchor, they began to unload her; and the merchants on board ordered their goods to be conveyed into the magazine. Casting my eyes on some bales, and on the writing which indicated to whom they belonged, I saw my own name; and, after having examined them more attentively, I was convinced that they were those which I had brought from Balsora. I also recognised the captain; but, persuaded that he believed me to be drowned, I went 'and asked him who owned the bales which I saw. "I had in my ship," replied he, "a merchant of Bagdad named Sindbad. One day, being near an island, as it appeared to us, he, with several other passengers, landed upon this supposed island, which was only a monstrous whale, that lay asleep upon the surface of the water. But he no sooner felt the heat of the fire they had kindled on his back to dress some victuals, than he began to move, and sunk in the sea. Most of the persons who were upon him perished; and with them the unfortunate Sindbad. Those bales belonged to him; and I am resolved to trade with them, until I meet with some one of his family, to whom I can return the profit I may have made with the principal." "Captain," said I, "I am that Sindbad, whom you believe dead; and those bales are my property."

When the captain heard me speak thus, "O Heaven!" cried he, "whom can we now trust? There is no faith left among men. I saw Sindbad perish with my own eyes; and the passengers on board saw the same; and you dare tell me that you are that Sindbad! What audacity! To look at you, one would suppose you to be a man of honour; and yet you state a horrible falsehood, in order to possess yourself of what does not belong to you." "Have patience, captain," replied I; "do me the favour to attend to what I have to say." "Well!" said he, "what have you to say? I am ready to hear you." I then told him how I had been saved; and by what adventure I had encountered the grooms of King Mihrage, who had brought me to his court.

He seemed staggered by my discourse: but he was soon persuaded that I was no cheat; for there came people from the ship who knew me, and made me great compliments, and testified their joy at seeing me alive. At length he also recollected me; and throwing himself at my knees, "Heaven be praised," said he, "for your happy escape from so great a danger! I cannot sufficiently express to you the joy I feel. There is your property; take it, it is yours; and do with it what you please." I thanked him, acknowledged his probity; and, in requital, begged his acceptance of some goods, as a present, but he refused them.

I selected what was most valuable in my bales, which I presented to King Mihrage, who, knowing my misfortune, inquired how I became possessed of such rarities. I related to him by what accident I had been led to recover them; and he had the goodness to testify his joy, he accepted my present, and made me a much more considerable return. After this, I took leave of him, and re-embarked on the same vessel: having first exchanged the remainder of my goods for the commodities of the country. I carried with me the wood of aloes and sanders, camphire, nutmegs, cloves, pepper, and ginger. We passed by several islands, and at last arrived at Balsora, whence I came to this city, with the value of about a hundred thousand sequins. My family and I met with all the transports that arise from true and sincere friendship. I bought slaves of both sexes, fine lands, and erected me a large house. Thus I settled myself, resolving to forget the miseries I had suffered, and to enjoy the pleasures of life.

Sindbad having stopped, ordered the musicians to proceed with their concert, which his story had interrupted. The company continued to eat and drink until the evening: and when it was time to retire, Sindbad sent for a purse of one hundred sequins, and giving it to the porter, "Take this, Hindbad," said he; "return to your own house, and come back to-morrow to hear the sequel of my adventures." The porter then retired, much confused at the honour and the present he had received. The relation of it which he gave at home was very agreeable to his wife and children, who did not fail to return thanks to God for the wealth sent them by the interposition of Sindbad.

On the morrow, Hindbad dressed himself more neatly than the day preceding, and returned to the house of the liberal traveller, who received him with a cheerful air, and caressed him a thousand times. When all the guests were arrived, the repast was served, which kept them at table a long time. As soon as it was finished, Sindbad, addressing himself to the company, said, "Gentlemen, be pleased to give me audience, and listen to the adventures of my second voyage; they are more worthy your attention than the first." Every one held his peace, and Sindbad thus proceeded:—

THE SECOND VOYAGE OF SINDBAD THE SAILOR.

I HAD resolved, after my first voyage, to pass the remainder of my days tranquilly at Bagdad, as I had the honour to tell you yesterday; but it was not long before I grew weary of an idle life. My inclination to trade by sea revived. I bought goods proper for the commerce I meditated, and set out a second time, with other merchants of known probity. We embarked on board a good ship; and after recommending ourselves to God, set sail on our voyage.

We traded from island to island, and made some exchanges with great advantage. One day we landed upon an isle, covered with several sorts of fruit-trees, but so desert, that we could not discover any habitation, nor even any person. We went to take the air in the meadows, and along the streams that watered them.

While some diverted themselves with gathering flowers, and others with plucking fruits, I took my provisions, and some wine that I had carried on shore, and sat down by a stream between two great trees which formed a fine shade. I made a sufficiently good repast with what I had; and afterwards sleep overpowered my senses. I cannot tell whether I slept long; but when I awoke the ship was not at anchor.

I was very much surprised at missing the ship; I arose, looked about everywhere, but could not see one of the merchants who landed with me. At length I perceived the vessel under sail, but at such a distance, that I lost sight of her soon afterwards.

You may conceive the reflections I made in this sad situation. I was likely to die with grief; I uttered dreadful cries; I beat my head, and threw myself upon the ground, where I lay a long time in terrible agony, one afflicting thought being succeeded by another still more distressing. I reproached myself a hundred times for not being contented with my first voyage, which ought for ever to have satisfied me. But all my lamentations were useless and my repentance unseasonable.

At last, I resigned myself to the will of God; and, not knowing what to do, I climbed to the top of a great tree, whence I looked about on all sides, to see if I could discover anything that would afford me hope. Casting my eyes towards the sea, I only distinguished sky and water; but perceiving something on the land side that appeared white, I descended from the tree, took up what provisions I had remaining, and went towards it, the distance being so great that I could not determine what it was.

When I approached nearer, it seemed to be a white bowl of a prodigious height and size. I proceeded close to it, and touching it, found it very smooth. I went round, to see if there were an opening, but could not discover any, and it appeared impossible to get to the top, it was so very even. It was probably fifty paces in circumference.

The sun was at this time nearly setting, when suddenly the air became as dark as if it had been covered with a thick cloud. But, if I was astonished at this sudden obscurity, I was much more so on finding it occasioned by a bird of monstrous size, that flew towards me. I remembered a fowl called roc, of which I had often heard mariners speak, and I conceived that the great bowl, which I had so much admired, might be its egg. In short, the bird alighted, and sat on it, as if to hatch it. Perceiving her approach, I crept close to the egg, so that I had before me one of the legs of the bird, which was as large as the trunk of a tree. I fastened myself strongly to it, with the cloth that surrounded my turban, in hopes that when the roc flew away next morning, she would carry me out of this desert island. In effect, having passed the night in this state, the bird, as soon as it was day, took wing, and carried me so high, that I could not see the earth; she afterwards descended suddenly with so much rapidity, that I lost my senses. But when the roc had settled, and I found myself on the ground, I speedily untied the knot with which I was fastened to her leg: I had scarcely released myself, when the bird, having seized a serpent of monstrous length in her bill, again took flight.

The place where she left me was a very deep valley, environed on all sides with mountains, so high, that their summits were lost in the clouds; and at the same time so steep, that there was no road by which they could be ascended. Thus was I again embarrassed; and when I compared this place with the desert island from which the roc had brought me, I found that I had gained nothing by the change.

Walking through this valley, I perceived that it was strewed with diamonds, some of which were of an extraordinary size. I took a great deal of pleasure in examining them; but I soon perceived, at a distance, objects that very much diminished my satisfaction, and which I could not observe without terror; they were a great number of serpents, so large and so long, that the least of them was capable of swallowing an elephant. They retired in the day-time to their dens, where they concealed themselves from their enemy the roc, and came out only during the night.

I passed the day in walking about the valley, resting myself occasionally in such places as I thought most commodious. In the meantime, the sun had set; and as night approached, I entered a cave, where I judged I should be in safety: and to preserve me from the serpents, I stopped the mouth of it, which was low and straight, with a great stone, though not so large as to entirely exclude the light. I supped on part of my provisions, but the dreadful hissing of the serpents, which began to appear, occasioned me extreme terror, and did not permit me, as you may suppose, to pass the night very tranquilly. When day appeared, the serpents retired; and I left the cave, trembling. I can justly say that I walked a long time upon diamonds, without having the least inclination to possess myself of any. At last I sat down; and notwithstanding my uneasiness, not having shut my eyes during the night, I fell into a doze, after having eaten a little more of my provisions. But I was scarcely asleep, when something that fell near me, with a great noise, awakened me: it was a large piece of fresh meat; and the same moment I saw several other pieces fall from the rocks in different places.

What I had heard mariners and other persons relate concerning the valley of diamonds, and of the stratagems used by some merchants to obtain the precious stones from thence, I always considered as fabulous; but I now found their representations were true. In effect, those merchants go to the neighbourhood of this valley, when the eagles have young; and throwing down great pieces of meat, the diamonds, upon the points of which they fall, stick to them, the eagles, which are stronger in this country than elsewhere, seize these pieces of meat, and carry them to their nests upon the top of the rocks, to feed their young ones; then the merchants, running to the nests, drive away the eagles by their cries, and collect the diamonds which they find attached to the meat. By this stratagem, diamonds are obtained from the valley, which is surrounded by precipices, which nobody can descend.

Till then, I thought it impossible for me to get out of this abyss, which I regarded as my grave; but my opinion was now altered; and what I had seen gave rise to a hope of yet saving my life.

I began to select the biggest diamonds I could find, and put them into a leathern bag, in which I used to carry my provisions. I then took the piece of meat that appeared largest, and fastened it closely round me with the cloth of my turban, laid myself upon the ground with my face downward; the bag of diamonds being secured to my girdle, in such manner that it could not fall.

I had no sooner placed myself in this situation, than the eagles came, and each of them seized a piece of meat; one of the strongest having taken me up, with the piece of meat on my back, carried me to his nest at the top of the mountain. The merchants did not neglect shouting, to frighten the eagles; and when they had obliged them to quit their prey, one of them approached the nest where I remained. He expressed much fear when he saw me; but recovering himself, instead of inquiring how I came thither, he began to quarrel with me, asking why I stole his goods. "You will treat me," said I, "with more humanity, when you know me better. Console yourself," I continued; "I have more diamonds for you, and myself likewise, than all the other merchants together. If they have obtained any, it is by chance; but I myself chose, in the bottom of the valley, all those that I carry in this

bag." Having said this, I showed them to him. I had scarcely done speaking, before the other merchants surrounded us, very much astonished to see me; but their astonishment was greatly augmented when I related my story; yet they did not so much admire the stratagem I had conceived, as my courage in carrying it into execution.

The merchants conducted me to the place where they associated together; and there, opening my bag, I surprised them by the largeness of my diamonds; they declared that, in all the courts where they had been, they never saw one that approached them. I prayed the merchant to whom the nest belonged whither I was carried, (for each merchant had his own,) to take as many for his share as he pleased. He contented himself with one, and that too the least of them; and when I pressed him to accept of more, without fear of doing me any injury, "No," said he, "I am very well satisfied with this, which is sufficiently valuable to save me the trouble of making any more voyages for the establishment of my little fotune."

I passed the night with these merchants, to whom I related my story a second time, for the satisfaction of those who had not heard it. I could not moderate my joy when I reflected

on the danger I had escaped: I fancied myself in a dream, and could scarcely believe I had nothing more to fear.

The merchants had for several days been occupied throwing their pieces of meat into the valley; and, as each appeared satisfied with the diamonds that had fallen to his lot, we left the place next morning all together, and travelled near high mountains, where there were serpents of prodigious length, which we had the good fortune to escape. We gained the first port; whence we sailed to the isle of Roha, where the trees grow that yield camphire This tree is so large, and its branches so thick, that a hundred men may easily sit under its shade; the sap of whic ·

                                                                                        h

camphire is made, flows from a hole bored in the upper part of the tree, and is received into a vessel, where it acquires consistency, and becomes what we call camphire. When the juice is thus drawn out, the tree withers and dies.

There are in the same island rhinoceroses, animals less than the elephant, but larger than a buffalo; they have a horn upon their nose, about a cubit long. This horn is solid, and cleft in the middle from one extremity to the other; and upon it are white strokes, representing the figure of a man. The rhinoceros fights with the elephant, runs his horn into his belly, and carries him off upon his head; but the blood and fat of the elephant running into his eyes, and rendering him blind, he falls on the ground; and, what is astonishing, the roc comes and carries them both away in her claws, to feed her young.

I omit several other particulars respecting this island, lest I should be troublesome to you. There I exchanged some of my diamonds for good merchandise. Thence we went to other islands; and, in fine, after touching at several trading cities on the *terra firma*, we landed at Balsora: whence I returned to Bagdad. There I first gave great alms to the poor; and lived honourably upon the vast riches I had acquired with so much fatigue.

Sindbad thus ended the story of his second voyage. He ordered that another hundred sequins should be given to Hindbad, and invited him to return next day to hear the account of the third.

The guests retired to their respective homes; and again presented themselves on the morrow, at the same hour, and with them the porter, who had already nearly forgotten his former poverty. They took their seats at the table, and after the repast, Sindbad, having demanded attention, related to them the history of his third voyage.

THE THIRD VOYAGE OF SINDBAD THE SAILOR.

IN the pleasures of the life I then enjoyed, I soon lost all remembrance of the perils which I had encountered during my two former voyages. Being then in the flower of my age, I grew weary of living without employment, and, hardened myself against the apprehension of danger, I set out for Bagdad, with the richest commodities of the country, for Balsora. There I again embarked with other merchants. We made a long voyage, and touched at several ports, where we drove considerable commerce.

One day, when in the main ocean, we were attacked by a horrible tempest, which made us lose our course. It continued several days, and forced us before the port of an island, in which the captain was very unwilling to enter: but we were obliged to anchor there. When we had furled our sails, the captain told us that this place, and some other neighbouring islands, were inhabited by hairy savages, who would soon assail us; and though they were but dwarfs, yet, such was our misfortune, we could make no resistance, for they were more numerous than locusts; and if we happened to kill one of them, they would all fall upon and destroy us.

The captain's discourse threw the whole company into great consternation; and we very soon found that what he had told us was but too true. An innumerable multitude of hideous savages, entirely covered with red hair, only about two feet high, swam towards us, and in a little time encompassed our vessel. They spoke to us as they approached, but in a language we did not understand; and climbed up the sides of the ship, and appeared upon deck, with astonishing agility and quickness.

We beheld all this with the utmost fear, without daring to attempt to defend ourselves, or to speak one word to divert them from the mischievous design we suspected. In short, they took down our sails, cut the cable without being at the trouble to weigh the anchor, and hauling to the shore, made us all disembark; and afterward carried the ship into another island, whence they came. All voyagers carefully avoided the island where they left us; and it was very dangerous to remain there, for a reason you will hear presently; but we were obliged to bear our affliction with patience.

Quitting the sea-side, we advanced into the island, where we found some fruits and herbs, of which we ate, to preserve our lives as long as we could, for all expected nothing short of certain death. As we went on, we perceived at a distance a large building, to which we proceeded. It was a palace, well built, and very high, with a

folding gate of ebony, which we thrust open. Entering the court, we saw before us a vast apartment, with a porch, on one side of which was a heap of men's bones, and on the other a great number of roasting-spits. We shuddered at this spectacle; and, being weary with travelling, our legs failed us; we fell to the ground, seized with a mortal fear, and lay a considerable time immoveable.

The sun went down; and while we were in the pitiable state I have just described, the door of the apartment opened with a great noise, and immediately there came out the horrible figure of a black man as high as a palm-tree. He had but one eye, in the middle of his forehead, but red and ardent as burning coal. The front teeth he had were very long and sharp, and appeared without his mouth, which was deep as that of a horse: and his lower lip hung down upon his breast. His ears resembled those of an elephant, and covered his shoulders; and his nails were long and crooked as the talons of the greatest birds. At the sight of this frightful giant, we lost all sense, and remained as if dead.

At length we recovered, and saw him sitting in the porch, examining us attentively. When he had considered us well, he advanced to us, and laying his hand upon me, took me up by the nape of my neck, and turned me round as a butcher would handle a sheep's head: after having viewed me thoroughly, and perceiving me to be so lean that I had nothing but skin and bone, he let me go. He took up all the rest, one by one, examining them in the same manner. The captain being the fattest of the ship's company, he held him with one hand, as I would hold a sparrow, and thrust a spit through his body. Having kindled a great fire, he roasted and ate him for supper in the apartment to which he had retired. His repast finished, he returned to the porch, where he lay down and slept, snoring louder than thunder; and his sleep continued till next morning. For our parts, it was impossible that we should taste th sweets of repose; and we passed the night in the most cruel inquietude that can be conceived. Day being returned the giant awoke, got up, went out, and left us in the palace.

When we thought him at some distance, we broke the melancholy silence we had preserved all night, and each grieving more than the other, we made the palace resound with our complaints and our groans. Though there were a great many of us, opposed to a single enemy, we had at first the presence of mind to think of delivering ourselves from him by his death. This enterprise, though difficult to execute, was, however, that which we ought naturally to have formed.

We deliberated on several other measures, but determined on none; and submitting to what it should please God to order concerning our fate, we continued running about the island, preserving our lives with fruits and herbs, as on the day preceding. When evening approached, we in vain sought for a place to repose in, and were forced, against our inclination, to return to the palace.

The giant failed not to appear, and supped again upon one of our companions; after which he slept and snored till day, when he went out and left us, as before. Our condition seemed so dreadful, that some of my company designed to throw themselves into the sea, rather than die so miserable a death; and invited the rest to follow his example. But one of the company thus addressed them:—"We are forbidden," said he, "to destroy ourselves, and if it were lawful, is it not more consistent that we should devise a means of destroying the barbarous tyrant, who has destined us to so cruel a death?"

A project for that purpose having occurred to me, I communicated it to my comrades, by whom it was approved. "Brethren," said I, "you know there is a great quantity of timber floating upon the coast; if you be advised by me, let us construct several rafts that will carry us; and when they are completed, leave them till we think proper to use them. In the meantime, we will execute the design that I have proposed to you, to deliver ourselves from the giant: if it succeed, we may remain here with patience till some ship pass by, that will convey us from this fatal island; but if, on the contrary, it should miscarry, we will speedily get to our floats, and put to sea. I confess that by exposing ourselves to the fury of the waves on such fragile security, we run a risk of losing our lives; but if we perish, is it not better to be buried in the sea, than in the entrails of this monster, who has already devoured two of our companions?" My advice was approved by all; and we formed rafts, each capable of carrying three persons.

We returned to the palace towards the evening, and the giant arrived soon after us. It was necessary we should resolve on seeing another of our comrades roasted; but we at last revenged ourselves on the cruel giant, thus:— After he had ended his detestable supper, he lay down on his back, and fell asleep. As soon as we heard him snore according to his custom, nine of the boldest amongst us, and myself, took each of us a spit, and putting the points of them in the fire till they were red-hot, we thrust them all together into his eye and blinded him.

The pain which the giant felt occasioned him to make a frightful cry. He arose quickly, and stretched out his hands on all sides, to seize one of us, to sacrifice to his rage; but we had time to get at a distance from him, and to throw ourselves on the ground, in places where he could not encounter us on his feet. After having vainly searched for us, he groped for the gate, and went out howling dreadfully.

Quitting the palace, after the giant, we proceeded to the shore, where we had left our rafts, which we launched immediately into the sea. We remained there till day, intending to get upon them, should the giant approach us with any guide of his own species; but we hoped, if he did not appear by sun-rising, and cease his howling, which we still heard, that he would die; and if that should be the result, we proposed to stay on the island, and not hazard our lives upon the rafts. But day had scarcely appeared, when we perceived our cruel enemy, accompanied by two other giants of almost the same height, conducting him; and a considerable number of others preceding him at a very quick pace.

Terrified at the discovery, we no longer hesitated, but threw ourselves upon the rafts, and rowed from the land. The giants, who saw this, furnished themselves with large stones, ran to the shore, and, entering the water up to the middle of their bodies, threw them so exactly, that they sunk all the rafts but that I was upon; and all my companions, excepting the two with me, were drowned. As for me, and my comrades, rowing with our utmost strength, we had got farther from the land, and were out of the reach of the stones.

When we had gained the open sea, we were exposed to the mercy of the winds and waves, which tossed us about sometimes on one side, sometimes on another; and we passed that day and the following night in cruel uncertainty as to our fate : but next morning we had the good fortune to be thrown upon an island, where we joyfully landed. We there found excellent fruit, which contributed greatly to the recovery of our strength.

In the evening, we fell asleep on the bank of the sea ; but were awakened by the noise that a serpent, long as a palm-tree, made with its scales, as it crept along. It was so near us, that it seized one of my comrades, and, notwithstanding his loud cries, and the efforts he made to disengage himself, the serpent shaking him several times, crushed him against the ground, and swallowed him. I and my other companion had taken to flight ; but, though we were at a considerable distance, we some time after heard what we judged to be the reptile disgorging the bones of our unhappy comrade. In truth, we next morning saw them with horror. " O Heaven!" cried I, " to what are we exposed! We yesterday rejoiced at having escaped from the cruelty of a giant, and the fury of the waves, and are now fallen into another danger not less terrible !"

As we walked about, we observed a large and very high tree, upon which, for security, we designed to pass the following night ; and having satisfied our hunger with fruit, as on the day preceding, at the approach of the evening we ascended it. Soon after we heard the serpent come hissing to the foot of the tree in which we were ; it raised itself against the trunk, and seizing my comrade, who sat lower than me, swallowed him at once, and then retired.

I remained upon the tree till it was day, and then descended, more dead than alive, expecting no other fate than that of my two companions. Shuddering with horror, I was going to throw myself into the sea ; but, as life is always desirable, I resisted this movement of despair, and submitted myself to the will of God, who disposes of our lives at his pleasure.

I now employed myself in collecting a great quantity of small wood, brambles, and dry thorns ; and making several faggots, I tied them together, and formed a great circle round the tree : I also fastened some of them to the branches over my head. This done, at the approach of night, I shut myself up in this circle, with the sad consolation of having neglected nothing that could preserve me from the cruel destiny with which I was threatened.

The serpent failed not to appear, and went round the tree, seeking for an opportunity to devour me ; but it was prevented by the rampart I had made : however, it remained till the return of day, like a cat watching in vain for a mouse, that has gained a place of safety. At length, day-light compelled the serpent to retire ; but I dared not venture to leave my fort before the sun arose.

I was so fatigued with the labour and anxiety I had encountered, and had suffered so much from the poisonous breath of the serpent, that I descended from the tree, and forgetting the resignation I had expressed on the preceding day, ran towards the sea, with the design of precipitating myself into it headlong. But God took compassion on my despair ; for, just as I was going to plunge into the sea, I perceived a ship at a considerable distance. I called as loud as I could ; and taking the linen from my turban, displayed it, that they might observe me. This had the desired effect ; all the crew perceived me, and the captain sent his boat. As soon as I was conveyed aboard, the merchants and seamen inquired, with much solicitude, what adventure had caused me to be left on that desert island. After relating to them all that had befallen me, the oldest among them said that they had several times heard of the giants who dwelt in that island ; that they had been assured they were cannibals, and ate men raw as well as roasted ; as to the serpents, they added, that there was an abundance in the isle ; that they concealed themselves by day, and appeared abroad at night. Having testified their joy at my good fortune in escaping so many dangers, and not doubting that I was in want of food, they brought me the best they had to eat ; and the captain remarking that I was in rags, generously gave me one of his own suits.

We continued at sea for some time, touching at several islands, and at last landed at that of Salahat, where sanders is produced, a wood of great use in medicine. Entering the port, we came to anchor. The merchants began to unload their goods, to sell or exchange them. In the mean time the captain called to me : " Brother," said he, " I have here a parcel of goods which belonged to a merchant who sailed some time in this ship : he being dead, I design to dispose of them for the benefit of his heirs, to whom I shall render an account, when I meet with them.' The bales of which he spoke were already on the deck ; and showing them to me, " There are the goods," said he, " I hope you will sell them to the greatest advantage, under the condition that you take the proper factorage." I accepted the employment ; thanking him for the opportunity he gave me of avoiding idleness.

The clerk of the ship took an account of all the bales, with the names of the merchants to whom they belonged. When he asked the captain whose name he should enter those that were in my charge, " Enter them," said the captain, " in the name of Sindbad the Sailor." I could not hear myself named without some emotion ; and looking stedfastly at the captain, I recognised him to be the person who, in my second voyage, had left me in the island where I fell asleep by a brook, and who had sailed without me, or sending to search for me. But he was so much altered in person that I did not at first remember him.

As for him, believing me dead, I could not wonder at his not knowing me. " Captain," said I, " was the merchant's name, to whom these bales belonged, Sindbad ?" " Yes," he replied, " that was his name : he came from Bagdad, and embarked on board my ship at Balsora. One day we landed at an island for water, and to take some refreshments ; and, I know not by what mistake, I set sail without observing that he had not re-embarked with us : neither I nor the merchants perceived it till four hours after. We had the wind in our stern, and so fresh a gale, that it was not then possible for us to tack about for him." " You believe him then dead ?" said I. " Certainly," he answered " No, captain," replied I ; " look at me, and you may remember that Sindbad, whom you left in the desert island. I fell asleep by the side of a brook ; and when I awoke, all the ship's company were gone." At these words, the captain considered me attentively. and, at last, knew me. " God be praised," exclaimed he, embracing me : " I am delighted that fortune has repaired my fault. There are your goods, which I have always taken care to preserve, and to turn to the best advantage at every port where I have touched. I restore them to you, with the profit I have made of them." I took them from him, at the same time acknowledging my gratitude.

From the Isle of Salahat, we shaped our course to another, where I furnished myself with cloves, cinnamon, and other spices. As we sailed from that island, we saw a tortoise that was twenty cubits in length and in breadth. We also observed a fish, which looked like a cow, and gave milk : its skin is so hard, that bucklers are usually made of it. I saw another, which had the shape and colour of a camel. In fine, after a long voyage, I arrived at Balsora, and thence returned to this city of Bagdad, with so much riches, that I knew not the value. I again distributed a considerable part to the poor ; and added great estates to those I had already acquired.

* * * * * * *

Thus Sindbad finished the history of his third voyage ; he ordered another hundred sequins to Hindbad ; and invited him to the repast next day, to hear the story of his fourth voyage. Hindbad and the company retired : the day following, being reassembled, Sindbad, after dinner, continued the relation of his adventures.

THE FOURTH VOYAGE OF SINDBAD THE SAILOR.

HE pleasures (said he) and amusements I experienced after my third voyage, had not charms sufficient to divert me from taking another. I had not yet satisfied my passion for traffic, nor my curiosity for novelties. I therefore arranged my affairs, and having provided a stock of goods proper for the places where I designed to trade, I set out on my journey. I took the route of Persia, travelled through several provinces of that country, and arrived at a sea-port, where I embarked. We set sail, and had already touched at several ports of the *terra firma*, and some of the eastern islands, when one day, having put out to sea, we were overtaken by such a sudden gust of wind, that the captain was obliged to furl his sails, and take all the necessary measures, to avert the danger that threatened us. But all our precautions were useless, and our manœuvres ineffectual. The sails were torn in a thousand pieces, the ship was stranded, a great many of the merchants and seamen were drowned, and the cargo perished.

I had the good fortune, with several other merchants and mariners, to seize a plank, and we were carried by the current, to an island that lay before us. There we found fruit and fountain water, which served to renovate our strength. We remained all night near the place where the sea had cast us ashore, without deciding how we should act, so much were we dispirited with our misfortune.

The day following, when the sun had risen, we walked from the shore, and, advancing into the island, saw some houses, to which we proceeded. As soon as we came thither, we were encompassed by a great number of blacks, who seized us, shared us among them, and carried us to their respective habitations.

Six of our company, including myself, were taken to the same place. The blacks, at first made us sit down, and gave us a certain herb, which they invited us by signs to eat. My comrades, not noticing that those who served it to us ate none of it themselves, consulted only the satisfying their hunger, and began to seize it with avidity. But I, suspecting some trick, would not so much as taste it : in which I was fortunate ; for, in a little time, I perceived my comrades had lost their senses, and that, when they spoke to me, they knew not what they said.

The blacks afterwards served us with rice, prepared with oil of cocoas ; and my comrades who had lost their reason ate of it greedily. I likewise ate of it, but in very small quantity. The blacks gave us the herb first, on purpose to deprive us of our senses, that we might not be aware of the sad destiny which awaited us ; and then the rice, to fatten us ; for, being cannibals, their intention was to eat us, as soon as we were become fat. Such was the unhappy lot of my comrades, who were unconscious of their fate ; being bereft of their senses. But my faculties continuing unimpaired, you will readily suppose, gentlemen, that instead of growing fat as the rest did, I became leaner every day. The fear of death, under which I incessantly laboured, turned all my food to poison. I fell into a languor, which proved my safety ; for the blacks, having killed and eaten my companions, seeing me withered, lean, and sickly, deferred my death till another time.

Meanwhile, I had so much liberty, that scarcely any notice was taken of my actions ; and this, one day, afforded me an opportunity of getting to a distance from the houses, and effecting my escape. An old man, who saw me, and suspected my design, called to me as loud as he could to return ; but, instead of obeying him, I redoubled my pace, and was quickly out of sight. At that time, there was only this old man about the habitations, all the other blacks being absent, and not expected to return before the evening, which was their frequent custom. Therefore, being assured they would not be home in time to pursue me, I proceeded till night, when I stopped to rest a little, and to eat some of the provisions with which I had provided myself. But I speedily set forward again, and travelled during seven days, avoiding those places which appeared to be inhabited, and living principally upon cocoa-nuts, which served me both for meat and drink.

On the eighth day I arrived near the sea, and suddenly perceived white people, like myself, gathering pepper, of which there was, in that place, great abundance. This occupation I considered a good omen, and I advanced toward them without hesitation.

As soon as the people who were gathering pepper saw me, they came to meet me, and inquired in Arabic, who I was, and whence I came. I was overjoyed at hearing them speak in my own language, and willingly satisfied their curiosity, by giving them an account of my shipwreck, and how I had fallen into the hands of the blacks. "But those blacks," replied they, "eat men : By what miracle did you escape their cruelty ?" I told them the same story I have related to you. at which they expressed the utmost astonishment.

I remained with them till they had collected the quantity of pepper they wished ; after which they took me on board the vessel, and we sailed to the island whence they came. They presented me to their king, who was a good prince. He had the patience to listen to the relation of my adventures, which surprised him ; he afterwards gave me clothes, and commanded that care should be taken of me.

The island was populous, with plenty of everything ; and the capital was a place of great trade. I found this agreeable asylum very comfortable after my misfortune : and the kindness of the generous prince toward me,

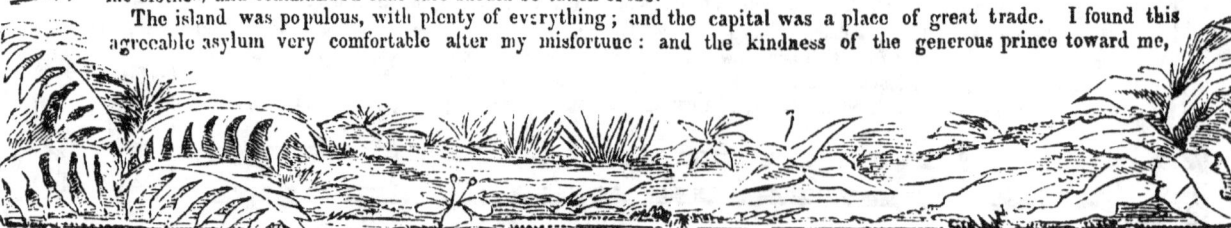

completed my satisfaction. In a word, there was not a person more in favour with him than myself; and consequently every man, in court and city, sought to oblige me; so that, in a very little time, I was considered rather as a native than as a stranger.

I observed one circumstance, which to me appeared very extraordinary:—all the people, the king himself not excepted, rode their horses without bridle or stirrups. Accordingly, I one day took the liberty of asking the king, why his majesty had not furnished himself with those articles. He answered, that I talked to him of things, of which nobody in his dominions knew the use.

Going immediately to a workman, I ordered him to make a saddle-tree by the model I produced. When that was completed, I covered it myself with velvet and leather, and embroidered it with gold. I afterwards went to a locksmith, who made me a bridle-bit agreeably to the pattern I showed him; and he also made me the stirrups.

When I had all the requisites perfect, I presented them to the king, and put them upon one of his horses. The prince mounted, and was so well pleased with the invention that he testified his joy to me by considerable presents. I could not avoid making several saddles for his ministers, and the principal officers of his household, who all of them gave me presents, by which I was soon enriched. I also made some for the people of quality in the city, which gained me a great reputation, and the regard of everybody.

As I paid my respects very regularly to the king, he said to me one day, "Sindbad, I love you, and all my subjects, who know you, treat you according to my example. I have one favour to demand of you, which you must grant." "Sir," answered I, "there is nothing I will refuse, as a mark of my obedience to your majesty, whose power over me is absolute." "I wish you to marry," said he; "that you may remain in my dominions, and think no more of your own country." I dared not resist the prince's will; and he gave me for wife one of the ladies of his court, a noble, beautiful, chaste

and rich lady. The ceremonies of marriage being over, I went and resided with the lady, with whom I lived for some time in perfect harmony. Nevertheless, I was not very well satisfied with my condition; and therefore determined to make my escape at the first opportunity and to return to Bagdad; which my present establishment, advantageous as it was, could not make me forget.

I was cherishing these sentiments, when the wife of one of my neighbours, with whom I had contracted a very strict friendship, fell sick and died. I went to his house to endeavour to console him, and found him a prey to the most acute affliction. "Heaven preserve you!" said I to him, on entering; "and grant you a long life." "Alas!" replied he, "how do you think I should obtain the favour you wish me? I have not above an hour to live." "Pray," returned I, "do not entertain such a melancholy thought; I hope it will not be so, but that I shall enjoy your company for many years." "I wish you," said he, "a long life; but as for me, my days are at an end, for I must be buried this day with my wife. Such is the custom which our ancestors have established in this island, and inviolably observed: the living husband is always interred with the dead wife, and the living wife with the dead husband. Nothing can save me; every one must submit to this law."

While he was giving me an account of this barbarous custom, with the mere representation of which I was very much alarmed, his kindred, friends, and neighbours arrived in a body to assist at the funeral. They dressed the corse in the woman's richest apparel, as if it had been her wedding-day, and decorated it with all her jewels; when, having put it into an open coffin, they lifted it up and began their march to the place of burial. The husband walked at the head of the company, following the corse of his wife. They proceeded to a high mountain, and, arriving there, they took up a great stone which covered the mouth of a very deep pit, and let down the corse with all its apparel and jewels. Then the husband, embracing his kindred and friends, suffered himself, without resistance, to be put in another open coffin, with a pot of water and seven little loaves by him, and was let down in the same manner as they had let down his wife. The mountain was of some length, bordering on the sea, and the pit was very deep. The ceremony completed, they again covered the hole with the stone.

It is unnecessary, gentlemen, for me to tell you that I was a very sad spectator of this funeral; while all the rest of the persons who assisted, frequently witnessing the same proceeding, appeared scarcely in the smallest degree affected.

I could not forbear speaking my thoughts on this matter to the king: "Sir," said I, "I cannot express my astonishment at the strange custom in this country of burying the living with the dead. I have been a great traveller and have associated with the inhabitants of many nations, but never heard of so cruel a law." "What do you mean, Sindbad?" replied the king; "it is a common law, and I am equally subject to it. If the queen my wife were to die first, I should be interred with her." But, sir, said I, "may I presume to inquire of your majesty if strangers are obliged to observe this custom?" "Certainly," answered the king, smiling at the occasion of my question; "they are not exempted, if they marry in this island."

I returned home very melancholy at this answer. The fear of my wife dying first, and that I should be buried alive with her, occasioned me very mortifying reflections. But what remedy was there? It was proper I should bear patiently, and submit to the will of God. Nevertheless I trembled at the least indisposition of my wife. Alas! my fears were very soon verified; she became seriously ill and died in a few days.

You may imagine my sorrow: to be interred alive appeared to me an end not less deplorable than being devoured by cannibals. But there was no alternative; the king and all his court determined to honour the funeral with their presence; and the most considerable people of the city likewise resolved to assist at my interment.

When all was ready for the ceremony, the corse of my wife was put into a coffin, with all her jewels and magnificent apparel. The procession advanced; and, as second actor in this doleful tragedy, I immediately followed the bier, with tears in my eyes, bewailing my unhappy destiny. Before our arrival at the mountain, I made an essay on the minds of the spectators: I first addressed myself to the king, and then to all the persons who surrounded me; and bowing before them to the earth, to kiss the border of their garments, I prayed them to have compassion on me: "Consider," said I, "that I am a stranger, and ought not to be subject to this rigorous law; and that I have another wife and children in my own country. Though I had pronounced these words with an air the most touching, the company were entirely unmoved; on the contrary, they hastened to lower my wife's corse into the pit, and the next moment let me down in an open coffin, with a vessel full of water and seven loaves. In short, the (to me) fatal ceremony being performed, they closed the mouth of the pit, notwithstanding the excess of my grief, and my lamentable cries.

As I approached the bottom, I discovered, by the help of the little light that came from above, the nature of this subterraneous place: it was a prodigiously large cave, and might be about fifty fathoms deep. I soon experienced an insupportable stench, proceeding from the multitude of dead bodies which I saw on the right and left: I even fancied that I heard some of those which had been recently entombed, breathe their last sigh. However, when I was down I immediately quitted my coffin, and, going to a distance from the corses, held my nose. I threw myself on the ground, where I remained a long time bathed in tears. Reflecting on my sad fate,—"It is true," said I, "that God disposes of all things according to his decrees; but, poor Sindbad, is it not thine own fault that thou art brought to die so miserable a death? Would to God thou hadst perished in one of those tempests which thou hast escaped! Then thy death would not have been so lingering and terrible in all its circumstances. But thou hast drawn it upon thyself by thy cursed avarice. Ah, unfortunate wretch! shouldst thou not rather have staid at home, and quietly enjoyed the fruits of thy labour?"

Such were the unavailing complaints with which I made the cave echo, beating my head and breast in rage and despair, and abandoning myself to the most distressing reflections. Nevertheless, I must admit, instead of calling for death to relieve me from my miserable condition, the love of life still prevailed, and induced me to endeavour to prolong my days. Accordingly I went groping about, with my nose stopped, to find the bread and water that were in my coffin, some of which I ate.

Though the darkness of the cave was so great that day and night were indistinguishable, yet I could always regain my coffin; while the cave seemed to be more spacious and fuller of corses than it at first appeared. I lived some days on my bread and water; until, they being all consumed, I at last prepared to die.

I was resigned, and thinking only of death, when I heard the stone removed from the mouth of the cave, and immediately the corse of a man was lowered down. It is natural for man, when reduced to extreme necessity, to adopt extraordinary resolutions. During the time the woman was descending I approached the place where her coffin would rest; and as soon as I perceived they were covering the mouth of the cave I gave the unfortunate wretch two or three violent blows on the head with a large bone that I had seized; which stunned, or, to speak the truth, killed her. I committed this inhuman action to obtain possession of the bread and water that were in her coffin, and thus I gained provisions for some days more. At the end of that time a dead woman and a living man were let down, and I killed the man in the same manner. Fortunately for me, there was then a species of mortality in the town; so that, continuing my assiduity, I did not want for provisions.

One day, when I had despatched another woman, I heard a breathing and the sound of footsteps. I advanced to that side whence the noise proceeded; and upon my approach, the breathing was more audible; and I thought I saw the glimpse of something that took to flight. I followed the indistinct object, which seemed occasionally to stop, but always blew, and receded in proportion as I approached. I followed it so long, and to so great a distance, that at length I perceived a light, resembling a star. I continued walking toward the light, losing sight of it at intervals, in consequence of obstacles that now and then intervened, but always finding it again; till at last I discovered that it came through a hole in the rock, large enough for a man to pass.

On this discovery I stopped some time, to get the better of the violent emotion I experienced; when, advancing to the opening, I went out at it, and found myself upon the bank of the sea. You may conceive the excess of my joy; it was such that I could scarcely persuade myself of the reality of my escape. When I recovered my senses, and was certain that I had not been deceived by my imagination, I considered that the thing which I had heard blow was an animal from the sea that was accustomed to enter at that hole to feed upon the dead carcases.

I examined the mountain, and perceived it to be situated between the town and the sea, but without communication by any road; it was so steep that nature had rendered it impassible. I prostrated myself upon the shore to thank God for this mercy, and afterwards entered the cave again to fetch bread and water, which I returned to eat by daylight, with a better appetite than I had felt since my dismal interment.

I went into the cave once more, and groped about among the biers to collect all the diamonds, rubies, pearls, gold, bracelets, and rich stuffs I could find; these I conveyed to the shore, and tying them up neatly into bales, with the cords that had lowered the coffins, of which I had a great quantity, I laid them together upon the bank, waiting some fortunate occurrence, without any fear of their being injured by the rain, as it was not then the season.

After two or three days, I perceived a ship leaving the harbour, and which passed near the place where I was. I made a sign with the linen of my turban, and called to them as loud as I could. They heard me, and sent a boat to carry me on board. When the sailors inquired by what misfortune I came thither; I told them, that I had suffered shipwreck two days before, and had contrived to get ashore with the goods they saw. Happily for me, these people, without examining the place where I was, or inquiring into the probability of what I told them, were satisfied with my reply, and took me to the ship, with the property I had secured.

When we arrived on board, the captain was so well pleased with having saved me, and so fully occupied with the care of the vessel, that he also took the story of my pretended shipwreck upon trust, and refused some jewels which I offered him.

We passed by several islands, one of which was called the Isle of Bells, about ten days' sail from Serendib, with a common regular wind, and six from the Isle of Kela, where we landed. This island has lead-mines, and produces Indian canes, and excellent camphire.

The king of the Isle of Kela is very rich and potent, and the Isle of Bells, which is about two days' journey in extent, and where the inhabitants are so barbarous that they still eat human flesh, is also subject to him. After we had had considerable commerce in that island we again put to sea, and touched at several other ports. In fine, I arrived happily at Bagdad, with infinite riches, of which it is unnecessary to trouble you with the detail. Out of thankfulness to God for his great mercies, I distributed considerable alms, as well for the maintenance of several mosques as for the subsistence of the poor; and I gave myself up wholly to the enjoyment and gratification of my kindred and friends.

*   *   *   *   *   *   *

Sindbad here finished the relation of his fourth voyage, which caused more admiration in his auditors than all the three preceding. He gave another present of a hundred sequins to Hindbad, whom he prayed to return, with the rest, next day, at the same hour, to dine with him, and to hear the detail of his fifth voyage. Hindbad and the other guests took leave of him and retired. Next morning, when all were reassembled, they sat down at table; and when the repast was finished, which occupied not less time than the former, Sindbad began the recital of his fifth voyage.

THE FIFTH VOYAGE OF SINDBAD THE SAILOR.

HE pleasures I enjoyed had again charms enough to efface the remembrance of all the troubles and calamities I had undergone, without having the power to obviate my inclination to make new voyages. I accordingly bought goods, which I ordered to be packed up and placed in carriages; and set out with them for the first sea-port. There, that I might not be obliged to depend upon a captain, but have a ship at my command, I remained till one was built on purpose at my own charge. When the ship was ready, I embarked with my goods; but not having sufficient to load her completely, I received several merchants of different nations, with their merchandise.

We put to sea with the first fair wind, and, after a long voyage, the first place we touched at was a desert island, where we found a roc's egg, equal in size with that I formerly mentioned, There was a young roc in it, ready to be hatched, and the bill of it began to appear.

The merchants whom I had taken on board my ship, and who landed with me, breaking the egg with hatchets, made a hole in it, whence they pulled out the young roc piece by piece, and roasted it. I had earnestly dissuaded them from meddling with the egg, but they would not listen to my advice.

Scarcely had they finished their repast when we saw in the air, at a considerable distance from us, two great clouds. The captain, whom I hired to navigate my ship, knowing, by former observation, what occasioned the appearance, cried out, that they were the male and female roc to which the young one belonged, and urged us to re-embark with the utmost expedition, to avoid the misfortune which would otherwise befal us. We immediately followed his advice, and set sail with all possible diligence.

In the mean time, the two rocs approached, with a frightful noise, which they redoubled when they saw the egg broken, and missed the young one. But designing to avenge themselves, they again took wing, flying toward the quarter whence they came, and disappeared for some time; while we made all the sail we could, to avert the threatened danger.

They returned, and we observed that each of them carried between its talons a piece of rock of an enormous size. When they were precisely over my ship, they stopped, and, hovering in the air, one of them let fall the stone which it held; but, by the dexterity of the steersman, who turned the vessel with the rudder, it missed us, and passing by the side of the ship into the sea, divided the water in such a manner that we could almost see to the bottom. The other roc, to our misfortune, dropped the stone which it carried so exactly upon the middle of the ship that it dashed it in a thousand pieces. The mariners and passengers were all killed or sunk by the violent concussion. The latter was my fate; but when I gained the top of the water, I had the good fortune to catch hold of a piece of the wreck; swimming first with one hand and then with the other, but always keeping fast hold of my board; the wind and tide being in my favour, I reached an island, the bank of which was very steep; however, I overcame that difficulty, and got on shore.

I sat down upon the grass, to recover myself a little from my fatigue, after which I arose and advanced into the island to examine it. It seemed as if I was in a delicious garden; I found trees everywhere, some of them bearing green, others ripe fruits, and streams of fresh, pure water, with agreeable windings. I ate some of the fruits, which were excellent, and drank of the water that was so inviting.

Night being arrived, I lay down upon the grass, in a place sufficiently convenient; but my sleep, which did not exceed an hour, was often interrupted by the dread I felt at being alone in so solitary a place. Thus I passed the greater part of the night in vexation and in reproaching myself for my imprudence in not remaining at home, rather than undertake this last voyage. These reflections carried me so far that I began to form a design against my own life. But daylight dissipated my despair; I arose and walked between the trees, though not without some apprehension.

When I had proceeded a little farther into the island, I perceived an old man, who appeared to be very feeble. He was seated upon the bank of a stream, and I imagined at first that he had suffered shipwreck, like myself. I approached and saluted him, but he answered only by a slight inclination of the head. I inquired his business there; but, instead of answering me, he made a sign for me to take him upon my back and carry him over the brook, giving me to understand that he was going to gather fruit.

I thought he really required my assistance; so, taking him upon my back, I carried him across the stream, when I desired him to get down, and for that purpose stooped to facilitate his descent; but instead of complying—I always laugh when I think of it—the old man, who to me had appeared very decrepit, crossed his legs nimbly about my neck, and then I perceived his skin was like that of a cow. He sat astride upon my shoulders, holding my throat so tight that I thought he would have strangled me; and the fright which seized me at the moment caused me to fall down in a swoon.

Notwithstanding my fainting, the ill-natured old fellow kept fast about my neck: he merely opened his legs a little to suffer me to breathe more freely. When I had recovered he pressed one of his feet against my stomach, and struck me so violently on the side with the other that he compelled me to rise against my will. Being up, he forced

me to walk under the trees, and stopped me now and then to gather and eat such fruits as we found. He never quitted me all day; and when I wished to rest at night, he laid himself down by me, still holding fast about my neck. Every morning he pushed me, to awaken me; and afterwards obliged me to get up and walk, by pressing me with his feet. Represent to yourselves, gentlemen, the trouble that I must have experienced, in seeing myself charged with such a burden, without the power of relief.

One day, having found in my road several dry calabashes which had fallen from the trees that bore them, I took a large one, and, after cleaning it, pressed into it the juice of some grapes, which the island producing in abundance, we met with at every step. When I had filled the calabash, I deposited it in a place where I had the address to make the old man conduct me some days after. I took up my calabash, and putting it to my mouth, drank of such excellent wine, that it made me forget for some time the miserable chagrin with which I was oppressed. It gave me strength; and I was even so light-hearted, that I began to sing and dance as I walked along.

The old man, perceiving the effect which this liquor had produced on me, and that I carried him with more ease than before, made a sign for me to give him some of the drink. I presented to him the calabash; he took it, and the liquor pleasing his palate, he drank it all off. There was enough of it to intoxicate him, and it very soon had that effect; when, the fumes of the wine rising into his head, he began to sing, after his manner, and to dance with his breech upon my shoulders. The jolting made him vomit; and he loosened his legs from about my neck by degrees; so, finding that he did not press me as before, I threw him upon the ground, where he lay without motion.

I then took up a great stone, with which I crushed his head to pieces.

Extremely rejoiced at being thus for ever freed from this cursed old fellow, I walked toward the seashore, where I met the crew of a ship, who had cast anchor, to take in water and refresh themselves. They were very much astonished at seeing me, and hearing the detail of my adventures. "You fell," said they, "into the hands of the old man of the sea, and are the first person who ever escaped being strangled by him. He never quitted those whom he had once mastered, till he destroyed them; and he has rendered this island famous by the number of people he has killed: the merchants and mariners who landed upon it, never dared to advance into the island but in strong companies.

After giving me this intelligence, they carried me with them to the ship; the captain of which, when he heard what had happened to me, received me with great satisfaction. He again put to sea; and, after some days' sail, we arrived at the harbour of a great city, where the houses were built with good stone.

One of the merchants of the ship, who had taken me into his friendship, obliging me to accompany him, conducted me to a place appointed for the reception of foreign merchants. He gave me a large bag, and having recommended me to some people of the town, who were provided in the same manner, he begged them to take me in their company to gather cocoa-nuts. "Go," said he, "follow them, and observe to act as they do; but be careful not to separate from them, otherwise your life will be endangered. He then furnished me with provisions for the journey, and I set out with them.

We reached an extensive forest of extremely straight and tall trees, the trunks of which were so smooth that it was impossible to climb up to the branches where the fruit grew. All the trees were cocoas; and our business was to fill our sacks with the fruit. On entering the forest, we saw a great number of apes, large and small, that fled as soon as they perceived us, and mounted to the tops of the trees with surprising agility.

The merchants with whom I was, collected stones, and threw them with all their strength at the apes on the tops of the trees. I did the same; and the animals in revenge hastily plucked the cocoa-nuts and flung them at us with such gestures as sufficiently testified their anger and resentment. We gathered up the nuts, and, from time to time, threw stones to irritate the apes; by this stratagem we filled our bags with the fruit, which it had been otherwise impossible for us to have obtained.

When we had got our quantity, we returned to the city, where the merchant who sent me to the forest gave me the value of the cocoa-nuts I brought. "Continue," said he, "to do the like every day, until you have gained money sufficient to carry you home." I thanked him for his good advice, and insensibly collected together so many nuts as produced a considerable sum.

When the merchants by whom I was carried to the island had loaded their vessel with the cocoa-nuts they had purchased, they set sail, and I waited the arrival of another ship, which soon entered the port for a similar cargo. I embarked on board this vessel all the cocoa-nuts that belonged to me, and when she was ready to sail, I went and took leave of the merchant from whom I had experienced so much kindness. He could not embark with me, because he had not finished his affairs.

We set sail, and directed our course towards the island where pepper is produced in the greatest abundance. Thence we steered to the isle of Comari, where the best sort of aloes-wood grows; and the inhabitants of which have established an inviolable law, to drink no wine, nor to suffer any place of debauch. I exchanged my cocoa-nuts in these two islands for pepper and aloes-wood, and accompanied other merchants to fish for pearls, when I hired divers, who brought me up a great number that were very large and pure.

I now joyfully embarked in a vessel, which happily arrived at Balsora, whence I returned to Bagdad, where I acquired vast sums of money by my pepper, aloes-wood and pearls. I distributed the tenth of my gains in alms, as I had acted at the close of my former voyages; and endeavoured to find relief from my fatigues in all kinds of diversions.

*   *   *   *   *   *   *

Having finished his story, Sindbad ordered that one hundred sequins should be given to Hindbad, who retired with the other guests. The next morning the same company reassembled at the house of the rich Sindbad, who, after treating them as before, demanded attention, and gave the following account of his sixth voyage:—

THE SIXTH VOYAGE OF SINDBAD THE SAILOR.

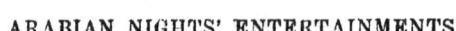

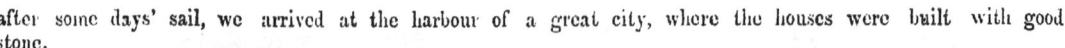

ENTLEMEN (said he), you are, without doubt, anxious to know how, after being shipwrecked five times, and having escaped so many dangers, I could resolve again to tempt my fortune, and expose myself to new hardships. When I reflect on the circumstance, I am myself astonished; and it would certainly appear that I was hurried away by my star. But, be that as it may, after one year's repose I prepared for a sixth voyage, notwithstanding the prayers of my kindred and friends, who tried by all possible means to prevent me.

Instead of taking my route by the Persian Gulf, I travelled once more through several provinces of Persia and the Indies, and arrived at a seaport, where I embarked on board a ship, the captain of which was resolved on making a long voyage. It was very long indeed; at the same time so unfortunate, that the captain and pilot lost their course, and knew not where they were. They at length found it; but the passengers had no reason to rejoice; and we were one day all very much astonished at seeing the captain quit his post in despair. He threw off his turban, tore his beard, and beat his head like a madman. We asked him the cause of his affliction; and he answered, that we were in the most dangerous place in all the sea. "A rapid current carries the ship along," said he, "and we shall all of us perish in less than a quarter of an hour. Pray to God to deliver us from this danger; we cannot escape if he do not take pity on us!" At these words he ordered the sails to be shifted; but the ropes broke, and the ship, without the possibility of prevention, was carried by the current to the foot of an inaccessible mountain, where she ran ashore and broke to pieces, yet so that we saved our lives, our provisions, and the most valuable of our merchandize.

This being effected, the captain said to us, "God has done what he thought proper! Every man may now dig his grave, and bid the world adieu; for we are in so fatal a place, that not one person of those who have been shipwrecked here before us, ever returned to his home." This discourse threw us all into the greatest distress, and we embraced each other with tears in our eyes, bewailing our deplorable fate.

The mountain, at the foot of which we were cast, formed the side of a very long and large island. This coast was covered with the fragments of vessels which had been there wrecked; and, by the vast quantity of men's bones we saw everywhere, and which filled us with horror, we concluded that numbers of people had perished, while the abundance of goods and riches that was presented to our view is incredible. All these objects served only to augment our grief. Instead, as in all other places, of rivers running from their source, and emptying themselves into the sea, here a large river of fresh water ran from the sea into a dark cave, the entrance of which was very high

and large. But what was most remarkable in this place, the mountain was composed of crystal, rubies, and other precious stones. There was also a fountain of a species of pitch or bitumen, that ran into the sea, which the fishes swallowing, afterwards vomit it up, changed into ambergris; and the waves threw it upon the beach in considerable quantities. Here were also trees, most of them al es-wood, equal in goodness to those of Comari.

To finish the description of this place, which may properly be called a gulf, since nothing ever returns from it, it is impossible for a ship to clear it, when once within a certain distance. If vessels be driven thither by a wind from the sea, the wind and the current ruin them; and if they approach it when a land-wind blows, which might seem to favour their escape, the height of the mountain intercepts the wind, and occasions a calm, so that the force of the current runs them ashore, where they are wrecked, as our ship was. To complete the misfortune, there is no possibility of gaining the summit of the mountain, which might afford a hope of safety.

We remained on shore like men out of their senses, expecting death every day. We had divided our provisions equally, so that every one lived a longer or shorter time, according to his temperance, and the use he made of his food.

Those who died first were interred by the rest: for my part, I paid the last duty to all my companions. Nor is this surprising; for, besides being more careful of the provisions that fell to my share, I had a stock of my own, which I did not divide with my comrades. Nevertheless, when I buried the last, I had so little food remaining, that I judged it would not hold out long; and accordingly I dug a grave, resolving to throw myself into it, since there was none left alive to inter me. I must confess to you, that, while I was thus employed, I could not avoid reflecting upon myself, as the cause of my own ruin; and repented that I had ever undertaken this last voyage. Nor did I stop at reflections, but had nearly hastened my own death, tearing my hands with my teeth.

But it pleased God once more to take compassion on me, and inspire me with the thought of going to the bank of the river which ran into the great cave. There, after examining the river with attention, I said to myself, "This water, which runs thus under ground, must come out somewhere or other. If I make a float, and abandon myself to the current, it will convey me to some inhabited country, or I shall perish. If I be drowned, I shall only change one kind of death for another; but if, on the contrary, I escape from this fatal place, I shall not only avoid the sad fate of my comrades, but, perhaps, find some new occasion of enriching myself. Who knows but Fortune waits, upon my getting away from this dreadful rock, to compensate my shipwreck with usury!"

After this reasoning, I immediately began to work on a raft. I made it of good pieces of timber, and large cables, of which I had choice; and tied them together so strongly, that I formed it sufficiently solid. When I had finished it, I loaded it with some bales of rubies, emeralds, ambergris, rock-crystal, and rich stuffs. Having balanced all my cargo exactly, and fastened it securely to the raft, I embarked, with two little oars that I had been careful to provide; and leaving it to the course of the river, I resigned myself to the will of God.

As soon as I entered the cave I lost all light; and the stream carried me I knew not whither. Thus I proceeded some days in perfect darkness; and one time the arch was so low, that it had nearly wounded my head; which rendered me very cautious afterwards to avoid a like danger. During this time I had eaten, of the provisions I had remaining, barely enough to sustain existence; yet, notwithstanding the utmost frugality, my provisions were all expended. A pleasing sleep then overcame me, in which I cannot tell how long I continued; but when I awoke, I was surprised to find myself in the middle of a vast country, at the brink of the river, where my raft was fastened, amidst a great number of negroes. I arose as soon as I saw them, and saluted them: they spoke to me in return, but I did not understand their language.

At this moment I became so transported with joy, that I knew not if I ought to believe myself awake. Being persuaded that I was not asleep, I recited the following words, in Arabic, aloud:—"Call upon the Almighty, and he will help thee; thou needest not perplex thyself with any other consideration: shut thine eyes, and while thou art sleeping, God will change thy bad fortune into good."

One of the blacks, who understood Arabic, hearing me speak thus, now approached me. "Brother," said he, "be not surprised at seeing us; we are inhabitants of this country, and came hither to-day to water our fields, by digging little canals from this river, which runs out of the neighbouring mountain. Perceiving something floating upon the water, we went speedily to see what it was; and distinguishing your raft, one of us swam to it, and brought it hither, where we fastened it as you see, until you should awake. Pray tell us your history, for it must be extraordinary. What induced you to venture yourself on this river; and whence did you come?" I begged of them first to give me something to eat, and then I would satisfy their curiosity.

They presented to me several sorts of food, and when I had satisfied my hunger, I gave them a faithful account of all that had befallen me, to which they apparently listened with admiration. As soon as I had ended my discourse, "This is," said they, through the person who spoke Arabic, and interpreted to them what I had related, "a most surprising history, and you must go and tell it to the king yourself; the matter is too extraordinary to be described by any other than the person to whom it happened." I replied, I was ready to do whatever they required.

The blacks immediately sent to search for a horse, which was brought them in a little time; and having assisted me to mount him, part of them walked in front to point out the road, while the others, who were the most robust, took my raft as it was, with the bales, and followed me.

We proceeded thus all together, till we reached the city of Serendib, for it was in that island I found myself. The blacks presented me to their king. I approached the throne on which he sat, and saluted him according to the custom of the Indies; that is to say, I prostrated myself at his feet, and kissed the earth. The prince ordered me to rise, and received me with an obliging air, desiring me to approach, and take a place near him. He first inquired my name; I answered, Sindbad, surnamed the Sailor, because of the many voyages I had undertaken, and that I was a citizen of Bagdad. "But," said he, "how came you into my dominions? and whence came you last?"

I concealed nothing from the king; I related to him all that I have now told you; with which his majesty was so surprised and charmed, that he commanded my adventure should be written in letters of gold, and laid up in the

archives of the kingdom. My raft was then brought to him, and the bales opened in his presence; he admired the quantity of aloes-wood and ambergris; but, above all, the rubies and the emeralds, for he had none in his treasury that approached them.

Observing that he considered my jewels with pleasure, and examined the most remarkable one after another, I fell prostrate at his feet, and took the liberty to say to him, "Sir, not only my person is at your majesty's service, but the cargo of the raft, and I beg you will dispose of it as your own property." He replied, smiling, "Sindbad, I shall be very cautious to avoid the least envy, or to take anything from you that God has given you. Far from diminishing your wealth, I intend to augment it, and will not suffer you to quit my dominions without carrying with you some marks of my liberality;" to which I could only reply, by wishes for the prosperity of the prince, and commendations of his goodness and generosity. He ordered one of his officers to take care of me, and to provide me with attendants at his expense. The officer then faithfully executed his master's commands, and had all the bales with which I had loaded the raft removed to the lodgings where he conducted me.

I attended every day at certain hours to make my court to the king, and employed the rest of my time in viewing the city, and in examining whatever was most worthy my curiosity.

The isle of Serendid is situated under the equinoctial line; so that the days and nights there are always of twelve hours each; it is eighty parasangs in length, and as many in breadth. The capital city stands at the extremity of a fine valley formed by a mountain, which is in the middle of the island, and is the highest in the world: it is distinguishable at sea at the distance of three days' sail from land. In this island are found rubies, several sorts of minerals; and the rocks, for the most part, are emerald, a stone impregnated with metal, used for the purpose of cutting or engraving other precious stones. It produced all sorts of rare plants and trees, especially cedars and cocoas. Pearls also are fished up along the shores, and at the mouths of the rivers; and in some of its valleys diamonds are found. I made, through devotion, a pilgrimage to the mountain, on which is the place where Adam was exiled, after his banishment from Paradise, and had the curiosity to ascend to the summit.

When I went back to the city, I solicited the king's permission to return to my own country, which he granted me in the most condescending and honourable manner. He obliged me to accept of a rich present, which he drew from his treasury; and when I attended to take leave of him, he gave me one much more considerable; and at the same time charged me with a letter for the Commander of the Faithful, our sovereign lord, saying to me, "I pray you give from me this present, and this letter, to Caliph Haroun Alraschid, and assure him of my friendship." I took the present and letter respectfully, and promised his majesty to be punctual in executing the commission with which he was pleased to honour me. Before I embarked, the prince sent for the captain and the merchants with whom I was going, and ordered them to treat me with every respect.

The letter from the king of Serendid was written on the skin of a certain animal of great value, on account of its scarcity; it was of a yellowish colour. The characters of this letter were of azure; and the contents, in the Indian language, were these:—

"The king of the Indies, before whom march a thousand elephants, who resides in a place that shines with a hundred thousand rubies, and who has in his treasury twenty thousand crowns enriched with diamonds, to the Caliph, Haroun Alraschid:

"Though the present we send you be inconsiderable, receive it, nevertheless, as a brother and a friend, in consideration of the hearty esteem we bear for you, and of which we are very glad to give you proof. We desire the same part in your friendship, believing that we merit it, being of the same dignity with myself. This we conjure you, in quality of brother. Adieu!"

The present consisted, first, of one single ruby formed into a cup, about half a foot high, an inch thick, and filled with round pearls of the weight of half a drachm each; secondly, of the skin of a serpent, the scales of which were as large as an ordinary piece of gold coin, and had the virtue to preserve from sickness those who lay upon it; thirdly, in fifty thousand drachms of the most exquisite aloes-wood, with thirty grains of camphire as large as a pistachio-nut; and, fourthly, of a female slave, of ravishing beauty, whose apparel was covered with precious stones.

The ship set sail; and, after a very long but fortunate voyage, we landed at Balsora, whence I returned to Bagdad; where the first thing I attended to, after my arrival, was to acquit myself of the commission with which I was charged.

I took the king of Serendid's letter, and went to present myself at the gate of the Commander of the Faithful, followed by the beautiful slave and some persons of my own family, who carried the presents. Having stated my business, I was immediately conducted to the throne of the caliph. I made my reverence, by prostrating myself; and, after a short speech, gave him the letter and present. When he had read the king of Serendid's demand, he asked me if that prince were really so rich and potent as his letter signified. I prostrated myself a second time; and rising again, "Commander of the Faithful," said I, "I can assure your majesty that he has not exaggerated respecting his riches and his grandeur, to which I have been witness. Nothing is more capable of raising admiration than the magnificence of his palace. When the prince appears in public, he has a throne fixed on the back of an elephant, and marches between two ranks, composed of his ministers, favourites, and other people of his court; before him, upon the same elephant, an officer carries a golden lance in his hand; and behind the throne is another, who stands erect, holding a column of gold, on the top of which is an emerald half a foot long, and an inch thick. He is preceded by a guard of a thousand men, clad in cloth of gold and silk, and mounted on elephants richly caparisoned.

"While the king is on his march, the officer who is stationed before him on the same elephant proclaims, from time to time, with a loud voice, *Behold the great monarch, the potent and redoubtable Sultan of the Indies, whose palace is covered with a hundred thousand rubies, and who possesses twenty thousand crowns of diamonds! Behold the crowned monarch, greater than the mighty Solomon, and the great Mihrage!* After he has pronounced these words, the officer behind the throne cries in his turn, *This monarch, so great and so powerful, must die, must die, must die!* The officer in front replies, *Praise be to Him who lives for ever!* Further, the king of Serendid is so just, that there are no judges in his capital, any more than in the rest of his dominions. His people have no occasion for them; they understand and observe justice strictly among themselves, and never swerve from their duty; consequently, tribunals and magistrates are unnecessary."

The caliph was much pleased with my discourse. " The wisdom of that king," said he, " appears in his letter; and after what you tell me, I must declare that his wisdom is worthy of his people, and his people deserve so wise a prince." Having thus spoken, he dismissed me, and sent me away with a rich present.

* * * * *

Sindbad now ceased speaking, and his company retired, Hindbad having first received a hundred sequins. The next day they returned to the house of Sindbad, who related to them an account of his seventh and last voyage, in these terms :—

THE SEVENTH AND LAST VOYAGE OF SINDBAD THE SAILOR.

 T my return from my sixth voyage, I absolutely abandoned all thoughts of travelling again; for, being now of an age that requires more rest, I had resolved not to expose myself to such perils as I had so often encountered. I therefore was determined to pass the rest of my life in quiet. One day, while regaling a number of my friends, a servant entered to inform me, that an officer of the caliph's demanded to see me. I arose from the table, and went to him. "The caliph," said he, "has sent me to tell you that he must speak with you." I followed the officer to the palace, where, being presented to the caliph, I saluted him by prostrating myself at his feet. "Sindbad," said he to me, "I stand in need of you: you must do me the service to carry my answer and presents to the king of Serendib. It is but just I should return his civility."

This command of the caliph to me was like a clap of thunder. "Commander of the Faithful," replied I, "I am ready to do whatever your majesty shall think fit to command; but I most humbly beseech you to consider, that I am disheartened by the inconceivable fatigues I have suffered; I have even made a vow never to go out of Bagdad." Hence I took occasion to give him a particular account of all my adventures, which he had the patience to hear to the end.

As soon as I had finished my relation, "I confess," said he, "that those are very extraordinary occurrences; yet you must, for my sake, undertake the voyage which I propose. You have only to go to the isle of Serendib, and deliver the commission that I give you: after which you will be at liberty to return. But you must go; for you know it would be incompatible with my dignity to be indebted to the king of that island." Perceiving that the caliph was disposed to insist on my compliance, I submitted, and signified to him that I was ready to obey. He was in consequence very well pleased, and ordered me a thousand sequins for the expenses of my journey.

I prepared for my departure in a few days; and as soon as the presents were delivered to me from the caliph, with a letter in his own handwriting, I set off, and took the route to Balsora, where I embarked, and had a very happy voyage. Arriving at the isle of Serendib, I acquainted the king's ministers with my commission, and prayed them to obtain me speedily audience. They did not neglect my request; and I was honourably conducted to the palace, where I saluted the king by prostration, according to custom.

The prince recognised me immediately, and testified very great joy at seeing me. "Ah, Sindbad!" said he, "you are welcome; I swear to you that I have many times thought of you since your departure. I bless this day since we see each other once more." I made my compliment to him; and after thanking him for his kindness, I delivered to him the caliph's letter and present, which he received with the greatest satisfaction.

The caliph's present consisted of a bed complete, of cloth of gold, valued at a thousand sequins; fifty robes of a very rich stuff; a hundred others of white cloth, the finest of Cairo, Suez, Cufa and Alexandria; another bed of crimson; and a third, of a different fashion: a vessel of agate, of which the breadth was greater than the depth of an inch thick, and half a foot wide, the bottom representing in bas relief, a man with one knee on the ground, who held a bow and arrow in the act of shooting at a lion. He sent him also a rich table, which, according to tradition, belonged to the great Solomon. The caliph's letter was conceived in these words:—

"Greeting, in the name of the Sovereign Guide of the right way, to the potent and happy Sultan, from Abdallah Haroun Alraschid, whom God hath stationed in the place of honour after his ancestors of happy memory:

"We have received your letter with joy, and send you this from the council of our port, the garden of superior wits. We hope, when you look on it, you will perceive our good intention, and that it will afford you pleasure. Adieu!"

The king of Serendib was much gratified by the caliph's acknowledgment of his friendship; and soon after this audience, I solicited leave to depart, which I obtained with difficulty. When, however, I at length received permission, the king dismissed me with a very considerable present. I embarked immediately, to return to Bagdad: but had not the good fortune to arrive there as I hoped: God ordered it otherwise.

Three or four days after our departure, we were attacked by corsairs, who easily secured our ship, it not being prepared for defence. Some of the crew offered resistance, which cost them their lives; but as for me and the rest, who were not so imprudent as to oppose the designs of the corsairs, we were made slaves.

After the pirates had stripped us, and they had exchanged our clothes for sorry habits, they carried us to a large island at a great distance, where they sold us.

I fell into the hands of a rich merchant; who immediately conducted me to his house, fed me well, and clad me neatly as a slave. Some days after, as he had not yet informed himself who I was, he asked me if I understood any trade. I answered, without otherwise discovering myself, that I was no mechanic, but a merchant; and that the corsairs, who sold me, had robbed me of all my property. "But tell me," said he, "can you shoot with a bow?" I replied, that the bow was one of my exercises during my youth, and I had not forgotten it. He then gave me a bow and arrows; and taking me behind him upon an elephant, carried me to a vast forest several hours' journey from the town. We proceeded a great way into the forest; and when he thought proper to stop, he bade me alight; then, showing me a large tree, "Climb up that tree," said he, "and shoot at the elephants as you see them pass; for there is a prodigious number of them in this forest. If any one of them fall, come and give me notice." Having thus spoken, he left me victuals, and returned to the town, while I continued upon the tree all night.

I perceived no elephant during that time; but next morning, as soon as the sun had risen, a great number appeared: I shot several arrows among them, and at last one of the elephants fell; the rest retired immediately, and left me at liberty to go and acquaint my patron with my success. When I had informed him of my good fortune, he gave me a hearty meal, commended my dexterity, and caressed me with warmth. We afterwards went together to the forest, where we dug a hole, and buried the elephant I had killed: my patron designing to return when it was decayed, for the teeth, in which he traded.

I continued this pursuit during two months, and killed an elephant every day; taking my station sometimes on one tree, sometimes on another. One morning, as I waited the arrival of the elephants, I perceived with extreme amazement, that, instead of passing by me across the forest, as usual, they stopped with a horrible noise, in such numbers that the earth was covered with them, and shook under their steps. They approached, and encompassed the tree where I was, with their trunks extended, and their eyes fixed upon me. At this alarming spectacle I continued immoveable, and was in such terror, that my bow and arrows fell from my hands.

I was not agitated without reason; for, after the elephants had regarded me for some time, one of the largest of them seized the lower part of the tree with his trunk, and making a great effort, he plucked it up by the roots, and threw it on the ground. I fell with the tree; but the elephant, raising me with his trunk, laid me on his back, where I sat, more dead than alive, with the quiver fastened to my shoulder. He then put himself at the head of the rest, which followed him in troops, and carried me to a place, where he laid me on the ground and retired with all his companions. Conceive, if it be possible, my apprehensions: I rather fancied myself in a dream. At last, after having lain some time, and seeing no more of the elephants, I arose, and found I was upon a long and broad hill, covered with the bones and teeth of those animals. I assure you this object furnished me with many reflections. I admired the instinct of the elephants; not doubting but that this was their burying-place, and that they had carried me thither on purpose to show it to me, that I might forbear persecuting them, since my only object was to obtain their teeth. I did not stay on the hill, but turned my steps towards the city; and, after having travelled a day and a night, I reached the house of my patron. I met no elephants in the way; which made me think they had retired farther into the forest, to leave me at liberty to go back to the hill without obstacle.

As soon as my patron saw me, "Ah, poor Sindbad!" said he; "I was in great trouble to know what was become of you. I have been at the forest, where I found a tree recently pulled up, and a bow and arrows on the ground; and after having sought for you in vain, I despaired of ever seeing you return. Pray tell me what has happened to you, and by what good fortune thou art yet alive." I satisfied his curiosity; and both of us going next morning to the hill, he found, to his great joy, that what I told him was true. We loaded the elephant upon which we rode with as many teeth as he could carry; and when we were returning, "Brother!" said my patron; "for I will no more treat you as my slave, after the pleasure you have afforded me, by making a discovery that will enrich me,— God bless you with all happiness and prosperity! I declare before him, that I give you your liberty. I have concealed from you what I am now going to confess:—

"The elephants of our forest have every year killed us a great many slaves, whom we have sent to obtain ivory. Notwithstanding all the cautions we could give them, they lost their lives, sooner or later, by those crafty animals. God has delivered you from their fury, and has bestowed that favour upon you alone. It is a proof that he loves you, and has occasion for your services in the world. You have procured me incredible gain: we could not get ivory formerly, without exposing the lives of our slaves; but now our whole city is enriched by your means. Do not think I pretend to have sufficiently rewarded you by restoring you to liberty: I will also give you considerable riches. I would engage all our city to contribute towards making your fortune; but it is a glory in which I will have no associate."

To this obliging discourse, I replied, "Patron, God preserve you! My liberty is sufficient to acquit you of every obligation; and I desire no other reward for the service I have had the good fortune to render you and your city but permission to return to my own country." "Very well," said he; "the monsoon will in a little time bring ships for ivory. I will then send you home, and give you wherewith to bear your expenses." I again thanked him for my liberty and his good intentions towards me. I stayed with him, expecting the monsoon; and during that time we made so many journeys to the hill that we filled our warehouses with ivory. All the other merchants who traded in that article did the same, for the discovery could not be long concealed from them.

At length the ships arrived; and my patron himself, having chosen that in which I could embark, loaded half of the vessel with ivory on my account; he laid in abundance of provisions for my passage; and, besides, obliged me to accept a present of the curiosities of the country, of great value. After I had made him every acknowledgment in my power for his kindness, I embarked. We set sail; while the adventure, which had procured me my liberty, being so very extraordinary, occupied all my thoughts.

We touched at several islands, to take in fresh provisions. Our vessel arriving at a port on the *terra firma*, in the Indies, we landed there; and, wishing to avoid the dangers of the sea to Balsora, I disembarked my proportion of the ivory, resolving to proceed on my journey by land. I disposed of my ivory for a considerable sum of money; purchased several rarities, which I intended for presents; and, when my equipage was ready, joined company with a large caravan of merchants. I was a long time on the way, and suffered much; but I endured all patiently, reflecting that I had no more to fear from the seas, from pirates, from serpents, nor all the other perils I had encountered.

My fatigues ended at last; I arrived safely at Bagdad. I immediately waited upon the caliph, and gave him an account of my embassy. That prince told me, that the length of my voyage had caused him some inquietude, but that he always hoped God would preserve me. When I related to him the adventure of the elephants, he appeared to be very much surprised, and would never have believed it, had he not known my veracity. He considered this story, and the other accounts I had given him, so curious, that he ordered one of his secretaries to write them in characters of gold, and lay them up in his treasury. I then retired, very well satisfied with the honours I received, and the presents which he made me; and gave up myself entirely to my family, kindred, and friends.

* * * * *

Sindbad here finished the recital of his seventh and last voyage; and addressing himself to Hindbad, "Well, friend," said he, "did you ever hear of any person who had suffered so much as I have undergone, or of any mortal who has encountered so many difficulties? Is it not reasonable, that, after such toil, I should enjoy a tranquil and pleasant life?" As he pronounced these words, Hindbad approached him: "I must acknowledge, sir," said he, kissing his hand, "that you have gone through terrible dangers. My troubles are not comparable to yours: if they afflict me during a time, I console myself with the little gains I acquire. You not only deserve a quiet life, but are likewise worthy of all the riches you enjoy, because you make such a good and generous use of them. May you, therefore, continue to live in happiness to the day of your death!"

Sindbad gave him a hundred sequins more, received him into the number of his friends, and desired him to discontinue his employment as a porter, and come every day to dine with him, that he might all his life have reason to remember Sindbad the Sailor.

THE THREE APPLES.

IR, (said Scheherazade) to the Sultan Schahriar, I have already had the honour to entertain your majesty with a ramble which the Caliph Haroun Alraschid made one night from his palace; I must now give you an account of one more:—

This prince, one day, commanded the grand-vizier Giafar to come to his palace the night following:—" Vizier," said he, " I will take a walk round the town, to inform myself what people say, and particularly if they are contented with my officers of justice. Should there be any against whom they have just reason to complain, we will discharge them, and supply their places with others, who may officiate better; if, on the contrary, there be any who have gained their applause, we shall entertain that esteem for them which they merit. The grand vizier attending at the palace at the hour appointed, the caliph, he, and Mesrour, the chief of the eunuchs, disguised themselves that they might not be known, and went out together.

They passed through several places, and by different markets; and, as they entered a little street, they perceived, by the light of the moon, a tall man, with a white beard carrying nets on his head; he had a folding basket of palm-leaves on his arm, and a club in his hand. " This old man," said the caliph, " does not seem to be rich; let us go to him, and inquire into his circumstances." " Honest man," said the vizier, " who art thou?" —" Sir," replied the old man, " I am a fisher, but one of the poorest and most miserable of the trade. I left my house about noon to go fishing; and, from that time to the present, I have not been able to catch a single fish; while I have a wife and small children, and nothing to maintain them."

The caliph, moved with compassion, replied to the fisherman, " Have you the courage to go back, and cast your nets once more? We will give you a hundred sequins for what you may bring up." At this proposal, the fisherman, forgetting all his day's toil, took the caliph at his word, and, with him, Giafar and Mesrour, returned to the Tigris; at the same time saying to himself, " These gentlemen appear too civil and reasonable not to reward my labour; and if they give me but the hundredth part of what they promised, it will be very handsome."

They arrived on the bank of the river, and the fisherman threw in his net; when he drew it out again, he brought up a trunk, closely shut, and very heavy. The caliph ordered the grand vizier to pay him a hundred sequins imme-

diately, and sent him away. Mesrour, by his master's command, took the trunk on his shoulder; and the caliph was so very eager to know what it contained, that he hastily returned to the palace. When the trunk was opened, they found in it a large basket, made of palm-leaves, closed up, the opening being sewed with red worsted. To satisfy the caliph's impatience, they would not spare time to unsew it, but cut the fastening with a knife, and took out of the basket a bundle wrapped in an old piece of hanging, and bound about with a rope. The cord being untied, they opened the bundle, and found, to their great amazement, the corse of a young lady, whiter than snow, cut in pieces.

Your majesty will conceive, much better than I am able to describe, the astonishment of the caliph at this horrid spectacle. But his surprise was instantly changed into passion; and darting a furious look at the vizier, "Ah! thou wretch!" said he, "is this your inspection into the actions of my people? Assassinations are committed, under your ministry, in my capital, with impunity; and my subjects are thrown into the Tigris, that they may cry for vengeance against me at the day of judgment! If you do not speedily revenge the loss of this woman by the death of her murderer, I swear, by Heaven, that I will cause you to be hanged, with forty of your kindred."— "Commander of the Faithful," replied the grand-vizier, "I beg your majesty to grant me time to make inquiry." "I will allow you no more than three days," said the caliph; "therefore, look to it."

The vizier Giafar returned home in great confusion of mind. "Alas!" said he, "how is it possible that, in so vast and populous a city as Bagdad I should be able to discover a murderer, who undoubtedly committed the crime without witness, and perhaps may be already gone hence? Any person but myself would take some wretched culprit out of prison, and put him to death, to satisfy the caliph; but I will not burthen my conscience with such a barbarous action; I will rather die, than save my life at that price."

Having ordered the officers of the police and justice to make strict search for the criminal, they dispersed their people in companies, while they themselves were not idle, for they were no less concerned in the affair than the vizier. But all their endeavours were ineffectual; whatever was their diligence, they could not discover the murderer; and the vizier considered his life as forfeited, without some remarkable interference of Providence.

The third day being arrived, a tipstaff proceeded to the house of the unfortunate minister, and summoned him to follow, which the vizier obeyed. The caliph having asked him where was the murderer, "Commander of the Faithful," answered he, with tears in his eyes, "I have not found any person who could give me the least information." The caliph, full of rage and fury, reproached him bitterly, and ordered that he, with forty Barmecides, should be immediately hung at the gate of the palace.

In the meanwhile, the gibbets were preparing, and orders were sent to seize forty Barmecides, in their houses, a public crier, by the caliph's order, proclaiming in all quarters of the city, "*Those who have a desire to see the grand-vizier Giafar hanged, with forty Barmecides, his kindred, let them come to the square before the palace.*"

When all things were ready, the criminal judge, and a great number of bailiffs belonging to the palace, brought out the grand-vizier with the forty Barmecides, and placed each of them at the foot of the gibbet designed for him; and the ropes with which they were to be suspended were put about their necks. The multitude of people who filled the square could not behold this tragical sight without grief and tears; for the grand-vizier and the Barmecides were loved and honoured for their probity, generosity, and impartiality, not only in Bagdad, but throughout all the dominions of the caliph.

Nothing remained to hinder the execution of this prince's too severe and irrevocable sentence; and the lives of the most honest people in the city were about to be sacrificed, when a young man of handsome mien, and good apparel, breaking through the crowd, penetrated to the grand-vizier; and after he had kissed his hand, "Most excellent vizier," said he to him, "chief of the emirs of this court, and friend of the poor, you are not guilty of the crime for which you stand here. Withdraw; and let me expiate the death of the lady who was thrown into the Tigris. I was the murderer, and I alone deserve to be punished."

Though these words occasioned great joy to the vizier, he could not refrain from pitying the young man, whose countenance, instead of being ominous, was somewhat engaging; and he was going to answer him, when a tall man far advanced in years, who had likewise forced his way through the crowd, approached:—"Sir," said he to the vizier, "do not believe what this young man tells you: I killed the lady who was found in the trunk; and upon me only this punishment ought to fall. I conjure you, in the name of God, not to punish the innocent for the guilty." "Sir," continued the young man, addressing the vizier, "I do protest that I am the person who committed this wicked action, and without any accomplice." "My son," said the old man, "despair has conducted you hither, and you would anticipate your destiny. As for me, I have lived long in the world, and it is time for me to depart; suffer me, therefore, to sacrifice my life for yours.—"Sir," continued he, again addressing the vizier, "I tell you once more, I am the assassin; let me die without further contention."

The controversy between the old man and the youth obliged the grand-vizier, Giafar, to carry them before the caliph, by permission of the criminal judge, who was very glad to serve the vizier. When he entered the presence of the prince, he kissed the ground seven times, and spoke after this manner:—"Commander of the Faithful, I have brought before your majesty this old man and this young man, each of whom declares himself to be the sole murderer of the lady." The caliph then asked the prisoners, which of them was the assassin who so cruelly murdered the lady and threw her into the Tigris? The young man assured him that he was the offender; but the old man, on his side, maintained the contrary. "Go," said the caliph to the grand-vizier, "and have them both hanged." "But, sir," replied the vizier, "if only one of them be guilty, it would be unjust to take the lives of both." At these words, the young man again spoke: "I swear by the great God, who has raised the heavens to the height they are, that I am the man who killed the lady, cut her in quarters, and threw her into the Tigris, four days ago. I renounce my share of happiness with the just at the day of judgment, if what I say be not truth; therefore, I am the person who ought to suffer." The caliph, surprised at this oath, believed him, particularly as the old man made no answer. Whereupon, turning to the young man, "Thou wretch!" said he, "what induced thee to commit that detestable crime? and what is it that moves thee now to offer thyself voluntarily to die?" "Commander of the Faithful," replied the young man; "if what has passed between that lady and me were put in writing, it would form a history that might be very useful to other men." "I command you, then, to relate it," said the caliph. The young man obeyed, and thus began his recital:—

THE STORY OF THE LADY WHO WAS MURDERED, AND OF THE YOUNG MAN, HER HUSBAND.

OMMANDER OF THE FAITHFUL, your majesty will be pleased to understand, that the murdered lady was my wife, daughter of this old man you see here, who is my paternal uncle. She was only twelve years old when he gave her to me in marriage; and eleven years have since elapsed. I have three children by her, all boys, who are living; and I must do her the justice to say that she never offered me the least offence: she was chaste, of good behaviour, and made it her whole study to please me. For my part, I loved her entirely, and rather anticipated her wishes, than opposed them.

About two months ago she fell sick: I took all imaginable care of her, and spared nothing to procure her a speedy recovery. After a month, she began to recover her health, and had a desire to go to the bath. Before she went out of the house, "Cousin," said she (for so she used familiarly to call me), "I long for apples; if you could get me some, you would please me extremely: I have had a desire for them a great while; and I must confess it is come to that height, that if I be not satisfied very soon, I fear some misfortune will befal me." "Very willingly," I replied; "I will do all that is in my power to render you contented."

I went immediately to all the markets and shops in the town to seek for apples; but I could not obtain one, though I offered to pay a sequin for it. I returned home very much vexed at my disappointment. As for my wife, when she returned from the bath, and saw no apples, she became so very uneasy that she could not sleep all night. I arose early in the morning, and searched all the gardens, with no better success than the day before, excepting that I happened to meet an old gardener, who told me that all my inquiries were useless, for I must not expect to find apples anywhere but in your majesty's garden at Balsora.

As I loved my wife passionately, and would not have to reproach myself with any neglect, I assumed the habit of a traveller; and, after telling her my design, set out for Balsora. I made my journey with such great diligence, that I returned at the end of fifteen days, with three apples, each of which cost me a sequin: there were no more in the garden, and the gardener would not let me have them cheaper. As soon as I reached home, I presented them to my wife; but her longing was over: so she satisfied herself with receiving them, and placed them by her side. In the mean time, she continued sickly, and I knew not what remedy to provide for her illness.

Some few days after I returned from my journey, while sitting in my shop in the public place, where all sorts of fine stuffs are sold, I saw an ugly, tall black slave enter with an apple in his hand, which I knew to be one of those I had brought from Balsora. I could not doubt it; since I was certain there was not one to be bought in all Bagdad, nor at any of the gardens in the neighbourhood. I called to him: "Good slave," said I, "pray tell me where you obtained that apple?" "It is a present," replied he, smiling, "from my sweetheart. I have been to visit her to-day, and found her a little unwell. I saw three apples lying by her, and asked her where she got them. She told me, the good man, her husband, had made a fortnight's journey to seek them, and had presented them to her. We had a collation together; and, when I took my leave of her, I brought away this apple that you see."

This discourse bereft me of my senses. I arose from my seat, shut up my shop, hastily ran home, and entering my wife's chamber, looked immediately for the apples; when seeing only a couple, I asked what was become of the third. Then my wife, turning her head towards the place where the apples lay, and perceiving there were but two, answered me coldly, "Cousin, I know not what has become of it." At this answer, I had no hesitation in believing what the slave told me to be true; and, at the same time giving myself up to madness and jealousy, I drew my knife from my girdle, and thrust it into the throat of the unfortunate creature. I afterward cut off her head, and divided her body into quarters, which I packed up in a bundle, and hiding it in a basket, sewed it up with a thread of red yarn; I put all together in a trunk, and at night carried it on my shoulder to the Tigris, where I sunk it.

The two younger of my children were already in bed and asleep: the third was from home; but, at my return, I found him sitting by the gate, weeping bitterly. I inquired the cause of his distress: 'Father," said he, "I took this morning, from my mother, without her knowledge, one of the three apples you brought her: I kept it a long while; but, as I was playing some time ago, in the street, with my little brothers, a tall slave who was passing, snatched it out of my hands, and carried it with him; I ran after him, demanding it back, and, besides, told him it belonged to my mother, who was sick, and that you had made a fortnight's journey to fetch it; but all to no purpose, he would not restore it. And, as I still followed, crying after him, he turned and beat me; and then ran away as fast as he could from one lane to another, till at length I lost sight of him. I have since been walking without the town, expecting your return, to pray you, dear father, not to tell my mother of it, lest it should make her worse." When he had said these words, he redoubled his tears.

During my son's discourse, my affliction was inconceivable; I then discovered the enormity of my crime; and, too late, repented of having so readily believed the calumnies of a wretched slave, who, from what he had learned of my son, invented that fatal lie. My uncle, who is here present, arrived just at the time to see his daughter; but, instead of finding her alive, he understood from me that she was no more, for I concealed nothing from him; and, without waiting for his censure, I declared myself the greatest criminal in the world. Nevertheless, so far from reproaching me, he joined his tears with mine, and we wept together three days without intermission; he, for the loss of a daughter whom he always tenderly loved; and I, for the loss of a dear wife, of whom I had deprived myself in so cruel a manner, by giving too easy credit to the report of a lying slave.

This, Commander of the Faithful, is the sincere confession your majesty has exacted from me. You now know all the circumstances of my crime, and I most humbly beg of you to order the just punishment; how severe soever it be, I shall not complain, but esteem it too lenient.

*   *   *   *   *   *

The caliph was very much astonished at the young man's confession. But this equitable prince, finding he was rather to be pitied than condemned, spoke thus in his favour: "The action of this young man," said he, "is

pardonable before God, and excusable with men. The wicked slave is the sole cause of this murder; he alone must be punished. Therefore," continued he, looking at the grand vizier, "I give you three days to find him; if you do not bring him to me within that space, you shall die in his stead."

The unfortunate Giafar, who thought himself out of danger, was terrified by this new order of the caliph; but as he durst not reply to that prince, whose hasty temper he well knew, he departed from his presence, and retired to his house with tears in his eyes, persuading himself he had but three days to live. He was so fully convinced that he should not be able to find the slave, that he made not the least search after him.

"It is not possible," said he, "that in such a city as Bagdad, where there is an infinite number of black slaves, I should be able to discover the guilty person. So that unless God be pleased to expose him, as he has already exposed the murderer, nothing can save my life."

He passed the first two days in affliction with his family, who sat round him weeping, and complaining of the caliph's cruelty. The third day being arrived, he prepared to die with firmness, as an honest minister, who had no cause to reproach himself. He sent for notaries and witnesses, who signed his last will, made in their presence. After which he took leave of his wife and children, and bade them the last farewell. All his family was drowned in tears; never was there a more sorrowful spectacle. At length, a tipstaff appeared, from the caliph, to express his impatience at not having heard from him, nor concerning the negro slave whom he had commanded him to find: "I am therefore ordered," continued the messenger, "to take you before his throne." The afflicted vizier prepared to follow the officer; but as he was going out, they presented to him his youngest daughter, about five or six years of age. The nurses who attended her had brought her to her father to receive his last blessing.

As he had a particular affection for that child, he prayed the tipstaff to permit him to stop for a moment; and taking his daughter in his arms, he kissed her several times. As he caressed her, he perceived she had something in her bosom, that appeared bulky, and had a sweet scent. "My dear little one," said he, "what have you in your bosom?" "My dear father," replied the child, "it is an apple, on which is written the name of our lord and master the caliph: Rihan, our slave, sold it me for two sequins."

At these words, apple and slave, the grand vizier cried out with surprise, mixed with joy; and putting his hand into the child's bosom, drew out the apple. He summoned the slave, who was not far off, to attend; and when he appeared, "Rascal!" said the vizier, "where did you get this apple?" "My lord," replied the slave, "I swear to you, that I neither stole it in your house, nor from the garden of the Commander of the Faithful. The other day, as I was passing along a street where three or four small children were playing, one of them having it in his hand, I snatched it from him and carried it away. The child ran after me, telling me it was not his own, but belonged to his mother, who was sick; and that his father, to satisfy her longing, had made a distant journey, and brought home three apples, whereof that was one, which he had taken from his mother without her knowledge. He said what he could to induce me to return it, but I would not; but brought it home and sold it, for two sequins, to the little lady, your daughter. This is the whole truth of the matter."

The astonishment of Giafar at the roguery of his slave was extreme; he had been the cause, not only of the death of an innocent woman, but nearly of his own. He took the slave with him, and, appearing before the caliph, gave that prince an exact account of what the slave had told him, and the chance that led to a discovery of his crime.

Never was surprise equal to that of the caliph; though he could not avoid falling into excessive fits of laughter. At length he recovered himself; and, with a serious air, told the vizier, that since his slave had been the occasion of a melancholy accident, he deserved exemplary punishment. "Sir," said the vizier, "I confess it, but his guilt is not unpardonable. I remember a still more surprising story of a vizier of Cairo, named Noureddin Ali, and Bedreddin Hassan of Balsora; and since your majesty delights in hearing such tales, I am ready to relate it, on condition that if your majesty find it more astonishing than that which gives me occasion to tell it, you will be pleased to pardon my slave." "I am content," said the caliph; "but you undertake a hard task; for I do not believe you can save your slave, the story of the apples is so very extraordinary." Giafar then commenced his story in these words:—

THE STORY OF NOUREDDIN ALI, AND BEDREDDIN HASSAN.

COMMANDER OF THE FAITHFUL, there was, in former days, a sultan of Egypt, a strict observer of justice, gracious, merciful, and liberal; and his valour rendered him formidable to his neighbours. He loved the poor, and protected the learned, whom he advanced to the highest dignities. This sultan had a vizier, who was prudent, wise, sagacious, and well versed in the fine arts, and in all the sciences. This minister had two sons, very handsome men and who constantly followed his own footsteps. The eldest was named Schemseddin Mohammed, and the younger Noureddin Ali. The last, especially, was endowed with every good quality and perfection.

Their father, the vizier, being dead, the sultan sent for them; and after having caused them both to put on the usual robes of a vizier, "I as much regret," said he, "the loss of your father as yourselves: of which I will give you proof. I know that you live together, and that you are perfectly united; I therefore bestow on each the same dignity: go, and imitate your father's conduct."

The two new viziers humbly thanked the sultan, and returned home to make preparations for their father's interment. At the end of a month, they left their house for the first time, and attended the council of the sultan; at which they afterwards continued to assist whenever it assembled. When the sultan took the diversion of hunting, one of the brothers always accompanied him; and this honour they received alternately. One evening, while conversing after supper, the next day being the elder brother's turn to attend the sultan to the chase, he said to his younger brother, "Since neither of us is yet married, and we live so happily together, a thought has just occurred to me:—Let us both marry on the same day; and let us choose two sisters from some family that may suit our quality: what think you of this idea?" "I confess, brother," answered Noureddin Ali, "that it is perfectly

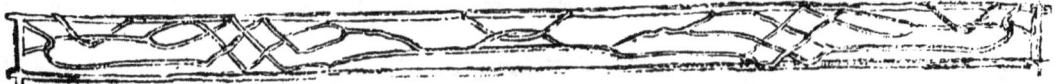

worthy our friendship: you could not have a better thought; for my part, I am ready to agree to whatever you think fit to propose." "But hold, this is not all," replied Schemseddin Mohammed; "my fancy carries me farther. Suppose both our wives should conceive the first night of our nuptials, and should happen to be delivered on the same day—yours of a son, and mine of a daughter—we will give them to each other in marriage, when they attain majority."—"Ah!" cried Noureddin Ali aloud, "that, I declare, is an admirable project! Such a marriage will perfect our union, and I willingly consent. But then, brother," continued he, "if this connexion should take place, would you require my son to settle a jointure on your daughter?" "That will be attended with no difficulty," replied the elder; "for I am persuaded, that, besides the usual articles of the marriage contract, you will not hesitate to promise, in his name, at least three thousand sequins, three good estates, and three slaves." "I will not consent to that condition," returned the younger. "Are we not brothers, and colleagues equal in title and dignity? Besides, we both know what is just:—the male being nobler than the female, it is your part to give a large dowry with your daughter. But, by what I perceive, you are a man who would have your affairs transacted at another's charge."

Although Noureddin Ali spoke these words in jest, his brother, being of an ill temper, was offended: "A mischief upon your son!" said he, passionately, "since you prefer him before my daughter: I wonder you had the assurance to believe him worthy of her! You must have lost your judgment, to think you are my equal, and that we are colleagues! I would have you to know, fool! that, since you are so impudent, I would not marry my daughter to your son, though you were willing to give him more than you are worth." This pleasant quarrel, between two brothers, concerning the marriage of children not yet born, proceeded to such a length, that Schemseddin Mohammed concluded with menaces: "Were I not to-morrow," said he, "to accompany the sultan, I would treat you as you deserve; but, at my return, I will make you sensible that it does not become a younger brother to speak so insolently to his elder brother, as you have to me." He then retired to his apartment, and his brother went to bed.

Very early next morning Schemseddin Mohammed arose and went to the palace to attend the sultan, who was going to hunt about Cairo, on the side of the pyramids. As for Noureddin Ali, he had passed the night in the greatest inquietude; and, being convinced that it would be impossible for him to live longer with a brother who treated him with so much haughtiness, he provided a good mule, furnished himself with money, jewels, and some provisions; and, having told his people that he was going a journey for two or three days, and would be alone, he departed.

When he had left Cairo, he rode by the desert toward Arabia, but his mule becoming tired on the road, he was forced to pursue his journey on foot. Fortunately a courier, who was on his way to Balsora, met him, and took him up behind him. When the courier arrived at Balsora, Noureddin Ali alighted, and returned him thanks for his kindness. As he went about the streets to seek for a lodging, he saw a person of quality, with a numerous retinue, approaching, to whom all the inhabitants paid great honour, respectfully standing still till he passed by; and Noureddin Ali stopped likewise. It was the sultan of Balsora's grand vizier, who walked through the city to maintain by his presence peace and good order.

This minister, casting his eyes by chance on Noureddin Ali, and perceiving that he had an engaging countenance, looked very attentively at him, and, as he came near him and saw his traveller's habit, he stopped, asking him who he was and whence he came. "Sir," replied Noureddin Ali, "I am an Egyptian, born at Cairo; and have left my country on account of the unkindness of a relation. I am resolved to travel through the world, or to die, rather than return home." The grand vizier, who was a venerable old man, after hearing these words, said to him,—"Son, beware how you pursue your design; there is nought but misery in the world, and you are ignorant of the hardships you must endure. Come, follow me; I may perhaps make you forget the cause that has forced you to leave your own country."

Noureddin Ali accompanied the grand-vizier, who soon perceived his good qualities, and became so warmly attached to him that, one day, talking with him privately, he thus addressed him:—"My son, I am, as you see, far advanced in years; and it is impossible I should live much longer. Heaven has bestowed upon me one daughter, who is as beautiful as you are handsome, and now of an age to marry. Several persons of the greatest distinction at this court have already demanded her for their sons, but I could not resolve to comply with their wishes. I have an affection for you, and think you so worthy of being received into my family, that, preferring you before all those who have sought her, I am ready to accept you for my son-in-law. If you are pleased with the proposal, I will acquaint the sultan my master that I have adopted you by this marriage, and I will pray him to grant you the reversion of my dignity of grand-vizier, in the kingdom of Balsora. In the mean time, as ease is highly necessary for me in my old age, I will not only put you in possession of my estate, but leave the administration of public affairs to your management."

The grand-vizier had no sooner ended his discourse, full of goodness and generosity, than Noureddin Ali fell at his feet; and expressing himself in terms that demonstrated the joy and gratitude with which his heart was penetrated, replied, that he was entirely at his command. Upon which the vizier summoned the principal officers of his house, and ordered them to decorate the great hall of his palace, and prepare a sumptuous feast; he afterwards sent to invite the nobility of the court and city to honour him with their company. When all were assembled, Noureddin Ali having informed him of his quality, the vizier addressed his friends (as he considered it proper to satisfy such of them to whom he had refused his alliance),—"I am very glad, my lords," said he, "to discover to you what hitherto I have kept a secret. I have a brother, who is grand-vizier to the sultan of Egypt, as I have the honour to be to the sultan of this kingdom. This brother has but one son, whom he would not marry to the court of Egypt, but sent him hither to espouse my daughter, that our branches may be reunited. His son, whom I knew to be my nephew the instant I saw him, and is to be my son-in-law, is this young gentleman I now present to you. I trust you will do me the honour to be present at his wedding, which I have resolved to celebrate this day." The noblemen, who could not be offended that he preferred his nephew before all the great matches which had been proposed to him, replied, that he had the best reason to form this connexion; that they would willingly be witnesses to the ceremony; and wished that God might prolong his days to see the fruits of the happy union.

The lords who had met in the house of the vizier of Balsora, having testified their satisfaction at the marriage of his daughter with Noureddin Ali, sat down to table, where they remained a long time. At the end of the repast, sweetmeats were served; of which, according to custom, each person took what he chose to carry away. The cadi then entered with the marriage contract; the chief lords signed it, and the company departed. When all had

retired, excepting the persons belonging to the house, the grand-vizier ordered his servants, whose province it was, to prepare the bagnio, to have it in readiness for Noureddin Ali to bathe, whom he furnished with new linen, of extraordinary fineness and beauty, and with every other necessary. When the attendants had washed and dried the bridegroom, he was going to dress himself in his former apparel; but they presented him with another suit of uncommon magnificence. Thus equipped, and perfumed with the most exquisite odours, he returned to the grandvizier, his father-in-law, who was charmed with his genteel mien; and having desired him to sit down, "My son," said he, "you have declared to me who you are, and the rank you held at the court of Egypt; you have also told me of a difference between you and your brother, which occasioned you to travel so far from your own country. I desire you to make me your entire confidant, and to acquaint me with the cause of your quarrel. You ought not now to have any reason either to doubt me, or to conceal any circumstance from me."

Noureddin Ali then recounted to him every particular relating to his difference with his brother; at which the vizier could not refrain from laughter: "This is," said he, "the most singular occurrence I ever heard! Is it possible, my son, that your quarrel should become so serious about an imaginary marriage? I am sorry you disputed with your elder brother on so frivolous a matter; but I find he was in the wrong to be angry at what you only spoke in jest; and I ought to thank Heaven for that difference which has procured me such a son-in-law. But," continued the old man, "it is late, and time you should retire: go to your bride, my son; she expects you. To-morrow I will present you to the sultan, and I hope he will receive you in a manner that will satisfy us both."

Noureddin Ali accordingly took leave of his father-in-law, and retired to the apartment of his spouse. It is remarkable (continued Giafar) that the very same day that these nuptials were solemnised at Balsora, Schemseddin Mohammed happened also to marry at Cairo, and these are the particulars of his marriage:—

In about a month after Noureddin Ali had left Cairo, with an intention never to return, Schemseddin Mohammed, his elder brother, who was gone to the chase with the sultan of Egypt (for the sultan was so extremely fond of hunting, that he continued his amusement all that time), re-entered his house, and immediately ran to Noureddin Ali's apartment; but was much astonished at learning, that under pretence of taking a journey of two or three days, he rode away on a mule the same day that the sultan went hunting, and had not appeared since. The information vexed Schemseddin so much the more, because he did not doubt but the hard words he had used to his brother were

the cause of his disappearance. He sent a messenger in search of him, who went to Damascus, and as far as Aleppo; but Noureddin was then at Balsora. When the courier returned, without having obtained any news of him, Schemseddin Mohammed proposed to extend his inquiry after him to other parts; and in the meantime resolving to marry, he espoused the daughter of one of the first and most puissant lords in Cairo, upon the same day that Noureddin married the daughter of the grand-vizier of Balsora.

But Commander of the Faithful, this is not all (said Giafar). At the end of nine months, Schemseddin Mohammed's wife was delivered of a daughter at Cairo; and on the same day, Noureddin Ali's spouse was brought to bed of a son at Balsora, who was named Bedreddin Hassan.

The grand-vizier of Balsora testified his joy by great gifts and public festivals, for the birth of his grandson. And, to shew his son-in-law the high esteem he entertained for him, he went to the palace, and most humbly begged of the sultan to grant Noureddin Ali the office he held, that he might have the comfort, before his death, of seeing his son-in-law settled in his place as grand-vizier.

The sultan, who had received Noureddin with much satisfaction, when his father presented him after his marriage, and had ever since heard his character mentioned with commendation, readily granted this old minister's request, and caused Noureddin immediately, in his presence, to put on the robe of the grand-vizier.

The next day, when the father saw his son-in-law preside in council, in his situation, and perform all the offices of a grand-vizier, his joy was complete: while Noureddin Ali conducted himself with so much judgment, that it might be supposed he had been all his life employed in such affairs. He continued afterwards to assist in council whenever the infirmities of age would not permit his father-in-law to attend. This good old man died about four years after the marriage, with the satisfaction of seeing a branch of his family, that promised long to support its lustre.

Noureddin Ali performed his last duty with all possible love and gratitude; and as soon as his son Bedreddin Hassan had attained to the age of seven years, he provided him an excellent tutor, who commenced his education in a manner worthy of his birth. It is true, that he found in the child a ready wit, penetration, and a genius capable of receiving all the good instructions which he gave him.

After Bedreddin Hassan had been two years under the tuition of this master, who taught him perfectly to read, he learned the Alcoran by heart. His father Noureddin Ali afterwards provided him other tutors, by whom his mind was so highly cultivated, that, when he had attained twelve years of age, he had no further occasion for their assistance. At that period, as his features were formed, he gained the admiration of all who beheld him.

Hitherto Noureddin Ali had confined him to his study, and had not yet introduced him to the world; but he now carried him to the palace, to have the honour of making his obedience to the sultan, who received him very graciously. The first persons who saw him in the streets were so charmed with his beauty, that they made exclamations of surprise, and gave him a thousand blessings.

As his father proposed to render him capable of one day supplying his place, he spared no exertions for that end, and made him enter into the most perplexing affairs, that he might at an early age be accustomed to trouble and difficulty. In short, he omitted nothing to advance a son so dear to him; and already began to enjoy the fruits of his labour, when he was suddenly seized with a fit of sickness, of such violence, that he was convinced he approached the end of his days. He could see no cause to flatter himself, and, therefore, prepared to die like a good Mussulman.

In this precious moment, Noureddin forgot not his dear son Bedreddin: he called for him: "My son," said he, "you see this world is transitory; nothing is durable, but the state in which I shall speedily appear. You must, therefore, soon think of fitting yourself for the situation in which you now see me: prepare to make this passage without regret, and without having reason to reproach yourself for neglecting your duties as a Mussulman, or those of a perfectly honest man. In regard to your religion, you are sufficiently instructed, by what you have learned from your tutors, and your own study; respecting the honest man, I shall give you some instructions, by which I hope you will profit. As it is necessary to know yourself, and you cannot have that knowledge unless you first learn who I am, I shall now tell you.

"I am," continued he, "a native of Egypt: my father, your grandfather, was first-minister to the sultan of that kingdom. I myself had the honour to be a vizier to that same sultan, with my brother your uncle, who, I suppose, is yet alive; his name is Schemseddin Mohammed. I was obliged to separate from him; and I came into this country, where I have raised myself to the high dignity I now enjoy. But you will understand all these matters more fully by a manuscript that I will give you."

At the same time, Noureddin Ali produced his pocket-book, which he had written with his own hand, and carried always about with him; and giving it to Bedreddin Hassan, "Take it," said he, "and read it at your leisure; you will there find, among other things, the day of my marriage, and that of your birth; these are circumstances that perhaps you may hereafter have occasion to know, and ought to induce you to preserve it with care." Bedreddin Hassan, sensibly afflicted at seeing his father in that condition, and touched by this discourse, received the pocket-book with tears in his eyes, and promised never to part with it.

At that moment, Noureddin Ali fainted, and it was thought he would have expired; but he recovered, and uttered these words,—

"My son," said he, "the first instruction I have to give you is, *Not to be familiar with all sorts of people. The way to live happy is to keep your thoughts to yourself, and not to open your mind easily.*

"Secondly, *Not to do violence to any person whatever; for, in that case, you draw upon you the hatred of every one. You ought to consider the world as a creditor, to whom you owe moderation, compassion, and forbearance.*

"Thirdly, *Not to reply when you are reproached; for, as the proverb says, 'He who keeps silence is out of danger.' And in this case particularly, you ought to practise forbearance. You also know what one of our poets has observed upon this subject, that 'Silence is the ornament and safeguard of life; that our speech should not be like a storm of rain, which spoils all.' Never did any man yet repent of having spoken too little; but many men have repented speaking too much.*

"Fourthly, *To drink no wine, for that is the source of all vices.*

"Fifthly, *To be careful of your wealth; if you do not squander it away, it will serve to support you in time of need. It is not necessary to amass great property, nor should you be avaricious; for though your means be slender, if you manage them properly, you will acquire many friends; while, on the contrary, should you have great riches, and make an ill use of them, all the world will abandon you, and leave you to yourself.*"

In short, Noureddin Ali continued, till the last moment of his life, to give good advice to his son; and when he was dead, he was interred, with all the honours due to his dignity.

Bedreddin Hassan of Balsora—so he was surnamed, because born in that town—was overwhelmed with grief at the death of his father. Instead of a month, according to custom, he had secluded himself, in tears and solitude, double the time, without seeing anybody, or even going to pay his duty to the sultan of Balsora; who, irritated by this neglect, and considering it as a mark of contempt for his court and person, suffered himself to be transported with anger. In his fury, he summoned the new grand-vizier (for he had created one as soon as he heard of the death of Noureddin Ali), and ordered him to go to the house of the deceased, to confiscate it, with all his other houses, lands, and effects, without leaving anything for Bedreddin Hassan, whom he also commanded him to seize.

The new grand-vizier, accompanied by a great many bailiffs, belonging to the palace, justices' attendants, and other officers, went immediately to execute his commission; but one of Bedreddin Hassan's slaves, who was accidentally in the crowd, no sooner understood the vizier's errand, than he hastily ran before, to give his master warning. He found him sitting in the porch of his house, as much afflicted as if his father had but just died. The slave, out of breath, threw himself at his master's feet; and after having kissed the hem of his garment, " My lord," cried he, " save yourself immediately!" "What is the matter?" said Bedreddin Hassan, lifting up his head. "What news dost thou bring?" "My lord," replied he, " there is no time to lose; the sultan is horribly incensed against you, and has sent people to confiscate all your property, and also to seize your person."

The words of this faithful and affectionate slave, occasioned Bedreddin Hassan great perplexity. "But have I not sufficient time," said he, " to re-enter my house, and take some money and jewels with me?" "No, sir," replied the slave, " the grand-vizier will be here in a moment. Begone immediately, save yourself!" Bedreddin Hassan, speedily quitting the sofa on which he sat, put his feet in his sandals; and, after he had covered his head with the tail of his gown, that his face might not be seen, he fled, without knowing on which side to turn his steps, to avoid the impending danger.

The first thought that occurred to him was, to gain the nearest gate of the town as soon as possible; he accordingly ran, without stopping, till he reached the public cemetery. As it was becoming dark, he resolved to pass the night on his father's tomb; which was a large edifice, in form of a dome, that Noureddin Ali had himself built; but Bedreddin, as he approached it, encountered a very rich Jew, who was a banker and merchant by profession, and was returning from a place where his affairs had called him to the city.

The Jew, whose name was Isaac, having recognised Bedreddin, halted and saluted him very courteously; and paying his respects to Bedreddin Hassan, by kissing his hand, "My lord," said he, " dare I be so bold as to ask whither you are going at this hour of night, apparently alone, and a little agitated? Has anything disquieted you?" "Yes," replied Bedreddin; " while I was asleep, my father appeared to me in a dream: his countenance was terrible, as if he were extremely angry with me: I started out of my sleep, very much frightened, and came immediately to go and pray upon his tomb." "My lord," said the Jew (who did not know the true reason of Bedreddin's leaving the town), " as the late grand-vizier, your father and my good lord, of happy memory, loaded with merchandise several vessels, which are yet at sea, and belong to you, I beg you will grant me the preference before any other merchant. I am able to lay down ready money for all the goods that are in your ships; and, to begin, if you will let me have the cargo of the first ship that arrives in safety, I will pay you a thousand sequins. I have the money here, in a purse; and am ready to deliver it to you in advance." At the same time, he drew a large purse from under his robe, and showed it to him sealed up with his seal.

Bedreddin Hassan, in the state he was, banished from home, and dispossessed of all he had in the world, considered this proposal of the Jew as a favour from Heaven, and therefore joyfully accepted it. "My lord," said the Jew, " then you sell to me, for a thousand sequins, the lading of the first of your ships that may arrive in this port?" "Yes," answered Bedreddin, " I sell it to you for a thousand sequins: it is settled." The Jew immediately delivered to him the purse of a thousand sequins, offering to count them; but Bedreddin Hassan saved him the trouble, by saying, he would take his word. "Since it is so, my lord," said he, " have the goodness to give me an acknowledgment, in writing, of the bargain we have made." On saying this, he pulled an ink-horn from his girdle, and taking out a small reed, neatly cut for writing, he presented it to him, with a piece of paper he found in his letter-case; and while he held the ink-horn, Bedreddin Hassan wrote these words:—

"This writing is to testify, that Bedreddin Hassan of Balsora, has sold to Isaac the Jew, for the sum of one thousand sequins, which he has received, the lading of the first of his ships that may arrive in this port.

"BEDREDDIN HASSAN of Balsora."

When he had written this note, he delivered it to the Jew, who put it in his letter-case, and took leave of him.

While Isaac pursued his journey towards the city, Bedreddin continued his road to his father Noureddin Ali's tomb. When he came to it, he prostrated himself, with his face to the ground; and, his eyes full of tears, deplored his miserable condition. "Alas!" said he, " unfortunate Bedreddin! what will become of thee? Where canst thou seek an asylum from the unjust prince by whom thou art persecuted? Was it not enough to be afflicted with the death of so dear a father? Must fortune add a new sorrow to my just complaints?" He remained a long time in this posture; but at length he arose; when, leaning his head upon his father's sepulchre, his grief returned more violently than before; and he sighed and mourned till, overcome with heaviness, he withdrew his head from the tomb, stretched himself upon the pavement, and fell asleep.

He had scarcely tasted the sweets of repose, when a geni, who had established his retreat in this cemetery during the day, and was preparing to range the world this night, according to his custom, perceived the young man in Noureddin Ali's sepulchre. He entered, and, as Bedreddin lay on his back, was dazzled with his beauty.

After the geni had attentively considered Bedreddin Hassan, he said to himself, "To judge of this creature by his good mien, he would seem to be an angel of the terrestrial paradise, whom God has sent to put the world in a flame with his beauty!" In fine, when he was satisfied with viewing him, he rose very high in the air, where, by chance, he met a fairy. They saluted each other; after which, he said to her, "Pray descend with me into the

cemetery where I stay, and I will show you a prodigy of beauty, who is not less worthy of your admiration than mine." The fairy consented, and they both descended in an instant; when, entering the sepulchre, "Well!" said the geni to the fairy, showing her Bedreddin Hassan, "did you ever see a young man of comelier stature, or more beautiful, than this."

The fairy, having attentively examined Bedreddin, turned to the geni: "I must confess," said she, "that he is very handsome; but I am now come from seeing an object at Cairo, still more admirable, of which, if you will attend to me, I will give you an account." "You will afford me great pleasure," replied the geni. "You must know, then," continued the fairy—"for I will relate it at length—that the sultan of Egypt has a vizier, named Schemseddin Mohammed, who has a daughter, of about twenty years of age, the most beautiful and accomplished person ever known. The sultan, having heard of this young lady's beauty, sent the other day for her father, and said to him, 'I understand you have a daughter to marry: I wish to espouse her: will you give your consent?' The vizier, unprepared for such a proposition, was a little troubled, but not flattered, by it; and instead of accepting

it joyfully, which others in his situation certainly would, he answered the sultan, 'Sir, I am not worthy of the honour your majesty would confer upon me; and I most humbly beseech you to pardon me, if I do not agree to your request. You know that I had a brother named Noureddin Ali, who had the honour, as well as myself, to be one of your viziers. We had some difference together, which was the cause of his leaving me suddenly; since that time I have received no account of him till within these four days, when I heard he died at Balsora, being grand-vizier to the sultan of that kingdom. He has left a son behind him; and, there being an agreement between us to match our children together, if ever we had any, I am persuaded he intended to fulfil that match when he died: anxious, therefore, to adhere to the promise on my part, I conjure your majesty to grant me permission. There are in your court many other lords who have daughters, whom you would honour by your alliance.'

"The sultan of Egypt, incensed to the highest degree at the refusal and boldness of Schemseddin Mohammed, replied to him, in a rage, which he could not restrain, 'Is this your requital of my goodness in offering so to degrade myself, as to form an alliance with you! I know how to revenge your daring to prefer another before me; and I swear that your daughter shall have, for a husband, one of the most vile and ugly of my slaves.'—Having spoken these words, he angrily bade the vizier be gone, who returned to his house full of confusion, and cruelly mortified·

"This day the sultan sent for one of his grooms, who is hump-backed, big-bellied, and as ugly as an hobgoblin; and after commanding Schemseddin Mohammed to consent to marry his daughter to this frightful slave, he caused the contract to be drawn out, and signed by witnesses in his own presence. The preparations for this fantastical wedding are completed; and at this moment all the slaves belonging to the lords of the court of Egypt are at the door of the bagnio, each with a flambeau in his hand, waiting for the hump-backed groom, who is there bathing, to conduct him to his bride who is already dressed. When I departed from Cairo, the ladies, who had assembled, were preparing to conduct her, in her nuptial attire, to the hall where she is to receive her hump-backed bride-groom, and she is now expecting him. I have seen her, and do assure you, no one could look on her without admiration."

When the fairy ceased speaking, the geni thus replied:—"Whatever you may say, I cannot be persuaded that the girl's beauty exceeds that of this young man." "I will not dispute the point with you," answered the fairy; "for I must confess he deserves to be married to that charming creature whom they design for hump-back; and I think it were a deed worthy of us, to oppose the injustice of the sultan of Egypt, and substitute this young man in the room of the slave." "You are in the right," replied the geni; "I am extremely gratified by your suggestion. Let us cheat, I agree to it, the vengeance of the sultan of Egypt; console a distressed father; and render his daughter as happy as she thinks herself miserable. I will use my utmost endeavours to effect this project; and I am persuaded you will not be backward: I will engage to carry him to Cairo before he awake; after which, when we have accomplished our design, I shall leave him to your care, to carry where you please."

The fairy and the geni having thus concerted what they were to do, the geni lifted up Bedreddin Hassan gently, and carrying him with inconceivable swiftness through the air, set him down at the door of a public lodgment next to the bagnio, whence hump-back was ready to appear with the train of slaves that attended him.

Bedreddin Hassan, awaking at this moment, was very much surprised to find himself in the middle of a strange city. He was going to cry out, and to inquire where he was; but the geni, touching him gently on the shoulder, forbade him to speak a word. He then put a torch in his hand: "Go," said he, "join the crowd at the bagnio-door, and follow them till you reach a hall, where a marriage is to be celebrated. The bridegroom is hump-backed, by which you will easily know him. Place yourself on his right hand as you enter; and immediately open the purse of sequins that you have in your bosom, and distribute them among the musicians and dancers in the way. When you are in the hall, give money also to the female slaves you see about the bride, when they approach you. But every time you put your hand in the purse, be sure you take out a whole handful of sequins, and mind you do not spare them. Act in everything precisely as I have directed, with great presence of mind; be not astonished; fear nobody; and leave the rest to a superior Power, who will order matters as he thinks fit."

Young Bedreddin, well instructed in all that he was to perform, advanced towards the door of the bagnio. He first lighted his torch, as that of a slave; and then mixing with the attendants, as if he belonged to some nobleman of Cairo, he accompanied them, following hump-back, who came out of the bath, and mounted a horse from the sultan's own stable.

Bedreddin Hassan, finding himself near the musicians, and male and female dancers, who walked immediately before the bridegroom, drew from his purse, time after time, handfuls of sequins, which he distributed among them. As he bestowed his gifts with an unparalleled grace and engaging air, he attracted the notice of all who received them; and when they had viewed him, they found him so comely and handsome, that they could not divert their observation.

At length they reached the gate of the vizier Schemseddin Mohammed, who little imagined his nephew was so near. The doorkeepers, to prevent disorder, kept back all the slaves that carried torches, and would not let them enter. Bedreddin was likewise repulsed; but the musicians, who had free entrance, stopped, and protested they would not go in, if he were hindered accompanying them. "He is not a slave," said they; "you need only look at him to be convinced. No doubt he is a young stranger, who is curious to see the ceremonies observed at weddings in this city." Saying this, they put him in the midst of them, and carried him with them in spite of the porters. They took his torch, and gave it to the first who presented; and having introduced him to the hall, they placed him at the right hand of the hump-backed bridegroom, who sat near the vizier's daughter on a throne magnificently decorated.

She appeared to advantage in all her dresses; but in her face was a languor, or rather mortal sadness, the cause of which is readily defined, by seeing at her side a husband deformed, and so little worthy of her love. The throne of the ill-matched couple was in the midst of a sofa: on each side of which, a little lower, were seated the wives of the emirs, viziers, the officers of the sultan's bedchamber, and several other ladies of the court and city, every one according to her quality; and all of them so advantageously and richly dressed, that it was a most agreeable spectacle: they held in their hands large wax-tapers lighted.

As soon as they saw Bedreddin Hassan enter the room, they all fixed their eyes upon him; and admiring his shape, his behaviour, and the beauty of his face, they could not refrain from looking at him. When he was seated, each of them left her seat, and approached him, to have a distinct view of his face; and almost all of them, as they returned to their places, found themselves moved with the tender passion.

The disparity between Bedreddin Hassan and the hump-backed groom, whose figure excited horror, occasioned murmuring in the company; insomuch that the ladies cried out, "We must give our bride to this handsome young man, and not to that ugly hump-back." Nor did they rest here; but dared to utter imprecations against the sultan, who, abusing his absolute power, would unite ugliness and beauty. They also upbraided the bridegroom, and put him quite out of countenance, to the great pleasure of the spectators, whose shouts for some time interrupted the concert of music in the hall. At length the musicians recommenced; and the women who had dressed the bride again attended her.

Each time that the bride changed her habit, she arose from her seat, followed by her women, and passing by hump-back without deigning to notice him, went toward Bedreddin Hassan, before whom she presented herself in her new attire. Then Bedreddin, agreeably to the instructions given him by the geni, remembered to put his hand in his purse, and drew out handfuls of sequins, which he distributed among the women who followed the bride; nor did he forget the players and dancers, but also threw money to them. It was pleasant to see how they pushed one another to gather it up; at the same time testifying their thanks, and making signs that the young bride should be for him, and not for hump-back. The women who attended her said the same, regardless of the groom's hearing them, for they put a thousand roguish tricks upon him, which very much diverted the spectators.

When the ceremony of changing habits was concluded, the musicians ceased playing, and retired, making a sign to Bedreddin Hassan to remain. The ladies likewise departed with all those who did not belong to the house. The bride entered a closet, whither her women followed to undress her; and the only persons remaining in the hall were the hump-backed groom, Bedreddin Hassan, and some domestics.

Hump-back, who was furiously exasperated against Bedreddin, suspecting him to be his rival, looked at him askant, saying. "And thou! what dost thou wait for? Why art thou not gone as well as the rest? Away!" Bedreddin, having no pretext to remain, withdrew, very much embarrassed. But he had not passed the porch, when the geni and the fairy met and stopped him. "Whither are you agoing?" said the geni. "Stay, for hump-back is not now in the hall; he has had occasion to leave it; therefore, you have only to return and introduce yourself to the bride's chamber. When you are alone with her, tell her boldly that you are her husband; that the

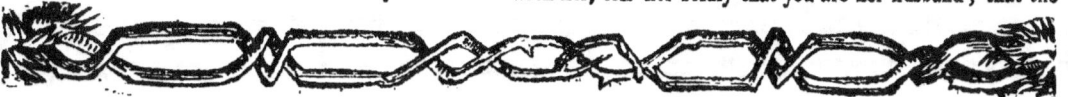

sultan's intention was merely to make sport with the groom; and, to render this pretended husband some amends, that you had caused to be prepared for him, in the stable, a good dish of cream. Then use all your arguments to persuade her; but as you are so handsome, that will be attended with little difficulty; she will think herself happy in being so agreeably deceived. In the meantime, we will give orders to prevent hump-back's return, to hinder your passing the night with your bride, for she is yours, and not his."

At the time the geni thus encouraged Bedreddin, and instructed him how he should conduct himself, hump-back had actually quitted the room; for the geni attacked him in the shape of a great black cat, mewing in a dreadful manner. Hump-back called to the cat, and clapped his hands to drive her away, but instead of flying the cat rose upon her hind feet, staring with her eyes like fire, looking fiercely at him, miauling louder than before, and increasing in size, till she was as large as an ass. At this appearance, hump-back would have cried out for help, but his fear was so great, that he stood gaping, unable to utter a word. That he might not have time to recover, the geni immediately changed himself into a mighty buffalo; in which shape he called to him, in a voice that redoubled his terror, "Thou hump-backed villain!" At these words the affrighted groom fell on the floor, and covering his face with his gown, that he might not see the dreadful beast, "Sovereign prince of buffaloes," said he, "what do you require of me?" "Wo be to thee!" replied the geni; "hast thou the temerity to dare marry my mistress?"

"Oh, my lord," said hump-back, "I pray you to pardon me; if I am criminal, it is through ignorance. I knew not that this lady had a buffalo for her sweetheart; command me in any manner you please, I give you my oath that I am ready to obey you." "By thy death," replied the geni; "if thou goest hence, or speakest a word till the sun rise, I will crush thy head to pieces—then I give thee leave to retire; but I warn thee to make despatch, and not to look back; and if thou hast the audacity to return, thy life shall be the forfeit." Having thus spoken, the geni transformed himself into the shape of a man, took hump-back by the legs, and after placing him against the wall with his head downwards, "If thou stir," said he, "before the sun rise, as I have already told thee, I will again take thee by the heels, and dash thy head in a thousand pieces against this wall."

To return to Bedreddin Hassan, who, encouraged by the geni and the presence of the fairy, re-entered the hall, whence he slipt into the nuptial chamber, where he sat down, waiting the success of his adventure. After some time the bride arrived, conducted by an old matron, who stopped at the door; and reminding the bridegroom of his duty, without observing whether it was humpback or another, closed it, and retired.

The young bride was extremely surprised, instead of hump-back, to find Bedreddin Hassan, who presented himself to her with the best grace possible. "What! my dear friend," said she, "by your being here at this hour of night, you must be my husband's comrade." "No, madam," replied Bedreddin; "I am of condition different from that of the ugly hump-back." "But," said she, "you do not consider that you speak degradingly of my husband." "He your husband, madam!" returned he. "Can you retain this opinion so long? Be convinced of your mistake; so much beauty could never be sacrificed to the most contemptible of mankind. I am, madam, the happy mortal for whom it is reserved. The sultan determined to divert himself, by thus deceiving the vizier, your father, and chose me to be your real husband. You might observe how the ladies, the musicians, the dancers, your women, and all the servants of your house, were entertained with this comedy. We have sent that hump-backed fellow to his stable again, where he is just now eating a dish of cream; and you may rest assured he will never again appear before your beautiful eyes."

At this discourse the vizier's daughter, who entered the nuptial chamber more dead than alive, changing countenance, assumed an air so gay, that she appeared still more handsome, and Bedreddin was perfectly charmed. "I did not expect," said she, "to meet with so agreeable a surprise; and I had already condemned myself to unhappiness all the remainder of my life; but my good fortune is so much the greater, as I shall possess in you a man worthy of my tenderest affection."

Having thus spoken, she unrobed herself, and stepped into bed. Bedreddin Hassan, on his part, overjoyed at finding himself possessor of so many charms, hastened to undress, placing his clothes upon a chair; and covering the purse that he received from the Jew, which, notwithstanding the money he had distributed, was still full, he then, removing his turban, put on a nightcap that had been intended for hump-back, and went to sleep in his shirt and drawers. His drawers were of blue satin, tied with a lace of gold.

While the two lovers were sleeping, the geni, who had rejoined the fairy, observed to her, that it was time to finish what they had so well begun, and so successfully conducted: "Let us not, then," said he, "be surprised by daylight, which will soon appear; go you, and bring away the young man without waking him."

The fairy entered the chamber where the two lovers were fast asleep, and raising Bedreddin Hassan in the state he was, namely, in his shirt and drawers, joined company with the geni, and conveyed her charge with wonderful swiftness to the gates of Damascus, in Syria, where they arrived precisely at the time when the ministers of the mosques, appointed to that function, were summoning the people to attend prayers, day beginning to appear. The fairy laid Bedreddin Hassan softly on the ground, and placing him near the gate, departed with the geni.

The city gates being opened, a great number of people, already assembled, passed through, who were extremely surprised at seeing Bedreddin Hassan in his shirt and drawers, lying on the ground. One said, "He has been so hard pressed to escape from the house of his mistress, that he could not gain time to dress!" "Look ye!" exclaimed another, "how people expose themselves! No doubt he has spent the greater part of the night in drinking with his friends: he has become inebriated, and then, perhaps, having occasion to leave the city, instead of returning, he had insensibly proceeded so far, when he was overcome with sleep." Others were of different opinions; but nobody could guess by what adventure he had been conducted thither. A gentle wind happening to arise at that time, by removing his shirt, exposed a breast whiter than snow; with which the by-standers were so astonished, that they uttered a cry of admiration, and awoke the young man.

His surprise was not less than that of the spectators, when he found himself at the gate of the strange city, and encompassed by a crowd of people gazing at him. "Gentlemen," said he, "pray tell me where I am, and what is required of me." One of the by-standers replied to him:—"Young man," said he, "the gates of the city were just now opened, and, as we came out, we found you sleeping in that state, and stopped to look at you: have you lain here all night? Do you know that you are at one of the gates of Damascus?" "At one of the gates of Damascus!" exclaimed Bedreddin: "surely you mock me. When I lay down to sleep last night, I was at Cairo." At these words, some of the people, touched with compassion for him, said it was a pity so handsome a young man should have lost his senses, and continued their road.

"My son," said an old man to him. "you know not what you say: how is it possible that you, being this morning at Damascus, could be last night at Cairo?" "It is nevertheless very true," said Bedreddin; "and I swear to you that I was all day yesterday at Balsora." He had scarcely uttered these words, when all the people roared with laughter—crying out, "He is a fool! He is a madman!" There were some, however, who pitied him on account of his youth; and one of the company thus addressed him: "My son, you must certainly have lost your senses; you do not consider what you say. Is it possible that a man could yesterday be at Balsora, the same night at Cairo, and the next morning at Damascus? Certainly you are not yet awake; come, rouse your spirits." "What I say," answered Bedreddin Hassan, "is so true, that last night I was married in the city of Cairo." At this observation, all those who laughed before could not forbear repeating their clamour. "Recollect yourself," said the same person who had just spoken; "you have surely dreamed all this, and the illusion still possesses your brain." "I am perfectly sensible of what I say," replied the young man. "Tell me yourself how it was possible for me to go in a dream to Cairo, where I am convinced I was in person, and where my bride was seven times brought before me, each time dressed in a different habit; and where, in fine, I saw an ugly hump-backed fellow to whom they pretended to give her? Besides, I want to know what is become of my gown, my turban, and the bag of sequins I had at Cairo."

Though he assured them that what he had stated was matter of fact, his auditors only laughed, which occasioned him such confusion, that he scarcely knew himself what he ought to think of his adventures.

At length Bedreddin Hassan, confidently affirming all that he said to be true, rose up to enter the town; and was followed by the crowd, exclaiming, "A madman! a fool!" At these cries, some looked out of their windows, some came to their doors, and others joined with those about him, calling out as they did, "He is a fool, who knows not how to act." While in this embarrassment, the young man arrived before the shop of a pastry-cook, who opening his door, Bedreddin entered to avoid the rabble.

This pastry-cook had formerly been captain of a troop of Arabian robbers, who plundered the caravans; and though he was become a citizen of Damascus, where he gave no offence, he was still dreaded by all who knew him: in consequence of which, as soon as he appeared to the populace that followed Bedreddin, they dispersed.

When all the people were gone, the pastry-cook put several questions to the young man; asking him who he was, and what had brought him thither. Bedreddin Hassan concealed neither his birth, nor the death of his father the grand-vizier: he afterwards told him why he quitted Balsora; how, falling asleep, the night following, upon his father's tomb, he found himself, when he awoke, at Cairo, where he had married a lady; and, lastly, his amazement at being at Damascus, without the power of comprehending these wonders.

"Your history is most surprising!" said the pastry-cook; "but if you follow my advice, you will not confess to any man those circumstances which you have revealed to me, but patiently wait till Heaven deign to end your misfortunes. Till that time, you may remain with me; and as I have no children, I will own you for my son, if you consent to it: after you are so adopted, you can freely walk through the city without being again exposed to the insults of the rabble."

Though this adoption was degrading to the son of the grand-vizier, Bedreddin was glad to accept of the pastry-cook's proposals, judging it the most prudent conduct he could pursue, in his then circumstances. The cook clothed him, summoned witnesses, and went to declare before a cadi that he acknowledged him for his son; after which, Bedreddin staid with him under the simple name of Hassan, and learned the pastry trade.

During the time these circumstances were passing at Damascus, Schemseddin Mohammed's daughter awoke; when finding Bedreddin had quitted the bed, she supposed he had risen gently for fear of disturbing her, and would soon return. While waiting his reappearance, her father the vizier, who was sensibly wounded by the affront he had received from the sultan, knocked at her chamber door, determined to join his tears with hers, in bewailing her sad destiny. He called her by name; and she no sooner heard his voice, than she arose and opened the door. She kissed his hand, and received him with so much satisfaction in her countenance that the vizier, who expected to find her drowned in tears, and as much grieved as himself, was astonished: "Unhappy wretch!" said he in a rage; "Do you appear before me thus? After the hideous sacrifice you have just consummated, can you look at me so contentedly?"

When the new bride saw her father was angry at the joy she could not avoid expressing, she said to him, "For Heaven's sake, sir, do not reproach me so unjustly; it is not hump-back, whom I abhor more than death—it is not that monster I have married: he was derided and ridiculed by every one, till he was forced to go and hide himself, to make room for a charming young man, who is my real husband!" "What fable do you tell me?" interrupted Schemseddin Mohammed. "How! did not crook-back sleep with you last night?" "No, sir," replied she; "I have not slept with any other person than the young man I mentioned, who has full eyes, and large black eye-brows." At these words the vizier lost all patience, and put himself in a furious passion with his daughter. "Ah, wicked woman!" said he, "would you render me distracted by your discourse?" "It is you, my father," returned she, "who will deprive me of my senses by your incredulity." "Is it not, then, true," said the vizier, "that hump-back—" "Let us talk no more of him," interrupted she quickly: "A curse upon hump-back! must I always be teased about him?—Father," continued she, "I tell you, once more, that I have not passed the night with him, but with my dear spouse, who cannot be far off."

Schemseddin Mohammed went out to seek him; but instead of finding him, he was extremely surprised at observing hump-back with his head on the ground, and his heels in the air, precisely in the situation where he had been placed by the geni. "What is the meaning of this?" said he; "who placed you in that state?" Crook-back, recognising the vizier, answered, "Alas! alas! it is you then that would marry me to the mistress of a buffalo, the sweetheart of an ugly geni! I will not be your dupe; you shall not trick me."

Schemseddin Mohammed, thinking hump-back crazed, bade him move, and stand upon his legs. "I will take care how I do that," said hump-back, "unless the sun be risen.—Know, sir, that when I came hither, last night, suddenly a black cat appeared to me, and became insensibly as large as a buffalo: I have not forgotten what he said

to me : therefore you may go about your business, and leave me here," The vizier, instead of retiring, took him by the heels, and obliged him to rise; when hump-back ran away as fast as he could, without once looking behind him, and presented himself at the palace of the sultan, whom he highly diverted by his account of the treatment he had received from the geni.

Schemseddin Mohammed returned to his daughter's apartment, more astonished, and in still greater perplexity, than when he left it. "Well, my abused daughter," said he, "cannot you furnish me with more information respecting this adventure ?" "Sir," replied she, "I can give you no other account than what I have already had the honour to relate. But here are my husband's clothes," continued she, "which he left upon this chair; they, perhaps, may afford you some satisfaction." She then presented to him Bedreddin's turban, which he took; and examining it attentively, "I should suppose this to be a vizier's turban," said he, if it were not made after the Mossoul fashion." But perceiving that something was sewed between the stuff and the lining he called for scissors : when, having unripped it, he found a folded paper, which was the pocket-book that Noureddin Ali had given to Bedreddin, his son, as he was dying, and which he had hidden in his turban for greater security.

Schemseddin Mohammed, having opened the book, recognised his brother Noureddin's handwriting, and read this superscription,—"*For my son Bedreddin Hassan.*" Before he could make any reflections upon it, his daughter delivered to him the purse that lay under his clothes. He opened it likewise, and found it was full of sequins; for, as I before stated, notwithstanding the unbounded liberality of Bedreddin, it was constantly refilled by the geni and the fairy. On a note, in the bag, he read these words,—"*A thousand sequins belonging to Isaac the Jew;*" and underneath the following lines, which the Jew wrote before he parted from Bedreddin Hassan ;—"*Delivered to Bedreddin Hassan, for the cargo, which he has sold to me, of the first of those ships formerly belonging to Noureddin Ali, his father, of happy memory, that arrives in this port.*" He had scarcely ended these words, when, with a loud cry, he fainted.

Being at length recovered from his swoon, by the assistance of his daughter, and the women she had summoned to her aid, "Daughter," said he, "do not be alarmed at this accident; the occasion of it is such as you will hardly believe—your bridegroom is your cousin, the son of Noureddin Ali. The thousand sequins that are in this purse remind me of a quarrel I had with my dear brother—they are, without doubt, the dowry he gives you. God be praised for all things; and particularly for this miraculous adventure, which so clearly demonstrates His almighty power!" He again looked at his brother's writing, kissed it several times, and shed abundance of tears. "Ah! that I cannot," continued he, "as well as I see these remains, which cause me so much joy, see also Noureddin, and reconcile myself with him !"

He read the book through, and found the date of his brother's arrival at Balsora, of his marriage, and of the birth of Bedreddin Hassan; when he afterwards compared these dates with the day of his own marriage, and the birth of his daughter at Cairo, he admired the union of every circumstance, reflecting that, as his nephew was his son-in-law, he should be happy. In fine, he took up the book and the ticket of the purse, and went to show them to the sultan, who not only pardoned what had passed, but was so much pleased with the recital of this affair, that he caused a particular account of it to be put in writing for the use of posterity.

Meanwhile the vizier Schemseddin Mohammed could not comprehend why his nephew had disappeared; he hoped, nevertheless, every moment to see him arrive, and was impatient to fold him in his arms. After having in vain expected him seven days, he searched through all Cairo, but could obtain no news of him, notwithstanding the strictest inquiry. "This is the most singular adventure," said he, "that ever man met with." In the incertitude of what might happen, he thought it proper to draw up an account, in his own handwriting, of the present state of his house, the manner in which the wedding had been solemnized, how the hall and his daughter's bed-chamber were furnished, and other circumstances. He likewise made a packet of the turban, the purse, and the remainder of Bedreddin's habiliments, and secured them under lock and key.

After the lapse of some days, the vizier's daughter perceived herself pregnant, and at the expiration of nine months was delivered of a son. A nurse was provided for the child, besides other women and slaves to wait upon him, and his grandfather named him Agib.

When young Agib had attained the age of seven years, the vizier Schemseddin Mohammed, instead of learning him to read at home, sent him to the school of a master who had obtained high reputation; and two slaves had the care of conducting him to and from the seminary daily. Agib was accustomed to play with his schoolfellows, who, as they were all inferior to him in quality, treated him with great respect; in this they were influenced by the example of their master, who often would tolerate faults in him that he would not pardon in the rest. This blind complaisance so spoiled Agib, that he became proud and insolent, and would have his playfellows submit implicitly to his caprices, while he would not bear from them the slightest offence. He domineered over all, and if any one had the hardiness to oppose his will, he would call him a thousand names, and many times go to blows. In short, he rendered himself insupportable to the scholars, who complained of him to the master of the school. He at first exhorted them to have patience : but when he found that Agib, in consequence, became more and more intolerant, and occasioned him a great deal of trouble, "Children," said he to his scholars, "this Agib is a little insolent gentleman; I will show you a way to mortify him, so that he shall never torment you any more; nay, I even think it will make him leave the school:—When he is here to-morrow, and you are disposed to play together, place yourselves round him, and one of you call out, "Come, let us play :—but upon this condition, that whoever desires to play shall tell his own name, and the names of his father and mother; and they who refuse shall be considered bastards, and not suffered to play in our company." The schoolmaster made them understand the embarrassment into which Agib would be thrown by this means, and they all joyfully retired.

Next day, when they were assembled, they proceeded to follow their master's instructions. Having encircled Agib, one of them called out, "Let us begin to play :—but on condition that he who cannot tell his own name, and that of his father and mother, shall not play at all." They all cried out, and so did Agib, with consent. Then he who had spoken first interrogated them, one after another; and all fulfilled the condition except Agib, who answered, "My name i Agib; my mother is called the lady of beauty, and my father, Schemseddin Mohammed, vizier to the sultan."

At these words, all the children cried out, "Agib! what do you say? That is not the name of your father, but your grandfather." "A curse on you!" said he in a passion: "What! dare you say that the vizier Schemseddin Mohammed is not my father?" "No, no," cried they, laughing heartily, "he is only your grandfather, and you shall not play with us; nay, we will take care how we come into your company." Saying this, they withdrew from him railing; and continued laughing among themselves. Agib was so mortified by their scoffs that he wept. The schoolmaster, who was near, and had heard all that passed, entered at this moment; and addressing himself to Agib, "Do not you yet know, Agib," said he, "that the vizier Schemseddin Mohammed is not your father? He is your grandfather, and the father of your mother, the lady of beauty. We are equally ignorant with yourself of the name of your father: we only know that the sultan is going to marry your mother to one of his grooms, a hump-back fellow, but that a geni slept with her. This is hard upon you; and ought to teach you to treat your school-fellows with less haughtiness than you have hitherto."

The little Agib, nettled at the behaviour of his companions, ran hastily out of the school, and returned home crying. He went immediately to his mother's chamber, who, alarmed at seeing him thus grieved, anxiously inquired the reason. He could only reply in words interrupted by sobs, so great was his distress; and it was not till after several attempts, that he became sufficiently recovered to state the cause of his affliction. When he had ended his complaint, "Mother," added he, "for the love of God be pleased to tell me who is my father?" "My son," replied she, "Schemseddin Mohammed, who is every day so kind to you, is your father." "You do not tell me truth," said Agib; "he is your father, and not mine. But whose son am I?" At this question the lady of beauty, calling to mind her wedding-night, which had been succeeded by a long widowhood, began to shed tears, repining bitterly at the loss of so amiable a husband as Bedreddin.

While the lady of beauty and Agib were both weeping, the vizier Schemseddin Mohammed entered, and demanded the reason of their sorrow. The lady told him of the mortification Agib had received at school, which so much affected the vizier, that he joined his tears with theirs; and judging from this occurrence, that everybody treated the character of his daughter with dishonour, he was almost in a state of despair. Wounded by this cruel thought, he went to the sultan, and, falling prostrate at his feet, humbly prayed him to grant him permission to make a journey into the provinces of the Levant, particularly to Balsora, in search of his nephew Bedreddin Hassan, saying, he could not bear to let the people of the town think a geni had slept with his daughter.

The sultan was much concerned at the affliction of the vizier, approved his resolution, and gave him the permission he demanded. He also caused a passport to be prepared for him, praying, in the most obliging terms, all kings and princes, in whose dominions the said Bedreddin might sojourn, to allow the vizier to take him with him.

Schemseddin Mohammed could not find words to express his acknowledgments to the sultan for this kindness; he therefore prostrated himself before the prince a second time; but the tears he shed gave him sufficient testimony of his gratitude. In fine, having wished the sultan every kind of prosperity, he took his leave and returned home,

No. 14.

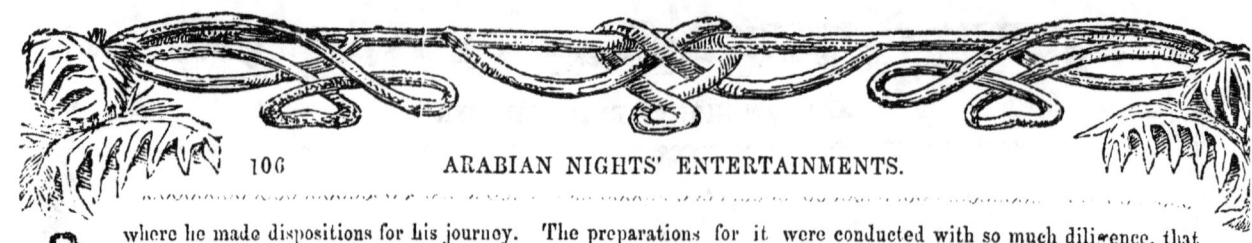

where he made dispositions for his journey. The preparations for it were conducted with so much diligence, that in four days after he left the city, accompanied by his daughter the lady of beauty, and his grandson Agib.

Taking the road to Damascus, they travelled nineteen days without stopping in any place; but on the twentieth, arriving in a very pleasant mead at a small distance from the gates of that city, they alighted, and pitched their tents upon the banks of a river that runs through the town, and renders the environs very agreeable.

The vizier Schemseddin Mohammed declared he would stay in that pleasant place two days; and on the third continue his journey. In the meantime, he gave his retinue leave to go to Damascus; and nearly all of them profited by the permission: some influenced by curiosity to see a city of which they had heard so much, and others by the opportunity of vending there the Egyptian goods they had brought with them, or buying stuffs, and the rarities of the country. The lady of beauty wishing her son Agib might also share in the satisfaction of viewing that celebrated city, ordered the black eunuch, who acted in the quality of governor, to conduct him thither, and take care he met with no accident.

Agib, in magnificent apparel, went with the eunuch, who had a large cane in his hand. They had no sooner entered the city, than Agib, fair as the day, attracted the eyes of the people. Some quitted their houses to obtain a nearer view of him; others put their heads out of the windows; and those who passed along the streets were not satisfied with stopping to look at him, but followed, to prolong the pleasure of the agreeable sight: in fine, every body admired him, and uttered a thousand benedictions on the father and mother who had given being to so fine a child. By chance, the eunuch and he arrived before the shop where Bedreddin Hassan was, and there the throng was so great, they were compelled to halt.

The pastrycook who had adopted Bedreddin Hassan, had been dead some years, and had left him his shop with all his other property. Bedreddin had therefore become master of the concern, and managed the pastry trade so dexterously, that he had obtained great reputation in Damascus. Observing a great crowd before his door, looking so attentively at Agib and the black eunuch, he stepped out to see them himself.

Bedreddin Hassan, having cast his eyes particularly upon Agib, immediately felt himself sensibly affected, without knowing the reason. He was not struck, like the people, with the shining beauty of the boy: his trouble and emotion had another cause, unknown to him: it was the force of blood that agitated the tender father, who, interrupting his occupations, approached Agib, and, with an engaging air, said to him, "My little lord, who has won my soul, have the kindness to walk into my shop, and eat something; that during the time I may have the pleasure of admiring you at my ease." These words he pronounced with such tenderness, that tears trickled from his eyes. Little Agib was moved when he saw it; and turning to the eunuch, "This honest man," said he, "has a face that pleases me; and he speaks in so affectionate a manner, that I cannot avoid complying with his request. Let us step into his house, and taste his pastry." "Truly," replied the slave, "it would be a fine sight to see the son of a vizier, like you, enter a pastry-shop to eat; do not expect I will suffer such a proceeding." "Alas! my little lord," cried Bedreddin, "your friends are very cruel to trust your conduct in the hands of a person who treats you so harshly." Then addressing himself to the eunuch, "My good friend," said he, "pray do not give me the mortification of hindering this young lord's granting me the favour I ask; rather do me the honour to walk in with him: by such behaviour you will convince the world, that though your outside is as brown as that of a chesnut, your inside is as white as the interior of the fruit. Do not you know," continued he, "that I am master of a secret to make you white, instead of being black as you are?" The eunuch laughed at this discourse, and then asked Bedreddin the nature of the secret. "I am going to tell you," replied Bedreddin, who repeated some verses in praise of black eunuchs, implying, that it was by their ministry that the honour of princes and of all great men was insured. The eunuch was charmed with these verses; and, without further opposition, he suffered Agib to enter the shop, and followed him also himself.

Bedreddin Hassan was overjoyed at having obtained what he had so passionately desired; and returning to the work Agib's appearance had interrupted, "I was making," said he, "cream tarts; and must beg of you, if you please, to eat of them: I am persuaded you will find them very good, for my own mother, who made them incomparably well, taught me the method, and the people from all quarters of the town send to purchase them of me." As he said this, he took a cream tart out of the oven, and, after strewing upon it some pomegranate-kernels and sugar, placed it before Agib, who found it delicious. The eunuch, to whom Bedreddin was not entirely inattentive, also passed the same judgment.

While they were both eating, Bedreddin Hassan examined Agib with great attention; and as he regarded him, he represented to himself that he might have such a son by his charming wife, from whom he had been so soon and so cruelly separated; and the very thought drew tears from his eyes. He had determined to put some questions to little Agib concerning his journey to Damascus; but the child had not time to gratify his curiosity, for the eunuch, pressing him to return to his grandfather's tents, took him away as soon as he had finished eating. Bedreddin Hassan, not contented with looking after him, shut up his shop immediately, and followed.

Bedreddin Hassan ran after Agib and the eunuch, and overtook them before they had reached the gate of the city. The eunuch, perceiving he followed them, was extremely surprised. "You impertinent fellow!" said he, in an angry tone. "What do you want?" "My dear friend," replied Bedreddin, "do not disturb yourself: a little business out of town, which I have just remembered, compels me to go to give orders." This answer did not appease the eunuch, who, turning to Agib, said, "You have brought this trouble upon me: I foresaw I should repent of my complaisance: you would enter the man's shop; though I acted unwisely in permitting you." "Perhaps," replied Agib, "he really has business without the town; and the road is free for every person." While this passed, they continued walking together, without looking back, till they approached the vizier's tents, when they turned to see if Bedreddin still followed them. Agib, perceiving he was within two paces of him, became red and pale alternately, according to the various emotions that affected him. He was afraid the vizier, his grandfather, would learn he had been in the pastry-shop, and had eaten there. Under the influence of this fear, he seized a large stone that lay at his foot, and, throwing it at Bedreddin Hassan, struck him on the forehead, which gave him such a wound that his face

was covered with blood; he then took to his heels, and ran under the tents, with the eunuch, who told Bedreddin he had no reason to complain of a mischance that he had merited, and brought upon himself.

Bedreddin turned towards the city, stanching the blood of the wound with his apron, which he had not put off: "I was wrong," said he to himself, "in leaving my house, to take so much trouble after this boy; for he would never have treated me in this manner, if he had not suspected me of some ill design against him." When he reached home, he had his wound dressed; and consoled himself by reflecting, that there was an infinite number of people upon the earth yet more unfortunate.

Bedreddin continued the pastry trade at Damascus; and his uncle Schemseddin Mohammed departed thence three days after his arrival. He travelled by way of Emaus, Hannah, and Haleph, where he stopped two days. He then crossed the Euphrates, entering Mesopotamia; and after passing through Mardin, Mossoul, Sengier, Diarbeker, and several other towns, at length arrived at Balsora, and immediately demanded audience of the sultan, who was no sooner informed of Schemseddin's quality, than he admitted him, received him very favourably, and inquired the occasion of his journey to Balsora. "Sir," replied the vizier Schemseddin Mohammed, "I come to make inquiry respecting the son of Noureddin Ali, my brother, who had the honour to serve your majesty." "Noureddin Ali," said the sultan, "has been dead a long time. As for his son, all I can tell you of him is, that he disappeared suddenly, two months after his father's death, and nobody has since seen him, notwithstanding all the search I have had made. But his mother, who is daughter of one of my viziers, is still living. Schemseddin Mohammed begged permission of the sultan to visit her, and carry her to Egypt; and having obtained his request, without waiting till the next day for the satisfaction of seeing her, he inquired her place of abode, and that very hour went to her house, accompanied by his daughter and grandson.

The widow of Noureddin Ali resided in the same house in which her husband had lived till his death. It was a fine stately building, adorned with marble pillars; but Schemseddin did not stop to admire it. On his arrival, he kissed the gate, and a marble upon which his brother's name was written in letters of gold. He demanded to speak with his sister-in-law; and was told by her servants that she was in a small edifice, in the form of a dome, which they showed to him, in the middle of a very spacious court. The truth was, this tender mother had accustomed herself to pass the greatest part of the day and night in that room, which she had built as a representation of the tomb of Bedreddin Hassan, whom she now believed to be dead. She was then occupied in lamenting the loss of that dear son; and Schemseddin Mohammed found her a prey to the most violent affliction.

He made his compliment; and, after beseeching her to suspend her tears and groans, informed her that he had the honour to be her brother-in-law, and acquainted her with the motive of his journey from Cairo to Balsora. He then gave her an account of all that passed at Cairo on his daughter's wedding-night, and of the surprise occasioned by the discovery of the paper sewed up in Bedreddin's turban; and concluded by presenting to her Agib and the lady of beauty.

The widow of Noureddin Ali, who had continued sitting like a woman totally indifferent to all worldly affairs, no sooner understood by his discourse that her dear son, whom she so bitterly lamented, might still be alive, than she arose, and ardently embraced the beautiful lady, and her grandchild Agib, in whom perceiving the features of Bedreddin, her eyes were filled with tears of quite a different nature from those she had been so long accustomed to shed. She could not forbear kissing the youth, who, on his part, received her embraces with all the demonstrations of joy he was capable of expressing. "Madam," said Schemseddin Mohammed, "it is time to dry your tears, and cease your groans: you must prepare to accompany us to Egypt. The sultan of Balsora permits me to conduct you thither, and I do not doubt obtaining your consent. I hope we shall at last discover your son, my nephew; and if that happen, his history, yours, that of my daughter, and my own adventures, will merit being put in writing to be transmitted to posterity."

The widow of Noureddin Ali heard this proposal with pleasure, and immediately commenced the preparations for her departure. In the meantime Schemseddin Mohammed desired a second audience; and having taken leave of the sultan, who treated him with the highest honours, and gave him a considerable present for the sultan of Egypt, he set out from Balsora, and took the road to the city of Damascus.

When he arrived in the neighbourhood of that city, he ordered his tents to be pitched without the gate at which he designed to enter, signifying that he should tarry three days, to give his equipage rest, and to purchase what he might find the most curious, and worthy of being presented to the sultan of Egypt.

While he was employed in selecting the finest stuffs which the principal merchants had brought to his tents, Agib begged the black eunuch, his governor, to take him through the city, saying, he wished to see what he had not leisure to view as he passed before; and he should be very glad also to know what was become of the pastry-cook whom he had wounded with a stone. The eunuch, complying with his request, proceeded with him towards the city after having obtained permission of his mother, the lady of beauty.

They entered Damascus by the palace-gate, which was the nearest to the tents of the vizier Schemseddin Mohammed. They walked through the great squares, and the public places, where the richest goods were sold; and saw the ancient mosque of the Ommiades, at the hour of prayer, between noon and sunset. Then they passed in front of the shop of Bedreddin Hassan, whom they found still employed in making cream-tarts: "I salute you, sir," said Agib: "observe me. Do you remember to have ever seen me before?" Bedreddin, at these words, threw his eyes upon him, and recognising him—surprising effect of paternal love!—expeirenced the same internal emotion as at their first interview. He was embarrassed; and, instead of answering, continued a long time without the power of uttering a word. Having at length recalled his spirits, "My little lord," said he, "be so kind as to come once more, with your governor, into my house, and taste a cream-tart. I beg your pardon for the trouble I occasioned in following you out of town: I was not myself at that time; I was unconscious of what I was doing. You drew me after you, and with so soft violence, that I could not withstand it."

Agib, astonished at what Bedreddin said, replied, "There is an excess in the friendship you indicate towards me; and I will not enter your house unless you pledge yourself, by oath, not to follow me when I go hence. If you give me your promise, and prove a man of your word, I will visit you again to-morrow; as the vizier, my grandfather'

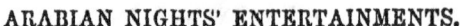

will be employed buying articles for a present to the sultan of Egypt." "My little lord," replied Bedreddin, "I will do whatever you desire." Agib and the eunuch then entered the shop.

Bedreddin placed before them a cream tart, which was not less delicate and excellent than what he had before presented to them. "Come," said Agib, addressing himself to Bedreddin, "sit by me, and eat with us." Bedreddin, being seated, made an offer to embrace Agib, as a testimony of the joy he conceived from sitting at his side; but Agib repulsed him, saying, "Be quiet; your friendship is troublesome. Content yourself with seeing and entertaining me." Bedreddin submitted; and began to sing a song, the words of which he composed extempore, in praise of Agib. He did not eat, but occupied himself in serving his guests. When they had finished eating, he brought them water to wash, and a very white napkin to wipe their hands. He then filled a large china cup with sherbet, and put snow into it, and offering it to the little Agib, "This," said he, "is sherbet of roses, and the most delicious you will meet with in all the town; I am sure you never tasted better." Agib having drank of it with pleasure, Bedreddin Hassan took the cup from him, and presented it to the eunuch, who drank the remainder.

In fine, Agib and his governor, well satisfied, returned thanks to the pastry-cook for their good entertainment, and retired briskly, it being somewhat late. When they arrived at the tents of Schemseddin Mohammed, they proceeded immediately to the ladies' pavilion. Agib's grandmother received him with transports of joy; but as her son Bedreddin was constantly in her mind, she could not restrain her tears, when caressing Agib: "Ah, my child!" said she, "my happiness would be perfect, if I had the pleasure of embracing your father, Bedreddin Hassan, as I now embrace you!" Then seating herself at table to supper, she made Agib sit by her, putting several questions to him relating to his walk, and, observing he ought not to want an appetite, gave him a piece of cream-tart, which she had made herself, and was excellent; for, I said before, she could make them better than the best pastry-cooks. She likewise presented some to the eunuch; but they had both eaten so heartily at Bedreddin's house, that they could not even taste it.

Agib had scarcely touched the piece of cream-tart that had been served to him, when he pretended he did not like it, and left it uncut; and Schaban (which was the name of the eunuch) did the same. The widow of Noureddin Ali noticed with regret the little appetite her grandson had for the tart: "What!" said she, "is it possible that my child should despise the work of my own hands? Know that no other person in the world can make such cream tarts, excepting your father Bedreddin Hassan, whom I myself taught to make them." "My good grandmother," replied Agib, "permit me to tell you, if you cannot make better, there is a pastry-cook in this town who surpasses you in this great art: we came from his shop, where we ate one, that was much better than yours."

At these words, the grandmother, frowning upon the eunuch, "How, Schaban!" said she, "was the care of my grandchild committed to you, to carry him to eat at pastry-shops like a beggar?" "Madam," replied the eunuch, "it is true we conversed a little while with a pastry-cook, but we did not eat with him." "Pardon me," interrupted Agib, "we entered his shop, and there ate a cream-tart." The lady, more incensed against the eunuch than before, rose quickly from the table, and going to the tent of Schemseddin Mohammed, informed him of the eunuch's crime; and in such terms as tended rather to inflame the vizier, than to dispose him to excuse the fault.

Schemseddin Mohammed, who was naturally passionate, was not slow on this occasion to display his anger. He went immediately to his sister-in-law's pavilion, and addressing the eunuch, "What!" said he, "you pitiful wretch! Have you the impudence to abuse the trust I repose in you?" Schaban, though clearly convicted by Agib's testimony, still denied the fact. But the child persisted in what he had affirmed. "Grandfather," said he, "I can assure you we both ate so heartily, that we have no occasion for supper; the pastry-cook even treated us with a great bowl of sherbet." "Well, wicked slave," cried Schemseddin, turning to the eunuch, "after all this, will you continue to deny that you entered the pastry-cook's house, and ate there?" Schaban had still the impudence to swear it was not true. "You are a liar!" said the vizier. "I must believe my grandchild in preference to you. Nevertheless," continued he, "if you can eat all this cream-tart which is on the table, I shall be persuaded that you tell the truth."

Schaban, though he had crammed himself to the throat before, submitted to that proof, and accordingly took a piece of the tart, but his stomach revolting, he was obliged to throw it from his mouth; yet he still persisted in the falsehood, pretending he had overeaten himself the day preceding, and that his appetite was not returned. The vizier, irritated with the eunuch's evasions, and convinced of his guilt, ordered him to be laid on the ground, and soundly bastinadoed. While undergoing this punishment, the poor wretch cried out frightfully, and confessed the truth. "I own," said he, "that we did eat a cream-tart at the pastry-cook's, and it was a hundred times better than that on the table."

The widow of Noureddin Ali thought it was in spite of her, and with a design to mortify her, that Schaban commended the pastry-cook's tart, and therefore said to him, "I cannot believe the cook's tarts are better than mine. I am, however, resolved to satisfy myself. You know where he lives; go immediately, and bring me one of his cream-tarts." The eunuch, having received of her the money necessary for the purchase, set out. Being arrived at Bedreddin's shop, "Good Mr. Pastrycook," said he, "take this money, and let me have a cream-tart, which one of our ladies wishes to taste." Bedreddin chose the best, and gave it to the eunuch. "Have this," said he, "I will engage it is excellent; and I can assure you that no person is capable of making such, unless it be my mother, who perhaps is still alive."

Schaban returned speedily to the tents with his cream tart. He presented it to Noureddin's widow, who took it eagerly, and broke a piece off; but she had no sooner put it into her mouth, than she cried out, and fainted. Schemseddin Mohammed, who was present, was extremely astonished at this incident—he threw water himself upon her face, and was very active in assisting her. As soon as she recovered, "My God!" exclaimed she, "it must be my son, my dear Bedreddin, who made this tart."

When the vizier Schemseddin Mohammed heard his sister-in-law declare that the maker of the tart brought by the eunuch must be Bedreddin Hassan, he was overjoyed; but reflecting that his joy was probably unfounded, as,

according to all appearances, the conjecture of Noureddin's widow was false, "Madam," said he, "why do you entertain that opinion? Do you imagine there is not a pastry-cook in the world who knows how to make cream-tarts as well as your son?" "I agree," replied she, "there may be many pastry-cooks who can make as good; but, as I make them after a peculiar manner, and not one person. excepting my son, is in possession of the secret, it must absolutely be him who made this. Let us rejoice, my brother," added she, with transport; "we have at length found what we so long sought and desired." "Madam," replied the vizier, "I entreat you to moderate your impatience; we shall quickly know the truth. All we have to do is, to bring the pastry-cook hither, and then you and my daughter will easily determine whether it is Bedreddin or not. But you must both be concealed, so as to see without being seen; for I would not have our reunion effected at Damascus. I purpose to delay the discovery till we return to Cairo, where I intend to give you a very agreeable diversion."

On concluding these words he left the ladies in their tent, and retired to his own. He then summoned fifty of his men, and said to them, "Take each of you a stick, and follow Schaban, who will conduct you to the house of a pastry-cook in this city. When you arrive there, break and destroy all you find in his shop. If he require to know why you commit that disorder, merely ask him whether he was not the person who made the cream-tart that was brought from his house; and if he say he was, seize his person, bind him, and bring him with you, but be careful not to do him the least harm. Go, and lose no time."

The vizier's orders were promptly executed. His people, armed with sticks, and conducted by the black eunuch, proceeded immediately to Bedreddin's house, where they broke in pieces the plates, kettles, copper pans, tables, and all the other moveables and utensils they met with, and inundated the shop with sherbet, cream, and comfits. Bedreddin, astonished at the proceeding, said in a pitiful tone, "Pray, good people, why do you treat me in this manner? What is the cause? What have I done?" "Was it not you," replied they, "who sold this eunuch the cream-tart?" "Yes," answered he, "I am the person; and who speaks against it? I defy any one to make a better." Instead of replying, they continued to destroy all they could find, and even the oven was not spared.

In the meantime, the neighbours, being alarmed at seeing fifty armed men commit such disorder, demanded the reason of such great violence; and Bedreddin said once more to the despoilers, "Pray tell me what crime I have committed, to merit this treatment?" "Was it not you," replied they, "who made the cream-tart you sold to the eunuch?" "Yes, it was me," cried he; "and I maintain it was good: I do not deserve the unjust usage you give me." Without listening to him, they seized his person, and snatching the cloth of his turban, tied his hands with it behind his back; then, dragging him by force out of his shop, they set off on their return.

The populace, who had assembled, touched with compassion for Bedreddin, took his part, and would have opposed the design of Schemseddin's men, but, at the moment, some officers from the governor of the city arrived, who dispersed the people, and favoured the carrying off of Bedreddin; for Schemseddin Mohammed had been at the governor's house, to acquaint him with the order he had given, and to demand support; and this governor, who commanded all Syria in the name of the sultan of Egypt, was anxious to oblige his master's vizier. So Bedreddin was forced away, notwithstanding his cries and his tears.

Bedreddin Hassan ineffectually inquired, on the road, of those who had him in custody, what fault had been found with his cream-tart: they gave him no answer. In short, they reached the tents, where they made him stay till Schemseddin Mohammed returned from the governor of Damascus's house.

The vizier being arrived, inquired for the pastry-cook, and Bedreddin Hassan was taken before him. "My lord," said Bedreddin, with tears in his eyes, "pray do me the favour to let me know wherein I have displeased you?" "Why, you wretch!" replied the vizier, "was it not you who made the cream-tart you sent me?" "I own myself the man," answered Bedreddin; "what crime have I committed in that?" "I will punish you as you deserve," said Schemseddin; "it will cost you your life, for sending me such a sorry tart." "Good God!" cried Bedreddin, "what do I hear? Is it a capital crime to make a bad cream-tart?" "Yes," replied the vizier; "and you ought not to expect other treatment from me."

During this conversation, the ladies, who were concealed, observed Bedreddin attentively, whom they knew readily, notwithstanding his long absence; and the joy they experienced was so great, that they fainted. When they recovered from their swoon, they would have run and fallen upon Bedreddin's neck; but the promise they had made to the vizier, of not discovering themselves, restrained the tender emotions of love and of nature.

As Schemseddin Mohammed had resolved to set out that night, he ordered the tents to be struck, and the carriages to be prepared for his departure. In regard to Bedreddin, he gave directions to have him put in a chest well secured, and placed on a camel. When all was ready, the vizier and his retinue began their march, and travelled the rest of that night, and all the next day, without stopping. In the evening they halted, and Bedreddin was then released from his cage, that he might have the necessary refreshment, but still carefully kept at a distance from his mother and his wife; and, during the whole journey, which lasted twenty days, he was treated in the same manner.

When they arrived at Cairo, they encamped in the neighbourhood of that town, by order of the vizier Schemseddin Mohammed, who sent for Bedreddin, and gave orders, in his presence, to a carpenter to provide some wood, and make a stake immediately. "My lord," said Bedreddin, "what is your intention with this stake?" "Why, to nail you to it," replied Schemseddin, "and then to have you carried through all quarters of the town, that the people may see in person a worthless pastry-cook, who makes cream-tarts without pepper." At these words, Bedreddin cried out in so whimsical a manner, that Schemseddin could hardly keep his countenance: "Good God!" said he, "must I suffer a death, as cruel as it is ignominious, for not putting pepper in a cream-tart? What! must I have all the property in my house broken and destroyed; must I be imprisoned in a chest, and at last nailed to a stake; and all for not putting pepper in a cream-tart? Good God! who ever heard of such a proceeding! Are these the actions of Mussulmen—of persons who make a profession of probity and justice, and who practise all kinds of good works?" At these words he shed tears; when, renewing his complaints, "No," continued he, "never was man used so unjustly, or so severely. Is it possible they should be capable of taking a man's life for not putting pepper in a cream-tart? Cursed be all the cream-tarts, as well as the hour in which I was born! Would to God I had died that minute!"

The disconsolate Bedreddin did not cease his lamentations; and when the stake was brought, and nails to fasten him to it, he uttered loud cries at sight of the terrific spectacle. "O Heaven!" said he, "can you suffer me to die an ignominious and painful death? And this, for what crime? Not for robbery, nor murder, nor renouncing my religion; but for not putting pepper in a cream-tart!"

Night being already somewhat advanced, the vizier Schemseddin Mohammed directed that Bedreddin should be again put in his cage, saying to him, "Remain there till to-morrow: that day shall not pass before I give orders for your death." They then carried the chest, and laid it upon the camel that had brought it from Damascus: at the same time all the other camels were reloaded; and the vizier, mounting his horse, ordered the camel that carried his nephew to march before him, and thus entered the city, followed by his equipage. After passing through several streets, where nobody appeared, the inhabitants being retired to rest, he arrived at his house, and then ordered the chest to be taken down, but not to be opened till he should direct.

While his attendants were unloading the other camels, he led Bedreddin's mother and his daughter aside; and addressing himself to the latter, "God be praised!" said he, "my child, for the meeting he has so happily effected with your cousin and your husband! You remember, no doubt, the state your chamber was in on your wedding-night: go and arrange everything as it was then: if your memory be unfaithful, I can assist you from a written account which I took at the time. I shall be careful to order the rest."

The lady of beauty went with joy to execute her father's directions; and he began also to dispose the things in the hall in the same manner as they were when Bedreddin Hassan was there with the sultan of Egypt's hump-backed groom. As he read his inventory, his domestics placed every article of furniture in its place. The throne was not forgotten, nor yet the lighted wax candles. When all was arranged in the hall, the vizier entered his daughter's chamber, and put on a chair, as before, Bedreddin's clothes, with the purse of sequins. This settled, he said to the lady of beauty, "Undress yourself, my child, and go to bed. As soon as Bedreddin enters your room, complain of his being so long from you; and tell him that, when you awoke, you were astonished at not finding him by you. Press him to return to bed; and to-morrow morning you will divert your mother-in-law and me, in relating to us what passes between you and him this night." At these words, he went from his daughter's apartment, and left her at liberty to undress, and go to bed.

Schemseddin Mohammed ordered all his domestics to quit the hall, excepting two or three, whom he had desired to remain. These he commanded to go and take Bedreddin out of the chest, to strip him to his shirt and drawers, and to conduct him in that state to the hall, there to leave him by himself, and shut the door.

Bedreddin Hassan, though overwhelmed with grief, was asleep during all this time; insomuch that the vizier's domestics had taken him out of the chest, and stripped him, before he awoke; and they conveyed him so suddenly into the hall that he had no time for reflection. When he found himself alone in the hall, he looked about, and the surrounding objects recalling to his memory the circumstances of his marriage, he perceived, with astonishment, that it was the same hall where he had seen the sultan's hump-backed groom. His surprise was augmented, when approaching softly to the door of a chamber, which he found open, he saw within his own clothes, in the same situation he remembered to have left them on his wedding-night. "Good God!" said he, rubbing his eyes, "am I asleep or awake?"

The lady of beauty, who, in the meantime, was diverting herself with his astonishment, suddenly opened the curtains of her bed, and bending her head forward, "My dear lord," said she, tenderly, "what are you doing at the door? Pray, come to bed again. You have been out a long time! I was quite surprised when I awoke, at not finding you by me." When he perceived that the lady who spoke to him was the charming person with whom he remembered to have slept, Bedreddin Hassan's countenance changed. He entered the chamber, but, instead of going to bed, his mind was occupied with the thoughts of what had passed during the ten years' interval; and, being unable to persuade himself that all could have happened in the space of one night, he approached the chair where his clothes lay, with the purse of sequins, and, after examining them very attentively, "By Heaven!" cried he, "these things I cannot comprehend!" The lady, who was amused by his embarrassment, said once more, "My lord, come to bed again. What detains you?" At these words, he advanced towards the bed. "Pray, madam," said he, "tell me, is it long since I left you?" "The question," answered she, "surprises me. Did not you rise from me just now? Certainly your mind is much engaged." "Madam," replied Bedreddin, "I do assure you it is not very tranquil. I remember, indeed, having been with you; but I remember also, that I have since lived ten years at Damascus. Now if I were actually with you this night, I cannot have been from you so long: these two circumstances are inconsistent. Pray, tell me what I ought to think—whether my marriage with you is an illusion, or my absence from you merely a dream?" "Yes, my lord," returned the lady of beauty, "doubtless, you were dreaming, when you thought yourself at Damascus." "This is the most whimsical occurrence," cried Bedreddin, laughing heartily. "I assure you, madam, this dream will be very diverting to you. Do but imagine, if you please, that I found myself at the gate of Damascus in my shirt and drawers, as I am at this moment; that I entered the town with the shouts of a mob that followed and insulted me; that I sought shelter in the house of a pastry-cook, who adopted me, taught me his trade, and left me all his property when he died; that, after his death, I continued his business. In fine, madam, I had an infinity of other adventures, too tedious to recount: and I shall only say, that it was fortunate I awoke, for they were just going to nail me to a stake." "How," cried the lady, feigning astonishment, "for what would they have used you so cruelly? Surely you must have committed some enormous crime!" "Not the least," replied Bedreddin; "it was for the most trifling and ridiculous thing you can imagine. The only crime I was charged with, was selling a cream-tart that had no pepper in it." "Ah!" said the lady of beauty, laughing heartily, "then I must declare they did you great injustice." "Oh, madam," continued he, "that was not all; for this cursed cream-tart, with which I was reproached, was every article in my shop broken and destroyed; myself bound with cords, and shut up in a chest, where I lay so close, that I can scarcely persuade myself I am not there still. In fine, a carpenter was summoned, and he was ordered to prepare a stake to hang me. But, thanks to God! all was no more than a perturbed sleep."

Bedreddin did not pass the night tranquilly, he awoke from time to time, and questioned himself, whether he dreamed or was awake. He distrusted his felicity; and wishing to be satisfied, opened the curtains, and looked round the room. "I certainly am not mistaken," said he; "this is the same chamber which I entered, instead of the hump-backed groom; and I am now in bed with the fair lady who was designed for him." Daylight, which began to appear, had not dissipated his inquietude, when the vizier Schemseddin Mohammed, his uncle, knocked at the door, and immediately entered to bid him good morning.

Bedreddin Hassan was extremely surprised at seeing, suddenly, a man whom he knew so well, but who had no longer the air of the terrible judge that pronounced his sentence of death. "Ah!" cried Bedreddin, "it was you who treated me so unjustly, and condemned me to a death which I still think of with horror, and all for making a cream-tart without pepper!" The vizier laughed; and, to ease him of his perplexity, told him how, by the ministry of a geni (for hump-back's statement had made him suspect the adventure), he had been at his house, and had married his daughter, instead of the sultan's groom: he then informed him that he had discovered him to be his nephew by the book in the handwriting of Noureddin Ali; and, in consequence of that discovery, had gone from Cairo to Balsora in search of him. "My dear nephew," added he, embracing him tenderly, "I ask your pardon for all I have made you suffer; I wished you to be conveyed to my house before you knew your happiness, which ought to be the more charming, as it has cost you so much trouble. Console yourself for all your afflictions, with the joy of being reunited to those who ought to be dearest to you. While you are dressing, I will prepare your mother, who is in the greatest impatience to embrace you; and will also bring your son, whom you saw at Damascus, and for whom you showed so much affection, without knowing him."

Words are of insufficient energy to express the joy of Bedreddin, when he saw his mother and his son. They embraced each other, and exhibited all the transports that love and the liveliest tenderness could inspire. The mother talked to Bedreddin in the most touching manner; she spoke of the grief his long absence had occasioned her, and the tears she had shed: little Agib, instead of flying, as at Damascus, his father's embraces, received them with pleasure; and Bedreddin Hassan, divided between two objects so worthy of his love, thought he could not show sufficient proofs of his affection.

While this passed at Schemseddin Mohammed's, the vizier was gone to the palace, to give the sultan an account of the happy termination of his journey; and the sultan was so charmed with the recital of the marvellous story, that he ordered it to be written, and carefully preserved among the archives of the kingdom. As soon as Schemseddin returned to his house, having prepared a sumptuous feast, he sat down to table with his family, and all the household passed the day in the greatest conviviality.

* * * * * * *

The vizier Giafar having thus ended the story of Bedreddin Hassan, told the caliph Haroun Alraschid, that it was what he had to relate to his majesty. The caliph thought the story so surprising, that without further hesitation he pardoned his slave Rihan; and to console the young man for the grief of having unhappily deprived himself of a woman whom he tenderly loved, he married him to one of his slaves, bestowed liberal gifts upon him, and entertained him till he died.

THE STORY OF LITTLE HUMP-BACK.

HERE was in former times, at Casgar, at the extremity Grand Tartary, a tailor, who had a very pretty wife, hom he tenderly loved, and was equally beloved by er. One day, as he sat at work, a little hump-back came and seated himself at the shop-door, and began to sing, at the same time playing upon a tabor. The tailor found pleasure in hearing him, and determined to take him to his house to amuse his wife. "With his humorous songs," said he, "he will divert us both very agreeably." He accordingly made the proposition; and hump-back accepted it, he shut up his shop, and conducted him home.

As soon as they arrived, the tailor's wife, who had already covered the table, it being supper-time, placed before them a good dish of fish, which she had prepared. They all sat down; but, in eating, hump-back unfortunately swallowed a large bone, which caused his death in a few moments, the tailor and his wife being unable to afford him any relief. They were both extremely frightened at the accident, more particularly as it had happened in their house; and there was reason to fear, if it should become known to the magistrates, they would be punished as assassins. However, the husband thought it expedient to get rid of the corse. He remembered there was a Jew doctor living in the neighbourhood; his wife and he, therefore, took the corse, the one by the feet, and the other by the head, and carried it to the physician's house. They knocked at the door, from which ascended a steep flight of stairs to his chamber; a female servant immediately came down without any light, and opening the door, demanded what they wanted. "Pray go up again," said the tailor, "and tell your master we have brought him a man who is very sick, and in want of advice." "Here," continued he, putting a piece of money into her hand, "give him this in advance, to convince him we have no intention to defraud him of his labour." While the servant was gone to acquaint her master with the welcome news, the tailor and his wife nimbly conveyed the corse of hump-back to the head of the stairs, and leaving it there, precipitately retreated.

In the interim, the servant having told the doctor that a man and a woman waited for him at the door, desiring he would go down and look at a sick man they had brought with them; at the same time, putting the money she had received into his hand; the doctor was transported with joy: being paid beforehand, he thought his visitor would be a good customer, and should not be neglected. "Take the light quickly," cried he to the servant, "and follow me!" Saying this, he advanced to the stairs with so much precipitation, that he left the light far behind him: and encountering the corse of little hump-back, gave it so violent a kick, that he tumbled it to the bottom of the staircase; with difficulty saving himself from rolling after it. "Bring me a light immediately!" cried he to his servant. At length she arrived, and he descended the stairs with her; but, finding that what he had kicked down was a dead man, he was so terrified at the spectacle, that he invoked Moses, Aaron, Joshua, Esdras, and all the other prophets of his law. "Unhappy man that I am!" said he, "what could induce me to descend the stairs without a light! I have killed the sick person who was brought to me to be cured! I have caused his death; and, if the good ass of Esdras do not assist me, I am ruined!—Alas! the officers of justice will be here, and drag me from my house as a murderer!"

But, notwithstanding his trouble, he had the precaution to shut the door; afraid that any one passing in the street might observe the misfortune of which he believed himself to be the cause. He then took the corse, and carried it into the chamber of his wife, who nearly fainted when she saw him enter with his melancholy burthen: "Alas!" cried she, "we are utterly ruined, unless we devise some means of putting the corse out of our house this night! Beyond all question, if we keep it here till morning, our lives will be forfeited. What a dilemma! How did you ct to kill this man?" "That is not the question," replied the Jew; "our business now, is to find a remedy for this unlucky accident." The doctor and his wife consulted together on the possibility of

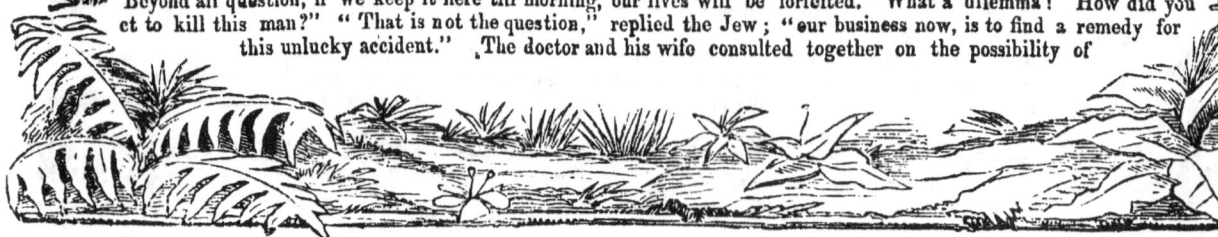

disposing of the dead body that night. The doctor considered to no purpose; he could not think of any stratagem that was likely to be successful; but his wife, more fertile in invention, said, "A thought has entered my head; let us carry the corse on the terrace of our house, and tumble it down the chimney into the house of the Mussulman, our neighbour."

This Mussulman was one of the sultan's purveyors: he was charged with the care of furnishing oil, butter, tallow, &c., and had a magazine in the house, where the rats and mice made a prodigious havoc.

The Jew doctor approving of the proposed expedient, his wife and he took little hump-back up to the roof of the house; and, after passing ropes under his arm-pits, they lowered him down the chimney, into the purveyor's chamber, so softly and dexterously, that he remained on his feet against the wall, as if he had been alive. When they found

w was at the bottom, they pulled up the ropes, and left him that attitude. They had scarcely reached their chamber, hen the purveyor entered his—being just returned from a wedding feast, to which he had been invited that night— with a lantern in his hand. He was greatly surprised when, by the aid of his light, he descried a man standing upright in the chimney; but being naturally courageous, and supposing it was a robber, he seized a large cane, and going directly to hump-back, "Ah, ah!" said he, "I thought the rats and mice ate my butter and tallow, while it is you comes down the chimney to rob me! I question if you will ever return on this errand" Saying this, he struck hump-back, giving him several heavy blows with his cane. The corse fell down with its nose against the ground, and the purveyor redoubled his blows: but at length, observing the body to be without motion, he paused a moment to consider it; and, perceiving it was a corse, fear succeeded to anger. "Wretched man that I am!" said he, "what have I done? I have killed a man! Alas, I have carried my revenge too far! Good God, unless thou pity me, my life is lost! Cursed, a thousand times, be the fat and the oil that have been the cause of my committing so criminal an action!" He stood pale and terrified: he thought he already saw the officers come to drag him to punishment, and he could not determine on what course he ought to pursue.

The sultan of Casgar's purveyor had not observed the little man's hump while he was beating him; but as soon as he perceived it, he uttered imprecations against him. "Ah, you cursed hump-back!" cried he; "you crooked villain! would to God I had not found you here, if you had robbed me of all my fat; I should not then have been in this perplexity, for the love of you and your filthy hump. Oh, stars that twinkle in the heavens, give light to none but me in this dangerous juncture!" As he uttered these words, he took little hump-back upon his shoulders, and carried him out of doors to the end of the street, where he placed him upright, resting against a shop, and returned home without once looking behind him.

A short time before the appearance of day, a Christian merchant, who was very rich, and furnished the sultan's palace with most articles it wanted, having passed the night in debauch, left his house to go to the bath. Though he was intoxicated, he was sensible that the night was far advanced, and the people would soon be called to morning prayers, which began at daybreak; he therefore quickened his pace, to reach the bath, for fear some Turk, going to the mosque, should meet him, and take him to prison as a drunkard. However, when he arrived at the end of the street, he stopped for some occasion, and leaned against the shop where the sultan's purveyor had put the corse of hump-back, which being shaken, tumbled on the merchant's back. The merchant, thinking it was a robber attacking him, struck him on the head with his fist, and knocked him down; and, after repeating his blows, cried out,—"Thieves!"

The watch being alarmed, immediately came up, and finding a Christian beating a Turk, (for hump-back was of our religion), "What reason have you," said he, "thus to abuse a Mussulman?" "He would have robbed me," replied the merchant; "and threw himself upon my back, for the purpose of seizing me by the throat." "If he did," said the watch, "you are sufficiently revenged: come, disengage yourself." At the same time, he presented his hand to little hump-back to help him to rise; but, observing he was dead, "Ah!" continued he, "is it thus that a Christian dares to assassinate a Mussulman?" Saying this, he arrested the Christian, and conveyed him to the house of the governor of police, where he was confined till the judge arose, and was ready to examine him. In the meantime, the Christian merchant became sober, and the more he reflected upon his adventure, the less could he conceive how simple blows with the fist could kill a man.

The police-officer having heard the report of the watch, and viewed the corse, which they had brought to his house, interrogated the Christian merchant, who could not deny the crime, though he was innocent. But the officer, as little hump-back belonged to the sultan—for he was one of his buffoons—would not put the Christian to death without asking the sultan's pleasure. For this purpose, he went to the palace, to acquaint the sultan with what had happened, who replied, "I can show no mercy to a Christian that kills a Mussulman: go, do your office." The judge accordingly ordered a gibbet to be erected, and sent criers through the city, to proclaim that they were going to hang a Christian, for killing a Mussulman.

In fine, the merchant was taken out of prison, and conveyed to the foot of the gallows; and the executioner having put the rope about his neck, was in the act of turning him off, when the sultan's purveyor, forcing through the crowd, advanced, calling to the hangman. "Stop! stop! do not be precipitate: it was not him who committed the murder; I am the guilty person." The officer who attended the execution interrogated the purveyor, who told him every circumstance relative to his killing little hump-back, and conveying his corse to the place where it was found by the Christian merchant. "You were going," added he, "to put to death an innocent person, since he could not be guilty of the death of a man who was dead before he saw him. I am sufficiently unhappy in having killed a Turk, without loading my conscience with the death of an innocent Christian."

The sultan of Casgar's purveyor having publicly charged himself with the death of little hump-back, the officer could not avoid rendering justice to the merchant: "Liberate the Christian," said he, "and hang this man in his stead, since it is evident, by his own confession, he is guilty." The hangman accordingly released the merchant, and immediately put the rope round the purveyor's neck; but, as he was preparing to launch him into eternity, his proceedings were arrested by the Jew doctor, who earnestly entreated him to suspend the execution, and make room for him to place himself at the foot of the gallows.

When before the police-judge, "My lord," said he, "this Mussulman, whom you were going to hang, is innocent; I alone am guilty. Last night, a man and a woman, strangers, brought a sick man to my door, and, knocking, my female servant went, without a light, and opened it, when they presented to her a piece of money, with a commission to return, and request me, in their name, to step down and examine the sick person. While she was delivering her message to me, they conveyed the sick person to the stair-head, and disappeared. I proceeded without waiting till my servant had lighted a candle; and, in the dark, happened to stumble over the patient, and threw him down stairs. In fine, I saw he was dead, and that it was the crooked Mussulman whose death you are prepared to avenge. So my wife and I took the corse, and conveying it up to the roof of our house, carried it thence to that of the purveyor, our neighbour, whom you were about unjustly to deprive of life, and let it down the chimney into his chamber. The purveyor, finding it in his house, supposed it to be a thief, and beating the little man concluded he had killed him; but it was not so, as you will be convinced by my deposition. I am, then, the sole author of the murder; and, though it was committed unintentionally, I have resolved to expiate my crime, by not having to reproach myself with the death of two Mussulmen, in suffering you to execute the sultan's purveyor, whose innocence I have established. Therefore, pray dismiss him, and put me in his place, since I alone am the cause of the death of little hump-back."

The police-justice, being persuaded that the Jew doctor was the murderer, ordered the executioner to seize him, and release the purveyor. Already was the cord round the physician's neck, and the hangman was preparing to do his duty, when the tailor appeared, calling to the executioner to stop, who made the populace stand aside, that he might approach the officer of police; before whom being arrived, "My lord," said he, "you have narrowly escaped taking away the lives of three innocent persons; but, if you will have the patience to hear me, you will know the real murderer of hump-back. If his death is to be expiated by another, my life must be the sacrifice. Yesterday, towards the evening, as I was at work in my shop, in a merry humour, hump-back came to my door half drunk, and sat down before it. He sang some time, and I invited him to pass the evening at my house: he accepted the invitation, and I conducted him there. We sat down to supper, and I served him a piece of fish; but, in eating, a bone stuck in his throat; and, though my wife and I did our utmost to relieve him, he died in a few minutes. His death afflicted us extremely, and in fear of being charged with it, we carried the corse to a Jew doctor's house and knocked. A female servant opening the door, I desired her to return immediately, and beg her master, from us, to come down and give his advice to a sick person whom we had brought; at the same time, that he might not refuse, I charged her to give him a piece of money, which I had put into her hand. While she was going to her master, I carried hump-back to the top of the staircase, and laid him on the uppermost step; when my wife and I hastened home. The doctor, in descending, threw the corse down stairs, which made him believe that he was the cause of his death. This being the case," continued he, "release the doctor, and let me die.'

The police-justice and all the speculators were greatly surprised at the strange circumstances that had followed the death of little hump-back. "Loosen the Jew doctor," said the judge to the executioner, "and hang the tailor, since he confesses the crime. This history is really very extraordinary, and deserves to be recorded in letters of gold." The hangman having dismissed the doctor, placed the cord round the neck of the tailor.

While the executioner was preparing to hang the tailor, the sultan of Casgar, wanting the company of his crooked jester, demanded what was become of him; and was answered by one of his officers thus—"Little hump-back, sir, after whom you inquire, being intoxicated yesterday, slipped out of the palace, contrary to his custom, to go sauntering in the city, and this morning was found dead. A man was brought before the police-justice charged with the murder; and the judge ordered a gibbet to be erected immediately. As they were preparing to hang the accused, a man advanced, and after him another, each of whom took the charge upon himself, and cleared the other. This business has been a long time on hand; and the judge is now actually examining a fourth man, who accuses himself with being the real assassin."

At this intelligence, the sultan of Casgar sent a messenger to the place of execution: "Go," said he, "make all the haste you can, and desire the police judge to bring the arraigned persons before me immediately; and likewise the corse of poor hump-back, that I may see him once more." Accordingly the messenger set off; and, arriving at the time the executioner was fastening the cord, to hang the tailor, he cried aloud to him to suspend the execution. The hangman, knowing the sultan's officer, dared not proceed, and untied the tailor. Then the messenger, having joined the police-justice, declared the sultan's pleasure. The judge obeyed; and took the road to the palace, with the tailor, the Jew doctor, the purveyor, and the Christian merchant, while four of his men carried the corse of hump-back.

When they were before the sultan, the police-judge threw himself at the prince's feet; and, on rising again, gave him a faithful relation of all he knew concerning the fate of little hump-back. The sultan thought the story so singular, that he ordered his private historian to write it, with all its circumstances. Then addressing himself to the persons present: "Did you ever hear," said he, "of an occurrence more surprising than this which has happened through my little crooked buffoon?" The Christian merchant after prostrating himself, by touching the earth with his forehead, replied thus: "Most puissant monarch, I know a story yet more astonishing than that which you have just heard: with your majesty's permission, I will relate it. The circumstances are such, that no person can hear them without being moved." The sultan having granted leave, the merchant proceeded in these terms:—

THE STORY TOLD BY THE CHRISTIAN MERCHANT.

IR.—Before I commence the recital of the story your majesty allows me to tell, I beg leave to remark, that I had not the honour of being born in a place pertaining to your empire. I am a stranger, a native of Cairo, in Egypt; a Copt by country; and a professor of the Christian religion. My father was a broker, and had amassed considerable wealth, which he left me at his death. I followed his example, and embraced the same calling. One day, at Cairo, as I was standing in the public apartment for corn-merchants, a handsome young man, well clad, and mounted on an ass, advanced toward me. He saluted me; and opening a handkerchief, in which he had a sample of sesame, asked me what a bushel of such corn would produce.

I examined the sesame that the young merchant showed me, and told him it was worth a hundred drachms of silver per bushel. "Pray," said he, "find some merchants to purchase it at that price, and go to the Victory-gate, where you will see a hut standing entirely alone; here I will attend you." Saying these words, he left me; and I exhibited the sample to several merchants of the town, who offered to take all I had to sell at a hundred and ten drachms of silver the bushel, by which I should gain ten drachms a bushel for my brokerage. Flattered by this profit, I went to the Victory-gate, where the young merchant was waiting for me: he conducted me into his granary, which was full of sesame. There were fifty bushels of it; which, having measured, I loaded upon asses and sold for five thousand drachms of silver. "Of this sum," said the young man, "five hundred drachms are your right, at the rate of ten drachms the bushel: I desire you will take them. As for the rest, which belongs to me, having no occasion for it at present, I wish you to receive it from the merchants, and preserve it till I demand it." I answered, "that it should be ready for him whenever he pleased to call or send for it;" and, kissing his hand, took leave of him and retired, well satisfied with his generosity.

A month had elapsed before I again saw him: at the end of that time he arrived. "Where are," said he, "the four thousand five hundred drachms of silver which you owe me?" "They are ready," replied I; "and I will count them to you immediately." As he was then mounted on his ass, I begged him to alight, and do me the honour to eat a mouthful with me before he received the money. "No;" said he, "I cannot dismount at present; I have urgent business that calls me near here; but I shall come back, and at passing will take the money, which I request you to have in readiness." This said, he disappeared, and I, in vain, expected his return for near a month, before I

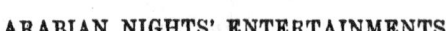

again saw him. I thought the young merchant reposed great confidence in me, a stranger, by leaving so large a sum in my hands; another would have been afraid I should have embezzled it. He again presented himself at the end of the third month; and was still mounted on his ass, but more magnificently dressed than on his former visits.

As soon as I saw the young merchant, I entreated him to alight; and asked him if he would not then receive his money. "It is not material," said he, with a gay and contented air: "I know it is in good hands. I will come and take it when I have spent all my other property. Adieu!" continued he; "expect me towards the end of the week." He immediately clapped spurs to his ass, and was out of sight in an instant. "Well," thought I to myself, "he says he shall see me at the end of the week, but it is more likely he will not appear for a long time; I will, in the interim, make use of his money, and shall turn it to good account."

I was not deceived in my conjecture; for a full year had passed, during which time I heard no tidings of the young man. He then appeared, as richly habited as before, but apparently dejected. I solicited him to do me the honour to walk into my house. "This time," replied he, "I will comply; but under the condition, that you put yourself to no extraordinary charge upon my account." "That shall be as you please," I answered; "pray, then, dismount." He accordingly alighted, and entered my house. I gave orders for the repast I wished him to take; and, while it was preparing, we entered into conversation. When the victuals were ready, we sat down to table. At the first mouthful, I observed he fed himself with the left hand, and was astonished that he did not use the right: I knew not what to think. "I have always considered this young man very polite," said I to myself; "is it possible he can do this in contempt of me? What can be the reason he does not use his right hand?"

When we had finished our repast, and the things were removed, we sat together on a sofa, and I presented to him a lozenge, which was excellent to sweeten the breath; and he took it likewise with his left hand. "My lord," said I then to him, "pray pardon the liberty I take in asking why you never make use of your right hand. You have, perhaps, received some hurt in that hand." Instead of answering, he heaved a deep sigh, and, exposing his right arm, which he had hitherto concealed under his garment, showed me, to my great astonishment, that his hand had been amputated. "Doubtless you were surprised," said he, "at seeing me constantly use the left hand: but you will now judge whether I had the power to do otherwise." "May I presume to ask," returned I, "by what misfortune you have lost your right hand?" At this demand, he shed tears; and, after restraining his grief, related his history thus:

THE STORY OF THE YOUNG MERCHANT OF BAGDAD.

YOU must know (said he) that I am a native of Bagdad, the son of a rich father, the most distinguished man in that city, by his property and by his rank. I had scarcely entered public life, when, frequenting the company of travellers, who represented the wonders of Egypt, and especially of Grand Cairo, I was interested by their discourse, and ardently wished to take a journey thither; but my father was still living, and would not grant me permission. At length he died; and, his death leaving me master of my actions, I resolved to go to Cairo. I employed a considerable sum of money in purchasing several sorts of fine stuffs of Bagdad and Moussol, and set off on my route.

Arriving at Cairo, I went to the inn called the khan of Mesrour, and there hired lodgings, with a warehouse for my bales, which I had conveyed upon camels. This settled, I retired to my chamber, to rest myself after the fatigue of my journey; and ordered my servants, to whom I gave money, to buy some provisions, and dress them. After my repast, I visited the castle, some mosques, the public buildings, and other places worthy of notice.

Next day I dressed myself neatly, and having selected a few of the finest and richest of my bales, I loaded some of my slaves, and sent them to the Circassian bezestein, whither I followed. I was no sooner there, than I was surrounded by a crowd of brokers and criers, who had been informed of my arrival. I gave patterns of my stuffs to several of the latter, who went and cried them, exhibiting them all over the bezestein; but none of the merchants offered nearly so much for them as they had cost me, with the carriage. This vexed me, and I expressed my dissatisfaction to the criers; "If you will take our advice," said they, "we will inform you of a means by which you may dispose of your stuffs without loss." I asked them, what proceeding they would have me adopt. "Divide your goods," replied they, "among several merchants, and they will sell them by retail; and twice a week, namely, Mondays and Thursdays, you may receive the money they have taken. By this mode, you will gain instead of losing, and the merchant will likewise have a profit: in the interim, you will be at liberty to divert yourself, and to walk in the town, or on the banks of the Nile.

I followed their advice, and taking them to my warehouse, I had all my goods conveyed to the bezestein, where I divided them among the merchants, whom they represented to me as the most reputable, and who gave me a proper receipt, signed by witnesses, under the condition that I should not make any demand upon them during the first month.

Having thus regulated my affairs, my mind was occupied with other considerations than ordinary pleasures. I contracted a friendship with many persons of nearly the same age with myself, who were careful my time should be well employed. The first month being elapsed, I began to visit my merchants twice a week, accompanied by a public officer to inspect their books of sale, and a banker to examine the money, and to regulate the value of the several species; so every pay-day I had a good sum of money to carry home to my lodging. I went, nevertheless, on the intervening days, to pass the morning, sometimes at one merchant's house, sometimes at another's: in fine, I diverted myself in visiting among them, and seeing the management of business in the bezestein.

One Monday, as I sat in the shop of a merchant, whose name was Bedreddin, a lady of quality, as might easily be perceived by her air, her habit, and by her being attended by a female slave neatly dressed, entered the shop, and sat down by me. Her exterior, joined to a natural grace which appeared in every action, inspired me with an ardent desire to be better acquainted. I was at a loss to guess whether she observed that I took pleasure in looking at her, and if my attention was displeasing; but she removed the crape which hung down over the muslin that covered her face, thereby giving me an opportunity of seeing her large black eyes, with which I was perfectly charmed. In fine, she completed her conquest by the agreeable sound of her voice, and her genteel and graceful manner in saluting the merchant, asking him if he had enjoyed his health since she last saw him.

After entertaining him some time on indifferent topics, she told him that she wanted a kind of stuff with a gold ground; that she came to his shop, as affording the best choice in the bezestein; and if he had any such as she described, he would oblige her by showing them. Bedreddin accordingly produced several pieces, one of which she selected, and demanded the price; he replied, eleven hundred drachms of silver. "I agree," said she, "to give you that sum; but I have not money sufficient about me; however, I hope you will give me credit till to-morrow, and permit me to take the stuff. I shall not forget," added she, "to send you to-morrow the eleven hunderd drachms you require for it." "Madam," replied Bedreddin, "I would willingly give you credit, and allow you to carry the stuff away, if it were mine; but it belongs to the young man you see here, and this is the day on which we settle our accounts." "Eh!" said the lady in astonishment, "whence arises this treatment? Am I not a regular customer at your shop? Often as I have bought stuffs of you, and carried them home without paying immediately, did I ever fail to send you the money next morning?" "Madam," answered the merchant, "what you say is true, but this very day I have occasion for the money." "Well, there is your stuff!" said she, throwing it at the merchant; "and may Heaven confound you, and all your fraternity! You are all alike; you respect nobody."

When I saw the lady walking away, I felt in my breast a strong interest for her; I therefore called her back. "Madam," said I, "do me the favour to return, perhaps I may discover a means of satisfying both." In fine, she returned, saying, it was affection for me that induced her to comply. "Mr. Bedreddin," said I to the merchant. "what do you demand for this stuff that belongs to me?" "I must have," replied he, "eleven hundred drachms of silver; I cannot take less." "Give it, then, to the lady," continued I; "let her take it home with her. I allow you a hundred drachms profit, and will draw up a note empowering you to deduct that sum from the produce of the other goods you have of mine." Accordingly I wrote, signed, and delivered, the note to Bedreddin, and then presented the stuff to the lady. "Madam," said I, "the stuff is at your service—as for the money, you may send it to-morrow, or another day; or, if you will, accept the stuff as a present from me." "That, sir," replied she, "was far from my thoughts; but you treat me with so much civility, and in so obliging a manner, that I should be unworthy of showing my face again in the world, if I did not express my gratitude to you. May God reward you, by augmenting your fortune; may you live many years after I am dead; may the gate of heaven be opened to you when you leave this world; and may all the city proclaim your generosity."

These words inspired me with some assurance: "Madam," said I, "I desire no other recompense for the service I have rendered you, than the pleasure of seeing your face; that will repay me with interest." She immediately turned towards me, and removing the muslin that covered her face, discovered to my eyes an incomparable beauty. I was so amazed, that I could not speak to her, to express my thoughts. I gazed at her with undiminished admiration. She quickly covered her face, afraid of being noticed; and having lowered the crape, she took the piece of stuff, and withdrew, leaving me in a state of mind quite different from that in which I entered the shop.

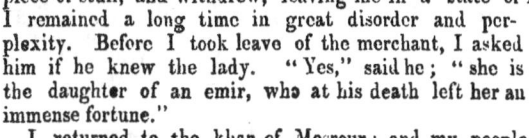

I remained a long time in great disorder and perplexity. Before I took leave of the merchant, I asked him if he knew the lady. "Yes," said he; "she is the daughter of an emir, who at his death left her an immense fortune."

I returned to the khan of Mesrour; and my people brought in supper, but it was impossible to eat: I could

not even shut my eyes during the night, which appeared the longest of my life. I arose as soon as it was day, in hopes of seeing once more the object that troubled my repose; and, to engage her attention, I dressed myself yet more neatly than I had the day preceding.

I had not been long in Bedreddin's shop, when I saw the lady approaching, more magnificently appareled than before, and attended by her slave. She did not regard the merchant, on entering; but addressing herself to me, "Sir," said she, "you see I am punctual to the promise I made you yesterday. I am come on purpose to pay the sum for which you were so kind as to pass your word for me, though a stranger to you—an act of generosity I shall never forget." "Madam," replied I, "such haste was unnecessary. I was perfectly satisfied respecting the money, and am sorry you have given yourself so much trouble about it." "I had been very unjust,' returned she, "if I had abused your civility." Saying this, she put the money in my hand, and sat down by me.

Profiting by the opportunity, I spoke of the love I had for her; but she arose, and left me very abruptly, as if angry with the declaration I had made. I followed her with my eyes till she was no longer visible, when I took leave of the merchant, and walked out of the bezestein, without knowing where I went. I was musing upon this adventure, when I felt somebody pulling me behind; and, turning about to see who it was, had the pleasure to recognise the slave of the lady who then occupied my thoughts. "My mistress," said the slave—"I mean the young lady with whom you talked in the merchant's shop—wants to speak a word with you; if you please to give yourself the trouble to accompany me, I will conduct you." Accordingly I followed, and found her mistress waiting for me at the house of a banker.

She desired me to sit by her, and thus addressed me:—"Dear sir, be not surprised that I left you rather abruptly: I judged it improper, before the merchant, to give a favourable answer to the disclosure you made of your regard for me. But, to confess the truth, so far from being offended at your declaration, I was pleased at hearing it; and I consider myself infinitely happy in having a man of your merit for my lover. I know not what impression the first sight of me made on you; but I assure you we no sooner met, than I entertained an affection for you. Since yesterday, my thoughts have been entirely engaged by what you said to me; and the haste with which I came to find you this morning may convince you of the pleasure I experienced in the meeting." "Madam," replied I, transported with love and joy, "Nothing could be more agreeable to me than what I now hear. It is impossible to love with a more fervent passion than that I have felt for you, since the happy moment when you appeared to my eyes; my senses were dazzled with so many charms, that my heart yielded without resistance." "Let us not trifle away the time in needless discourse," said she, interrupting me: I do not doubt your sincerity, and you shall quickly be convinced of mine. Will you do me the honour to come to my home? or, if you wish it, I will go to yours." "Madam," answered I, "I am a stranger, lodged in a khan, which is not a fit place for the reception of a lady of your quality and merit. It will be more proper, madam, for me to visit you at your home, if you will have the goodness to tell me where you reside." The lady consented: "I live," said she, "in Devotion-street: come the day after to-morrow, Friday, after noon-prayers; inquire for the house of Abon Schamma, surnamed Bercout, late chief of the emirs; there you will find me." This said, we departed, and I passed the next day in the greatest impatience.

On the Friday, I arose early, and having dressed in my best clothes, put fifty pieces of gold in my pocket: thus equipped, I mounted an ass that I had hired the day preceding, and set out, accompanied by the man to whom it belonged. When we arrived in Devotion-street, I directed the owner of the ass to inquire for the house I wanted; and, having found it, he conducted me thither. I paid him liberally, and dismissed him, desiring him to observe the house where he left me, and not to fail returning with the ass the next morning, to convey me back to the inn.

I knocked at the door, and immediately two little female slaves, white as snow, and neatly dressed, came and opened it. "Be pleased to walk in," said they; "our mistress expects you impatiently; for two days she has spoken only of you." I entered the court, and saw a great pavilion raised upon even steps, and surrounded with iron rails that parted it from a garden of admirable beauty. Besides the trees intended to embellish the prospect, and form an agreeable shade, there was an infinite variety loaded with all kinds of fruit; and I was charmed with the warbling of a vast number of birds, that joined their notes to the murmurings of a prodigiously high fountain which appeared in the middle of a grass-plot enamelled with flowers. This fountain was a very agreeable sight; four large gilded dragons adorned the angles of the basin, which was of a square form; and these dragons threw up water in abundance, clearer than rock-crystal. This delicious place gave me a high idea of a conquest I had made. The two little slaves conducted me into a parlour magnificently furnished; and, while one of them went to acquaint her mistress with my arrival, the other remained behind, and directed my attention to the ornaments of the room.

I had not waited long before the lady I loved appeared, adorned with pearls and diamonds; but the brilliancy of her eyes far outshone that of her jewels. Her shape, which was not now hidden by her walking habit, was extremely fine and charming. I will not attempt to describe the joy with which we received each other; words would very faintly express our mutual gratification: I shall only tell you, that after the first compliments, we both sat down upon a sofa, where we conversed with all the satisfaction imaginable. We had then the most delicious and exquisite meats served up to us; and, after the repast, continued our discourse till night. Then we had excellent wine brought in, and fruits proper to excite drinking; and we drank to the sound of instruments which the slaves accompanied by their voices. The lady of the house sang herself; and by her songs rendered me the most impassioned of men. In fine, I passed the night in the full enjoyment of every pleasure.

Next morning, after having adroitly conveyed under the bolster of the bed the purse with the fifty pieces of gold I had carried with me, I took leave of the lady, who asked me when I would see her again. "Madam," replied I, "I pledge myself to return this night." She seemed transported with my answer; and, conducting me to the door, conjured me at parting to be mindful of my promise.

The same man who had taken me thither, waited for me, with his ass; I accordingly mounted, and returned to the khan of Mesrour. On discharging the man, I told him I should not pay him then, that he might not neglect attending me in the afternoon, at an hour I mentioned.

My first care, when I arrived at my lodging, was to purchase a good lamb, and several sorts of cakes, which I sent, by a porter, as a present to the lady. I then attended to my serious affairs till the owner of the ass

arrived; when I set out with him for the lady's house, and was received by her with as much joy as on the day preceding, and entertained with equal magnificence.

On the morrow, at quitting her, I left another purse, with fifty pieces of gold. I continued to visit the lady every day, and at each time to leave her a purse containing the like sum, till the merchants whom I employed to sell my cloth, and whom I visited regularly twice a week, were no longer in my debt; in fine, I found myself without money, and even hopeless of obtaining any more.

In this desperate state, and ready to abandon myself to despair, I walked from the khan, not knowing what I should do, and proceeded towards the castle, where there was a great crowd of people assembled to witness a spectacle given by the sultan of Egypt. When I had reached the place, I entered the crowd, and happened to stand by a cavalier, well mounted and handsomely clothed, who had upon the bow of his saddle a bag, half open, with a string of green silk hanging from it. Putting my hand to the bag, I judged that the silk-twist might be the string of a purse within it. While this was passing in my mind, a porter with a load of wood upon his back, pressed by on the other side of the horse; and so near, that the gentleman was forced to turn his head towards him, to avoid being injured by the wood. At that moment the devil tempted me: I took the string in one hand, and with the other opening the mouth of the bag, pulled out the purse without being observed. It was heavy, and I did not doubt but there was gold or silver in it.

When the porter had passed, the cavalier, who had apparently some suspicion of what I had effected while his head was turned, put his hand into the bag, and discovering his loss, gave me so severe a blow with his battle-axe, that he felled me to the ground. All who were witnesses to this violence were offended; and some seized the horse's bridle to stop the gentleman, and to demand what reason he had for striking me, or how he dared so to ill-treat a Mussulman. "Why do you interfere?" said he, sharply; "I had sufficient reason for so acting; this fellow is a thief." At these words, I arose; and, influenced by my air, every one took my part, and cried he was a liar, for that it was not possible a young man of my appearance could be guilty of such an offence. In fine, they all maintained that I was innocent, and held his horse to favour my escape. Unfortunately for me, the police-judge, followed by his people, passed by; and, seeing a crowd about a gentleman and me, approached, and demanded what had happened. Every person, in reply, reflected on the gentleman for treating me so unjustly, under the pretence that I had robbed him.

The judge would not listen to all that was said in my defence; but asked the cavalier if he suspected any person besides me. The gentleman replied in the negative, and gave his reasons for believing his suspicions just. The judge then ordered his followers to seize and search me, which they accordingly did; and one of them finding the purse upon me, exposed it to the view of the people. I could not support this shame, but fainted away. In the meantime, the judge demanded the purse.

The police-justice having received the purse, asked the horseman if it was his, and how much money it contained. The cavalier knew it to be that he had lost, and assured the judge he had put twenty sequins into it. The judge opened it; and having found exactly twenty sequins, he returned it to him. He then summoned me before him: "Come, young man," said he, "confess the truth. Was it you who took the gentleman's purse? Do not put me to the trouble of employing torture to extort confession." Casting down my eyes, I thought within myself, that if I denied the fact, they, finding the purse in my possession, would convict me of a lie; so, to avoid a double punishment, I looked up, and confessed the crime. I had no sooner acknowledged my guilt, than the judge, summoning people to witness it, ordered my hand to be cut off; and the sentence was executed immediately, to the great regret of all the spectators: I observed even in the cavalier's countenance, that he was not less moved than the rest. The judge would likewise have ordered my foot to be cut off; but I begged the cavalier to intercede for my pardon, which he did, and obtained it.

When the police-judge had retired, the cavalier approached me, holding out the purse: "I see plainly," said he, "that it was necessity induced you to commit an action so disgraceful and unworthy of a handsome young man like you. Here, take the fatal purse; I give it you; and am very sorry for the misfortune you have suffered." Having thus spoken, he quitted me; and as I was very weak from loss of blood, some of the good people who lived in the neighbourhood had the charity to take me into a house, and give me a glass of wine: they likewise dressed my arm; and wrapped up the dismembered hand in a cloth, which I carried with me, attached to my girdle.

If I had returned to the khan of Mesrour in this sad condition, I should not have found there the relief I wanted; and to go to the young lady was encountering considerable hazard; "She will not be willing, perhaps, to see me again," said I, "when she has learned the extent of my infamy!" However, I resolved to venture; and, to escape the crowd that followed me, I walked through several by-streets, and at length arrived at the lady's house, so weak and fatigued, that I threw myself upon a sofa, keeping my right arm under my coat, for I was very anxious to conceal my misfortune.

In the meantime, the lady, hearing of my arrival, and that I was unwell, came to me hastily, and seeing me pale and confused, "My dear soul!" said she, "what is the matter with you?" I dissembled: "Madam," replied I, "I have a violent pain in my head." She appeared very much affected, and desired me to be seated; for I had risen to receive her. "Tell me," said she, "what has occasioned your illness; the last time I had the pleasure of seeing you, you were quite well. There must be something else, that you conceal from me; pray let me know what it is." As I remained silent, and instead of answering, tears trickled down my cheeks, "I cannot conceive," said she, "what afflicts you. Have I unintentionally offended you, and do you come on purpose to tell me you no longer love me?" "It is not that, madam," replied I, sighing deeply; "a suspicion so unjust aggravates my sufferings."

I could not resolve to discover to her the true cause of my uneasiness. Night being arrived, supper was served, and she pressed me to eat; but reflecting that I could only feed myself with my left hand, I begged to be excused, declaring that I had no appetite. "You would not want an appetite," said she, "if you were to confess what you so obstinately hide from me. Your aversion, no doubt, is owing to the difficulty you feel in determining." "Alas, madam!" I replied, "must I, then, discover at last!" I had scarcely spoken these words, when she filled me a cup of wine: "Drink that," said she; "it will give you courage." I presented my left hand, and, taking the cup, I redoubled my tears and sighs. "What occasions you to cry and weep so bitterly?" said the lady; "and why do you take the cup with your left hand rather than with your right?" "Ah, madam!" replied I, " excuse me, I beseech you! I have got a swelling in my right hand." " Let me see the tumour," said she: " I will open it." I excused myself, alleging that it was not sufficiently matured; and emptied the cup, which was very large. The vapours of the wine, added to my weakness and dejection, brought on a sound sleep, in which I continued till the morning.

In the meantime, the lady, solicitous to know with what disease my right hand was affected, lifted up my robe, which concealed it, and saw, to her extreme astonishment, that it had been amputated, and that I had it with me wrapped in a cloth. She then clearly saw my reason for resisting the pressing instances she made; and passed the night in afflicting herself for my disgrace, which she concluded had been occasioned by my affection for her.

When I awoke, I plainly discerned by her countenance that she was very much distressed. However, that she might not increase my uneasiness, she did not speak of my misfortune. She presented to me a jelly-broth of fowl, which she had ordered to be prepared, and made me eat and drink to recruit my strength. After the repast, I offered to take leave of her; but she held me by my robe, declaring that I should not leave her house. "Though you will not confess to me," said she, " I am persuaded that I have been the innocent cause of the fatal accident which has befallen you; and the unhappiness I experience in consequence will soon destroy me; but, before I die, I must execute a design I have meditated for your benefit. On saying this, she summoned an officer of justice and witnesses, and ordered a writing to be drawn up, entitling me to all her property. After dismissing the people, whom she satisfied for their trouble, she opened a large trunk, where were all the purses I had presented to her from the commencement of our amours. "There they are all entire," said she; " I have not touched one of them; take the key; the trunk is yours." I returned her thanks for her generosity and bounty. "I consider what I have done for you as nothing," continued she, " and I shall not be satisfied unless I die, to convince you how much I love you." I conjured her by all the influence of love to abandon so fatal a resolution; but my remonstrances were ineffectual; and the chagrin she felt at seeing me maimed, caused her an illness of five or six weeks, of which she died.

After mourning her death the usual period I took possession of all her property, of which she had given me an account, and the sesame you have taken the trouble to sell for me formed a part."

* * * * * *

The young man of Bagdad having finished recounting his history (said the Christian merchant), "What I have now related," continued he, " will plead my excuse for eating with my left hand. I am extremely obliged to you for the trouble you have have taken on my account. I cannot sufficiently acknowledge your fidelity; and, as I still retain, thank Heaven, competent wealth, though I have expended largely, I beg your acceptance of the sum you hold of mine, as a present from me. Besides which, I have a proposal to make to you:—As, in consequence of my misfortune, I cannot remain any longer in Cairo, I have resolved to leave it, never to return. If you are willing to accompany me, we will trade together, and equally divide the profits."

I made my acknowledgments, in the best manner I was able, for his present, and cheerfully accepted the proposal of travelling with him, assuring him that his interest should always be as dear to me as my own.

Having appointed a day for our departure, we set out on our travels. We passed through Syria and Mesopotamia, traversed all Persia; and, after stopping at several cities, came at last, sir, to your metropolis. Some time after our arrival in this place, the young man having expressed a design to return to Persia, and establish himself there, we settled out accounts, and parted, well satisfied with each other. Accordingly he went hence, and I, sir, remain here at your majesty's service. This is the story I had to relate. Is it not more surprising than that of hump-back?

* * * * * *

The sultan of Casgar was irritated against the Christian merchant. "You appear very bold," said he, " in daring to relate a story to me so little worthy my attention, and then comparing it to that of hump-back! Can you flatter yourself with persuading me that the silly adventures of a young debauchee are more interesting than those of my jester? I am resolved to hang you all four, to avenge his death."

At these words the terrified purveyor flung himself at the sultan's feet: "Sir," said he, I beseech your majesty to suspend your just wrath, and hear my story; and if it should appear to your majesty more admirable than that of your jester, I hope you will pardon us all." "I grant your request," replied the sultan,—"speak!" The purveyor then proceeded thus:—

THE STORY TOLD BY THE SULTAN OF CASGAR'S PURVEYOR.

IR,—A person of distinction invited me yesterday to the nuptials of one of his daughters; accordingly, I went to his house in the evening at the hour appointed, and found the company assembled, composed of doctors, ministers of justice, and other persons of the first consideration in this city. After the ceremony, we were entertained with a sumptuous feast, and each of the guests ate what was most agreeable to his palate. With other delicacies, a course was served up, seasoned with garlic, which was delicious, and agreeable to all the company excepting one, who, it was observed, did not taste it, though it was placed immediately before him; we, therefore, invited him to imitate us. But he conjured us not to urge him to an acquiescence so repugnant to his feelings. ' I will take good care," said he, " not to touch a dish containing garlic. I have not forgotten what the tasting of it once cost me. We entreated him to tell us the occasion of his great dislike to garlic. But before he had time to answer, "Is it thus," said the master of the house, " that you honour my table? This ragout is excellent; attempt not to excuse yourself from eating of it: you must do me that favour as well as the rest." "Sir," replied the gentleman, who was a Bagdad merchant, "I hope you do not think I refuse to eat of it from a false delicacy. If you insist upon my compliance, I will submit, but upon this condition, that, after eating of it, I may wash my hands, with your permission, forty times with alkali, forty times with the ashes of the same plant, and forty times with soap. I trust you will not be offended at this stipulation, when I assure you it is in conformity with an oath I have made, never to taste garlic without that ablution."

The master of the house would not dispense with the merchant's eating of the garlic ragout, and therefore commanded his servants to have ready a basin of water, with alkali, the ashes of the same plant, and soap, that the merchant might wash as often as he pleased. When he had given this order, "Now," said he to the merchant, "I hope you will join us. All that you required will be in readiness."

The merchant, apparently angry at the violence offered him, advanced his hand, took a piece, which he conveyed to his mouth, trembling, and ate with a repugnance that astonished us all. But our wonder was augmented, when we observed that he had only four fingers, and no thumb, which we had not not noticed before, though he had eaten of other dishes. "You have not a thumb!" said the master of the house. "By what accident did you lose it? Surely by some extraordinary occurrence, a relation of which would be an agreeable entertainment to the company." "Sir," replied the merchant, "I have neither a thumb on the right hand nor on the left." At the same time, he showed us his left hand.

to convince us of the truth of his assertion. "But this is not all," continued he; "I have not a great toe on either of my feet, for which you will take my word. I was thus maimed by an unheard-of adventure, which I will not refuse to relate, if you have the patience to hear me. The account will equally astonish you, and excite your pity. But permit me first to wash my hands. He then arose from the table; and after washing his hands a hundred and twenty times, took his place again, and recited his history in these words:—

THE STORY OF THE MERCHANT OF BAGDAD.

YOU must know, gentlemen, that under the reign of the Caliph Haroun Alraschid, my father resided at Bagdad, the place of my nativity, and was considered one of the richest merchants of the city. But as he was a man greatly addicted to his pleasures, who loved an irregular life, and neglected his private affairs, instead of leaving me a plentiful fortune at his death, I had occasion to adopt the most rigid economy, to enable me to liquidate his debts. However, with difficulty, I paid them all; and, with care, my little fortune began to assume a smiling aspect.

One morning, as I opened my shop, a lady mounted on a mule, accompanied by an eunuch, and followed by two female slaves, stopped near my door, and, with the assistance of the eunuch, alighted. "Madam," said he, "I was aware you would be too early; you see here is nobody yet in the bezestein; if you had taken my advice, you would have avoided the unpleasantry of waiting." The lady looked all around, and seeing no shop open but mine, approached saluting me, and requested leave to sit in my shop till the rest of the merchants arrived. I replied to her request' as I thought civility demanded.

The lady seated herself in my shop, and remarking that there was no person but the eunuch and me in the whole bezestein, she uncovered her face to take the air. I had never witnessed so ravishing a beauty: to see and to love were an effect of the same moment; and my eyes were constantly rivetted on her. She appeared not displeased with my attention, for she gave me a full opportunity to admire her at my ease; and she did not cover her face till she was afraid of being noticed.

When she had adjusted her veil as before, she told me she wanted several sorts of the finest and richest stuffs, and asked me if I had them. "Alas, madam!" I replied, "I am but a young merchant, just beginning the world; I am not sufficiently rich to deal in such valuable articles, and it is a mortification to me that I have nothing like what you want to show you. But, to save you the fatigue of going from shop to shop, as soon as the merchants come, I will, if you please, fetch from them what you desire, with the lowest prices; by which means you can settle your business without further trouble." She consented, and entered into discourse with me, which continued so much the longer as I made her believe the merchants who could furnish what she wanted were not yet arrived.

I was not less charmed with her wit than I had been with the beauty of her countenance; but it was at length necessary I should deprive myself of the pleasure of her conversation. I ran out to seek for the stuffs she wanted, and after she had chosen what she liked, we concluded the price at five thousand drachms of coined silver. I made a packet of the stuffs, and gave it to the eunuch, who put it under his arm; the lady then arose, and took leave. I continued to gaze after her till she had reached the bezestein-gate, and remounted her mule.

The lady had no sooner disappeared than I perceived that love had occasioned me to commit a serious fault. It had so deranged my thoughts, that I had suffered her to leave my shop without paying for the goods she had obtained, nor did I even inquire who she was, nor where she resided. I reflected at the same time that I was accountable for a large sum to several merchants, who, perhaps, would not have patience to wait for their money. However, I went to them, and made the best excuse I could, pretending that I knew the lady. In fine, I returned home equally troubled with love, and with the burden of so heavy a debt.

I had begged my creditors to withhold their demands for eight days, and when that time was elapsed, they did not fail to press me for payment. Then I entreated them to allow me eight days more, to which they consented; but the next day, I saw the lady enter the bezestein, mounted on her mule, with the same attendants, and at the same hour of the day, as before.

She came directly to my shop, "I have made you wait some time," said she; "but I have at last brought you the money for the stuffs I had the other day: take it to a banker, and see it is right and good." The eunuch, who had the money, went with me to the banker's, and we found it just. I immediately returned, and had again the happiness of conversing with the lady till all the shops of the bezestein were open. Though we talked but of ordinary occurrences, she gave them, nevertheless, a turn which made them appear new; and convinced me that I was not deceived in admiring her wit during our first conversation.

When the merchants were arrived, and had opened their shops, I carried what I owed to the persons from whom I had obtained the stuffs on credit; and was readily intrusted with more, which the lady had desired to see. In short, she selected goods to the value of a hundred pieces of gold; and again carried them away, without either paying for them, apologising, or giving me her address. I was astonished at her conduct; while she hazarded nothing, I remained without security, and in the certainty of being ruined if she did not return. "She has paid me," said I to myself, "a considerable sum, but she leaves me answerable for another much greater. Surely she is not a cheat!. Can it be possible she has a design to inveigle me to my ruin? The merchants are unacquainted with her; they will consequently look to me for payment.' My love was not sufficiently powerful to prevent unpleasant and mortifying reflections. My alarms increased daily during a whole month, in which time I had not heard of the lady. In fine, the merchants became impatient; and, to satisfy them, I was even going to dispose of all my property, when she returned one morning, attended as before.

"Take your scales," said she, "and weigh the gold I have brought you." These words dissipated my fear, and inflamed my love. Before we counted the money, she asked me several questions; and particularly if I was married. I answered negatively, telling her I never had been. Then giving the gold to the eunuch, "Let us have your interposition," said she, " to terminate our affair." The eunuch laughed; and, taking me aside, desired me to weigh the gold: while I was so doing, he whispered in my ear, "I see clearly that you love my mistress, and am surprised that you have not the courage to disclose your affection to her: she loves you yet more passionately. Do not imagine she has any real occasion for your stuffs: it is merely an excuse to come hither, because you have inspired her with a violent passion. Only ask her the question; and it will only be your own fault if you do not marry her." "It is true," I replied, "I have loved the lady from the first moment I saw her; but I durst not aspire to the happiness of thinking my love would be agreeable. I am entirely hers, and shall not fail to retain a grateful sense of the good offices you have rendered me."

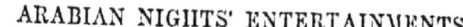

In fine, I finished weighing the gold; and while I was putting it again into the bag, the eunuch turned to the lady, and told her I was satisfied, that being the word they had agreed upon between themselves. Presently after, the lady arose, and took leave, telling me she should send the eunuch to me, and desiring that I would follow his directions in her name.

I carried to each of the merchants the money that was due to him, and waited impatiently some days for the eunuch. At length he came, when I entertained him very kindly; and inquired after the health of his mistress. "you are," replied he, "the happiest lover in the world; she is dying in love with you. She wishes very much to see you; and were she mistress of her own actions, would not fail to come here, and willingly pass all the moments of her life in your company." "Her noble mien and graceful carriage," said I, "convince me that she was a lady of consideration." "You are not deceived in that opinion," replied the eunuch: "she is the favourite of Zobeide, the caliph's spouse, who has the more sincere regard for her, as she brought her up, from her infancy, and intrusts her with all her affairs. In her design to marry, she has confessed to the caliph's lady her affection for you, and requested her consent. Zobeide has agreed to her demand, only desiring to see you first, that she may judge if her favourite has made a good choice; and, if satisfied, Zobeide means to defray the expenses of the wedding. Thus, you see, your happiness is certain; since you have pleased the favourite, you will be equally agreeable to the mistress, who is anxious to please her, and would by no means thwart her inclination. You have only, then, to accompany me to the place whither I am sent to conduct you; so you have merely to determine." "My resolution is already formed," said I; "and I will follow you wherever you please to direct." "That is well," replied the eunuch, "but you know that men are not permitted to enter the ladies' apartments in the palace; and therefore you must be introduced with great secrecy: the favourite has taken measures accordingly. On your side be careful in acting your part, and be very discreet, for your life is at stake."

I assured him that I would punctually perform whatever might be enjoined me. "You must then," said he, "in the evening be at the mosque built by Zobeide on the banks of the Tigris, and stay there till you are visited." I agreed to all he proposed; and, after passing the day in great impatience, went in the evening and assisted at the prayer an hour and a half after sunset, in the mosque, where I remained after all the people had retired.

But a short time had elapsed before I saw a boat approaching the mosque, the rowers of which were all eunuchs. They landed, and carried several large trunks into the mosque; after which they withdrew, one only of them staying behind, whom I perceived to be the same eunuch who had always accompanied the lady, and had been with me that morning. I likewise saw the lady enter the mosque. Immediately advancing towards her, I told her I was ready to obey her commands. "We have no time to lose," said she, opening one of the trunks, and desiring me to get into it: "this is a necessary caution, for your safety as well as mine. Fear nothing," added she; "leave to me the management of the rest." Considering that I had gone too far to recede, I complied with her orders, and she locked the trunk. The eunuch, her confident, then called the other eunuchs who had carried the trunks on shore, and ordered them to take them again on board. After which, the lady and her eunuch having re-embarked, the boatmen began to row, to convey me to the apartment of Zobeide.

In the meantime, reflecting very seriously on the danger to which I had exposed myself, I repented of my indiscretion, and offered up vows and prayers, though then too late.

The boat landed before the gate of the palace, and the trunks were carried to the chamber of the chief of the eunuchs, who keeps the key of the ladies' apartments, and suffers nothing to enter without a previous inspection. The officer being in bed, it was necessary to awaken him; at which he was much offended, and rebuked the favourite lady severely for returning home so late. "You shall not escape so easily as you expect," said he; "not one of these trunks shall pass till I have opened it, and examined its contents; at the same time commanding the eunuchs to bring them before him, and open them one after another. They began with that in which I was secreted; and, taking it up, carried it to the officer. At this proceeding I was seized with a terror I cannot describe; I believed my destruction inevitable.

The favourite, who had the key, protested she would not surrender it, nor should the trunk be opened. "You know very well," said she, "I bring nothing hither but what is for the service of Zobeide, your mistress and mine. This trunk in particular is filled with rich goods, which have been intrusted to me by some merchants lately arrived, besides a number of bottles of water from the fountain of Zemzem, sent from Mecca, and if one of these should happen to be broken, the goods will be spoiled, and you must answer for them. The wife of the commander of the faithful will know how to resent your insolence." In fine, she spoke with such firmness, that the officer had not the courage to open either of the trunks. "Take them away, then," said he, angrily; "go!" The ladies' apartment was accordingly opened, and all the trunks were carried in.

This was scarcely effected, when, suddenly, I heard the cry, "There is the caliph! there is the caliph!" These words threw me into such a state of horror, that I wonder I survived it; for, in truth, it was the caliph. "What have you in these trunks?" said he to the favourite. "Commander of the faithful," replied she, "they contain some stuffs, lately arrived, which your majesty's lady wished to see." "Open them," said he; "and let me also see your curiosities." She endeavoured to excuse herself, alleging that the stuffs were only proper for ladies; and that, by opening them, his lady would be deprived of the pleasure of seeing them first. "Open them, I say," cried the caliph; "I order you." She further represented to him, that, by a compliance with his commands, she should be exposed to the anger of her mistress. "No, no," replied he; "I will engage she shall not be offended with you. Come, open them; and do not keep me waiting."

It was necessary to obey; and I felt such dreadful alarms, that I shudder when I think of them. The caliph seated himself; and the favourite ordered the trunks to be brought before him, one after another. She opened them; and, to cause delay, described all the beauties of each particular stuff, thinking thereby to exhaust his patience, but her stratagem was ineffectual. As she was not less interested than myself in keeping the trunk in which I was hidden unopened, she hesitated to touch it; but as he had viewed all the rest, "Come," said the caliph, "let us see what is in that trunk." I could scarcely tell whether I was alive or dead at that moment; at least I thought it impossible to escape so serious a danger.

When Zobeide's favourite saw that the caliph would not relinquish the gratification of his curiosity, "As for this trunk," said she, "your majesty will please to dispense with my opening it: there are some articles in it which

I cannot show you, unless your lady were present." "Well, well," replied the caliph, "I am satisfied; let the trunks be taken away." She immediately ordered the attendants to carry them into her apartment; and I began to experience symptoms of returning respiration.

As soon as the eunuchs had retired, she opened the trunk in which I was confined: "Come out," said she; and showing me the door of a staircase which led to an upper room, she desired me to ascend, and await her coming. She had scarcely closed the door after me, when the caliph entered her chamber, and seated himself on the trunk in which I had been concealed. This visit was occasioned by a motive of curiosity, that had no reference to me. The prince wished to put some questions to the lady concerning what she had seen or heard in the city. They discoursed together a considerable time; after which he left her, and retired to his apartment.

When she found herself at liberty, she proceeded to the chamber where I was waiting, and made many excuses for the alarms she had caused me. "My uneasiness," said she, "was not less than yours, which you cannot doubt, since I have encountered equal danger through love for you. Another in my place would not have had the courage to act with such dexterity on so delicate an occasion. Presence of mind, as well as resolution—or rather my unbounded love for you—was requisite, to enable me to extricate myself from this embarrassment. But assume confidence; there is nothing more to fear." After we had discoursed for awhile with much tenderness, "It is time," said she, "you should go to rest: I shall not present you to Zobeide till to-morrow, which will be effected without trouble, as the caliph sees her only at night." Encouraged by this information, I slept tranquilly; or if my repose was sometimes interrupted by inquietudes, they were not unpleasant, being caused by the hopes of possessing a lady of so much wit and beauty.

The next day, before I was introduced to Zobeide, her favourite instructed me how to behave in her presence, telling me nearly the questions she would put to me, and dictating the answers I was to give: she then conducted me into a saloon of the utmost magnificence and richness. I had no sooner entered than twenty female slaves, advanced in years, richly and uniformly habited, came out from Zobeide's apartment, and very modestly arranged themselves before the throne in two equal rows: they were followed by twenty other ladies, all young, and clothed in the same manner as the former, with this difference—that their habits appeared somewhat gayer. Surrounded by these, appeared Zobeide, with a majestic air, and so loaded with jewels, that she could scarcely walk. She seated herself on the throne; and the favourite lady, who I forgot to mention accompanied her, stood at her right hand, while the slaves, a little distant, were assembled on each side of the throne.

As soon as the caliph's lady sat down, the slaves who first entered made a sign for me to approach. I accordingly advanced between the rows they formed, and prostrated myself, laying my head upon the tapestry that was under the princess's feet. She ordered me to rise; and did me the honour to inquire my name, my family, and the state of my fortune; to all which questions I gave her satisfactory answers, as I perceived, not only by her countenance, but by her expressions. "I am glad," said she to me, "that my daughter (so she called the favourite lady, for she regarded her as such, after the care she had taken of her education,) "has made a choice that pleases me: I approve of it, and consent to your marriage. I will myself order the necessary preparations, but I shall want my daughter for ten days; in which time I will speak to the caliph, and obtain his consent; and you may remain here, where you will be safe."

I accordingly stayed ten days in the ladies' apartment. During that period I was deprived of the pleasure of seeing the favourite lady; but was so well treated, by her orders, that I had no reason to be dissatisfied.

Zobeide mentioned to the caliph the resolution she had taken to marry her favourite; and the prince, leaving her at liberty to act as she pleased, granted to the favourite a considerable sum, as a contribution on his part towards her establishment. Zobeide then ordered the contract of marriage to be drawn up, which was properly executed; and preparations for the nuptials having been made, the male and female dancers were called in, and there were great rejoicings in the palace for the ten days. The tenth day being appointed for the completion of the marriage, the favourite lady was conducted to a bath on one side, and I to another. In the evening I sat down to table, and had all kinds of dishes served up to me; and, with others, a garlic ragout, like that of which you have forced me to eat. This ragout was so agreeable to my palate, that I scarcely touched either of the other dishes. But, such was my misfortune, when I arose from the table, I only wiped my hands, instead of well washing them—a negligence I had never before committed.

It was then night, but the apartment of the ladies was rendered as light as day, by means of a grand illumination. The music played, the company danced, and contrived a thousand different amusements; and the palace resounded with acclamations of joy. My bride and I were introduced to a great hall, where we were placed upon two thrones. The women who attended her made her change her habits several times, and painted her face in different manners, according to the usual custom on wedding-days; and at each alteration in her dress, they presented her to me.

In fine, all these ceremonies being concluded, we were conducted to the nuptial chamber. As soon as our attendants had retired, I approached to embrace my spouse; but instead of returning my transports, she forcibly repulsed me, crying out fearfully, which immediately brought all the ladies of the apartment into the chamber, to inquire the cause of her distress. For my own part, I was so astonished, that I remained immoveable, without the power even to ask in what I had offended. "Dear sister," said they to her, "what has happened so soon after our leaving you? Let us know, that we may endeavour to afford you relief." "Take," cried she, "that vile fellow out of my sight!" "How, madam," said I, "wherein have I had the misfortune to incur your displeasure?" "You are a villain!" she replied, furiously: "you have eaten garlic, and not washed your hands! Do you think I would suffer such a filthy creature to approach and infect me? Down with him on the ground," continued she, addressing herself to the ladies, "and let me have a good cat o'nine tails." They immediately threw me down, and, while some held my hands, and others my feet, my wife, whose orders had been promptly obeyed, beat me most unmercifully, till her strength was exhausted. She then said to the ladies, "Take him, send him to the police-judge, and let the hand be cut off with which he has eaten of the garlic ragout."

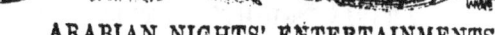
At this dreadful sentence, I exclaimed, " Great God ! I am beaten and bruised, and, to complete my affliction, am condemned to have my hand cut off ! And for what ? For eating of a garlic ragout, and forgetting to wash my hands ! What vengeance for so trifling an offence ! Plague on the ragout ! Cursed be the cook who dressed it ! and may he who served it up be equally unhappy !"

All the ladies who witnessed the punishment I had received, when they heard speak of the cutting off my hand, could not avoid pitying me. " Dear sister ! good lady !" said they to the favourite, " you carry your resentment too far. He is certainly a man who knows not the world, who is ignorant of your consequence, and the respect that is due to you; but we beseech you to overlook and pardon the fault he has committed." " I am not yet satisfied," replied she ; " I will teach him how to behave ; and he shall carry some sensible marks of his filthiness which will render him cautious hereafter how he eats garlic ragout without washing his hands." They, however, continued their solicitations : falling at her feet, and kissing her hand, " Good lady," said they, " in the name of God, moderate your anger, and grant the favour we request." Without answering them, she arose ; and after uttering a thousand reflections against me, quitted the chamber. All the ladies followed her, leaving me alone, in indescribable affliction.

I remained ten days, without seeing any person, excepting an old female slave, who brought me food : of her I inquired respecting the favourite lady. " She is sick," replied the old woman, " by the poisonous smell you infected her with. Why were you not careful to wash your hands after eating of that cursed garlic ragout ?" " Is it possible," thought I to myself, " that these ladies can be so delicate, and at the same time so vindictive for a trifling fault !" Nevertheless, I still loved my wife, notwithstanding her cruelty, and ceased not to regret her loss."

One day the old slave thus addressed me :—" Your spouse is recovered ; she is gone to the bath ; and she desired me to say, that she will come to see you to-morrow. So, be patient, and endeavour to accommodate yourself to her humour. Besides, she is a woman of great sense and discretion, and entirely beloved by all the ladies who attend on Zobeide, our admirable mistress."

Accordingly, my wife came the next day ; and accosting me, " I am too good," said she, " in seeing you again, after the offence you have committed. But I cannot resolve to be reconciled to you, till I have punished you as you deserve, for not washing your hands after eating the garlic ragout." Saying this, she called several ladies who, by her order, threw me on the ground ; and, after they had bound me, she had the barbarity herself to cut off my thumbs and great toes with a razor. One of the ladies applied a certain root to stanch the blood ; but, in consequence of the bleeding and pain, I fainted.

When I recovered from the swoon, they gave me wine to drink, to recruit my strength. " Ah, madam !" said I to my wife, " if ever I should eat of garlic ragout again, I swear to you, that, instead of once, I will wash my hands a hundred and twenty times—with the herb alkali, with the ashes of the same plant, and with soap." " Well," replied my wife, " on that condition, I am willing to forget what has passed, and to live with you as my husband."

This (continued the Bagdad merchant, addressing himself to the company) is the reason why I refused to eat of the garlic ragout that is now on the table.

The ladies (said he) applied to my wounds, not only the root I mentioned, but likewise some balsam of Mecca, which they were certain was genuine, since they had it from the caliph's own dispensatory. By virtue of that admirable

balsam, I was perfectly cured in a few days; and my wife and I lived together as happily as if I had never eaten of the garlic ragout. But as I had always enjoyed my liberty, I was very uneasy at being immured in the caliph's palace, though I did not mention it to my wife, for fear of displeasing her. However, she perceived my dissatisfaction, and was herself not less anxious to escape from her confinement: gratitude alone induced her to continue with Zobeide. Being a very sensible woman, she represented, in so impressive a manner, to her mistress, the constraint I was under by not living in the city with persons of my own condition, as I had been accustomed, that the good princess chose rather to deprive herself of the pleasure of having her favourite near her, than not to grant what we both equally desired.

In consequence of this permission, about a month after our marriage, my wife appeared with several eunuchs, each of them carrying a bag of silver. When they had retired, "You never told me," said she, "that you were dissatisfied with remaining in the court; but I clearly perceived it, and have happily accomplished the means of rendering you contented. My mistress, Zobeide, permits us to leave the palace; and here are fifty thousand sequins, of which she has made us a present, to enable us to live comfortably in the city. Take ten thousand of them, and purchase us a house."

I soon found a residence for the money; and, having furnished it magnificently, we took possession of it. We kept a great many slaves of both sexes, with a very fine equipage: in short, we began to live very agreeably. But our happiness was of short duration; for, at the end of a year, my wife fell sick, and died in a few days.

I might have married again, and continued to live honourably at Bagdad; but curiosity to see the world inspired me with other designs. I sold my house; and, after purchasing several sorts of merchandise, I joined a caravan, and went to Persia; from Persia I took the route to Samarcande, whence I came to settle in this city.

*   *   *   *   *   *   *   *

This, sir, (continued the purveyor to the sultan of Casgar), is the story that the Bagdad merchant related in the company where I was yesterday. "His history," said the sultan, "is somewhat extraordinary; but it is not comparable to that of my little hump-back." The Jew physician then advancing, prostrated himself before the sultan's throne; and rising again, "Sir," said he, "if your majesty will also have the goodness to listen to me, I flatter myself you will be pleased with the history I have to recount." "Well, speak," replied the sultan; "but if it be not more surprising than that of little hump-back, do not expect that I shall spare your life." The Jew physician, finding the sultan of Casgar disposed to hear him, spoke to this effect:—

THE STORY RELATED BY THE JEW PHYSICIAN.

 IR,—While I was a student of physic at Damascus, and commencing the practice of that noble profession with some reputation, a slave desired me to visit a patient in the house of the governor of the city. I accordingly went, and was introduced to a chamber, where I found a very handsome young man extremely depressed by his indisposition. Seating myself near him, I saluted him; but he made no reply to my compliments, only signifying by his looks that he heard and thanked me. "Pray, sir," said I, "give me your hand, that I may feel your pulse." Instead of offering his right hand, he presented his left, at which I was very much surprised. "This," said I to myself, "is the grossest ignorance, not to know that people present their right hand, and not their left, to a physician." However, I felt his pulse; and, after writing a prescription, retired.

I continued my visits during nine days; and every time I wished to feel his pulse, he presented to me the left hand; on the tenth day he seemed so well recovered, that I only judged it necessary to recommend bathing. The governor of Damascus, who was present, in testimony of his satisfaction, immediately invested me with a very rich robe, appointing me physician to the city hospital, and physician in ordinary at his house, where he said I might freely eat at his table whenever I pleased.

The young man likewise treated me with the utmost civility, praying me to accompany him to the bath. Accordingly, we went together; and, when his attendants had undressed him, I perceived that he had lost the right hand, and that it had recently been cut off, which had occasioned his illness, though concealed from me. As soon as his friends had applied the proper external remedies, they summoned me to prevent the ill consequence of the fever with which he was seized. I was very much surprised and concerned at seeing him in that condition; which he observed by my countenance. "Doctor," said he, "be not astonished at my misfortune; I will, some day, tell you the occasion of it; when you will hear a history the most extraordinary."

After we had quitted the bath, we sat down at table. Discoursing together, he asked me if it would be prejudicial to his health to take a walk out of town, to the governor's garden. I answered, that so far from being injurious, it would be salutary. "Well then," said he, "if you will honour me with your company, I will entertain you with my history." I replied, I was at his command the remainder of the day. He immediately ordered his servants to provide a collation, and we set out to the governor's garden. Arriving there, we made two or three turns; and then seating ourselves on a carpet that his servants had spread under a tree, which afforded a very agreeable shade, the young man related his history in these terms:—

STORY OF THE YOUNG MAN OF MOUSSOL.

I WAS born at Moussol, and my family is one of the most considerable in that city. My father was the eldest of ten brothers; all living, and married when my grandfather died. But of this number of brothers, my father alone was not childless, and he had only me. He took the greatest care of my education, and bestowed on me every accomplishment that was proper for a child of my quality.

I was already well grown, and beginning to frequent public society, when, one Friday, I happened to attend the noon-prayer with my father and my uncles, in the great mosque of Moussol. After prayer, all the people retired, excepting my father and my uncles, who continued sitting on the carpet with which the mosque was covered. I seated myself near them, and, discoursing of different subjects, the conversation fell insensibly on travels. They extolled the beauties and peculiar rarities of some kingdoms, and of their principal cities; but one of my uncles said, that if they might believe the uniform report of an infinite number of travellers, there was not in the world a more beautiful country than Egypt, with the Nile; and his representation made so great a impression on my mind, that from that moment I conceived a desire to travel. Whatever my other uncles could say, to support, in preference, Bagdad and the Tigris—calling Bagdad the true residence of the Mussulman religion, and the metropolis of all the cities on the earth, had not the least effect on me. My father joined his opinion with those who had spoken in favour of Egypt, which caused me much joy. "Say what you will," said he, "the person who has not seen Egypt has been deprived of the pleasure of viewing the most extraordinary country in the world. All the land there is golden, I mean so fertile that it enriches the inhabitants; the women of that country are all charming, whether we consider their beauty o their agreeable manners. If you speak to me of the Nile, where is there a more admirable river? What water was ever lighter or more delicious? The very slime it conveys in its overflowing, enriches the countries, which produce a thousand times more without cultivation, than others with the greatest labour. Recollect what a poet said of the Egyptians, when he was obliged to quit Egypt. "Your Nile loads you with wealth every day; it is for you only that it travels so far. Alas! in removing from you, my tears will flow as abundantly as its water! While you continue in the enjoyment of its sweetness, I am condemned to deprive myself of it against my inclination."

"If you look," continued my father, "towards the island that forms the two great branches of the Nile, what variety of verdure do you perceive! How enamelled with all sorts of flowers. What a prodigious number of cities, villages, canals, and a thousand other agreeable objects! If you turn your eyes to the other side, directing your attention towards Ethiopia, how many other objects of admiration. I cannot make a more appropriate comparison of the verdure of so many plains, watered with the different canals of the island, than to sparkling emeralds set in silver. Is not Grand Cairo the largest, the most populous, and the richest city in the universe? What a prodigious number of magnificent edifices, public and private! If you view the pyramids, you will be seized with astonishment; you will become immoveable at the sight of these enormous masses of stone, which reach to the skies; and you will be obliged to admit that the Pharaohs, who employed so much riches and so many men in the erection of them, must have surpassed all the monarchs that have since appeared, not only in Egypt, but in the whole world, in magnificence and invention, by leaving monuments so worthy of their memory. These fabrics, so ancient, that the learned cannot agree as to the time when they were built, exist to this day, and will endure for ages. I silently pass over the maritime towns of the kingdom of Egypt, as Damietta, Rosetta, Alexandria— where the number of nations that visit them, in quest of a thousand sorts of grains and cloths, with an infinite variety of other articles for the convenience and the delight of men is incredible. I speak of what I know; for I passed some years of my youth there, which, as long as I live, I shall always consider the most agreeable of my life."

My uncles could not reply to my father, and therefore acquiesced in all he had said relative to the Nile, to Cairo, and to the whole kingdom of Egypt. For my part, I was so impressed with what he had related, that I could not sleep that night. Shortly after, my uncles themselves declared how much they were interested by my father's discourse. They proposed to him, that they should altogether travel into Egypt. He agreed; and being rich merchants, they resolved to carry with them such goods as were in request there. I learned that they were making preparations for their departure; and thereupon went to my father, whom I supplicated, with tears in my eyes, to permit me to accompany him, and allow me a portion of goods to trade with by myself. "You are yet too young," said my father, "to encounter the journey into Egypt; the fatigue would be too great for you; besides, I am persuaded you would be a loser by your traffic." However, these words did not remove the earnest desire I had to travel; I employed my uncles' interest with my father, from whom they at length obtained permission for me to go as far as Damascus, where it was determined they would leave me, while they continued their journey to Egypt. "The city of Damascus," said my father, "has likewise its beauties; and he must be contented with going there." Notwithstanding the desire I had to see Egypt, after what I had heard him mention, I reflected that he was my father, and submitted to his will.

I accordingly set out from Moussol with him and my uncles. We traversed Mosopotamia, passed the Euphrates, and arrived at Halep, where we stayed some days; thence we went to Damascus, the first sight of which was a very agreeable surprise to me. We all lodged in the same khan; and I had the pleasure of viewing a city that was,

large, populous, gay, and very well fortified. We employed some days in visiting the delicious gardens in the environs; and we all agreed that Damascus was justly said to be seated in a paradise. My uncles at length determined to pursue their journey; but took care before their departure to sell my goods, which they effected so advantageously for me, that I gained five hundred per cent. This sale produced so considerable a sum, that I was transported with the possession of it.

My father and my uncles then left me in Damascus, and continued their journey. After their departure I was very cautious not to expend my money extravagantly; but I nevertheless engaged a stately house, built of marble, adorned with pictures of foliage in gold and azure; and in the garden were very fine fountains. I furnished it, not so richly, indeed, as the magnificence of the place deserved, but at least sufficiently handsome for a young man of my condition. It had formerly belonged to one of the principal lords of the city, whose name was Moudoun Abdalraham, but was then the property of a rich jewel-merchant, to whom I paid for it only two sherriffs a month. I engaged a number of domestics, and lived honourably: sometimes I gave entertainments to persons with whom I had become acquainted, and on other days I visited them. Thus I spent my time at Damascus, waiting my father's return. No passion disturbed my repose; and association with people of respectability formed my sole employment.

One day, as I sat at my gate, enjoying the cool breezes, a lady, well dressed, and who appeared very handsome, came to me, and inquired if I did not sell stuffs; at the same time walking into my house. I immediately arose, and, shutting the gate, conducted her into a parlour, requesting her to be seated. "Madam," said I, "I have had stuffs that were worthy your notice; but I have parted with them all, for which I am very sorry. She removed the veil that covered her face, and exhibited to my view a beauty so brilliant, that the sight of it affected me with emotions I had never before experienced. "I have no occasions for stuffs," replied she, "I came merely to see you, and to pass the evening with you, if it be agreeable: I require no more of you than a light refreshment.

Transported with such good fortune, I ordered my servants to bring in several sorts of fruits, and some bottles of wine. My commands were speedily obeyed; and we ate and drank, and made merry till midnight: in short it was the most agreeable night I had passed at Damascus. Next morning I would have put ten sherriffs in the lady's hand, but she withdrew it quickly: "I am not come to see you," said she, "with a view to interest; you insult me. So far from receiving money, I desire you to accept some from me, or I will see you no more." Saying this, she drew ten sherriffs from her purse, and forced me to take them. "You may expect me again," said she, "three days hence, after sunset." She then took leave of me; and I felt, as she departed, that she carried my heart with her.

Three days afterwards she failed not to return, at the appointed hour; and I received her with all the joy of tender impatience. The evening and the night we passed as before; and next morning, at parting, she promised to see me again on the third day; but she would not go until I had accepted ten sherriffs more.

She returned according to promise; and, when we were both elevated with wine, she thus addressed me:—"My dear heart, what is your opinion of me? Am I not handsome and agreeable?" "Madam," replied I, "these questions would appear unnecessary; all the marks of affection that I have given you ought to convince you of my love; I am charmed in seeing you, and delighted with your company. You are my queen, my sultaness; in you is all the happiness of my life." "Ah, sir," returned she, "I have no doubt your sentiments would alter, if you were to see a lady of my acquaintance, who is younger and handsomer than I. She has so pleasing a disposition, that she would excite laughter in persons the most melancholic. I must bring her hither. I have spoken of you to her; and, from the account I have given of you, she is dying of anxiety to see you. She entreated me to procure her that pleasure; but I could not venture to satisfy her, without first speaking to you." "Madam," said I, "you may act as you please; but, whatever you say of your friend, I defy all her charms to tear my heart from you, to whom it is so inviolably attached, that nothing can disengage it." "Take good care," returned she; "I confess to you, that I am going to put your love to a strong proof."

We passed the night together; and, next morning, at parting, instead of ten sherriffs, she gave me fifteen, which I was forced to accept. "Remember," said she, "that in two days you are to receive a new guest; pray give her a good reception: we shall come at the usual hour after sun set." I accordingly had my apartments embellished, and a handsome collation prepared for their arrival.

I waited for the two ladies with impatience; and, at length, in the evening, they appeared. They both unveiled; and, if I had been surprised with the beauty of the first, I had reason to be much more interested when I saw her friend. She had regular features, a perfect face, lively complexion, and such sparkling eyes, that I could scarcely support their splendour. I thanked her for the honour she had conferred on me, and entreated her pardon, if I did not give her the reception she merited. "No compliments," said she; "I ought to make them to you, for permitting my friend to bring me hither. But, since you were pleased to suffer it, let us lay aside all ceremony, and only think of being merry."

As I had given orders for the collation to be served up when the ladies arrived, we very soon seated ourselves at table. I sat opposite to the stranger lady, who never ceased regarding me with smiles; I could not resist her penetrating looks; and she rendered herself so firmly mistress of my heart, that I had not the power of defence. But, by inspiring me, she was herself ensnared; and, so far from being under embarrassment or constraint, she applied to me many tender expressions.

The other lady, who noticed us, at first only laughed at our behaviour. "I told you," said she, addressing herself to me, "that you would find my friend charming; and I perceive you have already violated the oath you made of being faithful to me." "Madam," replied I, laughing in my turn, "you would have reason to complain of me, if I were deficient in civility to a lady that you brought hither, and of whom you are so fond: both of you might then upbraid me with not knowing how to support the honours of my house.

We continued to drink, but, as the wine elevated our spirits, the stranger lady and I exchanged our regards with so little reserve, that her friend became violently jealous, of which disposition she quickly gave us a melancholy

proof. She arose from the table, and went out, saying she would soon return; but a few moments afterwards, the lady who remained with me, changing countenance, fell into violent convulsions; and, in fine, expired in my arms, while I was calling to the people to assist me in relieving her. I immediately left the room, and inquired for the other lady; my people told me, that she had opened the street-door, and had quitted the house. Then I suspected, what was really true, that she had been the cause of her friend's death. She had had the dexterity and the malice to put some very strong poison into the last glass, which she presented to her with her own hand.

I was seriously afflicted with this incident. "What shall I do?" said I to myself. "What will become of me?" Judging there was no time to lose, I made my servants, by the moonlight, and without noise, take up one of the great pieces of marble with which the court of my house was paved; under that I ordered them to dig a hole quickly, and there inter the

corpse of the young lady. After they had replaced the stone, I habited myself in a travelling dress, and taking all the money I had, I secured every part of the house, affixing my own seal on the door. I then went in quest of the jewel-merchant, my landlord; paid him the rent I owed, with a year's rent in advance; and, giving him the key, begged him to keep it for me. "A very urgent affair," said I, "obliges me to be absent for some time; I am under a necessity of going to seek my uncles at Cairo." In fine, I took leave of him; and that moment, mounting my horse, set out with my attendants.

I had a good journey, and reached Cairo without any ill accident. There I met with my uncles, who were very much surprised to see me. I excused myself by pretending I was tired of waiting for them; and not hearing from them, my inquietude had induced me to undertake the journey. They received me very kindly, and promised their good offices to prevent my father being angry with me for leaving Damascus without his permission. I lodged in the same khan with them, and saw all worthy of notice in Cairo.

Having finished their traffic, they spoke of returning to Moussol, and had already begun to make preparations for their departure. But, as I had not yet satisfied my curiosity in Egypt, I quitted my uncles, and went to lodge at a great distance from the khan, not appearing till they were gone. They had assiduously sought for me all over the

city; but not finding me, they judged that remorse, for having come to Egypt against my father's will, had induced me to return to Damascus without disclosing my intention to them; and they commenced their journey, in the hope of finding me there, and of taking me with them on passing.

I remained at Cairo, after their departure, three years, fully to satisfy my curiosity to see all the wonders of Egypt. During that time I was careful to send money to the jewel-merchant, desiring him to keep my house for me; for I designed to return to Damascus, and stay there yet some years. Nothing happened to me at Cairo, worthy your hearing; but doubtless you will be surprised at what I encountered after my return to Damascus.

Arriving in that city, I went to the jewel-merchant's dwelling, who received me joyfully, and insisted on

accompanying me to my house, to show me that nobody had entered it during my absence. In effect, the seal on the lock was still entire ; and when I entered, I found everything in the same order in which I had left it.

On sweeping and cleaning out the room in which I had entertained the ladies, one of my servants found a gold chain necklace decorated with ten very large and perfect pearls placed at certain distances. He brought it to me ; and I knew it to be the same I had seen on the neck of the young lady who was poisoned. I concluded it had been detached and had fallen off without my perceiving it ; but I could not look at it without shedding tears, when I remembered the lovely creature I had seen die in so dreadful a manner. I wrapped it up, and put it carefully in my bosom.

I passed some days in recovering from the fatigue of my journey ; after which I began to visit my former acquaintance. I abandoned myself to all kind of pleasure, and insensibly squandered away all my money. In this situation, instead of selling my furniture, I resolved to dispose of the necklace ; but I was so little acquainted with pearls that I acted very indiscreetly, as you shall hear.

I went to the bezestein, where, taking the crier aside, I showed him the necklace, told him I wished to sell it, and desired him to offer it to the principal jewellers. He conducted me to a shop, which proved to be my landlord's. " Wait here," he said, " I will soon return, and bring you an answer."

While in the most secret manner he went from merchant to merchant, I sat with the jeweller, and we began a conversation on different topics. The crier returned, and taking me aside, instead of telling me that the necklace was valued, at least, at two thousand sherriffs, he assured me that nobody would give me more than fifty. " The reason they assign is," added he, " that the pearls are false ; so it is for you to determine whether you will part with it at that price." Believing the crier to be a man of veracity, and wanting money, " Go," said I—" I trust to your word, and their better judgment—deliver it to them, and bring me the money immediately."

The crier had been directed to tender me fifty sherriffs by the richest jeweller of the bezestein, who had made that offer merely to ascertain if I knew the value of the article I exposed to sale. He had no sooner received my answer, than he took the crier to the police-judge ; and showing him the necklace, " Sir," said he, " here is a necklace which was stolen from me ; and the thief, disguised as a merchant, has had the impudence to offer it to sale, and is actually in the bezestein. He is willing," continued he, " to take fifty sherriffs for a jewel that is worth two thousand ; nothing could more clearly prove him a thief."

The justice sent immediately to apprehend me ; and when I appeared before him, he asked me if the necklace he held in his hand was not the same that I had offered for sale in the bezestein. I replied in the affirmative. " Is it true," continued he, " that you were willing to part with it for fifty sherriffs ?" I answered, it was. " Well," said he, scoffingly, " give him the bastinado ; he will soon acknowledge, with all his merchant's fine clothes, that he is an arrant thief ; let him be beaten till he confess." The violence of the blows made me tell a falsehood ; I declared, contrary to truth, that I had stolen the necklace, and immediately the judge ordered my hand to be cut off.

On the third day after this dreadful transaction, I saw with astonishment, a party of people belonging to the police-justice, accompanied by my landlord and the merchant, enter my house. I demanded what they wanted ; but, instead of answering, they bound me, applying to me the most opprobrious epithets, and telling me that the necklace belonged to the governor of Damascus, who had lost it about three years before, at which time one of his daughters had disappeared. " I will tell the governor the truth," said I to myself ; " he will then use his own discretion to put me to death, or to pardon me."

When I was conducted before him, I observed that he regarded me with an eye of compassion, whence I augured favourably. He ordered me to be unbound ; and addressing himself to the jeweller, my accuser, and to my landlord, " Is this the man," said he, " who exposed the pearl-necklace to sale ?" They had no sooner answered affirmatively, than he continued : " I am certain he did not steal the necklace, and am much astonished at the great injustice he has suffered." Encouraged by these words, " Sir," cried I, " I swear to you, I am, in effect, perfectly innocent : I am likewise persuaded that the necklace did not belong to my accuser, whom I never saw, and whose horrible perfidiousness has been the cause of my undeserved treatment." " I know enough already," replied the governor, " to accord you one part of the justice that is due to you. Take hence," continued he, " the false accuser, and let him undergo the same punishment he caused to be inflicted on this young man, whose innocence is known to me."

The governor's order was immediately executed ; the jeweller was taken away, and punished according to his desert. Then the governor, having ordered all the people to withdraw, said to me, " My son, tell me without fear how this necklace came into your possession ; conceal no part of the circumstance from me." I accordingly related to him candidly all that had passed ; and declared I had chosen rather to be considered a thief, than to reveal that tragical adventure. " Great God !" exclaimed the governor, when I had ceased speaking, " thy judgments are incomprehensible, and we ought to submit to them without murmuring !" Then directing his discourse to me, " Know," said he, " that I am the father of the two young ladies of whom you have been speaking. The first lady, who had the impudence to go to your house, was my eldest daughter. I had given her in marriage to one of her cousins. Her husband dying, she returned home, corrupted with all kinds of wickedness, which she had imbibed in Egypt. Before her arrival, her youngest sister was a very prudent woman, and had never given me the smallest occasion to complain of her conduct. But her eldest sister rendered her as wicked as herself.

The day after the death of the younger, not finding her at table, I inquired for her of her eldest sister, who had returned home. " My father," replied she, sobbing, " I can only tell you that my sister put on her best clothes yesterday, with her beautiful pearl-necklace, went abroad, and has not appeared since." I made search for my daughter all over the town, but could obtain no information respecting her unhappy fate. However, my son," added he, " since we are both equally unfortunate, let us unite our sorrows, and not abandon one another. I have a third daughter, whom I give you in marriage ; she is younger than her sisters, and bears no resemblance to them in her conduct. She has even more beauty than they had ; and, I assure you, she is of a disposition proper to render you happy. You shall reside in my house ; and, after my death, you and she shall be my sole heirs." He immediately called for witnesses ; and I espoused his daughter.

He was not satisfied with punishing the jeweller who had falsely accused me, but confiscated for my benefit all his goods, which were very considerable. I must tell you, further, that a man who was sent by my uncles to Egypt,

expressly to search for me, discovered me in passing through this city, and last night delivered me a letter from them. They apprised me of my father's death, and invited me to go and take possession of his estate at Moussol. But as the alliance and friendship of the governor have attached me to him, and will not permit me to leave him, I have sent back the express, with an order which will secure to me my right.

* * * * * * * * *

The sultan of Casgar was well pleased with this last story. "I must allow," said he to the Jew, "that what you have related is extraordinary; but I declare frankly that I think that of little hump-back yet more so; therefore, do not expect that I will grant you your life, any more than the rest :—I will hang you all four." "Stop, I beg, sir!" cried the tailor, advancing, and prostrating himself at the sultan's feet: "since your majesty is amused with pleasant stories, those which I have to recount will not, I trust, be disagreeable." Then, as if certain of success, he spoke in these terms :—

THE STORY TOLD BY THE TAILOR.

IR,—A citizen of this city did me the honour, two days ago, to invite me to a treat, which he proposed giving to his friends yesterday morning. Accordingly I went at an early hour, and found there twenty persons.

The master of the house had left home on some business; but he soon returned, accompanied by a young stranger, very well dressed, and handsome, but lame. As he entered, we all arose; and, to show respect to our friend, invited the young gentleman to sit with us upon the sofa. He was going to comply; when, perceiving a barber, who was in our company, he retired quickly, and approached the door. The master of the house, surprised at his conduct, stopped him: "Where are you going?" said he: "I brought you with me, to honour the entertainment; and you are scarcely here, when you would leave us!" "Sir," replied the young man, "for God's sake do not detain me; but permit me to leave you. I cannot see without horror that abominable barber: though born in a country where all the natives are whites, he resembles an Ethiopian; while his soul is yet blacker, and more horrible, than his face."

The master of the house having entreated the stranger to tell us what cause he had for hating the barber, "Gentlemen," he replied, "you must know that this cursed barber occasioned my lameness, through the most cruel proceeding that can be imagined: I have, in consequence, made an oath always to avoid him, and even not to remain in a town where he resides. It was for this reason that I quitted Bagdad, where he then dwelt; and travelled so far, to settle in this city. I find him here. This obliges me, gentlemen, much against my will, to deprive myself of the honour of being merry with you." On concluding these words, he would have departed; but the master detained him, entreating him to stay, and relate the cause of his detestation for the barber. We joined our solicitations, and at length the young man sat down on the sofa, and gave us the following account :—

STORY OF THE LAME YOUNG MAN OF BAGDAD.

Y father's consideration would have entitled him to the highest posts in the city of Bagdad; but he always preferred a quiet life to all the honours he might deserve. I was his only child; and when he died, I was of age to dispose of the great wealth he had left me.

I had not yet been disturbed with passion: I was so far from being sensible to love, that I cautiously avoided the conversation of women. One day, in the street, I saw a great company of ladies advancing towards me; and, that I might not meet them, turned down a narrow lane, and seated myself on a bench near a door. Opposite to me was a window, where stood a vase with very fine flowers; and my eyes were fixed upon this, when suddenly the window opened, and a young lady of dazzling beauty appeared. She immediately cast her eyes upon me, and regarded me with a smile that inspired me with as much love for her, as I formerly had of dislike for all women. She reclosed the window, and left me in inconceivable trouble and disorder.

I might have remained there a long time, if a noise in the streets had not recalled my faculties. Rising, I turned my head, and saw the chief cadi mounted on a mule, and accompanied by five or six attendants, approaching. He alighted at the door of the house at which the young lady had opened the window, and entered; whence I concluded he was her father.

I returned home agitated by a passion, of so much the more violence, as I had never before felt its effects. I went to bed with a violent fever, which caused all the family great affliction. My relations, who loved me, began to despair of my life, when an old lady of their acquaintance, hearing of my illness, came to visit me. She considered me with great attention; and, after having well examined me, ascertained, I know not how, the occasion of my illness. Taking my relations aside, she begged they would leave her alone with me, at the same time desiring the attendants to retire.

When everybody had quitted the room, she sat down at the side of my bed: "My son," said she, "you have hitherto obstinately concealed the cause of your illness; and I do not desire you to reveal it to me : I have sufficient experience to penetrate this secret which you will not disown, when I tell you that love has occasioned your indisposition."

In fine, the good lady told me so many other circumstances that I broke silence, declared to her my distress, informed her of the place where I had seen the object which caused it, and detailed all the circumstances of my adventure : "If you succeed," said I, "and procure me the happiness of seeing that charming beauty, and revealing to her the passion with which I burn, you may command my gratitude." "My son," replied the old lady, "I know the person of whom you speak; she is, as you rightly judged, daughter of the first cadi of this city. Would to God you had loved some other lady! then I should not have had so many difficulties to surmount as I anticipate. However, I will employ all my skill to accomplish your happiness: time only is required. In the meanwhile, take courage, and place confidence in me."

The old lady took leave of me. Next day she visited me again, and I read in her countenance that she had nothing favourable to impart. In effect, she thus addressed me :—" My son, I was not deceived in my opinion; I have more to conquer than the vigilance of a father; you love an insensible girl, who derives pleasure from making all burn with love that suffer themselves to be charmed by her. She heard me with satisfaction, while I spoke of the torment she had made you suffer; but I had no sooner attempted to induce her to allow of your seeing her, than she said, with a terrible look, " You are very bold to make such a proposal to me ! I desire you never to see me again, if you wish to introduce such discourse."

To shorten my narration (said the young man), this good comforter made several fruitless attempts in my behalf with the proud enemy of my repose. The chagrin I suffered in consequence inflamed my distemper to such a degree that I was absolutely abandoned by the physicians. I was then regarded as a man devoted to certain death, when the old lady came to give me life.

That no person might understand what was said, she whispered in my ear, " Remember, you owe me a present for the good news I now bring you. Yesterday, being Monday, I went to visit the lady you love, and I found her in good humour. When I arrived, I assumed a sad countenance, heaved many deep sighs, and let fall some tears. " My good mother," said she, " what distresses you? Why are you so afflicted ?" " Alas, my dear," replied I, " I am just returned from the house of the young gentleman, of whom I spoke to you the other day : his doom is fixed; love for you will cost him his life." The fear of your death alarmed her, and I saw her face change colour. " Is what you say true ?" she asked ; " and has he positively no other complaint than what is occasioned by his love for me ?" " Ah, madam!" replied I, " it is too true; would to God it were false!" " Do you believe," said she, " that the hope of seeing and speaking to me would contribute towards rescuing him from the danger he is in ?' " Perhaps it might," I replied ; " and, by your orders, I would try the remedy." " Well," said she, sighing, " give him the hope of seeing me, but he must not pretend to other favours, unless he aspire to marry me, and my father give his consent to our union." " Madam," replied I, " your goodness is very great : I will go to the young gentleman, and acquaint him that he is to have the happiness of an interview with you." " The most convenient time I can appoint," said she, " for granting him that favour, is next Friday during noon-prayer. Let him observe when my father goes to the mosque, and then place himself opposite the house. When he comes, I shall see him from my window, and will go down, and open the door to him. We can then converse together during prayer time; but he must quit the house before my father returns." " It now is Tuesday," continued the old lady, " you have from this time to Friday to recruit your strength."

Friday morning the old lady appeared as I was beginning to dress, and selecting the most elegant clothes from my wardrobe, " I do not inquire," said she, " respecting your health; your occupation clearly indicates an amendment. But will you not bathe before you go to the house of the first cadi ?" " That will occupy too much time," I replied; " I shall content myself with employing a barber to shave my head and beard.' I immediately ordered one of my slaves to fetch a barber, who was expert in his profession, and very expeditious.

The slave brought me this wretch you see here, who, after saluting me, said, " Sir, you appear to be unwell." I replied, I had just recovered from a fit of sickness. " I wish," said he, " God may deliver you from every misfortune, and that his grace may always accompany you. Now please to tell me what service I am to perform: I have brought my razors and my lancets. Do you desire to be shaved or to be bled ?"

The barber employed a long while opening his case, and preparing his razors, when, instead of putting water into the basin, he took a very handsome astrolabe from his pocket, and went very gravely out of my room to the middle of the court, to obtain the height of the sun. He returned with the same gravity, and entering my room, " Sir," said he, " you will be very glad to learn that this day is Friday, the 18th of the month Safœ, in the year 653, since the retreat of our great prophet from Mecca to Medina, and in the year 7320 of the epocha of the great Iskender with two horns; that the conjunction of Mars and Mercury signifies you cannot choose a better time than this day, and this very hour, for beings shaved. But, on the other hand, the same conjunction is a bad presage to you. I learn thence, that this day you run a great risk not indeed of losing your life, but of an inconvenience which will attend you while you live."

You may conceive my vexation at having fallen into the hands of such a prattling extravagant barber I was quite irritated. " I do not trouble my head," said I, angrily, " with either your advice or your predictions: I did not send for you to consult your astrology ; you came hither to shave me; therefore, shave me, or begone, and I will call another barber." " Sir," returned he, with an indifference that made me lose all patience, " what reason have you to be angry with me? Are you unapprised that all barbers are not like me; and that you will scarcely find such another, if you were expressly to search ? You wanted only a barber; and you have, in my person, the best barber in Bagdad; an experienced physician; a very profound chemist; an infallible astrologer; a finished grammarian; a perfect orator; a subtle logician; a mathematician perfectly versed in geometry, arithmetic, astronomy, and all the refinements of algebra; an historian, who is acquainted with the histories of all the kingdoms of the universe."

He did not stop there ; for, beginning another harangue, he spun it out for a full half-hour. Fatigued with hearing him, and distressed by seeing the time elapse, while I was yet undressed, I scarcely knew what to say " No," I exclaimed, " it is impossible there should be another such a man in the world, who finds pleasure, as you do, in driving people to distraction."

Thinking that I might succeed better if I dealt mildly with the barber, " In the name of God," said I, " cease your fine discourses, and despatch me quickly ; I am engaged to attend an affair of the last importance, as I have already told you." He then began to laugh : " It would be a happy circumstance," said he, " if our minds were always uniform—if we were constantly wise and prudent ; however, I am willing to believe, if you are angry with me, it is your distemper which has caused that change in your humour; you therefore need some instructions, and you cannot follow a better example than that of your father and your grandfather. They consulted me upon all occasions ; and I can say without vanity that they always extolled my counsels."

" What! cannot I prevail on you ?" said I, interrupting him ; " no more of these tedious discourses, which tend to nothing but to tear my head to pieces, and to detain me from attending my engagement. Shave me, or begone !" Saying this, I started up in a passion, stamping my foot on the ground.

When he saw I was seriously angry, " Sir," said he, " be not offended, we are going to begin." In effect, he washed my head, and began to shave me; but he had not taken four sweeps with his razor, when he stopped saying, " Sir, you are hasty; you should avoid these transports which come from the devil. Besides, my merit claims some respect, in consideration of my age, my knowledge, and my shining virtues."

" Go on shaving me !" cried I, again interrupting him, " and speak no more !" " That is to say," replied he, " as you have some urgent business to attend :—I will lay you a wager I have guessed right." " Why, I told you so two hours ago," said I ; " and you ought to have shaved me long since." " Moderate your warmth," replied he ; " perhaps you have not maturely considered the affair you are engaged in; when things are done precipitately, they generally bring repentance. I wish you would tell me what the concern is, in which you are so earnest; I would give you my opinion of it. Besides, you have time enough, as your appointment is not till noon, which is three hours hence."

He quitted his razor once more, and seizing the astrolabe a second time, left me half shaved to go and ascertain precisely what o'clock it was. Back he came : " Sir," said he, " I well know I was not mistaken ; it wants three hours of noon ;—I am sure of it, or all the rules of astronomy are false." " Just Heaven !" cried I, " my patience is exhausted ; I can refrain no longer. You cursed barber ! you barber of mischief! I can scarcely forbear throwing myself upon me, and strangling you." " Softly, sir," said he, very calmly, without being disturbed by my passion: " are you not afraid of a relapse? Do not be in a passion ; you will be finished in a minute." " You tell me what business you have at noon, I would give you some advice that might be of service to you." To satisfy him, I told him I was going to meet some friends, who were to regale me, and rejoice with me upon the recovery of my health.

When the barber heard me talk of regaling, " God bless you this day, as well as all other days!" cried he. " You remind me that yesterday I invited four or five friends to come and eat with me this day, at my house; I had forgotten it, and have as yet made no preparation." " Let not that trouble you," said I ; " though I dine abroad, my larder is always well furnished. I make you a present of what is in it; and I will order you as much wine as you can drink."

He was not satisfied with my promise merely : " God reward you, sir," said he, " for your kindness ! but pray show me the provisions now, that I may see if there will be sufficient to entertain my friends : I would have them contented with the good cheer I give them." " I have," replied I, " a lamb, six capons, a dozen of pullets, and the necessary accompaniments to form four services ;" at the same time ordering a slave to bring all before him, with four large pitchers of wine. " It is very well," said the barber; " but we shall want fruit, and sauce for the meat. I desired he might have what he demanded. He then ceased shaving me, to examine every article one after another ; and as this survey occupied nearly half an hour, I raged, I stormed; but to no purpose, the tormentor was totally unconcerned. He at length took up his razor again, and shaved me for some moments; when stopping suddenly, " I could not have believed, sir," said he, " that you were so liberal! Certainly I am undeserving the favours with which you have loaded me; and I assure you I shall hold them in perpetual remembrance. For, sir, to be explicit, I have nothing but what I receive through the generosity of obliging gentlemen, like you ; in which I may be compared to Zantout; who attends people in the bath ; to Sali, who sells parched peas in the streets ; to Salouz, who sells beans ; to Akerscha, who sells vegetables ; to Abou Mekarez, who waters the streets to lay the dust; and to Cassem, the caliph's lifeguardman. Of all these persons not one is ever melancholy; they are never peevish nor quarrelsome ; they are always gay, and ready to dance or to sing ; and they have their particular songs and dances with which they divert the city of Bagdad; but what I esteem most in them is, that

they are not great talkers, no more than your slave who has now the honour to speak to you. Hold, sir, here are the song and the dance of Zantout; observe me, and see if I do not imitate him exactly."

The barber sung the song, and danced the dance of Zantout; and, whatever I could say to induce him to end his buffooneries, he would not cease till he had imitated, in like manner, the songs and dances of the other people he had named. After which, addressing himself to me, "I have invited," said he, "all these honest persons to my house: if you take my advice, you will join us, and shun your friends, who perhaps are noisy prattlers, that will only tease you to death with their tiresome discourses, and cause you an illness worse than that from which you have so lately recovered; whereas at my house, you will have nothing but pleasure."

Notwithstanding my anger, I could not avoid laughing at the fellow's impertinence. "I wish I had no business upon my hands," said I, "and I would accept the proposal you make me; I would accompany you with all my heart; but I must beg to be excused to-day, I am too much engaged: another day I shall be more at leisure, and then we will make the party. Come finish shaving me, and hasten to return home; your friends are perhaps already at your house."

"Since you will not come to my house," replied the barber, "I beg you will permit me to accompany you. I will carry what you have given me to my house, where my friends may eat of them if they choose, and I will return immediately." "Heavens!" cried I, "cannot I, then, deliver myself from the persecutions of this troublesome man to-day! Go to your friends: drink, eat, and be merry with them; and leave me at liberty to see mine. I wish to be alone, I have no occasion for company; besides, I must tell you, at the place to which I am going, you would not be received; no person can be admitted besides myself." "You jest, sir," said he; "if your friends have invited you to a feast, why should you hinder me accompanying you? You will please them, I am certain, by taking thither a man so humorous as me, and who knows how to divert company agreeably. Whatever you say to me, the matter is determined. I will go with you in spite of opposition."

These words embarrassed me very much. "How shall I avoid this cursed barber!" thought I to myself; "unless I seriously quarrel with him, our contest will never be ended." Besides, I then heard the first call to noon-prayer, and it was time for me to set out. However, I resolved to dissemble, and appear as if I consented to his going. As he had now finished shaving me, I said to him, "Take some of my servants, to carry these provisions with you, and return hither; I will wait, and shall not go without you."

At length he went, and I quickly completed my dressing. I heard the last call to prayer, and hastened to get away; but the malicious barber, suspecting my intention, had proceeded with my servants only within sight of his house, where he stood till he saw them enter. He concealed himself at the turning of a street, to observe and follow me; in fine, when I reached the cadi's door, I looked back, and saw him at the entry of the street, which vexed me excessively.

The cadi's door was half open, and, on entering, I saw an old woman waiting for me, who after shutting the door, conducted me to the chamber of the young lady with whom I was in love; but I had scarcely begun the conversation, when we heard a noise in the street. The young lady put her head to the window, and saw through the blinds that it was the cadi, her father, returning already from prayer. I looked at the same time, and perceived the barber sitting opposite the house, in the same place whence I had first seen the young lady.

As soon as the cadi entered his house, he himself bastinadoed a slave who had offended. The slave uttered loud shrieks, which were heard in the street, and the barber thought it was me who cried out, and that I was maltreated. Prepossessed with this opinion, he screamed out horribly, rent his clothes, and threw dust upon his head, summoning all the people in the neighbourhood to his assistance. They assembled immediately, and inquired what afflicted him. "Alas!" answered he, "they are assassinating my master, my dear patron!" and without saying anything more, he ran, repeating the same cry to my house, whence he presently returned, followed by all my domestics, armed with clubs. They knocked with fury at the door of the cadi, who sent a slave to inquire the reason; but the slave being terrified, returned to his master, exclaiming, "Sir, above ten thousand men are forcibly breaking into your house!"

Immediately the cadi himself opened the door, and asked what they wanted. His venerable presence could not inspire my people with respect: "You cursed cadi!" said they, "what right had you to assassinate our master? How has he injured you?" "Good people," replied the cadi, "why should I assassinate your master, whom I do not know, and who has done me no offence? My house is open to you; come in, see, and search." "You bastinadoed him," said the barber; "I heard his cries not a minute since." "But pray," replied the cadi, "of what offence could your master be guilty, to occasion my abusing him in the manner you represent? Is he in my house? If he is, how came he in, or who could have introduced him?" "Ah! wretched cadi," cried the barber, "your long beard shall never make me believe you! What I say, I know to be true; your daughter is in love with our master, and gave him a meeting during the time of noon-prayer, of which you, without doubt, have been informed: you returned home and surprised him, and made your slaves bastinado him; but your wicked action shall not pass with impunity; the caliph shall know it, and he will give true and brief justice." "There is no occasion for so many words," replied the cadi, "nor for so great a noise. If what you assert be true, go in and seek for him; I give you permission." The cadi had scarcely uttered these words, when the barber and my domestics rushed into the house like furies, and commenced their search.

As I had heard all that the barber said to the cadi, I sought for a place to secrete myself; but could only find a large empty trunk, in which I lay down, and closed it upon me. The barber, after searching everywhere, entered the chamber where I was; when, having opened the trunk, and discovered me, he took it upon his head, and carried it away. He ascended a high staircase leading to a court, which he speedily crossed, and reached the street-door. While he thus carried me, the trunk unfortunately opened, and unable to endure the shame of being exposed to the view and shouts of the mob that followed us, I leaped out into the street with so much precipitation that I hurt my leg in such a manner that I have been lame ever since. I was not at first sensible of the extent of the injury, and therefore arose immediately, to avoid the populace by a hasty flight. I threw several handfuls of gold and silver of which my purse was full among them; and whilst they were gathering up the money, I escaped by cross-streets and alleys. But the cursed barber profiting by the stratagem to which I had had recourse to get away from the mob, followed without losing sight of me, calling out, as loud as he possibly could, "Stop, sir, why do you run so fast? Did I not truly inform you that you would expose your life, by your obstinate refusal to let me accompany you? All this happened through your own fault; and if I had not resolutely followed you, to see whither you went, what would have become of you?"

Thus the unlucky barber cried aloud in the street. My rage was so great that I had almost determined to wait for, and strangle him; but I should, by that proceeding, have only rendered my confusion more conspicuous. I adopted a different course; for perceiving that his calling after me exposed me to the rude gaze of numbers of people, I entered a khan, or inn, the chamberlain of which knew me. Finding him at the gate, "In the name of God!" cried I, "have the goodness to hinder that madman from following me here." He promised me, and kept his word, though not without great trouble; for the obstinate barber would enter in spite of him, and did not, at length, retire, without bestowing on him a thousand opprobrious names.

I quitted Bagdad, and came hither. I had reason to hope I should not meet with the pernicious barber in a country so distant from my own; and yet I find him in your company! Be not surprised, then, at my anxiety to retire : you may readily conceive how unpleasant to me is the sight of a man who was the occasion of my lameness, and of my being reduced to the melancholy necesssity of living far separated from kindred, friends, and country.

    *   *   *   *   *   *

As soon as the lame young man had finished his relation, (continued the tailor,) he arose, and went out, the master of the house conducting him to the gate, and expressing his regret that he had, though innocently, occasioned him so great mortification.

The young man having quitted the house, we remained in the utmost astonishment at his story. Casting our eyes on the barber, we told him he had acted very wrong, if what we had just heard was true. "Gentlemen," replied he, raising his head, which till then he had held down, "my silence during the young man's discourse is sufficient to testify that he advanced nothing untrue. But, notwithstanding all he has said to you, I maintain that I acted precisely as I ought. Has he any reason to complain of me, or to treat me with such harsh expressions? Those are the returns of ungrateful people! He accuses me of being a prattling fellow, which is a mere calumny. Of seven brothers, I am he who speaks the least, and who has most wit for his share. To convince you, gentlemen, of the truth of my assertion, I need only relate my own story, and the histories of my brothers. Honour me, I beseech you, with your attention.

THE STORY OF THE BARBER.

NDER the reign of the Caliph Monstanser Billah, ten highwaymen infested the roads about Bagdad, and for a long time committed the most atrocious robberies and cruelties. The caliph being apprised of these disorders, sent for the judge of the police, and ordered him, on pain of death, to apprehend the whole ten, and bring them before him.

The police-judge used so much diligence, and despatched so many people round the country, that the ten robbers were taken on the day of Bairam. I was then walking on the banks of the Tigris, and saw ten men, richly apparelled, enter a boat. I might have known they were robbers, had I observed the guards that accompanied them; but I looked only at them; and thinking they were people who had determined to pass the festival-day in jollity, I stepped into the boat with them, in hopes they would allow me to be one of the party. We proceeded down the Tigris, and landed before the caliph's palace. On quitting the boat, we were surrounded by police-guards, who bound us all.

As soon as we were before the caliph, "Let the heads of the ten highwaymen," said he, "be cut off." The executioner immediately arranged us in a row within reach of his arm, and by good fortune I was the last. He decapitated the ten highwaymen, beginning at the first; and when he came to me, he stopped. The caliph, perceiving that he hesitated to strike me, was angry: "Did I not command you," said he, "to cut off the heads of ten highwaymen, and why have you performed the sentence but on nine?" "Commander of the faithful," replied the executioner, "here are ten bodies on the ground, and as many heads which I cut off; your majesty may count them." When the caliph himself saw that the executioner had declared the truth, he looked at me with amazement; and perceiving that I had not the countenance of a robber, "Good old man," said he, "how came you with those wretches, who have deserved a thousand deaths?" "Commander of the faithful," I replied, "I will make a true confession. This morning I saw those ten persons take boat: I embarked with them, persuaded that they were going to regale themselves, in honour of this day, which is the most celebrated of our religion."

The caliph could not forbear laughing at my adventure; and, so different to the behaviour of the young man who treated me as a prattling fellow, he admired my discretion and constant silence. "Commander of the faithful,' said I, "your majesty need not be surprised at my keeping silence on an occasion that would have extorted speech from any one. I make a particular profession of holding my tongue, and, on that account, have acquired the glorious title of *Silent* : thus am I called, to distinguish me from my six brothers. "I am very well pleased," said the caliph, smiling, "that they have given you a title of which you make such good use. But tell me what sort of men were your brothers—were they like you?" "By no'means," replied I : "they were all of them addicted to prattling, and as to their persons, there was a still greater difference between us and me : —the first was hump-backed, the second was toothless, the third had but one eye, the fourth was blind, the fifth had his ears cut off, and the sixth had hare lips." As it appeared to me that the caliph wished to hear their stories, I proceeded without waiting his order :—

THE STORY OF THE BARBER'S ELDEST BROTHER.

IR (said I), my eldest brother, whose name was Bacbouc the Hump-back, was a tailor by trade. At the expiration of his apprenticeship, he hired a shop opposite a mill; but, as he had yet but few connexions, he could scarcely maintain himself. The miller, on the contrary, was wealthy, and had a very handsome wife. One day, as my brother was at work in his shop, he saw the miller's wife looking out of the window, and was charmed with her beauty. The woman did not notice him, but closed her window, and appeared no more at it all that day. In the evening, when it was necessary to close his shop, he could scarcely resolve to do so, still hoping to see the miller's wife once more; but he was forced to shut up, and retire to his little house, where he passed a very uncomfortable night. He arose early in the morning, and so impatient was he to obtain a sight of his mistress, that he ran all the way to his shop; but he was no happier than on the day preceding, for the miller's wife appeared at the window only for one moment during the day; but that moment rendered the tailor the most amorous of men.

No sooner had the miller's wife penetrated my brother's sentiments than she resolved to make them her diversion She accordingly regarded him with a smiling countenance, and my brother looked at her in the same manner, but so ridiculously that the miller's wife was compelled to close her window, lest her loud laughter should expose her humour.

The miller's wife then determined to amuse herself with my brother. She had a piece of very fine stuff, of which she had long designed to have a habit made. Having enclosed it in a handkerchief, she sent it to him by a young slave, who, being taught her lesson, proceeded to the tailor's shop. "My mistress presents her compliments," said she, "and begs you to make her a habit of this stuff, according to the pattern which I have brought. She often changes her clothes, so that her custom must be very profitable to you." My brother no longer doubted that the miller's wife loved him. Full of this opinion, he charged the slave to tell her mistress that he would lay aside all other work to attend to her order, and that the habit should be ready by the next morning. In effect, he worked at it with so much diligence that he finished it the same day.

Next morning the slave presented herself to see if the habit were ready. Bacbouc gave it to her neatly folded up, saying, "I have too much interest in pleasing your mistress, to neglect her business. I would engage her, by my assiduity, to employ no one but myself in future." The young slave receded some steps, as if going, but returning, she whispered my brother, "Apropos, I had forgotten part of my commission. My mistress charged me with her compliments to you, and to inquire how you passed the night; as for her, poor woman, she loves you so ardently that she could not sleep." "Tell her," answered my silly brother, with transport, "my passion for her is so violent that I have not closed an eye during the last four nights."

A quarter of an hour had not elapsed from the departure of the slave, when my brother saw her returning with a piece of satin. "My mistress," said she, "is very well pleased with her habit—nothing could fit her better; but, as it is very fine, she cannot wear it without new drawers, and she begs you to make her a pair directly of this piece of satin." "Enough," replied Bacbouc, "they shall be done before I leave my shop: you have only to fetch them in the evening." The miller's wife presented herself often at her window, was very prodigal of her charms, and to encourage my brother, appeared as if she found pleasure in seeing him work. The drawers were soon completed, and the slave fetched them, but brought the tailor no money, either for the trimming he had purchased, or for his labour. In the meantime, this unfortunate lover, whom they only amused, though he could not perceive the deception, had eaten nothing all that day, and was obliged to borrow money at night to buy his supper. Next morning, as soon as he entered his shop, the young slave arrived, to inform him that the miller wished to speak with him. "My mistress," continued she, "praised you so much, when she showed him your work, that he also has resolved to employ you." My brother was easily persuaded, and accompanied the slave to the mill. The miller received him very kindly, and presented to him a piece of cloth. "I want some shirts," said he; "there is the cloth; I wish you to make me twenty. If any of the stuff should remain, you will return it."

My brother had now work sufficient for five or six days, to make twenty shirts for the miller, who afterwards gave him another piece of cloth, to make him as many pairs of drawers. When they were finished, Bacbouc carried them to the miller, who asked him the amount of his demand. My brother replied, he would be content with twenty drachms of silver. The miller immediately called the young slave, and desired her to bring him the scales, that they might see the money he was going to pay was weight. The slave, who had learned her lesson, regarded my brother with an angry countenance, to signify he would ruin all if he received the money. He understood her meaning, and refused to take any, though so much distressed that he was obliged to borrow money to purchase the thread with which he sewed the shirts and drawers.

The miller's wife was both avaricious and wicked, for, not content with cheating my brother of his due, she incited her husband to be revenged for the love he showed to her, and they thus effected their determination. The miller invited Bacbouc one night to supper, and, after entertaining him in a very sorry manner, "Brother," said he, "it is too late for you to return home, you had best remain here." So saying, he conducted him to a place in the mill, where there was a bed; there he left him, and retired with his wife. At the middle of the night, the miller went to my brother, "Neighbour," said he, "are you asleep? My mule is ill, and I have a quantity of corn to grind, you would do me a great kindness if you would turn the mill in her stead." Bacbouc, to show his good nature, replied he was ready to perform what he required, if he would only instruct him how it was to be done. The miller then fastened him by the middle of the body, in the same manner as a mule, to turn the mill; and, giving him a severe lash on the back with a whip, "Go, neighbour!" said he. "Ho!" cried my brother, "why do you beat me?" "To make you active," replied the miller, "for without a whip, my mule will not move." Bacbouc was confounded at this treatment, but dared not complain. When he had proceeded five or six rounds, he wished to rest, but the miller gave him a dozen hearty lashes, saying, "Courage, neighbour! I beg you will not stop. You must continue your labour without delay, otherwise you will spoil my meal."

Bacbouc remained in this state for some time, till at length the young slave appeared and unfastened him. "Ah," cried the treacherous girl, "how my mistress and I have grieved for you. We had no concern in this wicked trick, which her husband has played you." The unhappy Bacbouc answered not a word, so much was he fatigued with work, and depressed by the treatment he had received, but crept home to his house, firmly resolving never more to think of the miller's wife.

The relation of this story (continued the barber) made the caliph laugh. "Go home," said he to me, "I have ordered something to be given you." "Commander of the faithful," replied I, "I beg your majesty not to require me to receive anything till I have recounted the history of my other brothers." The caliph having signified that he was willing to hear me, I thus proceeded :—

THE STORY OF THE BARBER'S SECOND BROTHER.

Y second brother, who was called Backbarah the Toothless, walking one day through the city, met an old woman in a by-street. She approached him. "If you have time to accompany me," said she, "I will conduct you to a magnificent palace, where you will see a lady fairer than the day. She will receive you with great pleasure, and present you with a collation and excellent wine. Backbarah having accepted the condition, they at length reached the gate of a large palace, where were many officers and domestics, some of whom would have stopped my brother; but, no sooner did the old woman speak to them, than they suffered him to pass. Then, turning to my brother, she said to him, "Remember, the young lady I conduct you to, loves mildness and discretion, and cannot endure to be contradicted: if you please her in your behaviour, you may be sure to obtain of her whatever you wish."

My brother, who had never before been in so superb a palace, gazed at the elegancies that were presented to his view, and was scarcely able to contain his joy. Presently he heard a great noise, occasioned by a troop of merry slaves, who came towards him with loud bursts of laughter, and, in the middle of them, he perceived a young lady of extraordinary beauty, who was easily known to be their mistress, by the respect they showed her. Backbarah, who expected a private conversation with the lady, was extremely surprised to find her surrounded by so much company. In the meantime, the slaves assumed a grave countenance as they approached; and, when the young lady was near the sofa, my brother, who had risen, made her a low bow. Having seated herself in the upper place, she begged him to sit down, and said to him, smiling, "I am extremely glad to see you, and wish you all the happiness you can desire."

She immediately commanded a collation to be brought, and a table was presently covered with baskets of fruit and confections. As he was placed opposite to her, when he opened his mouth to eat, she perceived his want of teeth, and, noticing it to her slaves, she and they laughed heartily. Backbarah, who occasionally lifted up his head to look at her, perceiving her merriment, thought it arose from the pleasure of his company, and flattered himself that she would soon send away her slaves, and remain with him alone.

The repast being finished, they arose from the table, when ten slaves, taking musical instruments, began to play and sing, while others danced. My brother, to render himself agreeable, likewise danced, and the young lady did the same. After they had continued this amusement some time, they seated themselves to recover breath; and the young lady, calling for a glass of wine, regarded my brother with a smile, to signify that she was going to drink his health. He rose up, and remained standing while she drank. When she had so done, instead of returning the

No. 18.

glass, she ordered it to be refilled, and presented it to my brother, that he might pledge her. He accordingly took the glass from the young lady's hand, which he kissed at the same time, and, standing, drank to her, in acknowledgment of the honour he had received. The young lady then made him sit near her, and began to caress him. She placed her hand behind his head, and patted him from time to time with her fingers. The young lady continued tapping him with her fingers, but at last gave him so rude a box on the ear, that he was offended. The colour appeared in his face, and he arose, to place himself at a greater distance from so unpleasant a playfellow. Then the old woman, who had conducted him thither, looked at him in a manner to signify he had acted wrong, and had forgotten the advice she gave him—to be very complaisant. He recollected his fault, and again approached the young lady. She drew him by the arm, made him reseat himself by her, and gave him a thousand malicious caresses. Her slaves, who only sought to amuse their mistress, took part in the diversion. One gave poor Backbarah fillips on the nose with all her strength; another pulled him by the ears, as if she would have torn, them off; and others boxed him, all which passed for raillery.

After this, the young lady commanded the slaves to renew their concerts. They obeyed; and, in the meantime, the lady called another slave, and ordered her to take my brother with her. "Do what you know," said she, " and, when you have finished, bring him back to me again." Backbarah, who heard this order, arose, and approaching the old woman, prayed her to tell him what they were going to do. "Our mistress is only a little curious," replied the old woman, softly. "She wishes to see how you will look in women's apparel; and this slave, who has orders to take you with her, is directed to paint your eyebrows, cut off your whiskers, and dress you like a female." "They may paint my eyebrows as much as they please," said my brother. "I consent to that, because I can remove the stain by washing; but, as to shaving me, that, you know, I ought not to permit." "Beware of refusing what is required of you," replied the old woman. Backbarah submitted, and, without saying a word, suffered himself to be conducted by the slave to a chamber, where they painted his eyebrows red, cut off his whiskers, and were proceeding to do the same with his beard. My brother's docility was now put to a severe trial. "Oh!" cried he "I absolutely will never part with my beard!" The slave told him that he had parted with his whiskers to no purpose, if he would not suffer his beard also to be removed, as a bearded visage would not accord with female habiliments. The old woman supported the slave's reasoning with fresh arguments, and concluded by menacing him with the loss of the young lady's regard. In fine, their reasoning prevailed, and he permitted them to act with him as they pleased.

When he was habited like a woman, they conducted him before the young lady, who laughed so heartily when she saw him, that she fell backwards on the sofa where she sat. The slaves also laughed, and clapped their hands, putting my brother quite out of countenance. The young lady recovered her seat, and, still laughing, said to him. "After the complaisance you have shown, I should be very much to blame not to love you with all my heart; but there is one thing more you must do for me, which is, to dance with us." He obeyed; and the young lady and her slaves danced with him, laughing as if they had been mad. After continuing this amusement some time, they all attacked the poor wretch, and gave him so many boxes on the ear, blows with the fist, and kicks with the foot, that he fell on the ground nearly deprived of his senses. The old woman assisted him to rise; "Console yourself," said she; "you have only one thing more to encounter, and that is trifling. My mistress has a whim, when she has drunk a little, as she has to-day, not to let those whom she loves approach her unless they be stripped to the shirt. When they are in that state, she takes a little advantage of them, running before them through the gallery, and from chamber to chamber, till they catch her. Whatever advantage she may have, your nimbleness will enable you soon to overtake her. Strip yourself, then, quickly to the shirt; undress yourself without ceremony."

My silly brother put off his clothes; and, in the meantime, the young lady was stripped to her chemise and under-petticoat, that she might run with the more facility. When they were ready to start, the young lady took an advantage of twenty paces, and began to run with surprising swiftness: my brother followed her as fast he could; while the slaves laughed aloud, clapping their hands. The young lady, instead of losing distance, gained upon my brother: she led him two or three times round the gallery; and then running into a long dark passage, escaped by a turning which she knew. Backbarah was obliged to slacken his pace on account of the darkness of the place: at length, perceiving a light, he directed his course towards it, and went out at a door, which was immediately shut upon him. You may conceive his astonishment at finding himself in a street inhabited by curriers, who were no less surprised to see him in his shirt, with his eyebrows painted red, and without either beard or mustaches. They began to hoot at him; and some of them ran after him, and lashed him with strips of leather. At length they stopped him, and placing him on an ass, which they met by chance, conveyed him through the town, exposed to the ridicule of the people.

To complete his misfortune, on passing the house of a justice of police, the magistrate desired to know the cause of the tumult. The curriers replied, that they saw my brother come out, in that condition, at the gate of the apartment of the grand-vizier's ladies, which opened into their street. At this information, the justice gave orders for the unhappy Backbarah to receive a hundred blows, with a cane, on the soles of his feet; and afterwards, sent him out of the town with an injunction never to return.

"Thus, commander of the faithful," said I, "I have given an account of the adventures of my second brother, who did not know that our greatest ladies sometimes divert themselves by putting such tricks upon young people, who are so foolish as to be caught in their snares.

*   *   *   *   *   *

THE STORY OF

THE BARBER'S THIRD BROTHER.

OMMANDER OF THE FAITHFUL (continued the barber to the caliph, without interrupting his discourse), my third brother, whose name was Bakbak, was blind, and his ill destiny reduced him to the hard necessity of begging from door to door. He had been so long habituated to walk through the streets alone, that he had no occasion for a conductor. His custom was to knock at people's doors, and not to reply till they were open to him. One day he thus presented himself at a house, the master of which was alone, who descended, opened the door, and asked my brother what he wanted. "That you would bestow your charity, for Heaven's sake!" replied Bakbak. "You appear to be blind," said the master of the house. 'Alas! too truly!" returned my brother. "Give me your hand," continued the housekeeper. My brother accordingly presented it, expecting to receive alms; but the man merely took it to assist him up to his chamber. Bakbak imagined he was taking him to eat with him, a treatment he had frequently experienced. When they reached the chamber, the man loosened my brother's hand, and sitting down, again asked him what he wanted. "I have already told you," replied Bakbak, "that I solicit something for the love of God." "Good blind man," returned the master of the house, "all that I can do for you, is to wish that God may restore you your sight." "You might have given me that answer at the door," said my brother, "and saved me the trouble of coming up. Assist me down stairs, then," continued Bakbak, "as you helped me up." "The stairs are before you," replied the housekeeper; "and you may descend alone, if you will." My brother attempted to do so; but, missing a step about the middle of the stairs, he fell to the bottom, and severely hurt his head and his back. Recovering his feet with much difficulty, he quitted the house, complaining and murmuring against the master, who only laughed at his misfortune.

As he went out, two blind men, his comrades, were passing, and knowing him by his voice, inquired what was the matter. He told them what had happened to him; and afterwards said, he had eaten nothing all that day: "I conjure you," continued he, "to go along with me to my house that I may take, while you are present, some of the money that we three have in common, to buy me something for supper." The two blind men consented, and accompanied him home.

You must know that the master of the house, where my brother had been so ill used, was a robber, naturally cunning and malicious. Having heard from his window what Bakbak had said to his companions, he descended and following them, entered, with them, a miserable house in which my brother resided. The blind men being seated, Bakbak said to them, "Brethren, it will be necessary to shut the door, and take care there be no stranger with us." At these words the robber was much perplexed; but perceiving a rope which chanced to hang from a beam, he caught hold of it, and suspended himself, while the blind men closed the door, and felt about the room with their sticks. When they had done this, and had retaken their places, the robber left the rope, and sat down softly by my brother, who thinking himself alone with his comrades, said to them, "Brothers, as you have deposited in my care the money which we all three have collected during a long time, I will convince you that I am not unworthy of your confidence. The last time we reckoned, you know we had ten thousand drachms, and that we put them into ten bags; I will prove to you that I have not touched one of them." So saying, he put his hand under some old lumber, and drawing out the bags, gave them to his comrades. "There they are," continued he, "you may judge by their weight that they are entire, or we will reckon them, if you please." His comrades having answered they did not doubt his honesty, he opened one of the bags, and took out ten drachms, each of the other blind men taking the same sum.

My brother then returned the bags to their place: after which one of the blind men told him there was no occasion to expend money for supper, as he had received as much victuals from charitable people as would serve all three. At the same time he drew from his bag, bread and cheese, and some fruit; and putting them all upon the table, they began to eat. The robber, who sat at my brother's right hand, picked out the best, and ate with them; but notwithstanding his care to avoid making a noise, Bakbak heard him eating, and immediately cried out, "We are undone! there is a stranger with us!" Saying this, he stretched out his hand, and seizing the robber by the arm, he threw himself on him, exclaiming, "Thieves!" at the same time beating him severely with his fist. The other blind men acted in like manner; while the highwayman, on his part, made the best defence he could; and having the advantage of sight, he dealt furious blows, calling out, "Thieves" louder than his antagonists. The neighbours were soon alarmed by the noise, and forcing open the door, demanded the cause of their quarrel. "Gentlemen," cried my brother, who had not quitted the robber, "this man is a thief, who entered here on purpose to deprive us of the little money we have." The robber, who had shut his eyes on the first appearance of the neighbours, feigned himself also blind; and said, "Gentlemen, he is liar. I swear to you that I am their associate, and they refuse to

give me my just share. They have all three conspired against me, and I demand justice." The neighbours would not interfere in their quarrel, but took them all to the police-judge.

When they were before the magistrate, the robber, without waiting to be interrogated, said, still feigning himself blind, "Sir, I declare to you that we are all equally criminal, but we have engaged, on oath, not to confess excepting we are bastinadoed ; so that you need only order us that punishment, and begin with me." My brother would have spoken, but was not permitted ; and the robber was put under the bastinado. He had the courage to bear twenty or thirty blows ; when, seeming to be overcome with pain, he first opened one eye, and soon afterwards the other ; and crying out for mercy, supplicated the judge to put a stop to the blows. The judge perceiving that he looked at him with his eyes open, was very much astonished. "Rogue !" said he, "what is the meaning of this miracle ?" "Sir," replied the robber, "I will discover to you an important secret, if you pardon me, and give me, as a pledge that you will keep your word, the seal-ring which you have on your finger."

The judge accordingly stopped the punishment, gave him his ring, and promised him pardon. "On the faith of this assurance," said the robber, "I will confess to you, sir, that I and my three comrades, all of us, see very well. We feigned ourselves blind, that we might freely enter people's houses. I will further confess to you that by this artifice we have gained ten thousand drachms. This day I demanded of my partners two thousand five hundred, which belongs to me as my share ; but when I insisted on having my right, they all three attacked and ill-treated me ; for the truth of which I appeal to those people who brought us before you. I expect from your justice, sir, that you will compel them to deliver me the two thousand five hundred drachms which are my due. If you desire that my comrades should corroborate what I have asserted, order them three times the number of blows I have received, and you will find they can see as well as myself."

My brother's asseverations were of no effect ; he and his comrades each received two hundred blows. The judge observed them attentively, expecting them to open their eyes, and ascribed to obstinacy what was in fact impossible. During this time the robber addressed the judge. "I perceive, sir," continued he, "that they will obstinately persist to the last, and will never open their eyes. It would, perhaps, be better to pardon them, and send some person with me to take the ten thousand drachms they have concealed."

The judge accordingly sent one of his people with the robber for the ten sacks ; and having counted out two thousand five hundred drachms for the informer, kept the rest himself. As for my brother and his two companions, he took pity on them, and only sentenced them to be banished.

* * * *

Thus I finished the sad adventure of my honest blind brother. The caliph laughed at it as heartily as at those he had before heard, and again ordered that something should be given to me ; but, without waiting, I began the history of my fourth brother.

THE STORY OF THE BARBER'S FOURTH BROTHER.

LCOUZ was the name of my fourth brother, who lost one of his eyes by an accident, of which I shall have the honour to acquaint your majesty. He was a butcher by profession, and had a particular talent for rearing and teaching rams to fight. He had likewise a very good trade ; and his shop was always full of the finest meat in the market, because he was very rich, and spared no expense to obtain the best.

One day, when he was in his shop, an old man, with a long white beard, entered, bought six pounds of meat of him, gave him money for it, and went away. My brother thought the the money so fine, so white, and so well coined, that he put it by in a chest, by itself. The old man continued to visit him every day, for five months successively, always buying a like quantity of meat, and paying for it in the same sort of money, which my brother carefully preserved.

At the end of five months Alcouz, wishing to purchase a number of sheep, and to pay for them in this fine coin, opened the trunk ; but, instead of finding the money, he was extremely surprised at seeing only a heap of leaves in the place where he had deposited it. In the greatest distress, he beat his head, and cried out aloud, which soon brought the neighbours about him, who were equally astonished when he related the circumstance. "Would to God," exclaimed my brother, weeping, "that this treacherous old fellow would come now, with his hypocritical looks !" He had scarcely ceased speaking, when he saw him approaching at a distance : he immediately ran to him, and seizing him, "Mussulmans," cried he, as loud as he could, "help ! hear what a deception this wicked fellow has practised upon me ;" at the same time telling a great crowd of people, who had assembled round him, what he had formerly related to his neighbours. When he had concluded, the old man very coolly said to him, "You would be wise to let me go, and by that means atone for the affront you have put upon me, before so many people, for fear I should be compelled, unwillingly, to retaliate." "How ?" replied my brother ; "what have you to say against me ? I am an honest tradesman, and fear you not." "You would have me tell it, then ?" said the old man, in the same tone ; and, turning to the crowd, "Know, good people," continued he, "that this fellow, instead of selling mutton, as he ought, sells human flesh." "You are a cheat !" exclaimed my brother. "No, no," replied the old man. "At this moment, while I am speaking to him there is a man, with his throat cut, hung up on the outside of his shop like a sheep. If any of you go thither, you will find what I say to be true."

Just before my brother had opened the chest, he had killed a sheep, dressed it, and exposed it without his shop, according to custom. He protested that what the old man said was false ; but, notwithstanding his asseverations the populace determined to investigate the truth of the accusation immediately. They ran like furies to his shop, where they saw a human body hung up, as the old man had represented ; for he was a magician, and deceived sight of all persons, as he had the eyes of my brother, when he made him take leaves instead of money.

At this spectacle one of the people who held Alcouz, said to him, giving him a severe blow with his fist, "So, you villain, it is thus you make us eat human flesh!" And the old man, who had not quitted him, gave him another blow, which beat out one of his eyes; while every person who could get near struck him; and, not content with this treatment, they took him before the police-judge. "Sir," said the old magician, "we have brought you a man who has the barbarity to murder people, and sell their flesh instead of mutton: the public expect that you will punish him in an exemplary manner." The judge heard my brother with patience; but his account of the money changed into leaves appeared so little worthy of credit, that he considered him as an impostor, and ordered him five hundred blows. He then, having obliged him to confess where his money was, seized it all, and banished him for ever, after making him ride three days through the town upon a camel, exposed to the derision of the people.

I was not at Bagdad when this tragical adventure happened to my fourth brother. He retired to a remote place, where he remained in concealment till he was cured of the terrible bruises. As soon as he was able to go abroad, he proceeded by night to a certain town, where he was entirely unknown, and there took lodgings which he seldom quitted. Becoming, at length, weary of this seclusion, he walked into one of the suburbs, where he was suddenly alarmed by the noise of horsemen approaching behind him. He was then near the gate of a large house; and apprehending that these horsemen were in pursuit of him, he opened the gate, in order to hide himself: after he had closed it, he entered a great court, where he had no sooner appeared, than two servants came, and taking him by the neck, "Heaven be praised," said they, "that you have surrendered yourself to us, of your own accord! You have terrified us so much during the last three nights, that we have had no sleep; nor would you have spared our lives, if we had not found means to guard against your wicked design."

You may well imagine my brother was much surprised at this address: "Good people," said he, "I cannot conceive what you mean; you certainly mistake me for another person!" "No, no," replied they, "we know very well that you and your comrades are arrant robbers. You were not contented with robbing our master of all he had, and reducing him to beggary, but you wished also to take his life!—let us see if you have not the knife about you, which you had in your hand when you pursued us last night." Saying this, they searched him, and found a knife. "Ho! ho!" cried they, "and dare you still say that you are not a robber?" "Why," replied my brother, "cannot a man carry a knife about him, without being a robber?" But, far from attending to his remonstrances, they fell upon him, trod him under foot, forced off his clothes, and tore his shirt. Then, seeing the scars on his back, "Ah, dog!" said they, redoubling their blows, "you would have us believe you an honest man, while your back proves the contrary." "Alas!" cried my poor brother, "my sins must be very great, since, after having been already abused so unjustly, I am ill-treated a second time, though not more culpable!"

The two servants, totally regardless of his complaint, took him before the police-judge, who gave orders that he should receive a hundred lashes over the shoulders, and afterwards be carried through the town on a camel, with a crier before him, proclaiming, *Thus are men punished, who enter people's houses by force.* This procession finished, they banished him the town, forbidding him ever to return.

The caliph (continued the barber) did not laugh so heartily at this story as at the others. He again expressed a wish to make me a compensation, and to send me away; but I continued my discourse. "My sovereign lord and master," said I, "since your majesty has been pleased to favour me with your attention so far, I beg you will likewise have the goodness to listen to the adventures of my two other brothers. You may make a complete history of them, which will not be unworthy of your library."

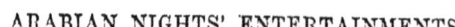

THE STORY OF THE BARBER'S FIFTH BROTHER.

ALNASCHAR, so long as our father lived, was extremely lazy: instead of working for his subsistence, he was in the habit of begging in the evening, and existing the next day on what he thus obtained. Our father died, and left among us seven hundred drachms of silver: we divided them equally, so that each of us had a hundred for his share. Alnaschar, who had never before possessed so much money at one time, was very much perplexed to determine what use he should make of it. After a long consultation with himself, he at last resolved to employ it in trade, and ventured it on glasses, bottles, and other similar articles. He put all in an open basket, and chose a very small shop, where he sat, with the basket before him, and his back against the wall, expecting customers to buy his ware. In this attitude he continued, with his eyes fixed on his goods; and, lost in a reverie, he pronounced the following words, loud enough to be heard by a neighbouring tailor: "This basket," said he, "cost me one hundred drachms, which is all the property I have in the world: I shall certainly make two hundred of it by retailing my glass; and of these two hundred, which I will again employ in glass, I shall make four hundred. Continuing thus, I shall at length amass four thousand drachms: of four thousand I can easily make eight thousand. When I have reached ten thousand, I will discontinue selling glass, and commence jeweller. I will trade in diamonds, pearls, and all sorts of precious stones. Nor will I stop here: I will, by the favour of Heaven, proceed till I am worth a hundred thousand drachms. When I have obtained so much, I shall think myself as great as a prince; and will send to demand the grand-vizier's daughter in marriage, representing to him that I have heard much of the wonderful beauty, modesty, wit, and all the other qualities of his daughter; in a word, I will give him a thousand pieces of gold the first night of our wedding. If the vizier be so uncivil as to refuse me his daughter, but which he cannot do, I will go and take her before his face, and carry her to my house in spite of him.

"As soon as I have married the grand-vizier's daughter, I will buy her ten young black eunuchs, the handsomest that can be found. I will clothe myself like a prince; and, mounted on a fine horse, with a saddle of pure gold, and housings of cloth of gold, enriched with diamonds and pearls, I will proceed through the city, attended by slaves before and behind: and I will go to the vizier's palace, in view of all descriptions of people, who will show me a profound reverence. When I reach the foot of the vizier's staircase, I will ascend in presence of all my people, ranged in files on each side; and the minister, receiving me as his son-in-law, will place me above him on his right hand, to do me the more honour. If this take place, as I hope it will, two of my people shall each of them carry a purse containing a thousand pieces of gold. I will present one of them to the grand-vizier:—'There,' I shall say to him, 'are the thousand pieces of gold which I promised for the first night of my marriage;' and then, offering him the other, 'There is as much more,' I shall say, 'to convince you that I am a man of my word, and that I give more than I promise.' After such an act as this, all the world will applaud my generosity.

"I shall always dress magnificently. When I retire with my wife in the evening, I will sit on the upper hand, and affect a grave air, without turning my head to either side. I will speak but little; and while my wife, beautiful as the full moon, stands before me in all her ornaments, I will appear as if I did not see her.

"Her mother will wait upon me, respectfully kiss my hands, and say to me, 'Sir' (for she will not dare to call me son-in-law, for fear of provoking me by such familiarity), 'I pray you not to disdain my daughter, or to refuse approaching her: I assure you that her whole study is to please you, and that she loves you with all her heart.'

"Then my mother-in-law will take a glass of wine, and putting it in the hand of her daughter, my wife, will say, 'Go, present him this glass of wine yourself: he will not, perhaps, be so cruel as to refuse it from so fair a hand.' My wife will approach with the glass, and stand trembling before me; and when she finds that I persist in disregarding her, and continue to treat her with disdain, she will say to me, with tears in her eyes, 'My heart! my dear soul! my amiable lord! I conjure you, by the favours which Heaven bestows so liberally upon you, to receive this glass of wine from the hand of your very humble servant.' But I will not yet notice her, nor make any reply. 'My charming spouse!' she will continue, redoubling her tears, and raising the glass to my mouth, 'I will not cease importuning you, till I prevail with you to drink.' Then, fatigued with her entreaties, I will dart a terrible look at her, and give her a severe blow on the cheek, at the same time repulsing her with my foot, in such a manner as to force her far from the sofa."

My brother was so absorbed in these chimerical visions, that he represented the action with his foot, as if it had been real; and, most unfortunately, he struck his basket with so much force, that he threw it down from his shop into the street, and broke all his glasses in a thousand pieces.

My brother, on this fatal accident, recovered his senses; and, considering that he had brought this misfortune upon himself by the insupportable pride he had encouraged, he beat his face, tore his clothes, and lamented so loud, that his neighbours assembled about him, while the people who were going to noon-prayer, stopped to inquire the cause of his distress; and, it being Friday, more persons attended prayer than on other days. Some of them pitied Alnaschar; others only laughed at his extravagance; in the meantime, his vanity being dissipated with the destruction of his property, he bitterly bewailed his loss; when a lady of consideration, mounted on a mule, richly caparisoned, passed by. My brother's cries having excited her compassion, she inquired who he was, and the occasion of his grief. The by-standers told her that he was a poor man who had employed the little money he possessed in purchasing a basket of glasses; and that the basket having fallen, all his property was destroyed. The lady immediately turned to an eunuch who attended her, "Give him," said she, "what you have about you." The eunuch obeyed, and put into my brother's hands a purse containing five hundred pieces of gold. Alnaschar had nearly died with joy when he received it; he gave a thousand blessings to the lady, and, shutting up his shop, where his attendance was no longer necessary, he returned to his house.

He was seriously reflecting on his good fortune, when he was roused by a knock at the door. Before he opened it, he asked who was there; and knowing, by the voice, that the person was a female, he no longer hesitated. "My son," said she, "I have a favour to beg of you:—it is the hour of prayer; have the goodness to let me wash myself, that I may be in a fit state to attend to my devotions. Suffer me, if you please, to enter your house, and give me a basin of water." My brother looked at the woman, and seeing that she was already advanced in years, though a stranger, he granted her request. As she was very meanly dressed, and behaved with much deference

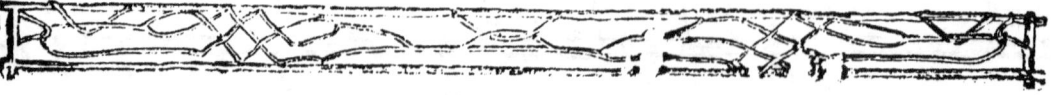

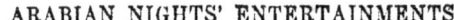

owards him, he thought she expected alms, and offered her two pieces of gold. The old woman retired from him with surprise, as if my brother had caused her a serious injury: "Heavens!" exclaimed she, "what is the meaning of this? Is it possible, sir, that you suppose me to be one of those miserable wretches who make a profession of impudently entering people's houses, to demand charity? Take back your money: thank Heaven, I have no need of it. I belong to a young lady of this city, who is a most charming beauty, and likewise very rich; she suffers me to want for nothing."

My brother had not sufficient penetration to discover the craft of the old woman, who only refused the two pieces of gold that she might obtain more. He asked her if she could not procure him the honour of seeing that lady. "With all my heart," replied she, "my mistress will be very glad to marry you, and to put you in possession of all her wealth, by making you master of her person. Take up your gold and follow me."

She walked before him, and he followed at a distance, till she reached the gate of a large house, where she knocked. He rejoined her at the moment a young Greek slave opened the gate. The old woman made him enter first, and crossing a well-paved court, conducted him into a hall, the furniture of which confirmed him in the high opinion he had conceived of the mistress of the house. In a short time the young lady appeared, who surprised him more by her extraordinary beauty, than by the richness of her habiliments. She signified her satisfaction at seeing him; and after some engaging expressions, "We are not agreeably situated here," added she; "come, give me your hand." At these words, she presented hers, and conducted him to an inner chamber, where she entertained him some time longer. She at length quitted him, desiring him to remain, and she would return in a moment. He accordingly waited her re-appearance; but, instead of the lady, a great black slave entered, with a scimitar in his hand; and regarding my brother with a terrible aspect, said to him fiercely, "What is your business here?" Alnaschar was so terrified that he had not power to answer. The slave stripped him, and carried off his gold, after giving him several cuts on the legs with his scimitar. My unhappy brother fell to the ground, where he lay without motion, though he still retained his senses. The black supposing him to be dead, called for salt; and the Greek slave brought him a basinful; with which they rubbed my brother's wounds, who had sufficient command of himself, notwithstanding the excessive pain he suffered, to lie still, apparently lifeless. The black and the Greek slave having retired, the old woman, who had inveigled my brother into the snare, entered, and taking him by the feet, dragged him to a trapdoor, which she opened, and threw him down. When he recovered his senses, he found himself in a subterraneous place, with the bodies of several persons who had been assassinated. The salt with which his wounds had been rubbed, preserved his life. He gained strength by degrees, so as to be able to walk; and after the lapse of two days, having opened the trapdoor during the night, he perceived a place in the court where he could conceal himself, and in which he determined to remain till daybreak. At that time the detestable old woman appeared, and opening the street-door, went out to seek other prey. That he might escape her observation, he remained in his hiding-place some minutes after she had left the house, and then sought shelter with me, when he informed me of his extraordinary adventures.

In about a month he was perfectly cured of his wounds, by medicines which I gave him; and he then resolved to avenge himself on the old woman who had so cruelly deceived him. For this purpose he took a bag, large enough to contain five hundred pieces of gold, and filled it with broken glass. Having fastened the bag round him, with his girdle, he disguised himself like an old woman, and concealed a scimitar under his gown. One morning he met the object of his detestation walking through the town, seeking an opportunity of defrauding some person. He appoached her, and, counterfeiting the voice of a female, said, "Can you lend me a pair of scales? I am a Persian woman, lately arrived; I have brought five hundred pieces of gold from my country, and wish to know if they are weight." "Good woman," replied the old cheat, "you could not have accosted a more proper person; follow me, and and I will conduct you to my son, who is a money-changer; he will with pleasure weigh them himself, and save you the trouble. Let us make haste, that we may meet with him before he leaves home." My brother followed her to the same house where she had formerly introduced him, and the door was opened by the Greek slave.

The old woman took my brother to the hall, where she requested him to wait a moment, while she fetched her son. The pretended son appeared, and proved to be the villanous black slave. "Thou cursed old woman!" said he to my brother, "rise, and follow me!" Saying these words, he went before, to lead him to the place where he designed to murder him. Alnaschar arose, and followed; when, drawing his scimitar from under his robe, he gave him so dexterous a blow on the neck, as cut off his head; taking it in one hand, and dragging the corse with the other, he threw them both into the place under ground. The Greek slave, accustomed to the business, soon presented herself with a bason of salt; but when she saw Alnaschar with the scimitar in his hand, and who had removed the veil with which he had covered his face, she let fall the basin, and fled; but my brother, quickly overtaking her, cut off her head likewise. The wicked old woman entered hastily at the noise, and my brother seized her before she had time to escape. She then fell on her knees, to beg his pardon, but he cut her in four pieces.

There remained only the lady, who was entirely unacquainted with what had passed in her house. He searched for her, and found her in a chamber, where she was ready to swoon when she saw him appear. She begged her life, which he generously granted. "Madam," said he, "how could you live with people so wicked as those on whom I have justly revenged myself?" "I was," replied she, "wife to an honest merchant; and the cursed old woman, with whose wickedness I was unacquainted, occasionally visited me. 'Madam,' said she to me one day, 'we have a very fine wedding at our house, the sight of which would afford you much pleasure, could I prevail on you to honour us with your company.' In short, I was persuaded by her; I put on my best apparel, and took with me a hundred pieces of gold. I followed her, and she conducted me to this house, where the black has kept me, by force, for three years, to my very great sorrow." "By the proceedings that detestable black has adopted," replied my brother, "he must have amassed considerable riches." "The quantity is so great," answered she, "that if you could convey them away, you would be enriched for ever. Follow me, and you shall see them." Alnaschar accompanied her to a chamber, where she showed him several coffers full of gold, which he beheld with an admiration he could not restrain. "Go," said she, "fetch people sufficient to remove it all." My brother did not wait to be told a second time; he went out, and stayed only till he had assembled ten men, whom he took with him to the house, when he was much surprised to find the gate open, but more so on discovering that the lady, yet more diligent, had disappeared, with all the coffers. However, resolved not to return empty-handed, he carried off all the furniture he could find in the house; of which there was much more than enough to produce the amount of the five hundred pieces of gold he had been robbed of. But when he quitted the house, he forgot to shut the door. The neighbours, who had observed my brother and the porters going backwards and forwards repeatedly, went and acquainted the police-justice with their suspicion of my brother's conduct. Alnaschar passed the night tranquilly; but the next morning, as he was leaving his house, he found at his door twenty of the magistrate's men, who seized him. "Come along with us," said they; "our master would speak with you." My brother prayed them not to be precipitate, and offered them a sum of money to let him escape; but, instead of listening to him, they bound him, and forced him to go along with them. "I desire to know," said the judge, "where you obtained all the goods which were conveyed into your house yesterday?" My brother then related to him all that had happened, without disguise, from the time the old woman entered his house to say her prayer, to that when the young lady made her escape, after he had killed the black, the Greek slave, and the old woman. And in regard to what he had carried to his house, he prayed the judge to leave him at least a portion of the furniture, as a compensation for the five hundred pieces of gold of which he had been robbed.

The judge, without making him any promise, sent his officers to bring away all his property; and when he understood that the whole had been removed, and deposited in his own store-house, he commanded my brother to quit the town immediately, and never to return; for he was afraid, if Alnaschar had remained in this city, he would by some means have represented this injustice to the caliph. Alnaschar obeyed the order without murmuring, and left the town, to seek refuge in another. On the road he was met by highwaymen, who stripped him entirely naked. I had no sooner learned this new misfortune, than I took a habit, and went in search of him; and after having given him all the consolation in my power, I brought him again secretly into the town, where I attended to his comfort with as much care as I had to that of his other brothers.

THE STORY OF THE BARBER'S SIXTH BROTHER.

IT now only remains for me to recount the history of my sixth brother, called Schacabac with the Hare-Lips. He was at first sufficiently industrious to increase the hundred drachms of silver which fell to his share, and lived in a very comfortable manner; but a reverse of fortune reduced him to the necessity of soliciting alms, in which, however, he acquitted himself with considerable address.

One day, as he was passing a magnificent house, the open gate of which exposed a very spacious court, where there was a crowd of servants, he approached one of them, and inquired of him to whom the house belonged. "Good man," replied the domestic, "whence do you come, to ask me such a question? Does not all that you see explain to you that it is the palace of a Barmecide?" My brother, who well knew the generosity of the Barmecides, addressed himself to one of the porters, and prayed him to bestow his charity. "Go in," said he, "nobody hinders you; and present yourself to the master of the house; he will send you back satisfied."

My brother entered the palace, which was so extensive, that he was a considerable time in finding the Barmecide's apartment. He at length reached an elegant square building, of excellent architecture; and entered by a porch, through which he saw a most beautiful garden, with gravel-walks of various colours, delightful to the sight. He advanced, and entered a saloon richly furnished, and adorned with paintings of gold and azure foliage, where he saw a venerable man, with a long white beard, sitting at the upper end of an alcove; whence he concluded him to be the master of the house. In truth, it was the Barmecide himself, who addressed my brother very politely, saying he was welcome, and asking him what he wanted. "My lord," answered my brother, in a supplicating tone, "I am a poor man, in need of the assistance of rich and generous persons like yourself."

The Barmecide appeared astonished at my brother's answer: "It is possible," cried he, "while I am at Bagdad, that there should be a man in the town so distressed as you represent! This I cannot suffer." At these demonstrations of pity, my brother, expecting he was going to bestow on him some singular mark of his bounty, blessed him a thousand times, wishing him every happiness. "It shall not be said," replied the Barmecide, "that I abandon you; nor will I suffer you to leave me." "Sir," said my brother, "I swear to you, I have not eaten a mouthful to-day." "Is it really true," replied the Barmecide, "that you are fasting till this time? Alas, poor man! he will die with hunger! Ho, boy!" cried he, raising his voice, "bring a basin and water quickly, that we may wash our hands." Though no boy appeared, nor did my brother see either basin or water, the Barmecide began to rub his hands, as if water had been poured on them, and bade my brother wash with him. Schacabac, supposing that his lordship loved to be merry, approached and acted as he desired. "Come," said the Barmecide, "bring us something to eat, and do not keep us waiting." Saying these words, though nobody appeared, he acted as if he had taken food on a plate, and, carrying his hand to his mouth, began to chew. "Eat heartily, friend, I beg," said he to my brother; "use the same freedom as if you were at home. Come, eat: for a starving man, you do not appear to have a very keen appetite." "Pardon me, my lord," returned Schacabac, perfectly imitating his gestures: "you see I lose no time, and that I am not deficient in my duty." "How like you this bread?" said the Barmecide; "do you not think it excellent?" "Ah, my lord," replied my brother, who saw no more bread than meat, "I never ate any so white or so fine." "Eat, then, your bellyful," said the Barmecide: "the baker-woman, who makes this bread, cost me, I assure you, five hundred pieces of gold."

The Barmecide, after boasting of his bread, which my brother ate only in idea, cried, "Boy, bring us another dish. My good friend," continued he to my brother, though no boy appeared, "taste this meat; and tell me if you ever ate better mutton-and-barley broth than this?" "It is extremely good," replied my brother; "and therefore you see I feed heartily." "I was certain," said the Barmecide, "you would like it." "Nothing in the world could be more exquisite," replied my brother: "it is the most delicious dish at your table." "Bring the ragout directly," cried the Barmecide; "Honour this ragout; eat heartily, I beg of you. Ho, boy!" continued he, "bring us another ragout." "No, my lord, with submission," interrupted my brother; "I cannot possibly eat any more."

"Let them take away then," said the Barmecide, "and bring the fruit." He waited a moment, as if to give time for the servants to remove the dishes; after which he continued to my brother, "Taste these almonds; they are good, and fresh gathered." Both of them feigned to peel the almonds, and eat them. Then advancing his hand, as if he had presented my brother something, "Hold," added he, "here is a lozenge, excellent to assist digestion." Schacabac appeared as if he took and ate it: "My lord," said he, "there is no want of music here." "These lozenges," returned the Barmecide, "are made at my own house, where no requisite is wanting to render everything good." He still solicited my brother to eat: "For a man," continued he, "who had not broken his fast when he entered my house, you seem to me to have eaten with very little appetite." "My lord," replied Schacabac, whose jaws ached with their inutile operations, "I assure you that I am so full, that I could not swallow another morsel."

"Well, then, friend," replied the Barmecide, "we must drink after our repast;" at the same time commanding some wine to be brought; but which no more appeared than the meats and fruits had before. "Drink my health," said he, presenting my brother with a glass. My brother motioned to take the glass, and

made a low reverence to the Barmecide, to signify that he took the liberty of drinking his health. "My lord," said he, "this is very excellent wine; but I think it has not sufficient strength." "If you would have stronger," replied the Barmecide, "you need only speak; I have several sorts in my cellar. Try how you like this." Upon which he appeared as if pouring out another glass to himself, and then to my brother; which he repeated so often that Schacabac, feigning intoxication, rose his hand, and gave the Barmecide a box on the ear, which felled him to the ground, when he cried out "What! are you mad?" Then my brother, seeming to recover your senses, said, "My lord, you have had the goodness to admit your slave, and to give him a handsome treat: I should have been satisfied in making me eat, without obliging me to drink wine for, as I told you before was afraid it might occasion me to be unguarded in my behaviour. I am very sorry for my conduct, and beg a thousand pardons.

Scarcely had he concluded those words, when the Barmecide, instead of being offended, laughed heartily. "I have long sought a man of your character," said he; "and I not only pardon you for the blow you gave me, but desire henceforward that we may be friends, and that you will make my house your home. You have had the complaisance to accommodate yourself to my humour, and the patience to support the jest to the last; we will now eat in reality." On finishing these words he clapped his hands, and commanded his servants, who then appeared, to cover the table. His order was promptly obeyed, and my brother was regaled with all those delicacies of which he had before only tasted in idea. In fine, Schacabac had every reason to be satisfied with the Barmecide's civility and goodness; for he treated him with the utmost familiarity, and ordered him a suit of clothes out of his own wardrobe.

The Barmecide found my brother to be a man of solid sense, and such general information, that, in a few days afterwards, he trusted him with the care of his household and all his affairs. Schacabac acquitted himself very well in his employment during twenty years; at the end of which period the generous Barmecide died, and, leaving no heirs, all his estate was confiscated to the use of the prince. My brother was dispossessed of all the property he had acquired, and therefore, seeing himself reduced to his first condition, he joined a caravan of pilgrims going to Mecca, designing to accomplish that pilgrimage on their charity; but unfortunately the caravan was attacked and plundered by a number of Bedouins. My brother was seized as a slave by one of the marauders, who put him under the bastinado several days, to oblige him to ransom himself. Schacabac protested his inability. "I am your slave," said he; "you may dispose of me as you please, but I declare to you that I am extremely poor, and totally unable to redeem myself." But the Bedouin was unmoved, and irritated at finding himself disappointed of a considerable sum on which he had reckoned, he took his knife and slit my brother's lips, to avenge himself for the loss he thought he had sustained.

The Bedouin had a very pretty wife, and frequently, during his excursions, he left my brother alone with her, when she endeavoured to console him under the rigour of his slavery. She gave sufficient indications that she loved him: but he shunned her company as much as she sought opportunities of being alone with him. She had so constant a habit of trifling and jesting with Schacabac, whenever she saw him, that she was one day guilty of that indiscretion in presence of her husband.

The Bedouin immediately attacked my brother in a rage, and, after mangling him in a barbarous manner, carried him on a camel to the top of a desert mountain, where he left him. The mountain was on the road to Bagdad, so that I received an account of his situation from some passengers who had met with him. I directly proceeded thither, where I found the unfortunate Schacabac in a deplorable state. I gave him the succour he required, and brought him back to the city.

This is what I related to the Caliph Monstanser Billah (added the barber), and that prince applauded me with repeated bursts of laughter. "Now," said he, "I am convinced they justly give you the surname of Silent. Nobody can contradict it. For certain reasons, however, I command you to depart this town immediately, and let me hear no more of your discourse." I yielded to necessity, and travelled during several years in distant countries. At length, hearing that the caliph was dead, I returned to Bagdad, where I found not one of my brothers alive. It was on my return to that town that I rendered to the lame young man the important service which you have heard. You are, however, witness to his ingratitude, and to the injurious manner in which he treated me. Instead of testifying his gratitude, he rather chose to fly from me, and to desert his own country. When I learned that he was not at Bagdad, though nobody could tell me whither he was gone, I set off in quest of him. A long time has elapsed, during which I have travelled from province to province, and, when I least expected, I have met with him this day. I did not suppose he would be so incensed against me.

The barber finished his story, and we had found that the young man was not to blame for calling him a great talker. Nevertheless we were willing that he should remain with us, and partake of the treat which the master of the house had provided. We sat down to table, and enjoyed ourselves till the prayer-time between noon and sunset, when the company separated, and I went to attend my business till evening.

It was during this interval that humpback, half drunk, presented himself before my shop, where he sung and tabored. Thinking that, by taking him home, I should divert my wife, I invited him to accompany me. My wife gave us a dish of fish, and I served some to humpback, who ate it without observing a bone. He fell down dead before us, after we had in vain endeavoured to relieve him. In the distress occasioned by this melancholy accident, and through fear of the consequences, we quickly carried the corpse from our house, and adroitly deposited it in that of the Jew doctor. The Jew doctor lowered it down the chimney into the chamber of the purveyor; and the purveyor conveyed it into the street, where the merchant was detected, as was supposed, in the act of assassination. This, sir (added the tailor), is what I had to say, to satisfy your majesty, who will now pronounce whether we be deserving of mercy or punishment, of life or death.

The sultan of Casgar gave the tailor and his comrades their lives. "I cannot but acknowledge," said he, "that I am more interested with the account of the lame young man, with that of the barber, and the adventures of his brothers, than with the story of my jester. But before you return to your respective homes, or that we inter the remains of humpback, I would see this barber who has obtained your pardon. Since he is in my capital, my curiosity may be easily gratified." At the same time he sent an officer, with the tailor, to fetch him.

The messengers soon returned with the barber, whom they presented to the sultan. He was an old man of ninety years, his eye-brows and beard were white as snow, his ears hanging down, and he had a very long nose. The sultan could not forbear laughing when he saw him. "Silent man," said he to him, "I understand that you are acquainted with marvellous histories—will you relate some of them?" "Sir," replied the barber, "let us leave the stories which I know, if you please, for the present. I most humbly beg your majesty's permission to ask what this Christian, this Jew, this Mussulman, and that dead humpback lying on the ground, do here before your majesty?" The sultan had the condescension to satisfy the barber's curiosity. He ordered that the story of humpback, which he appeared particularly anxious to learn, should be related to him. When the barber had heard it, he shook his head. "Truly," cried he, "this story is surprising; and I am glad to have an opportunity of examining the body more closely." He approached humpback, seated himself on the ground, and took his head

between his knees; when, after looking at him steadfastly, he suddenly fell into so violent a fit of laughter, that he lost all command of himself, and sunk backwards on the ground, without considering that he was before the sultan of Casgar. When he had recovered, "It is said, and not without reason," cried he, "that no man dies without a cause. If ever a history deserved to be written in letters of gold, it is this of humpback."

At these words all the people regarded the barber as a crazy old man. "Silent man," said the sultan, "speak to me—why do you laugh so loud?" "Sir," replied the barber, "I swear that humpback is not dead.: he is still alive; and you may consider me a madman if I do not convince you in an hour." He then produced a box, in which he had several remedies, that he carried about him, to make use of on occasion; and taking out a little phial of balsam, he anointed humpback's neck, rubbing it a long time. Afterwards he drew from the case a neat iron instrument, which he put between his teeth, when, opening his mouth, he thrust down his throat a pair of small pincers, and brought up a bit of fish and the bone, which he showed to all the people. Immediately humpback sneezed, stretched forth his arms and legs, opened his eyes, and exhibited other signs of life.

The sultan, ravished with joy and admiration, ordered the story of humpback, with that of the barber, to be written down, that the memory of it might be preserved for ever. Nor did he stop here; but, that the tailor, the Jew doctor, the purveyor, and the Christian merchant, might remember with pleasure the adventure which the accident of hump-back had occasioned to them, he did not send them away till he had given to each a very rich robe, which he caused to be put on in his presence. As for the barber, he honoured him with a considerable pension, and retained him near his person.

THE HISTORY OF ABOULHASSEN ALI EBN BECAR, AND OF SCHEMSELNIHAR, FAVOURITE OF THE CALIPH HAROUN ALRASCHID.

NDER the government of the Caliph Haroun Alraschid, at Bagdad, lived a druggist named Aboulhassen Ebn Thaher, a very rich, handsome, and agreeable man.

His good qualities, and the favour of the caliph, made his company sought by the sons of emirs, and of the other officers of the first rank; his house was the rendezvous of all the nobility of the court. But of the young lords who daily visited him, there was one whom he took more notice of than the rest, and with whom he had contracted a particular friendship, named Aboulhassen Ali Ebn Becar, who traced his origin from an ancient royal family of Persia. This family still existed at Bagdad, where it had remained ever since the Mussulmans conquered that kingdom Nature seemed to have taken pleasure in endowing this young prince with the most rare qualities of body and of mind. His face was extremely beautiful, his shape fine, his manners free from embarrassment, and his physiognomy so engaging that he gained the affection of every one at first sight.

Being a man of so amiable qualities, we need not wonder at Ebn Thaher distinguishing him from the other young noblemen of the court, most of whom had the vices opposed to his virtues. One day, when the prince was at the house of Ebn Thaer, there arrived a lady mounted on a piebald mule, in the midst of six female slaves, who accompanied her on foot, all very handsome, so far as could be judged by their air, and through the veils which covered their faces. She came to make some purchase; and as she had occasion to speak to Ebn Thaher, she entered his shop, which was neat and spacious, and he received her with demonstrations of the most profound respect, entreating her to sit down, and showing her with his hand the most honourable place.

In the meantime, the prince of Persia, unwilling to let pass such an opportunity of showing his politeness and gallantry, smoothened the cushion of cloth of gold, for the lady to lean on; after which he retired speedily, that she might sit down; and having saluted her, by kissing the tapestry at her feet, he arose, and remained standing before her at the bottom of the sofa. As she was accustomed to be at her ease with Ebn Thaher, she lifted up her veil, and discovered to the prince of Persia a beauty so extraordinary, that he was struck with it to the heart. On the other hand, the lady could not prevent herself from looking at the prince, the sight of whom had made on her the same impression. "Sir," said she to him, with an obliging air, "pray be seated." The prince of Persia obeyed, and sat down on the edge of the sofa. His eyes were constantly rivetted upon her, and he swallowed large draughts of the sweet poison of love. She quickly perceived what passed in his heart, and this discovery served to inflame her passion for him. She arose, and approached Ebn Thaher; and after whispering to him the motive of her visit, she inquired the name and country of the prince. "Madam," replied Ebn Thaher, "this young nobleman's name is Aboulhassen Ali Ebn Becar, and he is a prince of the blood-royal."

At this answer the lady bowed, and bade him farewell; and after she had glanced a favourable look towards the prince of Persia, she remounted her mule and departed.

The prince of Persia was so deeply enamoured of the lady, that he followed her with his eyes as far as he could see her; and for a long time after she had disappeared, he continued looking on vacancy. Ebn Thaher told him that he had observed several persons notice him, and began to laugh at seeing him in this attitude. "Alas!" said the

prince to him, "the world and you would have compassion on me, if you knew that the charming lady who has just quitted you carried with her the best part of me, and that the remainder seeks for an opportunity to follow. Tell me, I conjure you," added he, "what tyrannical lady this is, who forces people to love her, without giving them time for reflection?" "My lord," answered Ebn Thaher, "it is the famous Schemselnihar, the principal favourite of the caliph our master." "She is justly so named," interrupted the prince, "since she is more beautiful than the sun in a cloudless day." "That is true," replied Ebn Thaher; "and therefore the commander of the faithful loves, or rather adores, her. He expressly commanded me to furnish her with all she might require of me, and even, as much as possible, to anticipate her wishes."

While the prince of Persia was thus consecrating his heart to the fair Schemselnihar, that lady, when she had returned home, devised a means of seeing and freely conversing with him. She no sooner entered her palace, than she sent to Ebn Thaher the woman in whom she placed the utmost confidence, to desire him, with the prince of Persia, to visit her without delay. The slave entered Ebn Thaher's shop, while he was still speaking to the prince, and endeavouring to dissuade him, by the most forcible reasoning, from loving the caliph's favourite. Seeing them together, "Gentlemen," said she, "my honourable mistress, Schemselnihar, the chief favourite of the commander of the faithful, entreats you to come to her palace, where she waits your company." Ebn Thaher, to testify his obedience, rose up immediately, without answering the slave, and proceeded after her, though with some reluctance. As for the prince, he readily followed, not reflecting on the danger that might attend the interview. The presence of Ebn Thaher, who had liberty to enter the house of the favourite, freed the prince from all inquietude. They therefore followed the slave, who walked at a short distance before them, and entering the palace of the caliph, overtook her at the gate, which was already open. She introduced them to a large hall, where she prayed them to be seated.

Soon after Ebn Thaher and the prince had sat down, a very handsome black slave brought them a table covered with several very delicate meats, the exquisite odour of which proved the richness of the sauce. Other slaves brought them excellent wine after their repast; and when they had finished, presented to each of them an elegant gold basin, full of water, that they might wash their hands; after which they brought them perfume of aloes, in a vase likewise of gold, with which they perfumed their beards and their clothes. Odoriferous water was not forgotten; it was in a golden vessel, enriched with diamonds and rubies, made expressly for this purpose; and it was thrown upon their hands, which they passed over their beards and faces, according to custom. They then returned to their places; but they had scarcely sat down, when the slave begged them to rise and follow her. She opened a door of the hall where they were, and they entered into a large saloon of marvellous structure.

The prince of Persia and Ebn Thaher remained a long time admiring the magnificence of the place; and testified their surprise and delight at every object they saw, especially the prince, who had never witnessed any sight comparable. Ebn Thaher, though he had been several times in that beautiful palace, yet could not but observe many new beauties. In fine, they ceased not admiring so many singular curiosities; and were thus agreeably employed, when they perceived a company of ladies, richly apparelled, sitting without, at some distance from the dome, each of them upon a seat of Indian wood, inlaid with silver wire, in figures, with an instrument of music in their hands, expecting orders to play.

Advancing to the window, which fronted the ladies, they saw, on the right, a spacious court, with stairs leading to the garden, encompassed with beautiful apartments. The slave had quitted them, and being alone, they discoursed together. "As for you, who are a wise man," said the prince of Persia, "I doubt not but that you look with great satisfaction on all these indications of grandeur and power. For my part, I do not think there are in the world objects more surprising. But when I reflect that this is the glorious habitation of the too lovely Schemselnihar, and that she is retained here by the greatest monarch of the earth, I confess to you that I consider myself as the most unfortunate of mankind."

"Sir," replied Ebn Thaher, "I sincerely wish I could give you as good assurance of the happy success of your amour, as I can of the safety of your life. Though this superb palace belongs to the caliph, who erected it purposely for Schemselnihar, under the name of *the palace of eternal pleasures*, and it adjoins his own palace, nevertheless you must know this lady lives here in perfect freedom. She is not beset by eunuchs as spies upon her actions; this is her own house, and is absolutely at her disposal. She leaves it when she pleases to go into the city, and returns again without asking permission of anybody; and the caliph never visits her, without sending Mesrour, the chief of his eunuchs, to give her notice, that she may be prepared to receive him. Therefore, you may remain tranquil, and attend to the concert of music, with which I perceive Schemselnihar is going to entertain you."

As Ebn Thaher concluded these words, the prince of Persia and he saw the favourite's confidential slave approach, and give orders to their ladies to commence the concert. They all immediately began a prelude; and when they had played some time, one of them commenced a solo, which she executed admirably on her lute, accompanying the instrument with her voice. Having been before instructed in the subject on which she was to sing, the words were so agreeable to the prince of Persia's sentiments, that he could not refrain applauding her at the end of the couplet. When she had concluded, she and her companions rose up, and sung together, indicating by their words that the *full moon was about to rise in all her splendour, and that they should speedily see her approach the sun,* which signified, that Schemselnihar would soon appear, and that the prince of Persia would shortly have the pleasure of her company.

Schemselnihar approached, and, placing herself on the throne, saluted them both by inclining her head. But she fixed her eyes on the prince of Persia; and they spoke to each other in a silent language, intermixed with sighs; by which, in a few moments, they expressed more than they could have said in a great deal of time. The more Schemselnihar regarded the prince, the more she was convinced, by his looks, that he was enamoured of her; and, thus persuaded of his passion, she thought herself the happiest of women. At length she turned her eyes from him, to command the women who had sung to approach. They arose; and while they advanced, the black women, who came from the walk into which they had retired, brought their seats, and placed them near the window in front of the projection of the dome where Ebn Thaher and the prince of Persia had stationed themselves; and the seats were so disposed, on each side of the favourite's throne, as to form a semicircle before them.

When the women had retaken their places, with the permission of Schemselnihar, who ordered them by a sign, that charming favourite chose one of them to sing. After the woman had employed some moments in tuning her tute, she sung a song: the meaning of which was—that when two lovers had an unbounded affection for each other, their hearts, though in different bodies, were united; and, when any obstacle opposed their desires, they could say, with tears in their eyes, *If we love because we find each other amiable, ought we to be censured? Let destiny bear the blame.*

Schemselnihar so well discovered, by her eyes and gestures, that those words were intended to be applied to her and the prince of Persia, that he could not contain himself; but, rising, and advancing to a balluster, on which he leaned, he desired one of the women who came to sing, to attend to him. As she approached, "Listen to me," said he to her, "and do me the favour to accompany, with your lute, a song which you shall hear." He then sung with an air so tender and impassioned, as perfectly expressed the violence of his love. As soon as he had finished, Schemselnihar, following his example, said to one of her women, "Observe me likewise, and accompany my voice." She immediately sung, in such a manner, as still further pierced the heart of the prince of Persia, who replied by another air, as impassioned as the former.

The two lovers having declared their mutual affection by their songs, Schemselnihar arose from her throne, and advanced towards the door of the saloon. The prince precipitately arose to receive her. They met at the door, where, taking each other by the hand, they embraced with so much ardour that they fainted, and would have fallen, if the woman who followed Schemselnihar had not assisted them. The attendants having supported them to a sofa, they were recovered by throwing odoriferous water in their faces, and by presenting to them scents of various kinds.

Schemselnihar, turning towards the prince of Persia, who sat by her, and regarding him with some confusion, after what had passed between them, said to him, "Sir, I am very well assured you love me; and however great your affection for me may be, you need not doubt that mine is equally fervent for you. But let us not flatter ourselves; for though our sentiments are in perfect conformity, I see for you and me nought but troubles, anxieties, and tormenting griefs. "Madam," replied the prince of Persia, "you will render me the greatest injustice possible, if you for one moment doubt the continuance of my love. It is united to my soul so firmly, that I can justly say it forms the better part of it, and that I shall preserve it after death." On concluding these words he shed tears in abundance, and Schemselnihar was unable to restrain hers.

After this, she took a lute from one of her women, and accompanied it in so passionate a manner with her voice, that she seemed in a state of delirium; and the prince of Persia remained, with his eyes fixed upon her, immoveable as if he had been enchanted. In the meantime her trusty slave arrived in a fright, and, addressing herself to her mistress, "Madam," said she, "Mesrour and two other officers, with several eunuchs that attend them, are at the gate, and demand to speak with you from the caliph!" When the prince of Persia and Ebn Thaher heard these words, they changed colour, and began to tremble, as if their destruction had been certain; but Schemselnihar, who perceived their apprehension, encouraged them by a smile." She then ordered the slave, her confident, to return and entertain Mesrour, and the two other officers till she was prepared to receive them, and should send to her to introduce them. She immediately ordered all the windows of the saloon to be closed, and the painted cloths on the side of the garden to be let down; and after having assured the prince and Ebn Thaher that they might remain there without fear, she went out at the door leading to the garden, and shut it upon them. But, notwithstanding her assurances, they were much alarmed for their safety all the time they were left there.

As soon as Schemselnihar had entered the garden with the women who attended her, she ordered all the seats which had been occupied by the female musicians to be placed near the window whence the prince of Persia and Ebn Thaher had heard them; and everything being in the state she wished, she seated herself on a silver throne; and sent her confidential slave to conduct the chief of the eunuchs and his subaltern officers to her presence. They appeared, followed by twenty black eunuchs, all handsomely clothed, with scimitars by their sides, suspended by golden belts of four inches broad. The instant they perceived the favourite Schemselnihar, at a distance, they made her a profound reverence, which she returned them from her throne. When they approached, she arose, and went to meet Mesrour, who advanced first. She inquired what news he brought: to which he replied, "Madam, the commander of the faithful has sent me to signify that he cannot exist longer without seeing you; he designs to to visit you to-night, and I come to give you notice, that you may be prepared to receive him.

At this, the favourite Schemselnihar prostrated herself to the ground, as a mark of the submission with which she received the caliph's order. When she arose, "Pray tell the commander of the faithful," said she, "that I shall always consider it my glory to execute his majesty's commands, and that his slave will do her utmost to honour him with all the respect that is his due."

The chief of the eunuchs and his retinue being gone, Schemselnihar returned to the saloon, extremely concerned at the necessity she was under of parting with the prince of Persia sooner than intended. "Madam," said he to her, "I perceive you are come to announce that we must part. Provided there be nothing more to dread, I hope Heaven will give me the patience requisite to support your absence." "Alas!" interrupted the too tender Schemselnihar, "how happy do I think you, and how unfortunate do I consider myself, when I compare your lot with my sad destiny! No doubt you will suffer by my absence; but that will be all your trouble, and you may comfort yourself with the hope of seeing me again. But as for me, just Heaven! to what a terrible trial am I reduced! I must not only be deprived of the sight of the only person whom I love, but I must be tormented with the company of one whom you have rendered hateful to me." At these words, she tenderly embraced the prince of Persia, without being able to speak to him, and went to meet the caliph in a disorder that might easily be imagined.

In the meanwhile, the confidential slave took the prince and Ebn Thaher to the gallery; and having introduced them, left them there, and closed the door, after assuring them that they had nothing to fear, and that she would return at the proper time.

Schemselnihar waited for the caliph at the entry of an alley, accompanied by twenty women, all of surprising beauty, adorned with necklaces and ear-rings of large diamonds, with which some of them had their whole heads

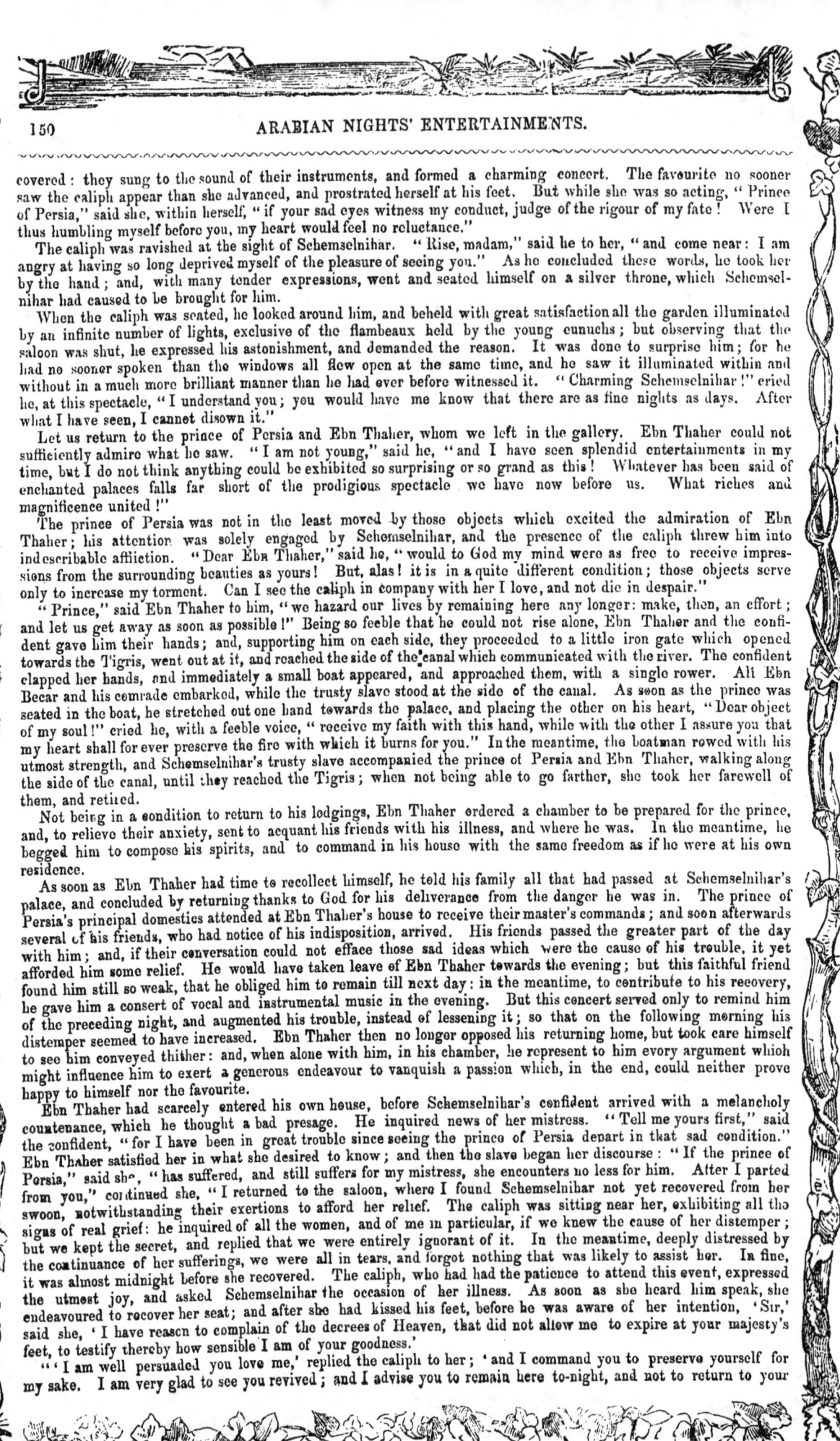

covered : they sung to the sound of their instruments, and formed a charming concert. The favourite no sooner saw the caliph appear than she advanced, and prostrated herself at his feet. But while she was so acting, " Prince of Persia," said she, within herself, " if your sad eyes witness my conduct, judge of the rigour of my fate ! Were I thus humbling myself before you, my heart would feel no reluctance."

The caliph was ravished at the sight of Schemselnihar. " Rise, madam," said he to her, " and come near : I am angry at having so long deprived myself of the pleasure of seeing you." As he concluded these words, he took her by the hand ; and, with many tender expressions, went and seated himself on a silver throne, which Schemselnihar had caused to be brought for him.

When the caliph was seated, he looked around him, and beheld with great satisfaction all the garden illuminated by an infinite number of lights, exclusive of the flambeaux held by the young eunuchs ; but observing that the saloon was shut, he expressed his astonishment, and demanded the reason. It was done to surprise him ; for he had no sooner spoken than the windows all flew open at the same time, and he saw it illuminated within and without in a much more brilliant manner than he had ever before witnessed it. " Charming Schemselnihar !" cried he, at this spectacle, " I understand you ; you would have me know that there are as fine nights as days. After what I have seen, I cannot disown it."

Let us return to the prince of Persia and Ebn Thaher, whom we left in the gallery. Ebn Thaher could not sufficiently admire what he saw. " I am not young," said he, " and I have seen splendid entertainments in my time, but I do not think anything could be exhibited so surprising or so grand as this ! Whatever has been said of enchanted palaces falls far short of the prodigious spectacle we have now before us. What riches and magnificence united !"

The prince of Persia was not in the least moved by those objects which excited the admiration of Ebn Thaher ; his attention was solely engaged by Schemselnihar, and the presence of the caliph threw him into indescribable affliction. " Dear Ebn Thaher," said he, " would to God my mind were as free to receive impressions from the surrounding beauties as yours ! But, alas ! it is in a quite different condition ; those objects serve only to increase my torment. Can I see the caliph in company with her I love, and not die in despair."

" Prince," said Ebn Thaher to him, " we hazard our lives by remaining here any longer : make, then, an effort ; and let us get away as soon as possible !" Being so feeble that he could not rise alone, Ebn Thaher and the confident gave him their hands ; and, supporting him on each side, they proceeded to a little iron gate which opened towards the Tigris, went out at it, and reached the side of the canal which communicated with the river. The confident clapped her hands, and immediately a small boat appeared, and approached them, with a single rower. Ali Ebn Becar and his comrade embarked, while the trusty slave stood at the side of the canal. As soon as the prince was seated in the boat, he stretched out one hand towards the palace, and placing the other on his heart, " Dear object of my soul !" cried he, with a feeble voice, " receive my faith with this hand, while with the other I assure you that my heart shall for ever preserve the fire with which it burns for you." In the meantime, the boatman rowed with his utmost strength, and Schemselnihar's trusty slave accompanied the prince of Persia and Ebn Thaher, walking along the side of the canal, until they reached the Tigris ; when not being able to go farther, she took her farewell of them, and retired.

Not being in a condition to return to his lodgings, Ebn Thaher ordered a chamber to be prepared for the prince, and, to relieve their anxiety, sent to acquaint his friends with his illness, and where he was. In the meantime, he begged him to compose his spirits, and to command in his house with the same freedom as if he were at his own residence.

As soon as Ebn Thaher had time to recollect himself, he told his family all that had passed at Schemselnihar's palace, and concluded by returning thanks to God for his deliverance from the danger he was in. The prince of Persia's principal domestics attended at Ebn Thaher's house to receive their master's commands ; and soon afterwards several of his friends, who had notice of his indisposition, arrived. His friends passed the greater part of the day with him ; and, if their conversation could not efface those sad ideas which were the cause of his trouble, it yet afforded him some relief. He would have taken leave of Ebn Thaher towards the evening ; but this faithful friend found him still so weak, that he obliged him to remain till next day : in the meantime, to contribute to his recovery, he gave him a consert of vocal and instrumental music in the evening. But this concert served only to remind him of the preceding night, and augmented his trouble, instead of lessening it ; so that on the following morning his distemper seemed to have increased. Ebn Thaher then no longer opposed his returning home, but took care himself to see him conveyed thither : and, when alone with him, in his chamber, he represent to him every argument which might influence him to exert a generous endeavour to vanquish a passion which, in the end, could neither prove happy to himself nor the favourite.

Ebn Thaher had scarcely entered his own house, before Schemselnihar's confident arrived with a melancholy countenance, which he thought a bad presage. He inquired news of her mistress. " Tell me yours first," said the confident, " for I have been in great trouble since seeing the prince of Persia depart in that sad condition." Ebn Thaher satisfied her in what she desired to know ; and then the slave began her discourse : " If the prince of Persia," said she, " has suffered, and still suffers for my mistress, she encounters no less for him. After I parted from you," continued she, " I returned to the saloon, where I found Schemselnihar not yet recovered from her swoon, notwithstanding their exertions to afford her relief. The caliph was sitting near her, exhibiting all the signs of real grief : he inquired of all the women, and of me in particular, if we knew the cause of her distemper ; but we kept the secret, and replied that we were entirely ignorant of it. In the meantime, deeply distressed by the continuance of her sufferings, we were all in tears, and forgot nothing that was likely to assist her. In fine, it was almost midnight before she recovered. The caliph, who had had the patience to attend this event, expressed the utmost joy, and asked Schemselnihar the occasion of her illness. As soon as she heard him speak, she endeavoured to recover her seat ; and after she had kissed his feet, before he was aware of her intention, ' Sir,' said she, ' I have reason to complain of the decrees of Heaven, that did not allow me to expire at your majesty's feet, to testify thereby how sensible I am of your goodness.'

" ' I am well persuaded you love me,' replied the caliph to her ; ' and I command you to preserve yourself for my sake. I am very glad to see you revived ; and I advise you to remain here to-night, and not to return to your chamber, for fear the motion should injure you.' He then commanded a little wine to be brought, to renovate her strength; when taking leave of her, he retired to his apartment.

"Next morning, as she was not commodiously lodged in the saloon, I assisted her to her chamber, where she no sooner arrived, than all the physicians of the palace came to visit her, by order of the caliph, who soon followed himself. The medicines which the physicians prescribed for Schemselnihar had not the least good effect, as they were ignorant of the cause of her indisposition, which the presence of the caliph augmented. She obtained a little rest, however, this night; and, as soon as she awoke, she charged me to come to you, to make inquiry respecting the prince of Persia." "I have already informed you of his condition," said Ebn Thaher; "therefore, return to your mistress, and assure her that the prince of Persia expects news from her with as much solicitude as she does from him. But pray exhort her to moderation, and to command herself, for fear she let some word escape her before the caliph, which may prove fatal to us all." "As for me," replied the confident, "I confess I dread her transports: I have taken the liberty to speak my mind freely to her on the subject, and am persuaded that she will not be offended if I tell her your opinion."

Ebn Thaher, who had but just returned from the prince of Persia's lodgings, thought it not prudent to go again so soon, and neglect his own important affairs, which required his attention: he did not, therefore, repeat his visit till the evening. The prince was alone, and no better than in the morning. Ebn Thaher then gave him a particular account of all that the trusty slave had related to him. The prince listened with every different emotion of fear, jealousy, tenderness, and compassion, which his discourse was capable of inspiring in so impassioned a lover; making, on all he heard, either afflicting or consolatory reflections, as the impulse of the moment suggested.

Their conversation continued so long, that the night was far advanced, and the prince of Persia obliged Ebn Thaher to remain with him. The next morning, as this faithful friend returned home, he met a woman whom he recognised to be Schemselnihar's confident, who immediately accosted him thus:—"My mistress salutes you; and I am come to entreat you, in her name, to deliver this letter to the prince of Persia." The zealous Ebn Thaher took the letter, and retraced his steps to the prince's residence, accompanied by the confidential slave.

When Ebn Thaher entered the prince of Persia's house with Schemselnihar's confident, he prayed her to wait one moment in the drawing-room. As soon as the prince saw him, he asked earnestly what news he had to announce. "The best you can desire," answered Ebn Thaher: "your affections are reciprocal. Schemselnihar's confident is in your drawing-room: she has brought you a letter from her mistress, and attends your orders to enter." "Let her come in!" cried the prince, with a transport of joy: speaking thus, he sat down, to receive her.

As the prince's attendants had quitted him on the appearance of Ebn Thaher, and left him alone with their master, Ebn Thaher went himself to open the door, and introduced the confident. "My lord," said she to him, "I am aware of the afflictions you have endured since I had the honour to conduct you to the boat which conveyed you from the palace; but, I hope, the letter I have brought will contribute to your cure. She then presented him the letter. He took it, and read as follows :—

FROM SCHEMSELNIHAR TO ALI EBN BECAR, PRINCE OF PERSIA.

THE person by whom I convey this letter to you, is capable of giving a more satisfactory account of me, than I am able to relate; for I have been insensible since I saw you. Deprived of your presence, I seek to deceive myself, by entertaining you with these ill-written lines, with the same pleasure as if I had the happiness of your company.

It is said that patience is a remedy for all ills; but it irritates my sufferings, instead of solacing them. Although your portrait be deeply engraven on my heart, yet my eyes incessantly desire to view the original; and they will totally lose their light, if they be long deprived of that satisfaction. May I flatter myself that yours experience the same impatience to see me? I would reckon as nothing all that opposes our love, were I only allowed to see you sometimes with freedom. Then I should possess you, and what more could I desire?

So much does this thought oppress me, that it would cause my death, were I not persuaded you love me. This sweet consolation balances my despair, and attaches me to life. Adieu! I salute Ebn Thaher, who has so much obliged us.

*　　*　　*　　*　　*　　*　　*　　*　　*

The prince of Persia was not satisfied with having read the letter once; he thought he had not perused it with sufficient attention, and therefore read it again more leisurely. In a word, he could not remove his eyes from characters drawn by so dear a hand; and was beginning to read it a third time, when Ebn Thaher reminded him of the confident's haste, and that he ought to think of preparing an answer. "Alas!" cried the prince, "my spirits are agitated by a thousand tormenting reflections, and my thoughts destroy each other the moment they are conceived, to make room for more."

The prince of Persia, before he began to write, gave Schemselnihar's letter to Ebn Thaher, and begged him to hold it open while he wrote, that, by casting his eyes upon it, he might conceive the better what to reply. At

length he finished his letter, and presenting it to Ebn Thaher, "Read it, I pray," said he to him, "and do me the favour to see if the disorder of my mind has permitted me to give a reasonable answer." Ebn Thaher took it, and read as follows :—

THE PRINCE OF PERSIA'S ANSWER TO SCHEMSELNIHAR'S LETTER.

WAS plunged in mortal grief when I received your letter, and, at the view of the characters traced by your lovely hand, my eyes experienced an accession of light more sensible than the diminution they suffered when yours were suddenly closed at the feet of my rival. I have not enjoyed one moment's repose since our cruel separation ; your letter alone has brought a solace to my troubles. I had preserved a mournful silence till the moment I received it, and then it restored to me the faculty of speech. I was buried in profound melancholy, but it inspired me with a joy, which was immediately visible in my eyes and countenance. You would have me declare that my affection for you is unalterable. Ah, though I did not love you so perfectly as I do, I should be compelled to adore you, after all the marks you have given me of an affection so uncommon. Yes, I love you, my dear soul! and shall account it my glory to burn all my life with the sweet fire that you have kindled in my heart. I will never complain of the lively ardour with which I feel it consumes me; and, how rigorous soever be the ills which I suffer, I will bear them courageously, in the hope of being again blessed with your presence. Would to Heaven it were to-day ! and that, instead of sending my letter, I might be allowed to go and assure you that I die for love of you. My tears hinder me from saying more. Adieu.

*   *   *   *   *   *   *   *

Ebn Thaher returned the letter to the prince of Persia, assuring him that it wanted no correction. The prince closed it, and, when he sealed it, "I beg of you to approach," said he to Schemselnihar's confidential slave, who was at some distance from him; "here is my answer to your dear mistress. I conjure you to carry it to her, and to salute her in my name." The slave took the letter, and retired with Ebn Thaher.

After Ebn Thaher had walked some time with the slave, he quitted her, and returned to his own house, when he began to reflect seriously upon the amorous intrigue in which he found himself unhappily engaged. He considered that the prince of Persia and Schemselnihar, notwithstanding their interest in concealing their correspondence, conducted themselves with such little discretion, that it could not long remain a secret, and he anticipated all the consequences from it which a man of good sense had a right to expect.

Next morning he went to the prince of Persia, in the design of making a last effort to oblige him to conquer his passion. He accordingly repeated to him the arguments he had, in vain, formerly represented—that it would be much better for him to exert all his resolution to overcome his passion for Schemselnihar, than to suffer himself to be conquered by it; while this passion was so much the more dangerous, as his rival was the more potent.

The prince listened to Ebn Thaher with much impatience; nevertheless, he suffered him to finish what he had to say ; when, speaking in his turn, "Ebn Thaher," said he, "think you I can cease to love Schemselnihar, who loves me so tenderly ? She is not afraid of exposing her life for me ; and would you desire that the care of preserving mine should engage my thoughts? No; whatever misfortunes befal me, I will love Schemselnihar to my last breath."

Ebn Thaher, offended at the obstinacy of the prince of Persia, left him rather abruptly ; and going to his own house, recalled to mind his reflections of the day preceding, and began to think seriously on the conduct he ought to adopt. In the meantime, a jeweller, one of his intimate friends, came to visit him. This jeweller had observed that Schemselnihar's confident was at Ebn Thaher's house oftener than usual, and that he constantly attended the prince of Persia, whose sickness was generally known, though the cause of it was still a secret. The jeweller became suspicious ; when finding Ebn Thaher very pensive, he justly concluded that he was perplexed with some important affair ; and fancying that he knew the cause, he asked what Schemselnihar's confident wanted with him. Ebn Thaher, embarrassed with the question, would have dissembled, telling him that it was for a trifle she came so frequently to his house. "You do not answer me sincerely," replied the jeweller; "and you give me reason to think, by your dissimulation, that this trifle is a more important affair than I at first conjectured."

Ebn Thaher, as his friend pressed him so closely, then said to him, "It is true, that this affair is of the greatest consequence. You know in what esteem I am held at court, and what a disgrace it would be to me should this rash intrigue be discovered. That is what perplexes me ; but I have just now formed the resolution I ought to take ; I will immediately endeavour to satisfy my creditors, and recover my debts ; and when I have secured my property, will retire to Balsora, where I will remain till the tempest which I foresee is blown over. The friendship which I have for Schemselnihar and the prince of Persia renders me very sensible to the dangers by which they are environed ; and which I pray Heaven to discover to them, and to avert. But if their evil destiny should expose their amours to the knowledge of the caliph, I shall, at least, be out of the reach of his resentment ; for I do not think them so wicked as to wish to involve me in their misfortunes."

The jeweller heard with extreme astonishment the recital of Ebn Thaher. "What you tell me," said he, "is of so great importance, that I cannot conceive how Schemselnihar and the prince could be capable of abandoning themselves to an amour so violent ; whatever attachment they may have to each other, instead of yielding, they ought to resist it, and make a better use of their reason. Is it possible they can be insensible of the danger attending their correspondence ? How deplorable is their blindness ! I appreciate all the probable consequences, as well as you. But you are wise and prudent, and I approve of the resolution you have formed, as the only means of delivering yourself from the fatal events which you have reason to dread." After this conversation, the jeweller arose, and took leave of Ebn Thaher, who conjured him by their mutual friendship, not to mention to any person what he had related. "Be under no apprehension," said the jeweller, "I will preserve the secret at the peril of my life."

On the second day following this interview, the jeweller passed by Ebn Thaher's shop ; and seeing it shut, he doubted not but that he had executed the design he meditated. To be certain, he inquired of a neighbour if he knew why his friend's shop was not open ; the neighbour answered that he supposed Ebn Thaher was gone a journey.

There was no need of further inquiry; and he immediately thought of the prince of Persia. "Unhappy prince," said he to himself, "how will you be grieved when you hear this news! By what means will you now continue your correspondence with Schemselnihar? I fear you will die of despair. I have compassion on you; I must supply the loss you have sustained in a too-fearful confident."

The business that had brought him from home being of little consequence, he determined, at this time, to neglect it; and though his only knowledge of the prince of Persia proceeded from having sold him some jewels, he went immediately to his house. He addressed himself to one of the domestics, requesting him to tell his master that he wished to speak with him concerning a business of very great importance. The servant returned immediately to the jeweller, and introduced him to the prince's chamber, who was leaning on a sofa, with his head resting upon a cushion. His features were not forgotten by the prince, who arose to receive him, said he was very welcome, and desiring him to be seated, asked him if he could be of any service to him, or if he came to announce news concerning himself. "Prince," replied the jeweller, "an anxiety to testify my zeal for your happiness has induced me to take the liberty of coming to your house, to impart to you some information that nearly concerns you."

After this introduction, the jeweller entered upon the subject of his visit, which he thus explained:—"I have e honour to tell you that conformity of humour, and several transactions we had together, long since united Ebn haher and me in strict friendship. I know that you are acquainted with him, and that he has been employed till his time in obliging you in all he could; I have understood this from himself, for he conceals nothing from me, nor

I from him. Passing by his shop, I was surprised to find it shut; and addressing myself to one of his neighbours to inquire the reason, he informed me that two days ago Ebn Thaher took his leave of him and other neighbours, offering them his services at Balsora, whither he is gone, (continued he,) about an affair of great importance. Not being satisfied with this answer, the interest I take in whatever concerns him determined me to come to your house, to ask if you know anything concerning his precipitate departure?"

The prince remained some moments absorbed in melancholy thoughts. At length he lifted up his head and addressing one of his attendants, " Go," said he, " to Ebn Thaher's house, and ask any of his domestics if it be true that he is gone to Balsora. Run! and return quickly, to let me know what you hear.'

At length the prince's domestic returned, and reported that he had spoken with one of Ebn Thaher's servants, who assured him that his master had set out two days before for Balsora. "As I came from Ebn Thaher's house,' added the domestic, " a slave accosted me; and, after asking me if I had not the honour to belong to you, she told me she wanted to speak with you, and begged, at the same time, that she might accompany me. She is in the antechamber; and I believe has a letter to deliver to you from some person of consideration." The prince desired that she might be immediately introduced, not doubting but it was Schemselnihar's confidential slave, and he was not mistaken. She could not have arrived more opportunely to save the prince from despair. They mutually saluted each other; when the jeweller, who had arisen at her appearance, stepped aside to leave them at liberty to speak together. After having conversed some time, the confident took leave, and departed, leaving him in a quite different state of mind from that in which she had found him; his eyes appeared brighter, and his counte-nance more gay, which convinced the jeweller that the good slave was the bearer of some news favourable to his amour.

The jeweller, having retaken his place near the prince, said to him, smiling, " I see, prince, you have important affairs at the caliph's palace." The prince of Persia, astonished and alarmed at this discourse, replied, "Why do you suppose I have affairs at the caliph's palace?" " I judge," answered the jeweller, " by the appearance of the slave who is just gone out." "And to whom, think you, belongs this slave?" said the prince. " To Schemsel-nihar, the caliph's favourite," replied the jeweller.

The jeweller's words very much troubled the prince of Persia. "He would not speak in these terms," said he to himself, " if he did not suspect, or rather know, my secret." The prince remained silent for some time, at a loss what to answer. At length he spoke: " You have mentioned circumstances which induce me to believe you know yet more than you have acknowledged," said he to the jeweller; " it is important to my repose that I be perfectly informed; I conjure you, therefore, not to dissemble with me."

Then the jeweller gave him a particular account of his conversation with Ebn Thaher, and forgot not to tell him that Ebn Thaher was terrified by the danger to which his quality of confident exposed him, which was partly the occasion of his retiring to Balsora, where he intended to remain until the storm, which he feared, should be dissi-pated. "This design he has executed," added the jeweller; " but I am surprised that he could resolve to abandon you, in the condition he informed me you were. As for me, prince, I confess I was moved with com-passion for you, and am come to tender you my services; and, if you do me the favour to accept of them, while I engage to be as faithful to you as Ebn Thaher, I promise to be more constant. "This discourse encouraged the prince, and consoled him for the absence of Ebn Thaher. " I am highly gratified," said he to the jeweller, " to find in you a reparation of my loss; I am incapable of expressing my sense of the obligation. I pray God to recom-pense your generosity, and I accept your friendly offer with all my heart. Would you believe,' continued he, " that Schemselnihar's confident came to speak to me concerning you? She told me it was you who advised Ebn Thaher to quit Bagdad: these were the last words she uttered on leaving me; and she had almost persuaded me that her information was correct."

They remained in conversation for some time, deliberating together on the most convenient means of conducting the prince's correspondence with Shemselnihar. They agreed to begin by disabusing the confident, who was so unjustly prepossessed against the jeweller. The prince promised to undeceive her the first time she returned, and to entreat her to address herself to the jeweller, when she was sent with letters, or other information, from her mistress to him. At length the jeweller arose, and, after again praying the prince of Persia to have an entire confidence in him, he retired.

The jeweller, returning to his house, perceived before him, in the street, a letter, which somebody had dropped. He took it up, and as it was not sealed, he opened it, and found it conceieved in these terms:—

LETTER FROM SCHEMSELNIHAR TO THE PRINCE OF PERSIA.

 Y confident has informed me of an occurrence which gives me no less affliction than it must occasion you. By losing Ebn Thaher, we have indeed lost much; but let not this hinder you, dear prince, from studying to preserve yourself. As our friend has abandoned us, let us console ourselves by the reflection that it is an unavoidable evil. Fortify your heart against this misfortune: the wishes of mankind are not to be obtained without trouble. Let us not discourage ourselves, but hope that Heaven will be favourable to us; and that, after so many sufferings, we shall attain a happy accomplishment of our desires. Adieu!

While the jeweller was conversing with the prince of Persia, the confident had had time to return to the palace, and announce to her mistress the ill news of Ebn Thaher's departure. Schemselnihar immediately wrote this letter, and sent back her confident in haste with it to the prince, but the slaves had dropped it by accident.

The jeweller was very glad to obtain possession of it, as it furnished him with the means of justifying himself in the mind of the confident, and bringing him to the point he desired. As he ended reading it, he perceived the slave, who sought it with great anxiety, looking about in every direction. He closed it again quickly, and put it

in his bosom; but the slave, having noticed the action, ran to him: "Sir," she said, "I dropped the letter you had this moment in your hand; I beseech you to restore it." The jeweller, appearing not to hear her, and without replying, continued his way till he arrived at his own house. He left the door open, that the confident, who was behind him, might enter; she accordingly followed; and when she reached his chamber, "Sir," said she to him, "you can make no use of the letter you have found; and you will not hesitate to return it to me, if you knew from whom it came, and for whom it is intended. Besides, permit me to observe, you cannot honestly retain it."

Before the jeweller answered the confident, he desired her to be seated; and then said to her, "It is not true that this letter is from Schemselnihar, and that it is addressed to the prince of Persia?" The slave, unprepared for such an interrogation, blushed. "The question embarrasses you," continued he; "but, I assure you, I do not propose it rashly. I could have returned you the letter in the street, but I wished to bring you here, that I might have an explanation with you. Is it just, tell me, to impute an unhappy accident to persons who nowise contributed towards it? Yet this you have done, in telling the prince of Persia that I counselled Ebn Thaher to leave Bagdad for his own safety. I do not intend to lose time in justifying myself to you: it is sufficient that the prince of Persia is fully persuaded of my innocence on this point. As soon as I knew certainly that Ebn Thaher had quitted Bagdad, I presented myself to prince, to inform him of the circumstance, and to offer him the same services which he rendered him. I succeeded in my application; and, provided you place the same confidence in me that you had in Ebn Thaher, you may benefit yourself by my assistance. Inform your mistress of what I have said to you, and assure her that, though my life should be forfeited for engaging in so dangerous an intrigue, I will not repent having sacrificed myself for two lovers so worthy of each other."

The confident begged him to pardon the ill opinion she had conceived of him, through zeal for the interests of her mistress. "I am extremely glad," added she, "that Schemselnihar and the prince have found in you a man so fit to supply the place of Ebn Thaher. I will not fail to explain to my mistress your good will towards her."

The jeweller then took the letter from his bosom, and restored it to her saying, "Go, carry it quickly to the prince of Persia, and come back this way, that I may see the answer. Forget not to give him an account of our conversation." The confident took the letter, and carried it to the prince, who replied to it immediately. She returned to the house of the jeweller to show him the answer, which contained these words:—

THE PRINCE OF PERSIA'S ANSWER TO SCHEMSELNIHAR.

OUR valuable letter produced on me a great effect; but not so great as I could wish. You endeavour to console me for the loss of Ebn Thaher: alas! sensible as I am of this misfortune, it is the least of my troubles. You know my sufferings, and that it is only your presence can alleviate them. When will the time arrive that I shall enjoy your company without the fear of deprivation? Oh! how distant it seems to me! But may we flatter ourselves that we shall see each other? You command me to preserve myself; I will obey, since I have renounced my own will to follow yours. Adieu!

* * * * * *

When the jeweller had read this letter, he gave it again to the confident, who said, as she was going away, "I will advise my mistress to place the same confidence in you that she did in Ebn Thaher. You shall hear of me to-morrow. Accordingly, next day she returned with a countenance that indicated satisfaction: "Your very look," said he to her, "informs me that you have removed Schemselnihar's apprehension. "You judge rightly," replied the confident; "and you shall hear how I effected it. Yesterday," continued she, "I found my mistress expecting me with impatience. I presented to her the prince of Persia's letter, which she read with tears in her eyes; and when she had concluded, as I saw that she was going to abandon herself to her ordinary sorrows, 'Madam,' said I to her, 'it is, doubtless, Ebn Thaher's removal that troubles you; but suffer me to conjure you to distress yourself no longer on that subject. We have found another Ebn Thaher, who offers to serve you with as much zeal, and, what is yet more important, with greater courage.' She appeared to me to be much relieved by my discourse. 'Ah! what obligations,' cried she, 'are the prince of Persia and I under to the honest man of whom you speak! I must see him, that I may hear from his own mouth what you tell me, and thank him for his extraordinary generosity towards persons or whom he is nowise obliged to concern himself. Do not fail to bring him here to-morrow.' Therefore, pray, sir, accompany me to the palace."

The jeweller submitted to the confident's arguments, and arose to follow her; but, notwithstanding his natural courage, he was seized with such violent terror, that his whole body trembled. "In the state you are," said she, "I perceive it will be better for you to remain at home, and that Schemselnihar should adopt other measures to see you; indeed, it cannot be doubted but that, to satisfy her desire, she will come hither herself. Such being the case, sir, I would not have you go; I am persuaded it will not be long ere you see her arrive. The confident justly anticipated this result; for Schemselnihar was no sooner informed of the jeweller's apprehensions, than she prepared to go to his house.

He received her with all the tokens of a profound respect. When she was seated, being a little fatigued with her journey, she unveiled herself, and displayed to the jeweller such beauty as compelled him to acknowledge that the prince of Persia was excusable in giving his heart to the caliph's favourite. She then saluted the jeweller with a graceful air, saying to him, "I could not learn with what zeal you have engaged in the interests of the prince of Persia, and in mine, without immediately forming a design to avow to you my gratitude.

Schemselnihar said several other obliging things to the jeweller, after which she returned to her palace. The jeweller went immediately to give an account of this visit to the prince of Persia, who said to him as soon as he saw him, "I have expected you impatiently. The trusty slave has brought me a letter from her mistress; but this letter affords me no consolation." "I see clearly," said the jeweller, "that the only means of affording you satisfaction, is to enable you to converse freely with Schemselnihar: this pleasure I will procure you, and will

to-morrow commence my operations. You must not expose yourself to enter Schemselnihar's palace ; you have found, by experience, the danger of that proceeding. I know a very convenient place for this interview, where you would be safe."

After the prince had thanked him for the zeal he had displayed, the jeweller returned home, where, early next morning, Schemselnihar's confident came in search of him. He told her that he had given the prince of Persia hopes he should very soon see Schemselnihar. "I am come expressly," answered she, "to devise measures with you for that purpose ; I think," continued she, "this house will be sufficiently commodious for their interview." "I could receive them here very well," replied he ; "but I think they will be more at liberty in another house of mine, where nobody resides at present : a short time will enable me to furnish it for their reception." "That matter settled," returned the confident, "I have only to obtain the consent of Schemselnihar : I will go and speak to her, and return in a little time with an answer."

She acted with the utmost diligence ; and returning speedily to the jeweller, told him that her mistress would not fail attending to the appointment in the evening. At the same time, she gave him a purse of money, which she told him was to purchase a collation

The joy of the prince of Persia, when the jeweller informed him of the object of his visit, may be easily conceived ; he totally forgot all his recent sufferings. Habiting himself in a magnificent robe, he without attendants accompanied the jeweller, who, to escape observation, conducted him through several by-streets, till they reached the house in which the interview was to be held, and where they awaited in conversation the arrival of Schemselnihar.

She came after evening prayer, with her confident, and attended by two other slaves. Words are inadequate to express the joy that seized the two lovers at sight of each other. Schemselnihar asked the jeweller if he had a lute, or other instrument. The jeweller, who had been careful to provide everything that could afford them pleasure presented to her a lute, with which she accompanied her voice, singing an air expressive of her passion.

While Schemselnihar was thus charming the prince of Persia, they were suddenly alarmed by a violent noise and immediately a slave entered in a fright to announce that persons were breaking down the gate. The jeweller, alarmed, quitted Schemselnihar and the prince, to ascertain the truth of this unpleasant information. He had already reached the court, when he perceived a troop of men, who had forced the gate, proceeding directly towards him. Placing himself against a wall, without being observed, he saw them pass, to the number of ten. From the place where he had found safety, he distinctly heard a confused noise, which continued till midnight ; when, as tranquillity appeared to be restored, he begged his neighbour to lend him a scimitar ; thus armed, he proceeded to the gate of his own house, and entering the court, perceived, with terror, a man, who demanded his business, but whom, by his voice, he directly knew to be his own slave. "By what means," said he to him, "did you avoid being taken by the watch ?" "Sir," replied the slave, "I concealed myself in a corner of the court, whence I came out as soon as the noise ceased. But it was not the watch that broke into your house ; they were robbers, who, a few days ago, pillaged another in this neighbourhood."

The jeweller examined the house, and found, in fact, that all the valuable furniture of the chamber, where he had received Schemselnihar and her lover, had been removed, with the vessels of gold and silver ; in a word, they had not left the most trifling article ; every place was stripped.

Daylight had scarcely returned, before the report of the robbery was circulated through the city, and his house was filled with friends and neighbours ; of whom the greater part, under pretence of consoling him for his loss, were brought by curiosity to hear the particulars. He thanked them for the affection they had shown him, and was at least gratified to find that nobody spoke of Schemselnihar or the prince of Persia, which afforded him reason to believe that they had regained their own residences, or were in some place of security.

About noon, one of his slaves informed him that there was a man, whom he knew not, at the gate, who desired to speak with him. The jeweller, unwilling to receive a stranger into his house, arose, and went to the door, to hear his business. "Though a stranger to you," said the man, "you are not unknown to me ; and I am come to talk with you concerning an important affair." The jeweller, at these words, begged him to enter. "No," replied the stranger ; "rather take the trouble, if you please, to accompany me to your other house. Follow me without apprehension ; I have something to communicate to you that will give you pleasure."

When they arrived before the house, and the stranger saw the gate had been half destroyed, "Let us pass by," said he to the jeweller ; "I see clearly that your statement is true ; I will conduct you to a place where we shall be better accommodated." Saying this, he proceeded ; and continued walking all the remainder of the day without stopping. The jeweller, fatigued with the journey, and vexed on observing the approach of night, and at the mysterious secrecy of his companion, who had not yet informed him where they were going, began to lose patience, when they arrived at a place that led to the Tigris. As soon as they reached the side of the river, they embarked in a little boat, and passed to the opposite shore. The stranger then conducted the jeweller through a long street, where he had never before been ; and after having traversed many by-streets, he stopped at a door, which he opened. He desired the jeweller to enter ; when closing the door, and securing it with a large iron bar, he showed him into a chamber, where were ten men unknown to the jeweller.

The men received the jeweller with very little ceremony. They desired him to be seated ; and he readily accepted the favour, for he was exhausted with his long journey. As they had waited supper for the arrival of their leader, he no sooner entered than it was served up. When the repast was ended, the men asked their guest if he knew with whom he spoke. He replied in the negative, and that he was even ignorant of what place he was in. "Relate to us your adventure of last night," said they ; "and do not attempt to disguise anything." The jeweller, astonished at their demand, replied, "Probably, gentlemen, you are already acquainted with it." "We are," returned they ; "the young man and young lady who were with you yesterday evening have mentioned it to us, but we wish to hear it from your own mouth. Nothing more was necessary to convince the jeweller that he was conversing with the robbers who had plundered his house. "Gentlemen," said he, "I am very much interested in the welfare of that young man and young woman ; can you give me any information concerning them ?" "Be under no apprehensions respecting them," replied the robbers ; "they are safe and well ;" at the same time showing him two closets, in which, they assured him, the young people were separately lodged. "They told us," continued the men, "that you only were acquainted with what relates to them. As soon as we knew this circumstance, we treated them with all possible respect, on your account ; and, so far from using the least violence, we have, on the contrary, afforded them the utmost indulgence. We will promise you the same security; and you may place the greatest confidence in us."

The jeweller, reassured by this discourse, and happy to find that the prince of Persia and Schemselnihar were safe, determined to engage the robbers still further in their interest. "Gentlemen," said he, "I must confess that I have not the honour of your acquaintance; but it affords me very great happiness to learn that I am not unknown to you; and I can never be sufficiently grateful for the favours which that knowledge has procured me on your part. With confidence in those qualities which are so justly your due, I will not hesitate faithfully to relate to you my history, together with that of the two persons whom you found in my house."

After the jeweller had taken these precautions to interest the robbers' fidelity in preserving the secret he had to reveal, which he thought could only produce a good effect, he recounted to them, without any omission, the detail of the amours of the prince of Persia and Schemselnihar, from their commencement to the interview at his house.

On receiving this information, the robbers went, one after another, to throw themselves at the feet of the prince and Schemselnihar, and to supplicate their pardon; protesting that they would not have forced the house of the jeweller, if they had been before informed of the quality of their persons. "But we will endeavour," continued they, "to repair the fault we have committed." Returning to the jeweller, "We are extremely sorry," said they, "that we are unable to restore to you the whole of the property which was taken from your house; part of it is no longer at our disposal. We must, therefore, beg you will be satisfied with the articles of silver which shall be immediately put into your hands."

The jeweller was delighted with his unexpected good fortune. When the robbers had delivered the silver plate, they introduced the prince of Persia and Schemselnihar, and promised them, together with the jeweller, that they should be conveyed to a place whence they might return to their respective homes; first requiring a pledge, on oath, not to betray them. Immediately the robbers set out with them.

On the road, the jeweller, uneasy at not seeing either the confident or the two slaves, approached Schemselnihar, and begged her to tell him what was become of them. "I know nothing of either," replied she; "all I can inform you is, that after being taken from your house, we were conveyed across the river, and thence conducted to the place where you found us."

Schemselnihar and the jeweller had no further discourse; but, proceeding with the robbers and the prince, they arrived at the border of the river, where their conductors took a boat, and accompanied them to the opposite side.

While the prince of Persia, Schemselnihar, and the jeweller were disembarking, they heard the sound of the horse-watch hastily approaching towards them; and it came up at the moment the robbers had quitted the land, rowing away with their utmost strength.

The commander of the brigade demanded of the prince, Schemselnihar, and the jeweller, who they were, and whence they came at so late an hour. Seized with terror, and fearful of saying what might be injurious to them, they remained confounded. It was, however, necessary to reply; and the jeweller, whose mind was rather more free from alarm, answered, "Sir, I can assure you that we are honest people of this town. The men who landed us from the boat, and then repassed to the other side, are robbers, who last night broke into the house where we were, and after having pillaged it, took us to their residence; from which through our solicitations and entreaties, we have been liberated, and they have reconveyed us here. They have likewise restored to us a part of the booty which they had obtained.

The commander of the watch, not satisfied with the statement of the jeweller, approached him and the prince of Persia, and looking steadfastly at them, one after the other, "Tell me truly," said he, "who is this lady, how did you become acquainted with her, and where do you reside?" This demand very much embarrassed them, and they knew not what to reply. Schemselnihar, at length, overcame the difficulty; taking the officer aside, she told him her quality; which he no sooner heard, than he dismounted, with the greatest marks of respect, and ordered his men to prepare two boats immediately.

When the boats were ready, the commander put Schemselnihar in one, and the prince of Persia and the jeweller in the other, with two of his people in each boat, whom he directed to accompany them wherever they wished to be conveyed. The two boats each taking a different course, I shall, at present, follow that in which were the prince of Persia and the jeweller.

The prince, to lessen the trouble of the jeweller and their conductors, told the latter that he should take his friend home with him, and named the place of his residence. On this information, their conductors landed them opposite the caliph's palace. The prince of Persia and the jeweller were thereby much alarmed, though they dared not show their apprehensions; notwithstanding they heard the order which the officer had given, they suspected that they were to be left in custody of the guard, and taken before the caliph next morning. But this was not the intention of the guides; who, having to rejoin their brigade, recommended them to the officer on duty, and he assigned them two soldiers, to conduct them to the prince of Persia's house, which was at some distance from the river, where they at length arrived, but so weak and fatigued that they could scarcely move.

But the prince of Persia was still so weak as to be unable to utter a word; he could only reply by signs, even to his friends who spoke to him. He continued in the same state next morning, when the jeweller took leave, to return home.

The jeweller's return had been anxiously expected by his family during the day on which he left home with the stranger; and as he did not appear, they concluded he had met with some fatal accident. His wife, his children, and his domestics were in the greatest alarm; and he found them all in tears when he arrived. They were overjoyed at seeing him safe, but his altered looks since he quitted them, gave them considerable inquietude. Finding himself very unwell, he remained in the house two days, to recruit his spirits, seeing only some of his most intimate friends, who had, by his orders, free entrance.

The third day, his strength appearing somewhat re-established, he went out to take the air. He proceeded to the shop of a rich merchant, one of his friends, with whom he conversed for a long time. As he arose to take leave, he observed a woman beckon to him, and whom he immediately recognised as the confident of Schemselnihar. She followed him, as he expected; because the place in which they were was not convenient for them to speak together.

He continued until he reached a mosque which was little frequented, and which he knew would not then be occupied; he entered, and was followed by the slave, with whom he had thus the liberty of conversing unobserved.

After reciprocally expressing their joy at meeting each other, the jeweller desired the confident to inform him how she and the two slaves had escaped, and inquired if she could give him any information respecting Schemselnihar since he had parted from her. But the confident expressed so earnest a wish to hear first what had occurred to him since their sudden separation, that he was obliged to comply with her request. Having concluded his relation, he begged she would, in her turn, satisfy him in what he had demanded.

"When I saw the robbers entering," said the confident, " I supposed that they were soldiers belonging to the caliph's guard; that the caliph had been apprised of the meeting, and had sent them to massacre the prince and all of us. I hastily ascended to the terrace at the top of your house, while the thieves were engaged in the chamber where we had left the prince of Persia and Schemselnihar, and was quickly followed by the two slaves. Going from terrace to terrace, we reached that of a house belonging to very civil people, who received us with the greatest kindness, and with them we passed the night.

"The next morning we returned to the palace of Schemselnihar, which we entered in the utmost perturbation; and what rendered our affliction the more poignant, we were unacquainted with the fate of the two unfortunate lovers. Schemselnihar's other female attendants were astonished at seeing us return without their mistress; we told them, as we had predetermined, that she had stopped at the house of a lady, one of her friends, and would send for us when she wished to be taken home; with which excuse they appeared to be satisfied.

"I passed the day in the greatest inquietude; and, at the approach of night, opening a little back-gate, I perceived a small boat on the canal, driving with the stream. Calling to the boatman, I begged him to row from side to side along the river; and if he should discover a lady, to bring her with him.

"I awaited his return with the two slaves, who were in as much trouble as myself, until midnight, when the same boat arrived, having two men in front, and a lady lying in the stern. As soon as the boat had reached the shore, the men assisted the lady to rise, and to land; when I had the inexpressible pleasure to recognise my mistress Schemselnihar. When she had landed, she whispered to me, to go and fetch a purse containing a thousand pieces of gold, and give it to the soldiers who had accompanied her. Leaving her, I soon brought the money, which I presented to them; and, having paid the boatman, I reclosed the gate, and followed Schemselnihar, whom I rejoined before she had reached her chamber. We lost no time in putting her to bed, where she remained all night in the most imminent danger of her life.

"When I perceived that she was able to converse, I begged of her to acquaint me by what good fortune she had escaped the hands of the robbers. 'Why do you require me,' she said, sighing heavily, 'to renew the subject of my grief?' 'Madam,' I replied, 'I beg you will not refuse my request. You are not ignorant that the unfortunate find a sort of consolation in relating their distresses.'

"'Listen then,' said she, 'to the most afflicting occurrence that could happen to a person impassioned as I am. When I saw the robbers enter, with scimitars and poniards in their hands, I believed the destruction of the prince of Persia and myself inevitable. But, instead of rushing upon us, and seathing their weapons in our hearts, two of them were appointed to guard us, while the others were employed packing up all the property in the house. When they had finished, and taken the booty on their backs, they departed, forcing us to accompany them.

"'The next day the jeweller was brought; and, thinking to oblige us, as in fact he did, he confessed to the robbers who we were. The thieves then came to beg my pardon; and I believe they acted in the same manner towards the prince of Persia, who was in another place; and they declared that they would not have forced the house where we were, if they had known it belonged to the jeweller. They immediately conducted the prince, the jeweller, and me, to the side of the river, where we embarked in a boat, by which we were conveyed to the opposite shore; but we had scarcely landed, when a brigade of the horse-watch galloped up to us. Taking the commander aside, I told him my name, and said that, on the preceding evening, while on my return from the house of a friend, the robbers, who were re-crossing the river, had seized me, and conveyed me to their residence; that having informed them who I was, they had released me, granting the same favour to the two persons you see here on my account. The officer immediately dismounted, to do me honour; and, after expressing his happiness in having the power to afford me assistance, he provided two boats, on board one of which I embarked, with two of his men, whom you have seen, who escorted me hither: he sent the prince of Persia and the jeweller in the other, also with two of his people to accompany them, and to conduct them safely to their respective homes.'

"I was obliged to be silent, and am come hither in compliance with her commands. I have been at your house; where not finding you, and in the uncertainty of meeting with you at the place to which your people directed me, I had almost determined to go to the prince's residence, but dared not undertake so long a journey. I left the two purses, in passing, with an acquaintance; wait for me here, and I will bring them in a few minutes."

The confident soon returned to the jeweller, who remained in the mosque, where she had left him; and presenting to him the two purses, "Take them," said she, "and satisfy your friends." He then agreed with the confident, that she should meet him at the house where they held their first interview, whenever she had anything to communicate from Schemselnihar, or wished to hear from the prince of Persia; after which they separated.

Next morning, the jeweller again waited on the prince, who desired him to take a seat: "You know," said he, "that everything must have an end: twice have I been near the completion of my wishes, when I was torn away from the idol of my soul, and in the most cruel manner imaginable. After what has passed, I can only look for death, as a solace from my troubles."

The jeweller, who knew no more effectual means of diverting his despair, than by recalling Schemselnihar to his mind, and giving him some shade of hope, told him, he was afraid the confident might be already at his house, and it would, therefore, be imprudent for him to remain longer from home. "I will suffer you to go," replied the prince; "and when you see her, I beg you will earnestly desire her to assure Schemselnihar, that if I am to die, which I very soon expect, I shall continue to love her till the last breath."

The jeweller then returned to his house, and anxiously awaited the arrival of the confident. After the lapse of some hours, she appeared, but in tears, and in very great affliction. The jeweller, alarmed, inquired with much solicitude the cause of her distress. "Schemselnihar, the prince of Persia, you, and I are all lost! Hear the

sad news I learned yesterday, on re-entering the palace, after having parted from you. Schemselnihar, for some offence, had chastised one of the slaves whom you saw with her at your other house: the slave, enraged by the punishment, and finding the door of the palace open, ran away, and took refuge with an eunuch of our guard, who has afforded her shelter, and to whom, we have no doubt, she has exposed everything. But this is not all : the other slave also has taken to flight, and found safety in the palace of the caliph; and we have reason to believe she has revealed to him all our proceedings; for, just before I came out, twenty eunuchs arrived, to conduct Schemselnihar to the palace. I found means to steal away, to give you intimation of the circumstance: I know not what will be the result ; but I augur no good. Whatever it be, I beg you to be secret. She said no more, but retired speedily, without waiting for an answer.

The jeweller remained immoveable, as if thunderstruck, with the news ; he, however, soon called to mind the urgency of the occasion, and summoning his faculties, went immediately to the prince of Persia. Entering with a countenance that indicated the unfortunate intelligence he had to announce, "Prince," said he, "prepare to encounter the most terrible assault you have ever had to oppose." "Tell me instantly," cried the prince, "what you have to relate; do not keep me in torture; if my life be required, I am prepared to surrender it." The jeweller then repeated to him the confident's information. "You see," continued he, "if you delay, your destruction is inevitable. Rise, then; save yourself quickly; time is precious."

At this moment, the prince appeared ready to expire with affliction, grief, and terror; but, recovering himself, he asked the jeweller what resolution he would advise him to adopt in so pressing a conjuncture. "There is no alternative," replied the jeweller, "but to mount on horseback immediately, take the road to Anbar, and get there before daybreak to-morrow. Let such of your people accompany you as you judge proper ; and permit me to save myself with you."

The prince, who saw no other means of safety, gave orders for such preparations as could be completed with the greatest facility ; furnished himself with money and jewels; and departed with the utmost expedition, accompanied by the jeweller, and the attendants he had selected.

They travelled during the remainder of the day, and all the night, without stopping, till within two or three hours of sun-rising next morning, when, both themselves and their horses being quite exhausted, they alighted to enjoy some repose. Scarcely had they time to breathe, before they were assailed by a strong band of robbers, against whom they defended themselves very courageously for some time ; but the prince's attendants being killed, he and the jeweller were compelled to lay down their arms, and submit at discretion.

When the thieves had quitted them, "What is to be done," cried the prince, "in this dilemma? Had I not better have remained at Bagdad, and encountered my fate, than be reduced to this extremity?" "Prince," replied the jeweller, "God pleases to add affliction to affliction, and we ought not to murmur at His will, but receive these chastisements from His hand with entire submission. Let us not remain any longer here; but let us seek some place of security, where we may find succour in our misfortunes." The jeweller persuaded him to comply ; and, after proceeding some time, they reached a mosque, which was open, where they entered, and passed the rest of the night.

At daybreak, a man alone entered the mosque. When he had said his prayer, and was turning to go out, he perceived the prince of Persia and the jeweller, who were sitting in a corner. He approached; and saluting them with great civility, "By what I observe," said he, "it would seem to me that you are strangers." "You are not deceived," replied the jeweller; "we have been robbed this night, on our way from Bagdad, and are in want of succour, but know not to whom to apply." "If you will take the trouble to accompany me home," said the man, "I will willingly afford you all the assistance in my power." The man, observing them consult together, imagined that they hesitated to accept his services, and therefore asked them how they meant to act. "We are willing to follow you," replied the jeweller; "the only circumstance that embarrasses us, is our being naked, and we are ashamed to be seen in this state." Fortunately the man could accommodate them with covering sufficient to enable them to proceed to his house; where they had no sooner arrived, than he presented to each of them very decent clothing; and, not doubting that they were in want of food, he sent them several dishes by a slave. But they ate little, particularly the prince, who was so languid and dejected, that the jeweller had the greatest fears for his life.

Their host visited them repeatedly during the day; and at night, as he knew they wanted repose, he took leave of them at an early hour. But the jeweller was very soon obliged to call him to assist in the last duties to the prince of Persia. He perceived that the prince breathed short, and with difficulty, which made him suppose he had not long to live; and approaching near him, "It is done," said the prince, "as you perceive; and I am happy that you are present to witness my last sigh. All the regret I feel, is, in not dying in the arms of my dear mother, who always loved me tenderly, and for whom I have constantly entertained the highest respect. Express to her the grief I suffer on that account, and beg her, in my name, to have my remains conveyed to Bagdad, that she may bedew my tomb with her tears, and assist my departed soul with her prayers." He forgot not the master of the house, to whom he made his acknowledgments for the hospitality he had experienced; and, after praying him to suffer his body to remain there till it should be demanded by his friends, he expired.

Early the day after the death of the prince of Persia, the jeweller took the opportunity of a numerous caravan which was going to Bagdad, and returned there in safety. He stopped at his own house merely to change his apparel, and immediately proceeded to the hotel of the deceased prince of Persia, at which his appearance, alone, excited great alarm. He requested the attendants to apprise the mother of the prince that he wished to speak with her; and he was soon introduced to the saloon where she was, with several of her women. "Madam," said the jeweller, with an air and in a tone which indicated the afflicting news he had to announce, "Heaven preserve you, and bestow on you its choicest blessings! You are sensible that God disposes of us all agreeably to his will."

The lady would not allow the jeweller to say more. "Ah!" cried she, "you come to tell me that my son is dead!" at the same time uttering the most lamentable cries, which, joined to those of her women, renewed the tears

of the jeweller. At length, she ceased her sighs and tears, and begged him to proceed, without concealing any circumstance relative to her sad loss. He then gave her a particular account of all that had passed, concluding with the prince's dying request. Accordingly, next morning, at daybreak, she set out from Bagdad, accompanied by her women, and the greater part of her slaves.

When the jeweller had taken leave of the mother of the prince of Persia, he returned to his own house very sad. As he proceeded, endeavouring to collect his wandering faculties, a woman presented herself, and stopped before him; he raised his eyes, and saw the confident of Schemselnihar, habited in black, weeping. The sight of her renewed his distress, and, without speaking, he continued his road, till he reached the place of his residence, where he, with the confident following, entered.

Being seated, the jeweller began the discourse by asking the confident, with a heavy sigh, if she had already heard of the prince of Persia's death, and if it was him she lamented. "Alas, no!" cried she. "What is, then, that charming prince dead? He has not long survived his dear Schemselnihar. Heavenly souls!" continued she, "wherever you remain, you ought to rejoice that your love will meet with no further obstacle."

The jeweller, who was unacquainted with the death of Schemselnihar, and who had not observed that the confident was dressed in mourning, experienced additional distress at this information. "Ah! is Schemselnihar no more?" cried he. "She is dead," replied the confident, her tears increasing; "and it is for her I mourn. You may remember that I informed you the caliph had sent for Schemselnihar to the palace: it was true, as we conjectured, that the caliph had been apprised of the amours of his favourite with the prince of Persia, by the two slaves, whom he had interrogated separately. The caliph received her with an open countenance. 'Schemselnihar,' said he, 'I cannot bear your appearing before me evidently under extreme affliction. You know with how fervid a passion I have always loved you: the continual demonstrations I have given, have proved my affection, and which is still unabated. You have enemies; and those enemies have made reports to injure your character; but their malice has had no impression on me. Shake off, then, this melancholy, and prepare, agreeably to your custom, to entertain me in the evening with something pleasant and diverting.' He continued to speak to her with the utmost kindness, and, at length, desired her to go into a magnificent apartment, where he begged her to wait for him.

"The caliph entered in the evening to the sound of instruments, and the collation was immediately served. The caliph took my mistress by the hand, and seated her near him on the sofa. She made so great an exertion to comply with his desire, that she was incapable of supporting it; in effect, she was scarcely on the seat, before she sunk backward and expired.

"The caliph thought she had fainted; and we were all of the same opinion, and endeavoured to assist her, but too late—she was no more! The caliph honoured her with his tears, which he could not restrain; and, before retiring to his apartment, he gave orders that all the musical instruments should be destroyed, which were accordingly executed. I continued with her remains all night, performing to them the last sad offices I had the power of rendering, and bathing them with my tears. The next day her body was interred, by order of the caliph, in a magnificent tomb which he had already built, in a place she had herself chosen. 'Since you tell me,' added the confident, "that the corse of the prince of Persia is to be brought to Bagdad, I am resolved to endeavour to obtain permission for it to be deposited in the same tomb."

The jeweller was much astonished at the confident's concluding observation:—"You will not surely attempt what you mention!" said he; "the caliph will never suffer it." "When I inform you," replied she, "that the caliph has given liberty to all her slaves, with a competent pension to each, and has charged me with the care of my mistress's tomb, allowing me a considerable annuity to preserve it, and for my own maintenance, you will not think it impossible to obtain his consent." The jeweller had nothing more to say; he therefore merely begged the confident to conduct him to the tomb, that he might offer up his prayer.

As the jeweller approached the place of Schemselnihar's interment, he was greatly surprised to find a crowd of people assembling from all parts of Bagdad. He was, consequently, obliged to say his prayer at a distance; and when he had finished, returning to the confident, "I am now persuaded," said he, "there will be no difficulty in executing what you have so well imagined. We have only to publish our knowledge of the tender connection between you, mistress and the prince, and that they died nearly at the same moment; and before the body of the prince of Persia arrives, all Bagdad will concur in demanding its interment with that of Schemselnihar." It happened precisely as the jeweller had anticipated; and on the day when the corse was expected to reach the city, an infinite number of people went out to meet it, to a distance of more than twenty miles. The confident attended at the city-gate, where, presenting herself before the prince's mother, she supplicated her, in compliance with the ardent wish of all the city, to consent that the bodies of the two lovers, whose hearts had been so firmly united, might rest in the same tomb. She willingly complied; and the remains of the prince were carried at the head of the procession, composed of an immense concourse of people of all ranks, and laid by the side of Schemselnihar.

THE AMOURS OF CAMARALZAMAN, PRINCE OF THE ISLE OF THE CHILDREN OF KHALEDAN, AND OF BADOURE, PRINCESS OF CHINA.

AT about the distance of twenty days' sail from the coast of Persia, in the main ocean, is an island, called the Isle of the Children of Khaledan. This island is divided into several large provinces, which contain flourishing and populous towns, forming together a potent kingdom. Formerly it was governed by a king named Schahzaman, who had four lawful wives, all daughters of kings, and sixty concubines.

Schahzaman esteemed himself the most fortunate monarch of the earth, in the tranquillity and and prosperity of his reign. One circumstance only troubled his happiness, which was, that, though already advanced in years, and notwithstanding he had so many wives and concubines, he was without children. He long dissembled the chagrin with which he was tormented, and which irritated his feelings the more as he considered the disguise necessary. At length, however, he broke silence; and one day, after complaining bitterly of his misfortune to his grand vizier, to whom he privately addressed himself, he asked if he knew by what means it might be remedied.

"If what your majesty demands of me," replied the sage minister, "depended on the ordinary rules of human wisdom, you should very soon have the satisfaction you so ardently desire ; but I confess that my experience and knowledge are insufficient to enable me to solve the difficulty. From God alone can we obtain assistance in wants of this description.

You have some subjects who particularly profess to honour, to serve, and to live in fear and love of Him ; my advice is, that your majesty should bestow alms upon them, and exhort them to join their prayers with yours ; perhaps, in the number, one may be found sufficiently pure and agreeable to God to obtain your wishes." The king Schahzaman highly approved of this counsel, for which he thanked the vizier. He ordered rich alms should be distributed liberally to all the religious communities ; he sent for their superiors, and having regaled them with a frugal repast, he declared to them his intention, and begged them to acquaint the members of their respective establishments.

164

In fine, Schahzaman obtained the object of his solicitude, in the birth of a son, and the event was celebrated, not only in his capital, but throughout his dominions, by public rejoicings for an entire week. The prince was presented to him as soon as born, and he appeared to him so beautiful, that he gave him the name of Camaralzaman, that is, *the moon of the age.*

The prince Camaralzaman was nursed with all imaginable care; and, as soon as he had attained the proper age, the sultan Schahzaman gave him a sage governor and able preceptors. These persons found in him a capacity to receive all the instructions they wished to inculcate, whether for the regulation of his manners, or in the knowledge more particularly appertaining to the education of a prince.

When he had reached the age of fifteen years, the sultan, who loved him tenderly, conceived the design of surrendering him his throne, and acquainted his grand vizier with his intention. "I am fearful," said he, "that my son should lose, in the heedlessness of youth, not only the advantages that nature has bestowed upon him, but likewise those he has acquired with so much success by the good education I have been anxious to afford him. As I am now of an age to think of retreating from the toils of state, I have resolved to abandon the government to him, and to pass the rest of my days in the satisfaction of seeing him reign."

The grand vizier seemed to enter into his views. "Sir," replied he, "the prince is yet very young, in my humble opinion, to take upon himself the weight of a burden so heavy as that of governing a powerful state. Your majesty very justly fears he may, in his early age, acquire habits of laziness; but, to correct that failing, would it not be advisable, first, to marry him? Marriage will render him more sedate, and prevent his giving way to dissipation."

Schahzaman thought his minister's advice very reasonable and just; and, therefore, having dismissed him, he summoned prince Camaralzaman into his presence. The prince was not a little surprised at this unexpected order; and, instead of appearing before him with his accustomed freedom, he saluted him with great respect, and remained motionless, with his eyes directed towards the ground. When the sultan observed the prince's embarrassment. "My son," said he, kindly, "do you know for what purpose I have called you?" "Sir," replied the prince, modestly, "God only can penetrate the hearts of his creatures; I attend with pleasure your majesty's commands." "I sent for you," returned the sultan, "to inform you of my determination that you should marry. What think you of it?"

Prince Camaralzaman heard these words with much uneasiness: he was disconcerted, his face glowed, and he knew not what to reply. After a silence of some moments, "Sir," said he, "I beseech your majesty to pardon me if I seem confounded at the declaration you have made; young as I am, I was unprepared for it. However, I humbly submit it is necessary I should have some time to consider your majesty's proposition."

After a year had elapsed, the sultan took prince Camaralzaman aside, "Well, my son," said he, "have you thoroughly considered the design I expressed, to marry you, about a twelvemonth since?" The prince seemed less disconcerted than before; and, with little hesitation, replied firmly, "Sir, I have not neglected to reflect seriously on what you indicated; but, after maturely weighing the subject in my mind, I am yet more confirmed in my determination not to enter into the state of marriage. In short, the infinite evils that women have occasioned at every period of the world, as I have fully learned in our histories, and what I every day hear of their malice, are the motives which persuade me to have no connexion with them." Concluding thus, he quitted the sultan his father without waiting his reply.

Sultan Schahzaman then went to the apartment of the mother of prince Camaralzaman, to whom he had long expressed his ardent desire for the marriage of his son. After relating to her, with sorrow, in what manner he had been a second time refused, "Madam," said he, "I know that Camaralzaman has more confidence in you than in me, and will listen to you with greater attention. I beg you will take an opportunity of speaking seriously with him, and give him to understand that, if he continue to oppose my determination, he will compel me to adopt measures for which I shall be very sorry, and which will cause him to repent his disobedience."

A long while afterwards, Fatima thought she had found an opportunity of speaking to him. "My son," said she, "I beg of you to inform me what is the reason that creates in your mind so great an aversion from marriage? If you have no other than the malice and wickedness of some women, nothing can be more weak. I will not undertake the defence of bad women, but it is the most intolerable act of injustice to decry all without exception."

"Madam," replied Camaralzaman, "I doubt not there are many women chaste, virtuous, good, affable, and of engaging manners. Would to God they all resembled you! Supposing I should submit to engage in marriage, as the sultan my father urges with so much impatience, what wife would he give me?—A princess, probably, the daughter of a neighbouring potentate, who would think himself honoured by the alliance; and, handsome or ugly, I must not refuse her. But, if she should be an incomparable beauty, who can assure me that her mind will be in unison with her exterior—that she will be affable, complaisant, entertaining—and of an engaging disposition—in a word, that she will not be haughty, proud, disdainful, peevish; and will not waste a state by her culpable extravagance in clothes, jewels, toys, and a train of ridiculous magnificence;—but should this princess even be so perfect and accomplished, as to be irreproachable on either of these points, I have a great number of reasons yet more weighty to confirm me in my sentiments and resolution."

"What, my son!" returned Fatima, "have you more objections than those you have already advanced? However, I could perhaps obviate them, and silence you in a moment. I would say that it is easy for a prince, when he has espoused a princess such as you have described, to put her away, and effectually prevent her ruining his state." "Ah, madam!" said prince Camaralzaman, "do you not perceive the terrible mortification a prince would suffer in being reduced to that extremity? Would it not have been better, for his glory and his repose, that he had never exposed himself to that alternative?" "But, my son," added Fatima, "if this be your opinion, I should suppose you wish to be the last of your race of kings, who have reigned so gloriously in the Isle of the Children of Khaledan." "Madam," replied the prince, "I do not desire to survive the king my father; and should I die before him, it will be by no means extraordinary, since many children have preceded their fathers in ceasing to exist."

After that time, Fatima had often similar conversations with prince Camaralzaman; and she omitted no opportunity or argument to endeavour to overcome his settled aversion. But he eluded all the reasons she could adduce, by advancing others to which she was unable to reply, and remained immoveable.

The year elapsed, and to the great regret of sultan Schahzaman, the prince Camaralzaman indicated not the least

change of sentiment. One day the solemn council was assembled, at which the prime-vizier, the other viziers, the principal officers of the crown, and the generals of the army, were present; when the sultan thus addressed the prince. "My son, a long time has passed since I first expressed to you my anxiety to see you married: and I expected you would have shewn more complaisance to a father who required from you nothing unreasonable. After a studied resistance on your part, which has almost exhausted my patience, I find it necessary to repeat the proposition in presence of my council. Declare then your determination; that I may, according with your reply, adopt such measures as I consider requisite." The prince answered with so little discretion, or rather with insult, that the sultan, justly irritated at the affront offered him in full council, exclaimed, "What! unnatural son! have you the insolence to speak thus to your father and your sultan!" and immediately ordered his guards to arrest him, and convey him to an ancient tower, long since abandoned, where he was confined, with a bed, a few articles of furniture, some books, and one slave only to attend upon him.

In this tower was a well, which, during the day, served as a retreat for a fairy named Maimoune, daughter of Damriat, king or chief of a legion of genii It was about midnight, when Maimoune arose lightly from the well, to traverse the world, according to her custom, wherever curiosity might lead her. Surprised at seeing a light in the chamber of Prince Camaralzaman, she entered, and without stopping to observe the slave who was lying at the door, approached the bed, to which she was attracted by its magnificence, when her astonishment was increased by the sight of a person sleeping.

Prince Camaralzaman lay with his face half covered with the bed-clothes; and Maimoune, having removed them a little, saw the most handsome young man she had ever beheld in her rambles through the habitable world. "How splendid," said she to herself, "or rather what a prodigy of beauty, must not this be, when the eyes, concealed by so well formed enclosures, are exposed! What occasion can a person of his high rank have given for so rigorous treatment!" She knew the prince, and was already partly acquainted with his history.

Maimoune could scarcely cease admiring Prince Camaralzaman; but at length, after having gently kissed him, she re-placed the bed covering as before, and took her flight into the air. As she mounted very high toward the middle region, she heard the clapping of wings, which induced her to fly to the same quarter; and, approaching, she knew it was a geni that occasioned the noise, but one of the tribe which is in rebellion against God. For Maimoune belonged to that class which the great Solomon had obliged to conform.

The geni, whose name war Danhasch, son of Schamarasch, also recognised Maimoune, but with great dread, as he knew the vast superiority she had over him, in consequence of her submission to God. He would gladly have avoided the rencontre; but he found himself so near her, that it was absolutely necessary either to fight or submit. He adopted the latter proceeding. "Brave Maimoune," said he, in a tone of supplication, "swear to me, in the great name of Heaven, that you will not do me injury, and I will make the same pledge to you, on my part." "Cursed geni!" replied Maimoune, "what ill canst thou do me? I fear thee not. However, I will grant you the favour you desire, and swear not to hurt you. Now tell me, whence you came, what you have seen, and the acts you have performed this night?" "Fair lady," answered Danhasch, "you have met me very opportunely, to learn something wonderful. I am come from the farthest limits of China, which look on the last islands of this hemisphere." "But charming Maimoune!" said Danhasch, interrupting himself, and so much terrified at the presence of the fairy, that he could scarcely speak, "promise, at least, that you will pardon me, and leave me at liberty when I have satisfied your demands." "Proceed, proceed, cursed spirit!" returned Maimoune, "and be under no apprehension."

Danasch, the country of China, whence I came, is one of the largest and most powerful kingdoms of the earth. The present king, whose name is Gaiour, has one daughter, the most beautiful woman ever seen since the creation of the world. Her hair is brown, and of so great length, that it would descend far beyond her feet; when dressed and buckled on her head, it not ill resembles a bunch of raisins of extraordinary size: her forehead is as smooth as the best polished mirror, and admirably formed; her eyes are black, brilliant, and full of fire: her nose is neither too long nor too short; her mouth small, and of a lively red; her teeth are like two rows of pearls, surpassing the most beautiful in clearness; and her voice is wonderfully soft and agreeable, while her expressions indicate the vivacity of her mind. Her neck is not excelled in colour by the whitest alabaster In a word, by this very inadequate sketch, you may easily judge that there is not a beauty in the world more perfect.

Any one not well acquainted with the king, father of this princess, would suppose from the marks of paternal tenderness which he continually shows her, that he was enamoured of his own daughter. Never did the most impassioned lover, or the most jealous husband, watch the object of his solicitude with greater care: and, that the restraint he feels it necessary to impose should not seem irksome to her, he has built for her seven palaces, of incomparable magnificence. The first palace is of rock-crystal; the second of bronze; the third of fine steel; the fourth of another kind of bronze, more precious than either of the two former; the fifth of touchstone; the sixth of silver; and the seventh of massy gold. He has furnished them all with unheard of sumptuousness, each in a manner suitable to the material of which it is composed. In a word, king Gaiour has exhibited to the world that he thinks no expense too considerable to gratify his paternal affection.

"The fame of the beauty of this unequalled princess had induced the most powerful neighbouring potentates to send solemn embassies to demand her in marriage; all of which the king of China admitted with equal ceremony; so, as he is resolved not to marry the princess against her inclination, and she did not agree to be united with either of the parties proposed, if the ambassadors retired little satisfied with the result of their application, they were, at least, gratified by the civilities and honours they received.

"'Sir,' said the princess to the king her father, 'you wish me to marry, and you think thereby to afford me great satisfaction: I am persuaded that is your opinion, for which I am very much obliged to you. But where, excepting with your majesty, can I find such superb palaces, and gardens so delicious? Under your kind protection, I have perfect freedom, and I receive the same honours as are paid to your own person: these are advantages that I should not find in any other part of the world, or with any spouse to whom I might be given.'

"After several embassies, there arrived one on the part of a king richer and more powerful than either of those who had been presented. The king of China spoke of him to his daughter, and urged how much it would be for her advantage to accept him as a husband: but the princess supplicated her father to permit her refusal, assigning the same reasons she had before advanced. The king, however, continued to press her compliance; and she, at length, in the vexation caused by his solicitations, forgot the respect and duty she owed him. "Sir," said she, "speak

no more to me of this marriage, nor of any other ; or I will plunge this poniard in my breast, and deliver myself from your importunities!" The king of China, extremely displeased at the conduct of the princess, replied, "Daughter, you are mad, and I will treat you as a lunatic :" and he accordingly had her shut up in an apartment of one of her palaces, allowing her only ten old women for her companions, and to attend upon her, of whom the principal had been her nurse. Afterwards, that the neighbouring kings might no longer think of her, he sent an ambassador to each, to announce her aversion from marriage ; and, as he doubted not she had lost her senses, he commanded his messengers to signify in the different courts, that if there were any physician sufficiently skilful to accomplish her recovery, he should have her for wife in recompense of his services."

Instead of replying to Danhasch, Maimoune burst into violent laughter, which she continued a long time ; and the geni, unconscious of the cause, remained in great astonishment. When she had, in some measure, recovered her serenity : " Good, good," said she ; " you would have me believe all that you have related ! Fie, fie ! what would you say, detestable geni ! if you had seen the beautiful prince I have this moment quitted, and whom I love with an affection equal to his merits !" "Agreeable Maimoune !" returned Danhasch, "may I presume to inquire the name of whom you speak?" "Know," answered the fairy, "that nearly the same circumstance has happened to him, as to the princess whose story you have mentioned. The king his father would have compelled him to marry ; but, after resisting long-continued importunities, he at length frankly declared his determination not to submit : and he is, in consequence, at this moment, confined in the old tower where I abide, and whence I am just come from admiring him." " I will not absolutely contradict you," said Danhasch ; " but, you must permit me to believe that no mortal can be comparable to my princess in beauty." "Hold your tongue, cursed geni !" replied Maimoune : " I tell you again, your judgment is ridiculous." " I will not oppose my opinion to yours," returned Danhasch ; " the only means by which you can be convinced whether what I have stated be true or false, is to see my princess, and then to show me your prince." " It is unnecessary I should take that trouble," said Maimoune ; " there is another method, by which we may be equally satisfied ; bring your princess, and place her on the bed by the side of my prince. Thus, we may compare them together ; and it will be easy to settle our dispute."

Danhasch then quitted the fairy, and flew directly to China, whence he returned with incredible diligence, conveying the beautiful princess with him, in a sound sleep. Maimoune received her from him, and having introduced her to the chamber of the prince Camaralzaman, placed her on the bed, by his side.

Maimoune struck the ground with her foot, the earth opened, and there arose a hideous geni, hump-backed, one-eyed, and lame, with six horns on his head, and claws to his hands and feet. As soon as he had quitted his subterraneous abode, the earth closed ; when perceiving Maimoune, he threw himself at her feet, and rising on one knee, inquired what humble service she wanted him to perform. " Rise, Caschcasch," said she ; " I have summoned you hither, to decide a dispute I have had with this cursed Danhasch. Cast your eye on this bed, and tell us without partiality, which you think the most beautiful, the young man or the young lady ?" Caschcasch regarded the prince and princess with extraordinary surprise and admiration ; and after he had well considered them, without the power of determining which deserved the preference, " Madam," said he to Maimoune, " I must confess I should deceive you, and betray myself, if I were to say that either appears to me handsomer than the other. But as a means to settle your controversy, I would advise that they be awakened, one after the other ; and that you agree the person who expresses the most love for the other, by ardour, eagerness, and passion, shall be pronounced least beautiful."

This proposal of Caschcasch was equally pleasing to Maimoune and to Danhasch. Maimoune then changed herself into a flea, and leaped on the neck of Camaralzaman, whom she pinched so acutely that he awoke, putting his hand quickly to the part bitten ; but Maimoune had immediately skipped away, and resumed her pristine form, which, like that of the two genii, was invisible.

In drawing back his hand, the prince let it fall on that of the princess of China. He opened his eyes, and was astonished at seeing a lady, and of so great beauty, sleeping by his side. He raised his head, and leaned on his elbow, the better to observe her ; when the youth of the princess, and her incomparable beauty, inflamed him in an instant with a fire of which he had never before been sensible, and which he had constantly guarded himself from with the utmost aversion. Love now seized his heart with so lively an impression that he could not avoid crying out, " What beauty ! what charms !—My heart, my soul !"—Saying these words, he kissed her forehead, her cheeks and her mouth, with so little precaution, that she would certainly have been awakened, had she not slept more profoundly, through the enchantment of Danhasch. "How ! my charming lady," said the prince, " do you not awake at these testimonies of love, given you by prince Camaralzaman ! Whoever you be, he is not unworthy of your affection." He was going to awaken her ; but suddenly checking himself, " Is not this the lady," said he, mentally, " that the sultan my father would have given me in marriage ?—He has acted unwisely, in not letting me see her before. Had he done so, I should not have offended him, by my disobedience.

" Perhaps the sultan wishes to surprise me. Without doubt, he has sent this young lady to prove if I am so averse to marriage as I have appeared to him. Who knows but that he brought her himself ; or that he is not concealed, to witness and expose my dissimulation ? This second crime would be much greater than the former. At all events, I will be contented with this ring in remembrance of her." It was a very elegant ring, which the princess had on her finger. He drew it gently off, and replaced it with his own. Immediately afterwards he turned his back, and was soon in as profound a sleep as before, through the enchantment of the geni.

Danhasch then, in his turn, transformed himself into a flea, and bit the princess on the lower lip so rudely, that she instantly awoke ; and rising up in bed, was very much astonished to find she had been sleeping with a man. But her astonishment was soon changed to admiration, and her admiration to joy when she had perfectly regained her sight, and saw that he was so handsome and agreeable.

" What !" cried she, " was it you whom my father destined for my husband ? I am most unfortunate in not having seen you before. The sight of you would have prevented the offence I have given to my father, and I should not

have been so long deprived of a husband whom I could not avoid loving with all my heart.—Awake! awake!" Saying this, she shook! prince Camaralzaman by the arm, and shook him so violently, that he must have been awakened, if at the moment Maimoune had not rendered his sleep more sound, by augmenting her enchantment. She then took his hand; when kissing it tenderly, she perceived the ring on his finger exactly resembled her own; and finding that she had another, she no longer doubted its being the same she had worn. She could not comprehend how the xchange had been made, bxt she was persuaded it was a certain proof of their marriage. She kissed him on each check, and composing herself, soon fell asleep.

When Maimoune perceived that she might speak without fear of disturbing the princess, "Well, cursed geni!" said she to Danhasch, "are you not now convinced that your princess is less beautiful than my prince?" then, turning to Caschcasch, after thanking him, she desired him to assist Danhasch in conveying the princess whence she had been brought. The two genii immediately executed the order they had received, and Maimoune retired to her well.

Early the next morning, prince Camaralzaman awoke, and looked for the young lady, when finding she was no longer present, "I justly conceived," said he to himself, "that it was a scheme of my father's to surprise me; and I have wisely escaped the snare." He then aroused the slave, who was still asleep, and desired his assistance in dressing without mentioning the subject of his meditations, the slave accordingly brought him a basin of water, he washed, and after having repeated a prayer, he took a book and read some time. After these usual exercises, Camaralzaman called the slave. "Come hither," said he, "and confess truly. How came the lady here who slept with me last night, and by whom was she introduced?" "My lord!" answered the slave in great astonishment, "of what lady do you speak?" "I speak of her," returned the prince, "who came, or was brought here last night." "My lord," replied the slave, I swear to you, that I have seen no lady; and how could she enter, without my knowledge, as I lay at the door?" "You are a liar, villain!" exclaimed the prince; and are confederated in afflicting and enraging me!" Saying this he gave him a box on the ear, which felled him to the ground; and, after kicking him repeatedly, he fastened the well-rope to his shoulders, and plunged him, head-foremost, several times in the water, "I will drown you, wretch," cried he, "if you do not immediately inform me, who the lady was, and who brought her here." The slave excessively distressed, and half-immersed in the water, said to himself, "no doubt, the prince's grief has bereft him of his senses, and I can escape only by a falsehood. My lord," continued he to the prince, in a suppliant tone, "grant me my life, I beseech you, and I promise to confess the truth." The prince then drew him up from the well, and commanded him to speak. "My lord," said he, trembling, "you will clearly perceive I cannot comply with your orders in this condition; suffer me first to go change my clothes." "I permit you to do so," replied the prince; "but be quick, and take care to inform me of all you know."

The slave immediately quitted the prince's apartment, and having fastened the door, ran directly to the palace in the state he was. The king was at that time in conversation with his grand-vizier, complaining to him of the unhappy night he had passed, in consequence of the disobedience and criminal behaviour of the prince his son in opposing his pleasure.

The grand-vizier had just ceased speaking, when the slave entered, and threw himself at the feet of Schahzaman. "Sir," said he, "I am very sorry to be the bearer of news which your majesty cannot hear without great affliction. The prince your son is distracted; he insists that a lady has slept with him during the night, and he has abused me for presuming to question the circumstance." The slave then related all that had passed, which his appearance tended to corroborate.

The king was unprepared for this new source of distress. "This is," said he to the vizier, "a most unfortunate result! very different from what you have given me reason to expect. Go immediately yourself, and examine into the truth of the statement, and let me know your opinion."

The grand-vizier obeyed; and entering the chamber of the prince, found him seated, tranquilly reading a book, which he held in his hand. He saluted him; and taking a seat by his side, "I would have your slave severely punished," said he, "who has much distressed your father, by a story he has related." "What story has he told my father," asked the prince, "to occasion him so much apprehension? I have very great reason to complain of my slave." "Prince," replied the vizier, "Heaven forbid what he has stated should be true! The good health in which I find you, and which may God preserve! convinces me of its falsehood." "Perhaps," returned the prince, "he did not clearly explain himself. As you, who are certainly capable of solving the difficulty, are here, permit me to inquire, where is the lady who slept with me last night?" The grand-vizier was confounded at this demand: "Prince," replied he, "be not surprised at the embarrassment in which I appear at your question. Can it be possible, think you, that a lady, that any person in the world, should enter this place last night, the only inlet to which is the door, and not trample on the body of your slave?" "Do not trifle with me in this manner!" exclaimed the prince in a high tone; "I will absolutely know what is become of the lady; and I am in a place where I can enforce obedience. At these menacing words, the vizier attempted to pacify the prince: and asked him in the most humble and conciliating terms, if he had, in reality, seen the lady. "Yes, yes," replied the prince, "I have seen her; and I very well perceive you were concerned in sending her, to tempt me. She played her part admirably, as you had prescribed. She did not speak a word; she pretended to sleep; and as soon as she found I had fallen into a slumber, she retired. But you, no doubt, are already informed; she has not failed to make her report." "Prince," answered the vizier, "I swear to you, that I am entirely innocent of what you accuse me; and that neither the king nor I had any concern in sending the lady you mention. "You, then, also, come to abuse me!" said the prince, again in a passion, when, seizing the vizier by the beard, he beat him till he was scarcely able to stand.

In the midst of the blows which the prince continued to bestow on him, he cried out, "My lord! I beseech you to give me a moment's respite." The prince then ceased beating him, and commanded him instantly to state what he had to say.

"I confess to you, my lord," said the grand-vizier, dissembling, "that your suspicions are not unfounded. But you are not ignorant of the duty a minister owes the king his master. If you will have the goodness to permit me,

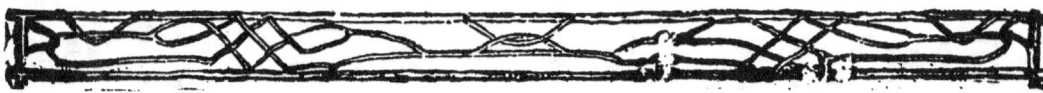

I am ready to convey to him any message you think proper to command." " Go then," replied Prince Camaralzaman, " and tell him that I am willing to espouse the lady whom he sent, or brought, and who slept with me last night ; be quick, and bring me his answer." The grand-vizier made a profound reverence on leaving the prince, and quitted the tower precipitately, not thinking himself safe till the door was closed behind him."

The grand-vizier presented himself before King Schahzaman with a sadness that alarmed him. " Well," said the monarch, " in what state have you found my son?" " Sir," replied the vizier, " the slave's report was too true!" He then repeated the conversation he had had with Prince Camaralzaman, described the treatment he had received, and the means by which he had effected his escape.

Schahzaman was the more mortified, as he had always tenderly loved the prince ; and he determined to ascertain the truth himself; accordingly, taking the grand-vizier with him, he proceeded to the tower.

Prince Camaralzaman received the king with great respect. The sultan, having taken a seat, desired the prince to sit by him, and asked him several questions, to which he gave immediate and sensible replies. As they conversed, the king repeatedly looked at the grand vizier, as if to upbraid him with having misrepresented the condition of the prince.

At length, the sultan said to Prince Camaralzaman, " My son, I request you will inform me, who was the lady that slept with you last night, and what did she say ?" " Sir," replied the prince, " I beg you will not augment the chagrin I have already experienced on that subject : rather grant me the favour of bestowing her on me in marriage. However averse I may have hitherto appeared to women, this young beauty has so charmed me, that I do not hesitate to acknowledge my weakness. I am ready to receive her from your hands with the utmost gratitude." King Schahzaman remained for some time in astonishment at his son's answer, so remote from the good sense he had before exhibited. When he had recovered from his surprise, " My son," said he, " your discourse confounds me. I swear to you that I am totally unacquainted with the lady of whom you speak ; and if any one has visited you, it was entirely unknown to me." " Sir," returned the prince, " I should be for ever unworthy of your majesty's goodness if I hesitated a moment to believe the pledge you have given me. But I beg you will have the patience to hear my statement, and then judge if what I shall have the honour to tell you be a dream." Prince Camaralzaman then recounted to the king all the occurrences of the night, extolling the charms of the lady, and declaring the love he had immediately conceived for her. He concluded by presenting to him the ring which he had taken from the princess's finger, in exchange for his own.

King Schahzaman was so well convinced of the truth of what his son had represented, that he was unable to make any reply.

The prince embraced the opportunity to renew his solicitation : " Sir," said he, " the passion I feel for this charming lady, whose precious image is impressed in my heart, is already so violent that I cannot resist it. I beseech you to have compassion on me, and to procure me the happiness of possessing her." " After what I have heard, my son, and after the sight of that ring," replied King Schahzaman, " I cannot doubt the reality of your passion, or of your having seen the lady who has given birth to it." On concluding these words, Schahzaman took the hand of the prince. " Come," added he, " let us go and grieve together : you, for love without hope ; and I at seeing your affliction, without having the power to afford you relief."

King Schahzaman then led his son from the tower, and conducted him to the palace, where the prince, in despair at loving with all his soul an unknown lady, took to his bed ; and the king, in the utmost distress, shut himself up with him, and continued weeping several days, unable to attend to the affairs of his kingdom.

While matters were thus passing in the capital of King Schahzaman, the two genii, Danhasch and Caschcasch, had conveyed the princess of China back to the palace, where the king, her father, had confined her, and replaced her in bed.

When she awoke next morning, and found, by looking to the right and to the left, that prince Camaralzaman was not by her side, she called to her women with such vehemence that they all immediately ran and surrounded her bed. Her nurse, who first presented herself, begged to know what she wished, and if anything had happened to her. " Tell me," said the princess, " what is become of the young man who slept with me last night, and whom I love with all my heart?" " Madam," replied the nurse, " we cannot understand your meaning, unless you be pleased more fully to explain yourself." " I mean," returned the princess, " that a young man, the most handsome and agreeable possible, has passed the night with me. I desire to be informed where he is?" " Madam," replied the nurse, " you are jesting with us. Will you be pleased to rise?" " I am perfectly serious," answered the princess, " and I will know what is become of him. " Madam," returned the nurse, " you were alone when you came to bed ; and we are certain no person has entered your chamber during the night." The princess of China now lost all patience, and, seizing her by the head, gave her several severe blows with her hand. The nurse struggled violently to get from her, and at length effected her escape ; when going immediately in search of the mother of the princess, she presented herself before her with tears in her eyes, to the great astonishment of the queen, who inquired what had occasioned her appearing in that state. " Madam," replied the nurse, " this treatment I have received from the princess your daughter ; she would have killed me, if I had not escaped from her hands." She then related the cause of the princess's rage, at which the queen was not less afflicted than surprised. " You see, madam," concluded the nurse, " that the princess is out of her mind ; of which you will be convinced, if you take the trouble to visit her."

The queen of China was too much interested in the welfare of her daughter to hesitate as to what course she ought to adopt ; but immediately, followed by the nurse, proceeded to the apartment where she was confined. On entering the chamber of the princess, the queen took a seat near her ; and, after being satisfied respecting her health, inquired the cause of her having ill-treated her nurse. " Daughter," said she, " such behaviour is unbecoming a great princess ; you should not give way to these excesses." " Madam," replied the princess, " I see clearly that your majesty is also come to abuse me ; but I declare to you that I shall not feel repose till I have the agreeable gentleman who lay with me last night for my husband." " Daughter," said the queen, " you surprise me ; I do not comprehend your discourse." " Madam," answered the princess, " the king my father and you have long persecuted me, to constrain me to marry against my inclination ; I am now inclined to marry, and I absolutely

will have the gentleman whom I mentioned for my husband, or I will destroy myself." The queen then endeavoured to gain the princess by mildness. "Daughter," said she, "you know very well that you are alone in this apartment, and no man could possibly enter." But, instead of attending to what she had to say, the princess interrupted her, and behaved so extravagantly, that she was obliged to retire in great affliction, and went to inform the king of their daughter's conduct.

The king of China determined to visit the princess his daughter himself; and, going to her apartment, demanded if what he had heard were true. "Sir," replied the princess, "let us speak no more on that subject; do me the favour only to give me for husband the cavalier who last night slept with me. "What, my daughter," said the king, "has some one lain with you last night?" "How, sir!" returned the princess, interrupting him, "you demand if some one has slept with me! your majesty is not unacquainted with that circumstance. He was the handsomest gentleman the sun ever shone upon, and I require him of you: I beseech you not to refuse me. But, that your majesty may not doubt I have seen the cavalier, be pleased to look at this ring. She advanced her hand, and the king knew not what to say, when he perceived a man's ring on her finger. However, as he could not comprehend her statement, and he had confined her on a supposition of being insane, he thought her madness was more confirmed; and, therefore, without again speaking to her, apprehensive she might be guilty of some act of violence on herself, or against her attendants, he ordered her to be chained, and secured with greater rigour, allowing only her nurse to wait upon her with a strong guard at the door.

Some days afterwards, the sultan, that he might not have to reproach himself with neglecting any means which could be of service to his daughter, had published in his capital, that any physician, astrologer, or magician, who thought himself able to effect her cure, should be at liberty to try his skill, on pain of losing his head in case of failure; at the same time he had the like offer announced in all the principal cities of his kingdom, and in the courts of the princes his neighbours.

The first who presented himself was both an astrologer and a magician, whom the king ordered an eunuch to conduct to the prison of his daughter. On his being introduced, he drew from a bag, which he carried under his arm, an astrolabe, a small sphere, a chaffing-dish, several sorts of drugs proper for fumigations, a brass vase, with other articles, and desired that a fire might be lighted. The princess of China demanded the reason of all these preparations; "Madam," replied the eunuch, "they are for the purpose of exorcising the evil spirit with which you are possessed, to enclose it in this vessel, and afterwards throw it to the bottom of the sea." "Foolish astrologer!" cried the princess, "your services are unnecessary; I am perfectly in my senses; you alone are mad. If you have the power to bring to me him I love, you will, indeed, render me a benefit." "Madam," replied the astrologer, "if that be your only trouble, it is not me, but the king your father solely, that can afford you relief." He then put his apparatus in the bag, and retired, very sorry that he had, with so little difficulty, engaged to cure an imaginary disorder.

When the eunuch had conducted the astrologer back to the king of China, the astrologer would not suffer his attendant to speak, but thus, with confidence, addressed the sultan: "Sir, judging from your majesty's proclamation, and which you yourself afterwards confirmed to me, I was persuaded that the princess laboured under a mental derangement, and I had no doubt of being able, by the secrets of my art, to restore her senses; but I very soon discovered that her only disorder is love, which my skill does not enable me to remedy; your majesty is the most capable of affording her consolation, by giving to her the husband whom she desires." The king, enraged at the boldness of the astrologer, ordered his head to be instantly struck off.

To avoid needless repetitions, it may be sufficient to mention that a hundred and fifty physicians, astrologers, and magicians presented themselves, all of whom shared the same fate, and their heads were arranged on the top of every gate of the city.

The princess of Persia's nurse had a son, named Marzavan, foster-brother to the princess, with whom he had lived in such great friendship during their childhood, that they were accustomed to call each other brother and sister, even after their more advanced age had obliged them to separate. Among several other sciences which Marzavan had cultivated from his earliest youth, his inclination had led him particularly to the study of judicial astrology, geomancy, and other occult arts, wherein he became exceedingly skilful.

After an absence of several years, Marzavan returned to the capital of China, and the appearance of a number of heads placed on the gate by which he entered, surprised him extremely. As soon as he reached his own house, he inquired the reason of the exhibition he had witnessed; and likewise concerning the welfare of the princess his foster-sister, whom he had not forgotten. They could not inform him of his first demand without apprising him of the second, and he therefore heard generally what he desired to know, and which caused him much grief, until he could learn the particulars from his mother, the princess's nurse.

Although Marzavan's mother was fully occupied in her attendance on the princess, she no sooner learned that her dear son was arrived, than she found time to go to embrace him, and to pass some moments in his company. When she had related to him, with tears in her eyes, the pitiable condition of the princess, and the reason why the king of China had thus treated his daughter, Marzavan asked if she could not procure him the means of seeing her mistress secretly, without the knowledge of the king. After some consideration, "My son," replied the nurse, "I cannot satisfy you immediately; but meet me here to-morrow, at the same hour, and I will bring you an answer."

The nurse, aware that no person could approach the princess without the permission of the eunuch who guarded the door, and judging, as he was young in the service, he could be but little acquainted with distant occurrences in the court of China, thus addressed him: "You know," said she, "that I suckled and nursed the princess, and you have, perhaps, heard that I had a daughter whom I brought up with her, and who has been long married. The princess, who always had a sincere affection for my daughter, wishes very much to see her; but she is anxious that the interview may take place without its being noticed." The nurse would have said more; but the eunuch stopped her: "It is sufficient," said he; "I shall always be happy to do anything in my power to oblige the princess. Fetch or send for your daughter to-night, after the king has retired; the door shall be open for her admittance."

As soon as night arrived, the nurse sought her son Marzavan; and having herself disguised him in female habiliments, in such a manner that no person could perceive the deception, she conducted him to the palace. The eunuch, who doubted not that it was her daughter, opened the door, and suffered them to enter together.

Before presenting Marzavan, the nurse approached the princess. "Madam," said she, "this is not a woman; it is my son Marzavan, lately returned from his travels, whom I have found means to introduce under this disguise; I hope you will allow him the honour of paying you his respects." At the name of Marzavan the princess expressed great joy. "Brother," said she, "come hither; and remove that veil, for surely brothers and sisters are not prohibited from approaching each other without that covering. Marzavan saluted her with great respect. "I am extremely glad," continued the princess, not giving him time to speak, "that you are returned in perfect health, after so many years absence, and without a word respecting your welfare having reached even your good mother." "Madam," replied Marzavan, "I am infinitely obliged by your kindness. I hoped to have heard, on my arrival, a very different account of your happiness from what I have been informed, and which I now witness with the utmost affliction."

"What, brother!" cried she, "you, then, also believe me mad? Undeceive yourself, and listen to what I have to say." The princess then related to Marzavan the whole of her history, not omitting the least circumstance; and concluded by showing him the ring which had been exchanged.

After the princess had ceased speaking, Marzavan, filled with admiration and astonishment, remained some time, his eyes fixed on the ground, without uttering a word; at length he looked up: "Madam," said he, "I do not despair of being able to procure you the satisfaction you desire. I have only to beg you will arm yourself with patience for some time, until I have travelled through the kingdoms which I have not yet visited; and when you hear of my return, you may assure yourself, that he for whom you sigh with so much ardour will not be far from you.' After these words, Marzavan took leave of the princess, and set out on the following day.

Marzavan journeyed from city to city, from province to province, and from island to island. Wherever he went, he heard continual reports of the princess Badoura, (thus was the princess of China called,) and of her extraordinary history. At the expiration of four months, he arrived at Torf, a large and populous maritime town, where he no longer heard of the Princess Badoura, but every person was talking of Prince Camaralzaman, who was said to be ill, and whose history was similar to that of the princess of China. Marzavan embarked in a merchant-vessel, which had a good voyage, till within sight of the capital of the kingdom of Schahzaman. But, unfortunately, through the unskilfulness of the pilot, as the vessel was entering the harbour, it struck on a rock, went to pieces, and sunk just in sight of the castle in which Prince Camaralzaman was confined. Marzavan could swim extremely well; he therefore did not hesitate to throw himself into the sea, and directed his course to the castle of King Schahzaman, where he was received, and every assistance afforded him, agreeably to the orders of the grand-vizier, who had received the king's commands to that effect. He had his dress changed, and was treated with the greatest kindness; when he had recovered from his fatigue, he was conducted before the grand-vizier, who had desired to see him.

Marzavan being a youth of good person and engaging air, this minister treated him with the utmost civility on his entrance, and soon conceived a great esteem for him, from the just and proper answers he made to all the questions he asked him; he discovered, almost insensibly, that he was possessed of a general knowledge. At length, he could not refrain from saying to him, "I plainly perceive, from your conversation, that you are not a man of common understanding; would to God, that in the course of your travels, you had learned some secret, that would enable you to cure a young man, whose illness has plunged this court in the deepest affliction for a long time!"

The grand-vizier then explained the state of Prince Camaralzaman. He concealed nothing; his so much wished-for birth; his education; the desire of King Schahzaman to have him married at an early age; the extraordinary aversion the prince had shewn from entering into an engagement of so serious a nature; his behaviour before the council; his subsequent confinement; the extravagances he committed in prison, which had suddenly changed into violent love for an unknown lady, for which there was no other foundation than a ring, which, as the prince pretended, had belonged to this lady, who probably was not in existence; in short, the vizier related every circumstance with scrupulous exactness.

This account gave Marzavan great joy. He felt convinced, beyond any doubt, that Prince Camaralzaman was the person with whom the princess of China was so deeply enamoured, and that this princess was no less the object of the prince's ardent vows. Nevertheless, he did not mention his thoughts to the grand-vizier; only saying to him, that if he saw the prince, he should be better able to judge what remedies it might be necessary to administer. "Follow me," replied the vizier; "you will find the king with him, who has lately expressed a wish to see you."

Marzavan approached Prince Camaralzaman, and speaking to him in a low voice, "Prince," said he, "the time is arrived when you should cease to afflict yourself so piteously. The lady for whom you suffer is well known to me; she is the Princess Badoura, daughter to the king of China, whose name is Gaiour. I can assure you of the fact, from what she herself has related to me of her adventure, and from what I have already learned of yours. The princess does not suffer less from her love for you, than you do from your affection toward her." He then related all that he knew of the history of the princess, since the fatal night of their almost incredible interview: nor did he omit to inform him of the punishment inflicted, by the order of the king of China, on all those who undertook to cure the princess Badoura of her supposed madness, and failed of success. "You are the only person," continued he, "who can accomplish her recovery, and you may, therefore, present yourself for that purpose, without fear of incurring the dreadful penalty. But before you can encounter so long a journey, you must be in good health yourself; we will then take the necessary measures for the performance of it. "Endeavour, therefore, to regain your strength as speedily as possible." Marzavan's discourse instantly produced a wonderful effect: Prince Camaralzaman was so comforted by the hope he had just experienced, that he felt sufficiently strong to rise, and he entreated the king his father, to permit him to dress himself, with an air and countenance which gave him indescribable joy.

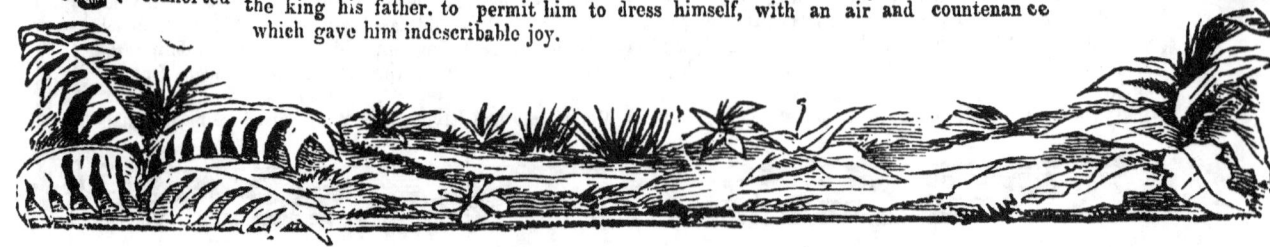

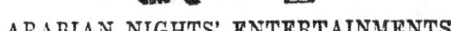
King Schahzaman embraced Marzavan, to express his thanks, without inquiring the means by which so surprising a change had been instantaneously effected; and immediately quitted the room, with the grand vizier, to proclaim this agreeable intelligence. He ordered public rejoicings for several days; he distributed presents to his officers and the populace, gave alms to the poor, and granted all prisoners their liberty. In short, nothing but joy and mirth reigned in the capital, and which very soon spread its influence throughout the dominions of king Schahzaman.

The next day, Prince Camaralzaman told the king his father how much he wished to take an airing, and begged his permission to hunt for a day or two with Marzavan. "I have no objection," replied the king; "provided, however, that you promise me not to remain out longer than one night. Too much exercise, at first, might be injurious; and a longer absence would be painful to me." The king gave orders for the best horses to be chosen for him, and took care himself that nothing should be wanting for his expedition. When everything was ready, he embraced; and having earnestly recommended him to the care of Marzavan, he suffered him to depart.

Prince Camaralzaman and Marzavan reached an open country; and, to deceive the two grooms who led the relay of horses, they pretended to hunt, and got as far from the city as possible. In the evening they stopped at a caravansera, where they supped, and slept till about midnight. Marzavan, who was first to wake, called Prince Camaralzaman without disturbing the grooms: he begged him to give him his dress, and to put on another, which one of the attendants had brought for him. They each mounted the relay of horses; and Marzavan having taken one of the groom's horses by the bridle, they set out in a quick pace.

At day break, the travellers found themselves in a forest, at a place where the road divided in four directions. At this place, Marzavan, begging the prince to wait for him a moment, rode into the forest. He here killed the groom's horse, tore the dress which the prince had worn the preceding day, and having dipped it in the blood, when he returned to the prince, he threw it into the middle of the cross-road. The prince asked Marzavan what was his design by so doing. "When the king your father," replied Marzavan, "finds that you do not return to-night, as you promised, or learns from the grooms that we set out without them, while they were asleep, he will send people in different directions in search for us. Those who find the bloody habit, will conclude that some beast of prey has devoured you, and that I have made my escape to avoid the anger of the king; who, thinking from their account that you are no longer in existence will desist from his researche after you.

The prince and Marzavan continued their journey by land and by sea, and encountered no other obstacle than the length of time which necessarily elapsed before they reached their place of destination.

At length they arrived at the capital of China, where Marzavan, instead of conducting the prince to his own house, made him alight at a public khan, for the reception of travellers. They remained there three days, to recover from the fatigue of the journey; and, during this interval, Marzavan had an astrologer's dress made, to disguise the prince. When the three days were elapsed, they went together to the bath, and Marzavan made the prince assume the astrologer's dress; quitting the bath, he conducted him within sight of the palace of the king of China, and there left him, to go and acquaint his mother, the nurse of Princess Badoura, of his arrival, that she might prepare the princess for the interview.

The prince, instructed by Marzavan how he should act, and furnished with every implement necessary for his assumed dress and character, approached the gate of the palace; and stopping before it, cried out, with a loud voice, in the hearing of the guard and porters, "*I am an astrologer; and I come to perfect the cure of the illustrious Princess Badoura, daughter of the great and puissant monarch Gaiour, king of China, according to the conditions proposed by his majesty,—to marry her, if I succeed; or to lose my life, if unsuccessful.*"

The novelty of this address instantly assembled a multitude of people round Prince Camaralzaman. In fact, a long time had passed since either physician, astrologer, or magician, had presented himself, after the many tragical examples of those who had failed in their enterprise.

The elegant figure of the prince, his noble air, and the extreme youth which was discernible in his countenance, excited compassion in the breast of every person present: "What are you thinking of, sir?" said those who were nearest to him; "what can be your motive for thus exposing a life which promises so flattering hopes? Have not the heads, which you have seen ranged on the top of the gates of the city, inspired you with horror? In the name of God, abandon this hopeless design, and withdraw."

Prince Camaralzaman remained firm, notwithstanding these remonstrances; and repeated the same words as before, with a vehemence which made all the people shudder. He called out a third time, when the grand-vizier presented himself, by order of the king of China.

This minister conducted Prince Camaralzaman into the presence of the king. The prince no sooner perceived the monarch seated on his throne, than he prostrated himself, and kissed the earth before him. Of all those men whose presumption had brought their heads to his feet, the king had not seen any one so worthy of his attention, and he felt unfeigned compassion for Camaralzaman. He even conferred greater honour on him; he desired him to approach and seat himself by his side: "Young man," said he, "I have some difficulty in believing that, at your early age, you can have acquired sufficient experience to dare undertake the cure of my daughter. I wish you may be able to succeed; I would bestow her on you in marriage, not only without repugnance, but, on the contrary, with the greatest pleasure and joy: but I should have felt truly unhappy, if either of those who have applied before you had obtained her. I must declare to you, nevertheless, although it gives me pain to inform you of this irrevocable condition, that if you fail, neither your youth, nor your noble and engaging appearance, can mitigate the penalty, but you must lose your head." "Sir," replied Prince Camaralzaman, "I owe infinite obligations to your majesty for the honour you confer on me, and for your kindness to an entire stranger. If, sir, I am to lose my life in the attempt, I shall at least die with the satisfaction of preserving your good opinion: I entreat you then to gratify my impatience, and let me prove the infallibility of my art by the means I am ready to employ."

The king of China commanded the eunuch who guarded the Princess Badoura, and was then present, to conduct Prince Camaralzaman to the apartment of his daughter; telling him, before he departed, he was still at liberty to relinquish his enterprise. The prince, however, was determined; he followed the eunuch with a resolution, or rather an ardour, truly astonishing.

Prince Camaralzaman accompanied the eunuch; and when they had reached a long gallery, at the end of which was the princess's apartment, the prince, finding himself so near the dear object which had caused him to shed so many tears, and heave so many fruitless sighs, hastened his pace, and proceeded before the eunuch, who had some difficulty to overtake him: "Where are you going so fast?" said he, seizing his arm: "you cannot obtain admittance without me. You must be very desirous to get rid of life, to run so eagerly into the arms of death! None of the astrologers I have seen and conducted where you will arrive but too soon, showed so much anxiety." "Friend," replied Prince Camaralzaman, looking at the eunuch, and slackening his pace, "the reason is, the astrologers of whom you speak had not the confidence in their science that I have in mine; they were certain of losing their lives if they did not succeed, and they were not sure of success; they had, therefore, some cause to tremble as they approached the place whither I am going, and where I am convinced I shall meet with happiness." As he pronounced these words, they reached the door; the eunuch opened it, and conducted the prince into a large room, which led to the chamber of the princess, and was divided from it only by a screen. Before he entered, the prince stopped, and speaking in a tone of voice much lower than before, lest he should be heard in her apartment, "To convince you," said he to the eunuch, "that neither presumption, caprice, nor the fire of youthful ardour, has stimulated me to this enterprise, I submit two modes of proceeding to your choice: which do you prefer—that I should cure the princess while in her presence; or here, without going farther, and without ever seeing her?" The eunuch, extremely astonished at the confidence with which the prince spoke to him, ceased to insult him; and speaking seriously, "It is, immaterial," said he; "in whatever manner you accomplish your undertaking, you will acquire immortal glory; not only in this kingdom, but over all the habitable world." "Then," replied the prince, "it will be better for me to cure her without seeing her, that you may witness my skill. As he was furnished with every article which distinguished the astrologer, he drew out his writing apparatus, and some paper, and wrote the following note to the princess of China:—

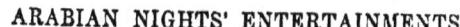

PRINCE CAMARALZAMAN TO THE PRINCESS OF CHINA.

 DORABLE PRINCESS,—The enamoured Prince Camaralzaman will not venture to describe to you the inexpressible woes he has endured since the fatal night when your charms deprived him of that liberty which he had resolved to maintain to the end of his life. He only assures you that he rendered to you his heart during your sweet sleep. He even had the presumption to place his ring upon your finger, as a token of his love, and to take yours in exchange, which he sends you enclosed in this note. If you condescend to return it to him as a reciprocal pledge of your affection, he will esteem himself the happiest and most fortunate of lovers. But should you not comply, your refusal will make him submit to the stroke of death with so much the more resignation, as he will receive it for the love he bears you. He awaits your answer in your antechamber.

* * * * * * *

When Prince Camaralzaman had finished this note, he made a small packet of it, with the princess's ring, which he enclosed in it, without letting the eunuch see what it contained ; then, giving it to him, " Take this, friend," said he, " and carry it to your mistress. If she be not cured the moment she has read this note, and seen its contents, I allow you to proclaim to the world that I am the most worthless and impudent astrologer, either of the past, the present, or the future age."

The eunuch went into the princess's chamber, and presenting the packet from Prince Camaralzaman, " Princess," said he to her, " an astrologer, who, if I am not mistaken, has more assurance than any who has yet appeared is just arrived and pretends that you will be cured as soon as you read this note, and see what it encloses. I wish he may be neither a liar nor an impostor." The Princess Badoura took the packet, and opened it with the utmost indifference ; but when she saw the ring, she could scarcely allow herself time to notice the writing. She started up precipitately, and, with an extraordinary effort, broke the chain which confined her, ran to the screen, and opened it. The princess instantly recognised the prince, and he immediately remembered her. They rushed into each other's arms with the tenderest embraces, and without being able to utter a word, from excess of joy.

The nurse, who had run out with the princess, made them return to the chamber, where the princess returned her ring to the prince. " Take it," said she, " I could not keep it without returning yours, which I am resolved not to part with during life. Neither of them can be more properly disposed of."

The eunuch, in the mean time, had departed hastily, to acquaint the king of China of what had passed. He related the manner in which Camaralzaman had proceeded ; and the king, most agreeably surprised, went immediately to the apartment of the princess, whom he tenderly embraced. He also embraced the prince, took hold of his hand, and joining it to that of the princess, " Happy stranger!" cried he, " whoever you be, I keep my promise, and give you my daughter in marriage. But I cannot be persuaded, that you are what you appear to be, and what you wished to make me believe."

Prince Camaralzaman thanked the king in the most submissive terms, the better to express his gratitude. " In regard to what I am, sir," continued he, " it is true, that I do not practise astrology as a profession. which your majesty has very rightly judged ; I merely put on the habit of that character to ensure my success in deserving and obtaining an honourable alliance with the most powerful monarch in the universe. I am a prince by birth, the son of a king and a queen ; my name is Camaralzaman, and my father is called Schahzaman, and reigns over the well-known isle of the Children of Khaledan."

The ceremony of the nuptials was performed on that very day ; and the most solemn rejoicings took place throughout the extensive dominions of China. Marzavan was not forgotten, the king granted him free access to the court ; bestowing on him an honourable charge, with the promise of raising him in future to other offices still more considerble.

Prince Camaralzaman and the Princess Badoura, arrived at the summit of their wishes, enjoyed the blessings of the marriage state ; and for several months the king of China did not cease from testifying his happiness by continual feasts and entertainments.

In the midst of these pleasures, Prince Camaralzaman had a dream one night, in which he thought he saw King Schahzaman his father in bed, on the point of death, and heard him say, " This son, whom I instructed, whom I have so tenderly cherished, has abandoned me, and he is the cause of my death!" He awoke with a deep sigh, which awakened the princess also, who demanded the occasion of his unhappiness. " Alas!" cried the prince, " perhaps at the moment I am speaking the king my father breathes no more!" He then told her the reason for submitting to such melancholy thoughts. The princess whose only desire was to afford him pleasure, and who knew that he earnestly wished to revisit his father once more, availed herself of an opportunity of speaking to the King of China in private. " Sir," said she, respectfully kissing his hand, " I have a favour to request of your majesty ; and I entreat you not to refuse me. It is to permit me to accompany the prince to see my father-in-law, King Schahzaman." " Whatever sorrow such a separation may occasion me," replied the king, " I cannot disapprove of the resolution. Go, I give my consent ; but only on condition, that you remain no longer than one year at the court of King Schahzaman. He will not, I hope, object to this proposal, and that we should each see you by turns :— he, his son and daughter-in-law ; and I, my daughter and son-in-law."

The king of China gave orders for the necessary preparations for the journey ; and when everything was ready, he set out with them, and accompanied them for several days. They at length separated, not without many tears being shed.

After they had been travelling about a month, they arrived on a plain of vast extent, planted at intervals with trees, which formed a very agreeable shade. As the heat on that day was excessive, Prince Camaralzaman thought it expedient to encamp, and asking the Princess Badoura if she had any objection, she replied, that she was at that moment going to make the same request of him. They immediately alighted in this beautiful spot, and, as soon as

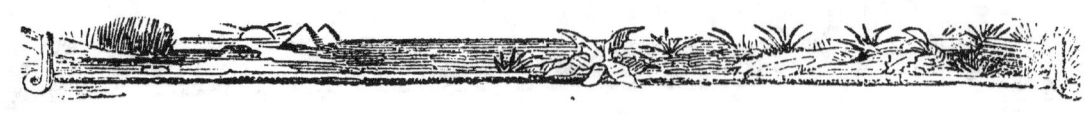

their tents were pitched, the princess, who had been resting in the shade, retired to hers, while Camaralzaman went to give orders to the rest of the party. That she might be more at her ease, she took off her girdle, which her women placed by her side. She then fell asleep, through fatigue, and her attendants left her.

When Prince Camaralzaman had made the necessary arrangements in the camp, he returned to the tent, and perceiving, as he entered, that the princess had fallen asleep, he sat down, without making any noise. While he was thus sitting, with an intention of sleeping also, the girdle of the princess caught his eye. He examined the different diamonds and rubies, with which it was enriched, one by one; and he perceived a small silk purse, sewn neatly to the girdle, and tied with a piece of twist. On touching it, he felt that it contained something hard. Curious to know what it was, he opened the purse, and took out a cornelian, upon which were different figures and characters engraven, all of them unintelligible to him. "This cornelian," said he to himself, "must certainly be of very great value, or my princess would not carry it about with her, and be so anxious to preserve it." In fact, this cornelian was a talisman, that the queen of China had given to her daughter, to ensure her happiness, and which she would ever enjoy, so long as she kept it in her possession.

The better to examine this talisman, as the tent was rather dark, Prince Camaralzaman went to the outside ; when, as he was holding it in his hand, a bird suddenly darted upon it, and carried it away.

Nothing could exceed the astonishment and grief of the prince, when the talisman was thus unexpectedly taken from him by the bird. This most afflicting accident, occasioned, too, by an ill-timed curiosity, had deprived the princess of a precious gift ; and the reflection rendered him for some minutes motionless.

The bird, having flown away with his prize, alighted on the ground at a little distance, with the talisman still in his beak. Prince Camaralzaman went towards him, in the hope of his dropping it ; but, as soon as he approached, the bird flew a little way farther, and then stopped again. The prince continued to pursue him ; the bird then swallowed the talisman, and took a longer flight. He again followed him, thinking, as he was very adroit, to kill him with a stone. The farther the bird got from him, the more was Camaralzaman determined not to lose sight of him, and to obtain the talisman.

Over hills and through valleys, the bird drew the prince after him for the whole day, still proceeding from the place where he had left the Princess Badoura ; and, in the evening, instead of perching in a bush, in which Camaralzaman might have surprised him during the night, he flew to the top of a high tree, where he remained in safety. The prince, extremely mortified at having taken so much useless trouble, deliberated whether he should return to his camp. "But," thought he, "how shall I return? Shall I climb the hills and traverse the valleys by which I came? Shall I not lose my way in the darkness, and will my strength support me? And, even if I could return, dare I venture to present myself before the princess without her talisman?" Absorbed in these disconsolate reflections, and overcome with fatigue, hunger, and thirst, and sleep, he laid down, and passed the night at the foot of the tree.

Next morning, Camaralzaman was awake before the bird had quitted the tree, and he no sooner saw him take flight than he arose to pursue him, and followed him the whole of that day with as little success as on the preceding, eating occasionally of the herbs and fruits he met with in his way. He continued his inutile pursuit till the tenth day, always keeping his eye on the bird, and sleeping at night at the foot of the tree in which it perched on the highest branches. On the eleventh day, the bird constantly flying onwards, and Camaralzaman as constantly pursuing, they arrived at a large city. When the bird was near the walls, he rose very high above them, and directing his flight to the other side, the prince entirely lost sight of him, and, at the same time, the hope of ever recovering the talisman of the Princess Badoura.

In the utmost affliction, and hopeless of relief, he entered the city, which was built on the seashore, with a very fine harbour. He walked for a considerable time along the streets, not knowing either where he was, or where to go ; and, at length, reached the harbour. Still more uncertain how to act, he proceeded along the shore, till he came to the gate of a garden, which was open when he stopped. The gardener, who was engaged with his labour, happened to raise his head at the same moment ; he scarcely perceived him, before, knowing him to be a stranger and a mussulman, he invited him to go in quickly, and shut the gate. Camaralzaman acted as he desired ; and, approaching the gardener, asked him, why he made him take this precaution. "Because," replied the gardener, "I see that you are a stranger just arrived, and a mussulman ; and this city is inhabited chiefly by idolaters, who have a mortal aversion against mussulmans; and treat even the few that are here, who profess the religion of our prophet, very ill."

Camaralzaman thanked this good man very gratefully, for the retreat he had so generously afforded him from insult. He would have said more ; but the gardener interrupted him. "No compliments," said he ; "you are fatigued, and must want food ; come and rest yourself." He conducted him into his little house ; and, after the prince had eaten a sufficiency of what the gardener had placed before him with a cordiality that won his heart, he begged of him to have the goodness to tell him the object of his visit.

Camaralzaman satisfied the gardener's curiosity ; and, when he had finished his story, in which he disguised nothing, he asked in his turn, by what means he might get back to the dominions of the king his father. The gardener, in reply, told him, that the city he was then in was a whole year's journey distant from the countries inhabited by mussulmans, and which were governed by princes of their religion ; but that, by sea, he might reach the Isle of Ebony in a much shorter time ; and it would be more easy to pass thence to the Isle of the Children of Khaledan ; that every year a merchant-ship sailed to the Isle of Ebony, of which opportunity he might avail himself to return thence to the Isle of the Children of Khaledan. "If you had arrived some days sooner," continued he, "you might have embarked in the ship which sailed this year. But, if you choose to wait till that of next year sails, and will live with me, I offer you my house, such as it is, with all my heart."

Prince Camaralzaman esteemed himself very fortunate in having thus met with an asylum in a place where he was an entire stranger. He therefore accepted the offer, and remained with the gardener; employing himself, while he waited the departure of a merchant vessel for the Isle of Ebony, working in the garden during the day ; and the nights, he passed in sighs, tears, and lamentations. We will leave him so circumstanced, to return to the Princess Badoura, whom we left sleeping in her tent.

The princess slept for some time, and, on waking, was surprised at the absence of Prince Camaralzaman. She summoned her women, and asked them if they knew where he was. While they were assuring her that they had seen him enter the tent, but had not seen him quit it, she perceived, on taking up her girdle, that the little bag was open, and the talisman missing. Not doubting that the prince had taken it out to examine it, and that he would soon return, she expected him till evening with the greatest impatience, and could not comprehend what induced him to be absent from her so long. When she perceived that night was arrived, that it was already quite dark, and yet he did not appear, she gave herself up to inconceivable affliction. Only the princess and her women knew of Camaralzaman's disappearance; for, at that time, his attendants had all retired, and were sleeping in their tents. She then changed her dress for one of Camaralzaman's, whom she so strongly resembled, that his people were completely deceived on the following morning, when she made her appearance, and commanded them to pack up the baggage, and proceed on their journey. When all was ready, she ordered one of her women to take her place in the litter; and having herself mounted on horseback, they set off.

After a journey of several months by land, and sea, the princess, who had continued the disguise of Prince Camaralzaman, in order to reach the Isle of the Children of Khaledan, arrived at the capital of the Isle of Ebony, the reigning king of which country was named Armanos. As those of her people who first disembarked to seek a lodging for her had published in the town that the vessel which had just arrived bore Prince Camaralzaman, who was returning from a long voyage, and whom bad weather had obliged to put into the port, the intelligence very soon reached the palace of the king.

King Armanos, accompanied by a great part of his court, immediately set out to receive the princess, and met her just as she had left the vessel, and was proceeding to the residence that had been engaged for her. He received her as the son of a king, who was his friend and ally, with whom he had always lived on terms of amity; and conducted her to his palace, where he lodged her and her whole suite, notwithstanding her earnest entreaties to be permitted to have a lodging to herself. He conferred upon her all the honours imaginable, besides regaling her for three days with extraordinary magnificence.

When the three days were expired, King Armanos finding that the princess whom he still supposed to be Prince Camaralzaman, intended to embark, and continue her voyage, and being quite charmed with a prince, as she appeared to him so handsome and agreeable, and possessed of so much sense, spoke to her in private: "Prince," said he, "at the advanced age to which you see I am arrived, with little hope of living much longer, I endure the mortification of not having a son, to whom I can bequeath my kingdom. Heaven has bestowed on me an only daughter, who is possessed of beauty that cannot be matched, but with a prince of such high birth, such mental and personal accomplishments, as distinguish you. Instead, therefore, of returning to your own country, accept her from my hands, together with my crown, which I from this moment resign in your favour, and remain with us.

This generous offer occasioned her a degree of embarrassment which she little expected. After having told the king that she was Camaralzaman, she thought it would be unworthy of a princess of her rank to undeceive him, and to declare that, instead of being the prince himself, she was only his wife; while, if she refused him, she had just reason to fear, that he might change his friendship and good-will towards her into hatred and enmity. These considerations determined Badoura to accept the proposals of King Armanos. Having, therefore, remained for some minutes without speaking, she thus replied:—"Sir, I am under infinite obligations to your majesty for the good opinion you have conceived of my person, and for the honour you do me, by conferring on me so great a favour, which, though I am by no means deserving, I dare not refuse. But, sir," added she, "I can only accept so great an alliance, on condition that your majesty will assist me with your counsels, and that I undertake nothing which you have not previously sanctioned."

King Armanos, overjoyed at having acquired a son-in-law, with whom he was so well satisfied, assembled his council on the morrow, and declared that he bestowed the princess his daughter, in marriage on Prince Camaralzaman, whom he had seated next to him, that he resigned his crown to him, and enjoined them to accept him as their king, and to pay him homage. When he had concluded, he descended from the throne, and made the Princess Badoura ascend and take his place, where she received the oaths of fidelity and allegiance from the principal nobles of the Isle of Ebony, who were present.

In the evening the whole palace was in festivity; and the Princess Haiatalnefous (this was the name of the daughter of the king of the Isle of Ebony) was conducted to the Princess Badoura, whom every one supposed to be a man, with a magnificence truly royal. The ceremonies being completed, they were left alone, and retired to rest.

The next morning, King Armanos and his queen repaired to the apartment of the new queen, their daughter, to inquire how she had passed the night. Instead of making any reply, she fixed her eyes on the ground; and, by the expression of sorrow which overspread her countenance, plainly showed that she was dissatisfied. To console the Princess Haiatalnefous, "My dear daughter," said the king to her, "be not afflicted; when Prince Camaralzaman landed here, he only sought to return, so soon as possible, to King Schahzaman his father. Although we have prevented him from putting his design in execution, by means with which he must be well satisfied, we must nevertheless conclude that he feels much disappointment at being so suddenly deprived even of the hope of ever seeing him again, or any one belonging to his family. You may, therefore, expect, when these emotions of filial tenderness are a little subsided, that he will behave towards you as a good husband."

The princess Badoura, under the name of Camaralzaman and king of the Isle of Ebony, passed the whole of that day, not merely in receiving the compliments of her court, but also in reviewing the regular troops belonging to the household, and in several other royal functions, with a dignity and ability which acquired her the approbation of all those who witnessed her conduct.

It was night when she entered the apartment of Queen Haiatalnefous; and she soon perceived, by the restraint with which the latter received her, that she had not forgotten the preceding night. She endeavoured to dissipate her sadness by a long conversation, in which she employed all her eloquence, of which she had a considerable share, to persuade her that she loved her excessively. She at last gave her time to go to bed, and during this interval,

she began to say a prayer: but she remained so long thus employed, that Haiatalnefous fell asleep. She then ceased from praying, and lay down by her side, without waking her, as much afflicted at the necessity she was under of acting a character which did not become her, as at the loss of her beloved Camaralzaman, whom she unceasingly lamented. She arose the next morning at break of day, before Haiatalnefous awoke, and went to the council, dressed in the royal robes.

King Armanos did not fail to visit the queen his daughter again on that day, and he found her in tears. He required no further indication to be satisfied of the cause of her grief. Indignant at this affront, for such he conceived it, the cause of which he could not comprehend, "Daughter," said he, "have patience for one night more. I elevated your husband to my throne, and I will make him descend from it, and banish him hence with shame and ignominy, if he do not behave to you as he ought. In my present anger, at seeing you treated with such neglect, I know not whether I shall be satisfied with so gentle a punishment."

The Princess Badoura returned to the chamber of Haiatalnefous as late that evening as on the preceding. She conversed with her in the same manner, and was then going to say her prayer, while she went to bed; but Haiatalnefous prevented her, and obliged her to sit down again. "What," said she, "I see you intend to treat me this night as you did on the two former. Tell me, I entreat, how I have displeased you, I—who not only love but adore you, and esteem myself the happiest of all the princesses of my rank, in having so amiable a prince as you for my husband. Any other person besides me would embrace the opportunity of revenge, by abandoning you to your luckless fate, for so indignant, so outrageous, an affront; but, though I had less affection for you, I am too compassionate for the misfortunes, even of those who are totally indifferent to me, not to warn you that the king my father is extremely irritated at your behaviour, and that he only suspends his anger till to-morrow, when you will feel its just effects, if you continue your unkind usage."

As Badoura had remained silent and confused, Haiatalnefous, becoming impatient, was about to proceed, when she prevented her by these words: "Amiable and charming princess," said she, "I am in fault; and I condemn myself; but I hope you will pardon me, and that you will not violate the secret that I am going to entrust you with for my justification." At the same moment, Badoura uncovered her bosom. "See, princess," continued she, "if a woman, and a princess, like yourself, does not deserve your forgiveness. I am persuaded you will grant it with good-will, when I have related to you my history; and, above all, when you are acquainted with the misfortune that has obliged me to act a deceitful part."

When the Princess Badoura had concluded her narration, she entreated her, a second time, not to betray her secret, and to agree to continue the deception, and pretend that she was really her husband, until the arrival of Prince Camaralzaman, whom she hoped shortly to see again. "Princess," replied Haiatalnefous, "be assured that I will most religiously preserve your secret. I shall feel the greatest pleasure in being the only person belonging to the great kingdom of the Isle of Ebony who really knows you for what you are, while you govern it with the wisdom you have displayed at the commencement of your reign. I asked you to love me; but now I declare to you that I shall be fully satisfied if you do not refuse me your friendship." After this conversation, the two princesses tenderly embraced, and, with a thousand demonstrations of reciprocal friendship, they lay down to rest.

During the time of these proceedings in the Isle of Ebony, between the Princesses Badoura and Haitalnefous King Armanos the queen, the court, and the rest of the people in that kingdom, Prince Camaralzaman still remained, in the City of Idolaters, with the gardener who had given him a retreat.

One morning, very early, as the prince was preparing to labour, the good old gardener prevented him. "The idolators," said he to him, "have a grand festival to-day; and as they abstain from all kinds of work, to pass it in public assemblies and rejoicings, they will not suffer mussulmans either to attend their business; and the latter, to preserve peace and amity with them, join in their amusements, and are present at the various spectacles, which are well worthy of notice; so you may allow yourself a little rest to-day. I shall leave you here; and as the time approaches for the merchant-vessel, which I mentioned to you, to sail for the Isle of Ebony, and I am going to see some friends, I will inquire of them what day it is to set sail, and at the same time arrange matters for your embarkation." The gardener put on his best dress, and went out.

When Prince Camaralzaman found himself alone, instead of partaking of the public rejoicings which enlivened the whole city, the state of inactivity he remained in brought to his mind in more vivid colours the sad recollection of his ever-beloved princess. Absorbed by his melancholy reflections, he sighed and moaned as he walked in the garden; when the noise made by two birds, which had perched on a tree near him, attracting his attention, induced him to lift up his head and stop. Camaralzaman observed that these birds were fighting desperately, and in a few minutes he saw one of them fall dead at the foot of a tree. The bird that had conquered then resumed his flight, and soon disappeared. At the same moment two other birds of a larger size alighted, one at the head, the other at the feet, of the deceased, looking at him for some time, shaking their heads in a manner which indicated their grief, and then dug a grave with their claws, in which they buried him. As soon as the two birds had refilled the grave with the earth they had removed, they flew away; and in a short time afterwards returned, holding in their beaks, one by the wing, and the other by a claw, the criminal bird, which uttered dreadful screams, and made violent efforts to escape. They forced him to the grave of the bird he had in his rage destroyed, and deprived him of life by pecking him with their beaks. They then tore open his body, drew out the entrails, and again took to flight.

Camaralzaman approached the tree where the scene had passed; and casting his eyes on the dispersed entrails, he perceived something red. He took up the mangled remains, and drawing out the red substance, found it to be the talisman of Badoura, which had cost him so much anxiety, pain, and regret, since this bird had flown away with it.

It is not possible to express the joy of Prince Camaralzaman: "Dearest princess!" he exclaimed, "this unfortunate moment is no doubt a happy presage that announces our meeting sooner than I dare to hope."

As he finished these words, Camaralzaman kissed the talisman, and wrapping it up, carefully tied it round his arm. During his affliction, he had passed every night in the midst of tormenting reflections, but he slept very tranquilly the whole of that which succeeded this happy event; and the next morning at daybreak, putting on his working dress, he went to the gardener for his orders, who begged him to cut and root up a particular tree, which he pointed out to him.

As he was cutting a part of the root, he struck something which resisted, and, on removing the earth, he discovered a large plate of brass, under which he found a staircase with ten steps. He immediately descended, and when he had reached the bottom, he found himself in a sort of cave, or vault, in which he counted fifty large bronze vases, ranged round it, each with a cover; he uncovered them all, one after the other, and found them filled with gold-dust. He then quitted the vault, overjoyed at having discovered so rich a treasure; and, replacing the plate over the staircase, continued to root up the tree, while he waited for the gardener's return.

The gardener had been informed on the preceding day that the vessel, which sailed annually to the Isle of Ebony, would depart in a very few days; but those who had given him this intelligence could not acquaint him with the precise time, promising, however, to obtain it on the morrow. He had been to gain the information he wanted, and returned with a countenance which displayed the joy he felt at being the bearer of good news to Camaralzaman: "My son," said he, "rejoice, and hold yourself in readiness to embark in three days; the vessel will certainly sail at that time, and I have agreed about your embarkation and passage with the captain." "In my present situation," replied Camaralzaman, "you could not announce to me anything more agreeable. In return, I have also to communicate to you news which must give you great pleasure. Take the trouble to follow me, and you will see the good fortune that Heaven sends you." Camaralzaman conducted the gardener to the place where he had rooted up the tree, and made him go down into the vault; when he had shown him the number of jars it contained, all filled with gold-dust, he expressed his joy, that God had thus recompensed his virtue, and all the troubles he had encountered during so many years. "What do you mean?" replied the gardener: "Do you suppose, then, that I will possess myself of this treasure? No, it is all your own; I have no pretensions to any part of it. Eighty years have I worked in this garden since my father's death, and never chanced to discover it. It is a sign that it was destined for you alone, since God permitted you to find it; and it is more appropriate to a prince, like you, than to me, who am on the brink of the grave, and want nothing more."

Prince Camaralzaman would not cede to the gardener in generosity, and they had a great contest on this point. He at length solemnly protested, that he would not touch any of the gold, unless the gardener retained half for his share, to which he with some difficulty consented; and they divided the vases, twenty-five to each.

The division being made, "My son," said the gardener, "this is not enough; we must now devise some plan for embarking these riches on the vessel, and taking them with you so secretly as not to excite suspicion, otherwise you might run a risk of losing them. There are no olives in the Isle of Ebony, and those which are taken from here are in great request. As you know, I have a good store of those I have gathered from my own garden, you must take the fifty jars, and fill them half way with the gold-dust, and the other half with olives up to the top, and we will have them conveyed to the ship, when you yourself embark. Camaralzaman employed himself the rest of the day in filling and arranging the fifty jars; and, as he feared that he might lose the talisman of the Princess Badoura by wearing it constantly on his arm, he had the precaution to secure it in one of the jars, on which he put a mark to know it again.

Whether it was on account of his great age, or that he had taken too much exercise that day, the gardener passed a bad night. His illness increased on the following day, and on the third morning he found himself still worse. As soon as it was day, the captain of the vessel himself, with some of his seamen, came and inquired for the passenger who was to embark on board their vessel. "I am the person," replied the prince. "The gardener who took my passage is ill, and cannot speak to you; however, carry those jars of olives, with my baggage, to the ship, and I will follow you as soon as I have taken my leave of him." The seamen accordingly took his jars and baggage, and, on leaving Camaralzaman, the captain desired him to follow them immediately. "The wind is fair," added he, "and I only wait for you to set sail."

As soon as the captain and seamen were gone, Camaralzaman returned to the gardener, but he found him dying, and had scarcely obtained from him the profession of his faith, when he saw him expire. The prince, being required to embark immediately, used the utmost diligence in performing the last duties to the deceased; and, having dug a grave, buried it himself, which employed him till the close of day. He then set out to embark, but when he reached the harbour, he was informed that the ship had weighed anchor some time, and that it was even out of sight.

Camaralzaman was in the utmost affliction at finding himself obliged to remain in a country where he had no motive for wishing to form any connexions, and to wait another year before the opportunity he had just lost would be again presented. What distressed him still more, was the reflection that he had parted with the talisman of the Princess Badoura, which he now considered as irrecoverably lost. In the meantime, he had no alternative but to return to the garden he had left, to rent it of the landlord, to whom it belonged, and to continue the cultivation of it. As he could not support the fatigue of all the labour it required, he hired a boy to assist him; and that he might not lose the remainder of the treasure, which was his right by the death of the gardener, who had died without heirs, he put the gold-dust into fifty other jars, which he filled with olives, intending to take them with him, when the time arrived for him to embark.

While Prince Camaralzaman was commencing another year, the vessel continued its course, and arrived at the capital of the Isle of Ebony.

As the palace was on the seashore, the new king, or rather the Princess Badoura, who perceived the vessel while sailing into port, inquired what ship it was, and was informed that it came every year from the City of Idolators at that season, and that it was in general laden with very rich merchandise. The princess, whose mind was constantly occupied with the remembrance of Camaralzaman, conceived that he might have embarked on board that vessel, and the thought occurred to her of going to meet him when he landed. Under pretence, therefore, of inspecting the merchandise, she ordered a horse to be brought her, and arrived at the moment that the captain landed. She desired to speak with him, and inquired whence he had sailed, how long he had been at sea, if he had with his passengers any stranger of distinction, and, above all, what goods he had on board his vessel. The captain gave satisfactory answers to all these questions; as for the passengers, he assured her they were all merchants, and that

they brought very rich stuffs from different countries, linens of the finest texture, painted as well as stained, precious olives, and several other articles. The Princess Badoura happened to be extremely fond of olives; and she had no sooner heard them mentioned, than she said to the captain, "I will take all you have on board; order them to be landed immediately."

The captain sent his boat to the ship, and it soon returned with the jars of olives. The princess asked what the value of the fifty jars might be, in the Isle of Ebony. "Sir," replied the captain, "the merchant is very poor; your majesty will confer a great favour on him by giving him a thousand pieces of silver." "That he may be perfectly satisfied," said the princess, "you shall have a thousand pieces of gold which you will be careful to deliver to him."

As night approached, the Princess Badoura went to the apartment, where she had the fifty jars of olives conveyed to her. She had one opened, for the princess to taste; and pouring some into a dish, her surprise may be conceived, at finding the olives mixed with gold-dust. "What a wonderful adventure!" exclaimed she; and immediately ordered the other jars to be opened, and emptied in her presence, and her astonishment increased, as she perceived that the olives in each jar were mixed with the gold-dust. But when that was emptied, in which Camaralzaman had deposited the talisman, her emotions were so violent that she fainted away. When she had regained her senses, she took up the talisman, and kissed it several times; but, as she did not choose to say anything before the princess's women, who were ignorant of her disguise, she dismissed them. "Princess," said she, "after what I have related to you, you no doubt guessed that the sight of this talisman caused me to faint. It is the fatal cause of the separation which has taken place between my husband and myself."

Next morning, the Princess Badoura sent for the captain of the vessel. When he appeared, "I beg you to give me a more satisfactory account of the merchant," said she, "to whom the olives belonged that I bought yesterday. I think you told me that you left him behind in the City of Idolators. Can you inform me what was his occupation there?" "Sir," replied the captain, "I can acquaint your majesty for certain, as I know it myself. I had agreed for his passage with a gardener, who was extremely old, and he told me that I should find him in his garden, where he worked under him: this made me say to your majesty that he was poor. "If this be true," said the princess, "you must set sail again to-day, and return to search for this young gardener, and bring him here, for he is my debtor: if you refuse, I declare that I will confiscate not only all the goods which belong to you, and those of the merchants you have on board, but your lives also shall be responsible for the performance of this service. This is what I had to say to you. Go and execute my commands."

The vessel had a very fortunate voyage, and the captain managed so well as to arrive by night at the City of Idolaters. When he had approached as near to the land as he thought proper, he took his boat, and landed at a little distance from the harbour, whence he went to the garden of Camaralzaman, accompanied by six of his seamen. The prince was not asleep, when he heard a knocking at the gate of the garden. He went half-dressed to open it, when the captain and sailors seized and forcibly conducted him to the boat, and conveying him to the ship, set sail again as soon as they had re-embarked. Camaralzaman, who had till then, as well as the captain and seamen, preserved silence, now asked the captain what reason he had for acting with so much violence. "Are you not a debtor to the king of the Isle of Ebony?" inquired the captain. "I, a debtor to the king of the Isle of Ebony!" exclaimed Camaralzaman, with amazement; "I do not know him, nor ever set my foot in his dominions." "You must be best acquainted with that matter," replied the captain; "but you will speak to him yourself; therefore, remain here quietly, and have patience."

The vessel had as fortunate a voyage in conducting Camaralzaman to the Isle of Ebony, as it had experienced in going for him to the City of Idolators. Although it was night when they got into port, the captain nevertheless did not delay going ashore, to take Prince Camaralzaman to the palace, where he requested to be presented to the king. The Princess Badoura was no sooner informed of the captain's return, and of the arrival of Camaralzaman, than she went out to them. She had no sooner cast her eyes on the prince, than she recognised him, even in his mean habiliments. As for Prince Camaralzaman, he had not the most distant idea that he was then before her whom he had desired so ardently to rejoin. If the princess had followed her inclination, she would have run to him, and discovered herself by her tender embraces; but she restrained her emotions, as she judged it for the interest of both that she should continue to sustain the character of king for some time longer, before making herself known.

After the lapse of two or three days, the Princess Badoura, to afford Camaralzaman more frequent access to her person, as well as to raise him to a higher distinction, bestowed on him the office of grand-treasurer, which had become vacant. He acquitted himself in his new office with so much integrity, at the same time conferring favours on every one, that he acquired not only the friendship of all the nobles belonging to the court, but even gained the hearts of the people by his rectitude and generosity.

Camaralzaman would have been the happiest of men, to find himself in so high favour, and in acquiring the esteem of all. But, in the midst of his good fortune, he never ceased lamenting her loss, and that he could gain no information respecting her. His suspicion might have been excited if the Princess Badoura had retained the name of Camaralzaman, which she assumed with his dress; but, when she ascended the throne, she changed it for that of Armanos, in compliment to the former king, her father-in-law, and was known only by the name of King Armanos, and there were only a few courtiers who remembered the name of Camaralzaman. Camaralzaman had not yet had sufficient intercourse with them to learn this circumstance; though he probably would have been informed of it. As the Princess Badoura feared that it might so happen, she resolved to put an end to her own torments, and to those she well knew he suffered.

The Princess Badoura had no sooner formed this resolution, than she spoke to Prince Camaralzaman in private, on the same day. "Camaralzaman," said she, "I wish to converse with you on an affair on which I want your advice. As I think I cannot attend to it more conveniently than at night, come to me in the evening, and desire your people not to wait for you."

Camaralzaman did not fail to repair to the palace at the hour appointed by the princess. She conducted him to the inner palace; and having told the chief of the eunuchs, who was preparing to follow her, that she did not require his attendance, and that he had only to keep the door fastened, she led him into a different apartment from that of the Princess Haiatalnefous, in which she was accustomed to sleep. When the prince and princess were in the chamber, she took the talisman out of a little box; and presenting it to Camaralzaman, "it is not long," said she, "since an astrologer gave me this talisman; and as I know you to be well informed in every science, you perhaps can tell me its peculiar properties." Camaralzaman took the talisman, and approached a light to examine it. He no sooner recognised it, than he exclaimed, "Ah, sir, your majesty asks me the properties of this talisman. Alas! its properties are to make me die with grief and sadness, if I do not shortly find the princess, to whom this talisman belonged and of whom it caused me the loss. The adventure was so extraordinary, that the recital of it would excite your majesty's compassion for a husband so unfortunate as I am, if you would have the patience to listen to it." "You may relate it to me some other time," replied the princess; "but I am very happy," added she, "to inform you that I am not entirely unacquainted with it. Wait for me here, I will return in a moment."

Saying this, the princess went into a closet, where she cut off the royal turban, and having shortly reassumed her female dress, with the girdle she wore on the day of their separation, she returned to the chamber where she had left the prince. Camaralzaman instantly ran to her, and embracing her with the utmost tenderness, "Ah," cried he, "how much I am obliged to the king, for having surpeisd me so agreeably!" "Do not expect to see the king again," replied the princess, returning his embrace, with tears in her eyes; "in me you behold the king. Let us sit down, that I may explain to you this enigma. They seated themselves, and the princess related to Camaralzaman the resolution she had formed in the plain, where they had encamped together for the last time, as he did not appear; in what manner she had executed it until her arrival at the Isle of Ebony, where she had been obliged to marry the Princess Haiatalnefous, and to accept the crown. When the Princess Badoura had concluded, she begged the prince to inform her by what accident the talisman had occasioned their separation. He satisfied her curiosity; and when he had finished, he complained to her, in an affectionate manner, of her cruelty, in keeping him so long in anxiety. She gave him the reasons already mentioned; after which, as the night was far advanced, they retired to rest.

They arose the next morning, as soon as it was day; when the princess, no longer continuing the royal robe, resumed her own habit, and, as soon as she was dressed, despatched the chief of the eunuchs to request King Armanos to take the trouble of coming to her apartment.

When King Armanos arrived, he was very much surprised to see a lady who was totally unknown to him, and the grand-treasurer, who was not allowed to enter the inner palace, any more than the other nobles of the court; therefore, seating himself, he inquired for the king. "Sir," replied the princess, "yesterday I was king; to-day I am only the princess of China, wife of Prince Camaralzaman. If your majesty will have the patience to listen, I trust you will not condemn me for having conceived so innocent a deceit." King Armanos listened to her with the utmost astonishment, from beginning to end. When she had concluded, "Sir," added she, "although the liberty granted by our religion to men to have several wives is not very agreeable to the sex, yet if your majesty will consent to give the Princess Haiatalnefous, your daughter, in marriage to Prince Camaralzaman, I will cheerfully resign the rank and quality of queen, which properly belong to her, and will myself be content with the second rank."

King Armanos listened to this discourse of the Princess Badoura, and, when she had concluded, he turned to Prince Camaralzaman. "My son," said he to him, "since the Princess Badoura, your wife, has offered to share your bed with my daughter, I have only to inquire if you also are willing to marry her, and to accept the crown?" "Sir," replied Camaralzaman, "the obligations I owe to your majesty and to the Princess Haiatalnefous have so great weight, that I cannot refuse you anything."

Camaralzaman was accordingly proclaimed king, and married the same day with the greatest magnificence.

The two queens continued to live together in uninterrupted friendship and union, and they each presented him with a son the same year, and nearly at the same period. The birth of the two princes was celebrated by public rejoicings. Camaralzaman gave the name of Amgiad to the first, whom the Queen Badoura had born; and that of Assad to him of whom the Queen Haiatalnefous had been delivered.

THE HISTORY OF PRINCE AMGIAD, AND OF PRINCE ASSAD.

HE two princes were nursed with great care; and, when they were of a proper age, they had the same governor, the same preceptors in all the sciences and polite arts which King Camaralzaman wished them to learn, and the same master also instructed them in each of their exercises. Camaralzaman, indeed, at length placed so implicit a confidence in their ability and rectitude, that, when they had attained the age of nineteen years, he did not hesitate to appoint them alternately to preside at the council, whenever he was for several days engaged in hunting.

As the two princes had always from their infancy been considered of equal beauty and elegance of stature, the two queens had conceived for them an almost incredible tenderness; yet it nevertheless happened that the Princess Badoura had a greater affection for Assad, the son of Queen Haiatalnefous, than she had for Amgiad, her own son; and, in like manner, Queen Haiatalnefous was more attached to Amgiad, than she was to her own son Assad.

The queens, at first, thought that this regard proceeded only from the great friendship they entertained for each other; but, as the princes advanced in age, this affection, which commenced in friendship, changed gradually to a more tender feeling, and at length became the most violent love; when the princes appeared, in their eyes, possessed of so many accomplishments that they were absolutely blinded by their attractions.

As the two queens had not entrusted each other with the secret of their passion, and as neither of them had the audacity openly to make a declaration of it in person to the prince whom she loved, they each determined to explain it by letter; and, to execute their pernicious design, they took advantage of the absence of King Camaralzaman, who was gone on a hunting party for three or four days.

The day after the king's departure, Prince Amgiad presided at the council, and was employed in administering justice for two or three hours after noon. At the breaking-up of the council, as he was returning to the palace, an eunuch took him aside, and presented to him a letter from Queen Haiatalnefous. Amgiad opened it, and read its contents with horror. "What, wretch!" cried he, to the eunuch, the moment he had perused it, and drawing his scimitar, "is this the fidelity you owe to your king and master?" And, in saying this, he struck off his head. Amgiad, transported with rage, then sought his mother, Queen Badoura; and, with an air that plainly showed his resentment, held the letter to her, and informed her of the contents, after telling her from whom it came. Instead, however, of listening to him, the queen herself was angry. "My son," she replied, "what you tell me is a calumnious falsehood. Queen Haintalnefous is chaste; and I consider it an act of great boldness in you to speak against her with this insolence."

Queen Badoura could easily judge, from Prince Amgiad's conduct, that Prince Assad, who was equally virtuous, would not receive more favourably the similar declaration which she intended to make to him. This, however, did not prevent her from persisting in her design; and the next day she wrote a letter to him, which she entrusted to an old woman, who had free admission into the palace. The old woman also chose the moment when Prince Assad left the council, where he went to preside in turn, as a convenient opportunity to execute her commission. The prince took the letter; and reading it, without giving himself time to finish the perusal, he was so exasperated, that he drew his scimitar, and punished the old woman as she deserved. He then ran to the apartment of Queen Haiatalnefous, his mother, with the letter in his hand, intending to show it her, but she did not give him time to speak. "I know what you want of me," she cried; "but you are as impertinent as your brother Amgiad. Go, retire, and never again appear in my presence." Assad was in the utmost astonishment at this reception, for which he was totally unprepared, and which put him into so violent a rage, that he was upon the point of exhibiting the most direful marks of it: but he restrained himself, and retired without reply.

The two queens, driven almost to desperation, renounced every natural and maternal feeling, and consulted together how they should destroy their sons. They made their women believe that the princes had endeavoured to violate their persons which they confirmed by the feigned tears they shed, and they slept in the same bed, as if the resistance they thus pretended to have made, had driven them to the greatest distress.

King Camaralzaman, when he returned from the chase, was in so great astonishment at finding the two queens bathed in tears, that it excited his compassion, and he eagerly inquired of them what had happened. To this question the dissembling queens only answered by increasing their sighs and groans; but, at length, after the greatest entreaty, Queen Badoura, broke silence: "Considering, sir," said she, "the just grief with which we are afflicted, we ought no more to see the day, after the outrage which the princes have attempted. By a conspiracy unworthy of their illustrious birth, your absence has given them the boldness and insolence to attempt our honour. We entreat your majesty not to make any further inquiries; our grief is sufficient to explain the rest."

The king then ordered the two princes to be called, and would have killed them with his own hand, if old King Armanos, his father-in-law, had not restrained him. "My son," cried he, "what are you going to do? Would you imbrue your hands, nay your very palace, with your own blood? There are other means of punishing them, if they are really criminal."

Camaralzaman had no difficulty in restraining himself from being the executioner of his own children; but, after having ordered them to be arrested, he desired an emir, called Giondar, to come in the evening to him; and he then commanded him to conduct the princes on the outside of the city, to what part, and to any distance, he pleased, and there to take their lives; and not to return without their clothes, as a proof of having executed his orders.

Giondar travelled the whole night, and the next morning, as he alighted from his horse, he informed the princes with tears in his eyes, of the order he had received. "Do your office," replied they, "we know well enough, that you are not the cause of our death, and we sincerely pardon you." In saying this, they embraced, and took an eternal farewell of each other. Prince Assad first prepared himself to receive the stroke of death. "Begin with me Giondar," said he, "that I may not experience the grief of seeing my dear brother Amgiad expire." Amgiad opposed his brother's wish; and they at length terminated this dispute, by entreating Giondar to bind them both together, and place them in such a manner that they might as nearly as possible, receive their death at the same moment.

Giondar promised to comply with their desire, and at the same instant drew out his scimitar; his horse which was fastened to a tree, startled at this action, broke his bridle, and galloped over the country at full speed. This horse was very valuable, and richly caparisoned, and Giondar vexed at this accident, instead of cutting off the the heads of the princes, threw down his scimitar, and run after his horse which led him to a wood, which he entered. Giondar followed; when the neighing of the horse disturbed a lion, which was asleep; the lion instantly darted forward, but, instead of pursuing the horse, he ran directly at Giondar, as soon as he perceived him. The emir endeavoured to avoid the attack of the lion, which never lost sight of him, and pursued him closely among the trees. In this extremity, "God" said he to himself, "would not have inflicted this chastisement upon me, if the princes whom I have been commanded to kill, were not innocent; and, to add to my misfortune, I have not my scimitar to defend myself with."

During the absence of Giondar, the two princes experienced the most burning thirst. Prince Amgiad then remarked that they were not far from a spring of water, and proposed to unbind themselves, and go and drink. "My brother," replied Prince Assad, "for the short time we have to live, it would be useless to quench our thirst; we shall have to support it only for a few moments longer." Without, however, paying any attention to this, Amgiad unbound both himself and his brother, when they went to the spring; and, after they had refreshed themselves, they heard the roaring of the lion, accompanied by the most piercing cries. Amgiad immediately took up the scimitar which Giondar had thrown down: "Brother," cried he to Assad, "let us hasten to the assistance of the unfortunate Giondar; perhaps we may arrive in time to deliver him from his danger."

The two princes lost no time, and arrived at the moment when the lion had pulled Giondar to the ground. No sooner did the animal observe Prince Amgiad approaching with his scimitar raised, than he let go his prey, and ran at him with the greatest fury; the prince received him with intrepidity, and gave him a blow with so much strength n d skill, that the lion instantly fell dead at his feet.

When Giondar perceived that he was indebted for his life to the two princes, he threw himself at their feet, and thanked them for the great favour they had afforded him, in terms that evinced the strongest gratitude. "Princes," said he to them, on rising, "God forbid that I should ever attempt to take your lives, after the succour you have afforded me! It shall never be said that the emir Giondar was capable of such black ingratitude." "The service we have rendered you," replied the princes, "ought not to hinder you from executing your orders. Go, take your horse; and let us return to the place where you left us." They had now no difficulty in securing the horse, but, as they approached the spring, neither by entreaty nor prayer could they persuade Giondar to be the instrument of their death. "The only thing that I take the liberty to require of you," said he, "is to accommodate yourselves as well as you can with my clothes between you, and to let me have yours; and then to seek your safety at such a distance, that the king may never again even hear your names mentioned." The princes were obliged to submit to his wishes; when, after having given him their habits, and put on what he could spare of his clothes, Giondar presented to them all the gold and silver he had about him, and departed.

While Camaralzaman was afflicting himself for the loss, the two princes wandered about the most desert places. for fear of encountering the people. They lived upon herbs and wild fruits, drinking the bad rain water which they found in the excavation of rocks; and during the night they slept by turns, in order to guard against the danger to be apprehended from wild beasts. After the lapse of about a month, they arrived at the foot of a frightfully steep mountain, composed of black stone, and, as it appeared to them inaccessible. At length, however, they perceived a path; but it was so narrow and difficult, that they durst not attempt to pursue it. In the hope of discovering another road less rugged, they continued walking round the foot of the mountain for about five days; but all their trouble was to no purpose, and they were compelled to return to the path they had neglected. It appeared to them so little practicable that they long deliberated before they attempted to ascend it; but at length, they began to mount. The farther they advanced, the higher and steeper the mountain appeared; and they were more than once tempted to abandon their enterprise. When either perceived that the other was tired, he stopped; and they took breath together. Sometimes they were both so exhausted, that their strength failed them: and they

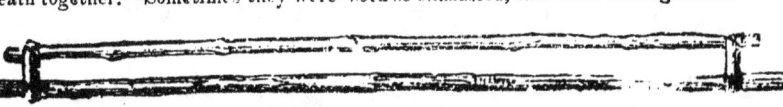

then gave up all thoughts of proceeding, expecting to die through weariness and fatigue. Again in a little time, as their strength returned, they acquired fresh courage, animated each other; and resumed their way.

In spite, however, of all their diligence, they were unable to reach the summit while it was day. Night overtook them, and Prince Assad found himself so completely exhausted, that he suddenly stopped: " My dear brother," said he to Amgiad, " I can proceed no farther." " Let us rest ourselves here," replied Amgiad, stopping at the same time, " as long as you please, and recover our strength. You may observe that we have not much farther to ascend, and the moon will favour our progress." After having reposed for above half an hour, Assad made a fresh effort, and they at length reached the summit of the mountain, where they again rested. Amgiad was the first to rise, and, advancing, he perceived a tree at a short distance. He approached, and found that it was a pomegranate-tree, the branches of which were loaded with fruit, and that a small stream washed the foot of the tree. Having refreshed themselves by eating a pomegranate, they soon fell asleep.

The brothers pursued their journey; and, at length, joyfully discovered a large city. " Do you not think," said Amgiad to Assad, " that it would be advisable for you to remain in some place without the town, while I go and learn in what country we are, the name of the place, and what language is spoken there? And when I come back, I shall be careful to bring provisions with me." " I approve of your counsel," replied Assad, " it is both prudent and wise; but, if one of us must separate himself from the other, I will never suffer you to be the person; you must permit me to undertake the charge." " But, brother," answered Amgiad, " ought not I to have the same apprehensions on your account, which you have for me? I entreat you, therefore, to suffer me to go; and do you wait patiently for me here." " I will never permit it," said Assad; " if any misfortune happen to me, I should at least have the consolation of knowing that you are in safety."

Prince Assad took some money, and continued his journey to the town. He had not proceeded far in the first street, before he met with a venerable-looking old man, well dressed, and with a cane in his hand. As he doubted not but that he was a person of some consequence, and therefore not likely to deceive him, he accosted him. " Sir," said Assad, " I beg you will inform me, which is the way to the market-place?" The old man looked at the prince with a smiling countenance: " My son," said he to him, " you seem to be a stranger; otherwise you surely would not put that question to me. Pray inform me, what concerns have you at the market-place?" " Sir," replied Assad, " nearly two months have passed since my brother and I set out from a very distant country. We have been all this time on our road, and arrived here only yesterday. My brother, fatigued with the length of the journey, remains at the bottom of the mountain, while I am come to obtain some provisions for us both." " My son," said the old man, " you could not possibly have arrived more opportunely; I have this day given an entertainment to several of my friends, and there is a great quantity of provisions left, untouched. Come with me, and I will give you abundance to eat; and when you have satisfied yourself, I will add as much more as will be sufficient for yourself and brother for some days. While you are satisfying your hunger, I can give you information respecting the peculiarities of our city." " I am obliged to you," returned Prince Assad, " for the kindness you express; I submit myself entirely to you, and am ready to go wherever you please."

The old man, walking on, with the prince by his side, laughed in his sleeve all the time, and, for fear Assad should perceive it, he conversed with him on many subjects, that he might preserve the good opinion he had at first formed. " I must confess to you," said he, " that it was fortunate you addressed me in preference to any other person. I thank God that I have met you; and you will know my reason when you have got to my house.'

At length the old man reached his residence, and introduced Assad into a large room, where he saw forty old men sitting, in a circle, round a blazing fire, to which they were paying their adorations. He felt not less horror at thus seeing human beings so far deprived of their reason, as to offer that reverence to the creature in preference to the Creator, than fear at seeing himself so deceived, and in such an abominable place.

While the prince, astonished, stood motionless, the artful old man saluted his forty associates: " Devout adorers of fire," said he to them, " this is a most happy day for us! Where is Gazban?" added he; " let him come in." At these words, spoken in a loud tone of voice, a black immediately appeared. This black no sooner perceived Assad than he understood for what purpose he was called. He ran to him, and, with a blow, felled him to the ground: he then bound his arms, with the most surprising quickness. When he had done this, " Carry him below," said the old man; " and do not fail to tell my daughters, Bostana and Cavama, to give him the bastinado well every day, with only one piece of bread night and morning for his subsistence; that will be enough to keep him alive till the departure of the vessel for the blue sea and the mountain of fire; we will offer him as an acceptable sacrifice to our divinity."

Immediately on the old man's giving these cruel orders, Gazban seized Assad, and forced him down under the room. After leading him through several doors, they reached a dungeon, when the black fastened him by his legs to a very large and extremely heavy chain. Gazban then went to inform the old man's daughters; but their father had already spoken to them himself: " My daughters," said he to them, " go down below, and bestow the bastinado in the manner you know every Mussulman whom I make captive ought to receive it; and do not spare him. You cannot more satisfactorily evince that you are the true worshippers of fire." Bostana and Cavama, having been educated in the greatest detestation of all Mussulmans, received this order with joy. They immediately went down to the dungeon, and having stripped Assad, they beat him so unmercifully, that he was covered with blood, and at last fainted. After this barbarous action, they placed a piece of bread and a jar of water by his side, and left him.

Prince Amgiad waited for his brother, at the foot of the mountain, till sun set, with the greatest impatience. When he saw two, three, and even four, hours of the night elapse, and that Assad did not return, he began to give way to despair. He passed the night in the most distressing inquietude, and as soon as day appeared, he set out towards the town. He was at first very much astonished at seeing so few Mussulmans; stopping the first he met, he asked him the name of the place. He learned, it was called the city of the Magi; because the Magi, who were idolators of fire, resided in great numbers in it, and there were very few Mussulmans. In walking about the town, he stopped at the shop of a tailor, whom, by his dress, he knew to be a Mussulman. After having saluted him, he sat down, and informed him of the cause of his great distress. When Prince Amgiad had finished, " If your brother," said the tailor, " has fallen into the hands of one of the Magi, you may make up your mind never to see him again.

He is gone, past recovery; and I advise you not to grieve, but only endeavour to preserve yourself from the same misfortune. To enable you to escape the danger, you may, if you choose, remain with me; and I will inform you of all the artful deceptions of the Magi, that you may be upon your guard against them, when you go out." Amgiad, greatly afflicted at the loss of his brother, accepted the tailor's offer, and thanked him a thousand times for the kindness he showed him.

Prince Amgiad did not quit the house for a whole month, except in company with the tailor; but at the end of this time he ventured to go alone to the bath. As he returned, he passed through a street, in which he only met a lady, who approached towards him. The lady lifted up her veil, and asked him, with a soft and smiling countenance where he was going. "Madam," replied he, "I am going to my own house or yours, whichever you choose." "Sir," answered the lady, with an engaging smile, "ladies of my description never take men home with them, they only accompany them to their houses." Amgiad was in the greatest embarrassment at this answer, which was totally unexpected. In this state of incertitude, he determined to abandon all to chance; so, without answering the lady, he went on and the lady followed him.

Prince Amgiad continued walking for a long time, from street to street, from one cross-way to another, and from square to square. At length, passing down a street which was terminated by a large door belonging to a house of handsome appearance, with a bench on each side of it, he sat down on one to take breath, and the lady sat down on the other. "Is this your house?" said she to Prince Amgiad, as soon as she was seated. "You see it is, madam," replied the prince. "Why do you not, then, open the door?" continued she. "What do you wait for?" "My charming creature," answered Amgiad, "I have not the key. I left it with my slave, whom I have charged with a commission, which he is not yet returned from executing." "What an impertinent slave is yours," said she, "to make you wait thus!" Saying this, she arose, and took a large stone, to break the lock, which, according to the fashion of that country, was made of wood, and not very strong.

Amgiad, alarmed, wished to prevent her design. "Madam!" cried he, "what are you going to do? I beg you you will have a little more patience." "What are you afraid of?" said she. "Is not the house your own? There is no great harm in breaking a wooden lock, as its place is easily supplied." She then forced the lock, and as soon as the door was open, she entered and walked on before. When the prince saw the house broken open, he gave himself up for lost. He hesitated whether he should enter, or endeavour to make his escape, in order to free himself from a danger which he believed to be inevitable; and he was going to adopt the latter plan, when the lady turning round, saw that he was not following. "What are you about," said she, "that you do not come into your own house?" "I am looking, madam," he answered, "to see if my slave appear; as I am afraid we shall find nothing ready." "Come, come," continued she, "we can wait his arrival much better within, than standing here." The prince, though much against his inclination, then entered into a very large and handsomely paved court; from which they ascended, by a few steps, to a grand vestibule where both he and the lady perceived a large open room handsomely furnished, and one table set out with numerous exquisite dishes, another covered with a variety of fine fruits, and a sideboard well supplied with wine. The lady was delighted with this agreeable sight. "What, sir!" cried she, "you were fearful that nothing was ready, but you now perceive that your slave has exceeded your expectations. But if I do not deceive myself, these preparations were intended for some other lady, and not for me. Well, never mind; let the lady come; I promise you not to be jealous."

Amgiad could not avoid laughing at the pleasantry of the lady. "Madam," said he, "I assure you that you are entirely mistaken in your conjectures: this is only my common fare." As he could not resolve to take a place at a table that had not been prepared for him, he was going to sit on a sofa, but the lady prevented him: "What are you about?" said she; "after having been in the bath, you ought to be hungry. Come, sit down at the table, let us eat, and enjoy ourselves." The prince was obliged to comply with the lady's desire: they sat down, and began to eat. After the first mouthful or two, she took a bottle and glass, and pouring out some wine, drank to the health of Amgiad. She then filled the same glass again and presented it to the prince, who returned her compliment.

They were beginning the fruit, when the master of the house entered: he was the grand equerry to the king of the Magi, and his name was Bahadar. This house belonged to him; but he had another, in which he commonly resided; this served him merely to receive a few chosen friends privately, for which purpose everything was brought from his other mansion. Not a little surprised at finding the door of his house open, he entered without making any noise; and crept round by the wall, and put his head half into the room, to see who was there. Observing only a young man and a lady eating at the table which had been prepared for himself and his friends, and that the mischief was not so great as he at first expected, he resolved to have some diversion.

The lady, whose back was turned towards the door, could not perceive Bahadar; but Amgiad saw him immediately, while in the act of drinking. At sight of him, he instantly changed colour, and fixed his eyes upon Bahadar, who made him a sign not to say a word, but to come and speak to him. The prince found Bahadar waiting for him in the vestibule; and they descended to the court, that the lady might not hear their conversation. Bahadar then asked the prince how he happened to be with the lady in his house, and why they had forced the door. "Sir," replied Amgiad, "I must appear culpable; but if you will have the patience to hear my story, I hope you will be convinced of my innocence." He then proceeded, and related, in a few words, every circumstance precisely as it was; and to prove that he was incapable of committing so disgraceful an action as that of breaking open a house, he did not even conceal from him that he was a prince, or his motives for coming to the city of the Magi.

Bahadar was highly delighted at having an opportunity of serving one of the quality and rank of Amgiad. In fact, his engaging manners left no doubt of the truth of his statement. "Prince," said he, "I am extremely happy at thus finding an occasion to oblige you, through a meeting so pleasant as what you have related. So far from disturbing your festivity, I shall take great pleasure in contributing to your satisfaction. You have made your lady believe that you have a slave, though in truth you have none. I will be that slave, and insist upon your compliance. Go then, retake your place, and continue to divert yourself; and when I return, and present myself before you dressed like a slave, quarrel well with me, and do not hesitate even to strike me. You shall both sleep here; and to-morrow morning you shall part with the lady in the most honourable manner."

The prince rejoined the lady. "Madam," said he, "I beg you a thousand pardons for my incivility, and the ill humour in which I feel myself on account of my slave's absence. The rascal shall suffer for it; I will let him see that he shall not be guilty of negligence with impunity." "Do not let this disturb you," replied the lady. "Trouble yourself no more about him; let us only think of enjoying ourselves."

They continued at table with much greater pleasure than before, because Amgiad was no longer rendered uneasy by the fear of consequences that might arise from the indiscretion of the lady, who ought not to have forced the door, had it even belonged to Amgiad. He now began to feel himself as much at his ease as the lady herself; and while they continued to drink more than they ate, they diverted each other with saying a thousand pleasant and humorous things, till the arrival of Bahadar, disguised as a slave. He was much mortified at finding his master with company before he returned; and throwing himself at his feet, he kissed the ground, and begged his pardon for being so late: when he got up, he stood still, with his hands crossed, and his eyes cast down, waiting for what he might be ordered to do. "Scoundrel!" cried Amgiad, with a look and voice of anger, "tell me, is there in the whole world a more impudent slave than yourself? Where have you been? What have you been about, not to come back till this time of day?" "My lord," replied Bahadar, "I entreat your pardon; I have executed the orders you gave me; and I did not think you would return so early." "You are a rascal," said the prince; "and I will teach you not to tell falsehoods, and be so negligent of your duty." He arose, and taking a stick, gave him two or three slight blows, after which he returned to the table. The lady, however, was not satisfied with this trifling punishment: she got up in her turn, and seizing the stick, she beat Bahadar so unmercifully, that the tears came into his eyes. She continued striking him with such fury, that Amgiad was forced to interfere, and take the stick out of her hands, which he effected with some difficulty.

Amgiad and the lady continued in conversation for half an hour longer; and, before they retired to repose, the latter, having occasion to pass through the vestibule, heard Bahadar already snoring very loud. As she had observed a scimitar hanging up in the saloon, "Sir," said she to Amgiad, on re-entering, "I beg of you to do one thing for love of me." "In what can I serve you?" inquired the prince. "Oblige me by taking this scimitar," replied she, "and go and cut off the head of your slave." Amgiad was extremely astonished at this proposition. "Madam," said he, "let us not regard my slave; he is unworthy of your thoughts: I have punished him, and you have chastised him also; let this be sufficient. Besides, I am very well satisfied with him, as he is not accustomed to be guilty of those faults." "That is of no consideration to me," replied the enraged female; "I wish the rascal dead; and if he is not to be killed by your hands, he shall by mine." Saying this, she took the scimitar, drew it from the scabbard, and ran to execute her design. The prince followed, and overtook her in the vestibule: "You must be satisfied, madam," said he, "since you insist upon it; but I should be sorry if any one besides myself were to kill my slave." When she had given him the scimitar, "Follow me," he continued; "and do not make a noise, for fear of waking him." They entered the chamber where Bahadar was lying; but, instead of striking him, Amgiad directed the blow at the lady, whose head fell upon Bahadar. Astonished at seeing Amgiad standing by him with the bloody scimitar in his hand, and the headless body of the lady on the ground, Bahadar demanded the cause. The prince related what had passed; and, in conclusion, added, "I could find no other means of preventing this enraged woman from taking your life, than by destroying her own. "Sir," returned Bahadar, impressed with the warmest gratitude; "you are my preserver, and I cannot sufficiently thank you." After he had embraced him, "Before the day breaks," said he, "this body must be carried out; which I will immediately do." Amgiad, however, opposed it; saying he would take that charge upon himself, as he had been the cause of her death. "A stranger in this place, like you, will not be so well able to manage it," replied Bahadar. "Leave it to me, and you retire to rest. If I do not return before daybreak, you may suppose that the watch has surprised me. In case this should happen, I will now make over to you, in writing, a donation of this house, with all the furniture, and here you can safely remain."

When Bahadar had written what was sufficient to transfer the house to Amgiad, and had delivered the security into his hands, he put the lady's body and head in a sack, and throwing it across his shoulders, walked along from street to street, towards the sea. He had not, however, proceeded far, before he encountered the judge of the police, who was going the rounds in person. His attendants stopped Bahadar, and, opening the sack, discovered the body and head of the murdered lady. The magistrate, who recognised the master of the horse, notwithstanding his disguise, conveyed him home with him; and next morning took Bahadar into the royal presence. The king had no sooner been informed of the inhuman action which it appeared Bahadar had committed, than he loaded him with abuse: "Is it thus," he cried, "that you murder my subjects, in order to plunder them, and then throw their bodies into the sea to prevent a discovery of your tyranny? Hang him, and let my people be freed from such a villain."

Prince Amgiad, who anxiously waited for Bahadar, was in the utmost consternation when he heard, from the house in which he was, the crier proclaiming this sentence. "If any person should suffer for the death of so wicked a woman," said he to himself. "I am that person, and not Bahadar; and I cannot bear that the innocent should be punished for the guilty." Without further deliberation, he went to the spot where the execution was to take place; and joined the crowd, which was collecting from all parts.

As soon as Amgiad saw the judge make his appearance, leading Bahadar to the gibbet, he went and presented himself before him: "My lord," said he, "I come to declare to you that the grand-equerry is entirely innocent of the death of that lady. I am the man who committed the crime, if crime it may be called, to deprive a detestable woman of life who was on the point of murdering the master of the horse."

When Prince Amgiad had informed the judge of the manner in which the lady had accosted him on his leaving the bath, how she caused his entering the house of Bahadar, and of all that had passed until he had found himself compelled to cut off her head to save the life of Bahadar; the officer suspended the execution, and took them both before the king. The monarch desired to be informed of the whole affair by Amgiad himself; who, the better to exculpate himself, as well as the grand-equerry, took advantage of the opportunity to relate the whole of his history together with that of Prince Assad his brother. When the prince had ended, "I am very much pleased, prince," said the king to him, "that this affair has afforded me the opportunity of becoming acquainted with you; I not only grant you your life, together with that of my equerry, but I also confer on you the dignity of grand-vizier, to console you for the unjust, although excusable, treatment you have experienced from the king, your father. As for Prince Assad, I permit you to exercise all the authority with which you are invested, to discover his abode."

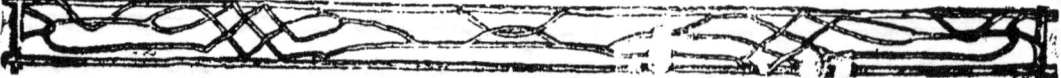

Assad, in the meantime, was constantly chained in the dungeon where he had been confined through the artifice of the old man; and Bostana and Cavama, his daughters, continued to treat him in the same cruel and inhuman manner. The solemn festival of the idolaters of fire approaching, the vessel which usually sailed to the mountain of fire was equipped for the voyage, and a captain named Behram, who was a zealous promoter of the religion of the Magi, superintended the lading it with merchandise. When it was ready to put to sea, Behram had Assad placed in a case half-full of merchandise, leaving sufficient space between the planks to admit air for him to breathe, and then caused the case to be lowered into the hold of the ship.

After some days' sail, the wind, which had before been favourable, suddenly changed, and increased to so violent a degree, that it at length produced a furious tempest. The vessel not only lost its track, but neither Behram nor the pilot could ascertain their course; and they were fearful every moment of striking on a rock, and being dashed to pieces. During the height of the storm, they discovered land, and Behram recognised it as the harbour and capital of Queen Margiana, which occasioned him great distress; in fact, Queen Margiana, who professed the Mahometan religion, was an avowed enemy to the idolaters of fire; she would not permit one to reside in her dominions, nor even suffer any of their vessels to land.

It was, however, totally out of the power of Behram to avoid making for the harbour of Margiana's capital, unless he had exposed himself to the danger of being cast away on the dangerous rocks which lined the shore. In this extremity, he held a council with his pilot and seamen: "My lads," said he, you see the necessity to which we are reduced. Of two alternatives, we must choose one;—either be swallowed up by the waves, or take refuge with Queen Margiana. I see but one remedy, which may perhaps succeed. I propose that we take off the chains from the mussulman who is with us, and dress him as a slave. When Queen Margiana sends for me to appear before her and asks me what I trade in, I will tell her that I am a merchant who sells slaves; that I have sold all I had, with the exception of one only, whom I have reserved for myself, to act as secretary, because he can read and write. She will desire to see him; and as he is well-looking, and of her religion, she will be solicitous to purchase him of me: to which I will only agree, on condition that we remain in her harbour until the weather be fair."

Behram having ordered Prince Assad's chains to be taken off, had him habited as a slave, in which character he wished him to appear before Queen Margiana. As soon as the queen perceived the ship at anchor, she sent for the captain; and, that she might sooner gratify her curiosity, went to meet him in the garden. Behram, landed with Prince Assad, having first exacted a promise from him that he would confirm what he might say, and they were conducted before the queen.

Margiana had felt a predilection for Assad, from the first moment she saw him; and she was delighted to hear that he was a slave. Determined, therefore, to purchase him at whatever price, she asked Assad his name. "Great queen," replied he, "does your majesty wish to known the name I formerly bore, or that by which I am now called?" "What!" said the queen, have you two names?" "Alas!" returned the prince, "it is but too true! My name was formerly Assad (*most happy*), but now I am called Motar (*destined for sacrifice*)."

The queen said no more to Behram; but taking Assad by the arm, made him walk before her, till they reached the palace, when she sent to acquaint Behram, that she should confiscate all his property, and set fire to his vessel in the middle of the harbour, if he attempted to pass the night there. He was consequently obliged to return to his vessel, and to make preparations for sailing, although the tempest had not entirely subsided.

Queen Margiana having ordered supper to be instantly served, conducted Prince Assad to her apartment, where she made him sit by her. Assad wished to decline it, saying that so great an honour was not to be conferred on a slave. "On a slave!" returned the queen: "a moment since you were a slave, but you are one no longer. Sit down next me, I tell you, and relate to me your history; for I judge by what you wrote just now, as well as by the insolence of that merchant, it must be extraordinary."

Prince Assad began by acquainting her of his royal birth, with that of his brother Amgiad; of their reciprocal friendship; of the odious passion conceived for them by their mothers-in-law, which suddenly changing into implacable hatred, became the origin of their strange adventures. He then told her of the anger of the king his father; of the almost miraculous manner in which their lives had been preserved; and lastly of the loss he had experienced in his brother, and the long and cruel imprisonment he was just released from, only to be immolated on the fiery mountain.

The repast lasted a considerable time, and Assad drank some glasses more than he could well support. When the table was cleared, Assad wished to recover himself, and took an opportunity of going out, unobserved by the queen. He descended to the court, when seeing the gate of the garden open, he entered it; and, attracted by the various beauties of the spot, walked about for some time. He at length went towards a fountain, and washed his hands and face in it, to refresh himself; then sitting down to rest on the lawn which bordered it, he fell asleep.

Night was approaching; and Behram had already weighed anchor, not a little vexed at having lost Assad, and being thereby frustrated in the hope of sacrificing his victim; but he endeavoured to console himself with the reflection that the storm had ceased, and that a land-breeze favoured his departure. As soon as he had got out of the harbour, with the assistance of his boat, before he drew it up to the ship, "My lads," said he to the sailors who were in it, "stop; do not come up yet, I am going to give you the casks to fetch water, and I will wait for you just off the shore."

The sailors went, and each having taken a cask on his shoulders, they easily got over the wall. As they approached the basin, they perceived a man lying asleep on the bank; and as they advanced nearer, they discovered him to be Assad. They divided into two parties; and whilst one set was hastily filling the casks as quietly as possible, their companions had surrounded Assad, watching to secure him in case he should awake. But he did not trouble them; and when the casks were filled, and hoisted on the shoulders of those who were to carry them, the others seized him, and took him away before he had time to recollect himself; put him in the boat, and rowed to the ship.

Queen Margiana, in the meantime, was in the greatest alarm. She did not feel uneasy when she first perceived the absence of Prince Assad, but finding that he did not make his appearance, she began to be very much disturbed. Her

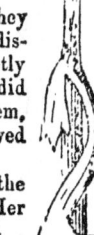

women searched for him, to no purpose; they could bring her no intelligence of him. Night came on, and she had him sought for with lights, but still ineffectually. In the state of impatience and alarm which Margiana experienced, she went herself to look by the light of flambeaux. Passing near the fountain, she observed a slipper on the bank, which, when examined, she knew to be one of those worn by the prince. This circumstance led her to believe that Behram might have taken him away by force. She immediately sent to inquire if his ship were still in the harbour; and being informed that he had sailed just before night, that he had stopped for some time off the shore, and that his boat had been seen to fetch water from her garden, she instantly despatched a messenger to the commander of ten ships of war, which were always kept in port fully equipped, and ready to sail, to acquaint him that she intended to embark the following day, about an hour after sunrise.

The commander was diligent in obeying her orders, and everything was ready by the appointed hour. She embarked; and when her squadron had got out to sea, and was in full sail, she declared her intention to the commander. "You must use the utmost expedition," said she, "to chase the merchant-vessel which sailed from the harbour yesterday evening. I give it up as your prize, if you take it; but if you do not succeed, your life shall be the forfeit." The ten ships accordingly chased Behram's vessel for two whole days, without being able to get within sight of it. On the third, at daybreak, they discovered it; and by noon they had so surrounded it, that it could not escape. No sooner did Behram perceive the ten vessels, than he concluded it must be the squadron of Queen Margiana, in pursuit of him, and he immediately inflicted the bastinado on Prince Assad; a practice he had continued daily, and which he now repeated with more violence than usual. When he found he was on the point of being surrounded on all sides, he was extremely embarrassed. He therefore had him unchained; and when the prince was brought up from the hold of the ship, and appeared before him, "It is thou," said he, "who art the cause of our being pursued!" and on saying this, he threw him into the sea.

Prince Assad could swim, and made so good use of his hands and feet, that, assisted by the waves, which bore him toward the shore, he had sufficient strength to hold out till he reached land. He thanked God for having delivered him from so imminent danger, and again favouring his escape from the hands of the idolaters of fire. He then undressed himself; and having wrung the water from his clothes, he spread them on a rock to dry. This was soon effected, as well from the direct heat of the sun, as from that acquired by the rock. He lay down for some time, deploring his miserable fate, equally ignorant of the country in which he was, and which way to turn. He then walked forward till he came to a road, which he followed, for ten days, through an uninhabited country, where he found nothing but wild fruits, and a few plants along the banks of rivulets, on which he lived. He at length reached a town, which he immediately recognised as the city of the Magi, where he had been so ill used. He resolved to stop in a cemetery close to the town, in which were many tombs, built like mausoleums. In looking about, he discovered one, the door of which was open. He entered, and determined to remain there during the night.

We will now return to the vessel of Behram. But a short time elapsed, after he had thrown Assad into the sea, before it was surrounded on all sides by the fleet of Queen Margiana. He was first boarded by the ship in which the queen herself had embarked; and as he was not able to make any resistance, Margiana immediately went on board the vessel, and asked Behram where the secretary was, whom he had had the audacity to seize in her palace. "Queen," replied Behram, "I swear to your majesty that he is not on board my vessel; if you will order it to be searched, you will be convinced of my innocence." Margiana directed the vessel to be searched, but the person whom she was so desirous of finding, could not be discovered. She was on the point of killing Behram with her own hand; but she restrained herself, and was satisfied with confiscating the vessel and all its cargo, and sending him and all the sailors ashore, in their own boat, which she gave them for that purpose. Behram, accompanied by his crew, arrived at the city of the Magi, on the same night in which Assad had stopped in the burial ground, and found shelter in the tomb. As the city-gate was shut, he also was obliged to have recourse to the cemetery, and to seek refuge in some tomb till day appeared, and the gate was again open. Unfortunately for Assad, Behram advanced to that in which he was reposing; and entering, saw a man asleep, with his head wrapped in his clothes. The prince awoke at the noise, and lifting up his head, demanded who was there. Behram immediately recognised him. "Ah, ha!" said he, "is it, then, you? You have escaped being sacrificed this year, but you shall not evade it again on the following." Saying this, he threw himself upon him, put his handkerchief into his mouth to prevent his calling out, and then made his sailors bind him.

Assad was extremely surprised at finding himself again in the same place where he had already suffered so much, and in expectation of the same tortures, from which he thought himself delivered for ever. He was lamenting the hardness of his destiny, when he saw Bostana enter the dungeon with a stick in her hand, a piece of bread, and a pitcher of water. But the lamentations, the complaints, and the continual supplications of the prince for mercy joined to his tears, were at length so powerful, that Bostana could not avoid being softened by them. "Sir," said she to Assad, as she again covered his shoulders, "I ask you a thousand pardons for the severity with which I have constantly treated you, and of which I have again made you feel the effects. Hitherto I have been afraid of disobeying my father, but I now detest and abhor this barbarity. Console yourself, therefore, for your sufferings are at an end, and I am going to repair all my crimes, by better treatment. You have always considered me as an infidel; you must, for the future, regard me as a Mahometan. I have already received some instruction from a female slave, who attends me; I hope you will complete what she has begun."

Some days after Prince Assad's return, Bostana happened to be at the door of her house, when she heard the public crier proclaiming something, which she could not understand, because he was so far off; but as she observed him approaching towards the house, she went in, leaving the door a little open, and saw him walking before the grand-vizier Amgiad, Prince Assad's brother, accompanied by several officers of state, and surrounded by a great multitude of people. The crier had only proceeded a few steps from the door, when he repeated this proclamation in a loud tone of voice :—"*The most excellent and illustrious grand-vizier, who is here in person, seeks for his dear brother, from whom he has been separated more than a year. If any person knows where he is, his excellency commands such person to give information, and he promises for such service a handsome reward. But if any one conceal him, and he shall be afterwards discovered, his excellency declares that he will punish such person with death, together with his wife, his children, and all his family, and will raze his house to the ground.*" Bostana had no sooner heard these words, than she shut the door, and went to the dungeon where Assad was confined. "Prince," cried she, with joy, "your misfortunes are at length terminated : follow me as quickly as possible." Assad, whom she had released from his chains on the day when he was reconducted to the dungeon, followed her into the street, where she cried out "Here, here !" The grand-vizier, who had not proceeded far, turned round ; and Assad instantly recognised him as his brother, ran towards him, and fell into his arms.

Bostana, after this event, was unwilling to return to her father's, whose house was razed to the ground the same day, and therefore followed Prince Assad till he arrived at the palace, when she was sent to an apartment belonging to the queen. The old man her father, and Behram, with their families, being brought next day before the king, were condemned to lose their heads; on which, they threw themselves at his feet, and implored his clemency. "No mercy shall be shown you," replied the king, "unless you renounce the adoration of fire, and embrace the Mussulman religion." By adopting this conduct they saved their lives; as also did Cavama the sister of Bostana, and all their families.

In consideration of Behram's being converted to the Mahometan religion, and as a recompense for the loss he had before sustained, Amgiad appointed him one of his principal officers, and lodged him at his own house. A few days after, when Behram was made acquainted with the adventures of Amgiad and his brother, he proposed to fit out a vessel, and to convey them back to their father Camaralzaman. The two brothers having accepted Behram's offer, they mentioned their design to the king, who not only approved of it, but gave orders for the equipment of a vessel. Behram hastened the preparations as much as possible; and when he was ready to sail, the princes went one morning to take leave of the king before they embarked. While they were paying their compliments they heard a great tumult, and at the same time an officer entered, to announce that a large army was approaching, and that no person could tell to whom it belonged. Observing the alarm that this news gave the king, Amgiad said to him, "Although, sir, I came for the purpose of resigning the office with which you have honoured me, I am, notwithstanding, ready to render you any service in my power; and I entreat you to suffer me to go and see who this enemy is.

Prince Amgiad soon discovered the army, which continued to approach. The advanced guards conducted him before a princess, who halted to hold a conference with him. Prince Amgiad inquired if she came as a friend or an enemy. "I come as a friend," she replied, "and have no cause for complaint against the king. I demand a slave, whose name is Assad, and who has been taken away from me by a captain, who is called Behram. I trust your king will afford me justice, when he shall know that my name is Margiana." "Mighty queen," replied Amgiad, "I am the brother of that slave whom you seek with so much solicitude. Come with me, and I will myself deliver him up to you.

Queen Margiana accompanied Prince Amgiad to the palace, where he presented her to the king; and when the monarch had received her as her dignity required, Prince Assad, who was present, advanced, and paid his compliments to her. While they were thus engaged, news was brought that another army, much more powerful than the former, had made its appearance on the other side of the city. The king of the Magi was now more terrified than before; "What will become of us, Amgiad?" cried he; "there is another army coming to overwhelm us!" The prince mounting his horse, rode as fast as possible to meet this second army. He demanded to speak to their commander, and they conducted him before a king, as he saw by the crown on his head. As soon as he perceived him, though at some distance, he alighted; and when he drew near him, he prostrated himself on the ground, and asked what he wished of the king his master. "My name is Gaiour," replied the monarch, "and I am king of China. The desire of obtaining some intelligence of a daughter, named Badoura, whom many years since I gave in marriage to Prince Camaralzaman, has occasioned my leaving my dominions. I gave this prince permission to visit his father, with injunction to spend every other year with me, and bring my daughter with him. A great length of time has elapsed, during which I have been unable to obtain intelligence of them." Prince Amgiad, who instantly knew, by his discourse, that the king with whom he was speaking was his grandfather, kissed his hand with great tenderness, saying to him, "Your majesty will pardon me, when you know that I take this liberty to render you my respects as my, grandfather. I am the son of Camaralzaman, now king of the Isle of Ebony, and of Queen Badoura. The king of China, delighted at seeing his grandson, embraced him, and this very unexpected and happy meeting drew tears from the eyes of both. On inquiring the occasion of his being thus in a foreign country, Prince Amgiad related his history, and that of his brother Assad. When he had finished, "My son," replied the king of China, "it is not just that two innocent princes, as you are, should experience any further ill-treatment. Console yourself; I will conduct back both you and your brother, and will ensure your peace."

While the king of China encamped his army in the place where Prince Amgiad had met him, the latter went back to make his report to the king of the Magi, who was waiting for him with the greatest impatience. The king was extremely surprised to hear that so powerful a monarch as the king of China had undertaken such a long and painful journey, excited by a desire to see his daughter, and that he should be so near his capital; he immediately gave orders for his reception, and prepared to go and receive him in person.

In this interval considerable clouds of dust were seen to rise from another side of the city, and news soon came that a third army was approaching. This circumstance obliged the king to stop, and to request Amgiad again to ascertain the cause of it. The prince departed, and his brother Assad accompanied him. They discovered that this was the army of Camaralzaman their father, who was searching for them. He had shown signs of so excessive grief at having destroyed them, that the emir Giondar at length informed him in what manner he had preserved their lives, which made the king resolve to endeavour to discover them, in whatever country they might reside.

This afflicted father embraced the two princes with tears of joy, which agreeably terminated the poignant affliction he had so long suffered. The princes had no sooner informed him of the arrival of his father-in-law, the king of China, on the same day, than he went with them to visit him in his camp. They had not proceeded far on their road, before they perceived a fourth army, which advanced in perfect order, and seemed to come from towards Persia. Camaralzaman desired his sons to go and see to whom that army belonged, while he waited their return. They departed immediately, and, when they had joined it, they presented themselves to the king to whom the army belonged. After saluting him with profound reverence, they asked him his motive for approaching so near to the capital of the king of the magi. The grand vizier, who was present, replied, "The monarch to whom you have addressed yourself, is called Schahzaman, king of the Isle of the Children of Khaledan, who has travelled for a great length of time, with the attendants you see, in search of his son Prince Camaralzaman, who left his dominions many years ago." To this the princes made no other reply than that they would return in a short time with an answer. A more tender and affectionate interview between a parent and son had scarcely ever been witnessed. Schahzaman affectionately chided Camaralzaman for his unkindness in leaving him in so cruel a manner, and Camaralzaman expressed a sincere regret for the fault which love alone had been the cause of his committing.

The three kings and Queen Margiana remained three days at the court of the king of the Magi, who entertained them in the most splendid manner. These three days were also remarkable for the marriage of Prince Assad with Queen Margiana, and Prince Amgiad with Bostana, in consideration of the service she had rendered Prince Assad. At length, the three kings, and Queen Margiana with Assad her husband, retired to their respective dominions. In regard to Prince Amgiad, the king of the Magi, who was at a very advanced age, felt so strong an attachment to him, that he placed the crown upon his head; and Amgiad used all his endeavours to abolish the idolatrous worship of fire, and to establish the Mahometan religion throughout his kingdom.

THE HISTORY OF NOUREDDIN, AND THE BEAUTIFUL PERSIAN.

HE city of Balsora had long been the capital of a kingdom tributary to the caliphs. The name of the king who governed it during the life of the caliph Haroun Alraschid, was Zinebi: the caliph and this king were cousins, sons of two brothers. Zinebi, not judging it proper to trust the administration of his states to one vizier only, made choice of two, Khacan and Saouy.

Khacan was mild, affable, generous; he took pleasure in obliging all who had transactions with him, by granting them every favour in his power, consistent with the justice he was bound to administer.

Saouy was a totally different character; he was sullen and morose; repulsing every one who approached him without distinction of rank or quality. Besides which, so far from doing good and deriving credit from the immense wealth he possessed, his avarice was so great, that he even denied himself the necessaries of life.

One day, after the council, the king of Balsora amused himself by talking familiarly with these two viziers, and some other members of the council. The conversation happened to turn upon those female slaves who are purchased and who are considered nearly in the rank of lawful wives. Some were of opinion that beauty and elegance o, form in a slave were of a sufficient compensation for the want of such qualifications in those females with whom af connection in marriage had been formed. Others maintained, and Khacan was of the number, that beauty and the charms of person were not the only attractions to be sought for in a slave; but that these qualities should be accompanied with great wit, understanding, modesty, and pleasing manners; and, if possible, withvarious elegant accomplishments. The king joined the latter party, which he evinced, by ordering Khacan to purchase for him a slave who was perfect in beauty, and in all personal charms, but who should, above everything, possess a well-cultivated mind.

Early one morning, as Khacan was going to the royal palace, a broker, taking hold of his stirrup with great eagerness, informed him that a Persian merchant, who had arrived very late the preceding evening, had a slave to sell, of infinitely greater beauty than he had ever beheld, and, with respect to understanding, the merchant assured him that she possessed every knowledge that was known in the world. Khacan, overjoyed with the news, desired that the slave might be brought to him on his return from the palace.

The broker did not fail to wait upon the vizier at the hour appointed, and Khacan found the handsome slave so much superior to his expectation, that he immediately gave her the name of the beautiful Persian. Being a man of great wisdom and penetration, he soon discovered, by his conversation with her, that he might search in vain for any slave who could surpass her in either of the qualifications required by the king. He inquired, therefore, what sum was demanded for her by the merchant. "Sir," replied the broker, "the merchant, who is a man of few words, protests that he cannot make the slightest abatement of ten thousand pieces of gold."

The vizier Khacan, who understood the merits of the fair Persian much better than the broker, was unwilling to defer the purchase; he, therefore, sent one of his people, by the broker's directions, in quest of the merchant, to desire his attendance. When he arrived, "It is not," said Khacan, "for myself that I wish to buy your slave, but for the king. You must, however, make a more reasonable demand than that which you have proposed." "Sir," replied the merchant, "I should consider myself infinitely honoured in being allowed to present her to his majesty, if it were compatible with my circumstances. I require no more than what I have actually expended in her education and support. I have only to say that I believe his majesty will be perfectly contented with the purchase."

The vizier Khacan was not inclined to delay the bargain; he ordered the sum to be paid to the merchant, who, before he withdrew, thus addressed him: "Since, sir, the slave you have purchased is intended for the king, allow me to inform you, that she is extremely fatigued with the long journey she has so lately encountered. Though her present beauty may well seem incomparable, yet she will appear quite a different person, if you retain her in your house about a fortnight. After this time, she will ensure you equal honour and reward, and entitle me, I hope, to your thanks."

Khacan thought the advice of the merchant very judicious, and determined to follow it. He allotted to the fair Persian an apartment near that of his wife, whom he requested to allow her a place at her own table, and treat her in every respect as a lady belonging to the king. He also desired his wife to cause the most magnificent dresses possible to be made, and such as might be peculiarly becoming to her beautiful charge, whom, before he quitted, he thus addressed: "The good fortune I have just procured you, could not possibly be greater: it is for the king that I have purchased you. I am anxious, however, to inform you that I have a son who, though not deficient in understanding, has all the inconsiderate rashness of youth: you will, therefore, when you meet him, be on your guard." The fair Persian thanked him for his advice; and assured him she would profit by it; after which the vizier withdrew."

Noureddin, for thus was the son called, was accustomed to enter, without restraint, the apartment of his mother with whom he usually took his meals. He was of an extremely handsome person, young, agreeable, and courageous. He saw the fair Persian; and from that moment, he put himself under no restraint whatever to guard against the effects of love. On the other hand, the fair Persian was extremely well satisfied with Noureddin. "The vizier does me great honour," said she to herself, "in purchasing me for the king of Balsora; but I should have esteemed myself very happy if he had designed me only for his son."

As, in consequence of her long journey, much time had elapsed since the fair Persian had bathed, about five or six days after she had been purchased, the wife of the vizier gave orders to have their own bath prepared. She sent her thither, accompanied with a train of female slaves, who were commanded to render to her the same services as to her mistress; and when she came out of the bath, to array her in the most magnificent dress, which had been provided for her.

On leaving the bath, the fair Persian, a thousand times handsomer than when Khacan purchased her, returned to the wife of the vizier, who scarcely knew her again; and gracefully kissing her hand thus addressed her:—"I know not, madam, how I may appear to you in the dress you have had the goodness to provide for me. Your women, who assure me it so well becomes me, that they scarcely know me again, are, I believe, inclined to flatter; it is to yourself that I wish to appeal. If, however, they should speak the truth, I am indebted to you, madam, for all the advantage it affords me." "My daughter," replied the vizier's lady, with an expression of great joy, "what my women have told you is no flattery. I am better able to judge; and, without considering your dress, which very much becomes you, be assured you have brought from the bath a beauty so infinitely superior to what you possessed before, that I scarcely knew you myself. If I thought the bath were still sufficiently warm, I would go and partake of it myself."

The wife of the vizier was desirous of profiting by the opportunity: and having declared this to her women, they soon provided all the requisites necessary. But, before she went to the bath, she commanded two little female slaves to remain near the fair Persian, who had retired to her apartment; ordering them not to permit Noureddin to enter it should he arrive during her absence.

While the vizier Khacan's lady was in the bath, Noureddin came; and not finding his mother in her apartment he went towards that of the fair Persian, where, in the antechamber, he found the two slaves. The chamber was only closed by a screen; and Noureddin advanced to go in, when the two slaves opposed themselves to prevent him. He immediately seized each of them by the arm, turned them out of the antechamber, and locked the door. They then ran to the bath, loudly complaining; and, in tears, informed their lady that Noureddin had driven them from their post, and, in contempt of their remonstrance, had entered the chamber of the fair Persian. The boldness of her son afflicted the good lady excessively. She instantly quitted the bath, and dressed herself with the utmost haste; but, before she had finished, and could arrive at the chamber of the fair Persian, Noureddin had quitted it and taken to flight. The fair Persian was extremely astonished at the appearance of the wife of the vizier. "Madam," said she, "may I presume to ask what so much afflicts you?" "What?" cried the vizier's lady, "can you ask this question, after my son Noureddin has been in your chamber alone with you?" "Has not my husband informed you that you were purchased for the king, and has he not cautioned you to avoid the company of Noureddin?" "I have not forgotten his injunction, madam," replied the fair Persian; "but Noureddin came to inform me that his father had changed his mind; and that, instead of reserving me for the king, he had presented me to him. I believed what he told me; and, slave as I am, you must be aware I could have as little will as power to oppose his inclinations. Permit me to add that I have submitted with the less repugnance, as I had conceived a passion for your son. I resign, without regret, the hope of belonging to the king, and shall esteem myself perfectly happy in being allowed to pass my whole life with Noureddin."

It is impossible to express the mortification of the vizier Khacan, when he was informed of the insolence of his son Noureddin. "Ah!" cried he, beating his breast, and tearing his beard, "is it thus, miserable son! that you precipitate your father from the highest degree of happiness to infamy and ruin, which must inevitably involve yourself!" His lady endeavoured to console him. "Do not afflict yourself," said she, "I can easily, by disposing of a part of my jewels, procure ten thousand pieces of gold, with which you may purchase a slave more beautiful, and more worthy of the king." "What!" returned the vizier, "do you believe that I am capable of being so unhappy at the loss of ten thousand pieces of gold? Surely, you are not ignorant that Saouy is my most inveterate enemy. Can you suppose, that when he is acquainted with the affair, he will not immediately go to the king to triumph at my expense?" "Sir," answered the lady, "the malice of Saouy is, I confess, very great, and he is capable of giving to the affair every injurious appearance. But how can he, or any other person, know what passes in your house? Even if it should be suspected, and the king should interrogate you on the subject, cannot you say that after having well examined the slave, you did not find her so worthy of his majesty's regard as she at first appeared; that the merchant has deceived you; that she is certainly of incomparable beauty, but extremely deficient in those qualities of the mind which it was boasted she possessed? The king will rely on your statement, and Saouy will have the mortification of not succeeding in his wicked intention of ruining you, which he has already so often in vain attempted. Take confidence then, send for the brokers, inform them that you are by no means satisfied with the fair Persian, and charge them to seek for another slave." This counsel appearing to the vizier Khacan very judicious, his mind became more tranquil, and he determined to adopt it, but his indignation against his son was not in the least abated.

Noureddin did not appear during the whole day; and afraid even of seeking an asylum with any of the young people whose houses he was in the habit of frequenting, from the apprehension that his father would search for him there, he went to some distance from the city, and took refuge in a garden where he had never before been, and where he was entirely unknown. He did not return home till very late, when he well knew his father had retired. He went out the next morning before his father had risen, and he was obliged to take the same precautions for a whole month. In fact, the women did not flatter him; they told him frankly that the vizier his father had conceived against him the greatest possible displeasure, and had protested that he would kill him whenever they might meet. The vizier's lady knew from her women that Noureddin returned home every night; but she had not the courage to solicit her husband to pardon him. At length she summoned resolution to mention the subject "Sir," said she, "I have not ventured hitherto to speak to you concerning your son. I entreat you now to allow me to ask what you intend to do with him? Do you wish absolutely to destroy him? Are you aware, that, in so doing, you will bring upon yourself a very heavy calamity, instead of the comparatively trifling injury which has been at present sustained?"

"Madam," replied the vizier, "what you have said has been dictated by perfectly good sense; but I cannot resolve to pardon Noureddin till I have chastised him as he deserves. "He will be sufficiently punished," replied the lady, "should you adopt what has at this moment entered my mind. Your son returns home every night after you have retired, and departs in the morning before you have risen Wait this evening for his arrival, and let him suppose that you intend to kill him; I will come to his assistance, when you, by appearing to grant his life to my prayers, may oblige him to take the fair Persian on any terms you desire. He loves her, and I know that the beautiful slave does not dislike him.

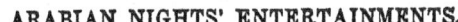
Khacan agreed to follow this advice; accordingly before Noureddin, who arrived at his accustomed hour, was allowed to enter the house, he placed himself behind the door, and immediately as it was opened, flew upon his son, and threw him under his feet. Noureddin, looking up, beheld his father with a poniard in his hand, ready to take his life. The mother of Noureddin arrived at this instant, and seizing the vizier by the arm, "What are you going to do, sir?" cried she. "Quit me," said he, "that I may kill this unworthy son." "Ah, sir!" replied the mother, "rather shall you kill me; never will I permit you to imbrue your hands in your own blood." Noureddin took advantage of this moment: "Father," cried he, with tears in his eyes, "I entreat your pity and forbearance."

Khacan, having suffered the poniard to be wrested from him quitted his hold of Noureddin, who instantly threw himself at his father's feet, which he kissed, to express how sincerely he repented of having given him offence. "Noureddin," said he, "thank your mother, respect for her has induced me to pardon you. I will even give you the fair Persian, on condition, however, that you engage on oath, not to consider her as a slave, but as your lawful wife, whom you will never, on any account, either sell or repudiate." Noureddin, who had not dared to hope for so much indulgence, thanked his father, and readily took the oath he desired. The fair Persian and he were perfectly contented with each other, and the vizier was very well satisfied with their happy union.

More than a year had elapsed, during which this business had been conducted much more fortunately than Khacan could have expected, when one day being in the bath, some very urgent affair obliged him to quit it, heated as he was; and the air, then rather cold, struck him so forcibly, as to bring on an immediate inflammation on the lungs, which confined him to his bed. His illness continuing to increase, he soon became sensible that his last moments were approaching; and he therefore addressed Noureddin in these terms:—"My son, the only thing that I am anxious to impress upon your mind, at this awful moment, is, that you will remember the promise you have made me, respecting the fair Persian. In confidence of your honour, I die content." These were the last words which the vizier uttered: he expired shortly afterwards, to the inexpressible grief of his family, the city, and the court.

Noureddin gave every proof of the utmost affliction for the loss he had sustained; suffering no person, for a long time, to have access to him. At length, he one day gave permission for one of his intimate friends to be admitted. This friend endeavoured to console him; and finding him disposed to attend, represented to him that, as every respect which duty and affection could claim had been paid to the memory of his father, it was time for him to reappear in the world, and to maintain that rank which his birth had acquired him. "We offend," added he, "against the laws of nature and civilized life, if we do not render to our deceased parents every respect which tenderness dictates; but when we have acquitted ourselves in such manner as to be above reproach, we should then resume our former habits, and live in the world like other persons."

The counsel of this friend was very reasonable; and Noureddin would have avoided many misfortunes which ensued, if he had followed it with the consistency which it required. By degrees he formed a society of ten persons, all nearly of his own age, with whom he passed his time in continual feasts and scenes of pleasure; and not a day passed, on which he did not dismiss every one of them with some present.

A prey to dissipation and extravagance Noureddin would sometimes introduce the beautiful Persian to their party. But, though she had the complaisance to comply with his commands, she much disapproved of his excessive profusion; on which subject she freely gave him her opinion: "I have no doubt," said she, "that your father has left you great riches; but be not displeased if I remind you that, however great they be, you will assuredly very soon see the end of them, if you continue in your present style of living. It were much better, sir, for your reputation and honour, that you followed the steps of your deceased father, and thereby put yourself in the way of obtaining those offices in which he acquired so much glory."

In the meantime, the] friends of Noureddin were very constant at his table, and lost no opportunity of profiting by his easy temper. They praised and flattered him; extolling as merits his most trifling actions: but, especially, they never neglected highly to commend everything that belonged to him; and they found their account in so doing. "Sir," said one of them, "I passed the other day by the estate which you have in such a place; nothing can be more magnificent, or better furnished, than the house; and the garden belonging to it is an absolute paradise of delights." "I am gratified to hear that you are pleased with it," answered Noureddin. "Here, bring me pen, ink, and paper. The place is yours—let me have no words—I give it you." Others had no sooner commended one of his houses, baths, or public buildings, than it was instantly given away. The fair Persian represented to him the injury he did himself; but, instead of regarding her admonitions, he continued in the same course of extravagance, till he had squandered away his all. Noureddin, in short, attended to nothing for the space of a year, but feasting and merriment, lavishing away the vast property which his ancestors, and the good vizier his father, had acquired, or preserved, with so much care and attention.

The year had scarcely elapsed, when one day, while he was at table, his attention was arrested by a rapping at the door of the hall. He had dismissed his slaves, and shut himself up with his friends, that they might enjoy themselves without restraint. One of his companions offered to rise; but Noureddin advanced before him, and went to open the door himself. It was his steward; and Noureddin, to hear what he wanted, withdrew a little way out of the hall, leaving the door partly open.

The friend who had risen, having perceived the steward, and curious to hear what he had to say to Noureddin, placed himself between the hangings and the door, when he heard him thus address his master: "My lord," said he, "I beg a thousand pardons for interrupting you in the midst of your pleasures; but what I have to communicate to you is, that I could not avoid taking this liberty. I have been arranging my accounts, and find, what I have long foreseen, is now arrived; that not more than a single coin remains, of all the sums I have received from you, to defray your expenses. The other funds which you assigned me, are also exhausted; and your tenants have so clearly convinced me that you have transferred to others whatever they held of you. that I can demand nothing in your name." Noureddin was so astonished at this disclosure, that he was unable to utter a word.

The friend who had been listening, and who had heard all that passed, returned immediately, and communicated it to the rest of the company: "You will act as you please," said he, "to profit by this information; with regard to myself, I declare to you that this is the last time you will ever see me in Noureddin's house." "Nay," replied they, "if circumstances be as you have represented, we have no more business here than yourself; and he shall not see us again."

The next day, Noureddin failed not to visit his ten friends, who all resided in the same street. He knocked at the first house he came to, where one of the richest of them lived. A female slave came to the door, but before she would open it, she inquired who was there. "Tell your master," said Noureddin, "that it is Noureddin, son of the late vizier Khacan." The slave, having admitted him, went to the chamber where her master was, to inform him that Noureddin was come to wait upon him. "Noureddin!" said he, in a tone of contempt, and so loud that Noureddin, with great astonishment, heard him. "Go, tell him I am not at home; and, whenever he may call, give him the same answer." The slave returned, and informed Noureddin that she had thought her master was within, but that she had been mistaken. Noureddin left the house in confusion. "Ah!" cried he, "base, perfidious wretch! it was but yesterday that he protested to me I had not a sincerer friend than himself, and now he treats me so unworthily!" He proceeded to the door of another friend, who ordered the same reply to be given. He received a similar answer from the third; and so, in succession, from all the rest.

As soon as the fair Persian saw the wretched Noureddin, she doubted not that he had been deceived in his expectations of assistance. "Well, sir," said she to him, "are you now convinced of the truth of what I foretold?" "Ah, my love," cried he, "your prediction was too true! Not one of them would know me, see me, speak to me! Never should I have believed it possible, that persons who owe me so many obligations, and for whom I have ruined myself, could treat me so cruelly." "Sir," replied the fair Persian, "I see no other remedy for your misfortune, than that of selling your slaves and furniture, on which you may subsist, till Heaven shall point out some other way of extricating you from your misery." The resource appeared to Noureddin extremely severe; but what could he do to supply his present necessities? He first sold his slaves, now an incumbrance, and whose maintenance he could no longer support. He lived for some time upon the money thus produced; and when this fund was nearly exhausted, he ordered his furniture to be conveyed to the public market, where it was sold very much below its real worth, as some of it was extremely valuable, and had cost immense sums. From the receipts of this sale he was enabled to live for a considerable time; but at length all was expended; and now, having nothing more to turn into money, he vented his excessive griefs in the bosom of the beautiful Persian.

Noureddin did not in the least expect the reply he received from this prudent and generous woman. "Sir," said she, "I am your slave, and you know that the late vizier, your father, purchased me for ten thousand pieces of gold. Perfectly aware that I am not so valuable as I was at that time, I, however, flatter myself that I may yet produce a sum not much short of it. Lead me, then, to the place of sale, and immediately dispose of me. With the money you will thus obtain, which will be very considerable, you may commence merchant in some place where you are unknown, and thus procure the means of living, if not in great opulence, at least in a way that may render you happy and contented." "Ah! charming beautiful Persian!" cried Noureddin, "is it possible that you can entertain such a thought? Have I given you so trifling proofs of my affection, that you believe me capable of such meanness? And even if I could be so unworthy, must I not add to my baseness the foulest perjury, after the oath I made to my late father never to sell you, which I would sooner die than break." "Sir," replied the fair Persian, "your love for me is, I am convinced, equal to what you have expressed; and Heaven is my judge, whether I do not regard you with an equal affection, and with what extreme repugnance I prevailed on myself to make the proposal which has so much displeased you. The necessity to which we are now reduced, is, I confess, extremely severe; but, alas! I see no other means to extricate us from the misery in which we are involved."

Noureddin, who knew too well the truth of what the fair Persian had represented, and having no other resource whatever to avoid the most abject poverty, was compelled to adopt the measure she proposed. He, therefore, though with inexpressible regret, conveyed her to the market-place where female slaves were sold; and addressing himself to a broker, "Hagi Hassan," said he to him, "here is a slave whom I wish to sell; I beg of you to learn what price may be obtained for her." Hagi Hassan desired Noureddin and the beautiful Persian to enter a chamber; when, as soon as the latter had removed the veil that concealed her face, "Sir!" said Hagi Hassan, with much astonishment, "am I deceived? Is not this the slave that the late vizier, your father, purchased for ten thousand pieces of gold?" Noureddin assured him it was the same; and Hagi Hassan, having given him reason to expect a large sum, promised to exert all his ability to obtain for her the best price possible.

Hagi Hassan and Noureddin then quitted the chamber, leaving the fair Persian, whom Hagi Hassan locked up. They went immediately in search of the merchants who were occupied in purchasing various slaves. When they had finished, and were re-assembled together, "My good gentlemen," said Hagi, "In the course of your lives, you have seen and purchased many slaves; but never have you beheld one who could in the least compare with her I have to show you. She is the pearl of slaves. Come, follow me, and look at her: I wish you yourselves to fix the price which I ought to demand."

The merchants accompanied Hagi Hassan, who admitted them into the apartment where was the beautiful Persian. They beheld her with astonishment; and immediately agreed unanimously, that they could not set a less price upon her at first than four thousand pieces of gold. They then left the room; and Hagi Hassan having closed the door, followed them, proclaiming with a loud voice, "The Persian slave for four thousand pieces of gold."

Neither of the merchants had yet spoken, and they were consulting together about the sum they should offer for her, when the vizier Saouy appeared. As he advanced, Hagi Hassan cried out a second time, "The Persian slave for four thousand pieces of gold."

Saouy, concluding from this high price that the slave to be sold must possess extraordinary beauty, immediately felt an anxious desire to see her. He accordingly pushed his horse forward, and riding up to Hagi Hassan, who was surrounded by the merchants, "Open the door," said he, "and let me see this slave." It was contrary to custom to exhibit a slave to any person after the merchants had seen her, and were bargaining for her; but they had not the courage to urge their right against the authority of the vizier. Hagi Hassan then, obliged to open the door, made a sign to the fair Persian to approach that Saouy might see her without alighting from his horse. When Saouy beheld a slave of such extraordinary beauty, his admiration was excessive; and knowing the name of the broker with whom he had occasionally transacted business, "Hagi Hassan," said he, "you have, I think, put her up at four thousand pieces of gold?" "Yes, my lord," replied he, "the merchants whom you see have just agreed that I should cry her at that price. I now wait their bidding, and expect they will tender considerably more." I will give you the money," said Saouy, " if no one offer a larger sum :" at the same time casting at the merchant I look that sufficiently indicated that he did not expect to be outbidden. When the vizier had waited some time and found that none of the merchants opposed him. "Well," said he to Hagi Hassan, "what do you wait for? Go afind the seller, and conclude the bargain for four thousand pieces of gold, or learn if we have any further demand." He knew not, at present, that the slave belonged to Noureddin.

Hagi Hassan then went to talk over the affair with Noureddin. "Sir," said he, "I am very sorry to have to communicate very unpleasant intelligence: your slave is going to be sold for absolutely nothing." "How so?" returned Noureddin. "Sir," said Hagi Hassan, "the business, at first, was in a very good train. The merchants without hesitation desired me to put her up at four thousand pieces of gold. Just as I cried her at this price, the vizier Saouy arrived, whose presence immediately shut the mouths of all the merchants, who were evidently disposed to raise her to at least the same price which she cost the late vizier your father. Saouy will give only four thousand pieces of gold. The slave is yours, but I will not advise you to part with her at that price." "Hagi Hassan," replied Noureddin, "I am much obliged to you for your advice; do not imagine, that I will ever permit my slave to be sold to the enemy of my house. It is true, I have great need of money; but sooner would I die in the extremest poverty, than part with her to Saouy. I have a single favour to request of you—that, as you are perfectly acquainted with the customs of this sort of business, you will tell me how I should act to prevent it." "Sir," replied Hagi Hassan, "nothing is more easy.—Pretend that, having been exasperated against your slave, you swore you would expose her in the public market; that you have done so not with an intention of selling her, but merely to acquit yourself of your oath. Come, then; and in the moment when I present her to Saouy, do you seize upon her, giving her several blows, and lead her to your house." "I thank you," said Noureddin; "you shall see that I will follow your counsel."

Hagi Hassan returned to the chamber, and having cautioned the fair Persian not to be alarmed, whatever might happen, he took her by the arm, and led her to the vizier Saouy. "Sir," said he, "there is the slave; take her, she is yours." Hagi Hassan had scarcely uttered these words, when Noureddin seized hold of the fair Persian, and, drawing her towards him, gave her a box on the ear: "Come here, you impertinent!" said he, in a tone sufficiently loud to be heard by every one, "and return home. Your unbearable temper compelled me to take an oath to expose you in the public market; but I did not intend to sell you. I have yet occasion for you; and it will be time enough to part with you, when every other resource fails."

The vizier Saouy was extremely enraged at this action of Noureddin. "Worthless libertine!" he exclaimed "would you wish me to believe that you have anything left to dispose of besides this slave?" at the same time, pushing his horse directly against him, he endeavoured to carry off the beautiful Persian. Noureddin, violently irritated by the affront which the vizier had put upon him, quitting the fair Persian, and desiring her to wait, immediately seized the horse's bridle. and compelled him to fall back three or four paces. As the vizier Saouy was not loved by any person, all present were delighted at the mortification he had received, which they indicated to Noureddin by various signs; giving him to understand, that he might revenge himself in any way he pleased, without experiencing opposition from them. Saouy endeavoured by every effort to oblige Noureddin to quit his horse's bridle! but the latter encouraged by the good wishes of the by-standers, pulled the vizier from his horse into the kennel, and after giving him many severe blows, dashed his head against the pavement till it was covered with blood. Noureddin having ceased beating the vizier, left him in the middle of the kennel, and again taking charge of the beautiful Persian, returned home amidst the acclamations of the people, who much commended him for what he had done.

Saouy, bruised by the blows he had received, got up, assisted by his attendants. Supporting himself upon the shoulders of two of his slaves, he went immediately to the palace. When he arrived near the apartment of the king, he began to cry out, and to implore justice, in the most pathetic manner. The king ordered him to be admitted; and desired to know by whom he had been so ill-treated, and put in that lamentable state. "Sir," said Saouy, taking care to relate all in his own favour, "I was going to the female slave-market, to purchase a cook, for whom I had occasion. On my arrival there, I heard them crying a slave for four thousand pieces of gold; I desired to be conducted to this slave, and found her the most beautiful that was ever beheld. I inquired to whom she belonged, and was informed that Noureddin, the son of the late vizier Khacan, wished to part with her.—Your majesty may remember, that, about two or three years since, you ordered ten thousand pieces of gold to be advanced to that minister, with which he was charged to procure a slave. He employed it in purchasing the one in question; but, instead of bringing her to your majesty, he presented her to his son. I sent to speak with him; when, without noticing the perfidy, of which his father was guilty toward your majesty, 'Noureddin,' said I to him, with the utmost civility, 'the merchants, as I understand, have put up your slave at four thousand pieces of gold. I wish to purchase her as a present for the king. It will afford me a good opportunity of recommending you to his majesty's favour; which you will find of infinitely more value than anything you can obtain from the merchants.' Instead of answering me with civility, the insolent wretch regarded me fiercely, 'Detestable old man,' said he, 'sooner than sell my slave to you, I would give her to a Jew for nothing!' Directly flew upon me like a madman; and without any regard to my age or dignity, pulled me off my horse, beat me till he was weary, and then left me in the condition in which your majesty now sees me."

The king deceived and incensed against Noureddin by his artful relation, showed in his countenance marks of great anger; and turning round to the captain of the guard who was near him, "take," said he, "forty of your men; go and plunder Noureddin's house, and when you have ordered it to be raised to the ground, bring him and his slave hither." The captain of the guard did not quit the apartment of the king so expeditiously, but that an officer of the chamber, who had heard the order

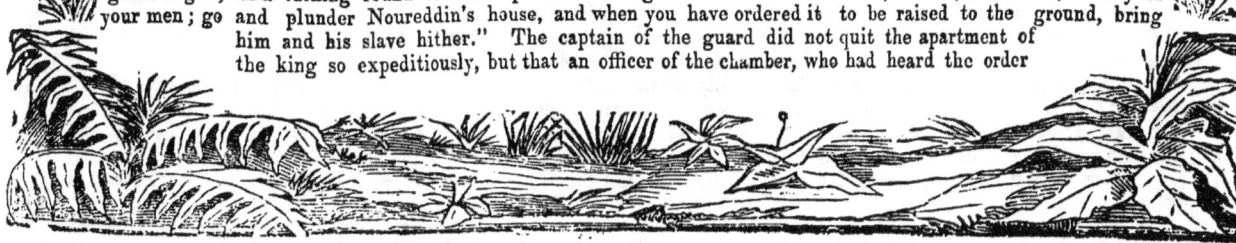

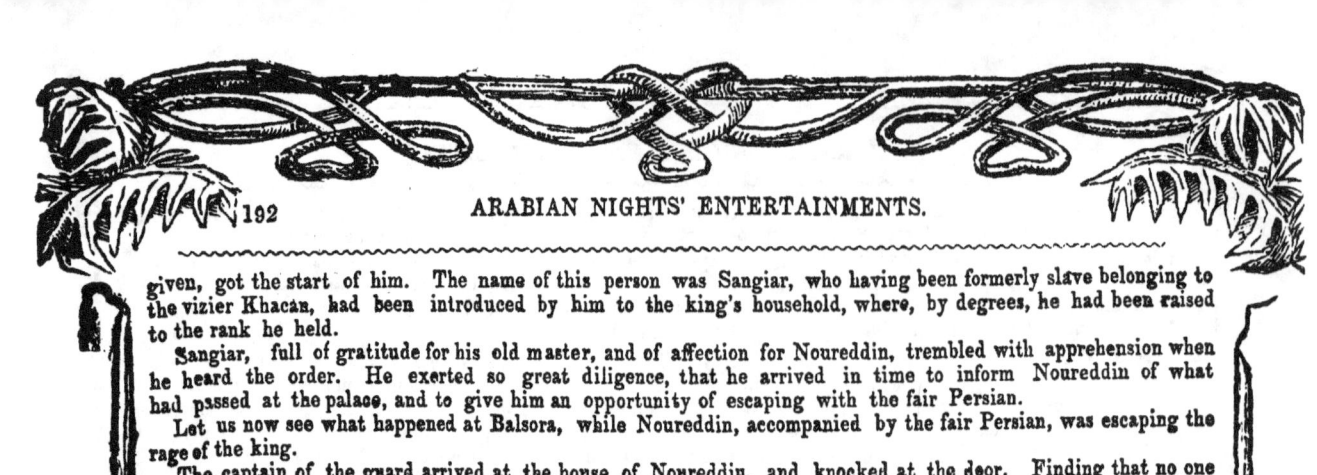

given, got the start of him. The name of this person was Sangiar, who having been formerly slave belonging to the vizier Khacan, had been introduced by him to the king's household, where, by degrees, he had been raised to the rank he held.

Sangiar, full of gratitude for his old master, and of affection for Noureddin, trembled with apprehension when he heard the order. He exerted so great diligence, that he arrived in time to inform Noureddin of what had passed at the palace, and to give him an opportunity of escaping with the fair Persian.

Let us now see what happened at Balsora, while Noureddin, accompanied by the fair Persian, was escaping the rage of the king.

The captain of the guard arrived at the house of Noureddin, and knocked at the door. Finding that no one answered, he caused it to be broken open, and immediately the soldiers entered in a body, and searched every part of the house, but could find neither Noureddin nor his slave. While the men were plundering and destroying the house, their commander went to inform the king of his want of success. " Let them search every place where it is possible they may be concealed," said the king ; " I must have them found."

That no means might be left untried, the king ordered to have proclaimed throughout the city, that he would reward any one with a thousand pieces of gold, who should apprehend Noureddin and his slave ; and that he would severely punish whoever might conceal them. But, notwithstanding all his care and diligence, he could obtain no account of them ; so that the vizier Saouy had no other consolation than that the king had taken his part.

In the meantime, Noureddin and the beautiful Persian continued their flight with all the good fortune possible ; and, in due time, arrived at the city of Bagdad.

They walked for a considerable time by the side of the gardens that bordered the Tigris, one of which was bounded by a long and handsome wall. When they had reached the end of it, they turned into a long well-paved street, in which they perceived the garden gate, near a handsome fountain. The gate, which was extremely magnificent, was locked ; but before it was an open vestibule, having on each side a sofa. " Here is a most convenient place," said Noureddin to the beautiful Persian; " night is approaching, and I recommend that we remain here. To-morrow morning we shall have ample time to seek a lodging." They then each took a draught from the fountain, and seating themselves on one of the sofas, conversed together for some time, till lulled by the agreeable murmur of the waters, they sunk into a profound sleep.

The garden, which belonged to the caliph, had, in the middle of it a large pavilion, called the pavilion of paintings. The grand and superb saloon was lighted by eighty windows, having each a lustre ; but these lustres were only lighted when the caliph came there to pass the evening. They then made a most brilliant illumination, which could be seen at some distance in the country, and in a great part of the city. This garden was inhabited only by the keeper, a very aged officer, named Scheich Ibrahim, to whom the caliph had given this post as a reward for former services. He had received with it an injunction not to admit people indiscriminately ; and particularly not to allow persons to sit or rest upon the sofas placed without the gate, that they might be constantly kept in the neatest condition, but to punish all those he found offending. Business had obliged the keeper to go out, but arriving before the day closed, he perceived two persons sleeping on one of the sofas, their heads covered with linen to protect them from the gnats. " So, so !" said Scheich Ibrahim to himself, " you thus disobey the commands of the caliph ; but I will teach you to respect them." He then, without noise, opened the gate, and soon afterwards returned with a large cane in his hand, and his sleeve tucked up. He was just preparing to strike them with all his force, when he restrained himself. " Scheich Ibrahim," said he, " you are going to chastise these people, without considering, that, perhaps, they are strangers, who knew not where to lodge, and are ignorant of the caliph's order. It will be better first to learn who they are." He then gently raised up the linen, which covered their heads, and was much interested when he saw a young man of an extremely good person, and a young woman so very beautiful. He then awakened Noureddin, pulling him softly by the feet. Noureddin immediately lifted up his head, and seeing an old man, he rose up on the sofa in a kneeling position, and taking him by the hand, which he kissed, " Good father," said he, " may Heaven preserve you ! what do you desire of me ?" " My son," returned Scheich Ibrahim, " who are you ? whence come you ?" " We are strangers, who are just arrived,' replied Noureddin ; " and we wish to remain here till to-morrow morning." You will be very badly off here," said Scheich Ibrahim. Come in with me ; I will accommodate you with a much more convenient place to sleep in ; and the sight of the garden, which is very beautiful, will delight you during the short portion of day that remains."

Noureddin arose, and having expressed how much he was obliged, went, with the beautiful Persian, into the garden.

While Scheich Ibrahim was going to purchase provisions for supper, as well for himself as his guests Noureddin and the beautiful Persian walked about, till they reached the pavilion. They stopped for some time to contemplate its admirable constructure, size, and loftiness; and after they had gone round it, surveying it on all sides, they ascended, by a grand flight of steps, formed of white marble, to the door of the saloon, which they found locked. They had just descended the steps, when Scheich Ibrahim returned laden with provisions. " Scheich Ibrahim," Noureddin with astonishment, " did you not say that this garden belonged to you ?" " I did say so, and I say it again," replied Scheich Ibrahim. " And is this superb pavilion," continued Noureddin, " yours, also ?" " My son," said he, " the pavilion does not go without the garden : both of them belong to me." " As such is the case," replied Noureddin, " I entreat you to grant us the favour of a sight of the interior of it ; for to judge from its external appearance, it must be of extraordinary magnificence."

Scheich Ibrahim thought he should be guilty of incivility in refusing Noureddin's request. He considered, too, that as the caliph had not sent him any notice, according to his custom, he would not be there that night ; and that, therefore, his guests, as well as himself, might safely take their repast in the pavilion. Having, then, placed the provisions he had brought upon the first step of the staircase, he went to his apartment to find the key, and, returning with a light, opened the door. Noureddin and the fair Persian entered the saloon, which they found so splendid, that they were wholly engrossed in admiring its riches and beauty. The sofas, to say nothing of the pictures, were magnificent; and, besides the lustres which hung at every window, there were between the frames silver branches, each containing a wax-taper. Noureddin could not behold these objects without calling to mind the splendour in which he himself had lived, and heaved a sigh.

In the meantime, Scheich Ibrahim, having brought the provisions, prepared a table upon one of the sofas; and when everything was ready, Noureddin, the beautiful Persian, and himself sat down to supper. When they had finished, Noureddin opened one of the windows, and calling the fair Persian, "Come hither," said he, "and admire, with me, the charming view, and the beauty of the garden by the light of the moon. Nothing can be more delightful." She approached, and they together enjoyed the sight, while Scheich Ibrahim was clearing the table.

About this time, the fair Persian noticed that there was only one light on the table: "Scheich Ibraham," said she to the good old officer, "you might have allowed us no more than one taper, while there are so many handsome ones about the room. Do us the pleasure, I beseech you, to light them, that we may see a little more clearly." Scheich Ibrahim, using the freedom which wine inspires, when the head becomes a little heated, and that a conversation he was then engaged in with Noureddin might not be interrupted, answered the beautiful lady, "Light them yourself; it is an office more suited to youth like yours; but take care not to light more than five or six, which will be sufficient." The fair Persian arose, taking a wax-taper in her hand, and proceeded, without regarding Scheich Ibrahim's injunction, to light up the whole eighty.

Some time after, while Scheich Ibrahim was conversing with the beautiful Persian upon a different suject, Noureddin, in his turn, requested him to light up some of the lustres. Without observing that all the tapers were burning, "You must," said he, "be very lazy, or have less vigour than I have, if you cannot light them yourself; go then and light them; but, remember, not more than three." Instead of confining himself to this number, he lighted up the whole, and afterwards opened the fourscore windows, unobserved by Scheich Ibrahim, who was earnestly engaged in conversation with the fair Persian.

The caliph Haroun Alraschid was not yet retired to rest; he was in a saloon of his palace, which fronted the Tigris, whence he had a side-view of the garden and the pavilion of paintings. By accident, he opened a window

on this side, and was astonished on seeing the pavilion entirely illuminated; and the more, as, from its great splendour, he at first imagined that it was a fire in the city. The grand-vizier Giafar was still with him, waiting the moment when the caliph should retire, to return to his own home. The caliph called to him in a great rage, "Come here, you careless vizier! approach this way; look at the pavilion of paintings, and tell me why it is now lighted up, and I not there?" The grand-vizier trembled excessively, fearing some calamity; but his confusion was still greater, when he approached, and found it really as the caliph had represented. It was necessary, however, to find some pretence to appease him: "Commander of the faithful," said he, "I can give your majesty no other information respecting this appearance, than that, about four or five days since, Scheich Ibrahim came and informed me that he had an intention of holding an assembly of the ministers belonging to his mosque, to observe some ceremony which he was anxious to perform under the happy reign of your majesty. I asked him in what way he expected me to serve him in the business; upon which he entreated me to obtain permission of your majesty to hold the meeting and perform the ceremony in the pavilion. I dismissed him, telling him he might act as he pleased, and that I would not fail to speak to your majesty on the subject; and I entreat your pardon for having forgotten to do so." "Giafar," replied the caliph, in a tone that indicated he was somewhat appeased, "it appears, from your own account, that you have committed three unpardonable faults; first, in having given permission to Scheich Ibrahim to perform this ceremony in my pavilion; secondly, in having neglected to speak to me on the subject; and thirdly, in not having penetrated the real object of this good old man. In truth, I am persuaded that he had no other motive in his application to you, than to try if he could obtain some gratuity towards assisting him in his expenses. That, you had not the wit to conceive; and I think him not to blame in avenging himself of your omission by the greater expense of this illumination."

The grand-vizier, overjoyed at the caliph's treating the affair with such good humour, confessed that he was very wrong in not having presented Sheich Ibrahim with a few pieces of gold. "That being the case," added the caliph, smiling, "it is just you should be punished for those faults; your punishment, however, will not be very severe; it shall be to pass, which I also intend, the remainder of the night with these good people, whom I should much like to see. While, therefore, I go and assume the dress of a citizen, you and Mesrour disguise yourselves in the same manner, and accompany me."

The caliph then, in the disguise of a citizen, with the grand-vizier Giafar, and Mesrour, chief of the eunuchs, left the palace, and proceeded through the streets of Bagdad, until he arrived at the garden, the gate of which he found open, through the negligence of Scheich Ibrahim, who had forgotten to lock it. The caliph was much offended at it. "Giafar," said he to the grand-vizier, "what excuse have you for the gate being open at this late hour? Is it possible that Scheich Ibrahim should make it a custom to leave it open thus all night? I would rather hope that the neglect has been occasioned by the confusion arising from the entertainment." The caliph entered the garden; and, when he was arrived at the pavilion, being unwilling to go up to the saloon before he knew what was passing there, he consulted with the grand-vizier as to the propriety of mounting one of the nearest trees to obtain the information he desired. But, in looking towards the door of the saloon, the grand-vizier perceived that it was not entirely closed. The caliph then abandoned his first design, and ascended softly to the door of the saloon, which he found so far open, that he could see those who were in the room, without being himself observed. His surprise was extreme, when he saw a lady of incomparable beauty, and a young man of the most handsome figure, with Scheich Ibrahim, sitting at table. Scheich Ibrahim was holding a cup in his hand, and addressing the beautiful Persian: "My charming lady," said he, "a good drinker should never empty his cup without adding music to his wine. Do me the honour to listen to me, and I will sing you a very pleasant song." He then began singing, at which the caliph was the more astonished, as he had been till then ignorant that Scheich Ibrahim ever indulged in wine, and had always believed him the grave, sober man he appeared. The caliph withdrew from the door as cautiously as he had approached, and returned to the grand-vizier, who was upon the staircase a few steps below: "Come up," said he, "and see if the persons who are within are ministers of the mosque, as you wished me to believe." From the tone in which the caliph pronounced these words, the grand-vizier knew too well that affairs were going on badly for him. He went up, and looking through the opening of the door, trembled with alarm for himself, when he saw the three persons in the situation and state they were. "What irregularity is this," said the caliph, "that these people should presume to come to divert themselves in my garden, and in my pavilion? I do not, however, believe that one can easily find a young man and a young woman more handsome, or better matched; before, therefore, I give way to my indignation, I wish to know more about them, and to learn who they are, and for what purpose they are here." He returned to the door, to observe them again; and the vizier, who followed, remained behind him, while he was looking at them. They both heard Scheich Ibrahim's conversation with the beautiful Persian: "My lovely lady," said he, "is there anything you can desire to render our pleasure this evening more complete?" "It appears to me," replied the fair Persian, "that all would be perfect, if you had an instrument on which I could play." "Madame," returned Scheich Ibrahim, "can you play on the lute?" "Bring me one," said the beautiful Persian, "and you shall hear." Without going far from his place, Scheich Ibrahim took a lute out of a closet, and presented it to the fair Persian, who began to put it in tune. The caliph, in the meantime, turned round to the grand-vizier: "Giafar," said he, "the young lady is going to play upon the lute. If she play well, I will pardon her, and also the young man for her sake; but, as for you, you shall certainly be hanged."

The fair Persian was already preluding in such a manner, that the caliph immediately perceived she was perfectly mistress of the instrument. She then began to sing an air, accompanying her voice, which was admirable, on the lute, and performed it with such exquisite skill, that the caliph was quite charmed.

As soon as the beautiful Persian had finished her song, the caliph descended the stairs, the vizier Giafar following him. When he was at the bottom, "On my life," said he, "I never heard a finer voice, nor a better player on the lute. I am so well satisfied that I wish to go in, and hear her play; but the difficulty is to find an excuse for effecting it." "Commander of the faithful," replied the vizier, "if you were to enter, and Scheich Ibrahim to know you, he would certainly die with terror." "This is what occasions the difficulty," returned the caliph; "I should be sorry to be the cause of the old man's death, after his having served me so many years. A scheme enters my mind, which may succeed: remain here with Mesrour, and wait in the first walk till I return."

The vicinity of the Tigris had afforded the caliph an opportunity of forming in his garden, by means of a large arch, well-terraced, a very handsome piece of water, to which many of the finest fish in the river retired. The fishermen were well acquainted with this circumstance, and had often wished to have the liberty of fishing there; but the caliph had expressly forbidden Scheich Ibrahim to permit them. Nevertheless, that same night a fisherman, passing the garden gate after the caliph entered, who left it open as he found it, had taken advantage of the opportunity, and, creeping into the garden, had proceeded as far as the piece of water. He had thrown in his nets, and was preparing to draw them out, when the caliph, who, after the negligence of Scheich Ibrahim, had suspected what might happen, and resolved to avail himself of the occurrence, reached the place. Notwithstanding his disguise, the fisherman knew him immediately, and, throwing himself at his feet, entreated his pardon, pleading his poverty as an excuse. "Rise, and fear nothing," said the caliph; "only take up your nets, and let me see what fish you

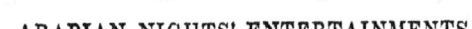

have got." The fisherman, resuming courage, quickly performed what the caliph desired, and drew up five or six very fine fish, of which the caliph chose the two largest, and fastened them together, by means of a twig passed through their heads. He then said to the fisherman, "Give me your clothes, and take mine." The exchange was made in a few moments; and as soon as the caliph had assumed the dress of the fisherman, from the turban to the boots, "Take up your nets," said he to the man, "and go about your business."

The caliph ascended to the saloon, and advancing that he might be seen, "Scheich Ibrahim," said he, "I am Kerim, the fisherman; I was told that you were entertaining your friends, and, as I have this moment caught two very fine fish, I come to ask you if you would like to have them." Scheich Ibrahim, no longer in a state to think of asking this pretended fisherman how or whence he came, was wholly devoted to the beautiful Persian; turning, therefore, his head towards the door, but with great difficulty, from the quantity of wine he had drunk, with a stammering voice he called to the caliph, whom he took for a fisherman: "Come hither," said he, "good thief of the night, come hither, and let me see you." The caliph advanced, counterfeiting perfectly well the manners of a fisherman, and presented his two fish. "They are very fine," said the fair Persian; "and I should like to partake of them, if they were properly cooked." "The lady is right," said Scheich Ibrahim; "what can we do with your fish in this state? Go, get them ready yourself, and bring them to us; you will find everything you want in my kitchen."

The caliph returned to find the grand-vizier. "Giafar," said he, "I have been extremely well received, but they require the fish to be dressed. I am so very desirous to accomplish my purpose that I will even take the trouble myself. Since I have acted the fisherman so well, I can surely personate the cook." Saying this, he proceeded towards Scheich Ibrahim's apartment, and was followed by the grand-vizier and Mesrour.

They all three set to work, and though the kitchen of Scheich Ibrahim was not very large, yet, as it contained everything necessary, the fish were soon prepared. The caliph carried up the dish, and, in serving it, placed before each of them a lemon, to squeeze if they thought proper. When they had finished, Noureddin looked at the caliph: "Fisherman," said he, "it is impossible to eat better fish, and you have afforded us the greatest pleasure in the world;" at the same time putting his hand into his bosom, and drawing out his purse, in which were thirty pieces of gold, the remainder of the forty which Sangiar, the attendant of the king of Balsora, had given him before his departure. "Take it," continued he, "if I had more I would give it you. Had I known you before I expended my fortune, I would have placed you beyond the reach of poverty; receive this, however, with as much good will as if the present were more considerable." The caliph took the purse, and perceiving that it contained gold, "Sir," said he, "I cannot enough thank you for your liberality. I am particularly fortunate to have dealings with such noble gentlemen as you; but, before I go away, I have one request to make, which I entreat you to grant. I see a lute there, from which I conclude that the lady plays; if you could obtain her consent to favour me with a single tune, I should return home the most contented man in the world, for it is an instrument of which I am passionately fond. "Beautiful Persian," said Noureddin immediately, addressing himself to her, "I beg this favour of you, which I hope you will not refuse me." She took the lute, and, having tuned it in a few moments, she played and sung an air that charmed the caliph. When the beautiful Persian had ceased playing, "Ah," cried the caliph, "what a voice! what a hand! what execution! Was there ever a better singer, or a better player on the lute? No, never was seen or heard her equal!" Noureddin was accustomed to give whatever belonged to him to those that flattered. "Fisherman," replied he, "I see clearly that you understand music; since she pleases you so much, she is yours, I make you a present of her."

The beautiful Persian, extremely astonished at the liberality of Noureddin, stopped him. "Sir," said she, looking at him tenderly, "whither are you going? Resume your place, I beseech you, and listen to what I am going to sing and play." He complied with her desire; when, touching the lute, and regarding him with tears in her eyes, she sung some extempore verses, in which she keenly upbraided him with his want of affection, since he could so readily, and even unfeelingly, abandon her to Kerim. When she had finished, she laid down the lute by her side, and put a handkerchief to her face, to conceal the tears she was unable to restrain. Noureddin answered not a word to her reproaches, but seemed to express, by his silence, that he did not repent the donation he had made. The caliph, surprised at what he had heard, then said to him, "From what I see, sir, this beautiful, rare, and accomplished lady, whom you have just presented to me with so much generosity, is a slave, and you are her master." "Exactly so, Kerim," replied Noureddin; "and you would be much more astonished than you appear, if I relate to you all the misfortunes I have suffered on her account." He recounted to him his whole history, beginning with the purchase of the beautiful Persian, by the vizier his father, for the king of Balsora; and omitted nothing of what he had done, or encountered, from that time till his arrival at Bagdad, and even to the very moment he was speaking.

When Noureddin had concluded, the caliph said to him, "To what place do you intend to go now?" "Where Heaven shall direct me," replied he. "If you will take my advice," continued the caliph, "you will proceed no further; "it is, on the contrary, necessary that you should return to Balsora. I will write you a short note, which you may give the king from me; you will find, after he has read it, he will receive you very graciously, and that no one will say anything against you." "Kerim," replied Noureddin, "what you say to me is very extraordinary; who ever heard of a fisherman, like you, corresponding with a king?" "This ought not to surprise you," resumed the caliph; "we pursued our studies together under the same masters, and have always been the best friends in the world. He has often wished to take me out of my present condition, which he has urged with all the kindness imaginable. I am, however, satisfied with his esteem, in not refusing anything I ask for the benefit of my friends. Leave the affair to me, and you shall see the consequence."

Noureddin consented to act as the caliph desired; and, there being in the saloon all the requisites for writing, the caliph wrote this letter to the king of Balsora; on the top of which, near the edge of the paper, he added, in very small characters—*In the name of the most merciful God*—a form to signify that he expected implicit obedience.

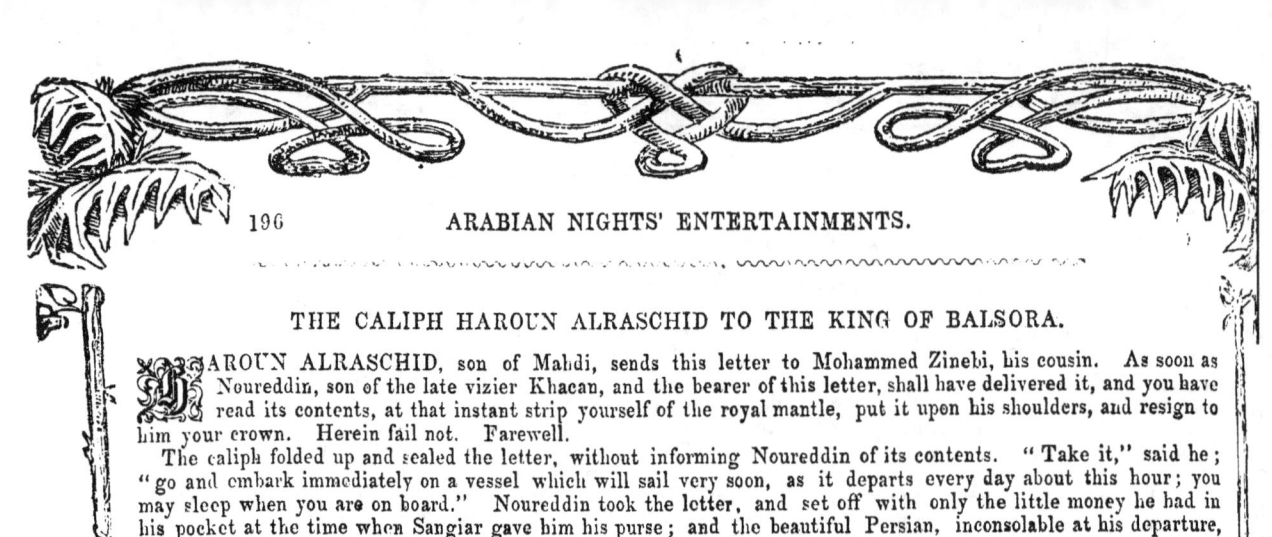

THE CALIPH HAROUN ALRASCHID TO THE KING OF BALSORA.

HAROUN ALRASCHID, son of Mahdi, sends this letter to Mohammed Zinebi, his cousin. As soon as Noureddin, son of the late vizier Khacan, and the bearer of this letter, shall have delivered it, and you have read its contents, at that instant strip yourself of the royal mantle, put it upon his shoulders, and resign to him your crown. Herein fail not. Farewell.

The caliph folded up and sealed the letter, without informing Noureddin of its contents. "Take it," said he; "go and embark immediately on a vessel which will sail very soon, as it departs every day about this hour; you may sleep when you are on board." Noureddin took the letter, and set off with only the little money he had in his pocket at the time when Sangiar gave him his purse; and the beautiful Persian, inconsolable at his departure, withdrew to a sofa, where she resigned herself to the most poignant grief.

Scarcely had Noureddin quitted the saloon, when Scheich Ibrahim, who had been silent during the whole transaction, looked steadfastly at the caliph, whom he still believed to be the fisherman Kerim: "Hark you, Kerim," said he; "you came here to bring two fish, which, at most, were not worth more than twenty pieces of copper, and for them you have obtained a purse and a slave. Do you imagine you are to have all this for yourself? I declare that I will have half the value of the slave, and with respect to the purse, show me what it contains;—if it be silver, you shall have one piece for yourself: if gold, I will take the whole, and give you some pieces of copper I have in my pocket."

[To render what follows sufficiently intelligible, it is necessary to remark that the caliph, before he served up the fish, had ordered the grand-vizier to repair with all diligence to the palace, and bring back with him a dress, with four of his personal attendants; and to wait on the other side of the pavilion, till he should strike one of the windows with his hands. The grand-vizier had acquitted himself of this commission; and he, Mesrour, and the four servants, were waiting at the place appointed, till the signal should be given.]

The caliph replied, "I know not what there may be in the purse; whether gold or silver, I will share it with you with all my heart, but in regard to the slave, I shall keep her myself. If you will not agree to these conditions, you shall have nothing." Scheich Ibrahim, furious with rage at this insolence, as he deemed it, took the candle which was upon the table, and staggering from his seat, went down the back stairs to find a cane.

The caliph profited by this interval; and, striking one of the windows with his hands, the grand-vizier, Mesrour, and the four attendants, were with him in an instant. The servants had very soon taken off the fisherman's dress, and put on that they had brought. They had not, however, quite finished, and were still employed about the caliph, who was seated on the throne which he had in the saloon, when Scheich Ibrahim, stimulated by interest, re-entered the room with a large cane in his hand, with which he promised himself to give the pretended fisherman a sound beating. Instead of finding the object of his wrath, he could perceive only his clothes lying in the middle of the saloon, while he beheld the caliph seated on his throne, with the grand-vizier and Mesrour at his side. He started at the sight, scarcely knowing whether he was awake or asleep. The caliph laughed at his confusion: "Scheich Ibrahim," said he, "what do you want? Who are you looking for?" Scheich Ibrahim, who could no longer doubt that it was the caliph, immediately threw himself at his feet, his face and long beard touching the ground: "Commander of the faithful," cried he, "your vile slave has offended you; he implores your mercy, and entreats your forgiveness." As the attendants had now finished dressing him, he said, while descending from his throne, "Rise, I pardon you."

The caliph then addressed himself to the beautiful Persian. "Beautiful Persian," said he, "rise and follow me. After what you have witnessed, you need not be informed who I am, or that I am not of a rank to take advantage of the present which, with unexampled generosity, Noureddin has made me of your person. I have sent him to ascend the throne of Balsora; and you shall follow him to be queen, as soon as I shall have forwarded the despatches necessary for his establishment. In the meantime, I will order you an apartment in my palace, where you shall be treated with all the respect due to your merit." This discourse reanimated the hopes of the beautiful Persian by the most lively consolation, and she was now fully repaid for her affliction by the joy she felt in learning that Noureddin, whom she passionately loved, was about to be raised to so high a dignity.

Noureddin's return to Balsora was fortunate, though sooner, by some days, than for his sake was to be wished. On his arrival, he visited neither relation nor friend, but went directly to the palace of the king, who was then giving audience. He pressed through the crowd, holding the letter up in his hand, every one giving way; he presented it to the king, who took it, opened, and read it, showing his emotion by the frequent changes in his countenance. He kissed it thrice, and was going to execute the order, when it occurred to him to show the letter to the vizier Saouy, the irreconcileable enemy of Noureddin.

Saouy, who had recognised Noureddin, and was conjecturing in his own mind, with much anxiety, what possible design he could have, was not less surprised than the king at the contents of the letter. Feeling equally interested, he devised, in a moment, a means of evasion. Pretending not to have read the letter attentively, and to peruse it a second time, he turned himself a little on one side, as if to take advantage of the light. Then, without being perceived by any one, and so that the effect could not be seen, unless on a very close examination, he dexterously tore off the top of the letter containing the words which expressed the caliph's injunction of implicit obedience, conveyed it to his mouth, and swallowed it. After this perfidious action, Saouy turned round to the king, and giving him the letter, "Well, sir," said he, in a very low voice, "what is your majesty's intention?" "To comply with the caliph's command," answered the king. "Be on your guard, sir," returned the wicked vizier; "the writing is indeed the caliph's, but the important form is wanting." The king had before observed it, but in his perturbation he imagined that he might have been deceived, since it was not now to be seen. "Sir," continued the vizier, "it cannot be doubted that the caliph has given Noureddin this letter, in consequence of the complaint he has been urging against your majesty and me, merely to get rid of his importunity; but he has not intended that you should

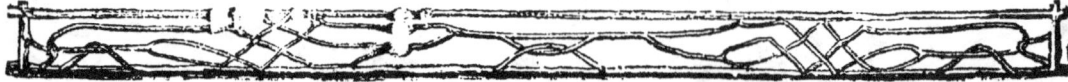

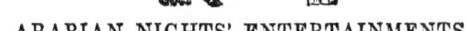

execute what it contains. Again, it is to be considered, that no express has been sent with the patent, without which the letter is useless."

King Zinebı suffered himself to be persuaded, and abandoned Noureddin to the discretion of the vizier Saouy, who had him conducted to his own house. As soon as he arrived there, Saouy ordered him the bastinado, which was inflicted till he was to all appearance dead, and in this state directed him to be conveyed to a prison, there to be confined in the darkest and deepest cell, with strict orders to the keeper to give him nothing but bread and water. When Noureddin, half dead with the blows he had received, began to recover his senses, and saw the dismal place he was in, he gave way to the most bitter lamentations, deploring his unhappy fate. "Ah, fisherman!" cried he, "how you have deceived me! and how ready was I to believe you! Could I expect so cruel a return for the benefits I had bestowed on you? God bless you, nevertheless; I cannot believe that your intention was so wicked, and I will wait patiently for the end of my misfortunes."

The afflicted Noureddin remained six whole days in this state, though not forgotten by the vizier. Resolved to put him to an ignominious death, and not daring to act from his own authority, the vindictive minister, to accomplish his design, loaded a number of his own slaves with rich presents, and placing himself at their head, went before the king; "Sir," said he, with the blackest malice, "behold the present which the new king entreats your majesty to accept, on his ascension to the crown." The king fully comprehended Saouy's meaning : "What!" said he, "is that wretch still living? I thought you had put him to death." "Sir," replied Saouy, "it is not my duty to order the execution of any person; that power belongs to your majesty." "Go, then," returned the king, "order his head to be cut off; I give you permission." "Sir," said Saouy, "I am infinitely obliged to your majesty for the justice you render me; but, as Noureddin gave me the affront, with which your majesty is acquainted, so very publicly, I request the favour that you will permit the sentence to be executed before the palace, and that the criers may go and proclaim it in every part of the city: as all were witnesses of the indignity I received, I wish all may witness the reparation." The king granted his request; while the criers, in performing their duty, occasioned general sadness through the whole city. The recollection, still recent, of the father's virtues made them learn with indignation that the son was going to be ignominiously sacrificed, at the solicitation, and through the revengeful malice, of the vizier Saouy.

Saouy went to the prison in person, accompanied by twenty of his slaves, ministers of his cruelty. They led away Noureddin, and obliged him to mount a miserable horse, without a saddle.

Saouy, implacable in his hate, now surrounded by a part of his armed slaves, ordered Noureddin to be conducted before him by the rest, and proceeded towards the palace. The people were on the point of attacking Saouy; and, if any one had set the example, would certainly have stoned him. When he had led Noureddin to the open space before the palace, in sight of the king's apartment, he left him in the hands of the executioner, and went immediately to the king, who was already in his cabinet, eager to feast his eyes with the bloody spectacle which was preparing.

The king's guard, and the slaves of the vizier Saouy, forming a large circle about Noureddin, had great difficulty to retain the populace, who made all possible efforts, though in vain, to force through them, and bear him away.

The vizier Saouy, perceiving their delay, cried out to the executioner from the window of the king's cabinet: "Strike! what do you wait for?" At these barbarous and inhuman words, the whole place resounded with the most lively imprecations against the minister; while the king, jealous of his authority, disapproved of this boldness in his presence, as evidently appeared from his immediately desiring them to stop. He had, indeed, another reason; for at this moment, directing his eyes towards a wide street before him, which led to the place of execution, he perceived in the middle of it, a troop of horsemen, who were approaching at full speed. "Vizier," said he immediately to Saouy, "look, what is that?" Saouy saw that it was the grand-vizier Giafar, with his suite, who was come from Bagdad in person, by order of the caliph.

To explain the occasion of this minister's arrival at Balsora, it is necessary to remark that, after the departure of Noureddin with the caliph's letter, the caliph forgot, not only the next day, but for some days afterwards, to send an express with the patent, of which he had spoken to the beautiful Persian. Happening to be in the inner palace, which belonged to his women, and passing one of the apartments, his attention was arrested by a very fine voice; he stopped, and had no sooner heard some words, which expressed grief at absence, than he demanded of an officer of the eunuchs, who followed him, what lady resided in that apartment. The officer replied it was the slave belonging to the young lord whom he had sent to Balsora to be king in the room of Mohammed Zineby: "Ah! poor Noureddin, son of Khacan!" cried the caliph, "I had, indeed, forgotten thee. Make haste," added he, "and desire them to send Giafar to me instantly." The minister arrived. "Giafar," said the caliph, "I have forgotten to send the patent, to confirm Noureddin king of Balsora. There is now no time to prepare one; therefore take some of your servants, with post-horses, and repair to Balsora as expeditiously as possible. If Noureddin no longer live, and they have caused his death, order the vizier Saouy to be hanged; but if still alive, bring him hither, with the king and his vizier." The grand-vizier Giafar mounted his horse immediately, and departed with a considerable number of the officers of his house. He arrived at Balsora at the time, and in the manner, already mentioned.

The king of Balsora recognised the prime minister of the caliph, and going out to meet him, received him at the entrance of his apartment. The grand-vizier first asked if Noureddin were yet alive, and, if he were, desired that he might be sent for. The king ordered him to be brought before them. He appeared, tied as a culprit; but was immediately liberated, by the desire of the grand-vizier, who ordered the vizier Saouy to be secured, and bound with the same cords.

The grand-vizier Giafar left the next day, and took with him Saouy, the king of Balsora, and Noureddin; whom, on his arrival at Bagdad, he presented to the caliph. When he had given an account of his journey, and particulars of the state in which he found Noureddin, and of the treatment he had received, through the counsel and animosity of Saouy, the caliph proposed that Noureddin should, himself, cut off the vizier's head. "Commander of the faithful," replied Noureddin, "whatever injury this wicked man has done me, or attempted to do my deceased father, I should esteem myself the most infamous of men, were I to stain my hands with his blood." The caliph, well pleased with Noureddin's generosity, ordered this act of justice to be performed by the executioner.

The caliph was desirous of sending Noureddin back to Balsora to reign there, but Noureddin humbly solicited permission to decline the honour: "Commander of the faithful, I wish to place my whole glory in the performance of such services as may not remove me from your majesty's person, if you will grant me so great an honour." The caliph placed him in the number of his most intimate courtiers, restored to him the beautiful Persian, and bestowed on him so ample a fortune, that they constantly lived together in the enjoyment of all the happiness they could desire.

With regard to the king of Balsora, the caliph, satisfied with having made him sensible how circumspect he ought to be in the choice of his viziers, sent him back to his kingdom.

THE HISTORY OF BEDER, PRINCE OF PERSIA, AND OF GIAUHARE, PRINCESS OF THE KINGDOM OF SAMANDAL.

 ERSIA is a portion of the earth of so great extent that its ancient monarchs did not assume, without reason, the haughty title of king of kings.

One of these powerful kings, who had commenced his reign by very fortunate and extensive conquests, continued to govern for many years with a happiness and tranquillity which rendered him the most contented of sovereigns. There was only one circumstance in which he esteemed himself unfortunate; he was far advanced in years, and not one of all his wives had given him a prince to succeed to the throne after his death. He had, nevertheless, more than a hundred women, all separately lodged in the most magnificent apartments, with female slaves to attend, and eunuchs to guard them; but, notwithstanding all his cares to render them happy, and even to anticipate their desires, not one of them gratified his anxious solicitude.

One day, he had an assembly of his courtiers, to which were admitted all the embassadors and foreigners of distinction who attended his court. The conversation was not confined to business of state, but regarded the sciences, history, literature, poetry, and every other topic that could agreeably interest the mind. On this day, an eunuch came to inform the king that a merchant who had just arrived from a very remote country with a slave whom he had bought, requested permission to present her to his majesty. The merchant was accordingly introduced, and placed so that he was able not only to see the king perfectly, but to hear him converse freely with those who were near his person.

When the assembly was concluded, and all but the merchant had retired, he prostrated himself before the throne, his face to the earth, praying for the accomplishment of all his majesty's desires. As soon as he arose, the king asked if he had brought him a slave, as had been stated, and if she were handsome. "Sir," replied the merchant, "your majesty has, I doubt not, many very beautiful slaves, since they have been sought for with so much care in every part of the world; but I can assure, without fear of too highly estimating the slave I have to dispose of, that you have never seen one comparable to her, either in point of beauty, figure, captivating manners, or all the various accomplishments of which she is mistress. I left her in the care of an officer belonging to your eunuchs. Your majesty can, if you please, command her appearance."

The slave was introduced; and the king, immediately on seeing her, became charmed with her fine figure and graceful manner. He then entered his cabinet, whither the merchant, and some of the attendant eunuchs, followed him. The slave had on a veil of red satin, striped with gold, which concealed her face: the merchant removed it, when the king of Persia beheld a lady who surpassed in beauty all he then possessed, or had ever seen. He instantly became passionately enamoured of her, and desired the merchant to name his price. "Sir," replied the merchant, "I gave to the person of whom I purchased her a thousand pieces of gold; and I calculate that I have expended an equal sum in the three years that I have been on a journey to your court. But it would be unbecoming in me to fix a price; I entreat, if it be agreeable to your majesty, that you will accept of her as a present." "I am much obliged to you," returned the king; "but it is not my custom to take gifts of merchants. I shall give orders for you to receive ten thousand pieces of gold. Will that satisfy you?" "Sir," answered the merchant, "I should have esteemed myself very happy, if your majesty had deigned to accept her for nothing; but I dare not reject your liberality. I shall not fail to proclaim it in my own country, and in whatever place I may chance to travel." The sum was paid to the merchant; and, before he withdrew, he was clothed, in the king's presence, by his majesty's order, in a robe of gold brocade.

The king gave directions that the beautiful slave should be lodged in the most magnificent apartment of the palace, that excepted which was appropriated to his own use. He appointed several matrons and other female slaves to wait upon her, whom he ordered to conduct her to the bath, and to dress her in the most magnificent habit that could be obtained; also to procure the most beautiful pearl necklaces, and diamonds of the greatest brilliancy, with other precious stones of the highest value, in order that she herself might choose such as she most approved. The officious matrons, who had no other object than to please the king, were themselves struck with admiration at the sight of the beautiful slave. Being perfectly skilled in their business, "Sir," said they, "if your majesty will have patience to grant us only three days, we engage so much to improve the lady's appearance, that you shall scarcely know her again." The king, though very unwilling to be so long deprived of the pleasure of her company, granted their request. "I agree," said he, "but on condition that you punctually keep your promise."

The capital of the king of Persia was situated in an island; and his palace, which was extremely superb, was built on the shore. The apartment of the king overlooked the sea, and that of the beautiful slave, which was but at a little distance, commanded a view of the same element, so much the more agreeable, as it rolled its waves to the foot of the walls.

At the end of three days, the beautiful slave, most magnificently dressed and adorned, was alone in her chamber, seated on a sofa, and resting her arm on one of the windows which opened towards the sea, when the king, informed that she was prepared to receive him, entered the room.

The king of Persia was extremely astonished to find a slave so beautiful and engaging, entirely unacquainted with the customs of the world. He attributed this defect to the bad education she had received, and to the little care which had been taken to instruct her in the rules of good manners. He advanced towards her as far as the window, when, notwithstanding the cold and careless manner in which she had received him, she suffered him to view, admire, and even to caress and embrace her, as much as he pleased. In the midst of these delights, the monarch paused a moment, looking at her as if enraptured. Whatever protestations of love the king of Persia could make, the slave preserved complete taciturnity; with her eyes fixed on the ground, she never cast a look on the king, nor uttered a single word.

The king of Persia, delighted with the acquisition he had made, did not press her further, in hopes that the kind treatment he meant to show her would produce a change. He clapped his hands, and immediately several females entered, whom he ordered to provide supper. As soon as it was served, " My love," said he to the slave, " come this way, and take your supper with me." The slave partook with him of the repast, but always with downcast eyes, and without replying a single word to his inquiries whether the dishes were suited to her taste. The king, not knowing what to think, at length imagined that she was probably dumb. " But," said he to himself, " is it possible that God should have formed so beautiful, so perfect, so accomplished a creature, and have left her with so great a defect? It would indeed be a great misfortune; but, nevertheless, I cannot cease from loving her." When the king rose from table, he retired to one side of the room to wash his hands, while the slaves was washing hers at the other. He availed himself of this opportunity to inquire of the women who presented the basin and napkin, if she had spoken to them. " Sir," said one of them, who replied for the rest, " we have not, any more than your majesty, heard her utter a syllable. We have attended her at the bath, have waited on her in her chamber, have combed and dressed her hair, and assisted in putting on her apparel, but she has never opened her lips. Whether it be owing to contempt, sorrow, stupidity, or that she is absolutely dumb, we can can only assure your majesty that we have never been able to draw a single word."

The king of Persia was more than ever surprised at what he now heard. As he thought the slave might have some cause for affliction, he endeavoured to soothe her, and, with other amusements, gave a ball to the ladies of his palace. The beautiful slave alone took no part in their diversions; she remained in the same place, her eyes constantly fixed on the ground, and with a tranquillity which was not less astonishing to the ladies than to the king himself. They retired each to her apartment, and the king, who alone remained, slept with the beautiful slave.

The next morning the king of Persia rose, more pleased than he had ever been with any other female he had hitherto seen, and more enamoured of the beautiful slave than on the preceding day. He did not fail to make known his affection; in short, he resolved to attach himself altogether to this lady, and he kept his resolution. On the same day, he dismissed all his other ladies, presenting them with rich dresses, diamonds, and jewels, in which they were accustomed to appear, and giving to each of them a large sum of money, with permission to marry whoever they pleased, retaining only the matrons and other aged females, whose attendance was necessary on the beautiful slave. During the space of a whole year, he had not the consolation to hear her utter a single word; he did not, however, lessen his assiduities, but, with all the complaisance imaginable, continued to give her the most signal proofs of his ardent attachment.

The year had elapsed, when the king, sitting one day by the side of his beloved fair, warmly protested to her that his love, instead of diminishing, daily increased: " My queen," said he, " I cannot guess what passes in your mind on the subject; nothing, however, is more true, and which I solemnly swear, than that I have not known what it is to form a wish since I had the happiness of possessing you. I consider my kingdom, great and powerful as it is, as of no value, when I have the pleasure of seeing you, and of telling you a thousand times how much I love you. I do not desire you to believe my declaration only; but surely you cannot doubt it, after the sacrifice I have made to your charms of all the numerous females who were in my palace. You may remember that a year has passed away since I dismissed them all, and which I as little repent at this moment as I did at the instant I sent them away, nor shall I ever repent it. Nothing would be wanting to my satisfaction, my happiness, my delight, would you but utter a single word, to inform me that you are not insensible to my attentions. But how can you comply with my desire, if you are dumb? Alas! I am too much afraid that such is the case; and how can I avoid entertaining those fears, when, after a lapse of a whole year, every day of which I have entreated you a thousand times to speak, you still preserve a silence so afflicting to me. If it be impossible that I should obtain this happiness from you, may Heaven at least grant that you may give me a son to succeed me on the throne! I perceive myself every day growing older, and even at the present time I have occasion for some one to assist me in sustaining the heavy weight of my crown. But again I cannot avoid expressing my ardent desire to hear you speak; something whispers me that you are not dumb. For Heaven's sake, madam, I conjure you, put an end to this long reserve; speak to me a single word, and I shall die content." At this discourse, the beautiful slave, who, according to her custom, had listened to the king with downcast eyes, and who had given him reason to suspect, not only that she was dumb, but that she had never laughed in her life, suffered her countenance to be illumined with a smile. The king of Persia perceived it with a surprise which made him utter an exclamation of joy; and, as he doubted not that she was going to speak, he waited the moment with an eagerness and impatience not easy to be expressed. The beautiful slave at length put a period to her taciturnity: " Sir," said she, " I have so many things to tell your majesty, now I have broken my silence, that I know not where to begin. I think, however, that it is my first duty to thank you for all the favours and honours you have so profusely heaped on me, and to beg of Heaven to make you prosperous, to avert from you all the ill intentions of your enemies, and to permit you, instead of dying after having heard me speak, to lead a long and happy life. After this, sir, I cannot give you greater satisfaction than by informing you that I am pregnant: I wish, with you, that it may be a son. I have only further to say, sir," added she—" and I entreat your majesty to pardon my sincerity—that, were it not for the circumstance which I have just mentioned, I had resolved never to love you, and to maintain a perpetual silence; but that at present I love you as much as is my duty. The king of Persia, enchanted at hearing her speak, and at receiving information which so highly interested him, tenderly embraced her. " Dearest light of my eyes," said he, " I could not have received a greater joy than what you bestow upon me. You have spoken, and you have declared yourself with child. I am scarcely in my senses, after two such unexpected occasions of delight."

The king of Persia, in the excess of his joy, said no more to the beautiful slave; he left her, but in a manner that made it sufficiently apparent he meant soon to return. Desirous that the cause of his happiness might be made public, he announced it to his officers; and having summoned his grand-vizier, he charged him to distribute a hundred thousand pieces of gold among the ministers of his religion who had made a vow of poverty, to the hospitals, and to the poor, as an act of thanksgiving to Heaven; which was punctually performed by the minister.

This order being given, the king of Persia returned to the beautiful slave. Tell me, I entreat you, my dear soul, what motive could possibly have operated with you so strongly, that having seen me, heard me speak, eaten and slept with me, every day and night for a twelvemonth, you could preserve so unshaken a resolution, I do not say of not opening your lips, but of not even permitting me to know whether you understood what I said to you. This surpasses my comprehension, as I cannot conceive how you could possibly but yourself under so great a restraint. The cause must be very extraordinary." To satisfy the king's curiosity, the beautiful female thus replied :—" Sir, to be a slave; to be far removed from one's country, without hope of ever returning thither; to have a heart pierced with grief, at seeing myself separated for ever from my mother, my brother, my relations, and my acquaintances—are they not motives of sufficient weight to produce that silence which has appeared to your majesty so strange ? " Madam," replied the king of Persia, "I am convinced of what you say; but still it appears to me that a person, beautiful, engaging, of excellent sense, and refined understanding, such as yourself, who has been, by ill fortune, destined to slavery, might think herself happy in finding a king for her master." " Sir," returned the lady, " If the slave be of inferior condition, and infinitely raised by such regard, I am willing to believe that she may think herself happy in her misfortune. But, after all, what is her happiness ? She cannot but consider herself as a slave, torn from the arms of her parents; and, perhaps, from a lover, whom, during her whole life, she will never cease to lament. But if we suppose this slave in no respect inferior to the king who has obtained her, your majesty may easily conceive the rigour of her destiny, her misery, her grief, and affliction, and what resolutions she may be able to maintain." The king of Persia was astonished at this discourse. "What, madam !" replied he, " is it possible, as you give me to understand, that you yourself are of royal descent ? Tell me who are the happy parents that gave existence to such a prodigy of charms; who are your brothers, your sisters, your relations—but, above all, what is your name ?"

" Sir," answered the beautiful slave, " my name is Gulnare, of the Ocean; my father, who is dead, was one of the most powerful kings of the sea. At his death, he left his kingdom to my brother, named Saleh, and to the queen my mother. My mother, also, was a princess, being the daughter of another powerful king of the sea. We were living tranquilly in our kingdom, and in profound peace, when an enemy, envious of our happiness, invaded our states with an immense army, and penetrated even to our capital, of which he soon made himself master; affording us scarcely time to save ourselves, attended by some faithful officers, who would not abandon us. In this retreat, my brother was not negligent in endeavouring to discover some means of expelling the unjust usurper of his authority; and during this interval he one day took me aside: ' Sister,' said he, ' I may fail in the execution of a design I have formed for the recovery of our states; but I should be less concerned on my own account, than at the misfortunes which may befal you. To guard against disasters, and to place you in security, I wish you could be prevailed on to marry some prince of the earth; and, to effect it, I am ready to give you every assistance in my power. With the beauty you possess, I am confident there is not one of them, however powerful, who will not be delighted to share with you his crown.' This proposal of my brother excited my extreme indignation: ' Brother,' said I, ' I am, as well as you, both on my father's and mother's side, descended from kings and queens of the sea, without any alliance with the kings of the earth; and I do not intend, any more than they, to form a disgraceful connexion; I took an oath to avoid so acting from the moment I attained sufficient knowledge to perceive the grandeur and antiquity of our house. The state to which we are now reduced will not induce me to change my resolution; and if you should perish in the execution of your project, I am ready to die with you, rather than to follow a counsel which I little expected you could give. My brother, infatuated with the thoughts of this marriage, however unpleasant it was to me, wished me to believe that there were many kings of the earth who were not inferior to those of the sea. This threw me into a violent rage, which drew some severities from him that stung me to the quick. He departed, as little satisfied with me, as I was displeased with him. In my paroxysm of anger, I darted from the bottom of the sea, and landed on the island of the moon.

" Notwithstanding the piercing discontent which had induced me to throw myself upon this island, I lived tolerably content, taking care to withdraw myself into the most retired places. My precautions, however, were ineffectual : a man of some distinction, accompanied with his servants, surprised me while I was sleeping, and conveyed me to his house. He expressed much love for me, and neglected nothing to persuade me to accede to his wishes. When he found he gained nothing by gentle means, he imagined that he should succeed better by force ; but I soon made him repent of his insolence : he, in consequence, resolved to dispose of me, and sold me to the merchant who brought me to your majesty. This merchant was a prudent, gentle, and humane man; and in the long journey which he made me take, gave me no reason but to speak of him in terms of gratitude.

" As to what regards your majesty," continued the Princess Gulnare, " if you had not shown me all those obliging attentions; if you had not given me so many marks of your affection, with a sincerity which left no room for doubt, when, without hesitation, you dismissed all your women; I will not affect to conceal that I should not have remained with you. I should have thrown myself into the sea, through that window where you addressed me when you first visited me in this apartment, and should have gone to seek my brother, my mother, and my other relations. I even persevered in this intention, and should have executed it, if after a certain time I had lost the hope of being a mother. In my present state, I have entirely relinquished the design: whatever I might say to my mother and my brother would be insufficient to make them believe that I had been the slave of a king like your majesty; and they would incessantly upbraid me with

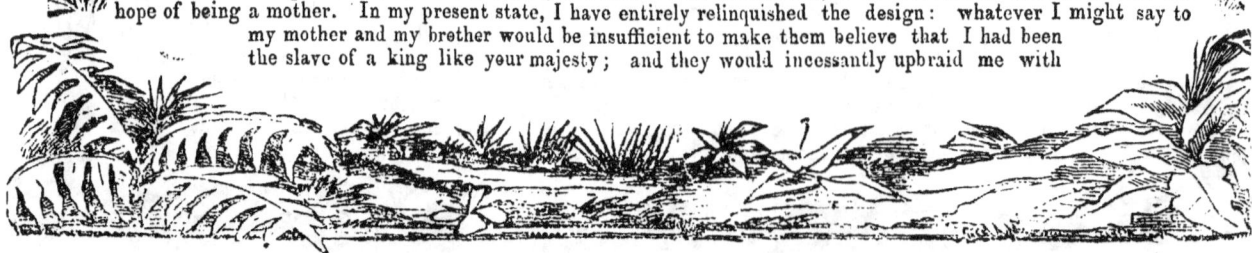

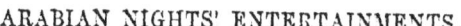

having made a voluntary sacrifice of my honour. Such being the case, sir, whether it be a prince or princess, which I may bring into the world, it will be a constant pledge for my attachment to your majesty: and I hope you will cease to regard me as a slave, but consider me as a princess not unworthy of your alliance."

It was in these terms that the Princess Gulnare made herself and her history known to the king of Persia. "My charming, my adorable princess," exclaimed the monarch, "what wonders have I heard! what ample matter to excite my curiosity, and to overwhelm you with questions in regard to things so wholly new! But first let me thank you for your goodness, and for your patience in proving the sincerity and constancy of my affection. I thought it impossible to love more ardently than I have loved you; yet since I have been informed that you are so great a princess, I love you a thousand times more than ever. Why do I say—princess? Madam, you are no longer so you are my queen, the queen of Persia, in the same manner as I am king; and this title shall very soon

resound through my whole dominions. Early, to-morrow, madam, it shall be proclaimed in my capital, with such rejoicings as have never been seen—such as shall make your splendid descent known, and that you are my lawful wife. There is still one thing that seems unaccountable, and of which I beg you to inform me :—I cannot comprehend how you are able to live, act, or move in the water without being drowned. Among us there are but few persons who have the art of remaining under water; and they likewise perish, if they do not quit it in a certain time, according to their respective ability and strength."

"Sir," replied the Queen Gulnare, "I will satisfy your majesty with the greatest pleasure. We walk at the bottom of the sea in the same manner as people do upon the earth, and we breathe in the water as they respire in the air; instead, therefore, of our being suffocated, as would be the case with you, the water contributes to our existence. What may seem also very remarkable, it does not wet our clothes; and, of course, when we visit the earth, we have no occasion to dry them. Our ordinary language is the same as that in which the inscription on the seal of the great prophet Solomon, the son of David, is written. I ought not to omit telling you, that the water does not, in the least, prevent our seeing, as we open our eyes in it without sustaining any inconvenience; and as our sight is excellent, we can, notwithstanding the depth of the sea, perceive objects in it as clearly as persons see

upon earth. It is same during the night; we have the moon to enlighten us, and the planets and stars are not hidden. I have already spoken of our kingdoms; as the sea is much more spacious than the earth, it affords a greater number, and some of them are considerably larger. They are divided into provinces, and in every province are many well-peopled towns. In short, there is an infinity of nations, of different manners and customs, the same as upon the earth. The palaces of our kings and princes are superb amd magnificent; they are formed of marble of various colours, of rock-crystal (with which the sea abounds), of mother-of-pearl, coral, and other more valuable materials. Gold, silver, and every sort of precious stones are in greater abundance there than they are upon the earth. I speak not of pearls; the very largest that are seen on the earth would be of no estimation in our countries, and are worn only by the lowest rank of citizens. As we have the power of transporting ourselves wherever we wish, with incredible agility, we have no occasion for either carriages or horses. None of our kings, however, are without their stables, and studs of sea-horses; but they are, in general, only made use of for amusements, or during feasts and public rejoicings. Some, after using great pains in training them for riding, will mount them, to show their dexterity in the race; others will harness them to cars of mother-of-pearl, ornamented with a thousand different sorts of shells, all of the most brilliant colours. These cars are made open, with a throne in the middle, of which our kings are seated when they show themselves to their people. They are all expert in the management of them, and therefore have no need of drivers. I pass over an infinity of other very curious particulars, respecting these marine countries," added the queen, "a recital of which would afford your majesty very great pleasure; but you must allow me to defer the conversation till I am more at leisure, that I may consult you respecting a matter of greater importance. It is, then, necessary to inform you, sir, that the women of the sea, when in my condition, are treated in a different manner from the women of the earth; and I have reason to think it would be imprudent to trust to the assistance which this country affords. As your majesty is in this affair not less interested than myself, I judge it advisable, if consonant with your good pleasure, to bring hither the queen my mother, and several of my female cousins; at the same time I should like to see the king my brother, with whom I much wish to be reconciled. They will be delighted to see me again, when I have informed them of my history, and that I am wife to the most powerful king of Persia. I entreat your majesty to grant my desire; they will be extremely glad to pay you their respects, and I can promise that you will be well satisfied with the interview."

"Madam," replied the king of Persia, "you are here sole mistress; act as you please: I will endeavour to receive them with all the honours due to their merit. But I request to know, by what means you are to make them acquainted with your desire, and when they will arrive, that I may order everything necessary for their reception, and may myself attend in person to introduce them." "Sir," replied Gulnare, "ceremonies are unnecessary; they will be here in an instant, and your majesty shall see the manner of their arrival. Only take the trouble to enter this little closet, and look through the lattice." When the king of Persia had retired to the closet, the queen ordered a perfuming-pot; and some fire to be brought her by one of her women, whom she then dismissed, charging her to fasten the door after her. Being now alone, she took a small piece of aloes-wood from a box, and put it in the perfuming-pot: as soon as she saw the smoke arise, she pronounced some word wholly unknown to the king of Persia, who observed her proceedings with great attention; and she had scarcely finished, before the sea became agitated. The closet, which the king had entered was so situated, that he could view the sea through the lattice.

In fine, at some distance, the sea began to open, and immediately there arose from it, a tall, handsome, young man, with mustachoes of a sea-green colour. A lady, somewhat advanced in years, but of a majestic air, rose at the same time a little behind him, with five young females, whose beauty equalled that of Queen Gulnare herself. Gulnare, who immediately presented herself at one of the windows, recognised the king her brother, the queen her mother, and her other relations, who instantly saw her. The party advanced, not walking, but as if borne on the surface of the sea, and, when they were all on shore, they bounded lightly, one after another, through the window at which Queen Gulnare had appeared, and whence she had retired to give them room. King Saleh, the queen his mother, and all her relations embraced her as soon as they entered, with the greatest tenderness, and their eyes suffused with tears. When Gulnare had received them with all possible honour, and made them sit down on a sofa, the queen her mother thus addressed her:—"I have very great joy, my daughter, in seeing you again after so long an absence, and I am sure that your brother and your relations do not feel less than myself. Your departure, without having acquainted any one with your intention, occasioned us all inexpressible affliction, and we cannot now tell you how many tears we shed. We could conceive no cause for your having acted so unaccountably, unless it were in consequence of a conversation with your brother, of which he informed us. But let us not renew a subject that will only bring to our recollection causes of complaint and sorrow, which we ought mutually to forget. Do you rather inform us of what has happened to you during the long time we have been separated, and of the state in which you now are; but, above everything, tell us if you are happy."

Queen Gulnare immediately threw herself at the feet of the queen her mother, and, after she had kissed her hand, "Madam," said she, rising, "I have, I confess, been guilty of a great fault, and I owe to your goodness the pardon you have been so kind as to grant me." She then related all that had happened to her, since her indignation had induced her to quit the bottom of the sea. When she had proceeded in her history, to inform them of her being sold to the king of Persia, with whom she then was, "Sister," interrupted the king her brother, "you have been much in the wrong to suffer so many indignities, and have had no one to blame but yourself. You have the power of extricating yourself, and I am astonished at your patience in continuing so long in slavery. Rise this moment, and return with us to my kingdom, which I have conquered from my fierce enemy, who had made himself master of it." The king of Persia, who had head these words from the closet where he was concealed, was in the greatest alarm. "Ah," said he to himself, "I am lost, and my death is certain, if my queen, my Gulnare, should listen to this cruel advice. She is now absolutely essential to my existence, and they wish to deprive me of her." Gulnare, however, did not leave him long in this state of painful apprehension. "My dear brother," replied she, smiling, "what I have just heard convinces me more fully than ever of the sincerity of your regard for me. Formerly, I could not endure the advice you gave me to marry a prince of the earth. To-day I am almost angry with you for having recommended me to quit the engagement I have contracted with the most powerful and most renowned of all princes.

The monarch with whom I am united, has given me the most unequivocal marks of his affection ; of which he could not possibly afford me a more distinguished proof, than that of having dismissed, at the very commencement of our acquaintance, the great number of females in his possession, to attach himself solely to me. I am his wife, and he has just declared me queen of Persia, and a sharer in his government. I have also to inform you that I am pregnant ; if I have, by the favour Heaven, the happiness to give him a son, it will unite me to him still more inseparably. Thus, my dear brother," continued Queen Gulnare, "far from following your advice, all these considerations, as you will readily perceive, oblige me not only to love the king of Persia, as much as he loves me, but even to remain and pass my life with him, as well from gratitude as from duty. I hope that neither my mother, you, nor my good cousins, will disapprove of my resolution, any more than of the alliance I have accidentally made, which does honour equally to the monarchs of the sea, and of the earth."

"My dear sister," said King Saleh, "for these reasons, I cannot, for my own part, but highly approve of the very laudable resolution you have have taken, and which is so worthy of you, after what you have told us of the king of Persia your spouse, and of the great obligations you owe him. With respect to the queen our mother, I am persuaded that she is not of a different sentiment." This princess confirmed what her son had said : "My daughter," replied she, addressing herself to Gulnare, "I am quite delighted you are so happy ; and I have nothing to add to what the king your brother has represented. I should be the first to condemn you, if you did not feel the utmost gratitude to a monarch who loves you with so much ardour, and who has made so great sacrifices on your account."

In proportion as the king of Persia, who was still in the closet, had been afflicted by the fear of losing Queen Gulnare, so great was his joy to find that she had resolved never to abandon him as he could no longer doubt of her affection, after so open a declaration, he loved her, if possible, more than ever, and resolved within himself to show his gratitude by every means in his power.

While the king of Persia, was, with extreme pleasure, making these reflections, Queen Gulnare had clapped her hands, and had commanded some slaves, who entered immediately, to serve up refreshments. When they were brought, she invited her mother, her brother, and her other relations to partake of them ; but they were all of opinion that, as they were then without permission in the palace of a most potent monarch, whom they had never seen, and to whom they were entirely unknown, it would be a mark of the greatest incivility to sit down to his table without him. The colour mounted into their cheeks ; and so great was their emotion, that they threw fire from their nostrils and their mouths, and their eyes seemed in flames.

The king of Persia was in extreme terror at this appearance, so entirely unexpected, and of which he did not know the cause. Queen Gulnare, aware of his sensations, and perfectly comprehending the intention of her friends rose from her seat, saying she would soon return. She accordingly went to the closet, and the king was much comforted by her presence. "Sir," said she, "I doubt not that your majesty is fully satisfied with the proof I have just given of my regard, and of the grateful sense I feel of the vast obligations I owe you. It rested entirely with myself to follow the wishes of my friends, and to return with them to our country ; but I am incapable of ingratitude, which I should be the first to condemn. The queen my mother, and the king my brother, are very anxious to see you, and to assure you themselves of their high esteem. I had intended to make a party with them at the table I have had furnished with refreshments, before soliciting this interview ; but I now entreat your majesty to have the goodness to enter, and to honour them with your presence." "Madam," replied the king of Persia, "I shall have great pleasure in saluting persons so nearly connected with you ; but the flames which I have observed proceeding from their mouths and nostrils somewhat terrify me." "Sir," replied the queen, smiling, "let not these flames give you the least uneasiness ; they merely express their unwillingness to eat in your palace unless your majesty honour them with your presence, and partake with them."

The king of Persia, encouraged by this declaration, rose from his place, and entered the chamber with Queen Gulnare, who presented him to the queen her mother, to the king her brother, and to her cousins, who immediately prostrated themselves with their faces to the earth. The king of Persia ran to them immediately, compelled them to rise, and embraced each of them in turn. After they were all seated, King Saleh thus spoke :—"Sir," said he to the king of Persia, "we cannot sufficiently express to your majesty the joy we feel at the good fortune Queen Gulnare my sister has experienced in her disgrace, in being placed under the protection of so potent a monarch. Permit us to assure you she is not unworthy the high rank to which she has the honour to be raised. We have ever felt so great an affection and tenderness for her, that we could not resolve to part with her to one of the most powerful princes of the sea, who solicited her in marriage even before she was of age. Heaven reserved her for you, sir ; and we cannot better return thanks for the favour it has rendered her, than in offering up our prayers that your majesty may live many years with your queen, and enjoy every prosperity and happiness." "It is evident," replied the king of Persia, "that Heaven reserved her for me, as you have observed. In fact, the ardent passion I feel for her makes me fully sensible that, till I saw her, I never loved. I cannot sufficiently express my gratitude to the queen her mother, to you, prince, nor your family, for the generous manner with which you have received me into an alliance that confers on me so much glory." On concluding these words, he invited them to be seated at the table, where he also placed himself with Queen Gulnare.

The king of Persia entertained his illustrious guests with perpetual feasts, in which were displayed the utmost grandeur and magnificence, and thus insensibly induced them to continue at his court till the time of the queen's delivery. As she perceived it approach, he gave orders that nothing should be wanting which could possibly be necessary on so important an occasion. She was at length brought to bed, and gave birth to a son, to the infinite joy of the queen her mother, who assisted, and who, as soon as the child was arrayed in the magnificent clothes prepared, went and presented it to the king his father. The king of Persia received the present with an excess of delight, which it is more easy to conceive than express ; and, as the countenance of the young prince his son was open, and of transcendent beauty, he thought he could not give him a more appropriate name than that of Beder. To express his thanks to Heaven, he assigned considerable alms to the poor, released the prisoners from their confinement, gave liberty to all his slaves of both sexes, and distributed great sums of money amongst the and holy men of his religion. He also made largesses to his court and to the people, and public festivals were held ministers by his order, for several days, in all parts of the city.

After Queen Gulnare had recovered from her confinement, the king of Persia, and the queen her mother, King Saleh her brother, and the princesses her relations, were one day conversing together in the chamber of the queen,

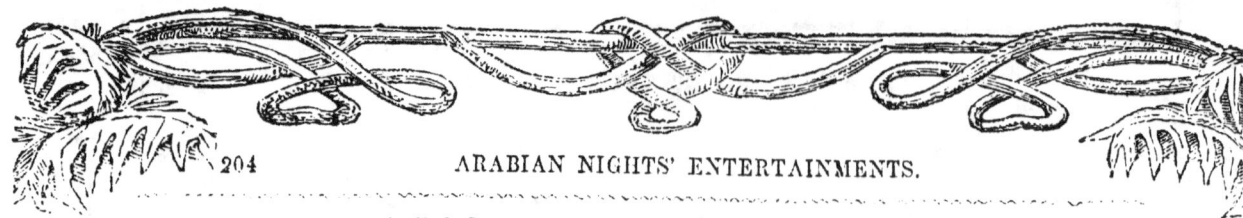

when the nurse entered with the little Prince Beder in her arms. King Saleh rose immediately from his place, ran to the prince, and taking him from her arms, began to caress him with the greatest marks of tenderness. He continued playing with him, making several turns about the chamber, and holding him up between his hands; when suddenly, in a transport of joy, he darted through a window which was open, and plunged with the prince into the sea. The king of Persia, totally unprepared for this event, gave a lamentable shriek, in the belief that he should never again see his beloved son, or, at least, that he would not be restored to him alive. His affliction, which had nearly deprived him of his senses, was only alleviated by his tears. "Sir," said Gulnare, with a countenance, and in a manner that were calculated to inspire hope, "may it please your majesty to dismiss your fears. The little prince is my son as well as yours, and I love him with equal fervour; but you see, nevertheless, that I am not in the least alarmed; indeed I have no occasion to be so. He runs, I assure you, no risk whatever; and you will soon see the king his uncle re-appear, and restore him to us in perfect safety. Although he is descended from you, yet, as he belongs to me likewise, he will not fail to have the advantage which we enjoy, of being able to live equally in the sea or on the earth." The queen her mother, and the princesses her relations, gave him the same assurances; but their assertions had little effect in removing his fears, which kept possession of him so long as Prince Beder was absent from his sight.

The sea at length became agitated, and soon afterwards King Saleh re appeared, rising from the waves, with the little prince in his arms: he then, glancing through the air, returned by the same window at which he went out. The king of Persia was delighted, but very much surprised, to see Prince Beder as tranquil as when he left the room. "Was not your majesty alarmed," asked King Saleh, "when you saw me plunge into the sea with the prince my nephew?" "Ah! prince," replied the king of Persia, "I cannot express to you my fears. From the moment he disappeared, I believed him irrecoverably lost: in bringing him back to me, you have given me new life." "Sir," replied King Saleh, "I was apprehensive you would be terrified, but there was not the least occasion for alarm. Before I plunged into the sea, I pronounced over him some mysterious words, that were engraven on the seal of the great King Solomon, the son of David. We follow the same proceeding with regard to the children who are born among us in the regions at the bottom of the sea; and in virtue of these words, they obtain the privilege that we possess above all the men who reside on the earth."

King Saleh, after these words, having restored the little Prince Beder to the arms of his nurse, opened a box, which he had brought from his palace during the short time of his absence:—it contained three hundred diamonds, each as large as a pigeon's egg; the like number of rubies, of extraordinary size; as many rods of emerald, each six inches long; and thirty pearl necklaces, every necklace comprised of ten pearls. "Sir," said he to the king of Persia, presenting to him the box, "when we were summoned hither by the queen my sister, we were ignorant in what part of the world she resided, and that she had the honour of being married to so great a monarch; on which account we came with empty hands. As it was not then in our power to give your majesty any mark of our gratitude, we humbly entreat that you will now deign to accept this trifling return for the singular favours you have confered on her, and of which we are all equally sensible." It was impossible to express how great was the king's surprise when he saw such abundance of riches contained in so small a space.

A few days after this, King Saleh addressed the king of Persia, assuring him that the queen his mother, the princesses his relations, and himself, could not possibly have greater pleasure than to pass their lives at his court; but as they had not been long absent from the kingdom, and as their presence there was become necessary, he begged him not to be displeased, if they took their leave of him and Queen Gulnare. The king of Persia replied that he was extremely sorry not to have it in his power to render the same civility, by visiting their states. "But as I am persuaded," added he, "that you will not forget Queen Gulnare, but will come to see her occasionally, I hope to have the honour of your company many times before I die."

When the moment of separation arrived, many tears were shed on all sides. King Saleh first withdrew; but the queen his mother, and the princesses, were obliged, in order to follow him, to tear themselves from the embraces of Queen Gulnare, who could not prevail with herself to suffer them to depart.

Prince Beder was brought up in the palace under the immediate inspection of the king and queen of Persia, who witnessed his increasing growth and beauty with the most lively satisfaction. Their gratulation augmented daily as he advanced in age, by his continual good humour, his constantly agreeable manners, and by an indication of correct judgment and vivacity of understanding in all he said; and their happiness was rendered complete, by its being frequently shared with King Saleh, his uncle, the queen his grandmother, and the princesses his cousins. No difficulty was experienced in teaching the young prince to read and write, and he learned with equal facility all the sciences suitable to a prince of his rank.

When the prince of Persia had attained the age of fifteen years, he already acquitted himself in all his exercises with infinitely more skill and address than his master; besides which, he was endowed with admirable wisdom and prudence. The king of Persia, who had observed in him, almost from his birth, those virtues so necessary to a sovereign, and had seen them augment with his years, perceiving, moreover, the infirmities of age daily increasing upon himself, was desirous that the prince's succession to the throne should not be delayed till his death, but proposed immediately to resign him the kingdom.

The day for the ceremony was fixed, when, surrounded by his council, which was more numerous than usual, the king of Persia descended from his throne, on which he had been sitting, and, having taken the crown from his own head, placed it upon that of Prince Beder; he then assisted him to ascend to the place he had quitted, kissed his hand, as a token that he had resigned to him all his authority, and took a seat beneath him with the viziers and emirs. Immediately the viziers and emirs, and all the principal officers, approached to prostrate themselves at the feet of the new king, each taking the oath of fidelity according to his rank. The grand-vizier then made a report to him of some important affairs of government, on all which he gave judgment with so much wisdom as gained him the admiration of the council.

During the first year of his reign, King Beder acquitted himself of all the royal duties with the greatest assiduity. Above all things, he took care to instruct himself in the real state of affairs, and in every matter which could contribute to the happiness of his subjects. The following year, having previously arranged the administration of government with his council, and sanctioned by the approbation of the old king his father, he left his capital, under pretence of taking the diversion of hunting; but in reality to visit all the provinces of his kingdom, in order to correct abuses, to establish everywhere good order and discipline, and to deprive the ill-intentioned princes his neighbours of the hope of effecting anything against the peace and security of his states, by showing himself upon the frontiers.

An entire year was necessary to enable the young king to execute a design so worthy of him. He had not long returned, before the old king his father became so dangerously ill, as to be convinced from the first he should not recover; but he looked forward to his last moments with the most perfect tranquillity, having no other care than to recommend to the ministers and lords of the court, to preserve always the fidelity they had sworn to his son; when they all renewed their oath with the same good will they had before shown. He soon afterwards died, to the great affliction of King Beder and of Queen Gulnare, who had his body deposited in a superb mausoleum, with a pomp suited to his exalted dignity. After the funeral obsequies were concluded, King Beder had no difficulty in complying with the custom of Persia, of bewailing the deceased for one entire month, and not seeing in this interval any person whatever. He would have lamented the loss of his father during his whole life, had he attended merely to the dictates of his heart, and had it been consistent with the duties of so great a king to abandon himself wholly to grief. In the meantime, the queen, mother of Gulnare, and King Saleh, with the princesses their relations, arrived and shared the affliction of her son, before they spoke to them of consolation.

When the month was elapsed, the king could no longer dispense with granting admittance to the grand-vizier and all the lords of his court, who entreated him to lay aside his mourning, to appear before his subjects, and to undertake, as before, the charge of public affairs. King Beder could not resist their pressing entreaties; he put off his mourning from that moment; and having resumed the habiliments and ensigns of royalty, began to provide for the necessities of his kingdom and of his subjects, with the attention he had always shown before the death of his father. He acquitted himself in all, with universal approbation; and, as he was very exact in following the ordinances of his predecessors, the people were scarcely sensible of the change of sovereign.

King Saleh, who had returned to his kingdom of the sea, with the queen his mother, and the princesses, finding that King Beder had resumed the reins of government, revisited alone, at the end of the year, King Beder and Queen Gulnare, who were delighted to see him. One evening, the conversation turned on a variety of subjects. King Saleh fell insensibly on the praises of the king his nephew, and remarked to his sister how perfectly he was satisfied with the wisdom with which he governed. Beder, embarrassed at hearing himself so highly commended, turned himself on one side, and pretended to sleep, while he rested his head upon a cushion that was placed behind him. After noticing the extraordinary prudence of King Beder, and his superior understanding, King Saleh proceeded to notice his personal perfections, and spoke of him as a prodigy which had never been equalled on earth, nor in any of the kingdoms he had known beneath the waters of the sea. "Sister," he exclaimed, "if I am not mistaken, he is now in his twentieth year—an age at which it is not permitted to a prince like him to remain without a wife. I will undertake myself to find a spouse for him in some princesses of our kingdoms, whom I may deem worthy of him." "Brother," replied Queen Gulnare, "you bring to my notice what has never till the present moment occupied my thoughts. As my son has never expressed a desire to be married, it never occurred to me, and I am extremely glad that you have put me in mind of it, and I beg you to select one who is so handsome and accomplished that my son may be compelled to love her." "I know one," replied King Saleh, "but, before I tell you who she is, I must request you to observe whether the king my nephew be really asleep. I will give you my reason why it is proper to take this precaution." The queen turned herself, and, seeing Beder in the same situation as before, she had no doubt he was in a profound sleep. King Beder, however, far from being in that state, redoubled his attention, that he might not lose anything of what his uncle was going to impart with so much secrecy. "You may speak freely," said the queen to her brother, "without fear of being overheard." "It is not desirable," returned King Saleh, "that the king my nephew should be made acquainted immediately with what I am going to say. Love sometimes gains admission by the ear, and it is not proper he should love on report the lady I am about to propose, as I foresee great difficulty to be surmounted, not, I hope, on the part of the princess, but on that of the king her father. I have only to mention to you the Princess Giauhare, and the king of Samandal." "What say you, brother?" replied Queen Gulnare; "is not the Princess Giauhare yet married?" "Sister," answered King Saleh, "the vanity of the king of Samandal is so excessive, that he considers himself as superior to all other kings, and there seems little probability of success in treating with him on the subject of this alliance. I will, however, myself wait upon him, to demand the princess his daughter, and, if he refuse us, we will address ourselves where we may expect to be more favourably heard." They continued to converse some time longer on this subject, and it was agreed that King Saleh should return immediately to his kingdom, and demand of the King of Samandal the hand of the Princess Giauhare for the king of Persia.

Queen Gulnare and King Saleh, who had no doubt that Beder was really asleep, roused him as they were about to retire, and the king perfectly succeeded in making them believe he had awoke from a sound sleep. The fact, however, was, that he had not lost a single word of their conversation, and that the picture they had drawn of the Princess Giauhare had excited in his breast a passion altogether new.

Next day, King Saleh proposed to take leave of Queen Gulnare and of the king his nephew. The young king of Persia, who was well aware that his uncle's only motive for leaving them so soon was to carry into effect the scheme he had formed for his happiness, could not hear of his departure without change of countenance. He formed the resolution of requesting his uncle to take him with him; but as he was unwilling his mother should be acquainted with the matter, that he might have an opportunity of speaking to him in private, he engaged him to defer his journey, to be of a hunting-party with him on the day following, resolving to profit of this opportunity to make his wishes known. The party accordingly took place, and King Beder found himself several times alone with his uncle; but he could not summon courage to utter a word of what he had before determined to say. In the height of the chase, King Saleh had separated himself from him, and alighted near a brook; and having fastened his horse to a tree, he reclined upon the grass, and gave free course to his tears; in this state he remained a long time, wholly absorbed in reflection, without uttering a single word. In the meantime, King Saleh, was extremely

anxious to know what was become of his nephew, but could find no person who could give the least information: He had observed the day before, and more evidently on the present day, that his nephew had not his usual spirits; that he was pensive; and that, if a question were asked him, he either did not reply, or gave an irrelevant answer. As soon as he saw him in the situation described, he doubted not that the king had overheard the conversation between himself and the queen his mother, and that he was in love. He alighted from his horse at some distance, and having tied him to a tree, approached in a circuitous manner, and without making the least noise, till he came sufficiently near to hear the young king pronounce these words:—"Amiable princess of the kingdom of Samandal!" he exclaimed, "doubtless I have only heard a feeble sketch of your beauty; which I am persuaded excels that of all the princesses in the world more than the splendour of the sun is superior to that of the moon and stars. I would this moment make you an offer of my heart, did I but know where to find you: it is yours; and never shall any princess but yourself possess it."

King Saleh did not wish to hear more; he advanced, and presenting himself to King Beder, "I see, nephew," said he, "you have overheard what the queen your mother and myself were yesterday saying about the Princess Giauhare. We have been deceived, as we believed you were asleep." "My dear uncle, returned King Beder, "I did not lose a word of your conversation: and I have fully experienced the effect you foresaw, and which you were so anxious to prevent: but the confusion I felt when I wished to acknowledge my weakness, if, indeed, it is a weakness to love a princess so worthy of my affection, closed my lips. I entreat you to extend your pity to me, and not defer procuring me a sight of the divine Giauhare till you have obtained the consent of the king her father to our marriage, if you wish to prevent my dying for the love of her before I see her. This discourse of the king of Persia extremely embarrassed King Saleh, who represented to him the great difficulty there would be in giving him the satisfaction he desired; as he could not do it without taking him with him, while his presence in his own kingdom was so necessary, that much inconvenience might be apprehended from his absence: he therefore entreated him to moderate his passion till matters could be properly arranged. The king of Persia was deaf to all these arguments; "Cruel uncle!" he exclaimed, "I see clearly that you do not love me so much as I believed, and that you would rather see me die than grant me the first prayer that I ever made you in my life." King Saleh, compelled to yield to the king of Persia's solicitation, drew from off his finger a ring, on which were engraven the same mysterious names of the Deity as were upon the seal of Solomon, and which, by their virtue, had produced such miraculous effects. In presenting it to him, "Take this ring," said he, "put it on your finger, and fear neither the waters nor the depth of the sea." The king of Persia took the ring; and when he had put it on his finger, "Follow me," said King Saleh; at the same time they proceeded towards the sea, and plunged into it.

His marine majesty was not long in reaching his palace, accompanied by the king of Persia his nephew, whom he immediately conducted to the apartment of the queen, and presented him to her. The king of Persia kissed the hand of the queen his grandmother, who embraced him with the most lively demonstrations of joy. "I do not inquire after your health," said she; "I perceive that you are well, and am very happy to find you so; but pray give me some intelligence of my daughter, Queen Gulnare." The king of Persia was careful not to divulge that he had left his palace without taking leave of her. On the contrary, he assured his grandmother that she was in perfect health, and that he was charged to present her most dutiful and affectionate regards. The queen then presented him to the princesses; and while they were engaged in conversation together, she entered a closet with King Saleh, who informed her of the love which the king of Persia had conceived for the Princess Giauhare, on the mere description of her beauty, and contrary to his intention; that, unable to resist the solicitations of the king, he had been compelled to bring him; and that he was going to concert measures to procure the princess for him in marriage.

"I hope," continued he, "you will approve the resolution I have taken, to wait upon the king of Samandal myself, to offer him a rich present of jewels, and to demand the princess his daughter for the king of Persia your grandson. I entertain some confidence that he will not refuse me, and that he will consent to an alliance with one of the most powerful monarchs of the earth." "It were to be wished," said the queen, "that we had not been reduced to the necessity of making this demand, for the happy success of which we have so great reason to fear; but as the object in view is to give repose and satisfaction to the king my grandson, I shall not withhold my consent. But take care to address him with all that high respect which is due to him, and in terms so obliging that he may not be offended."

The queen herself prepared the present, which consisted of diamonds, rubies, emeralds, and strings of pearls; and were deposited in an extremely rich and beautiful casket. Next day, King Saleh took leave of the queen his mother, and the king of Persia, setting off with a small and select retinue of his officers and servants. He very soon reached the kingdom, the capital, and the palace, of the king of Samandal, who, as soon as he heard of his arrival, gave him audience. He rose from his throne when King Saleh first made his appearance, who determined for a few moments to forget his rank, and prostrated himself at the feet of the monarch, wishing him the accomplishment of all he could desire. The king of Samandal immediately stooped to raise him; and having given him a place near him, he assured him of the satisfaction he had in seeing him, and requested to know if there were anything he could do for his service. "Sir," replied King Saleh, "though I had no other motive than to render my respects to one of the most powerful princes the world has known, a prince equally distinguished by his wisdom and his valour, I should but feebly express to your majesty how much I honour you. If you could penetrate to the bottom of my heart, you would perceive the great veneration I entertain for your majesty, and the ardent desire I have to give you some proofs of my attachment." In saying these words, he took the casket from the hands of one of his attendants, opened it, and, presenting it to him, entreated that he would have the goodness to accept it. "Prince," said the king of Samandal, "you would not offer a present of this value, if you had not some proportionate favour to ask. If it be anything within my power to grant, it will give me the greatest pleasure to accede to your wish. Speak, and tell me freely how I may oblige you." "It is true, sir," replied King Saleh, "that I have a favour to ask of your majesty, and as your majesty has encouraged me to place so great confidence in your good will, I will no longer dissemble that I am come hither to entreat you to honour us with your alliance by the marriage of the Princess Giauhare, your illustrious daughter, and thus to confirm the good intelligence which has so long subsisted between our two kingdoms."

At this proposal, the king of Samandal burst into a violent fit of laughter, highly insulting to King Saleh: "King Saleh," said he, with an air of contempt, "I always regarded you as a wise and considerate prince, possessed of good sense, and I am sorry to find I have been deceived. Tell me, I beg, where was your discretion when you formed to yourself so extravagant a chimera as that of which you have been speaking? Could you conceive even a thought of aspiring to the hand of a princess descended from so great and powerful a monarch as I am? You ought previously to have considered the immense distance there is between you and me, before you came hither to sacrifice, in a moment, the esteem I have been accustomed to entertain for your person."

King Saleh was extremely offended at this insolent answer, and had great difficulty in restraining his just resentment: he replied, however, with all possible moderation, "May God reward your majesty as you deserve! Allow me the honour to tell you that I do not solicit the princess your daughter in marriage for myself; though, had such been the case, so far from its being an insult, either to your majesty or the princess herself, I cannot but think it would have done equal honour to all parties. Your majesty need not be told that I, as well as yourself, am one of the kings of the sea; that the kings my predecessors yield in the antiquity of their house to no royal family whatever; or that the kingdom which I inherit from them is not less flourishing or powerful than it has ever been. But if your majesty had not interrupted me, you would very soon have been informed that the favour I asked you was not for myself, but for the young king of Persia, my nephew. The world admits that the Princess Giauhare is the most beautiful female beneath the heavens; but it is not less true that the young king of Persia is the finest figure, and most accomplished young man that lives on the earth. The princess is worthy of the king of Persia, and the king is not less worthy of her. There is neither king nor prince in the world who can dispute the justice of his pretensions."

The king of Samandal would not have given King Saleh an opportunity of speaking for so long a time, had not his rage deprived him of the power of utterance. It was yet some time before he could recover his speech. He at length broke out in terms of the grossest abuse, and unworthy of a great king. "Dog!" cried he, "dare you speak to me in this manner, and even to utter the name of my daughter before me! Do you imagine that the son of your sister Gulnare can enter into comparison with my daughter? Who are you? Who was your father? Who is your sister? and who is your nephew? Was not his father a dog, and the son of a cur, like yourself? Seize the insolent wretch this moment, and cut off his head!" A few officers, who were about the person of the king of Samandal, prepared immediately to obey his orders; but as King Saleh was in the full vigour of life, light and active, he escaped before they had drawn their scimitars, and gained the palace-gate, where he met a thousand men of his relations and friends, well armed and equipped, who had just arrived. The queen his mother, considering how few attendants he had taken with him, and having a presentiment of the ill reception the king of Samandal might give him, had sent off this party entreating them to proceed with the greatest diligence. Those of his relations who were at the head of the troop were much gratified at having arrived so opportunely, when they saw him approach in haste, with his people following in great disorder, and others pursuing them. "Sir," cried they, the moment he joined them, "what is the matter? We are ready to avenge you; you have only to command us." King Saleh, in a few words, informed them of the affair; when putting himself at the head of a considerable party, he left the rest in possession of the gate which they had seized, and returned back towards the palace. The few officers and guards that had pursued him being dispersed, he re-entered the apartment of the king of Samandal, who, having been abandoned by those about him, was instantly seized. King Saleh, leaving a sufficient number of his party about the king, to secure his person, then went from room to room in search of the Princess Giauhare; but this lady had, at the beginning of the confusion, accompanied by the females her attendants, darted to the surface of the sea, and escaped to a desert island.

During the time these things were passing at the palace of the King of Samandal, some of King Saleh's people, threw the queen his mother into great alarm, by informing her of the danger in which they had left him. The young King Beder, was so much the more disturbed, as he considered himself the primary cause of all the mischief which might ensue. He did not feel himself sufficiently in spirits to support the presence of the queen his grandmother, after hearing of the dilemma in which King Saleh was placed, entirely on his account; and therefore, while she was occupied in giving such orders as she judged necessary on the occasion, he darted from the bottom of the sea, and, being ignorant of the road to Persia, ascended to the same island to which the Princess Gianhare had made her escape.

The prince, in a very perturbed state of mind, seated himself at the foot of a great tree. While endeavouring to recover his spirits, he heard the sound of a voice; he arose from his seat, and advancing to the place whence the sounds came, he perceived through the foliage a beauty that dazzled him. "Without doubt," said he to himself, stopping, and considering her with admiration, "it is the Princess Giauhare, whom terror, perhaps, has compelled to abandon the palace of the king her father; but, if it be not her, she seems not less to deserve that I should love her with my whole heart." He did not pause any longer, but, discovering himself, approached the princess with a profound reverence: "Madam," said he, "I cannot sufficiently thank Heaven for the favour it has now done me, in presenting to my view so much beauty: no greater happiness could possibly befal me, than the opportunity of offering to you my most humble services." "Sir," replied the Princess Giauhare, sorrowfully, "I am a princess, daughter of the king of Samandal, and am called Giauhare. I was residing tranquilly in his palace, when suddenly I heard a dreadful noise. My people came immediately to inform me that King Saleh had forced the palace, and seized the king my father, after having laid violent hands on those of his guard who had made resistance. I had only time to save myself, and to seek in this place an asylum from his violence."

At this discourse of the princess, King Beder felt great confusion for having so abruptly quitted the queen his grandmother, without waiting the arrival of further information; but he was delighted to find that the king his uncle had rendered himself master of the king of Samandal's person not doubting that the latter, for the sake of regaining his liberty, would readily agree to his union with the princess. "Adorable princess," he replied, "your concern is just; but it is easy to put a period both to it and to the captivity of the king your father. You will certainly agree with me when you know that my name is Beder, that I am king of Persia, and that King Saleh is my uncle. I can confidently assure you that he has no intention of seizing on the dominions of the king your father; nor has he any other object in view, than to obtain for me the honour and happiness of being his son-in-law, by receiving you from

his hand. I dare hope that you will not refuse me, and that you will consider a king who has quitted his states solely to make you an offer of his love, as having some claims on your gratitude. The king your father will have no sooner given his consent to our marriage, than he will be left master of his kingdom, as before.

This declaration of King Beder did not produce the effect which he had expected from it. The princess, at the first view of him, struck with his fine figure, his air, and the grace with which he had accosted her, could not behold him without partiality. "The king my father was very wrong in so violently opposing our union. He will no sooner see you, than he will consent to render us both happy. After thus addressing him, she presented her hand, in token of friendship."

King Beder now imagined himself at the summit of human happiness. He extended his hand, and taking that of the princess, bowed forward to kiss it respectfully. The princess did not allow him time: "*Wretch!*" said she, repulsing him, and spitting in his face, for want of water, "*quit the form of a man, and take that of a white bird, with a red beak and feet.*" As soon as she had pronounced these words, King Beder, to his infinite chagrin and astonishment, was changed into a bird of that description. "Take it," continued she, to one of her women, "and convey it to the dry island." "It would be a pity," said the woman to herself, "that a prince so worthy to live should die of hunger and thirst. The princess, so kind and so gentle, will probably herself repent having given the cruel order, when she has a little recovered from her anger. It will be much better that I should carry him to some place where he may die a natural death."

Let us now return to King Saleh. After he and his people had sought in vain throughout the palace for the Princess Giauhare, he ordered the king of Samandal to be secured in his own palace, under a strong guard; when, having given the necessary orders for the government of the kingdom during his absence, he returned to the queen his mother, to inform her of his proceedings. On his arrival, he inquired after the king his nephew, and learned, with the greatest surprise and concern, that he had disappeared. "They came to inform us," said the queen, "of the great danger you were in at the palace of the king of Samandal; and while I was giving orders to send fresh troops to succour or avenge you, he disappeared. He must have been terrified at hearing of your danger, and perhaps thought himself not in safety with us." This news gave great affliction to King Saleh, who now repented of his too great facility in submitting to the wishes of King Beder, without having previously communicated the affair to Queen Gulnare. He sent in every direction to search for him; but, notwithstanding all the diligence he could use, no information concerning him could be obtained: the pleasure, therefore, he had experienced, in having so far promoted a marriage which he considered as his own work, was changed, by this unexpected event, into the most mortifying concern. In the meanwhile, till he should obtain some intelligence, good or bad, he left his kingdom under the administration of the queen his mother, and went to preside over that of the king of Samandal, whom he continued to guard with much vigilance, though with every respect due to his character.

The same day on which King Saleh departed to return to the kingdom of Samandal, Queen Gulnare, mother to King Beder, arrived at the court of the queen her mother. This princess had suffered little concern on the first day of her son's absence: she imagined that the ardour of the chase, as sometimes happened, had led him on farther than he intended. But when she found that he returned not the next, nor on the following day, she felt all those serious alarms which her maternal tenderness necessarily inspired. These alarms were greatly increased when she learned from the officers who accompanied him, and who had been obliged to return after a long and fruitless search that something disastrous must have happened to him and King Saleh, or that they were together in some place which the officers could not possibly discover; that they had even found their horses; but with respect to themselves, notwithstanding all their diligence, they could not gain the least information. The queen, on hearing their report, judged it prudent to dissemble, and conceal her affliction; and ordered them once more to pursue their former route, making the strictest inquiry possible. In the meantime she had formed her resolution; and without mentioning her intention to any person, but telling her women that she wished to be alone, she plunged into the sea, to clear up a suspicion she had formed, that King Saleh had drawn away the king of Persia with him.

This great queen would have been received by her mother with the utmost satisfaction, if she had not, the first moment she saw her, conceived the occasion of her visit. She gave her an account of the zealous manner in which King Saleh had undertaken in person to solicit the hand of the Princess Giauhare, and of what had afterwards happened, to the time of King Beder's departure; "I have sent many persons in search of him," added she; "and the king my son, who is just set off to assume the government of the kingdom of Samandal, has also used the utmost diligence on his part, but all hitherto without success; however, let us hope that we shall see him again, when we least expect it." The disconsolate Gulnare could not at first console herself with this feeble hope; she regarded the king, her dear son, as lost, and wept bitterly, imputing the whole blame to the king her brother. The queen her mother urged her to consider the necessity she was under of endeavouring to subdue in some measure, her affliction. "It is true," said she, "that the king your brother ought not to have spoken to you of this marriage with so little precaution, nor ever to have consented to bring away the king my grandson, without your previous assent; but, as it is not absolutely certain that the king of Persia has perished, you ought to neglect nothing to preserve his kingdom for him. Do not then lose time, but return to your capital. Your presence there is necessary, and you will find little difficulty in retaining all things in their present tranquil state, by reporting that the king of Persia has left his dominions merely for the purpose of paying us a visit." This argument had its full effect on Queen Gulnare. She took leave of her royal mother, and regained the palace of the capital of Persia, before even her absence had been perceived. She immediately despatched some of her people to recal the officers whom she had sent in search of the king her son, and informed them that she knew where he was, and that he would soon return. She also caused this report to be circulated through the whole city, and, in concert with the first minister and the counsel, she conducted the affairs of government with the same tranquillity as if King Beder had been present.

To return to King Beder, who was exceedingly astonished when he found himself alone, and in the form of a bird. He considered himself the more unhappy, as he knew not where he was, nor in what part of the world the kingdom of Persia was situated.

A few days afterwards, a peasant, who was very skilful in catching birds, came with his nets to the place where the king was, and was much delighted on perceiving so beautiful a bird, of a species quite unknown to him, although he had during many years followed the occupation in which he was then engaged. He employed all the address of which he was master, and took his measures so well, that he at length secured the bird. Overjoyed with his capture, which on account of its rarity, he esteemed infinitely more valuable than the birds he usually caught, he put it in a cage, and conveyed it to the city.

The king being near a window, whence he could see all that passed in the court, soon perceived the beautiful bird, and sent one of the officers of his eunuchs with orders to purchase it. The officer accosted the peasant, and inquired what price he would take for the bird: "If you want it for his majesty," replied he, "I entreat that he will allow me to make him a present of it." The officer carried the bird to the king, who found it so curious, that he desired the officer to take ten pieces of gold to the peasant, who retired perfectly content: after which the bird was put into a magnificent cage, and ordered various kinds of food, that it might choose what it most liked. As the table was already prepared, and they were serving up the repast when the king gave this order, the bird as soon as they had arranged the dishes, clapping his wings, flew upon the table, where he began to peck at the viands, at which the king was so much surprised, that he sent the officer of the eunuchs to entreat the queen to come and witness this marvellous sight, who, when she saw the bird, covered her face with her veil. The king wondered at this action—the more so

as there were only eunuchs in the chamber, with some of her women, who had followed her. " Sir," replied th
queen, "your majesty's astonishment will cease when you learn that this is not a bird, as you suppose, but a man."
" Madam," said the king, "you are without doubt, amusing yourself with me." " God forbid, sir," replied she, " that
I should deceive your majesty! Nothing is more true than what I have the honour to tell you: and I assure you
that you behold Beder, king of Persia, son of the celebrated Gulnare, princess of one of the most powerful kingdoms
of the sea, nephew of Saleh, the reigning monarch and grandson of Queen Farache, the mother of Gulnare and
of Saleh; and that it was the Princess Giauhare daughter of the king of Samandal, who thus metamorphosed
him." To remove all scepticism from the mind of his majesty, she then related to him how and why the Princess
Giauhare had so avenged herself of the ill treatment which the king of Samandal, her father, had received from
King Saleh.

The king had less difficulty in believing all that the queen related to him of this history. He had compassion on
the king of Persia, and entreated the queen with much importunity to dissolve the enchantment. The queen readily
consented: " Sir," said she to the king, " will your majesty be pleased to take the trouble of retiring to your cabinet
with the bird; and I will, in a few moments, make him appear before you in his proper form. The bird, which had
ceased eating to attend to the conversation of the king and queen, did not give his majesty the trouble of taking him;
but passed first into the cabinet, where the queen soon afterwards arrived, having in her hand a vessel full of water.
She pronounced over this vessel some words unknown to the king, till the water began to boil; she then immediately
took some in her hand, and throwing it on the bird, *"By virtue of the holy and mysterious words I have just pronounced,"* said she, *" and in the name of the Creator of heaven and earth, who revives the dead, and supports the
universe, quit the form of a bird, and resume that which you received from your Maker.',* The queen had scarcely
concluded these words, when, instead of a bird, the king saw before him a young prince of fine figure. The king then
desired that he would join him at table. After they had finished their repast, he requested to know for what reason
the Princess Giauhare could have been so inhuman as to transform into a bird so amiable a prince.—" But let us relinquish this unpleasant subject," he added, " and tell me if there be anything in which I can further serve you." " Sir,"
replied King Beder, " the obligation I am under to your majesty is so great, that I ought to remain with you during
the rest of my life: but, since you put no bounds to your generosity, may I presume to request that you will grant
me a vessel to take me back to Persia, where I fear my absence may occasion disorder; and even that the queen my
mother, may fall a sacrifice to her grief, in the painful uncertainty she must be under with regard to my fate." The
king granted his request with all the kindness imaginable, and as soon as the wind became fair, King Beder embarked,
after having thanked him for his numerous favours.

On the eleventh day from their departure, the wind augmented, and at length increased to a furious storm: the
vessel was, in consequence, not only driven out of its course, but so violently agitated by the tempest, that all its
masts at length gave way; when it struck upon a rock, and was dashed to pieces. The greater part of the crew
instantly sunk to the bottom; of the remainder, some, confiding in the strength of their arms, endeavoured to save
themselves by swimming, while others trusted to a plank or piece of the wreck. King Beder was with the latter;
and was carried about by waves and currents, till he at length perceived that he was near land, and not far from a
city of magnificent appearance.

King Beder reached the city, where he saw several handsome and spacious streets; but was much astonished at
at not meeting a single inhabitant. Proceeding, nevertheless, he observed that many shops were open, which led
him to conclude that the city was not so destitute of inhabitants as he at first imagined. He approached one of these
shops, where various fruits, displayed to much advantage, were exposed to sale, and accosted an old man, whom he found
there. The old man, who was at that moment occupied, immediately raised his head; and seeing before him a youth
of a commanding aspect, he desired to know whence he came, and what had brought him there. King Beder informed him in few words; when the old man inquired whether he had met any person in his way. " You," replied
the king, " are the first I have seen: and I cannot comprehend why so beautiful and magnificent a city as this should
be thus deserted." " Come in, remain no longer at the door," returned the old man, " lest evil befal you. At leisure,
I will satisfy you, and tell you the reason why you should take this precaution."

King Beder did not require a second invitation; he entered, and seated himself near the old man, and the latter
presented to him such food as he thought would best restore his strength; and although King Beder entreated him to explain for what reason he had urged him so earnestly to quit the street, he would not say a word till the repast was
finished. At length, when he saw that he would eat no more, " You ought to return thanks to God," said he, " that
you reached my house." " How! for what reason?" returned King Beder. " You must know," replied the old man,
" that this city is called the City of Enchantments; and that it is governed, not by a king, but by a queen. This
queen, is likewise a crafty and dangerous enchantress; of which you will be convinced, when I inform you, that all
the horses, mules, and other animals, which you may meet, were so many men, like you and me, whom, by her art, she
has thus transformed. Every handsome young man, like yourself, who enters the city, is intercepted by some of her
emissaries, who, conduct him before the queen. She receives the persons so brought in the most obliging manner
possible; regales them with dainties; lodges them well; and gives them so many reasons to believe that she is really in
love, that she rarely fails to succeed: but she does not long permit them to enjoy their imagined good fortune; for
not one, at the end of forty days, escapes being changed into some beast or bird, as suits her fancy."

This discourse very sensibly afflicted the young king of Persia: " Alas!" cried he, " scarcely am I delivered from
one enchantment, on which I look back with horror, than I see myself exposed to another still more terrible!"—This
recollection gave him occasion to relate to the old man his history more at length.

When the prince had concluded his narrative, by speaking of his good fortune in having found a queen who had destroyed the enchantment, he exhibited marks of the greatest distress, from the apprehension he entertained of falling
into a worse evil, and the old man became anxious to appease his fears: " Although," said he, " what I have told
you of the sorceress queen, and of her cruel proceedings, is perfectly true, it yet ought not to occasion the great disquietude which seems to have possessed you. I am beloved throughout this whole city, and am not unknown even to
the queen herself, who I may venture to add, has much regard for me. It is therefore a happiness for you, that your
good fortune directed you to me rather than to any other person. You are perfectly safe here, where I would advise
you, if it be agreeable, to continue."

King Beder thanked the old man for his hospitality, and for the protection he, with so much kindness, had ex-

tended to him. He seated himself at the entrance of the shop, where his youth and fine person attracted the eyes of all that passed; several of whom stopped to compliment the old man upon his having obtained so well-looking a slave, for such they supposed him to be. "Do not imagine," replied the old man, "that he is a slave; I am not, as you know, sufficiently rich, or in a condition of life, to assume such consequence: the young man is my nephew, the son of a diseased brother."

The old man was delighted to hear the praises bestowed on the young king of Persia, and he conceived for him a friendship, which, as he became better known, increased during his continuance with him. They had been living together about a month, when King Beder, sitting one day, at the entrance of the shop, saw the retinue of Queen Labe, (thus was the royal enchantress called,) approaching the house with great pomp. King Beder no sooner perceived the head of the guards that were advancing before her, than he arose, and re-entered the shop, to inquire what it signified. "The queen is going past," replied he; "but remain and fear nothing,".

The guards of Queen Labe, uniformly habited in a purple dress, marched in four files, with their scimitars drawn: they were about a thousand in number. These were followed by a like number of eunuchs, dressed in brocade. After those, as many young ladies, all of nearly equal beauty, richly dressed and ornamented with jewels, proceeded on foot, with a solemn step, having each of them a short pike in her hand; and in the midst of them appeared Queen Labe, seated on a horse glittering with diamonds, and with a saddle of gold and housings of inestimable value. The queen, struck with the fine person of King Beder, stopped. "Abdallah," (so was the old man called,) said she to him, "tell me, I beg, does this beautiful and charming slave belong to you?" Abdallah, before he replied to the queen, prostrated himself to the earth; and on rising, "Madam," he replied, "he is my nephew, the son of a brother who died not long since."

Queen Labe, who had never yet seen any person that could be compared with King Beder, and who had already conceived a very violent passion for him, was considering, after what she had heard, how she might address the old man, so as to prevail with him to give up his nephew: "My good father," returned she, "will you not do me the kindness to make me a present of him. I swear by the fire and by the light, I will make him so great and powerful that he shall enjoy a more exalted fortune than has ever fallen to the lot of mortal." "Madam," replied the good Abdallah, "I am infinitely indebted to your majesty for all your favours to me, and for the honour you wish to confer on my nephew. He is not worthy to approach so great a queen." "Abdallah," returned the queen, "I had flattered myself that your love for me was more sincere. I again swear by the fire and by the light, and even by whatever is most sacred in my religion, that I will not proceed a step farther till I have subdued your opposition. I give you my promise, that you shall not have the least cause to repent having obliged me."

Abdallah was mortified, both on his own account, and that of King Beder. "Madam," he replied, "I should be very sorry to give your majesty the least reason to harbour so ill an opinion of the respect I owe you; I place an entire reliance on your word, which you will, I doubt not, strictly keep. I only entreat you to defer bestowing on my nephew the great happiness you intend him, till you again pass this way." "That, then, will be to-morrow," answered the queen; inclining her head as she spoke, and she then resumed her road to the palace.

When Queen Labe, had passed: "My son," said the good Abdallah to King Beder, "I was not able, as you yourself witnessed, to refuse the queen what she solicited with so much earnestness. She would indeed be the most accursed being, if she deceived me: but she should not do so with impunity; I should find a means of being revenged."

These assurances appeared too vague to have much effect in tranquillising the mind of King Beder: "After all that you have told me of the wicked actions of this queen," he replied, "I will not conceal from you how much I dread approaching her. The condition to which I was reduced, through enchantment, by the Princess Giauhare, and from which it seems I have been delivered only to be brought again, almost instantly, into a similar state, makes me regard my fate with horror." "My son," said old Abdallah, "do not afflict yourself: though I confess to you, that little faith is to be put in the promises, or even the oaths, of so wicked a queen. I wish you, however, to know, that she is not able to extend her power over me: of this she is not ignorant; and it is principally for this reason that she confers on me so many marks of esteem. I well know how to prevent her doing you the least injury."

The sorceress queen did not fail, the next day, to pass by the shop of Abdallah. "My good father," said she to him, stopping, "you may judge of my impatience to have the pleasure of your nephew's company, by my punctuality in waiting upon you, to claim the performance of your promise." Abdallah, who had prostrated himself to the earth as soon as he saw the queen approaching, arose when she ceased speaking. "Most potent queen," said he, "I am persuaded that your majesty will not be offended at the unwillingness I yesterday expressed, to part with my nephew. To-day, I resign him to your majesty with perfect good will; but I entreat you to lay aside all the secrets of that wonderful science which you possess in so high a degree." "I again declare, by the same oath I took yesterday, that both you and he shall have every reason to be satisfied with my behaviour.—I clearly perceive," added she, "that you do not sufficiently know me; but if I find your nephew deserving of my friendship, I will convince you that I am not unworthy of his." While thus speaking, she exhibited to King Beder, who had attended Abdallah, her incomparable beauty; which, however, he little regarded. "It is not," said he to himself, "enough to be handsome; it is requisite that the actions should be as pure as the features are beautiful." As King Beder was making these reflections, the venerable Abdallah turned towards him, and taking him by the hand, presented him to her majesty: "Madam," said he, "I entreat that you will not forget he is my nephew; and that you will sometimes permit him to come and see me." The queen promised compliance; and, to convince him of her gratitude, presented to him a purse. She had ordered a horse as richly caparisoned as her own, to be brought for the king of Persia, and while he was putting his foot in the stirrup, "I forgot," said the queen to Abdallah, "to inquire of you your nephew's name." When he answered, "that he was called Beder."

As soon as King Beder had mounted on horseback, he was going to take his station behind the queen; but she obliged him to advance on her left hand, and desired that he would keep by her side. King Beder, instead of remarking in the countenance of the people a certain satisfaction, accompanied with respect, at the sight of their sovereign, perceived, on the contrary, that they beheld her with scorn. "The sorceress," said some, "has found a new subject on whom to exercise her malice."

The sorceress queen arrived at her palace; and, having alighted from her horse, she obliged King Beder to give her his hand; with whom, accompanied by her women and the officers of the eunuchs, she entered her splendid resi-

dence. She herself showed him all the apartments, where nothing was to be seen but massive gold, precious stones, and furniture of extraordinary magnificence. When she had conducted him into her cabinet, she advanced with him to a balcony, whence she directed his attention to a garden of enchanting beauty. King Beder praised everything he saw. They conversed on a variety of indifferent subjects, till it was announced to her majesty that dinner was ready.

The queen, and King Beder, immediately arose, and proceeded to the dining-room, and they continued to drink to the health of each other during the whole of the evening, and at length they retired to rest.

In this manner Queen Labe amused and regaled King Beder for the space of forty days. The fortieth night, while they were in bed together, believing King Beder to be asleep, she arose without making any noise; but the king, who was awake, and perceived that she had some design, feigned himself asleep. As soon as she had risen, she opened a casket, whence she drew a box full of yellow powder; she took some of this powder, and with it made a train across the chamber, which was instantly changed into a stream of transparent water, to the great astonishment of King Beder. Queen Labe took up some of the water of this stream in a vessel, and pouring it into a basin in which was some flour, made a paste, which she continued to knead for a long time: she then added to it certain drugs, from different boxes, and composed of the whole a cake, which she put into a covered baking pan. As she had been careful at first to light a good fire, she drew from it some of the burning coals, on which she placed the pan, and, on her pronouncing certain words, the stream, which was flowing in the middle of the chamber, disappeared. When the cake was sufficiently baked, she removed it, and deposited it in a closet; after which she returned to bed with King Beder.

King Beder, whom luxury and pleasure had caused to forget the good old Abdallah, his host, from the time he quitted him, now called him to remembrance and began to think, after what he had seen of Queen Labe's conduct during the night, that he had need of his counsel. As soon as he arose, he expressed to the queen a desire to visit him. "What! my dear Beder," said the queen, "are you already tired of the company of a queen." "Great queen," answered the king, "how can I be tired of the many and great favours which your majesty has had the goodness to heap upon me? Far from it, madam: I ask leave to pay this visit, rather to give an account to my uncle of the infinite obligations I owe your majesty, than to convince him that he is not forgotten." "Go," replied the queen, "I freely consent: but you will not be long ere you return."

Old Abdallah was delighted to behold King Beder again, whom, without regard to his quality, he tenderly embraced. When they were seated. "Well," said Abdallah to the king, "how do you find yourself? and how have you passed your time with that sorceress?" "Hitherto," replied King Beder, "I must own, she has shewn for me the utmost regard. But I last night observed a proceeding, which leads me to suspect that her whole conduct is guided by dissimulation." Continuing his story, he related to Abdallah how, and with what circumstances, he had seen her prepare the cake. "You are not deceived," replied old Abdallah, with a smile, which expressed that he himself never imagined she would pursue a different conduct; "nothing will ever produce amendment in this perfidious woman: but do not fear, I know a way to make the evil, which she intends to inflict upon you, recoil on herself. As she never retains her lovers more than forty days, and, instead of dismissing them in a handsome manner, changes them into so many animals, with which she furnishes her forests, parks, and the country in general I yesterday took measures to prevent her treating you in the same manner." Abdallah, on concluding these words, put into the hands of King Beder two cakes, which he desired him to preserve, and to use them as he was going to direct: "You have told me," continued he, "that last night the sorceress prepared a cake: be assured she intends you to eat of it; but take particular care not to taste it. Nevertheless, take some; but instead of putting it in your mouth, secretly break one of those I have given you, and eat instead of it. As soon as she believes you have swallowed a portion of your cake, she will not fail to attempt transforming you into some animal; when, not succeeding in her design, she will endeavour to turn into pleasantry, as if she were only in jest, and designed to put you little in fear, while she will in her heart be extremely chagrined. With respect to the cake you will have remaining, make her a present of it, and press her to eat it: she will immediately comply, though it be only to show her confidence in you. When she has eaten some of it, take a little water in the hollow of your hand, and throwing it in her face, say to her, quit your present form and take that of ———, adding the name of what animal you please, then bring the animal to me, and I will instruct you how to proceed."

King Beder signified to the old man, in the most expressive terms, how much he felt obliged for the interest he took in hindering so dangerous a sorceress from exercising her wicked power against him; and after conversing together for a short time, King Beder quitted Abdallah, and returned to the palace. He went to seek the queen, and she no sooner saw him, than she approached with extreme eagernesss: "My dear Beder," said she, "nothing is more true, than that the absence of an adored object best discovers the force and excess of love." "Madam," replied King Beder, "I can assure your majesty that my impatience to see you has been at least equal. I have been contented to bring you a single cake." King Beder, who had wrapped up one of the two cakes in a clean handkerchief, which he unfolded, then presenting it to the queen, added, "This is the cake, madam, I entreat you to accept of it." "With all my heart," said the queen, taking it; "but I wish that you should first oblige me, by eating of this, which I have made during your absence." "Beautiful queen," returned King Beder, "from your majesty's hands nothing can be produced but what is excellent." King Beder substituted, in the room of the cake the queen had produced, the other he had received from Abdallah, of which he broke off a piece, and conveyed it to his mouth. "Ah, queen!" he exclaimed, "I never tasted anything so exquisite!" As they were near a fountain, the sorceress, who perceived that he had swallowed the piece, took up some water in the hollow of her hand, and throwing it in his face, "wretch!" said she, "quit the form of a man, and take that of a miserable horse, one-eyed and lame!"

These words produced no effect, to the great astonishment of the sorceress, who saw before her King Beder remaining in the same state. The colour flew into her cheeks; "My dear Beder," said she, "do not be alarmed; I had no intention to injure you: I only wished to see how you would be affected. Judge for yourself whether I should not be the most abandoned and execrable of women, if I could be guilty of so base an action." "Most potent queen," replied King Beder, "however persuaded I may be that your majesty merely intended to divert yourself, I could not, nevertheless, wholly guard myself from surprise. Do me the favour now to taste of my cake." Queen Labe, who had no better way of justifying herself, than by thus showing her confidence in the King of Persia, broke off a small piece of the cake, and ate it. As soon as she had swallowed it, she appeared exceedingly troubled, and became as it were, immoveable. King Beder lost not a moment; he took some water from the same fountain, and throwing it in her face, "*Abominable enchantress!*" he exclaimed, "*depart from your present form, and assume that of a mare!*"

At the same instant, Queen Labe became transformed into a very handsome mare; and so great was her confusion and sorrow at seeing herself metamorphosed, that she shed abundance of tears. He led the mare to the stable of the palace, where he put her into the hands of a groom to saddle and bridle her; but, of all the bridles which the groom tried, not one was found that would answer. He then ordered two horses to be equipped, one for himself and one for the groom, whom he commanded to follow him to the house of Abdallah, leading the mare in hand. Abdallah, perceived at a distance King Beder and the mare: "Cursed sorceress!" said he to himself at the same time, with great satisfaction, "Heaven has at length chastised you as you deserve." King Beder alighted on his arrival, and entered the shop of Abdallah. He related to him in what manner everything had passed, and observed, that he could find no bridle to suit the mare. Abdallah, who had one of every sort, bridled the mare himself; and as soon as King Beder had sent away the groom with the two horses, "Sir," said he, "you have no occasion to remain any longer in this city; mount the mare, and return to your kingdom. The only thing I have to recommend you is, that, in case you are disposed to part with the mare you take particular care to give her up with the bridle on her." King Beder promised that he would not forget; and he departed.

Three days after his departure, he arrived at a large city; and passing through the suburbs, was met by an old man of consideration, who was going to his country-house. "Sir," said the old man, "may I presume to ask whence you come?" The king likewise stopped; and while the old man proceeded with several more questions, an elderly woman approached, who advancing up to them, and looking at the mare, began to weep.

King Beder and the old man ceased their conversation, and King Beder inquired the occasion of her grief: "Sir," said she, "your mare so perfectly resembles one lately belonging to my son, and which, for his sake, I yet regret, that I should believe her to be the same, were his still alive. Sell her to me, I entreat you." "My good mother," replied King Beder, "I am very sorry it is not in my power to grant your request. "Ah, sir!" urged the old woman, "I beseech you, in the name of God, not to refuse me." "My good mother," replied King Beder, "I should agree to it very willingly, if I had an intention to part with so valuable a mare; I certainly would not dispose of her for less than a thousand pieces." "Why not give it?" returned the old woman: "I am ready to pay the money." King Beder, who saw that the old woman was dressed very meanly, could not imagine that she was in circumstances to raise so large a sum. To prove, therefore, if she could conclude the bargain, "Give me the money," said he, "and the mare is yours." Immediately the old woman untied a purse, and presenting it to him, "Take the trouble to alight," said she, "that we may reckon whether the sum is here If it be not, I can very soon provide the rest." The astonishment of King Beder, when he saw the purse, was extreme: "My good mother," said he, "do not you perceive that I have been merely joking?" The old man, who had witnessed the whole conversation, then spoke: "My son," said he to King Beder, "it is necessary that you should be made acquainted with a matter of which I find you are ignorant:—it is not permitted in this city to use falsehood on any occasion whatever, under pain of death. Therefore, you must take this good woman's money and give up your mare."

King Beder, much afflicted at having thus inconsiderately involved himself in so disagreeable an affair, descended from his mare with great regret. The old woman was instantly ready to seize the bridle and strip it off; and, if possible, yet more alert in taking some water in her hand from a stream that flowed in the middle of the street, which she threw on the mare, pronouncing at the same time these words: "*My daughter, quit this strange form, and resume your own.*" The change was instantaneously made; and King Beder, who swooned at the reappearance of Queen Labe before him, would have fallen to the ground, if the old man had not supported him.

The old woman, who was the mother of Queen Labe, and had been instructed by her in all the secrets of magic, had no sooner expressed her joy, by embracing her daughter, than she summoned, by whistling, a hideous geni, of gigantic stature. The geni immediately took King Beder upon one arm, while he embraced the old woman and the sorceress queen with the other, and in a few moments transported them to the palace of Queen Labe, in the City of Enchantments. When the queen had regained her palace, she furiously reproached King Beder: "Ungrateful wretch!" said she, "is it thus that your unworthy uncle and you give proofs of your gratitude, after all that I have done for you?" She ceased speaking, and, taking some water in her hand, threw it upon his face, "*Quit your present form,*" said she, "*and take that of an ugly owl.*" The words were followed by their effect; and she immediately commanded one of her woman to confine the animal in a cage, and to give it nothing to eat or drink. The woman took the cage; but without regarding the commands of the queen, placed it both food and water; and being attached to old Abdallah, she sent secretly to inform him of the queen's treatment of his nephew.

Abdallah saw that he could no longer keep terms with Queen Labe. He had only to whistle in a particular manner, and an enormous geni with four wings appeared before him. "Lightning," (thus was the geni called,) "it is our present business," said Abdallah, "to preserve the life of King Beder. Go to the palace of the sorceress, and transport instantly to the capital of Persia the compassionate woman to whom she has given the cage in charge, that she may inform Queen Gulnare of the danger to which her son is exposed. Lightning disappeared, and at the same instant arrived at the palace of the sorceress. He instructed the woman as he had been ordered, and raising her in the air transported her to the capital of Persia, where he placed her on a terraced roof which communicated with the apartment of Queen Gulnare. The woman descended the staircase which led to this apartment, where she found Queen Gulnare, and Queen Farache her mother. She saluted them with profound reverence; and by her recital convinced them of the urgent necessity for affording King Beder succour.

King Saleh her brother assembled an army. He called also to his assistance the genii his allies, who appeared with another army more numerous than his own. When the two armies had joined, he placed himself at their head with Queen Farache, Queen Gulnare, and the princess, who were desirous to partake of the action. They mounted in the

air, and very soon descended on the palace, and on the City of Enchantments, where the sorceress queen, her mother, and all the worshippers of fire, were instantaneously destroyed. Queen Gulnare had ordered that Queen Labe's woman who conveyed the news of her son's transformation and imprisonment, should attend her : and whom she strictly charged to have no other care in the confusion, than to secure the cage and bring it to her. The queen opened the cage herself, and drew thence the owl, on which she threw some water, which she had commanded to be brought. "*My dear son*," said she, "*quit this strange form, and resume that of a man, your natural figure.*" In the same moment the hideous owl disappeared; and the queen saw King Beder her son, whom she immediately embraced with an excess of joy.

The first care of Queen Gulnare was to make inquiry after old Abdallah. As soon as he was conducted to her, "The obligation I am under to you," said she, "is so great, that there is nothing I am not ready to do." "Great queen," he replied, "if the lady whom I sent to your majesty will consent to accept in marriage him who now offers himself to her, and the king of Persia will permit me to remain at his court, I will, with my whole heart, devote the remainder of my life to his service." Queen Gulnare immediately turned towards the lady, who was present; and her modest blushes expressing how little repugnance she felt at the proposal, the queen joined their hands together.

This marriage occasioned the King of Persia thus to address himself to the queen his mother : "Madam," said he smiling, "I am delighted with the marriage you have just concluded; there is, however, another which demands your attention." Queen Gulnare did not immediately comprehend to what marriage he alluded; but having reflected for a moment, she conceived his meaning. "My son," replied Queen Gulnare, "if there be in the world no one but the Princess Giauhare who can render you happy, and she be agreeable, it is not my intention to oppose your union. The king your uncle has only to bring the king of Samandal hither, and we shall soon learn whether he remain as intractable as before."

King Saleh ordered a chafing-dish, containing fire, to be brought him, upon which he threw a certain composition pronouncing at the same time some mysterious words. As soon as the smoke began to ascend, the whole palace shook, when the king of Samandal, with the officers of king Saleh who attended him, appeared. The king of Persia immediately threw himself at his feet, and remained with his knee on the ground. "Sir," said he, "it is no longer King Saleh who solicits your majesty to honour the king of Persia with your alliance." The king of Samandal no longer suffered the king of Persia to continue at his feet. "Sir," said he, "I should be very sorry to contribute in the least to the death of so worthy a monarch." On concluding these words, he charged one of his own officers, that by King Saleh's desire had remained about his person, to go in search of the princess, and instantly to bring her to them.

The Princess Giauhare had not quitted the island where the king of Persia met with her : the officer found her there, and soon returned, accompanied by her and her woman.

The nuptials were celebrated in the palace of the City of Enchantments, with so much the greater pomp, as all the lovers of the sorceress queen, who had regained their proper form at the moment of her death, and who had come to return their thanks to the king of Persia, Queen Gulnare, and King Saleh, attended on the occasion. They were all sons of kings, princes, or persons of very high quality.

THE HISTORY OF GANEM, OR THE SLAVE OF LOVE, SON OF ABOU AIBOU.

 HERE lived formerly at Damascus a merchant, who, by his industry and attention to business, had acquired great wealth, on which he lived very honourably. Abou Aibou, for that was his name, had a son and a daughter. The son was originally called Ganem, but afterwards surnamed the Slave of Love. The daughter was named Alcolomb, signifying the Vanquisher of Hearts, because her beauty was so captivating. that all who saw her were enamoured with her charms.

Abou Aibou died, leaving immense riches.

At that time, Mohammed, surnamed Zinebi, the son of Soliman, reigned at Damascus, the capital of Syria. His relation, Haroun Alraschid, who resided at Bagdad, had bestowed upon him his tributary kingdom.

Shortly after the death of Abou Aibou, Ganem was conversing with his mother on the affairs of their family, when the goods in the warehouse being mentioned, he asked her the meaning of the writing which he observed on each bale: "My son," replied his mother, "as your father travelled into various provinces, it was his custom, before his departure, to write upon each bale the name of the place to which he purposed to go. He had arranged everything for his journey to Bagdad, and was ready to set off when death———." Ganem could not see his mother affected without experiencing a reciprocal feeling. But at length Ganem recovered himself: "Since my father destined this merchandise for Bagdad, and has not been permitted to execute his design, I will prepare to take the journey." "My son," replied she, "I cannot but applaud your anxiety to imitate your father; but consider your youth and inexperience, and how entirely unaccustomed you are to the fatigue of long journeys. Is it not better to dispose of these goods to the merchants of Damascus, and content ourselves with a moderate profit."

He went to the market at which slaves were sold, and purchased some of the most robust; having hired a hundred camels, and being provided with everything necessary, he at length set off with five or six merchants of Damascus, who were going to trade at Bagdad.

These merchants, followed by all their slaves, and accompanied by several other travellers, formed so large a caravan, that they were under no apprehensions from the Bedouins. They came in sight of the city of Bagdad, where they arrived in perfect safety. They alighted at the most magnificent and best frequented khan in the city; but Ganem, who wished to be lodged more privately and commodiously, did not take up his abode there, and hired, in the neighbourhood, a very handsome house.

Some days after this young merchant had established himself in his house, he dressed himself very neatly, and attended the public place where the merchants assembled to buy and sell. He was followed by a slave, who carried a parcel containing several pieces of rich stuffs and fine linens. The merchants received Ganem with much civility; and their chief, or syndic, to whom he first addressed himself, bought his whole parcel. Ganem continued his traffic with so much success, that he sold every day whatever merchandise he exposed. One bale only remained, which he had ordered to be taken out of the warehouse, and carried to his own home. When he one day attended the public market, he found all the shops shut, which appeared to him very extraordinary: on inquiring the cause, he was told that one of the principal merchants, who was not unknown to him, was dead.

It was nearly night before all the ceremonies were finished. Ganem, who had not expected they would occupy so long a time, began to be uneasy: and his inquietude augmented, when he saw them serving a repast in honour of the deceased, according to the custom of Bagdad. He was also told that the tents had been pitched, not merely to guard against the heat of the sun, but to protect them from the night-damp, as they were not to return to the city till the next morning. This account alarmed him: "I am a stranger," said he to himself, "and I am accounted rich: thieves may take advantage of my absence, and pillage my house." Fully occupied by these reflections, he hastily ate a few morsels, and stole away from the company. He set out with the utmost diligence. To complete his misfortune, he found the city gate shut: he was now obliged to search for some place where he might pass the remainder of the night. He entered a cemetery, so extensive, that it reached from the city to the place he had just quitted; and advancing, he came to some high walls, that surrounded a small field. being the private burying-ground of a particular family, and in which was a palm-tree. There were a great many other private cemeteries, the doors of which had not been carefully secured. Finding that open where he had seen the palm-tree, Ganem entered. After walking several times backward and forward before the door, he opened it, without any particular motive, and immediately perceived at a distance, a light which seemed to approach. Alarmed at the sight, he quickly closed the door again, which was only confined by a latch, and hastily ascended the palm-tree, which, in his agitation, appeared to be the most secure asylum he could find. He was no sooner in the tree, than he saw, by means of the light which had terrified him, three men, whom he knew by their dress to be slaves, enter the burying ground. One of them walked before with a lantern, and the two others followed, with a chest about five or six feet long. "Brothers," said one, "I would advise that we leave the chest here, and return to the city." "No, no," replied another, "the orders of our mistress will not be properly executed in this manner: let us bury the chest, since she has commanded it." The other slaves consented; having made a deep hole, they put in the chest, and covered it with the earth. They then left the burying-ground.

Ganem, who had heard, from the top of the palm-tree, the slaves' conversation, knew not what to think of this adventure. He imagined that the chest must contain something very precious. He descended the palm-tree. The departure of the slaves had relieved him from his fears. He began to work at the place, and so well employed his hands and feet, that he soon uncovered the chest; but he found it fastened by a large padlock. Nevertheless, he was not discouraged; and the light, now beginning to appear, enabled him to discover several large flints, which were lying about. He chose one of them, with which he had little difficulty in forcing the padlock. Then he opened the chest, but, instead of finding money in it, as he expected, Ganem was inexpressibly surprised at beholding a young lady of incomparable beauty. By the fresh and beautiful bloom on her cheeks, and still more by her soft and regular respiration, he discovered her to be alive, but he could not comprehend the reason of her not waking, if she were only asleep. She was magnificently dressed, with bracelets and ear-rings of diamonds, and a necklace of the largest and finest pearls. His first care was to shut the door of the burying-ground; he then returned to the lady, took her in his arms, and lifting her out of the chest, laid her upon the earth. The lady was scarcely in this situation, and exposed to the open air, before she sneezed; and, by a slight effort she made in turning her head, a liquid flowed from her mouth, with which it appeared her stomach was oppressed; then, half opening her eyes, and rubbing them, she cried, "Zohorob, Bastan, Schagrom Marglan, Cassabos, Souccar, Nourounihar, Nagmatos Sobi, Nouzhetos Zaman, speak, where are you?" These were the names of the female slaves who usually attended her. She at length opened her eyes, and, finding herself in a cemetery, was seized with terror.

Ganem was unwilling to leave the lady any longer in this state of disquietude. He immediately presented himself before her, with all possible respect and politeness. To inspire the lady with confidence in him, he first told her who he was, and by what accident he had entered the cemetery. He afterwards gave her an account of the arrival of the three slaves, and of the manner in which they had buried the chest. The lady, who had covered her face with a veil the instant Ganem appeared before her, was greatly affected when she learned the extent of her obligation to him. "I thank God," said she, "for having sent so worthy a person as yourself, to deliver me from death. Go, I beseech you to the town, and find a muleteer, who may come and convey me, concealed in this chest, on a mule to your house. When I am in your house, you shall hear my whole history." The young merchant, before he quitted the lady, drew the chest from the hole, in which it had been left, and which he again filled up with the earth. He then replaced the lady in the chest, and closed it in such a manner as to make it appear as if the padlock were still secure; but, for fear she might be suffocated, he did not shut the chest so close as to prevent an admission of air. On leaving the burying-ground, he closed the door after him; and, the city-gate being opened, he soon found what he sought. He returned to the cemetery, where he assisted the muleteer in placing the chest across his mule; and, to remove any suspicion he might entertain, told him that he had arrived late in the night with another muleteer, who, being in haste to go back, had left the chest in the burying-ground.

His joy was extreme, when, fortunately reaching his own house, he saw the chest safely deposited. He opened the chest, and assisted the lady out of it, when, presenting her his hand, he conducted her to his apartment, lamenting how much she must have suffered in so close an imprisonment. "I am well recompensed," said she to him, "for all I have encountered, by your kindness."

She sat down on a sofa, and, as an earnest to the merchant of her sense of the great services he had rendered her, took off her veil. Whatever might be her obligation to him, he thought himself more than rewarded by so singular an honour. Supposing that she must be in need of refreshment, and not choosing to trust any one to provide for so charming a guest, he himself went, followed by a slave, to order a repast from a neighbouring tavern; and, after they had eaten some trifles, Ganem, remarking that the lady's veil, which she had placed near her on the sofa, was embroidered at the edge with letters of gold, asked permission to look at it. The lady took up the veil immediately, and, presenting it to him, inquired if he could read, "Madam," replied he, modestly, "a merchant would badly conduct

his affairs, if he did not, at least, know how to read and write." "Well, then," said she, "read the sentence that is written upon this veil. It will offer an occasion for me to relate to you my history." Ganem took the veil, and read these words : "I AM YOURS, AND YOU ARE MINE, O DESCENDANT OF THE PROPHET'S UNCLE!" This descendant of the uncle of the prophet, was the Caliph Haroun Alraschid, the then reigning monarch, who was descended from Abbas the uncle of Mahomet.

When Ganem had comprehended the meaning of these words, "Ah, madam," he exclaimed in a melancholy tone, " I have been the means of preserving your life, and this writing will prove my death. I do not quite understand the mystery; but, I too clearly perceive that I am the most unhappy of men." He could not utter these words without shedding tears. The lady was affected by them. She, however, disguised her feelings; and, as if she had not attended to Ganem's discourse, " I should have been very cautious," replied she, " in showing you my veil, if I had thought it could cause you so much uneasiness.

" You must know, then," continued she, "that I am called Fetnab. You can scarcely be unacquainted with this name, since there is no person in Bagdad who does not know that the Caliph Haroun Alraschid, my sovereign master and yours, has a favourite so called. I was brought to his palace in my infancy. I was not deficient in acquiring those accomplishments which they were at the pains to learn me ; and my capacity, joined to some share of beauty, gained me the friendship of the caliph. The prince did not confine himself to this mark of distinction. He appointed twenty women, and as many eunuchs, to attend on me. Hence, you will readily imagine, that Zobeide, the wife and relation of the caliph, could not behold my good fortune without jealousy. Hitherto, I had successfully guarded against her snares ; but I have at length fallen under this last effort of her jealousy, and, but for you, should have been at this moment awaiting inevitable death. Zobeide, the better to execute her wicked design, has taken advantage of the absence of the caliph, who quitted the palace a few days since, to put himself at the head of his troops. Without this opportunity my rival, furious as she is, would not have ventured to undertake anything against my life. You are yourself interested in not disclosing my adventure ; for, were Zobeide to learn the obligation I owe to you, she would punish you for having preserved me. A the return of the caliph, I shall have less occasion for caution "

As soon as the beautiful favourite of Haroun Alraschid had ceased to speak, "Madam," said he, "I return you a thousand thanks for having given me the information I took the liberty of requesting. I well know, and I shall never forget it, that *what belongs to the master is forbidden to the slave*. I wish that your august, and too-happy lover, may revenge the malignity of Zobeide by recalling you to his presence ; and, when you are restored to his wishes, that you may sometimes think o the unfortunate Ganem."

Fortunately for them both, some one at this moment knocked at the door. Ganem arose to see who it might be, and found it was one of his slaves, who came to announce to him the arrival of the master of the tavern.

When the female slaves had retired to an adjoining apartment, into which the young merchant had sent them, he sat down on the same sofa with Fetnab. He again turned the conversation on his passion, and made many affecting remarks in regard to the invincible obstacles which bereft him of all hope. " I dare not flatter myself," said he, " that you have not observed with indifference the excess of my passion." "My lord," replied Fetnab—— " Ah, madam," interrupted Ganem, " this is the second time you have done me the honour to address me with that appellation. In the name of God, madam, do not show me a respect to which I have no claim." "No, no," interrupted Fetnab, in her turn, " I shall be cautious of treating thus a man to whom I owe my life ; and I will confess to you that I do not see with an eye of indifference the attentions you have shown me."

Night approaching, he arose to fetch a light, which he brought himself, together with a collation, according to the custom in Bagdad. They both placed themselves at table. The excellence of the wine insensibly led them to drink ; and they had no sooner taken two or three cups each, than they agreed to drink no more without previously singing an air. The repast was of long continuance ; and the night was already far advanced before they thought of separating. Ganem then retired to another apartment, and left Fetnab in that she already occupied, where the female slaves he had purchased entered to attend her.

While Fetnab, snatched as it were, from the jaws of death, passed the time so agreeably with Ganem, Zobeide was not free from embarrassment, in the palace of Haroun Alraschid. The three slaves, the ministers of her vengeance had no sooner conveyed away the chest, ignorant of what it contained, than a thousand importunate reflections disturbed her repose. " My husband," she said, "loves Fetnab more than he has ever loved any of his favourites. What shall I say to him on his return, when he asks for her?"

She had with her an old lady, who had attended her from her earliest infancy ; and after having confided her secret to her, "My good mother," said she, "you have always assisted me with your excellent advice ; if ever it were necessary to me, it is on the present occasion." "My dear mistress," replied the old lady, " it would have been much better had you not brought yourself into this embarrassment; but as the affair has taken place, we must say no more about it, and only think of some artifice to deceive the commander of the faithful. I am of opinion that you should immediately get a piece of wood carved to look like a corse : we will wrap it up in some old linen ; and, after having enclosed it in a coffin, will order it to be buried in some place belonging to the palace ; then without the least loss of time, you must cause a marble mausoleum, in the form of a dome, to be erected over the place of burial, and also an effigy to be raised covered over with black cloth, and surrounded with chandeliers and large wax lights. You must go into mourning, and order your own women, with those of Fetnab, to do the same. When the caliph returns, and finds the whole palace in mourning, and yourself also, he will not fail to ask the reason of it. You will then have an opportunity of recommending yourself by saying, that from respect to him, you were anxious to render the last offices to Fetnab. As his passion for her was most ardent, he will no doubt go and shed tears over her grave. He will then feel himself much obliged to you for what you have done and will express his gratitude. Do you, madam, order the woman who gave Fetnab her lemonade last night, to tell her companions that she has just found her mistress dead in her bed ; and that they may only lament her, without wishing to enter the chamber ; let her add that she has informed you of the event, and that you have already commanded Mesrour to prepare for her immediate interment."

The wooden image was prepared with all the diligence Zobeide could wish, and conveyed by the old lady herself into the apartment of Fetnab, where she attired it like a corse, and placed it in a coffin. Then Mesrour, who was himself deceived, ordered the coffin, and the figure representing Fetnab, to be carried away; and they were buried, with the customary ceremonies. The same day Zobeide sent for the architect of the palace and various mansions belonging to the caliph; and the mausoleum was very soon finished.

Ganem was one of the last to hear of Fetnab's death; for, as before mentioned, he scarcely ever went from home; he was, however, at length informed of it. "Madam," said he to the beautiful favorite of the caliph, "your death is generally believed in Bagdad; and I doubt not but Zobeide is herself perfectly persuaded that the belief is well founded. Would to God that, taking advantage of this false report, you were willing to unite your fate with mine, and going far from hence, to reign solely in my heart! But would you accompany me, ought I consent to it? No! it must be my duty constantly to remember, that *what belongs to the master is forbidden to the slave.*"

The amiable Fetnab assumed sufficient command over herself merely to reply: "My lord, we cannot hinder the triumph of Zobeide. The caliph will ere long return, and we shall find means privately to inform him of all that has passed."

At the end of three months the caliph re-entered Bagdad, having vanquished all his enemies. Impatient to

return to Fetnab, he proceeded to his palace; but how great was his astonishment at seeing all the officers he had left behind him clothed in mourning! He shuddered involuntarily at the sight; when, on reaching the apartment of Zobeide, he perceived that princess, as well as her women, habited in the same manner. He instantly asked the reason of this melancholy appearance. "Commander of the faithful," answered Zobeide, "I have taken this dress for your slave Fetnab." She would have proceeded, but the caliph did not allow her time; he was so much affected at the intelligence that he uttered a shriek, and fell senseless into the arms of his vizier Giafar. He, however, soon recovered, and desired to know where his dear Fetnab had been buried. "My lord," replied Zobeide, "I have myself taken care of the funeral; I have caused a marble mausoleum to be erected at the place of her interment. I will conduct you thither, if you wish it." The caliph did not choose to give Zobeide the trouble, and was satisfied with the attendance of Mesrour. He went thither in his military habit, without delaying to make any alteration in his dress. When he saw the effigy covered with black cloth, the tapers burning round it, and the magnificence of the monument, he was astonished that Zobeide should have performed the obsequies of her rival with so much pomp; and, as he was naturally suspicious, began to distrust the generosity of his wife. In order to satisfy himself of the truth, the prince ordered the effigy to be taken down, and the grave and coffin to be opened in his presence; but, when he saw the linen which enveloped the piece of wood, he did not dare to proceed any further. No longer doubting the death of Fetnab, he ordered the coffin to be reclosed, the grave to be filled up, and the effigy to be placed in the situation it before stood.

The caliph, judging it necessary to pay some tribute of respect at the tomb of his favourite, sent for the ministers of religion, those of the palace, and the readers of the Koran; and during the time they were assembling, he remained in the mausoleum. When all the ministers whom he had summoned were arrived, he placed himself at the head of the effigy, and they, ranging themselves around it, recited long prayers. The same ceremony was repeated every day for a month.

On the last day of the month, the prayers and reading of the Koran continued from morning till day break on the following day; when, the whole being finished, every one returned to his own house. Haroun Alraschid, fatigued by watching so long, went to rest himself in his apartment, and fell asleep upon a sofa, between two of the ladies of his palace. She who sat at the head, and who was called Nouronnihar, perceiving the caliph to be asleep, said in a low voice, "Nagmatos Sobi, there is great news. The commander of the faithful will be delighted when he wakes and hears what I have to communicate. Fetnab is not dead; she is in perfect health." "Heavens!" cried Nagmatos Sobi, "is it possible that the beautiful Fetnab be still alive?" Nagmatos Sobi spoke these words in so loud a voice, that the caliph awoke. "Ah, my lord," replied Nagmatos Sobi, "pardon my indiscretion, I could not hear without emotion that Fetnab still lives." "How!—what, then, is become of her?" said the caliph. "Commander of the faithful," replied Nouronnihar, "I have received this evening a note without a signature, but in the handwriting of Fetnab, giving an account of her melancholy adventure, and desiring me to inform you of it." "Give me—give me the note," interrupted the caliph, with great earnestness. Nouronnihar immediately presented the note to him. Fetnab had detailed all that had happened to her, but enlarged a little too much on the attentions she had received from Ganem. The caliph, naturally jealous, instead of being moved by the inhumanity of Zobeide, was only sensible to the infidelity of which he imagined Fetnab to have been guilty. "What!" said he, "after having lived four months with a young merchant, has the perfidious wretch the effrontery to boast of his attentions to her? Ungrateful creature! while I was consuming whole days in lamenting her, she passed them in betraying me. I will revenge myself on the faithless wretch, and on the presumptuous youth who has dared to injure me." The prince arose as he concluded these words. The hall-door being opened, the couriers, who were waiting for admission, immediately entered. The grand-vizier Giafar approached and prostrated himself before the throne; he then rose, and stood before his master, who, in a tone which demanded prompt obedience, said, "Giafar, your presence is necessary in the execution of an important commission. Take with you four hundred men of my guards; and having informed yourself where a merchant of Damascus, called Ganem, the son of Abou Aibou, resides, rase his house to the ground; but first seize Ganem, and bring him hither, with Fetnab my slave, who has been living with him these four months."

The grand-vizier put his hand on his head, to signify that he would rather lose it than be remiss in his duty. His first care was to send to the syndic of the merchants who dealt in foreign silks or fine cloths, to inform himself of the house and street in which Ganem lived. The officer to whom this order was given soon returned with an account that for some months Ganem had scarcely ever made his appearance. The same officer also informed Giafar of the situation of Ganem's house, and of the widow's name of whom he had hired it. Having gained this intelligence, the minister, at the head of the soldiers, began his march; he went to the house of the police-judge, whom he desired to accompany him, and then, followed by a great number of masons and carpenters, furnished with the necessary implements for demolishing buildings, he arrived before Ganem's house. He commanded the soldiers to surround it.

Fetnab and Ganem were just finishing their dinner. The lady was seated near the window, which opened towards the street, and hearing a noise, she looked through the lattice; when seeing the grand-vizier approaching with his train, she conjectured there was some design against Ganem, as well as herself. She was persuaded that her note had been received, but she little expected such an answer. She knew not that the prince had been so long returned; and therefore experienced, though aware of his disposition to jealousy, no apprehension on that account. With regard to Ganem, whom she loved less through gratitude than from inclination, she foresaw that his irritated rival would probably see him, and then condemn him to death. Full of this idea, she turned towards the young merchant. "Ah, Ganem," said she, "we are ruined! They are in search of us. There is no time to be lost. If you love me, quickly put on the dress of one of your slaves, and rub your face and arms with soot; then place one of these dishes upon your head, and they will take you for the waiter from the tavern, and will let you pass." The young merchant was so much afflicted, that he knew not on what to determine; and would doubtless have suffered himself to be surprised by the caliph's soldiers, had not Fetnab pressed him to disguise himself. He submitted to her entreaties; and having put on a slave's dress, besmeared himself with soot; he was barely in time, for a knocking was now heard at the door. Ganem went out with some dishes on his head, and being taken for the waiter of the tavern, was allowed to pass without interruption.

While, by this stratagem, Ganem was flying from the pursuit of the grand-vizier Giafar, that minister entered the apartment of Fetnab, whom he found seated on a sofa, and where there was also a great number of chests full of merchandise belonging to Ganem, and money which he had made by the sale of his goods. Fetnab prostrated herself with her face to the ground; and remained in that posture, as if prepared to receive the stroke of death. "My lord," said she, "I am ready to submit to the sentence that the commander of the faithful has pronounced against me; you have only to declare it." "Madam," replied Giafar, "God forbid that any person should dare to touch you with profane hands! I have no design to occasion you the least displeasure; my orders are merely to request you to accompany me to the palace, and to conduct you thither with the merchant who inhabits this house." "My lord," said the favourite, rising, "let us depart; I am ready to attend you. With regard to the young merchant, to whom I owe my life, he is not here; nearly a month has elapsed since he set out for Damascus, whither his affairs called him; and he has left me the care of the chests, you see, till his return. I beseech you to permit them to be carried to the palace, and to give orders that they may be put in a place of safety, that I may keep the promise I have made, of preserving them with all possible attention." "You shall be obeyed, madam," replied Giafar, and he immediately sent for some porters, whom he directed to take up the chests, and to carry them to Mesrour. As soon as the porters were gone, he whispered to the police-judge, and commissioned him to see that the house was completely rased to the ground; but not till a thorough search had first been made after Ganem, whom he suspected to be still concealed in it, notwithstanding what Fetnab had said. He then set out on his return, and conducted with him the young lady, followed by the two female slaves who had attended her.

"Well," said Haroun Alraschid, when he saw him enter his cabinet, "have you executed my orders?" "Yes, my lord," replied Giafar; "the house which Ganem inhabited is levelled with the ground, and I have conducted hither your favourite Fetnab; she is at the door of your apartment, and I will bring her in, if you please to order me. The young merchant could nowhere be found, though the strictest search was made for him." Never did rage equal that of the caliph, when he learned that Ganem had escaped him. With regard to his favourite, persuaded that she had been unfaithful to him, he would neither see nor speak to her. "Mesrour," said he to the chief of the eunuchs, "take away the ungrateful Fetnab, and shut her up in the dark tower." This tower was within the enclosure of the palace, and usually served as a prison for those favourites who had offended the caliph. Mesrour, though accustomed to execute every order of his master, however violent, without reply, obeyed this with regret. He expressed his sorrow to Fetnab, who was the more afflicted, as she had persuaded herself that the caliph would not refuse to speak with her. But she was compelled to submit to her sad destiny; and following Mesrour, he conducted her to the dark tower.

In the meantime, the enraged caliph dismissed his grand-vizier; and, attending only to the suggestions of his passion, wrote with his own hand a letter to the king of Syria, his cousin, and who was tributary to him at Damascus, for the arrest of Ganem.

The caliph's messenger travelled night and day, to gratify the impatience of his master; and when he arrived at Damascus, he proceeded immediately to the palace of Zinebi, who received the caliph's letter seated on his throne. The courier presented it to the king, who immediately recognising the writing, he arose from his seat, as a mark of respect, kissing the letter, and putting it to his head, to signify that he was ready to execute, with all submission, whatever order it might contain. He opened it; and having read it, descended from his throne, and mounted his horse without delay, attended by the principal officers of his household. He also sent the police-judge, who came to him; and, followed by his own guard, proceeded to Ganem's house.

When King Mohammed Zinebi knocked at the door, a female slave having opened it, he hastily entered, asking for Ganem, the son of Abou Aibou.

"My lord," replied she, "Ganem, whom you inquire for, is dead. My mistress is now at his tomb, which you see before you, lamenting his loss." The king ordered his guards to make strict search for Ganem throughout the house. He then advanced himself towards the tomb, where he beheld the mother and daughter, seated upon a mat, their countenances bathed in tears. As soon as he perceived a man at the door of the building, these unfortunate women covered themselves with their veils. But the mother, who recognised the King of Damascus, arose, and ran to throw herself at his feet. "My good lady," said the prince to her, "I am in search of your son Ganem: is he here?" "Ah, sir," cried she, "he has long been dead."

The guards, whom the king had sent to seek for Ganem, now came to inform him that their search had been fruitless. "My good lady," said he to Ganem's mother, "leave this tomb; you are neither of you here in safety." When they came out, he, to secure them from insult, took off his robe, which was very large, and covered them both with it, recommending them to keep near him. This being done, he ordered the populace to be admitted; and the pillage commenced with extreme eagerness, and accompanied by shouts, at which the mother and sister of Ganem were the more terrified, as they were entirely ignorant of the cause of these proceedings.

Mohammed, after the pillage of the house, ordered the police-justice to have it utterly rased, together with the tomb; and while this work was proceeding, he conducted Alcolomb and her mother to his palace. The king there redoubled their affliction, by declaring to them the will of the caliph: "He orders," said he, "that you should be stripped, and exposed naked before all the people, during three days. It is with extreme repugnance that I must execute this cruel and ignominious sentence." Although the fear of being dethroned prevented his following the suggestions of his pity, he nevertheless softened, in some degree, the rigour of Haroun Alraschid's command, by causing coarse horse-hair covering, without sleeves, to be made for Alcolomb and her mother.

The next day these two victims were stripped of their clothes, and dressed in their horse-hair garments. Their head-dresses were also taken off and their dishevelled hair suffered to hang loose over their shoulders. In this state, they were exposed to the rude gaze of the people. The police-judge, followed by his attendants, accompanied them, and led them through the city. They were preceded by a crier, who from time to time proclaimed in a loud voice, "*Such is the punishment of those who draw upon themselves the indignation of the commander of the faithful.*"

It was almost night before this dreadful scene concluded. The mother and daughter were then taken back to the palace of the king, where they no sooner arrived, than overcome by the fatigue they had suffered, they fainted away. But let us here leave Alcolomb and her mother, and return to Fetnab.

The favourite had been strictly confined in the dark tower from the day which proved so fatal to her and Ganem; but, however disagreeable her prison might be to her, she was much less afflicted by her own sufferings, than at Ganem's, whose fate caused her the most poignant anguish; there was scarcely a moment in which she ceased to lament him. One night, as the caliph was walking alone in the environs of his palace, according to his usual custom, he passed near the dark tower; and, thinking he heard a voice, he stopped: approaching the door in order to listen, he distinctly heard these words, which Fetnab, still a prey to the sad remembrance of Ganem, uttered very intelligibly: "O Ganem! too unfortunate Ganem! What is become of you? Whither has your unhappy destiny conducted you? The commander of the faithful, who ought to have recompensed you, is your prosecutor; in requital for having always regarded me as a person consecrated to his love, you lose all your property, and are obliged to seek your safety in flight!"

The caliph had heard sufficient to induce reflection: he clearly perceived that, if what Fetnab said were true, she must be innocent, and that he had been too precipitate in the orders he had issued against Ganem and his family. I order to investigate thoroughly an affair in which his character for equity seemed to be involved, he, instantly returned to his apartment, and ordered Mesrour to go to the dark tower, and bring Fetnab before him. The chief of the eunuchs inferred from this order, and still more from the caliph's manner, that he intended to pardon and recal his favourite. He immediately flew to the tower: "Madam," said he, in a tone expressive of his joy, "have the goodness to follow me; I hope you will never again return to this gloomy dismal place."

Fetnab followed Mesrour, who conducted and introduced her to the caliph's cabinet. "Fetnab," said the caliph, without desiring her to rise, "it appears that you accuse me of violence and injustice. Who is the man that, notwithstanding the respect and attention he has preserved towards me, is reduced to so miserable a situation?" "Commander of the faithful," she replied, "if any expression has escaped me which displeases your majesty, I humbly entreat your pardon. But the man with whose innocense and sufferings you desire to be made acquainted, is Ganem, the unfortunate son of Abou Aibou, a merchant of Damascus. It was he who saved my life, and gave me an asylum in his house. I will confess that, when he first saw me, he might perhaps entertain the thought of devoting himself to me, in the hope that I would repay his attention; at least, I inferred this from the earnestness he betrayed in affording me relief, and in rendering me every assistance of which I then stood in need. But as soon as he learned that I had the honour to belong to you, "Ah, madam," said he, "*what belongs to the master is forbidden to the slave.*"

This ingenious confession would perhaps have irritated any other than the caliph; but it completely softened this prince. He commanded her to rise, and, seating her near him, desired her to relate her story from beginning to end. She passed slightly over what regarded Zobeide; she enlarged more upon her obligations to Ganem, upon the expense he had been put to on her account, and she particularly extolled his discretion, wishing by that means to make the caliph understand that she was under the necessity of remaining concealed in Ganem's house, in order to deceive Zobeide.

"It is enough, Fetnab," replied the caliph: "I acknowledge my error, and am willing to repair it by conferring the greatest favours on the young merchant of Damascus." "Commander of the faithful," said she, "after thanking your majesty for Ganem, I humbly beseech you to give orders to have proclaimed throughout your dominions, that you pardon the son of Abou Aibou, and that he is only to present himself before you." "I will do more," replied the prince, "I will give him to you for a husband." Fetnab was unable to find words sufficiently strong to express her gratitude to the caliph for his generosity.

The next day, Haroun Alraschid gave orders to the grand-vizier to have proclaimed in every town of his dominions, that he pardoned Ganem, the son of Abou Aibou; but this proclamation was without effect; for a considerable time passed, and no account was obtained of the young merchant. Fetnab begged the caliph's permission to go herself in search of Ganem; which having obtained, she took from her casket a purse, containing a thousand pieces of gold, and left the palace one morning, mounted on a mule very richly caparisoned, which she had from the stables of the caliph. Two black eunuchs attended her, one on each side. She employed the whole day, and expended her thousand pieces of gold in acts of charity at the mosques, and in the evening returned to the palace.

The following day she took another purse, containing the like sum, and, with the same equipage, repaired to the place where the jewellers associated. She stopped at the entrance; and, without dismounting, sent one of the black eunuchs to desire the syndic to come to her. The syndic immediately attended on Fetnab, whom he knew by her dress to be a lady belonging to the palace. "I address myself to you," said she, putting her purse into his hands, "as a man whose piety is much commended through the whole city. I beg you will distribute these pieces of gold to the poor strangers you are accustomed to assist." "Madam," replied the syndic, "I will execute your commands with pleasure; but if you are desirous of exercising your charity in person, and will take the trouble of coming to my house, you will there see two women worthy of your compassion. I conducted them both to my house, and placed them under the care of my wife, who immediately formed the same judgment of them that I had done. Fetnab, without being able to assign a cause, felt some curiosity to see them. Arriving at the door, she alighted from her mule, and followed the syndic's slave, who had first entered to announce her to his mistress, whom he found in the apartment occupied by Alcolomb and her mother; for they were the persons of whom the syndic had spoken.

The syndic's wife, having learned from her slave that one of the ladies of the palace was in the house, was coming out of the chamber to receive her; but Fetnab followed the slave so closely as not to give her time, and entered the apartment, saying, "My good lady, I entreat your permission to speak to the two strangers who arrived at Bagdad last evening." "Madam," replied the wife of the syndic, "they are now lying in the two little beds that you see standing together." The favourite immediately approached that in which the mother was, and, looking at her attentively, "My good woman," said she, "I am come to offer you my assistance; I am not without interest in this city, and I may perhaps be useful to you and your companion." "I see, madam," replied the mother of Ganem, "by your kind offers, that Heaven has not yet abandoned us." On concluding these words, she began to weep so bitterly, that Fetnab and the wife of the syndic could not restrain their tears. The caliph's favourite, having dried her eyes, said, "I beseech you to relate to us the history of your life and misfortunes." "Madam," replied the disconsolate widow of Abou Aibou, "a favourite of the commander of the faithful—a lady called Fetnab—has caused all our sufferings. I am the widow of Abou Aibou, a merchant of Damascus; I had a son named Ganem, who, being brought by his business to Bagdad, has been accused of carrying off this Fetnab. The caliph caused him to be sought for everywhere, to put him to death; and, not being able to find him, he wrote to the king of Damascus, to have our house plundered and destroyed, my daughter and myself exposed naked to the people for three successive days, and then to banish us both for ever out of Syria. But, with whatever indignity we have been treated, I might still be happy, could I again meet my son alive. Alas! I am persuaded that he is only the innocent cause of our misfortunes, and that he is as free from guilt towards the caliph as his sister and myself." "No, unquestionably," interrupted Fetnab, "he is no more criminal than you are. I can assert his innocence; for I am that very Fetnab of whom you have so much reason to complain. Consider me, then, as your daughter, and receive my pledge of eternal friendship."

Fetnab was proceeding, when the syndic of the jewellers arrived. "Madam," said he, "I have just witnessed a very affecting sight. It is a young man whom a camel-driver has brought to the hospital at Bagdad. He was fastened with cords upon the camel, not having sufficient strength to support himself; I accordingly had him brought hither by my slaves, who placed him in a separate apartment, giving him, by my order, some of my own linen, and attending him in the same manner as I should be attended myself." Fetnab started at the jeweller's discourse, and felt an emotion for which she could not account. "Show me," said she, "into the sick man's chamber; I wish to see him."

The favourite of the caliph, as soon as she had entered the apartment to which the syndic's slaves had conveyed the sick person, approached the bed, where she saw a young man, whose eyes were closed, his face pale and disfigured, and bathed in tears. She looked at him attentively; her heart palpitated; she thought she beheld Ganem, but at the same moment distrusted her eyes. Unable to ressist her desire of being satisfied, "Ganem," said she, with a trembling voice, "is it you I see?" Ganem (for it was in truth he) opened his eyes, and, turning towards the person who addressed him, recognised the favourite of the caliph. "Ah, madam," said he, "can it be you? By what miracle ——"He could not proceed, for he fainted.

The young man, having recovered his senses, looked around, and, not perceiving the object he sought, "Beautiful Fetnab," cried he, "what has become of you? Were you not presented to my eyes, or was it only an illusion?" "No, sir," said the syndic, "it was not an illusion; I have prevailed on the lady to retire, but you shall see her as soon as you are in a condition to bear the interview. Think only of re-establishing your health, and I will contribute all in my power towards effecting it." On concluding these words, he left Ganem to his repose, and went to order the remedies he judged necessary to restore his strength, exhausted by want of nourishment and fatigue.

Fetnab did not fail, very early the next morning, to repair to the house of the syndic of the jewellers, impatient to learn the state of Ganem's health; and to communicate to the mother and daughter the good news which she had to announce. The first person she met was the syndic, who told her that Ganem had passed a very good night; and that, as his disorder proceeded entirely from melancholy, the cause being removed, he would very soon recover. The son of Abou Aibou was in reality much better. It was determined, therefore, that Fetnab should first enter Ganem's apartment alone, and make a sign to the two other ladies to enter, when she judged it proper. Things being thus arranged, Fetnab was introduced by the syndic to the sick man, who was so delighted at her appearance, as again to be very near fainting. "Well, Ganem," said she, approaching his bed, "you see your Fetnab again, whom you imagined you had lost for ever." "Ah, madam," interrupted he, eagerly, "what miracle has restored you to my sight? I thought you were in the palace of the caliph; no doubt the prince has listened to you; you have dissipated his suspicions, and are restored to his affection." "Yes, my dear Ganem," replied Fetnab, "I am justified in the mind of the commander of the faithful, who, to repair the evils he has caused you to suffer, bestows me on you as a wife." "Ah, beautiful Fetnab!" he exclaimed, "may I give credit to what you tell me?" "Nothing is more certain," replied the lady; "this prince now wishes to see you."

In fine, when they had all related the circumstances that had respectively befallen them, "Let us thank Heaven," said Fetnab, "for having thus reunited us; and think only of our future happiness. As soon as Ganem's health is re-established, it will be necessary for him to appear before the caliph, with his mother and sister; but as they are not at present in a proper state to be seen by him, I must remove this obstacle, and therefore beg you will excuse me for a moment." Saying these words, she went out and proceeded to the palace, whence she soon returned to the syndic's house with another purse containing a thousand pieces of gold. She gave it to the syndic, begging him to purchase suitable dresses for Alcolomb and her mother. They were finished in three days; when Ganem, finding himself sufficiently recovered to go abroad, prepared for the visit. But on the day he had appointed to attend the caliph, as he was making ready with his mother and sister, the grand-vizier Giafar arrived at the house of the syndic. The minister was on horseback, attended by a great number of officers: "My lord," said he to Ganem, as he entered, "I come from the commander of the faithful, my master and yours; the commission with which I am now intrusted is very different from that which I do not wish to recal to your remembrance. I am ordered to accompany and present you to the caliph, who much wishes to see you." Ganem only replied to the complaisance of the grand-vizier by a very profound inclination of his head, and mounted a horse that had been brought for him from the stables of the caliph. The mother and daughter were placed on mules from the palace; and while Fetnab, mounted also on a mule, conducted them to the residence of the caliph by one private road, Giafar led Ganem by another, and introduced him to the hall of audience.

When the grand-vizier had conducted Ganem to the foot of the throne, the young merchant made his reverence by prostrating himself with his face to the ground; the caliph desired him to approach, and said, "I am very happy to see you; and wish to hear, from yourself, where you found my favourite, and all that you have done to serve her." Ganem obeyed, and with such apparent sincerity, that the caliph was convinced of his rectitude. The prince ordered a very rich robe to be presented to him, according to the custom always observed towards those admitted to audience. He then said, "Ganem, I wish you would remain in court." "Commander of the faithful," replied the young merchant, "the slave has no other will than that of his master, on whom his life and fortune depend." The caliph was well satisfied with Ganem's answer, and gave him a large pension. The prince afterwards descended from his

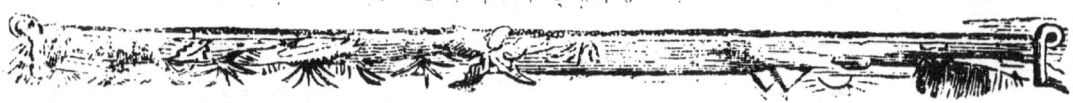

throne, and, desiring Ganem and the grand-vizier only to follow him, entered his own apartment. As he had no doubt that Fetnab was at the palace with the mother and daughter of Abou Aibou, he ordered them to be introduced ; when they prostrated themselves before him. He desired them to rise ; and was so struck with the beauty of Alcolomb, that, after having looked at her with great attention, he said, " I am extremely sorry for having treated your charms with such indignity, and I owe some reparation to them, which may exceed the offence I have committed. I take you for my wife; and by that means I shall punish Zobeide, who will thus become the remote cause of your happiness, as she has been of your misfortunes. This is not all," added he, turning towards the mother of Ganem; "you, madam, are still young, and, I think, will not disdain an alliance with my grand-vizier; I give you to Giafar, and you, Fetnab, to Ganem."

THE HISTORY OF PRINCE ZEYN ALASNAM, AND OF THE KING OF THE GENII.

 KING of Balsora, who possessed immense riches, and was beloved by his subjects, having no children, engaged, by considerable presents, all the holy men of his kingdom to petition Heaven to grant him a son; nor were their prayers ineffectual: the queen was happily delivered of a prince, who was named Zeyn Alasnam, signifying the Ornament of Statues.

The king summoned all the astrologers in his kingdom, and ordered them to calculate the nativity of his child. They discovered by their observations that his life would be long; that he would be courageous; but that he would need all his courage to sustain, with fortitude, the evils with which he was menaced. Having rewarded the astrologers, he then dismissed them.

He caused the young prince to be brought up with all the care imaginable ; and able masters were provided as soon as he was of an age to profit by their instructions. In short, he determined to give to the world an accomplished prince ; when the good king was suddenly attacked by a disease which his physicians were unable to cure. Perceiving himself on his death-bed, he sent for his son, whom he recommended, among other things, to make himself loved rather than feared by his people ; never to listen to flatterers ; and to be equally slow in rewarding as in punishing, since it frequently happened that monarchs, seduced by false appearances, heaped benefits on wicked men, and oppressed the innocent.

As soon as the king was dead, Prince Zeyn clothed himself in mourning, which he wore for seven days. On the eighth he ascended the throne, and began to taste the sweets of empire. He plunged into all kinds of debauchery, with a set of voluptuous young men, on whom he conferred the first offices of the state, and who, of course, neglected them. As he was naturally prodigal, he put no restraint upon his bounties; and his women and favourites insensibly exhausted his treasures.

The queen, his mother, was a wise and prudent princess ; and had many times attempted to check the licentious courses of her son, by representing to him, that, unless he very soon changed his conduct, he would not only dissipate his riches, but even alienate the affection of his people. What she predicted had nearly taken place : the people began to murmur against the government ; and their discontents would have been followed by a general revolt, if the queen had not had the address to prevent it.

In the meantime, Zeyn, finding all his riches dissipated, regretted his not having made a better use of them, and sunk into a profound melancholy. One night, in a dream, an old man appeared to him, and advancing toward him, thus addressed him :—" *Know, O Zeyn ! there is no sorrow which may not be succeeded by joy ; no misfortune that may draw some happiness in its train. If thou wishest to see the end of thy affliction, arise: depart for Egypt. and visit Cairo ;—good fortune there attends thee.*" The prince, when he awoke, was much struck with this dream. He spoke of it very seriously to the queen his mother, who ridiculed it, and attempted to dissuade him from his purpose, but was unable to succeed. The prince, having left to her the care of his kingdom, quitted the palace one night very secretly, and took the road to Cairo.

After encountering much fatigue and trouble, he arrived in this famous city, with which, either in extent or beauty, few cities can be compared. He alighted at the door of a mosque, where, overcome with weariness, he lay down to rest. Scarcely was he asleep, when he saw the same old man, who said to him, " *O my son ! I am satisfied with thee ; thou hast had faith in my words. Thou camest hither without suffering the length or difficulties of the way to abate thy resolution ; but learn that I have engaged thee in this long journey merely to prove thee. I see that thou hast courage and firmness. Thou deservest that I should render thee the most rich and happy prince in the whole world. Return to Balsora ; thou wilt find in thy palace immense riches : no king has ever possessed so much.*"

The prince was not pleased with this dream : " Alas ! " said he to himself, after he awoke, " how great was my error ! this old man, whom I believed to be our venerable prophet, is only the creature of an agitated mind. He then retook the road to his kingdom ; and as soon as he arrived there, the queen asked him if he returned contented. He related to her all that had passed. " Cease to afflict yourself, my son," she said to him, " if God destines you riches, you will acquire them without trouble."

Zeyn protested that he would in future constantly follow the counsels of his mother, and of the sage viziers whom he had chosen to assist him. But on the first night after his return to his palace, he again, for the third time, saw the old man in a dream, who said to him, " *O courageous Zeyn ! the time of thy prosperity is at length arrived. To-morrow morning, as soon as thou risest, take a pickaxe, and dig with it in the cabinet of the deceased king ; thou wilt there discover a great treasure,*" The prince was no sooner awake than he arose, and provided himself with a pickaxe, and entered alone the cabinet of the deceased king. He began his work, and raised more than half the squares of the pavement, without perceiving the least appearance of treasure. However, he resumed courage, and continued his labour. He had no cause to repent, for he discovered a white stone, which he raised, and found beneath it a door, secured by a steel padlock ; this he broke with the axe, and opened the door, under which was a staircase of white marble. Immediately lighting a small taper, he descended by this staircase into a chamber, inlaid with China porcelain, and the ceiling and wainscot of which were of crystal. But his attention was particularly arrested by four shelves, upon each of which were ten urns of porphyry. Approaching one of the urns, he took off the cover, when he saw the vessel was full of pieces of gold. He examined all the urns on the

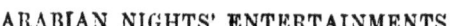

four shelves, one after another, and found them full of sequins: of which he took a handful, and went in search of the queen. This princess felt all the astonishment that may be imagined, when she heard the king's account of what he had seen: "My son," she cried, "take care not to dissipate these riches foolishly, as you have already wasted the royal treasure." "No, madam," replied Zeyn: "I will hereafter live in such a manner, as to afford you satisfaction."

The queen begged her son to show her into that subterraneous place. Zeyn led her to the apartment which contained the urns. She observed in a corner of the room a small urn of the same material as the rest which the prince had not seen. He took it up, and having opened it, found within a small golden key. "My son," said the queen to him, "this key, doubtless, secures some new treasure."

They examined the chamber with extreme attention, and at length discovered in the middle of one of the panels of the wainscot a lock, which they supposed was that to which the key belonged. The king immediately made trial of it, when the door opened in an instant, and discovered another apartment, in the middle of which were nine pedestals of massive gold, eight of which supported each a statue formed of a single diamond, the splendour of which was so great as completely to illuminate the room. 'The ninth pedestal redoubled his astonishment, for above it was placed a piece of white satin, on which was written these words:—'*My dear son, the acquisition of these eight statues has cost me considerable labour; but though they are of great beauty, know that there is in the world a ninth statue, which surpasses them; it is alone of a thousand times more value than all you behold. If you wish to render yourself master of it, go to the city of Cairo, in Egypt, where resides one of my old slaves, called Mobarec; you will have no trouble in finding him, the first person you meet will inform you of his abode. Find him and tell him all that has happened. He will know you to be my son, and will conduct you to the place where this marvellous statue is to be found, and instruct you how to obtain it with safety.*' The prince, after having read these words, said to the queen, "I will not be without this ninth statue, it must be a very rare piece since all these together do not equal it in value." The prince accordingly ordered his equipage to be got in readiness, but would only take with him a small number of slaves.

He pursued his journey without any unpleasant accident, and arrived at Cairo, where he inquired after Mobarec, and was informed that the person whom he sought was one of the richest men of the city. Zeyn requested to be conducted to his house he knocked at the door, which was opened by a slave, who demanded his name and business. "I am a stranger," replied the prince, "and having heard of the generosity of the Lord Mobarec, am come to take up my abode with him." The slave requested Zeyn to wait a moment, while he went to speak to his master, who ordered the stranger to be admitted. Zeyn then entered, and having crossed a large court, passed into a hall magnificently ornamented, where Mobarec, who was waiting for him, received him with much civility. The prince after having replied to this compliment, thus addressed him:—"I am a son of the late king of Balsora, my name is Alasnam."

"This king," said Mobarec, "was formerly my master, but, sir, I never knew he had a son. How old are you?" "I am twenty years of age," replied the prince. "But how will you convince me that you are his son?" "My father," returned Zeyn, "had a subterraneous place under his cabinet, in which I have found forty urns of porphyry, all filled with gold; there are nine pedestals of massive gold, upon eight of which are diamond statues, and on the ninth is a piece of white satin, upon which my father has written what it is necessary I should do to obtain another statue. You know where this statue is, since it is expressed upon the satin that you would conduct me to it." He had not finished these words when Mobarec threw himself at his knees, and repeatedly kissed one of his hands. "I return thanks to God," he exclaimed, "for having directed you hither. "If you wish to visit the place where the marvellous statue is to be found, I will lead you to it. I am this day giving an entertainment to the principal people of Cairo, we were at table when I was informed of your arrival. Will you condescend, my lord, to come and join our party?" Zeyn complied, and stayed with Mobarec all night.

The next day he said to Mobarec, "I have had sufficient repose, and it is time we set off in quest of the ninth statue." "My lord," replied Mobarec, "I am ready to comply with your desire; but you are not aware how many dangers you must encounter." "Whatever be the peril," replied the prince, "I am resolved to brave it: I will succeed or perish. Do but accompany me and let your fortitude equal mine."

Mobarec, seeing him determined to depart, summoned his domestics, and ordered them to provide equipages. They remarked on their route an infinity of rare and surprising objects; and continuing their journey during many days, at length reached a very delicious retreat, where they alighted from their horses. Mobarec then said to the domestics who attended them, "Remain in this place, and guard carefully our equipages, till we return." Addressing himself to Zeyn, "Come, my lord," said he, "let you and I advance by ourselves." They soon arrived at the margin of a large lake. Mobarec seated himself on the bank, saying to the prince, "It is necessary that we should pass this water." "How is that possible?" returned Zeyn; "we have no boat." "You will see one appear in a moment," replied Mobarec. "The enchanted bark, belonging to the king of the genii, will come to receive you; but forget not what I now tell you:—You must preserve a profound silence. Do not utter a syllable to the boatman. I tell you beforehand that, if you pronounce a single word, the vessel will sink to the bottom." While he was speaking, he perceived on the lake a bark of red sandal-wood, having a mast of fine amber, with a streamer of blue satin. There was only one waterman in it, whose head resembled that of an elephant, and his body was in the form of a tiger's. The vessel having approached, the boatman took them, one after the other, by his trunk, and placing them in the boat, passed to the other side of the lake in an instant.

"We are now permitted to speak," said Mobarec. "This island belongs to the king of the genii, and has not its equal in the world."

They at length arrived in front of a palace of fine emeralds, surrounded with a large moat, on the borders of which, at certain distances, were planted trees, so high as to cover the whole palace with their shade. Opposite the gate, which was of massive gold, was a bridge formed of a single shell of a fish, though it measured, at the least, twelve yards in length, and six in breadth. At the head of the bridge appeared a troop of genii, of immeasurable height, who defended the entrance of the castle. "Let us advance no farther," said Mobarec, "or these genii will destroy us." At the same time he drew from a purse, which he had under his robe, four bands of yellow taffetta, one of which he passed round his waist, and another across his back. The remaining two he gave to the prince, who made a similar use of them. After this, he spread upon the earth two large cloths, upon the borders of which he scattered some precious stones, with musk and amber. He then sat down on one of these cloths, and Zeyn on the other, when Mobarec thus addressed the prince :—" I am now going, my lord, to bring hither the king of the genii, who inhabits the palace before you. If our arrival in his island be displeasing to him, he will appear under the figure of a frightful monster ; but if he approve of our design, he will assume the appearance of a well-looking man. As soon as he comes before us, it will be necessary for you to rise and salute him. You must say to him, " Sovereign lord of the genii, my father, who was your servant, has been summoned away by the angel of death. May it please your majesty to extend to me the same protection you always bestowed on my deceased parent. It is, sir, the ninth statue, which I most humbly entreat you to give me."

Mobarec, after having thus instructed Prince Zeyn, began his magic arts. Immediately their eyes were struck by a vivid flash of lightning, which was followed by a clap of thunder. "Take confidence, my prince," said he, " all goes well." In effect, at that moment the king of the genii made his appearance under the form of a handsome man. Prince Zeyn, as soon as he perceived him, delivered the compliment which Mobarec had dictated. The king of the genii, smiling, replied,—" Oh, my son, I loved your father ; and every time he came to pay me his respects, I presented him with a statue, which he carried away. Some days before your father's death, I obliged him to write what you have read upon the piece of white satin. I promised him to take you under my protection, and to give you the ninth statue, which surpasses in beauty all those in your possession. But it is first necessary that you should swear by everything which renders an oath sacred, that you will return to this island, and bring back with you a girl in the fifteenth year of her age, who shall never have known, nor wish to know, the enjoyments of love. It is further necessary that she possess perfect beauty, and that you be so completely master of yourself that, in conducting her hither, you form no desire inconsistent with the most rigid virtue."

Zeyn took the rash oath which the king of the genii required. "But, my lord," said he afterwards, " suppose I should be fortunate enough to meet with a female such as you have described, how shall I be able to ascertain what you require ?" " I confess," replied the king of the genii, smiling, "that appearances may deceive ; nor do I intend to rely altogether on your sagacity. I will give you a mirror, which will be more certain than your conjectures. When you see a perfectly beautiful girl of the age required, you will have only to look in your mirror, where you will behold her image. If the glass remain perfectly pure and unsullied, you may be assured the damsel is chaste ; but if, on the contrary, it receive the least tarnish, it will be a certain proof that she has not been always virtuous. The king of the genii then put a mirror into his hands. "My son," said he, " you may return whenever you please." Zeyn and Mobarec took leave, and proceeded towards the lake. The boatman with the elephant's head appeared to them with his bark, and conveyed them over in the same manner as he had brought them. They rejoined the persons of their suite, with whom they returned to Cairo.

Prince Alasnam reposed some days at Mobarec's house. At length he said to him, " Let us depart for Bagdad, to seek a damsel for the king of the genii." " What !" replied Mobarec, " are we not in grand Cairo ? Do you suppose we cannot here find many handsome females ? Give yourself no concern on that account, my lord ; I know a very clever old woman, whom I will employ on the occasion ; she will acquit herself very skilfully." The old woman had, in truth, the address to give the prince a sight of a great number of very beautiful girls of the age of fifteen ; but when, after having observed them, he came to consult his mirror, the glass was constantly clouded. All the females of the court and of the city, who were in their fifteenth year, in succession, underwent the scrutiny ; and in no instance did the glass remain pure and unsullied.

When they saw that they could meet with no damsels of sufficient purity at Cairo, they went to Bagdad. They hired a magnificent palace, and began to live with great hospitality.

In the part of the city where they resided, was an iman named Boubekir Muezin. Having heard of Zeyn Alasnam, he clothed himself in his dress of ceremony, and set off to wait upon the young prince, who received him very graciously. After many compliments on both sides, Boubekir said to the prince, " Do you purpose, my lord, to remain long at Bagdad ?" " I shall continue here," replied Zeyn, " till I have found a female, in her fifteenth year, and possessed of perfect beauty, who shall be so chaste, that while she has never known the delights of love, she must never have even wished to know them." " You are in search of a great rarity," said the iman ; " and I should much fear that your labour will be useless, if I did not myself know a young lady of the character you describe. Her father was formerly vizier, but has long since quitted the court, and resided in a very retired situation. I will, my lord, with your permission, wait upon him in your behalf." " Not so fast," replied the prince ; " I shall not marry this young lady till I am convinced she answers the description I have given." " Eh ! what assurances do you require ?" said Boubekir. " It is necessary," replied Zeyn, " that I should see her face ; I wish nothing more to satisfy me." " Well, come with me to her father's house, and I will beg permission for you to see her one moment in his presence." Muezin conducted the prince to the vizier's residence, who was no sooner informed of the birth and intentions of Zeyn, than he ordered his daughter to appear, and to remove her veil. Never had the young king of Balsora beheld so perfect and captivating a beauty ; he remained for some time in fixed astonishment. He drew forth his mirror, the polished surface of which remained pure and unsullied.

Finding that he had at last met with a damsel such as he sought, he begged of the vizier to grant her to him. A cadi was immediately sent for, who attended ; the marriage-contract was prepared, and the nuptial-prayer recited. When all the company had retired, Mobarec said to his master, " Let us depart, my lord ; we should not remain longer at Bagdad." " Let us set out this instant," replied the prince ; " it is necessary that I should acquit myself with fidelity. I will, however, confess to you, my dear Mobarec, that in obeying the king of the genii I do no small violence to my own feelings." " Ah, my lord !" replied Mobarec, " learn to subdue your passions ; and whatever it may cost you, keep your engagement with the king of the genii."

They turned to Cairo, and thence took the route to the island of the king of the genii. When they arrived there, they presented her to the king of the genii, who

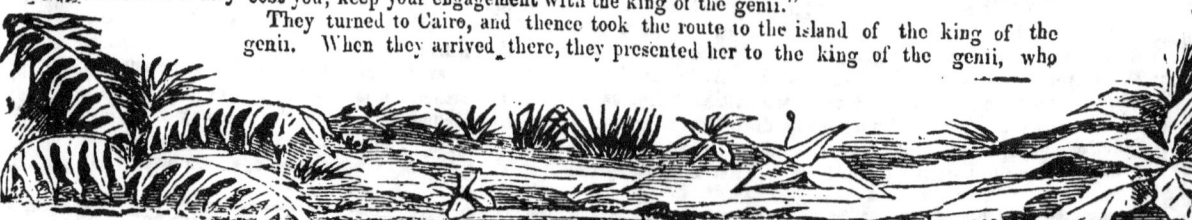

said to Zeyn, " I am satisfied, prince, with your conduct. The damsel you have brought me is equally chaste and beautiful ; and the effort you have made to keep your word is highly pleasing to me. Return to your dominions ; and when you enter the subterranean apartment containing the eighth statue, you will there find the ninth which I promised you." Zeyn thanked the king, and again set out with Mobarec, on the route to Cairo, in which city he mode a short stay, his impatience to possess the ninth statue urging him to precipitate his departure.

Prince Zeyn at length reached Balsora, where his subjects, delighted at his return, made great rejoicings. He went first to the queen, who was overjoyed on learning that he had obtained the ninth statue. "Come, my son," said she, " let us go and see it." The young king and his mother, full of impatience to see this marvellous statue, descended into the vault, and entered the statue-chamber together. But hew great was their surprise, when, instead of a diamond statue, they perceived on the ninth pedestal a young female of perfect beauty, whom the prince immediately recognised as the damsel he had conducted to the island of the genii. " You are much surprised, prince," said the young lady, " at seeing me here ; you expected to find something much more precious." " No, madam," replied Zeyn, " Heaven is my witness that I have more than once thought of breaking my promise to the king of the genii, to preserve you to myself."

As he was concluding this speech, a clap of thunder was heard, which shook the whole subterraneous building. The mother of Zeyn was terrified ; but the king ef the genii, who instantly appeared, dissipated her fears. "Madam," said he, " I protect and love your son. I was desirous to know whether, at his age, he would be able to subdue his passions. This is

the ninth statue I destined for him ; it is more rare and more precious than all the others." The king of the genii disappeared at these words ; and Zeyn, enchanted with his bride, had her proclaimed queen of Balsora on the same day.

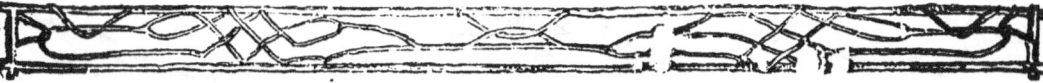

THE HISTORY OF CODADAD AND HIS BROTHERS.

THE historians of the kingdom of Diarbekir inform us, that in the city of Harran formerly reigned a very magnificent and powerful monarch, whose regard for his subjects was equalled by their affection for him. Although he had in his seraglio the most beautiful women in the world, he was yet destitute of children. He incessantly prayed to Heaven for them; and one night, while he was enjoying the sweets of sleep, a man of comely person appeared to him : " Your prayers are heard," said he, "you have obtained what you so ardently desire; rise as soon as you awake, betake yourself to prayer, and make two genuflexions; after which, go into the gardens belonging to your palace, call the gardener, and desire him to bring you a pomegranate; eat as many of the seeds as may be agreeable to you, and your wishes will be fulfilled."

The king, as soon as he awoke, arose, addressed himself to prayer, and made two genuflexions; he then went into the gardens, took fifty pomegranate-seeds, and ate them. He had fifty wives, who shared his bed, all of whom became pregnant; but there was one, named Pirouze, whose condition did not appear. He conceived, in consequence, a dislike to this lady, and was desirous to put her to death. He formed his cruel resolution; but his vizier dissuaded him from it. "Well," replied the king, "let her live; but she must quit my court." "Your majesty," returned the vizier, "might send her to Prince Samer your cousin." The king approved this advice; he sent Pirouze to Samaria, with a letter, in which he desired his cousin to treat her well, and if she were pregnant, to give him information of it as soon as she should be brought to bed.

Pirouze at length became the mother of a prince, beautiful as the day. The prince of Samaria wrote immediately to the king of Harran, to make him acquainted with the happy birth of his son, and to congratulate him on the event. This information gave very great pleasure to his majesty, who, in reply, wrote to Prince Samer in these terms :—"Dear cousin, all my other wives have each of them been delivered of a prince; so that we have here a great number of children; I beg, therefore, you will take care of Pirouze's infant, giving him the name of Codadad; and send him to me, when I demand him."

The prince of Samaria spared nothing in the education of his charge. He was taught to ride, to shoot with the bow, and all other accomplishments suitable to the son of a king. This young prince said one day to his mother, " I begin, madam, to be tired of Samaria; I feel in myself an ardent love of glory; permit me, then, to go in search of occasions to acquire it amidst the dangers of war. The king of Harran, my father, has enemies. Why does he not require my aid? I die with the desire of seeing the king, and am tempted to go and offer him my services as a young stranger." Pirouze approved this generous resolution; and, lest Prince Samer should oppose it, Codadad, without imparting to him his intention, one day quitted Samaria, under the pretence of taking the pleasures of the chase.

He soon found an opportunity of being presented to the king, who, charmed with his beauty and fine figure, gave him a favourable reception, and demanded of him his name and quality. " Sir," replied Codadad, "I am the son of an emir at Cairo—a desire to travel has induced me to quit my country; and as I learned, in passing through your dominions, that you are at war with some of your neighbours, I am come to your court to offer my services to your majesty." The king overwhelmed him with caresses, and gave him an employment in his army.

The young prince was not slow in making his valour known. Every day the ministers and other courtiers attended to pay their respects to Codadad, while they wholly disregarded the other sons of the king. These young princes could not observe this neglect without chagrin; and imputing it entirely to the stranger, they all conceived for him an extreme hatred. "What!" said they, "is not the king contented with loving this stranger more than us, but must he also make him our governor, so that we are to do nothing without his permission? We must rid ourselves of this stranger." "We have only," said one of them, "to go all of us together in search of him, and make him fall with our blows." "No, no," said another, "let us not sacrifice him ourselves. Let us destroy the stranger more adroitly. I propose that we ask permission to go to the chase; and when we are at a considerable distance from the palace, let us take the road to some other city, where we will go and remain for some time. Our absence will astonish the king; who, not seeing us return, will lose all patience, and most likely condemn the stranger to death.

They departed, but returned not. They had already been absent three days, when the king said to Codadad, " Where are the princes? It is a long time since I saw them." " Sir," replied he, making a profound reverence, " they have been out on a hunting party for the last three days; they promised that they would return much sooner." " Imprudent stranger !" said he to Codadad, " how dare you permit my sons to go away without yourself accompanying them? Go and find them instantly, and bring them to me, or be assured your life shall be the forfeit !" He immediately armed himself, mounted his horse, and left the city, and inquiring in every village if they had been seen, but obtaining no information whatever, he abandoned himself to the most poignant grief.

After some days employed in a fruitless search, he arrived in a plain of vast extent, in the middle of which was a palace, built of black marble. He approached it, and saw at the window a beautiful lady. As soon as she perceived Codadad, she addressed him in these words :—"Oh, young man ! fly from this fatal palace, or you will soon be in the power of him who inhabits it. A negro who makes his repast on human blood has here his abode; he seizes all persons whose ill fortune occasions them to pass through this plain, and shuts them up in dark dungeons, whence they are never released but to be devoured."

She had not finished these words, when the negro appeared, a man of gigantic size, and terrific aspect. He was mounted on a powerful horse, and carried a scimitar so large and heavy that none but himself could wield it. The prince was astonished at his monstrous stature; he then drew his scimitar, and waited in a posture of defence for the negro, who summoned him to surrender without conflict, but Codadad made him sensible by his countenance, that he intended to defend his life, for he approached and gave him a violent blow. The negro, perceiving himself wounded, uttered a dreadful cry. He became furious, he foamed with rage, and rising up in his stirrups, prepared in his turn to strike Codadad with his tremendous scimitar. The blow was directed with so great violence that the young prince's destruction would have been inevitable, if he had not had the address to evade it by the management of his horse. Before the negro had time to aim a second blow, Codadad discharged one on his right arm with so

much force that he severed it from his body. The scimitar fell with the hand that held it, while the negro, yielding to the violence of the blow, lost his stirrups, and made the earth quake with his fall. The prince alighted from his horse, threw himself on his enemy, and cut off his head. At this moment the lady uttered a shriek of joy, and said to Codadad, "Prince—for your noble air fully persuades me that you are of no common condition—the negro has the keys of the castle, take them, and come and release me from prison." The prince searched the pockets of the miserable wretch as he lay extended in the dust, and found several keys. Opening the first gate, he entered a large court, where he met the lady, who approached to receive him; she commended his valour, and extolled him above all the heroes of the world.

Their conversation was interrupted by cries and groans. "What do I hear?" exclaimed Codadad. "Sir," said the lady, pointing to a low door, "they arise from that place, where are confined I know not how many unhappy persons. They are all in chains; and every day this monster drew forth one of them for his horrid repast." In the meantime, the prince opened the door, and discovered a very steep staircase, by which he descended into a vast cave, receiving a feeble light from a small aperture; and in which were more than a hundred persons, fastened to stakes, with their hands tied. "Unfortunate travellers," said he, "I have killed the negro, of whom you were destined to be the prey, and am come to break your chains." The prisoners had no sooner heard these words, than they sent forth all together a cry of surprise and joy. Codadad and the lady began to unbind them; and those who were released from their chains assisted in giving freedom to the rest; so that in a short time they were all at liberty. When they reached the court, how great was the astonishment of the prince, at finding among the prisoners, his brothers, of whom he was in search, and whom he had despaired of ever seeing again. "Ah, princes," he exclaimed, on observing them, "am I not deceived? Do I really behold you? May I flatter myself that I shall be able to restore you to the king your father, who is inconsolable for your loss? Are you all in safety? Alas! the death of one only would be sufficient to poison all the joy I feel at having saved you!"

The forty-nine princes all presented themselves to Codadad, who embraced them one after another, and informed them of the uneasiness which their absence had occasioned the king. Afterwards, Codadad, with the rest of the party, examined the castle, in which he found immense riches that the negro had taken from the caravans he had pillaged; and of which a great part belonged to the prisoners whom Codadad had just released, who each knew and claimed his own property. The prince restored to each his own bales, and afterwards divided equally between them the rest of the merchandise. The merchants, overjoyed at having recovered their goods, with their liberty, prepared to continue their journey; but, before they departed, they again made their grateful acknowledgments to their deliverer.

When they were gone, Codadad addressed himself to the lady. "Whither, madam," said he, "do you wish to go? To what quarter were you directing your steps, when you were surprised by the negro? I intend to conduct you to the place you have chosen for your retreat; and I doubt not that these princes have formed the same resolution." The sons of the king of Harran protested to the lady that they would not leave her till they had restored her to her friends. "Princes," said she to them, "I am of a far distant country, and am for ever separated from my home. I have already told you that I was a lady of Cairo; but, after the kindness you have shown me, my lord," added she, directing her speech to Codadad, "it would ill become me to conceal from you the truth.—I am the daughter of a king." On this avowal, Codadad and his brothers entreated the princess to relate her history. After having thanked them for their new offers of service, as she could not refuse to gratify their curiosity, she thus began the recital of her adventures:—

THE HISTORY OF THE PRINCESS OF DERYABAR.

THERE is, in a certain island, a large city called Deryabar. It was for a long time governed by a monarch, who, had he been blessed with children, would have been completely happy. He unceasingly offered up prayers to Heaven, and Heaven granted his desire, but by halves; for the queen, after long expectation, gave to the world only a daughter. I am this unhappy princess.

One day, as he was taking the diversion of hunting, he perceived a wild ass, which he pursued, separating himself from the rest of his party. His ardour carried him so far, that he continued the chase till night. He then alighted, and seated himself at the entrance of a wood, into which the ass had fled. Scarcely was the day closed, when he perceived a light between the trees, which led him to believe that he was not far distant from some village. Much pleased at the hope of passing the night there, he arose, and proceeded towards the light, which served as a guide to conduct him. He very soon discovered that he had been deceived, and that this light was merely the fire in a hut. He approached it, and beheld with astonishment a great black man, or rather a horrible giant, who was sitting upon a sofa. The monster had before him a large pitcher of wine, and was roasting, upon some coals, an ox which he had just flayed. But what most engaged the attention of my father was a very beautiful woman, whom he saw in the hut. She appeared to be absorbed in profound grief; her hands were tied; and at her feet was a little child, two or three years of age, who, as if he already felt for the misfortunes of his mother, wept without intermission. In the meantime, the giant, after having emptied the pitcher, and eaten more than half the ox, turned himself towards the lady, and said, "Beautiful princess, why will you, by your obstinacy, compel me to treat you with so much rigour?" "Thou hideous Satyr," "hope not that time will diminish the horror I have for thee; ever wilt thou be a monster in my eyes." "This is too much!" he exclaimed, in a furious tone, "my love, thus scorned, turns to rage." On concluding these words, he seized the unhappy woman by her hair, and holding her with one hand in the air, while he drew his scimitar with the other, was preparing to cut off her head, when my father discharged an arrow, which pierced his breast: the giant staggered, and instantly fell down lifeless.

My father entered the hut; he untied the lady's hands, requesting to know who she was. "My lord," she replied, "there are on the sea-shore some Saracenic families, whose chief is a prince, my husband. The giant, whom you have just killed, was one of his principal officers: the wretch conceived a violent passion for me, which he took great pains to conceal, till he should find a suitable opportunity for executing a scheme which he had formed. One day the giant surprised me and my child in a retired place, when he carried us both off." "Indeed, madam," replied my father, "I am much interested by your misfortunes; nor shall it be my fault, if your condition be not ameliorated. To-morrow we will leave this wood, and seek the road to the great city of Deryabar, of which I am sovereign; and if it be agreeable to you, you shall reside in my palace till your husband comes to demand you." The lady accepted the proposal, and the next day followed my father, who, on quitting the wood, met the whole of his officers: they had passed the night in search of him, and were in great anxiety on his account.

They arrived at the palace of my father, who assigned an apartment to the fair Saracen, and had her son brought up with the greatest attention.

In the course of time, the son of this lady attained manhood: he was very handsome; and as he did not want understanding, he found the way to please my father. All the courtiers, perceiving this affection, imagined that the young man would be my husband. Possessed of this opinion, and considering him heir to the crown, they made their court to him. He penetrated the motive of their attachment; he congratulated himself with it; and flattered himself with the hope, that my father had conceived so much love for him, as to prefer his alliance to that of all the princes of the world. He did more: he presumed to demand it. Whatever punishment his audacity deserved, my father contented himself with telling him that he had other views for me. The haughty youth was irritated by this refusal, and felt himself offended at the slight put upon his addresses. He did not stop here: he conspired against him, struck a poniard in his breast, and got himself proclaimed king of Deryabar. His first care was to come himself to my apartment, at the head of a band of conspirators. His design was either to take away my life, or to compel me to marry him. But I had time to escape. While he was employed in murdering my father, the grand-vizier came and tore me from the palace, conveying me to a place of safety, where he kept me concealed till a vessel was ready to sail. It was the intention of the grand-vizier to conduct me to the courts of the neighbouring monarchs, in order to implore their assistance, but Heaven did not approve a resolution which appeared to us so reasonable. After some days' sailing, there arose so furious a tempest, that in spite of the skill of the sailors, our vessel struck upon a rock. I became insensible; and when I recovered my senses, I found myself on the shore.

Far from lamenting the death of the crew, I envied their fate, and formed the resolution of precipitating myself into the sea. I was going to rush forward, when I heard behind me a great noise of men and horses, and I beheld a party of cavaliers, one of whom was mounted upon an Arabian horse. Though his dress had not convinced me that he was the chief of the party, I should have discovered it from the air of grandeur which was diffused over his whole person. He was a young man, perfectly well-featured, and handsome as the day. He sent forward some of his officers to inquire who I was. I still continued to weep and afflict myself without being able to reply to those who interrogated me, when he thus addressed me:—"Madam, I entreat you to moderate your affliction. Summon, I entreat you, more fortitude. I offer you an asylum in my palace; you shall reside near the queen my mother, who will endeavour, by every kind attention, to soften your troubles." I thanked the young king for his goodness, and accepted his obliging offers. The prince, after I had ceased speaking, resumed the conversation, and again assured me that he took a great interest in my misfortunes. He then conducted me to his palace, where he presented me to his mother. The queen showed herself extremely sensible to my affliction. On the other hand, her son became passionately in love with me, and soon offered me his hand and his crown. Penetrated with gratitude, I could not refuse to promote his happiness; and our marriage was solemnised.

While all the people were engaged in celebrating the nuptials of their sovereign, a neighbouring hostile prince came one night with a considerable army, and made a descent on the island. This formidable enemy was the king of Zanguebar: he attacked us entirely by surprise, and cut in pieces all the subjects of my husband. We had both nearly fallen into his hands, when we found means to save ourselves, and gain the seashore, where we threw ourselves into a fisherman's bark. During two days we drove before the wind, uncertain what would be our fate: on the third, we perceived a ship, which approached us. We at first rejoiced at the sight, supposing it to be some merchant vessel, coming to our relief, but were thrown in the utmost consternation, when, on its nearer approach, we perceived ten or twelve armed corsairs on the deck. They immediately boarded us; five or six threw themselves into the bark, seized us both, bound my husband, and forced us into their own vessel: they all seemed charmed with my person; and, instead of drawing lots for me, each insisted on a preference, and resolved that I should be his prey. The controversy became violent, and they soon proceeded to blows, fighting like madmen. In a moment the deck was covered with dead bodies; nor did the conflict cease, till the whole party was slain, with the exception of one man, who thus addressed me:—"You are now my property, I shall conduct you to Cairo, and present you to a friend of mine, but," added he, observing my husband, "who is that man? How is he connected with you?" "Sir," I replied to him, "he is my husband." "If that is the case," said the, "I must in pity put him out of the way." At these words he took the unhappy prince, who was bound, and threw him into the sea.

We had already been several days on our journey, when yesterday, in passing through this plain, we perceived the negro who inhabited this castle. He drew his enormous scimitar, and summoned the pirate to yield himself prisoner. The corsair was courageous, and he attacked the negro. The combat was long continued, but the pirate at length fell under the blows of his enemy. The negro afterwards conveyed me to this castle, whither he also brought the body of the pirate, which he ate for supper. When he had ended, he conducted me to a chamber, and then retired to his own.

*   *   *   *   *   *

The princess had no sooner concluded the recital of her adventures than Codadad assured her that he most sincerely sympathised in her misfortunes. "The sons of the king of Harran offer you an asylum in their father's court," added he; "let me entreat you to accept it, and allow me to offer you my hand." The princess yielded, and the marriage was on the same day solemnised in the castle. There was also a variety of provisions, all excellent of their kind. They all sat down to table, and, after having eaten and drunk plentifully, they packed up the rest of the provisions, and quitted the castle. They continued their route many days, encamping in the most agreeable places they could find. Being arrived within a few day's journey of Harran, they halted, and drank the remainder of their wine, when Codadad thus addressed the party:—"Princes," said he, "I can no longer conceal from you who I am. You behold in me your brother Codadad; I owe my being, as well as you, to the king of Harran, and the Princess Pirouze is my mother." The princes congratulated Codadad on his birth, though in their hearts their

hatred for their amiable brother incessantly augmented. They assembled in the night, and withdrew to a retired place; while Codadad and the princess were enjoying, in their tent, the sweets of repose, they formed the horrid resolution of assassinating him. "This is our only alternative," said one of the villains. "The king will load him with caresses, will be incessant in his praise, and appoint him his heir." To these words he added others, which made so strong an impression on their jealous minds, that they instantly proceeded to the tent of Codadad, and, finding him asleep, pierced him with a thousand strokes of their poniards; after which, leaving him apparently dead in the arms of the princess, they departed, directing their course to the city of Harran.

In the meantime Codadad, weltering in his blood, lay stretched in his tent, attended by the princess his wife, who seemed little less to be pitied than himself. She filled the air with her cries.

He was not, however, dead. The princess observed him to breathe, and she instantly ran to a large town which appeared in the plain to provide a surgeon. She found one, who returned with her immediately; but, when they arrived at the tent, Codadad could nowhere be found. Concluding that some wild beast had seized and devoured him, the princess again gave way to the most bitter cries and lamentations. The surgeon proposed to her to return to the town, making her an offer of his house and services. She suffered herself to be persuaded; the surgeon, therefore, conducted her to his house, and treated her with all possible attention and respect. He endeavoured, by his discourse, to enforce consolation. "Madam," said he to her one day, "inform me, I entreat, of all your distresses; tell me, what is your country, and what your condition?" The princess immediately complied with his desire.

When she had finished the recital, the surgeon again addressed her. "Madam," said he, "I am ready, if you choose, to serve as your attendant. Let us go to the king of Harran's court; he is a good and equitable prince." "I submit," replied the princess. "Yes, I feel that I ought to revenge the fate of Codadad; and, as you are so generous as to offer to accompany me, I am ready to depart." The surgeon provided two camels, on which they commenced their journey, and soon arrived at the city of Harran. They alighted at the first caravansera they met with, where they inquired of the master the news of the court. "It is," replied he, "at present in very great distress. The king had a son, who was living with him here for a long time under an assumed character, and no one knows what is become of him. A wife of his majesty, named Perouze, the mother of the prince, has had a thousand inquiries made, but all have hitherto proved fruitless."

The surgeon was of opinion that the proper plan for the princess of Deryabar to pursue, would be to go to Pirouze; but this step could not be taken without danger. Having made these reflections, and being sensible of the danger to which he himself might be exposed, he was anxious to conduct the affair with all prudence; he therefore begged the princess to continue at the caravansera while he went to the palace to observe how he might introduce her to the mother of Codadad. He then directed his course to the city, when he perceived a lady mounted upon a mule, richly caparisoned; she was followed by several females, and by a great number of guards and black slaves. The surgeon saluted her, after which he inquired of a calender, who was near him, whether this lady was not wife to the king. "Yes, brother," replied the calender, "she is one of the king's wives; she is the mother of Prince Codadad."

The surgeon followed Pirouze as far as a mosque, which she entered, for the purpose of distributing alms. He forced his way through the multitude, and advanced near the guards of Pirouze, where he heard all the prayers. When this princess departed, he accosted one of her slaves, "Brother, I have a very important secret to reveal to the Princess Pirouze. Can I not, by your means, be introduced to her apartment? It is respecting her son that I wish to address her." "If that be the case," returned the slave, "you have only to follow us to the palace, and you shall very soon have the opportunity you desire." Accordingly, as soon as Pirouze had re-entered her apartment, the slave informed her that a strange man had something of importance to communicate to her, and that it concerned Prince Codadad. He had no sooner pronounced these words, than Pirouze showed the most lively impatience to see this unknown person. The instant she saw the surgeon, she demanded of him what it was that he had to communicate respecting her son. "Madam," answered the surgeon, "I have a long story to relate, in which are many events that will doubtless surprise you." He then gave her a full account of everything that had happened between Codadad and his brothers, which she listened to with the most eager attention. When he had finished, the princess said to him, "Return to the princess of Deryabar, and inform her, from me, that the king will soon acknowledge her for his daughter-in-law."

After the surgeon had departed, the king entered the apartment, and inquired of Pirouze whether she had heard bad news of Codadad. He did not give Pirouze time to finish her recital, and giving way to his passion, "Madam," said he, "these perfidious wretches, who have occasioned your tears, and caused me the most poignant affliction, shall soon experience the punishment they deserve." Having thus spoken, the king repaired to the hall of audience, where were his courtiers, and such of the people who had any petitions to prefer. He ascended his throne, and desiring his grand-vizier to approach, "Hassan," said he to him, "I have an order to give you; go immediately and take a thousand soldiers of my guard, and arrest all the princes, my sons; confine them in the tower destined for assassins, and let it be performed without delay." He was still in the hall when the vizier returned. "Well," vizier," said he, "are all my sons in the tower?" "Yes, sir," replied the minister. "But that is not all," replied the king; "I have another order to give you." Saying this, he left the hall of audience, and returned to the apartment of Pirouze, followed by the vizier. He desired to know of the princess where the widow of Codadad was lodged, of which Pirouze's women informed him. The king then turning towards his minister, said, "Go to that caravansera, and conduct hither a young princess who lodges there; but observe to treat her with all the respect due to a person of her rank."

The princess of Deryabar found the king waiting at the palace-gate to receive her. He took her by the hand, and conducted her to the apartment of Pirouze. These three persons, mingling their sighs and tears, preserved for a long time a tender and mournful silence. The princess of Deryabar, being at length somewhat recovered from her oppression, related the adventure of the castle, and the cruel fate of Codadad. "Madam," said the king to her, "these ungrateful wretches shall perish."

The king's determination was, that on the ninth day the princes his sons should be beheaded. The scaffolds were about being prepared; but they were obliged to defer the execution till another time, because it was suddenly discovered that the neighbouring princes, who had already made war on the king of Harran, were advancing with a more numerous army than before, and that they were at no great distance from the city. This news caused a general consternation, and furnished fresh matter of regret for the fate of Codadad, as this prince had greatly signalized himself in the preceding war against the same enemies. In the mean time, the king, instead of giving way to fear, made a hasty levy of his people; and, having formed a considerable army, he sallied out, and marched forward to meet them. The enemy, having learned by their spies that the king of Harran was advancing to engage, waited in the plain, and disposed their army in order of battle. The king had no sooner perceived them, than he also arranged and disposed his troops for combat. He ordered the charge to be sounded, and made his attack with great vigor; the enemy resisted with equal ardour. Much blood was shed on both sides, and victory long continued doubtful. But at length it was about to declare itself for the enemies of the king of Harran, when there suddenly appeared in the plain a large body of horsemen, approaching the combatants in good order. This troop advanced, and attacked the enemies of the king of Harran in flank, charging with so much fury, that they instantly put them in disorder, and very soon to the rout. They did not rest there; they pursued them briskly, and cut almost the whole of their army in pieces.

The king of Harran, who had observed all that had passed with great attention, admired the intrepidity of the horsemen. He had been particularly charmed with their leader, whom he had seen combating with extraordinary valour. Impatient to see and to thank him, he sought to join him. The two princes approached; when the king of Harran, recognising in this brave warrior his beloved son Codadad, remained motionless with surprise and delight. "Sir," said Codadad to him, "your majesty has much reason to be astonished at thus suddenly meeting with a man whom you have probably supposed to be dead." "I know all, my son," said the king, after he had, for a long time, held him in his arms. "Your mother is waiting to rejoice with me at the defeat of our enemies. What joy will she not receive, when she learns that I am indebted to you for my victory!" Codadad was also transported with joy, on learning that the princess his wife was at the court. "Come, sir," he exclaimed in ecstacy, "let us wait on my mother." The king immediately returned toward the city at the head of his army. These two princes found Pirouze and her daughter-in-law waiting to congratulate the king; but it is impossible to express the transports of delight with which they were agitated, when they saw the young prince. After these four persons had indulged in all the delightful emotions which the tenderest affection inspired, the king and the ladies were anxious to know of Codadad by what miracle his life had been preserved. He informed them that a peasant, mounted on a mule, accidentally entered the tent where he lay senseless; when seeing him alone, and pierced with so many wounds, he placed him on his mule, and conveyed him to his house, where he applied a variety of bruised herbs, which cured him in a very short time. "When I felt myself recovered," added he, "I thanked the peasant, and presented to him all the diamonds I possessed. I then approached the city of Harran; but having learned on the road that some neighbouring princes had assembled an army, and were advancing to attack his majesty, I made myself known in the villages, and excited the zeal of the people to rise in his defence. I armed a great number of young people; and, putting myself at their head, arrived at the time when the two armies were engaged. As to my brothers I pardon them their crime, and presume to request of you the same favour for them." These noble sentiments drew tears from the king, who caused the people to be assembled, and declared Codadad his heir. He then ordered them to bring forth the princes, who appeared loaded with irons. The son of Pirouze loosened their chains, and embraced them all, one after another, with as much cordiality as he had shown in the court of the negro's castle.

THE STORY OF THE SLEEPER AWAKENED.

UNDER the reign of the Caliph Haroun Alraschid, there lived at Bagdad a very rich merchant, whose wife was far advanced in age. They had only one son, named Abou Hassan, who had been educated with the utmost strictness.

The merchant died, and Abou Hassan took possession of the vast wealth his father had amassed. The son, whose views and inclinations were different from those of his father, made a very different use of his property. As his father had not allowed him, in his youth, more than was barely sufficient for his maintenance, he determined to distinguish himself in a manner equal to the great wealth with which fortune had favoured him. For this purpose he divided his wealth into two parts. One he employed in purchasing estates, which would produce a revenue sufficient to enable him to live at his ease; the other half, which consisted of a considerable sum in ready money, was destined to repair the time he thought he had lost under the severe restraint in which his father had kept him till his death.

With this design, Abou Hassan soon formed a society of young men, and he thought only of making their time pass agreeably. These amusements were so extremely expensive to Abou Hassan, that he could not continue so profuse a style of living beyond one year. From the moment he ceased giving these entertainments, his friends disappeared; in short, they constantly shunned him, and, if by accident, he joined any one of them, and wished to stop him, he excused himself under various pretences.

Abou Hassan was more affected by the strange conduct of his friends, who abandoned him, after all the demonstrations and protestations of friendship they had made him, than at the loss of all the money he had so foolishly expended with them. Melancholy and thoughtful, he entered his mother's apartment, and seated himself at the end of a sofa, at some distance from her. "What is the matter, my son?" said his mother, on seeing him in this state. "Why are you so altered, so cast down, and so different from yourself?" Abou Hassan burst into tears at these words, and, in the midst of his grief, "My dear mother," he cried, "I at length know, from woeful experience, how insupportable poverty is. Yes, I feel very sensibly, that as the setting of the sun deprives us of the splendour of that luminary, so poverty deprives us of every enjoyment. You know," continued he, "how I have conducted myself

toward my friends for a year past, I have entertained them until my finances are exhausted; and now, as I cannot continue the same profusion, I find myself abandoned by them all. I thank God for having inspired me with the idea of reserving what I call my income, under the condition and oath I made not to touch it. I will strictly adhere to this oath, and I have resolved on the good use I shall make of what remains; but first, I wish to see to what extremity my friends, if they deserve that appellation, will carry their ingratitude. I will see them all, one after another, and, when I have described to what a length I have proceeded, I will solicit them to raise amongst them such a sum of money as may serve in some measure to relieve me from the unhappy situation to which I am reduced. "My son," replied the mother of Abou Hassan, "I do not take upon me to dissuade you from executing your plan; but, I can tell you beforehand, that your hope is unfounded." "My dear mother," returned Abou Hassan, "I am well persuaded of the truth of what you tell me."

Abou Hassan set out immediately, and he timed his visits so well, that he found all his friends at home. He represented to them his great distress, and besought them to lend him money to such an amount as would effectually assist him. He did not forget to hold out to them the hope that he might one day be again in a situation to entertain them as he had done. Neither of his convivial companions was in the least affected by the lively colours in which Abou Hassan painted his distress. He had the still greater mortification to be plainly told by many of them, that they did not know him, and that they did not even remember ever to have seen him. He returned home with his heart filled with grief and indignation. "Ah, my mother!" cried he, "you have told me the truth; instead of friends, I have only found perfidious, ungrateful, and wicked men, unworthy of my friendship! It is enough; I renounce them for ever, and I promise never to see them more."

Abou Hassan remained firm in the resolution of keeping his word; for which purpose he took every prudent precaution to avoid being tempted to break it; and, that he might not again be subjected to the same inconvenience, he made an oath, never during his life to entertain an inhabitant of Bagdad. He resolved to draw for the expenses of each day, only a sufficient sum to enable him to invite one person to sup with him; and he took a second oath, that that person should not be an inhabitant of Bagdad, but a stranger who should have arrived there the same day; and that he would send him away the next morning, after giving him only one night's lodging. Abou Hassan rigidly observed this rule; he never regarded, or spoke to, the strangers whom he had once received in his house; when he met them in the streets, the square, or public assemblies, he appeared not to see them. For a long time conducted himself in this manner; when one day a little before sunset, as he was seated in his usual manner at the end of the bridge, the Caliph Haroun Alraschid appeared, but so much disguised, that he could not be known. That day, the first of the month, he appeared in the disguise of a Moussol merchant, who had just landed on the opposite side of the bridge, and was followed by a slave of a large and stout figure. As the caliph had, under his disguise, a grave and respectable air, Abou Hassan, rose from the place on which he was seated; and after having saluted him with a courteous air, "Sir," said he "I congratulate you on your happy arrival; I entreat you will do me the honour to sup with me." And, in short, to induce him to comply with his request, he briefly told him the rule he had laid down to himself, of every day receiving, if possible, and for one night only, the first stranger who presented himself. The caliph found something so singular in the whimsical taste of Abou Hassan, that he felt an inclination to know the foundation of it. He signified that he could not better reply to so great and unexpected a civility on his arrival at Bagdad, than by accepting his obliging invitation.

When the pretended merchant of Moussol and Abou Hassan were seated at table, the latter before he touched the fruit, took a cup, which he first filled for himself, "Sir," said he, "you know as well as I do, that the cock never drinks until he has called his hens about him, to come and drink with him, I invite you, then, to follow my example." Abou Hassan had no sooner drunk, than he filled the cup which the caliph held out, "Taste it, sir," said he, "you will find it good." "Of that I am well persuaded," returned the caliph, laughing.

The night was already far advanced, and the caliph, pretending to be greatly fatigued with his day's journey, said to Abou Hassan, that he was much inclined to repose himself. "Before we part, (for perhaps I shall leave your house to-morrow, before you are awake), I have the satisfaction of declaring how sensible I am of the civility the good cheer, and the hospitality, with which you have treated me. I am only concerned to determine in what manner I can best prove my gratitude." At these offers of the caliph, whom Abou Hassan had no doubt of being a merchant, "My good sir," he replied, "I am thoroughly persuaded that it is not out of mere compliment you so generously address me. But, upon the word of an honest man, I can assure you that I have no trouble, I will admit nevertheless, that one thing gives me some concern. You know the city of Bagdad is divided into quarters, and that in each quarter there is a mosque, with an iman, who assembles all the people of his division, at the accustomed hours to join with him in prayer. The iman here is a very old man, of an austere countenance, and a complete hypocrite, if ever there was one in the world. He assembles four other dotards, my neighbours, persons of a similar character, for a council, who meet regularly, every day, at his house; whence there is no kind of slander, calumny, and mischief, which they do not propagate against me, and against all the division, to disturb our quiet, and stir up dissensions among us." "So, then," replied the caliph, "you would find some means to check this disorder?" "You are right," answered Abou Hassan; "and the only thing I would beg of God, for this purpose, is, that I were caliph in the room of the commander of the faithful, our sovereign lord and master, Haroun Alraschid, for one day." "What would you do," demanded the caliph. "One very important thing, I would do," replied Abou Hassan, "which would give satisfaction to all good people.—I would order a hundred strokes on the soles of the feet to be given to each of the four old men, and four hundred to the iman, to teach them not to disturb and vex their neighbours."

The caliph was much diverted with Abou Hassan; it suggested to him a desire to amuse himself with him in a very singular manner. "Your wish pleases me the more," said the caliph, "because I see it springs from an upright heart. I am persuaded that the caliph would readily trust his power in your hands for twenty-four hours, if he were informed of your good intention, but let us drop this conversation: it is near midnight, and time to go to bed."

While Abou Hassan was speaking, the caliph seized the bottle and the two cups. He helped himself first, and made Abou Hassan understand that he drank to him a cup of thanks. When he had so done, he secretly threw into Abou Hassan's cup a little powder which he had by him, and poured upon it the remainder of the bottle. Presenting it to Abou Hassan, "You have had the trouble," said he, "of helping me during the whole evening; the least I can do, in return, is to spare you that trouble." Abou Hassan took the cup, and swallowed the whole at a breath. But scarcely had he put the cup on the table, before the powder began to take effect, and he fell fast asleep. The slave by whom the caliph was attended, had returned as soon as he had supped, and had been during some time on the spot, ready to obey his master's commands. "Place this man upon your shoulders," said the caliph to him; but take care to notice the situation of the house, that you may bring him back hither, when I order you."

The caliph, followed by his slave, with Abou Hassan on his shoulders, quitted the house, but intentionally without closing the door, as Abou Hassan had requested him. When he arrived at his palace, he entered by a private door, and desired the slave to follow him to his apartment, where all the officers of the bed-chamber were in waiting: "Undress this man," said he to them, "and lay him on my bed; I will afterwards tell you my intentions." The officers undressed Abou Hassan, and clothing him in the caliph's night-dress, put him to bed. The caliph commanded all the other officers of the court, and all the ladies to attend; and when they were assembled in his presence, "I desire," said he to them, "that all those who usually come to me, when I rise, do not fail in their attendance here to-morrow morning upon this man. I desire also, that the same respect be observed toward him, as is due to my own person; and that all his commands be strictly obeyed. Let him be refused nothing he may require, nor be contradicted in anything he shall say or do." The officers and ladies, who immediately perceived that the caliph wished to amuse himself, answered only by a profound inclination.

As day-light already began to appear, and it was time to get up for prayer before sun-rise, the officer who was nearest Abou Hassan's pillow, applied to his nose a small piece of sponge dipped in vinegar. Abou Hassan opened his eyes; and saw himself in a large and magnificent chamber. He found himself surrounded by young females of enchanting beauty, several of whom had different musical instruments. Casting his eyes on the coverlid of the bed, he saw it was a beautiful crimson and gold brocade. At the sight of these splendid objects, Abou Hassan was inexpressibly astonished and confounded. He considered the whole as a dream. "Well," said he to himself, "I am, then, caliph. But," added he, "I must not deceive myself; it is a dream—merely an effect of the wish I formed in conversation with my guest." At the same time an eunuch approached: "Commander of the faithful, your majesty will be pleased not to sleep again. It is time to rise for early prayer." Abou Hassan, very much astonished at what he heard, said again to himself, "Am I awake, or do I sleep?" "Commander of the faithful," resumed the eunuch, a moment afterwards, "your majesty will allow me to repeat that it is time to rise." He again opened his eyes, and saw it was now broad day. The young women of the palace then prostrated themselves before Abou Hassan; and those of them who had instruments of music, saluted him with a concert of soft-toned flutes, hautboys, lutes, and other harmonious instruments. "What does all this signify?" he muttered to himself; "Whose is this palace? What mean these eunuchs, these officers, these damsels, these musicians? Is it possible that I should not be able to distinguish whether I am dreaming?"

At this moment, Mesrour, the chief of the eunuchs, entered, prostrating himself before Abou Hassan; and, as he arose, "Commander of the faithful," said he, "your majesty will permit me to represent, that you have not been accustomed to rise so late, and that you have suffered the time of morning-prayer to pass unregarded. The generals of your armies, the governors of your provinces, and the other great officers of your court, only wait the moment when the door of the council-chamber shall be opened to them." By this address of Mesrour, Abou Hassan was persuaded that he was not asleep, and that the state in which he found himself was not a dream. At length he fixed his eyes upon Mesrour, and in a serious tone, demanded of him, "Who is it that you call commander of the faithful?—you, of whom I know nothing: you must certainly take me for some one else." "My most honoured lord and master," cried he, "your majesty surely talks thus to me to-day, in order to prove me. Is not your majesty the commander of the faithful, the monarch of the universe."

Abou Hassan, after having laughed a long time, again sat up in his bed; and speaking to a little eunuch, as black as Mesrour, "Hark you!" said he; "tell me who I am." "My lord," replied the little eunuch, with a respectful air, "your majesty is the commander of the faithful." "Thou art a little liar, sooty face!" returned Abou Hassan.

He then called one of the females, who was nearer to him than the rest: "Come hither, fair lady," said he, presenting his hand to her; "take the end of my finger, and bite it, that I may feel whether I am asleep or awake." The damsel, who knew the caliph saw all that passed in the chamber, was delighted with an opportunity of showing her zeal to afford him amusement: she approached Abou Hassan with the most serious air imaginable, and closing her teeth gently upon the end of his finger, which he had held out to her, she occasioned him to feel a little pain. Quickly withdrawing his hand, "I am not asleep!" said Abou Hassan immediately.

The chief of the eunuchs, perceiving that Abou Hassan meant to rise, offered his hand to assist him in getting out of bed. Mesrour led the way, and Abou Hassan followed. The arras was drawn back and the door opened by an usher. Mesrour entered into the council-chamber, and went on before him quite to the foot of the throne, where he stopped to assist him in ascending it; this he did by lifting him under the shoulder on one side, while another officer, who followed, assisted him in the same manner on the other.

In the mean time, the caliph went to another closet which overlooked this chamber, and whence he could see and hear all that passed in the council. He was highly amused at seeing Abou Hassan representing him upon the throne.

Abou Hassan, after all that had happened to him since he awoke, and what he had just heard from the mouth of the grand-vizier, no longer doubted of his being the caliph. Accordingly, looking at the grand-vizier, he asked him, whether he had any thing to say to him. "Commander of the faithful," returned the grand-vizier, "the emirs, the viziers, and the other officers, who have seats in your majesty's council, are at the door, and wait only the moment when you shall give them permission to enter." Abou Hassan immediately ordered it to be opened. The door was opened, and at once the viziers, the emirs, and the principal officers of the court, all in their magnificent habits of ceremony, entered in exact order. When this ceremony was ended, and they were all in their places, there was a profound silence.

Then the grand-vizier, constantly standing before the throne, began to make his report of various matters, in the order of the papers which he held in his hand.

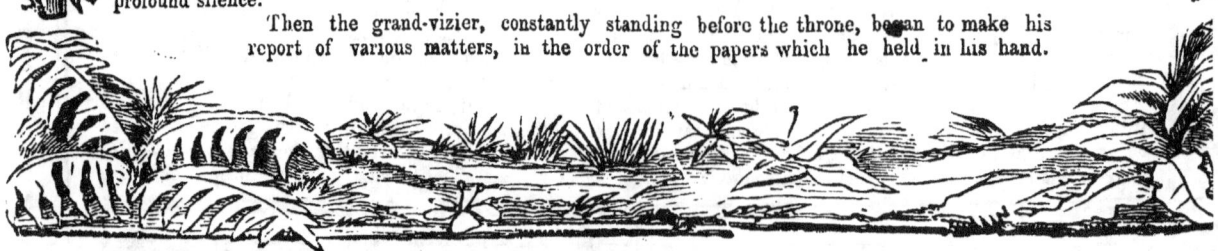

Before the vizier had finished his report, Abou Hassan perceiving the police-judge, whom he knew by sight, sitting in his place, "Stay a moment," said he, interrupting him, "I have an order of importance to give immediately to the officer of the police. Judge, go this moment, without loss of time, into—such a street, in such a quarter of the town," both which he named to him. "In this street is such a mosque, where you will find the iman, and four old grey-beards; seize their persons, and let the four old men have each a hundred lashes, and let the iman have four hundred. After that, cause all the five to be mounted, each on a camel, clothed in rags, and with their faces toward the tail. Thus equipped, have them conducted through the different quarters of the town,

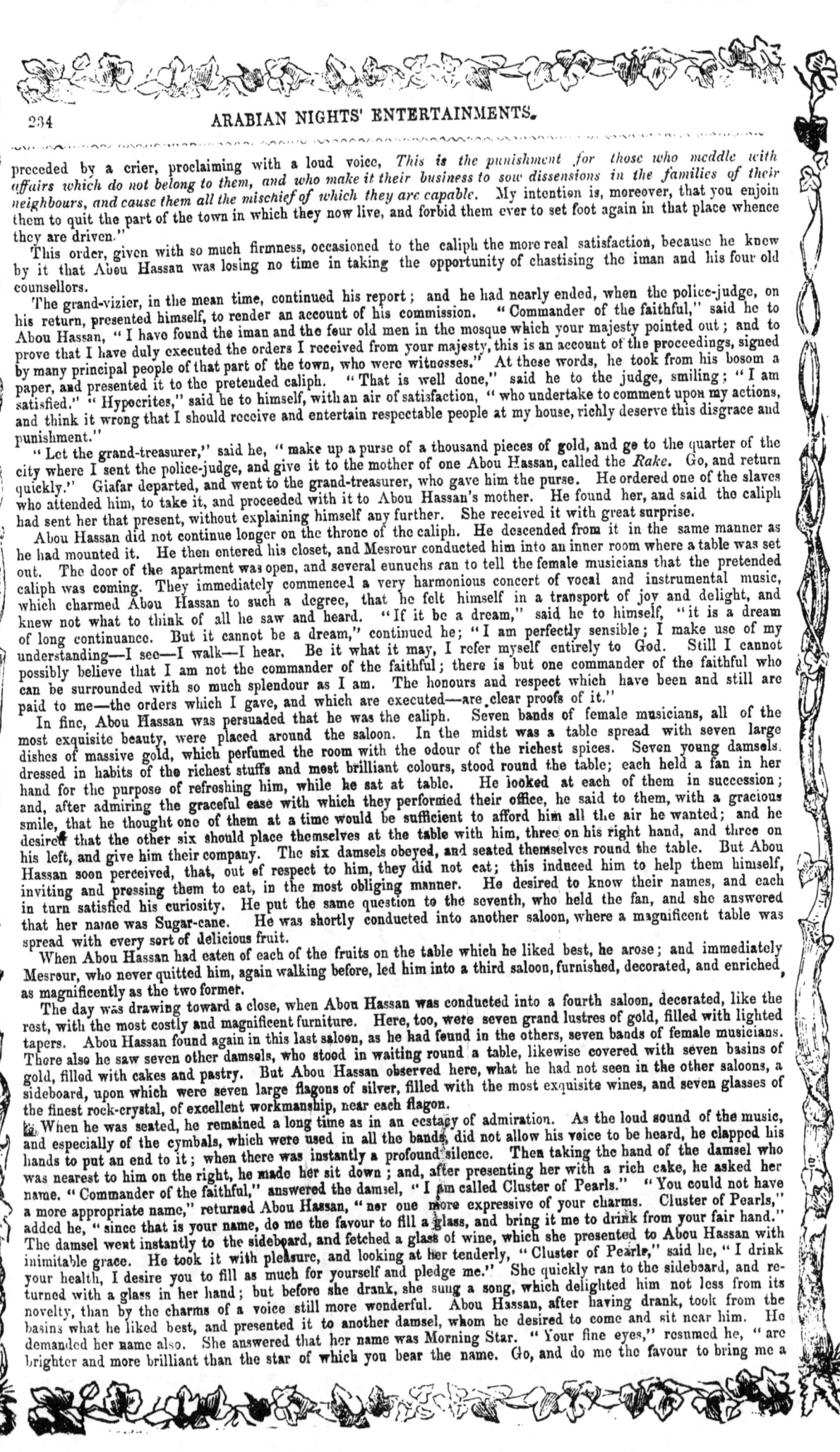

preceded by a crier, proclaiming with a loud voice, *This is the punishment for those who meddle with affairs which do not belong to them, and who make it their business to sow dissensions in the families of their neighbours, and cause them all the mischief of which they are capable.* My intention is, moreover, that you enjoin them to quit the part of the town in which they now live, and forbid them ever to set foot again in that place whence they are driven."

This order, given with so much firmness, occasioned to the caliph the more real satisfaction, because he knew by it that Abou Hassan was losing no time in taking the opportunity of chastising the iman and his four old counsellors.

The grand-vizier, in the mean time, continued his report; and he had nearly ended, when the police-judge, on his return, presented himself, to render an account of his commission. "Commander of the faithful," said he to Abou Hassan, "I have found the iman and the four old men in the mosque which your majesty pointed out; and to prove that I have duly executed the orders I received from your majesty, this is an account of the proceedings, signed by many principal people of that part of the town, who were witnesses." At these words, he took from his bosom a paper, and presented it to the pretended caliph. "That is well done," said he to the judge, smiling; "I am satisfied." "Hypocrites," said he to himself, with an air of satisfaction, "who undertake to comment upon my actions, and think it wrong that I should receive and entertain respectable people at my house, richly deserve this disgrace and punishment."

"Let the grand-treasurer," said he, "make up a purse of a thousand pieces of gold, and go to the quarter of the city where I sent the police-judge, and give it to the mother of one Abou Hassan, called the *Rake*. Go, and return quickly." Giafar departed, and went to the grand-treasurer, who gave him the purse. He ordered one of the slaves who attended him, to take it, and proceeded with it to Abou Hassan's mother. He found her, and said the caliph had sent her that present, without explaining himself any further. She received it with great surprise.

Abou Hassan did not continue longer on the throne of the caliph. He descended from it in the same manner as he had mounted it. He then entered his closet, and Mesrour conducted him into an inner room where a table was set out. The door of the apartment was open, and several eunuchs ran to tell the female musicians that the pretended caliph was coming. They immediately commenced a very harmonious concert of vocal and instrumental music, which charmed Abou Hassan to such a degree, that he felt himself in a transport of joy and delight, and knew not what to think of all he saw and heard. "If it be a dream," said he to himself, "it is a dream of long continuance. But it cannot be a dream," continued he; "I am perfectly sensible; I make use of my understanding—I see—I walk—I hear. Be it what it may, I refer myself entirely to God. Still I cannot possibly believe that I am not the commander of the faithful; there is but one commander of the faithful who can be surrounded with so much splendour as I am. The honours and respect which have been and still are paid to me—the orders which I gave, and which are executed—are clear proofs of it."

In fine, Abou Hassan was persuaded that he was the caliph. Seven bands of female musicians, all of the most exquisite beauty, were placed around the saloon. In the midst was a table spread with seven large dishes of massive gold, which perfumed the room with the odour of the richest spices. Seven young damsels, dressed in habits of the richest stuffs and most brilliant colours, stood round the table; each held a fan in her hand for the purpose of refreshing him, while he sat at table. He looked at each of them in succession; and, after admiring the graceful ease with which they performed their office, he said to them, with a gracious smile, that he thought one of them at a time would be sufficient to afford him all the air he wanted; and he desired that the other six should place themselves at the table with him, three on his right hand, and three on his left, and give him their company. The six damsels obeyed, and seated themselves round the table. But Abou Hassan soon perceived, that, out of respect to him, they did not eat; this induced him to help them himself, inviting and pressing them to eat, in the most obliging manner. He desired to know their names, and each in turn satisfied his curiosity. He put the same question to the seventh, who held the fan, and she answered that her name was Sugar-cane. He was shortly conducted into another saloon, where a magnificent table was spread with every sort of delicious fruit.

When Abou Hassan had eaten of each of the fruits on the table which he liked best, he arose; and immediately Mesrour, who never quitted him, again walking before, led him into a third saloon, furnished, decorated, and enriched, as magnificently as the two former.

The day was drawing toward a close, when Abou Hassan was conducted into a fourth saloon, decorated, like the rest, with the most costly and magnificent furniture. Here, too, were seven grand lustres of gold, filled with lighted tapers. Abou Hassan found again in this last saloon, as he had found in the others, seven bands of female musicians. There also he saw seven other damsels, who stood in waiting round a table, likewise covered with seven basins of gold, filled with cakes and pastry. But Abou Hassan observed here, what he had not seen in the other saloons, a sideboard, upon which were seven large flagons of silver, filled with the most exquisite wines, and seven glasses of the finest rock-crystal, of excellent workmanship, near each flagon.

When he was seated, he remained a long time as in an ecstasy of admiration. As the loud sound of the music, and especially of the cymbals, which were used in all the bands, did not allow his voice to be heard, he clapped his hands to put an end to it; when there was instantly a profound silence. Then taking the hand of the damsel who was nearest to him on the right, he made her sit down; and, after presenting her with a rich cake, he asked her name. "Commander of the faithful," answered the damsel, "I am called Cluster of Pearls." "You could not have a more appropriate name," returned Abou Hassan, "nor one more expressive of your charms. Cluster of Pearls," added he, "since that is your name, do me the favour to fill a glass, and bring it me to drink from your fair hand." The damsel went instantly to the sideboard, and fetched a glass of wine, which she presented to Abou Hassan with inimitable grace. He took it with pleasure, and looking at her tenderly, "Cluster of Pearls," said he, "I drink your health, I desire you to fill as much for yourself and pledge me." She quickly ran to the sideboard, and returned with a glass in her hand; but before she drank, she sung a song, which delighted him not less from its novelty, than by the charms of a voice still more wonderful. Abou Hassan, after having drank, took from the basins what he liked best, and presented it to another damsel, whom he desired to come and sit near him. He demanded her name also. She answered that her name was Morning Star. "Your fine eyes," resumed he, "are brighter and more brilliant than the star of which you bear the name. Go, and do me the favour to bring me a

glass of wine." She immediately complied with the best grace possible. He acted in the same manner with regard to the third damsel, who was called Light of the Day, as well as with all the rest, who each presented him wine, which he drank, to the high entertainment of the caliph.

When Abou Hassan had drank as many glasses as there were damsels, Cluster of Pearls went to the sideboard, took a glass, which she filled with wine, and after having thrown into it a little of the powder which the caliph had made use of the day before, she advanced and presented it to him. "Commander of the faithful," said she, "I entreat your majesty to accept this glass of wine; and, before you drink it, to hear a song, which, I dare flatter myself, will not be disagreeable to you." "I grant you this favour with pleasure," said Abou Hassan, as he took the glass which she offered to him. The damsel took her lute, and sang a song to the accompaniment of this instrument, with so much accuracy, grace, and expression, that she kept Abou Hassan in an ecstacy from beginning to end. When she had finished, Abou Hassan first drank off the glass completely at a draught; when turning his head toward the damsel, in order to speak to her, he was prevented by the sudden effect which the powder had taken, and could merely open his mouth. His eyes were presently closed; and he let his head fall upon the table. The caliph, who had derived much satisfaction from this amusement, and who saw all that passed upon this occasion, quitted his closet, and appeared in the saloon. He first ordered that Abou Hassan should be dispossessed of the caliph's habit in which he had been dressed, and that he should be re-clothed with that he had worn before. He summoned the same slave; and upon his appearing, "Take this man again," said he, "and carry him back to his own sofa." The slave took up Abbou Hassan, carried him off by the secret door of the palace, placed him in his own house, and returned in haste to give an account of what he had done. "Abou Hassan," said the caliph, "wished to be caliph for one day only, that he might punish the man of the mosque in his neighbourhood, and the four scheiks, whose conduct had displeased him. I have procured him the opportunity of doing what he desired."

Abou Hassan having been replaced on his sofa by the slave, slept till very late; nor did he awake before the powder which was put into the last glass he drunk had taken its full effect; when, opening his eyes, he was much surprised to find himself in his own house. "Cluster of Pearls!" cried he, "Morning Star! Break of Day! Coral-lips! Moonshine!" calling the damsels of the palace, who had been sitting with him, by their names, as he could recollect them, "where are you?" Abou Hassan cried out so loud, that his mother, who heard him from her apartment, ran to him alarmed. "What is the matter with you, my son?" she asked. At these words Abou Hassan raised his head, and looking at his mother with an air of haughtiness and disdain, "Good woman," asked he in his turn, "who is the person you call your son?" "It is yourself," replied the mother, with much tenderness; "are not you my son, Abou Hassan?" "I your son! execrable old woman!" returned Abou Hassan; "you know not what you are saying, I am not the Abou Hassan you speak of; I am the commander of the faithful. I am not out of my senses, as you suppose; I tell you again, I am commander of the faithful." "Ah, my son!" cried the mother, "is it possible that I hear you utter words which clearly prove that you are not in your senses! You are my son, Abou Hassan, and I am your mother." After some consideration,

"I believe you are right," said he; and his mother thought her son was cured of the malady which had disturbed his mind, and which she attributed to a dream. She was preparing to laugh with him, when suddenly sitting up, and looking at her crossly, "Old witch, old sorceress," said he, "you know not what you are saying; I am not your son, nor are you my mother. I am commander of the faithful." "For Heaven's sake, my son," cried she, "refrain from holding this sort of language." "I am no longer your son," resumed he; "I am assuredly the commander of the faithful. Know, it was by my orders that the iman and the four scheiks were punished. I am, then, I tell you, in good truth, the commander of the faithful." His mother, who could not guess why her son maintained, with so much obstinacy, that he was the commander of the faithful, no longer doubted his having lost his understanding. Under this persuasion, "My son," said she, "I pray God to pity you, and show you mercy. What would be said of you if you should be heard talking in this manner?"

These remonstrances, far from softening Abou Hassan's spirit, served only to irritate him still more. "Old woman," said he, "I have already cautioned you to be quiet. I am the caliph, the commander of the faithful, and you ought to believe me when I tell you so." The good lady, instead of replying, gave way to tears and lamentations, and striking her face and bosom, she uttered exclamations which testified her deep sorrow at the dreadful deprivation of understanding to which her son was reduced. Abou Hassan, instead of being softened by his mother's tears, forgot himself so far as to lose all natural respect for her. He rose suddenly, and, seizing a stick, advanced toward her like a madman. "Cursed old woman!" said he in his fury, "tell me this moment who I am!" "My son," answered his mother, looking most kindly at him. "I am most honest in telling you, that you are Abou Hassan, and that you are quite wrong in assuming a title which belongs only to the Caliph Haroun Alraschid. In fact, the grand-vizier Giafar took the trouble to seek me, and putting into my hands a purse of a thousand pieces of gold, bade me pray to God for the commander of the faithful, who made me this present." At these words, Abou Hassan lost all self-command. The circumstance persuaded him more firmly than ever that he was the caliph, because the vizier carried the purse only by his own order. "Well, old sorceress!" cried he, "will you not be satisfied when I tell you that I am the person who sent the thousand pieces of gold by the grand-vizier Giafar?" Saying which, in the height of his phrenzy, he beat her most unmercifully with the stick he held in his hand.

. The poor mother, who did not expect her son would put his threats into execution, began to cry out for help, as loud as she could. The first that appeared threw himself immediately between his mother and him. "What are you doing?" said he; "have you lost the fear of God, and your understanding? And are you not ashamed thus to ill-treat your mother, who so tenderly loves you?" "You are very impertinent," returned Abou Hassan; "I neither know her nor you. I am the commander of the faithful; and if you are ignorant of it, I will make you know it to your cost." Two of the company hastened immediately to the hospital for lunatics, to inform the keeper of what was passing: he came directly, followed by a considerable number of his people, who brought with them chains, hand-cuffs, and a cat-o'-nine-tails. At their arrival Abou Hassan made great efforts to free himself; but the keeper, by two or three strokes of his whip, soon brought him to reason. This treatment had such an effect, that he was quiet, and the keeper and his people did with him what they pleased. They chained him, and put hand-cuffs and fetters on him, and conveyed him to the hospital for lunatics.

There he was lodged, and shut up in an iron cage. But, before he was confined, the keeper treated his back and

shoulders most unmercifully, with fifty strokes of his whip; and continued, for more three weeks, to give him every day the same punishment.

In the meantime, Abou Hassan's mother came regularly every day to see her son. His mother was desirous of conversing with him, to console him, and to endeavour to learn whether he still continued in the same opinion respecting his pretended dignity of caliph. "My dear mother," answered Abou Hassan, with a settled and composed mind, and in a tone that marked the concern he felt for the violent manner in which he had behaved to her, "I acknowledge my error, and entreat you to forgive the horrid crime of which I have been guilty toward you. I have been deceived by a dream. However strange it may appear, I must think it a dream, or an illusion. I am even convinced that I am not that phantom of a caliph, but your son Abou Hassan." At these words, the tears of grief and distress, which she had shed during so long time, were changed into tears of pleasure, of comfort, and of tender affection. "My son," cried she, in a transport of joy, "I am not less delighted to hear you talk so rationally, than if I had this moment brought you into the world. I must tell you my opinion of your adventure, and make you remark a circumstance to which, perhaps, you may have paid no regard. The stranger whom you brought home to supper went away without shutting your chamber door as you desired him; and that, I believe, gave an opportunity to the evil spirit to come in, and throw you into that dreadful illusion, under which you have laboured." "You have discovered the source of my misfortune," answered Abou Hassan: "and it was on that very night that I had the dream which has so turned my head. In the name of God, Mother, I entreat you to liberate me from this place of torment." His mother gladly consented.

Abou Hassan returned to his house, and remained there several days, to recover his health by better food than he had received in the hospital for madmen. But as soon as he had a little regained his strength, he began to think it tiresome to pass his evenings without company. For this reason, he soon returned to his usual mode of living, that is to say, to provide sufficient every day to entertain a new guest at night. The day on which he recommenced his custom was the first of the month—the day, as before observed, on which the caliph amused himself with walking, in disguise, through a part of the suburbs of the city, according to the practice he had adopted from the commencement of his reign. Abou Hassan had not long taken his seat, when casting his eyes toward the other end of the bridge, he saw the caliph advancing to him, disguised as before, and attended by the same slave. "God preserve me!" said he to himself. "This, if I am not mistaken, is the very sorcerer who laid his spell upon me!" He immediately turned his head, and looked over the parapet, that he might not see him as he passed. The caliph, who wished to derive still further amusement, had taken great care to be informed of all that he had said and done the day after he awoke, and of everything that had happened to him. But, as this monarch was very just and generous, he thought fit, with the design of bringing him again near his person, to disguise himself, on the first day of the month, like a merchant of Moussol, as he had before acted. As he approached him, he stooped down, and looking in his face, "It is you, then, brother Abou Hassan!" said he; "I salute you. Permit me, I beseech you, to embrace you." "Not I!" answered Abou Hassan, bluntly, without regarding the pretended merchant of Moussol. "I do not wish to salute you. I want neither your salutation nor your embraces. Go on your way." "My good friend," returned the caliph, embracing him, "you treat me with a harshness I did not expect. I beseech you to be persuaded of my friendship. Do me the favour to relate to me what has befallen you." Abou Hassan submitted to the entreaty; and, after having made him take a seat near him, "Your earnestness and incredulity," said he, "have exhausted my patience. What I am going to tell you, will show you whether I complain of you without reason."

The caliph seated himself by Abou Hassan, who related to him an account of all the adventures in which he had been engaged, from the time of his waking at the palace to that of his second waking at his own chamber; and he told everything as if it were really a dream, not omitting a multitude of circumstances, which the caliph knew as well as he did himself, and which afforded him fresh pleasure. He then expatiated on the impression which this dream had left upon his mind, of his being the caliph and commander of the faithful.

The caliph, who knew all that had passed, was delighted within himself at having so well succeeded in bringing him into that state of illusion in which he still saw him; but he could not hear this narrative detailed with so much artlessness, without bursting into a fit of laughter. Abou Hassan, who thought his story ought to excite compassion, and that all the world must be of the same opinion, was highly offended. "Are you jesting with me," said he, "or do you think I am trifling? Do you wish for proof of what I advance? Here, look and convince yourself, and then tell me if I'm jesting." Saying this, he bent himself forward, and, uncovering his breast and shoulders, he exposed to the caliph the scars and bruises occasioned by the blows he had received. The caliph felt compassion, and was extremely sorry the joke had been carried so far. He ceased laughing, and cordially embracing Hassan, "Rise, my dear brother, I beseech you," said he, with a serious air, "let us go to your house; I wish to have again the pleasure of enjoying myself with you this evening. To-morrow, if it please God, you will see all things go well."

Abou Hassan, contrary to the oath he had taken not to entertain a stranger a second time at his house, could not withstand the caresses of the disguised caliph. "Well, I consent," said he, "but on one condition, which you shall engage by an oath to observe. It is, that you shut my chamber-door when you leave my house, that the devil may not come to turn my brain, as he did before." The pretended merchant promised all, when they both of them arose, and walked towards the town.

Abou Hassan and the caliph, followed by his slave, drew near Abou Hassan's house, by which time the day began to close. In a short time supper was served on a table that was placed before them, and they ate without ceremony. When they had finished, Abou Hassan's mother cleared the table, and placed the fruit upon it, with the wine and glasses. Abou Hassan helped himself to wine first, and then served the caliph. When the caliph saw that Abou Hassan began to grow warm, he led him to the subject of his amours, and asked him if he had even been in love. "Brother," replied Abou Hassan, very familiarly, "I have never considered either love or marriage but as a slavery, to which I have always felt a reluctance to submit; and to this moment, I will confess to you, I have never loved anything but the pleasures of the table."

They pushed their conversation on this subject to great length, when the caliph, perceiving that Abou Hassan was worked up to the point he wished, said, "Leave the matter to me; and, since you have a good taste, and are an honest fellow, I will find a person to your mind, without its being either cost or trouble to you." At this moment he took the bottle and Abou Hassan's glass, into which which he dexterously put a small quantity of the powder he had before made use of, and filled him a bumper. "Here," continued he, "drink beforehand to the health of the beauty who is to constitute the happiness of your life. Abou Hassan took the glass with a smile, and, shaking his head, "Let it be so," said he, "since you will have it. I will, then, drink to the health of this beauty you promise me, although, contented with my present situation, I build but little upon your assurances."

Abou Hassan had no sooner swallowed his bumper, than a profound sleep deprived him of his senses, the caliph immediately ordered the slave that attended him, to take Abou Hassan, and convey him to the palace. The slave carried him off; and the caliph, who did not intend to send Abou Hassan back as on the former occasion, shut the door of the chamber on quitting it. The slave followed with his burthen, and when the caliph reached the palace, he ordered that Abou Hassan should be laid upon the sofa, in the fourth saloon, whence he had been carried back to his own house, fast asleep, a month previously. Before they left him to his sleep, he directed the same dress to be put upon him, which he had already worn, to make him support the character of the caliph. He then bade them all go to bed ; and ordered Mesrour, and all the eunuchs, the officers of the bed-chamber, the female musicians, and the same ladies who were in this saloon when he had drunk the last glass of wine which had occasioned his sleep, to be in waiting. The caliph went to bed, after having desired Mesrour to awaken him before they went into the closet, where he had already been concealed.

Mesrour did not neglect to wake the caliph precisely at the hour he had appointed. He found the officers of the eunuchs, those of the bedchamber, the ladies, and the female band of music, at the door, attending his arrival. Having told them in a few words his intention, he entered, and stationed himself in the closet. Every thing being thus arranged, and the caliph's powder having taken all its effect, Abou Hassan awoke. At this moment, the seven choirs of female singers joined their delightful voices to the sound of hautboys, soft flutes, and other instruments, making a most agreeable concert. He opened his eyes, and his wonder was extreme on perceiving the damsels and the officers who stood around him, and whom he recollected. The saloon appeared to be the same as that which he had seen in his first dream : he observed there the same lights, the same furniture, and the same ornaments. "Alas!" he cried, "here am I again fallen into the same dream, and the same illusion, which I experienced a month ago ! and what have I to expect, but the same punishment at the hospital for madmen, and the iron cage." After these words, he shut his eyes, and remained lost in intense thought, with a mind entirely confused. Heart's Delight, one of the damsels whom he had seen the first time, advanced to him, and seating herself at the end of the sofa, "Commander of the faithful," said she, in a very respectful manner, "I beseech your majesty to pardon me, if I take the liberty of advising you not to sleep any more, but to endeavour to rouse yourself and get up, because the day is beginning to appear." Get thee hence, Satan !" exclaimed Abou Hassan, when he heard this voice. "Do you call me commander of the faithful ? you certainly take me for another person," "It is to your majesty," returned Heart's Delight, "that I give this title, which belongs to you as sovereign of all the mussulman world, whose very humble slave I am, and to whom now I have the honour of speaking."

Heart's Delight said so many other things which appeared probable, that he at length arose, and sat up. He opened his eyes, and recognised her, as well as the Cluster of Pearls, and the other damsels. They then all at once approached him, and Heart's Delight resumed her discourse. "Commander of the faithful," she said, "your majesty will allow us to remind you again, that it is time to rise." Abou Hassan cast his eyes around him, and felt as it were under enchantment, but he attributed it all to a dream, and of which he dreaded the miserable consequences.— "God have mercy upon me !" he said; "into his hands I resign myself." The caliph, who heard his exclamations, felt so strong an inclination to laugh, that he had some difficulty to prevent discovering himself. Abou Hassan, in the mean time, lay down, and reclosed his eyes. "Commander of the faithful," said Heart's Delight, "since your majesty does not rise after we have told you it is day-light, we shall make use of the permission you have given us on such occasions." On which she took him by the arm, and called the other damsels to assist her in removing him from the sofa where he was laid, and they carried him into the midst of the saloon, where they placed him on a seat.

Abou Hassan was inexpressibly perplexed. "Can I be really caliph and commander of the faithful?" said he to himself. He beckoned to Cluster of Pearls and Morning Star. "Let me have no falsehood," said he, with great simplicity; "but tell me truly who I am." "Commander of the faithful," answered Morning Star, "your majesty chooses to surprise us, by putting this question. If this be not the case, some extraordinary dream must have made your majesty forget who you are." She then related to him the punishment of the iman, and the four old men, by the police-judge; the present of a purse of gold sent by his vizier to the mother of a person called Abou Hassan; what was done in the interior of the palace, and what passed at the four tables of refreshment. "Well, well," returned Abou Hassan, shaking his head, "you would willingly deceive me, if I would hearken to you, but know, that since I saw you, I have been at my own house—have ill-treated my mother—have been carried to the lunatics' hospital, where I remained more than three weeks, during which time the keeper never failed to treat me every day with fifty lashes.—And would you persuade me that all this was nothing but a dream ?" "Commander of the faithful," replied Morning Star, "we are ready to swear that what you tell us is merely a dream. You have not quitted this saloon since yesterday; and you have not ceased sleeping the whole night, till this moment."

In the confused state of Abou Hassan's mind, he called one of the caliph's officers, who was near him. "Come hither," said he, "and bite the tip of my ear." The officer approached, and bit it so hard that Abou Hassan uttered a dreadful cry. At this cry all the instruments sounded at the same time, and the damsels and the officers began to dance, to sing, and skip about with so much noise, that he lapsed into a kind of phrensy. He began to sing with the rest; he stripped off the fine dress of the caliph, with which they had clothed him; he sprang from his seat, threw himself between two damsels, whom he took by the hand, and began to dance with them so actively, and with so many whimsical and ludicrous contortions of his body, that the caliph could no longer restrain himself in his hiding-place. The sudden merriment of Abou Hassan occasioned him such a fit of laughter, that he fell backward, and was heard above all the noise of the musical instruments. At length he rose up, and opening the lattice, "Abou Hassan, Abou Hassan," cried he, "are you determined to kill me with laughter?" At the caliph's voice all were silent, and the loud music ceased. Abou Hassan turning his head towards the place whence the voice came, immediately recognised the caliph, and at the same time the merchant of

Moussol. He was not disconcerted at this discovery; he knew, in a moment, that he was quite awake, and that all which had befallen him was perfectly real, and no dream. He entered into the humour and design of the caliph. "Ah, ah!" cried he, looking at him with an air of confidence, "you are there, merchant of Moussol." "You are in the right, Abou Hassan," replied the caliph, still continuing to laugh; "but for your comfort, and to make amends for all your sufferings, I am ready to recompense you in any manner you desire, and shall think proper to demand."

On concluding these words, the caliph entered the saloon. He directly ordered one of his best habits to be brought, and bade the damsels do the functions of the officers of the chamber, and dress Abou Hassan with it. When they had so done, "You are my brother," said the caliph, "ask of me whatever will afford you satisfaction, and I will grant it." "Commander of the faithful," replied Abou Hassan "I beseech your majesty to have the goodness to inform me, how you contrived to turn my brain, and what was your design in so doing?" The caliph was very ready to give this satisfaction. "You must, in the first place, understand then," said he, "that I frequently disguise myself, and especially by night, to learn whether proper order be preserved in the city of Bagdad. I was on my way the evening you invited me to sup with you. In the course of our conversation, you observed, that the chief thing you desired was to be caliph and commander of the faithful only during the space of twenty-four hours, that you might punish the iman of the mosque in your neighbourhood, and the four scheiks his counsellors. Your desire appeared likely to afford me amusement. I had in my possession a powder, which occasions deep sleep the moment it is taken, and from which the person will not awake for a certain time. I put a dose of it into the last glass I presented to you; you were immediately seized with a sleepy fit, and I ordered the slave who attended upon me to take you and carry you to my palace. I need not tell you what happened to you at my palace after your waking. I did not imagine you would have to undergo so much; but, as I have given you my word, I will do everything to console all your troubles. See, then, what I can do for your gratification, and freely ask whatever you wish." "Commander of the faithful," returned Abou Hassan, "the favour I shall presume to ask, is to allow me free access to your person, that I may have the happiness, all my life, of admiring your greatness." This last proof of disinterestedness completely secured the caliph's esteem. "I most readily comply with your request," said he; "and at the same time grant you free access to me in my palace at all hours, and in whatever part I may be;" and he immediately assigned him an apartment in the palace, and ordered a thousand pieces of gold to be paid him from the privy purse.

Abou Hassan's newly-acquired distinction, rendered him extremely attentive about the caliph's person. As he was naturally of a good temper, and occasioned much cheerfulness, the caliph scarcely knew how to live without him, and he never engaged in any scheme of amusement, but he made him of the party. Zobeide observed, that whenever he attended the caliph in his visits to her, he had always his eyes upon one of her slaves, called Nouzhatoul-aouadat which she determined to communicate to the caliph. "Commander of the faithful, you have not observed, perhaps, that every time Abou Hassan comes hither with you, he constantly fixes his eyes upon Nouzhatoul-aouadat. You will scarcely doubt of this being a sure sign she is not disagreeable to him. If, therefore, you take my advice, we will conclude a marriage between them." "Madam," returned the caliph, "you bring to my recollection a matter I ought not to have forgotten. I know Abou Hassan's opinion on the subject of marriage, and I have always promised to give him a wife. I am glad you have spoken to me about it, and I cannot conceive how the thing should have escaped my memory. But it is better that Abou Hassan should follow his own inclination. At the same time, since Nouzhatoul-aouadat does not seem averse to the match, we ought not to hesitate about this marriage.—Here they are both, they have only to declare their consent."

The marriage took place, and the nuptials were celebrated in the palace with great rejoicings, which continued many days.

Abou Hassan and his wife were charmed with each other. Their mutual regard was so perfect, that, except during the time they were employed in paying attendance, one on the caliph, the other on the Princess Zobeide, they lived entirely together, nor for a moment ever quitted each other. With such dispositions, they could not fail of passing their time together most agreeably. Their table was always covered with the most delicious and high-seasoned dishes, which a cook had the charge of furnishing. There they enjoyed themselves most agreeably in private, and entertained each another with a thousand pleasantries, which made them laugh more or less, according to the degree of their wit and humour.

Abou Hassan and Nouzhatoul-aouadat passed a long time in the enjoyment of this mirth and good cheer, never once considering the expense of their mode of living. It was but just the cook should receive some money; he accordingly presented his account to them. There was, besides, a demand to settle for bridal garments of the richest stuffs for the use of both, and for jewels of high value for the bride.

Abou Hassan well remembered, that the caliph promised that he should never want for anything. But when he reflected that he had squandered in so little time the liberal bounty he had received, he could not bear to expose himself to shame of avowing the ill use he had made of it, and his occasion for a fresh supply.

At length he broke silence, and looking at Nouzhatoul-aouadat, "I see plainly," said he, "that you are in the same embarrassment as myself, and that you are considering what course we ought to pursue. I know not what you may think of the matter; for my part, whatever may be the consequence, I am determined not to retrench my usual expenses; and I believe you, on your side, will agree with me The difficulty is, to find means to provide for them, without the degradation of applying either to the caliph or Zobeide, and I think I have discovered the means." This speech gave Nouzhatoul-aouadat much satisfaction, and some degree of hope. "I was not less engaged than you with this thought," said she, "and if I did not speak out, it was because I could see no remedy. I must confess that the declaration you have just made gives me the greatest pleasure possible. But since you have discovered the means, and my assistance is necessary, you have only to tell me what to do, and I will exert myself to the utmost." "I expected," replied Abou Hassan, "that you would not fail in an affair which concerns you equally with myself. This, then, is the scheme I have devised. It consists in a little deception, which we must practise, me to the caliph, and you to Zobeide; and which, I am assured, will cause them amusement, and not be unprofitable to us.—The deceit, then, which I propose, is, that we should both of us die. You must understand, I do not mean to talk of a real, but a feigned death." "Ah! good!" interrupted

Nouzhatoul-aouadat; "since we are only to feign death, I am at your service." "Very well," continued Abou Hassan, "you must immediately take a sheet, and envelope me with it; then place me in the middle of the chamber, in the usual way, with a turban on my face, and my feet turned toward Mecca; and make every preparation for carrying me to the grave. When all this is done, do you set up a cry, and shed tears, rending your garments and tearing your hair—at least, pretending to do so:—and in this state, go and present yourself to Zobeide. The princess will inquire the reason of your tears; and when you have informed her, she will pity you, and make you a present of a sum of money to assist in defraying the expenses of my funeral. As soon as you have returned with the money, and what you can get, I will rise from where I have been lying, and you must take my place. You then must pretend to be dead; and after you have been placed properly, I will go in my turn to the caliph, and play the same part as you have performed with Zobeide."

"I believe," said Nouzhatoul-aouadat immediately, "that the trick will be very diverting; and I am deceived if the caliph and Zobeide will not be much obliged to us for it. Let us lose no time. While I am getting a sheet, do you equip yourself in your shirt and drawers." Abou Hassan was soon in the state Nouzhatoul-aouadat recommended. He lay down, on his back, in the middle of the chamber, crossed his arms, and suffered himself to be wrapped up, appearing as if nothing more were necessary but to place him on the bier. His wife covered his face with the finest muslin, and placed his turban over it, in such a manner as not to prevent his breathing.

Nouzhatoul-aouadat played her part to perfection. The moment she perceived Zobeide, she redoubled her cries, tore off her hair, and threw herself at her feet, bathing them with her tears. Zobeide, astonished at seeing her slave so extraordinarily afflicted, asked her what was the matter, and what misfortune had happened to her. "Alas! my ever-honoured lady and mistress," cried she, her voice broken with sobs, "what greater or more fatal evil could befal me, than that which obliges me to throw myself at the feet of your majesty Abou Hassan, the poor Abou Hassan, whom you have honoured with your bounty, and whom you and the commander of the faithful gave me for a husband is no more!" Zobeide was extremely surprised at this news. "Is Abou Hassan dead?" cried she, "I did not indeed expect so soon to hear of the death of such a man."

In fact, Zobeide had always observed in her slave the same even temper, the same unaffected sweetness, a great docility, and a zeal in all she undertook in her service, which clearly proved it arose more from inclination than duty. She did not, therefore, hesitate to believe her; and she ordered her female treasurer to fetch a purse of a hundred pieces of gold, and a piece of brocade," which, by Zobeide's order, she delivered to Nouzhatoul-aoudat. On receiving this handsome present, she threw herself at the princess's feet, making her the most humble acknowledgments, with great inward satisfaction at having so well succeeded. "Go," said Zobeide, "let the piece of brocade be used to cover your deceased husband, and employ the money in defraying the expense of a funeral. Afterwards, endeavour to moderate your affliction; I will take care of you."

Nouzhatoul-aouadat was no sooner out of the presence of Zobeide, than she returned as speedily as possible to render an account of the good success of her part. As she entered, Nouzhatoul-aouadat burst into a violent fit of laughter, at finding Abou Hassan still in the same situation, ready prepared for interment. "Get up," said she, still laughing, "and behold the fruits of my imposition upon Zobeide. We shall not die of hunger to-day." Abou Hassan quickly arose, and heartily rejoiced with his wife.

Nouzhatoul-aouadat, delighted at having so well succeeded, could not contain her joy. "But this is not enough," said she, "I must pretend to die in my turn; and see whether you will be clever enough to get as much from the caliph as I have obtained from Zobeide." Abou Hassan laid out his wife in the same manner as he himself had been before, and then he proceeded to the caliph uttering exclamations expressive of the greatest grief. The caliph, who was accustomed to see Abou Hassan with a countenance always cheerful, was greatly surprised at his appearing in so melancholy a state; he withdrew his attention from the business on which they were engaged in the council, to ask him the occasion of his grief. "Commander of the faithful," answered Abou Hassan, "a greater misfortune could not possibly befal me, than what now causes my affliction. Nouzhatoul-aouadat, is, alas!—" At this exclamation, Abou Hassan pretended to be so much distressed, that he could not utter another word. In short, Abou Hassan counterfeited grief so perfectly, that the caliph gave credit to all he said. The treasurer of the palace was present; and the caliph ordered him to give Abou Hassan a purse of a hundred pieces of a gold, with a fine piece of brocade. Abou Hassan immediately threw himself at the feet of the caliph, to express his gratitude. "Follow the treasurer," said the caliph: "the piece of brocade will serve you to lay over your dead wife, and the money to furnish a funeral worthy of her."

Abou Hassan followed the treasurer; and when the purse and the piece of brocade were delivered to him, he returned to his house perfectly satisfied at having so readily found means to supply his present necessity. Nouzhatoul-aouadat, as soon as she heard the door open, ran towards him. "Well," said she, "has the caliph been as easily imposed upon as Zobeide was?" "You see," replied Abou Hassan, showing her the purse and the piece of brocade, "that I know how to counterfeit affliction for the death of a wife."

Although there were affairs of importance to settle in the council which was then holding, the caliph, impatient to condole Zobeide on the death of her slave, rose soon after Abou Hassan's departure, and adjourned the council to another day. As soon as they were gone, the caliph said to Mesrour, "Follow me, and share with me in the grief of the princess for the death of her slave Nouzhatoul-aouadat. They proceeded together to Zobeide's apartment. When the caliph was at the door, he removed the tapestry, and perceived the princess sitting upon her sofa in great affliction, with her eyes still bathed in tears. "Madam," said he, "it is unnecessary to say how great a share I take in your affliction, since you are not ignorant that I am as sensible to all that gives you pain, as I am to whatever affords you pleasure. Nouzhatoul-aouadat, your faithful slave, had, in truth, qualities, which deservedly merited your esteem; and I very much approve of your giving proofs of it after her death."

If the princess was charmed with the tender sentiments which accompanied the caliph's compliment, she was, at the same time, much surprised to hear of the death of Nouzhatoul-aouadat. This intelligence occasioned her such astonishment, that she remained some time unable to reply. At length, upon recovering herself, and regaining her voice, "Commander of the faithful," said she, "I am very sensible to all the tender sentiments you express for me; but allow me to say, that I do not in the least understand the intelligence you bring me of the death of my slave; if you see me afflicted, it is at the death of Abou Hassan, her husband, your favorite, whom I esteem.

The caliph, who was fully persuaded there could be no doubt of the death of the slave, began to laugh heartily, at hearing Zobeide talk in this manner. "Madam," said he, "shed no more tears for Abou Hassan, he is perfectly well. Weep rather for the death of your slave; it is scarcely a moment since her husband entered my apartment all in tears, to announce to me the death of his wife. I ordered a purse of a hundred pieces of gold, and a piece of brocade to be given to him, towards defraying the funeral expenses of the deceased."

"Commander of the faithful," replied she, "I must say, your raillery is ill-timed. What I have been saying is quite a serious matter; the death of my slave is not the consideration, but the death of her husband, Abou Hassan." "And I, madam," replied the caliph, becoming much more grave, "tell you, without jesting, that you are mistaken. It is Nouzhatoul-aouadat who is dead; and Abou Hassan is alive, and in perfect health." "Commander of the faithful," resumed she earnestly, "may God preserve you from long remaining under this error! Allow me to repeat once more, that it is Abou Hassan who is dead; and that Nouzhatoul-aouadat, my slave, widow of the deceased, is certainly alive. Not an hour has elapsed since she left me."

Fire sparkled in the caliph's eyes from anger. He was sitting on the sofa, but at a great distance from the princess; and speaking to Mesrour, "Go immediately," said he, "and see which of the two is dead." The caliph had not ended, before Mesrour was gone.—"You will learn in a moment," continued he, speaking to Zobeide, "who is right, you or I." "Do not think thus to carry your point," replied Zobeide; "I propose a wager. I am so convinced of the death of Abou Hassan, that I am ready to stake whatever I hold most precious against what you please. You are not unacquainted with my disposition, and therefore know what I love best; you have only to choose and propose." "Since this is the case," said the caliph, "I stake, then, my garden of delights against your palace of pictures."

While the caliph and Zobeide were contending so earnestly, and with so much warmth, Abou Hassan, who had foreseen their altercation on this point, was very attentive to whatever might happen. Consequently, when he saw Mesrour coming straight to their apartment, he immediately conceived the purport of his mission. He told his wife to feign dead once more, as they had before agreed, as quickly as possible. Scarcely was this performed, before Mesrour entered the chamber. The spectacle that presented itself gave him secret pleasure, so far as regarded the commission with which he was charged by the caliph. As soon as Abou Hassan saw him, he arose to meet him, and respectfully kissing his hand, "My lord," said he, sighing, "you see me in the deepest affliction, for the death of my dear wife Nouzhatoul-aouadat, whom you honoured with your kindness." Mesrour lifted the covering a little way from her head that he might look at her face, which was then exposed, and letting it fall again after he had taken a slight view, with a deep sigh, he said, "There is no other god but God!" He then turned towards Abou Hassan. "It is not said without reason," continued he, "that women sometimes disregard what they say, which cannot be excused. Zobeide, my most excellent mistress, is now in this predicament. She would maintain to the caliph, that it was you who were dead, and not your wife. I will return and assist at the interment."

Mesrour was leaving the house to render an account of his commission, when Abou Hassan, who conducted him to the door, observed, that he had no claim to the honour he intended him. Lest Mesrour should turn back to say something more, he followed him with his eyes for some time, and when he saw him at a considerable distance, he re-entered his chamber, and freeing Nouzhatoul-aouadat from her covering. "This, then," said he, "is a new scene in our play; certainly the Princess Zobeide will not regard Mesrour's report, but, on the contrary, will laugh at him. Her reasons are too strong against giving credit to him; so that we must expect some new occurrence."

In the meantime, Mesrour reached Zobeide's apartment; he entered her cabinet laughing like a man who had something agreeable to communicate. The caliph was naturally of an impatient temper. As soon, therefore, as he saw Mesrour, "Wicked slave!" cried he, "this is not a time for laughing; you say not a word: speak out boldly—Who is dead?" "Commander of the faithful," answered Mesrour, "it is Nouzhatoul-aouadat that is dead; and Abou Hassan is still as much afflicted as when he lately appeared before your Majesty." Without giving time for Mesrour to proceed, the caliph interrupted him, "Good news!" cried he, "It is not a moment since Zobeide, your mistress, was possessed of the palace of pictures; it is now mine. I will take care to reward you. But no more of this; tell me every particular of what you have seen." "Commander of the faithful," proceeded Mesrour, "when I reached Abou Hassan's apartments, I found him still weeping, and very much afflicted at the death of his wife Nouzhatoul-aouadat. He was seated near the head of the deceased, the body covered with the piece of brocade which your majesty lately presented to Abou Hassan." Then addressing the Princess Zobeide, "Well, madam," enquired the caliph, "have you any further opposition to make? Do you continue to think that Nouzhatoul-aouadat is still living? Do not you confess that you have lost your wager?" Zobeide could by no means admit that Mesrour had reported the truth. "How, sir!" replied she, "can you imagine that I shall believe this slave? I am neither blind nor deprived of my senses; I have seen with my own eyes, Nouzhatoul-aouadat under the greatest affliction; I have myself spoken to her: and I heard perfectly what she told me." She immediately summoned her women, by clapping her hands; and they entered in great numbers. "Come hither," said the princess to them; "tell me the truth—Who was the person that spoke to me a short time before the commander of the faithful appeared?" The women all answered, that it was the poor afflicted Nouzhatoul-aouadat. "And you," continued she, speaking to her treasuress—"What did I order you to give to her on retiring?" "Madam," replied the treasuress, "I gave to Nouzhatoul-aouadat, by your majesty's command, a purse of a hundred pieces of gold, and a piece of brocade."

During this altercation, the caliph—who had heard the statements on both sides, laughed heartily at seeing Zobeide in such a rage. "Madam," said he to Zobeide, "I know not who says, that women are sometimes beside themselves; but allow me to repeat, you make it appear that nothing is more true. Mesrour is this moment returned from Abou Hassan's apartments; he tells you he has seen with his own eyes, Nouzhatoul-aouadat lying dead; and, notwithstanding this testimony, you will not believe it." "Commander of the faithful," resumed Zobeide "I see plainly that you are leagued with Mesrour in a design to tease me, and to try my patience to the utmost. And as I perceive that the report which Mesrour has made

was concerted between you, I beg you will allow me to send also a person." The caliph consented, and the princess charged her nurse with this important commission. "Nurse," said she, "you know the subject of my dispute; there is no occasion to say any more to you; clear up the whole; and if you bring me back a good account, you shall have a valuable present; go quickly, and return as soon as possible."

In the meantime, Abou Hassan, who remained sentinel at the lattice, perceived the nurse at some distance and immediately conceived that her errand was on the part of Zobeide. He called his wife, and, without a moment's hesitation. "Here comes," said he, "the princess's nurse, it is now my turn to appear dead." Every thing was ready; Nouzhatoul-aouadat dressed Abou Hassan instantly, threw over him the piece of brocade, and placed the turban on his face. The nurse in her eagerness to execute her commission, was already at the house. She perceived Nouzhatoul-aouadat sitting at the head of Abou Hassan in tears, with her hair dishevelled, and uttering

loud lamentations. She approached the pretended widow. "My dear Nouzhatoul-aouadat," said she, "I am not come to disturb your grief." "Ah, my good mother!" interrupted the pretended widow, and in a tone to excite compassion, "you see to what a wretched situation I am reduced. Abou Hassan! my dear husband?" cried she again, "what have I done that you should so soon abandon me? Alas! what will become of the poor Nouzhatoul-aouadat!" The nurse was in the greatest astonishment at seeing everything contrary to what the chief had reported to the caliph.

Much affected by the tears of Nouzhatoul-aouadat, she seated herself near her, and, shedding tears imperceptibly approached the head of Abou Hassan, raised his turban a little, and uncovered his face, to see if she knew him: "Ah, poor Abou Hassan!" said she, immediately replacing his turban, "I pray God to have mercy upon you!—Adieu, my child! if I could stay longer with you, I would with all my heart: but I must not delay a moment to return and deliver our good mistress from her distressing anxiety." She had scarcely closed the door, before Nouzhatoul-aouadat, relieved Abou Hassan from his irksome confinement, and they again took their places on the sofa, near the lattice tranquilly waiting the event of their artifice, and prepared to combat every difficulty that might occur.

Zobeide's nurse, in the meantime, returned at a still quicker pace than she came. The pleasure of carrying to the princess a satisfactory account, accelerated her steps: she entered the cabinet of the princess almost out of breath; and related in an artless manner all she had seen. Zobeide heard the nurse's report with a satisfaction she could not conceal; she said to her in an exulting tone of voice, "Repeat the same account before the commander of the faithful. Tell it to this wicked black slave, who has the insolence to maintain to my face, what I know to be a falsehood."

Mesrour, who had no doubt that the nurse's expedition and reports would prove favourable to him, was excessively mortified: "Toothless old woman!" said he to the nurse, "I tell thee plainly, thou art a liar; I saw, with my own eyes, Nouzhatoul-aouadat lying dead." "Thou art a liar, an abominable liar, thyself," retorted the nurse, "to dare to maintain such a falsehood to me." "I am not an imposter," replied Mesrour; "it is thou who art trying to lead us into an error." "What impudent effrontery!" exclaimed the nurse.

The caliph, who had heard all this altercation, could not reconcile such striking contradictions. The princess for her part, as well as Mesrour, the nurse, and female slaves, who were present, knew not what to think. The caliph at length spoke: "Madam," said he, addressing himself to Zobeide, "it appears evident we are all liars;—I, first; you next; then Mesrour, and then the nurse." He then decided that they would go in person and ascertain the truth.

The apartment which the caliph and Zobeide quitted, although at some distance, was directly opposite to the residence of Abou Hassan and Nouzhatoul-aouadat. Abou Hassan who saw them approaching, immediately apprised his wife of it, observing, that he never was more mistaken, if they were not to be soon honored with a visit from them. "What shall we do?" cried she;—"we are ruined!" "Be not alarmed," returned Abou Hassan very coolly; "have you already forgotten what we have said upon this subject?—Let us both pretend to be dead, and all, you shall see, will turn out well. At the rate they walk, we shall be ready before they reach the door." In fine, Abou Hassan and his wife determined to cover themselves as well as they could; and in this state, after they had placed themselves one beside the other, in the middle of the chamber, each under the piece of brocade, they waited quietly for the arrival of the company.

Mesrour opened the door, and the caliph and Zobeide entered the chamber, followed by all their people. They were much surprised, and stood motionless, at the dismal spectacle which was presented to their sight. No one could form an opinion on the subject. Zobeide at last broke silence: "Alas!" said she to the caliph, "they are both dead —You have well done," she proceeded, looking at the caliph and Mesrour, "by obstinately endeavouring to persuade me that my dear slave was dead—as indeed she is, and, without doubt, for grief at having lost her husband." "Say rather, madam," replied the caliph, with a contrary prejudice, "that Nouzhatoul-aouadat died first, and that poor Abou Hassan fell under the affliction of witnessing the death of his wife. So, you must allow that you have lost your wager, and that the palace of pictures is now fairly mine." "And I," returned Zobeide, animated by the contradiction of the caliph, "maintain, that you have lost, and that your garden of delights belongs to me. Abou Hassan died first, since my nurse told you as well as me, that she saw his wife alive, and lamenting her husband's death."

At last the caliph, reflecting upon all that had passed, agreed that Zobeide had not less reason than himself to maintain that she was the winner. He approached the two bodies, and seated himself near their heads, secretly endeavouring to devise some expedient which might give him the victory over Zobeide. "Yes," cried he a moment afterwards, "I swear that I will give a thousand pieces of gold to the person who shall prove to me which of the two died first."—The caliph had scarcely uttered the last word, when he heard a voice from under the brocade which covered Abou Hassan, that cried, "Commander of the faithful, it was I who died first;"—At the same time he saw Abou Hassan, who freed himself from the brocade which covered him, and prostrated himself at his feet. His wife disengaged herself in the same manner, and ran to throw herself at the feet of Zobeide.

The caliph, far from being alarmed, when he heard Abou Hassan's voice, was near bursting with laughter on seeing them both freeing themselves from their coverings. "What, then, Abou Hassan," said the caliph, "have you determined to kill me with laughter? How came you to think of this surprising Zobeide and me—in a way we could not possibly guard against?" "Commander of the faithful," replied Abou Hassan, "I will tell you all without disguise. Your majesty well knows, that I was always fond of good living. The wife you gave me has not occasioned me to relax in this particular, on the contrary. In fine, the shame of seeing ourselves reduced to a wretched condition of poverty, and our not daring to inform your majesty of it, made us invent this plan to supply our wants, which we entreat your majesty to forgive."

The caliph and Zobeide, were very well satisfied with the sincerity of Abou Hassan, they did not seem in the least angry at what had passed; on the contrary, Zobeide could not avoid laughing in her turn, at the recollection of all that Abou Hassan had devised to accomplish his design. The caliph, who had scarcely ceased laughing, said to Abou Hassan and his wife, as he rose, "Follow me, both of you; I will give you the thousand pieces of gold that I offered, for the joy I feel, that neither of you is dead." "Commander of the faithful," resumed Zobeide, "content yourself, I beseech you, with causing the thousand pieces of gold to be given to Abou Hassan, you owe them only to him, as to his wife, that is my business," at the same time she ordered her treasuress, who accompanied her, to give a thousand pieces of gold also to Nouzhatoul-aouadat, in proof of the joy she felt, on her part, that she was yet alive.

Thus did Abou Hassan, and Nouzhatoul-aouadat, preserve a long time the favour of the Caliph Haroun Alraschid and acquired enough to supply all their wants, for the remainder of their lives.

THE HISTORY OF ALADDIN, OR THE WONDERFUL LAMP.

IN the capital of one of the richest and most extensive kingdoms in China, lived a tailor named Mustafa. He was very poor; and the profits of his trade were scarcely sufficient to provide subsistence for himself and his wife, and one son, whose name was Aladdin, who had been brought up in a very negligent manner, and had consequently imbibed the most vicious inclinations: he was mischievous, obstinate, and disobedient to his father and mother, who as he grew up could no longer keep him in the house; he went out early in the morning, and passed the whole day playing in the streets and public places.

As soon as he was old enough to learn a trade, his father took him to his shop, and began to instruct him how to use his needle. But neither kindness nor the fear of punishment had any effect in restraining his restless disposition.

As soon as Mustafa's back was turned, Aladdin decamped, and returned no more during the whole day. This conduct of his son caused him great uneasiness, and the vexation of not being able to bring him to his duty, occasioned so obstinate a disease, that at the end of a few months it put a period to his existence. Aladdin's mother, who saw that her son would never follow the trade of his father, shut up the shop, and converted all his stock and implements of trade into money; upon which, added to what she could earn by spinning cotton, she and her son subsisted.

Aladdin abandoned himself entirely to licentiousness. He was in this state, when, as he was one day playing with a troop of vagabonds, a stranger, who was passing stopped and looked at him. This stranger was a famous magician distinguished by the appellation of the African magician, and had arrived from that part of the world only two days before. Whether or not this African magician had remarked in the countenance of Aladdin the requisites necessary for the execution of the purpose which had occasioned his journey, is uncertain, but he adroitly informed himself of his family, who he was, and what disposition he possessed. When he had ascertained all he wished, he approached the young man, and taking him to a little distance from his companions, "My son," said he, "was not your father called Mustafa the tailor?" "Yes sir," replied Aladdin, "but he is dead." At these words, the African magician threw his arms round Aladdin's neck, embraced and kissed him several times, and shed many tears. Aladdin asked him what reason he had to weep. "Ah my child!" replied the magician, "how can I refrain? I am your uncle; I have been several years on my journey hither, desiring to see my brother, and at the instant of my arrival at this place, you inform me of his death." He then asked Aladdin where his mother lived, and as soon as he was answered, the African magician gave him a handful of small money, saying to him, "My son go to your mother, and tell her that I shall visit her to-morrow, to afford myself the consolation of seeing the spot where my brother lived so long, and where he finished his days."

The magician had no sooner quitted, than Aladdin ran to his mother, highly delighted with the money his pretended uncle had given him. "Pray tell me, mother," he cried, the instant of his arrival, "whether I have not an uncle?" "No, my child," replied she; "you have no uncle." "I have just parted from a man," continued Aladdin, "who told me, he was my father's brother. He even cried and embraced me, when I told him of my father's death. And to prove to you, that he spoke the truth," added he. showing her the money, "see what he has given me." "It is true, my son," returned Aladdin's mother, "that your father had a brother, but he has been dead a long time."

The next day the magician again accosted Aladdin, while he was playing with some other boys. He embraced him as before; and putting two pieces of gold into his hand, "Take this, my son," said he; "I intend to sup with your mother this evening, and this will procure what is necessary for the repast." Aladdin carried the two pieces of gold to his mother; and when he had told her of his uncle's intentions, she went out, and procured a supply of good provisions. She employed the whole day in preparing for the supper; and in the evening, when everything was ready, she desired Aladdin, as his uncle might not know where to find the house, to go into the street, and if he should see him to show him the way. Although Aladdin had given the magician a clear direction to his mother's house, he was nevertheless very ready to go, when some person knocked at the door. Aladdin opened it, and recognised the African magician, who entered, loaded with bottles of wine, and several sorts of fruit.

When the magician had placed himself where he chose, he entered into conversation with Aladdin's mother. "Be not surprised, my good sister," said he, "at never having seen me during the whole of the time you have been married to my brother. It is forty years since I left this country, of which I am a native, as well as my deceased brother. I went into Africa, where I made a long stay. At last, as it is natural to man, the desire of seeing and once more embracing my dear brother, fastened so strongly on my mind, that I felt myself sufficiently bold and strong again to undertake the fatigue of so long a journey. It is unnecessary to describe the various obstacles I had to encounter, before I arrived here; but nothing occasioned me so much pain, as the intelligence of the death of my poor brother, whose memory I must ever regard with a friendship truly fraternal."

The African magician, who perceived that the recollection of her husband renewed her grief, changed the subject; and turning towards Aladdin, he asked him his name. "I am called Aladdin," he answered. "Well, then, how do you employ yourself?" At this interrogation, Aladdin hung down his head, and was much disconcerted; but his mother thus replied: "Aladdin is a very idle boy. His father did all he could to make him learn his business, but entirely without effect; and in spite of all I can say, he will only lead the life of a vagabond." "This is very bad, nephew," said the magician; "you must think of working to support yourself. There are many trades; consider, if there is not one you have an inclination to learn. If you are averse from learning a trade, and yet wish to be an honest man I will procure you a shop, and furnish it with rich stuffs, you may sell the goods, and buy other merchandise: and in this manner will pass your life very respectably." This offer flattered the vanity of Aladdin, whom manual labour displeased so much the more, as he had sufficient sense to perceive that the shops which contained goods of this sort were much frequented, so that he was much more inclined to the latter plan, and said he should all his life continue sensible of the obligation. "Since this employment is agreeable to you," replied the magician, "I will take you with me to-morrow, and have you properly and handsomely dressed, and then we will see about procuring a shop of the description I propose."

The African magician did not fail to return the next morning as he had promised. He took Aladdin with him, and conducted him to a merchant's, where ready-made clothes of all kinds were sold. "Nephew," said he, "choose, among all these habits, that which you like best." Delighted with the liberality of his new uncle, Aladdin chose one; which the magician bought, together with every necessary to complete the dress.

He then conducted Aladdin to the most frequented parts of the city, where the shops of the more opulent merchants were situated; and when he reached the street in which fine stuffs and linens were sold, he said, "as you will soon become a merchant, it is proper that you should frequent this place, and become acquainted with them." In fine, after having viewed all parts of the city most worthy notice, they arrived at the khan were the magician had hired an apartment. They there found several merchants, and whom he had now invited to partake of a repast, for the purpose of introducing his pretended nephew to them.

The next morning, Aladdin arose and dressed himself, that he might be ready to set out the moment his uncle called. After waiting some time, he became so impatient, that he opened the door, to watch for his arrival. The moment he saw him approaching, he informed his mother of it, took leave of her, shut the door, and ran to meet him. The magician treated Aladdin in the most affectionate manner. "Come, my dear boy!" said he, with a smile, "I will to-day show you some very fine things." At each palace they came to, he asked Aladdin if he did not think it

very beautiful; while the latter often prevented this question, by exclaiming " O uncle ! here is one much more beautiful than those we have before seen." In the mean time, they continued proceeding into the country, and sat down by the side of a large basin of pure water. "My dear nephew," said he, "you must be fatigued. Let us rest ourselves here a little while." When they were seated, the magician took from a piece of linen cloth, that was attached to his girdle, various sorts of fruits and some cakes. When they had finished their slight repast, they got up and pursued their way by the side of the gardens. The African magician insensibly led Aladdin on much farther than the gardens extended; and they continued walking through the country, till they reached the neighbourhood of the mountains. Aladdin felt himself very much tired "Where are we going, my dear uncle?" said he; "I can see nothing but hills and mountains before us." "Take courage, nephew," replied the pretended uncle; "I wish to show you another garden, that greatly surpasses all you have hitherto seen."

They at length arrived in a narrow valley, situated between two moderately high mountains. This was the precise spot to which the magician wished to lead Aladdin, for the execution of a grand project. "We shall now," said he, "go no farther; and I shall here discover to your view some extraordinary things. While I strike a light, collect all the brambles that you can find, in order to make a fire." There were so many of these brambles about the place, that Aladdin had collected more than was sufficient by the time the magician had lighted his match. He then set fire to them; and as soon as they were in a blaze, the African threw on them a certain perfume. A dense smoke immediately arose, which unfolded itself on each side, in consequence of some mysterious words pronounced by the magician. At the same instant the ground slightly trembled, and opening before them, discovered a square stone about a foot and a half across, with a brass ring fixed in the centre.

Aladdin was greatly terrified at what he saw, and was about to run away, when the magician stopped him in an angry manner, giving him at the same moment a blow, which knocked him down, and very nearly beat out some of his teeth. "You have observed," he said, "what I have done by virtue of my perfumes, and the words I pronounced. You are now to be informed, that under this stone is a concealed treasure; and which will one day render you richer than the greatest monarch of the earth." Rapt in astonishment at all he had seen and heard, Aladdin forgot everything else that had passed: "Well, my dear uncle," he exclaimed, as he got up, "what must I do ? tell me, I am ready to obey you." "I heartily rejoice, my boy," replied the magician, "that you have made so good a resolution. Come here; take hold of this ring, and lift up the stone." "But I am not strong enough, uncle," said Aladdin; "you must help me." "No, no," answered the magician, "you have no occasion for my assistance; we shall not do any good if I attempt to help you: you must lift it up entirely by yourself. Pronounce only the name of your father and your grandfather as you take hold of the ring, lift it, and you will see it rise without difficulty." Aladdin followed exactly the magician's directions, and easily raised the stone.

When the stone was removed, a small excavation was visible, at the bottom of which appeared a small door, with steps to go down still lower. "My son," said the African magician, "observe very exactly everything I now tell you.—Go down into this cavern; and when you have reached the bottom of the steps, you will perceive an open door, which leads into a large vaulted space, divided into three successive halls. Before you enter the first hall, take up your robe, and bind it round you: then go in; pass on to the second without stopping; and thence, in the same manner to the third. Above everything avoid approaching the walls: for if you touch them even with any part of your dress, your instant death will be the inevitable consequence. At the extremity of the third hall is a door, which leads to a garden, planted with beautiful trees. Go straight forward, and pursue a path which will bring you to the bottom of a flight of fifty steps, at the top of which is a terrace. When you have ascended to the terrace, you will observe a niche before you, in which is a lighted lamp: take the lamp and extinguish it; and after throwing out the wick and the liquid, bring it to me. If you should feel very desirous of gathering any of the fruit in the garden, you may do so." On concluding these directions to Aladdin, the magician took off a ring from one of his fingers, and put it on his pretended nephew; telling him that it was a preservative against every evil that might otherwise happen to him. "Go, my child," added he, " descend boldly; we shall now both of us become rich."

Aladdin jumped into the opening, and descended to the bottom of the steps. He there found the three halls, which the magician had described: he passed through them with the greatest precaution possible. He crossed the garden without stopping; ascended to the terrace; took the lighted lamp from the niche, threw out its contents, and put it into his bosom. He then came down from the terrace, and stopped in the garden to examine the fruit. The trees of this garden were all loaded with the most extraordinary fruit: each tree bore a sort of a different colour;—some were white; others sparkling. and transparent like crystal; some were red, and of different shades; others green, blue, violet; some of a yellowish hue. The white were pearls; the sparkling and transparent diamonds; the deep red were rubies; the paler, a particular sort of ruby, called balass; the green, emeralds; the blue, turquoises; the violet, amethysts; those tinged with yellow, sapphires : and so of the others. As he was not yet of an age to be acquainted with their worth, he thought they were only pieces of coloured glass. The variety, however of so many beautiful colours, as well as the brilliancy and extraordinary size of each fruit, nevertheless tempted him to gather some. In fine, he took so many of every colour, that he filled his pockets, as well as the two purses which the magician had bought for him at the time he made him a present of his dress. Thus loaded with immense treasure, though ignorant of its value, Aladdin hastened through the three halls, that he might no longer detain the African magician : and having passed through them began to mount the steps he had descended, and presented himself at the entrance of the cave. As soon as Aladdin reached there, "Pray, uncle," said he, "lend me your hand, to help me up." "You had better," replied the magician, "first give me the lamp." "Pardon me, uncle, it is not at all in my way," said Aladdin; "I will give it you when I am out." The magician obstinately insisted on having the lamp, before he lent Aladdin any assistance : but the latter had, in fact, covered it with the fruit with which he was surrounded, and he absolutely refused to give it till he had got out of the cave. The magician put himself into the most violent rage : he threw a little perfume on the fire, and had scarcely pronounced two magic words, before the stone, which served to close the entrance of the cavern, resumed its place, with all the earth over it, precisely as it was when the magician and Aladdin first arrived.

It is certain that this magician was not the brother of Mustafa, as he had affirmed, and consequently not the uncle of Aladdin. He was born in Africa; and, as that is a country where magic is more studied than in any other, he had addicted himself to it from his earliest youth. After nearly forty years, spent in reading books of magic, he had at length discovered, that there was in the universe a wonderful lamp, the possession of which would render him more powerful than any monarch of the universe. But though the lamp was certainly in the place of which he had obtained a knowledge, yet he was not, nevertheless, permitted to take it away himself, nor to enter in person the subterraneous place where it was to be found: it was absolutely necessary that another person should descend to fetch it, and then put it into his hands. It was for this reason that he had addressed himself to Aladdin, who appeared to be well calculated to perform the service he expected from him; and he resolved, as soon as he had obtained the lamp, to raise the fumigation, pronounce the two magic words to produce the effect already seen, and sacrifice poor Aladdin to his avarice and wickedness, that he might not have existing witnesses of his acquisition.

Aladdin, who did not expect this treatment from his pretended uncle, experienced a surprise and astonishment much easier to conceive than describe. When he found himself, as it were, buried alive, he called aloud a thousand times to his uncle, telling him he was ready to give him the lamp: but his cries were useless, and he had no other means of making himself heard: he therefore remained in perfect darkness.

He remained two days in this state, without either eating or drinking. On the third day, regarding his death as inevitable, he lifted up his hands, and joining them, resigned himself wholly to the will of Heaven, uttering, in a loud voice, "*There is no strength or power, but in the high and great God!*" In this action of joining his hands, he happened to rub the ring which the magician had put upon his finger, and of the virtue of which he was as yet ignorant. Immediately a geni of a most enormous figure, and horrid countenance, arose out of the earth before him. He was so tall, that his head touched the vaulted roof; and he addressed these words to Aladdin. "*What do you wish? I am ready to obey you as your slave; as the slave of all who possess the ring on your finger, I and the other slaves of the ring.*" At any other time, Aladdin would have been so terrified at the sight of this extraordinary figure, that he would have been unable to speak; but now, entirely occupied with the danger of his situation, he answered, "Whoever you are, take me if you have the power, out of this place." He had scarcely pronounced these words, before the earth opened, and he found himself on the outside of the cave, at the very spot to which the magician had brought him. He could not comprehend in what manner he had been so suddenly disinterred. There was only the place where the fire had been made, which he recollected was close to the entrance of the cave. Looking round towards the city, he perceived it, and returned home, thanking God for having restored him to the world, which he thought he had quitted for ever. Aladdin had scarcely entered the house, when the joy experienced from again seeing his mother, added to his weak state, in consequence of not having eaten anything for nearly three days, caused him to faint. His mother, seeing him in this condition, did not omit any attention to restore him. At length he revived; and Aladdin then related to his mother all that had happened to him and the magician on the day when the latter took him to see the palaces and gardens round the city. He did not forget the blow he received from the magician. He omitted no circumstance of all that he had seen in passing and repassing through the three halls, in the garden, or on the terrace, whence he had taken the wonderful lamp, which he drew from his bosom, and showed to his mother, as well as the transparent and differently coloured fruits that he had gathered. He finished the recital of his adventure by telling her, that, when he returned and presented himself at the mouth of the cave to get out, upon refusing to give the lamp to the magician, the entrance to the cave was instantly closed, by means of the perfume that the magician threw on the fire. Aladdin had no sooner ended, than she uttered a volley of abuse against this impostor. "Yes, my child," she exclaimed, "he is a magician; and magicians are public evils; they hold communications with demons, by means of their sorceries and enchantments." She added many other observations; but, as she was thus speaking, she perceived that Aladdin, who had not slept for three days, wanted repose; she made him therefore, retire to rest.

Aladdin, who had not been able to obtain any repose in the subterraneous place in which he had been as it were buried, passed the whole of that night in the most profound sleep, and did not awake until very late the next morning. When he arose, the first words he uttered to his mother were, that he was very hungry. "Alas, my child!" replied his mother, "I have not a morsel of bread to give you. Have, however, a few moment's patience; it shall not be long before I will obtain you some. I have a little cotton of my own spinning; I will go and sell it, to purchase bread." "Keep your cotton, mother," said Aladdin, "for another time, and give me the lamp which I brought with me yesterday. I will go and sell that." Aladdin's mother took the lamp from the place where she had placed it. "Here it is," said she to her son; "but it is very dirty. If I clean it a little, perhaps it may sell for something more." She then took some water and a little fine sand to clean it with; but had scarcely begun to rub this lamp, when instantly a hideous and gigantic geni rose out of the ground before her, and cried with a thundering voice, "*What do you wish? I am ready to obey you as your slave, and the slave of all those who have the lamp in their hands, I and the other slaves of the lamp.*" The mother of Aladdin, was unable to endure the sight of a figure so hideous and alarming as that of the geni; and her terror was so great, that he had no sooner begun to speak than she fainted. Aladdin, who had before seen a similar appearance in the cavern, instantly seized the lamp; and supplied his mother's place, by answering for her in a firm tone of voice, "I am hungry; bring me something to eat." The geni disappeared, and returned the next moment with a large silver tray, and twelve covered dishes of the same metal, filled with excellent meats, six loaves as white as snow, on as many plates, two bottles of exquisite wine, and two silver cups in his hand.

All this passed so quickly, that Aladdin's mother had not recovered from her swoon before the geni had disappeared the second time. Aladdin, who had already thrown some water in her face without effect, was again preparing to endeavour to bring her to herself; but at the very instant, whether her scattered spirits returned of themselves, or that the smell of the dishes which the geni had brought produced the effect, she quite recovered. "My dear mother," cried Aladdin, "there is nothing the matter. Get up, and come and eat; here is what will put you in good spirits." His mother was extremely astonished, when she beheld the large tray, the twelve dishes, the six loaves, the two bottles of wine and two cups, and perceived the delicious odour that exhaled from them. "My child," she asked, "how came all this abundance here?" "My dear mother," replied Aladdin, "come and sit down, and begin to eat; I will tell you all when we have broken our fast."

When Aladdin's mother had put aside what they had not consumed, she seated herself on the sofa, near her son:

"I am waiting," said she, "for you to satisfy my impatient curiosity." Aladdin then described to her all that had passed between him and the geni, from the moment her alarm caused her to faint, till she recovered her senses. "But what do you tell me, child, about your genii? Never, in my life, have I heard of any person of my acquaintance that has seen one. Why did he not rather address himself to you, to whom he had before appeared?" "Mother," replied Aladdin, "the geni who just now appeared to you, is not the same that I had already seen. If you recollect, the geni whom I first saw called himself the slave of the ring, and he who appeared to you said he was the slave of the lamp." "What!" cried Aladdin's mother, "Is it then your lamp that caused this cursed geni to address himself to me?—Ah, child! take the lamp out of my sight, and put it where you please. If you follow my advice, you will also put away the ring; we ought to have no commerce with geni." "With your permission," replied Aladdin, "I shall now take good care not to sell this lamp, which has already been so useful to us both. Do you not see what it has procured us? and it will also continue to furnish us with whatever we want. Since chance has discovered its virtues to us, let us profit by them; but in such a manner as not to make any bustle. I shall take care to remove it out of your sight, and put it where I shall be able to find it whenever I may have occasion for it." As the arguments appeared very just, his mother had nothing to object. "Do as you like, my son," she cried; "as for me, I wish to have no commerce with genii. I declare to you, that I wash my hands of them, and will never mention them to you again."

After supper, the next evening, no part of the good provisions which the geni had brought remained. The following morning, Aladdin took one of the silver plates under his robe, and went out early, in order to sell it. He addressed himself to a Jew. Aladdin took him aside; and showing him the plate, asked him if he would buy it. The Jew took out of his purse a piece of gold, worth not more than one seventy-second part of the plate, and offered it to Aladdin. The latter eagerly took the money.

In his way, Aladdin stopped at a baker's shop, where he bought enough bread for his mother and himself, which he paid for out of his piece of gold. When he reached home, he gave what remained to his mother, who went to the market, and purchased provisions sufficient to last them for some days. They thus continued to live in an economical manner; that is, till Aladdin had sold all the twelve dishes to the Jew, for the same sum as he had given for the first; the Jew durst not offer him less for fear of losing so good a bargain. When the money received for the last dish was expended, Aladdin had recourse to the tray, which was, at least, ten times as heavy as one of the dishes. He wished to carry this to his ordinary merchant, but its great weight prevented him; he was in consequence obliged to seek for the Jew, and bring him to his mother's house. After having examined the weight of the tray, the Jew immediately counted out ten pieces of gold, with which Aladdin was satisfied.

When his ten pieces of gold were all expended, Aladdin had recourse to the lamp. Taking it up, he looked for the particular part that his mother had rubbed; and as he easily perceived the place where the sand had been used, he applied his hand to the spot, and the same geni whom he had before seen, instantly appeared. "*What do you wish?*" said he to him, in the same words as before—"*I am ready to obey you, as your slave, and the slave of those who have the lamp in their hands, I and the other slaves of the lamp.*" "I am hungry," replied Aladdin. The geni disappeared, and in a short time returned, loaded in the same manner as before. He placed all upon the sofa, and instantly vanished. Aladdin and his mother placed themselves at the table; and, after their repast, there still remained sufficient food to last them the two following days.

When Aladdin again saw that all his provision were expended, and that he had no money to purchase more, he took one of the silver dishes, and went to seek for the Jew with whom he had before formed an acquaintance, in order to sell it. As he walked along, he happened to pass the shop of a goldsmith, whose probity and honesty were unimpeachable. The goldsmith called him into the shop. "My son," said he, "I have seen you pass several times, loaded as you are at present, and join company with a Jew; and return shortly after, empty-handed. I have thought, that you went and sold him what you carried. But, perhaps, you are not aware that this Jew is a very great cheat. Now, I should be glad to serve you—if you will show me what you are carrying."

The hope of selling his silver dish for more money, induced Aladdin to take it from under his robe, and show it to the goldsmith. The old man asked him if he had sold any of the same kind to the Jew, and how much he had received for them. Aladdin ingenuously told him, that he had sold twelve, and that the Jew had given him a piece of gold for each. "Ah, the thief!" cried the merchant. "But, my son," added he, "what is done cannot be undone; let us, therefore, think no more of it; but, in letting you see what your dish, which is made of the finest silver that we ever use in our shops, is really worth, we shall know to what extent the Jew has cheated you." The goldsmith took his scales, weighed the dish, and after explaining to Aladdin how much a mark of silver was, what it was worth, and the different divisions of it, he made him observe, that, according to the weight of the dish, it was worth seventy-two pieces of gold, which he immediately counted out to him. Aladdin thanked the goldsmith, and for the future, carried all his dishes to him, as well as the tray, and always received the full value, according to weight.

Though Aladdin and his mother had an inexhaustible source for money in their lamp, they nevertheless continued to live with the same frugality as before, except that Aladdin reserved a little for decent apparel, and to procure some articles necessary in the house. With such economy, it is easy to conjecture how long the money, arising from the sale of the twelve dishes and the tray to the honest goldsmith, must have lasted them. They lived in this manner for some years, with the profitable assistance which Aladdin occasionally procured from the lamp.

During this interval, Aladdin did not fail to resort frequently to those places where persons of distinction associated. It was at the jewellers', more particularly, that he became undeceived in the idea he had formed respecting the transparent fruits he had gathered in the garden, and that he learnt they were jewels of inestimable price. By means of observing the dealings in all kinds of precious stones, he acquired a knowledge of their value; and as he did not see any that could be compared with those he possessed, he concluded, that, instead of bits of common glass, he was, in fact, possessed of an invaluable treasure.

One day, as he was walking in the city, Aladdin heard a proclamation, by order of the sultan, commanding all persons to shut up their shops and doors, and retire into their houses, until the Princess Badroulboudour, the daughter of the sultan, had passed by in her way to the bath. The public order created in Aladdin a curiosity to see the princess; but this he could only accomplish by going to some house where he was acquainted, and looking through the lattices. He at last thought of a scheme, in which he was completely successful. He went and placed himself behind the door of the bath, which was so disposed, that he could not fail of seeing her face. Aladdin did not wait

ong before the princess made her appearance; and he saw her distinctly through a crevice. She was accompanied by a great crowd of females and eunuchs, some walking on each side of her, others following. When she was within three or four paces of the door of the bath, she lifted up the veil, and thus gave Aladdin an opportunity of seeing her. He had no sooner beheld the Princess Badroulboudour, than he forgot that he had ever supposed all women to be like his mother; and he could not help surrendering his heart to the object whose appearance had so charmed him. Her eyes were large, well placed, and full of fire, yet the expression of her countenance was sweet and modest. When she had entered the bath, Aladdin remained some time as in an ecstacy, retracing and impressing more strongly on his mind the image of a person by whom he had been so charmed. He at length came to himself, and recollected that the princess had passed, and that it would be useless for him to keep his station to see her come out, as her back would then be towards him.

It is unnecessary to inquire how Aladdin passed the night, struck as he was with the beauty and charms of the Princess Badroulboudour; but the next morning as he was sitting upon the sofa, he said, " I will now, mother, break the silence I have preserved since my return from the city yesterday morning. I was not ill, nor am I at this time, yet I can assure you that what I feel, and what I shall ever feel, is worse than any illness. It was not known in this quarter of the city," continued Aladdin, " and therefore you of course are ignorant of it, that the Princess Badroulboudour, daughter of the sultan, went yesterday after dinner to the bath; an order was in consequence published that all shops should be shut, and every person remain at home. As I was not far from the bath; at the time, curiosity to see the princess's face induced me to take it into my head to place myself behind the door of the bath, supposing that she would remove her veil before she entered. She did in fact, and I had the happiness of seeing this charming princess. This, my dear mother, is the true cause of the state in which you saw me yesterday, and the reason of the silence I have hitherto preserved. I entertain so violent a passion for the princess, that I know not how to express it." " My son," she cried, " of what are you thinking? You must surely have lost your senses to talk thus." " Mother," replied Aladdin, " I do assure you! I have not lost my senses, I am perfectly collected. I foresaw that you would reproach me with folly and extravagance; but, nevertheless, nothing will prevent me from again declaring to you that my resolution to demand the Princess Badroulboudour, of the sultan her father, in marriage, is absolutely fixed." " Truly, my son," returned his mother, " I cannot help telling you, that you have entirely forgotten yourself. And pray, son, who do you suppose you are?" she continued, " to aspire to the daughter of your sultan? Have you forgotten that you are the son of one of the poorest tailors in his capital." " My dear mother," replied Aladdin, " I have already told you that I perfectly foresaw all your objections, but neither your arguments nor your remonstrances will cause an alteration in my sentiments. I have told you that I would through you, demand the Princess Badroulboudour in marriage, I require the favour of you, and I entreat you not to refuse unless you would rather see me die, than by granting it, give me life a second time."

Aladdin's mother was very much embarrassed, when she saw with what obstinacy her son persisted in his mad design, " My dear son," said she, " I am your mother, and like a good mother, am willing to undertake anything that is reasonable, and consistent with our situation in life. If this business were merely to ask the daughter of a neighbour, whose condition was similar to yours, I would readily exert all the means in my power; though to hope for success even in such a case, you ought to possess some fortune, or at least know a trade. There is also another reason, my son, of which you have not yet thought, which is, that no person ever appears before the sultan to ask a favour, without offering him some present; but what have you to offer?"

Aladdin listened with the utmost tranquillity to all his mother said, and having reflected on every point of her remonstrance, he said, " I confess, my dear mother, that it is a great presumption in me, to dare carry my pretensions so high, and that I am also very inconsiderate in requesting you to go and propose this marriage to the sultan without having first taken the proper steps to obtain an audience and a favourable reception. I am much obliged to you for the hints which you have suggested, and I consider this beginning as the first step toward procuring me the happy success I promised myself. I agree with you respecting the present, and I also confess that I never once thought of it. But, with regard to what you say about my having nothing to offer him, do you not suppose, mother, that what I brought home with me on the day when I was, as you know, so wonderfully delivered from a seemingly inevitable death, would not be an agreeable present to the sultan? I mean what I brought home in the two purses, and in my sash, and which we have both hitherto supposed to be coloured glass, but I am now undeceived, and I can inform you that they are precious stones of inestimable value; I am persuaded the present will be very agreeable to the sultan. You have a porcelain dish sufficiently large to contain them; bring it here, and let us see the effect they will produce when we have arranged them according to their different colours."

Aladdin's mother brought the dish, in which, taking the precious stones from the two purses, Aladdin arranged them. The effect they produced, in broad daylight, by the variety of their colours, by their lustre and brilliancy, was so great, that both mother and son were absolutely dazzled. After having for some time admired the beauty of the present, " You cannot now, mother," said Aladdin, " excuse yourself any longer from going and presenting yourself to the sultan. Here is a present which will procure for you the most favourable reception." " I cannot, my son," said she, " readily believe that this present will produce the effect you wish, and that the sultan will look upon me with a favourable eye. But, if it be absolutely necessary for me to undertake the mission you propose, I am convinced I shall not have courage to speak, and thus lose, not only my labour, but the present; and, after this, I shall have to return and inform you that all your hopes are frustrated." She advanced many other reasons to her son, in order to induce him to change his mind; but the charms of the Princess Badroulboudour had made too strong an impression on the heart of Aladdin. He persisted in requiring his mother to execute what he had resolved upon; and her tenderness for him at length conquered her repugnance, and she acceded to his wishes.

As it was already late, and the period of attendance at the palace to be presented to the sultan was passed for that day, they were obliged to defer the execution of their project till the morrow. They then separated, to take some repose. He arose before daybreak, and went immediately to awaken his mother, whom he urged to dress herself, that she might repair to the gate of the sultan's palace, and enter at the same time that the grand-vizier and all the great officers of state went into the divan.

She took the porcelain dish containing the present of jewels, and folded it up in a very fine and clean linen cloth, which she covered with another not so fine, tying the four corners of it together, that she might carry it the more easily. She then set out, to the great joy of Aladdin, and took the road towards the palace. The grand-vizier, and distinguished noblemen of the court, had already entered when she arrived at the gate. She stopped, and stationed herself in such a manner, that she faced the sultan, the grand-vizier, and other officers, who formed the council on both sides. They called up the parties one after another, according to the order in which their petitions had been presented; and their affairs were reported, pleaded, and determined, till the usual hour of closing the sitting. The sultan then arose, took leave of the members, and returned to his apartment.

Aladdin's mother, who saw the sultan get up and retire, rightly imagined that he would not appear any more that day: she therefore determined to return home. When Aladdin saw her with the present in her hand, he knew not, at first, what to think of the success of her journey. The good woman very soon relieved her son by saying to him, with an air of great simplicity, "I have seen the sultan, my son; and am persuaded he saw me also. I placed myself directly opposite to him; and there was no person in the way to hinder his seeing me; but he was so much engaged with those on each side of him, that I really felt compassion to see the patience and trouble he gave himself in listening to them. This continued so long, that I believe he was, at length, quite exhausted; for he got up before any one expected it, and quickly retired, without staying to hear a great many other persons; this, indeed, gave me great pleasure. I will not fail to return to-morrow: the sultan will not then, perhaps, be so much engaged."

The next morning, his mother set out for the palace with the present of jewels; but her journey was useless: she found the gate of the divan shut, and learned that the council never sat two days together, but alternately, and that she must come again on the following morning. She returned with this intelligence to her son, who was again obliged to exert his patience. She went again to the palace six different times, on the appointed days, always placing herself before the sultan, but still with as little success as on the first; and she would probably have attended a hundred times to no more purpose, if the sultan, who saw her standing opposite to him every day the divan sat, had not taken notice of her.

She was now so habituated to attending at the council before the sultan, that she totally disregarded the trouble, provided she could by this means convince her son that she had neglected nothing which depended upon her to afford him satisfaction. She accordingly returned to the palace the next day the council met, and placed herself at the entrance of the divan, opposite the sultan. The grand-vizier had not yet commenced his report of any affair, when the sultan perceived her. Touched with compassion at the excessive patience she had shown, "In the first place," said he to the grand-vizier, "there is the woman of whom I spoke to you; order her to come here, and we will begin by hearing and expediting her business." The grand-vizier immediately pointed out this woman to the chief of the ushers, and desired him to go and conduct her before the sultan. The officer having made a sign to her, she followed him to the foot of the throne, where he left her, and returned to his place near the grand-vizier.

Aladdin's mother prostrated herself, with her face to the carpet which covered the steps of the throne, and remained in that situation till commanded to rise. "Good woman," said the sultan, "for a long time past I have seen you regularly attend my divan, and remain during the whole sitting. What is the business that brings you here?" She prostrated herself a second time, and thus answered:—"High monarch, before I inform your majesty of the extraordinary subject that causes me to appear before your sublime throne, I entreat you to pardon the boldness, I might say impudence, of the request I am going to make to you." That she might have full liberty to explain herself, the sultan commanded every one to quit the divan, and leave him alone with his grand-vizier; he then told her she might speak, and explain herself without fear. "Sir," said she, "I venture once more to entreat your majesty to assure me of your pardon beforehand." "Whatever it may be," replied the sultan, "I pardon you from this moment; speak, therefore, with confidence."

When Aladdin's mother had taken all these precautions, she faithfully related by what means Aladdin had seen the Princess Badroulboudour, the violent passion with which this fatal sight had inspired him, his declaration of it to her, and every argument she had used to divert his thoughts from the passion. The sultan heard her with great mildness and good humour, and without shewing the least sign of anger or indignation; but before he gave an answer, he asked her what she carried tied up in a cloth. Immediately she took up the porcelain dish, and having uncovered it, presented it to the sultan. It is impossible to express the surprise and astonishment of the monarch, when he saw collected in that dish, such a quantity of the most precious, perfect, and brilliant jewels, the size of which was greater than any he had ever till then seen. At length he took the present from the hand of Aladdin's mother, and exclaimed, in a transport of joy, "Ah, how beautiful! how rich!" After having admired them all, one after another, he turned to his grand-vizier, and showing him the dish, "Look here!" said he; "did you ever see jewels richer or more perfect?" The vizier was himself delighted with them. "Well," continued the sultan, "what do you say to such a present? Is not the donor worthy of the princess, my daughter?" These words of the sultan very much agitated the grand-vizier; because the former had, some time before, signified an intention of bestowing the hand of the princess upon his son. He was fearful that the sultan would be dazzled by so rich and extraordinary a present, and would, in consequence, change his mind. He therefore approached the sultan, and whispering in his ear, "Sir," said he, "it must be allowed that this present is not unworthy of the princess; but I entreat your majesty to grant me three months before you finally determine." Although the sultan was well persuaded that it was not possible for his grand-vizier to enable his son to make so valuable a present to the princess, he nevertheless listened to his request, and even granted him this favour. "Go, my good woman," said he, "and tell your son that I agree to the proposal he has made through you, but that I cannot bestow the princess, my daughter, in marriage, until I have provided a variety of furniture, which will not be ready in less than three months."

The mother of Aladdin returned to her house with so much the greater joy, as she had at first conceived an access to the sultan, for a person of her condition, impossible.

When Aladdin saw his mother enter the house, two circumstances led him to suppose she brought him good news; the one was, that she had returned that morning much sooner than usual; and the other, that her countenance expressed pleasure and good humour. "Well, mother," said he, "what have I to hope?" "My son," said she, "not to keep you too long in suspense, I will, in the first place, tell you, that so far from thinking of dying, you have every reason to be satisfied." She then proceeded, and related to him in what manner she had obtained an audience, in preference to every other person; the precautions she had used in making her request to the sultan, that he might not be offended when he knew that it was to demand of him the Princess Badroulboudour in marriage for her son; and the very favourable answer the sultan had given her from his own mouth. When Aladdin received this intelligence, he esteemed himself the happiest of mortals. Impatient, however, as he was to possess the object of his affections, three months appeared to him an age; he nevertheless endeavoured to wait with patience, as he relied upon the word of the sultan. In the meantime he not only reckoned the hours, the days, and the weeks, but even every moment, as this period elapsed.

When about two months of this time had expired, as Aladdin's mother was one evening going to light her lamp, she discovered that she had no oil in the house. She therefore went out to purchase some; and, on advancing into the city, found that all the shops, instead of being shut, were open, and ornamented with boughs, and that preparations were making for an illumination; in fine, every one endeavoured to demonstrate his pleasure and his joy. Seeing this, she asked the merchant of whom she bought the oil, what it all signified. "Whence do you come, my good woman," said he, "not to know that the son of the grand-vizier is this evening to be married to the Princess Badroulboudour. She will

return presently from the bath, and the officers whom you see, are assembling to escort her back to [the palace. Aladdin's mother did not want to hear any more. She found her son, who was totally unprepared for the bad news she had brought him: "Everything, my son," she exclaimed, "is lost!" Aladdin was alarmed at these words: "On what account, mother?" said he; "will not the sultan keep his word?" "This very evening," answered she, "the son of the grand-vizier is to marry the Princess Badroulboudour at the palace."

He instantly remembered the lamp, which had hitherto been so useful to him; and, without uttering vain reproaches, only said, "The grand-vizier's son, mother, will not, perhaps, be so happy to-night as he expects.

No. 32.

While I am gone for a few moments into my chamber, do you prepare our supper." Aladdin was no sooner in his own room, than he took the wonderful lamp, and rubbing it in the usual place, the geni instantly stood before him: "*What do you wish?*" said he. "*I am ready to obey you as your slave, and the slave of those who have the lamp in their hands; I and the other slaves of the lamp.*"

"Attend to me," answered Aladdin. "You have hitherto only brought me the sustenance I wanted: I have now an affair for you of much greater importance. I have demanded of the sultan the Princess Badroulboudour, his daughter, in marriage. He promised her to me, and merely requested a delay of three months. Instead, however, of keeping his word, he has this evening, given his daughter to the son of his grand-vizier. What, therefore, I have to require of you is this: as soon as the bride and bridegroom have retired to repose, take them up and bring them both here in their bed." "*Master,*" replied the geni, "*I will obey you. Have you any further commands?*" "Not at present," answered Aladdin; at the same moment the geni disappeared.

In the meantime, the nuptials of the princess were celebrated, in the sultan's palace till the night was far advanced. When all was concluded, the son of the grand-vizier, at a sign privately made him by the chief of the eunuchs belonging to the princess, retired unperceived; and this officer then introduced him to the apartment, where the nuptial couch was prepared. He retired to bed first. Shortly afterwards the sultana, accompanied by her own women and those of her daughter, brought in the bride. The sultana assisted in undressing her, and placed her in bed almost by force; and after embracing her, and wishing her a good night, she retired with all the other families. Scarcely was the door closed, before the geni, as the faithful slave of the lamp, took up the bed with the bride and bridegroom in it, and, to the great astonishment of them both, in an instant transported them to Aladdin's chamber.

Aladdin, who was impatiently waiting this event, did not suffer the son of the grand-vizier to remain long in bed with the princess: "Take this bridegroom," said he to the geni, "and shut him up, and return to-morrow morning, soon after day break." The geni instantly took the grand-vizier's son out of bed, and transported him to the place Aladdin had commanded, where he left him.

However violent the passion which Aladdin felt for the Princess Badroulboudour, he did not hold a long conversation, when he found himself alone with her: "Fear nothing, adorable princess!" he exclaimed; "you are here in safety; and, notwithstanding the excessive love I feel for you, and the ardour with which I idolise your beauty and your charms, be assured that I will never exceed the limits of the profound respect I owe you. She was no longer in a condition to answer him. The terror and astonishment into which she had been thrown, had such an effect upon her, that she could not obtain a single word in reply. Aladdin did not remain long in this state; he determined to lie down in the place of the grand vizier's son, with his back turned towards the princess; having first taken the precaution to place a sabre between the princess and himself, to indicate that he deserved to be punished if he attempted her honour.

Aladdin had no occasion to rub the lamp next morning to call the geni. He returned at the appointed hour, while Aladdin was dressing. "*Here I am,*" said he; "*what are your commands?*" "Go, and bring back the son of the grand-vizier from the situation in which you left him, place him again in this bed, and transport it back to the palace of the sultan." The geni instantly went to relieve the grand-vizier's son from his post; and as soon as he reappeared, Aladdin took away his sabre. He placed the bridegroom by the side of the princess, and the next moment conveyed the bed to the same chamber of the palace whence he had before taken it. The geni had no sooner returned the nuptial couch to its place, than the sultan entered the chamber, to wish her a good morning. The son of the grand-vizier, half dead with the cold he had suffered during the night, when he heard some person opening the door, jumped out of bed, and went into the closet where he had undressed himself. The sultan advanced to the bed-side of the princess, and kissed her, as is the usual custom in wishing a good morning. She regarded him with the most sorrowful looks, which showed that she laboured under severe affliction. The sultan again spoke to her; but as he found he could not obtain an answer, he retired.

When the sultana was dressed, she went to the apartment of the princess. She approached the bed, and, wishing her a good morning, embraced her; but her surprise was excessive, when she observed that the princess was not only silent, but that she was in the greatest distress. "My dear daughter," said the sultana, "is it thus you act towards your mother? Something must certainly have taken place, which I do not understand. Confess to me, then, candidly, and do not suffer me to remain longer in an inquietude that distresses me beyond measure." At length, the Princess Badroulboudour broke silence. "Alas!" she cried, "pardon me, if I have failed in the respect I owe to you. My mind is so entirely absorbed by the extraordinary occurrences of this night, that I have not yet recovered from my astonishment and my fears, and have some difficulty in recollecting myself. She then related how, the instant after she and her husband were in bed, they had been taken up and transported into an ill-furnished and dismal chamber, where she found herself alone; that she found in this apartment a young man, who lay down in her husband's place, having first put his sabre between them; and that, at daybreak, her husband was restored to her, and the bed again brought back to its place in an instant of time."

The sultana listened with great attention, but she could not attach the least credit to the account. "You have done well, my child,' said she to the princess, "not to inform the sultan of this matter. Take care that you mention it to nobody, unless you wish to be supposed to be bereft of your reason." "Madam," replied the princess, "I assure you that I am in my right senses, and know what I say; you may ask my husband." "I will make the inquiry," answered the sultana; "but even if he give me the same account, I shall still continue equally incredulous. In the meantime, get up, and drive this phantasy from your mind."

The festivities in the palace continued during the day; and the sultan forgot nothing that he thought would inspire her with joy; but the recollection of the preceding night's occurrences had made so strong an impression, that it was very perceptible her mind was entirely occupied. The son of the grand-vizier was not less afflicted at the wretched night he had passed.

Aladdin, who was well informed of all that had passed in the palace, did not doubt but the new-married couple would again sleep together. He did not choose to suffer them to repose in quiet; and therefore he had again recourse to his lamp. The geni instantly appeared, and offered his services in the usual terms. "The grand-vizier's son and the Princess Badroulboudour," replied Aladdin, "are again to sleep together this night. Go, and so soon as they have lain down, bring the bed hither." The geni obeyed Aladdin with equal fidelity and exactness to the night pre-

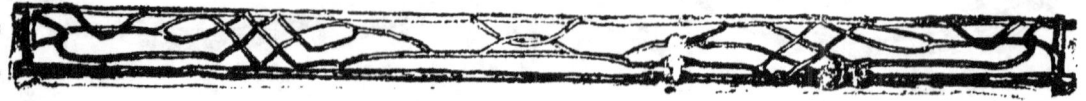

ceding, and the vizier's son passed this night in as cold and unpleasant a situation as he did the former; while the princess experienced the same mortification of having Aladdin for her bed-fellow. In the morning, the geni came, according to Aladdin's orders, replaced the bridegroom by the side of his spouse, and conveyed the bed, with the new married pair, back to the chamber of the palace.

The sultan approached the bedside, and wished the princess a good morning. "Well, my daughter," said he, "are you in as bad a humour this morning as you were yesterday?" The princess retained the same silence, and the sultan perceived that she was still more dejected and uneasy than before. Irritated at her secrecy, "Daughter," said he, in an angry tone, raising his scimitar, "tell me candidly what you thus conceal, or I will instantly strike off your head." "My dear father," she exclaimed, with tears in her eyes, "if I have offended your majesty, I earnestly entreat your pardon, and I hope, from your known goodness and clemency, I shall change your anger into compassion." After this, she described all that had happened to her on both these nights, and in a manner so affecting, that he was penetrated with grief. She thus concluded:—"If your majesty has the least doubt respecting any part of what I have said, you can easily inquire of the husband you have bestowed upon me."

As soon as the sultan re-entered his apartment, he sent for the grand-vizier, "Have you seen your son?" he asked him; "and has he mentioned anything in particular to you?" When the latter replied in the negative, the sultan stated to him everything he had heard from the Princess Badroulboudour, adding, "I have no doubt but that my daughter has told me the truth. I wish, nevertheless, to have this matter confirmed by the testimony of your son. The grand-vizier instantly went to his son; he informed him of what the sultan had said, and commanded him not to disguise the truth. "I will conceal nothing from you, my father," replied his son; "all that the princess has told the sultan is true. Since my marriage, I have passed two of the most dreadful nights it is possible to conceive; and I cannot express to you all the various evils I have suffered. Not to describe my fright at finding myself lifted up in my bed four different times without perceiving any one, and being transported from one place to another, you will yourself judge of the dreadful state I was in, when I tell you that I passed both nights standing upright in a sort of closet, with nothing upon me but my shirt, and deprived of the power of stirring, although there seemed to be no obstacle whatever to prevent me. After telling you this, I have no occasion to enter into a more minute detail of my sufferings; but I must declare that, notwithstanding the honour and splendour I derive from having married the daughter of my sovereign, I would much sooner die than enjoy this high alliance, if I must continue to undergo the treatment I have already encountered. I have no doubt the princess must be of the same opinion; I entreat you, therefore, my dear father, to endeavour to prevail with the sultan to have our marriage declared null and void."

However great might be the ambition of the grand-vizier to have his son so nearly allied to the sultan, yet the fixed resolution which he had formed to separate from the princess made him think it necessary to desire his son to have patience, in order to see whether this unpleasant business might not terminate. He then left him, and returned with the answer to the sultan, and then, without waiting till the sultan himself spoke about annulling the marriage, he requested permission for his son to leave the palace and return to him, under the pretext that it was not just the princess should be exposed for one moment longer to so terrible a persecution. The grand-vizier had no difficulty in obtaining his request, and in a short time every mark of public joy and festivity within the kingdom ceased.

Aladdin suffered the three months to elapse, which had been proposed by the sultan, before urging the marriage of the Princess Badroulboudour and himself; and, when the whole period had expired, he did not omit to send his mother to the palace to remind the sultan of his promise. She accordingly went, and stood at her usual place, near the entrance of the divan. The sultan no sooner saw her, than she brought to his recollection the request she had made, and the exact time to which he had deferred it. "Vizier," said he, stopping him, "I perceive the woman who presented us with the valuable present some time since; desire her to come forward." The grand-vizier immediately called to the chief of the ushers, and, pointing her out to him, desired him to bring her forward. Aladdin's mother advanced to the foot of the throne, where she prostrated herself, according to custom. After she had risen, the sultan asked her what she wished. "Sir," replied she, "I again present myself before the throne of your majesty, to represent to you, in the name of my son, Aladdin, that the three months which you desired him to wait are expired, and to entreat you to recal the circumstance to your remembrance."

The sultan, in desiring a delay of three months, thought he should hear no more of a marriage which appeared to him so little suited to the princess, judging only from the poverty and low condition of Aladdin's mother, who always appeared before him very meanly dressed. The application, therefore, which she now made greatly embarrassed him, and he did not think it prudent to give her an immediate answer. He consulted his grand-vizier, and told him the repugnance he felt at concluding a marriage between the princess and and an unknown person. The grand-vizier did not hesitate to give his opinion. "Sir," said he, "it seems to me that there is a very easy and yet certain method to elude this unequal marriage, and of which this Aladdin could not complain. It is, to set so high a price upon the princess, that all his riches, however great they may be, cannot amount to the sum." The sultan approved of the advice, and, after some little reflection, he said to Aladdin's mother, "Sultans, my good woman, ought always to keep their word, and I am ready to adhere to mine, and render your son happy by marrying him to my daughter; but, as I cannot bestow her in marriage without knowing how she will be supported, tell your son that I will fulfil my promise as soon as he sends me forty large basins of massive gold, quite full of the same sort of things which you have already presented to me, brought by an equal number of black slaves, each conducted by a white slave, young, well made, and of good appearance. Go, my good woman; I will wait till you bring me his answer."

Aladdin's mother again prostrated herself before the throne, and retired. When she entered the house, "My son," said she, "I advise you to think no more of a marriage with the Princess Badroulboudour. The sultan certainly received me with great goodness; but the grand-vizier, if I am not mistaken, made him alter his opinion, as you will yourself think, when you have heard my account." She then gave him an exact detail of all the sultan had said, and of the conditions on which he consented to the marriage of the princess his daughter with him. "He is even now, my son," continued she, "waiting for your answer; but, between ourselves, he may wait long enough." "Not so long as you may imagine, mother," replied Aladdin; "and the sultan deceives himself if he supposes by

such exorbitant demands to prevent my thinking any more of the Princess. While I am considering how to comply with his demands, leave me to myself."

As soon as his mother was gone out to purchase provisions, Aladdin took the lamp, and having rubbed it, the geni instantly presented himself. "The sultan agrees to give me the princess his daughter in marriage," said Aladdin; "but he first demands of me forty large heavy basins of massive gold, filled to the very top with the various fruits of the garden whence I took the lamp. He requires also from me, that these forty basins should be carried by as many black slaves, preceded by an equal number of young, handsome, and well-made white slaves. Go, and procure me this present as soon as possible." The geni replied his commands should be instantly executed. In a very short time the geni returned with forty black slaves, each carrying upon his head a large golden basin, of great weight, full of pearls, diamonds, rubies, and emeralds, even more valuable, for their brilliance and size, than those which had been already presented to the sultan. Every basin was covered with a cloth of silver embroidered with flowers of gold. All these slaves, with their golden basins, entirely filled the house, as well as the court in front, and the garden behind it.

Aladdin's mother now returned from market, and was in the greatest surprise, on entering, to see see so many persons and so much riches. "My dear mother," he cried, "there is no time to lose. It is of consequence that you should return to the palace before the divan breaks up." Without waiting for his mother's answer, Aladdin opened the street door, and ordered all the slaves to go out, one after another; placing a white slave before each of the black ones, who carried the golden basins on their heads.

As it was necessary to pass through several streets, to arrive at the palace, the inhabitants of every rank and condition were witnesses to this spectacle. When the first of the eighty slaves reached the gate of the outer court of the palace the porters were in the greatest haste to open it. As the sultan had been informed of the march and approach of these slaves, he gave orders for their admittance. Accordingly, when they arrived, they found the door of the divan open; and they entered in regular order, dividing to the right and to the left. After they were all within the saloon, and had formed a large semicircle before the throne, each of the black slaves placed the basin, which he carried upon the carpet. They then all prostrated themselves, with their foreheads to the ground. The white slaves also made a similar reverence. They then all arose; and in so doing, the black slaves skilfully uncovered the basins which were before them, and remained standing, with their hands crossed upon their breast.

Aladdin's mother advanced to the foot of the throne, and thus addressed the sultan:—"My son Aladdin, sir, is not ignorant that this present which he has sent your majesty, is very much below the inestimable worth of the Princess Badroulboudour. He nevertheless hopes that your majesty will accept it favourably. He has the greater reliance that his expectations will be fulfilled, because he has studied to conform himself to the conditions you were pleased to impose." The sight alone of such immense riches, and the wonderful celerity with which Aladdin had complied with his demand, easily persuaded him that Aladdin could not be deficient in anything, to render him as accomplished and deserving as he wished. That he might, therefore, send back Aladdin's mother as well satisfied as she could possibly desire, he said to her, "Go, my good woman, and tell your son, that I am waiting with open arms to receive and embrace him."

Aladdin's mother reached home, with an air that showed she was the bearer of good news. "You have every reason, my dear son," she said, "to be satisfied. You have accomplished your wishes. Not to keep you any longer in suspense, I must inform you, that the sultan has announced that you are worthy to possess the Princess Badroulboudour, and he is now waiting to embrace you, and conclude the marriage. You should, therefore, immediately think of making some preparations for the interview with your prince; but, after what I have seen of the wonders you have brought about, I am persuaded you will not fail in anything."

Aladdin scarcely answered his mother, but instantly retired to his chamber. He then seized the lamp, and had no sooner rubbed it, than the geni again showed his ready obedience to its power, by instantly appearing. "Geni," said Aladdin to him, "I have called you to convey me immediately to a bath; and, when I have finished bathing, I desire you to have in readiness for me, a richer and more magnificent dress than was ever worn by any monarch." Aladdin had no sooner concluded his speech, than the geni rendered him invisible, like himself, took him in his arms, and transported him to a bath, formed with the finest marble. Without being able to distinguish who waited upon him, Aladdin was undressed in a large and handsome saloon; and thence he was conducted into the bath, moderately heated, and rubbed and washed with various sorts of perfumed waters. His skin was white and fresh, his countenance blooming, and his whole body felt lighter and more active. He then returned to the saloon, where, instead of the dress he had left, he found another, the magnificence of which astonished him. By the assistance of the geni, he dressed himself, expressing the greatest admiration at each part of it as he put it on. This completed, the geni transported him back into the same chamber of his own house, and then inquired if he had any further commands. "Yes," replied Aladdin, "I wait till you, as quickly as possible, bring me a horse, surpassing in beauty and excellence the most valuable horse in the sultan's stables. I desire you to furnish me also, at the same time, with twenty slaves, as well and richly clothed as those who carried the present, and twenty more to proceed in two ranks before me. Also, procure six female slaves to attend upon my mother, all, at least, as well and as richly clothed as those of the Princess Badroulboudour, and each of them carrying a complete dress, suitable in splendour and magnificence for a sultana. I want, likewise, ten thousand pieces of gold, in ten separate purses." Aladdin had no sooner given those orders to the geni, than he disappeared, and soon after returned with the horse, the forty slaves, of whom ten had each a purse containing ten thousand pieces of gold, and the six female slaves, each carrying on her head a different dress, for Aladdin's mother, enveloped with a piece of silver tissue, and presented the whole to him. Aladdin took only four of the ten purses, and presented them to his mother. He left the other six in the hands of the slaves who carried them, desiring them to keep them, and to throw out the money by handfuls to the populace. In fine, he presented the six female slaves to his mother, informing her, that they were her property, and would, in future, consider her as their mistress.

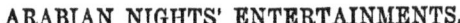

Aladdin instantly mounted his horse, and began his march in the order he had appointed. The streets through which he passed were filled with crowds of people, who made the air resound with their acclamation, their shouts of admiration and benedictions, particularly when the six slaves who carried the purses scattered handfuls of gold among them. It was soon known, that the sultan had bestowed upon Aladdin the hand of the Princess Badroulboudour; but no one ever considered his birth, or envied him, so well did he appear to deserve his fortune and elevation.

Aladdin at length arrived at the palace, where all was ready for his reception. When he reached the second gate he wished to alight, but the chief of the ushers prevented him, and accompanied him to the hall of audience, where he assisted him in dismounting from his horse. In the mean time all the ushers formed a double row at the entrance to the hall; and their chief, placing Aladdin on his right, advanced through the midst of them, and conducted him to the throne. As soon as the sultan perceived Aladdin he was surprised at seeing him more richly and magnificently clothed than he had ever been himself. His astonishment and surprise, however, did not prevent him from rising, and embracing him with the most evident marks of affection. Aladdin then addressed the sultan: "I receive the honours which your majesty has the goodness to bestow upon me, because it is your pleasure; but you must permit me to say, I have not forgotten that I was born your slave. If there be any reason from which I can in the least merit so favourable a reception, I candidly avow, that I am indebted to it from a boldness which chance alone inspired, and in consequence of which I have raised my eyes, my thoughts, and my desires to the divine princess who is the sole object of my eager wishes." As he concluded this speech, the air was immediately filled with the sound of trumpets, hautboys, and tymbals, and the sultan then conducted Aladdin into a magnificent saloon, where a sumptuous feast was served up. This being over, the sultan gave orders for the grand judge to attend, and commanded him to draw up, and instantly write out a contract of marrrage between the Princess Badroulboudour and Aladdin. When the judge had completed the contract, the sultan asked Aladdin, if he wished to remain in the palace and conclude all the ceremonies that day. "Sir," replied Aladdin, "however impatient I may be to possess the entire enjoyment of your majesty's goodness, I request you to permit me to defer my happiness until I have built a palace for the reception of the princess, suitable to her merit and dignity." "I will neglect nothing to have it finished with all possible diligence, my son," replied the sultan, "take all the ground you judge proper. The open space before my palace is too great, and I have already entertained thoughts of filling it up." Saying this, he again embraced Aladdin, who took leave of the sultan with much politeness.

Aladdin then mounted his horse, and returned home in the same order he had left it. The instant he arrived he alighted from his horse, and retired to his own chamber; where, rubbing the lamp, he again summoned the geni. "Geni," said Aladdin to him, "I have hitherto had every reason to praise the precision and promptitude with which you have executed whatever I have required of you by the power of your mistress, this lamp. You must now, if possible, show more zeal and make greater dispatch than has yet appeared. I command you to build me a palace immediately opposite to that belonging to the sultan; and let this palace be in every respect proper for the reception of the Princess Badroulboudour, my bride."

The sun had retired to rest when Aladdin concluded his orders to the geni respecting the construction of the palace he had thus imagined. The next morning Aladdin had scarcely risen before the geni presented himself. "Sir," said he, "your palace is finished, come and see if it is as you wished." Aladdin had no sooner signified his assent, than the geni transported him to it; and he found it so greatly to exceed his expectation, that he could not sufficienlty admire it. The geni led him through it, and he everywhere found the utmost splendour applied with strict propriety; with the proper officers and slaves, all dressed according to their rank, and suited to their different employments. When Aladdin had examined the palace throughout, from the top to the bottom, particularly a saloon with four-and-twenty windows, and had found riches and magnificence, with every convenience: "Geni," said he, "I am perfectly satisfied; and therefore I should be very wrong to make the least complaint. There is one thing only, which I did not mention to you, because it escaped my recollection;—it is, to have a carpet of the finest velvet, laid from the gate of the sultan's palace, up to the door of the apartment destined for the princess in this palace." "I will return in a moment," replied the geni; and he had scarcely disappeared before Aladdin saw what he wished, though without knowing by what means it had been effected. The geni again presented himself, and carried Aladdin back to his own house, just before the gate of the sultan's palace was opened.

When Aladdin had returned home, and dismissed the geni, he found that his mother was up. About the time that the sultan quitted the council, Aladdin requested his mother to go to the palace, attended by the female slaves that the geni had procured for her use. He begged her also, if she should see the sultan, to inform him that she came for the purpose of having the honour to accompany the princess in the evening, when it was proper for her to retire to her own palace. Aladdin himself mounted his horse, and left his paternal house, never more to return, not forgetting his wonderful lamp, which had been the cause of all his happiness.

As soon as the porters perceived the mother of Aladdin, they gave notice to the sultan. Immediately an order was sent to the bands of trumpets, cymbals, tabors, and fifes, and hautboys, which were already stationed in different parts of the terrace, and in a moment the air resounded with their flourishes. The merchants began to decorate their shops with rich carpets and cushions, adorned with foliage. The artificers quitted their labour, and the people thronged to the great square that still was left between the palace of the sultan and that of Aladdin. Aladdin's mother met with an honourable reception, and was introduced by the chief of the eunuchs into the apartment of the Princess Badroulboudour. As soon as the princess perceived her, she ran and embraced her, making her take a place upon her own sofa.

When night arrived, the princess took leave of the sultan her father. Their parting was tender, and accompanied by tears. They embraced each other several times, without uttering a word; and the princess at length quitted her apartment, and began her march, followed by a hundred female slaves, magnificently dressed. Four hundred young pages belonging to the sultan, who marched in two troops on each side, with flambeaux in their hands, caused a great light; which, joined to the illuminations in both palaces, well supplied the absence of day. The princess at length reached the new palace, and Aladdin ran, with every expression of joy, to the entrance of the apartment destined for her, to welcome her arrival, "Adorable princess," said he, accosting her in the most respectful manner, "if I should have had the misfortune to displease you by the temerity with which I have aspired to possess so amiable a person, and the daughter of my sultan, I must avow that it was to your beautiful eyes, to your charms that you ought to attribute it, and not to myself." "Prince,—for it is thus I must now call you," replied the prin cess,—"I obey the will of the sultan my father; and it is enough to have seen you, to own that I obey him without reluctance." Aladdin took her by the hand, which he kissed with the greatest demonstrations of joy, and conducted her into a large saloon, illuminated by an immense number of tapers, where, by the attention of the geni, was at table sumptuously covered. The dishes were of massive gold, and filled with the most delicious viands. The vases, the basins, and the goblets, with which the sideboard was amply furnished, were also of gold. The other ornaments, and all the embellishments of the saloon, perfectly corresponded.

The next morning, when Aladdin awoke, his chamberlains presented themselves to dress him. They clothed him in a quite different habit from that he wore on the day of his marriage, but equally rich and magnificent. They then brought him one of the horses that were appropriated to his use. He mounted it, and rode to the palace of the sultan. The sultan received him, embraced him, and invited him to breakfast. "Sir," said Aladdin to the sultan, "I beseech your majesty to dispense with my having this honour to-day; I come for the express purpose of entreating you to go and partake of a repast in the palace of the princess." The sultan granted his request with pleasure. He arose, and as the distance was not great, he determined to go on foot. He proceeded, therefore, in this manner with Aladdin on his right hand, and the grand-vizier on his left, followed by the nobles, with the principal officers of his palace. The nearer the sultan approached the palace of Aladdin, the more was he struck with its beauty. Yet this was trifling, to what he felt when he entered. But when they came to the saloon with twenty-four windows, to which Aladdin had invited him to ascend, and he had seen its ornaments, and, above all things, cast his eyes on the lattices, enriched with diamonds, rubies, and emeralds, all of the finest sort and most appropriate size, he stood absolutely motionless. The sultan wished to examine more closely the beauty of the twenty-four lattices, when, on reckoning them, he found only twenty-three that were equally rich. "Vizier," said he, "I am surprised that so magnificent a saloon should remain unfinished in this particular." "Sir," replied the grand-vizier, "Aladdin apparently was pressed for time, and therefore was unable to finish this window like the rest."

Aladdin, who had quitted the sultan to give some orders, rejoined him during this conversation. "My son," said the sultan, "this saloon is truly deserving the admiration of the world. One thing only surprises me; which is, that this lattice remains unfinished." "Sir," answered Aladdin, "it was intentionally left so, by my orders; that your majesty might have the glory of finishing this saloon and palace at the same time. And I entreat your majesty to think well of my intention, that I may ever remember the favour I have thus received from you." "If it be with that view," replied the sultan, "I take it in good part, and will immediately give the necessary orders concerning it." In effect, he ordered the jewellers who were best furnished with precious stones, and the most skilful goldsmiths in his capital, to be summoned.

The sultan descended from the saloon, and Aladdin conducted him into that where he had entertained the Princess Badroulboudour. The princess herself entered the moment after, and received the sultan her father in such a manner as plainly indicated that she was quite satisfied with her marriage. In this saloon were two tables furnished with the most delicious viands, all served up in utensils of gold. The sultan sat down at the first, with the Princess, Aladdin, and the grand-vizier. All the nobles of the court were regaled at the second.

When the sultan quitted the table, he was informed that the jewellers and goldsmiths were arrived. He re-ascended to the saloon with twenty-four windows; and when there, he showed to the jewellers and goldsmiths the window that was imperfect. "I have sent for you," said the sultan, "to finish this window in the same perfection as the rest." The jewellers and goldsmiths examined all the other twenty-three lattices, and after having consulted together, they presented themselves to the sultan, and the jeweller in ordinary to the palace thus addressed him:— "We are ready, sir, to employ all our care and diligence to obey your majesty, but, amongst all our profession, we have not jewels, either sufficiently valuable or numerous, to complete so great a work." "I have, then," cried the sultan, "and more than will be necessary. Come to my palace."

When the sultan had returned to his palace, he exhibited to the jewellers all his jewels; and they selected a very great quantity of them, particularly of those which had been presented by Aladdin. They used all these, without appearing to have made much progress. They went back for more; and, in the course of a month, they had not finished half their work. They employed all the sultan's jewels, with as many of the grand-vizier's as he could spare; and still, with all these, they could not finish more than half the window.

Aladdin, who knew that the sultan's endeavours to render the lattice of this window like the others were vain, and that he would never obtain that honour, at last went up to the workmen, and desired them not only to cease their labour, but even to undo what they had finished, and carry back all the jewels to the sultan. The work, which the jewellers and goldsmiths had been more than six weeks in performing, was destroyed in a few hours. They then went away, and left Aladdin alone in the saloon. He took out the lamp, which he had with him, and rubbed it, when the geni immediately appeared. "Geni," said Aladdin to him, "I ordered you to leave one of the twenty-four lattices of the saloon imperfect. I now inform you I wish it to be made like the rest." The geni disappeared, and Aladdin descended from the saloon. He returned to it again in a few moments, and found the lattice in the state he wished, and similar to the others.

In the meantime, the jewellers and goldsmiths arrived at the palace, and were introduced and presented to the sultan. The principal jeweller then presented to him the precious stones he had brought back, saying, "Sir, your majesty knows for what length of time we have worked, to finish the business with which you charged us. It was already very far advanced, when Aladdin obliged us, not only to cease our exertions, but even to destroy what we had already done. The sultan asked them if Aladdin had assigned any reason; and when they had answered in the negative, the sultan immediately ordered his horse to be brought. On his arrival at Aladdin's palace, he dismounted at the foot of the flight of stairs that led to the saloon with twenty-four windows, which he ascended, without inquiring for Aladdin; but the latter happened luckily to be in the saloon, and had barely time to receive the sultan at the door. The sultan said, "My son, I am come myself to ask the reason why you wish to leave this magnificent and singular saloon in an unfinished state?" Aladdin dissembled the true reason, which was, that the sultan was not sufficiently rich. But, to let him see how the palace, as it was, surpassed not only his, but also every other palace in the world, he replied, "It is true, sir, that your majesty did behold this saloon incomplete; but I intreat you to examine if at this moment there be anything wanting." The sultan immediately went to the window, where he had observed the lattice imperfect; and when he saw it was like the rest, he thought he was mistaken. He not only examined the window on each side of it, but looked at them all one after another; and when he was convinced that the lattice which had cost the jewellers and goldsmiths so many days' labour was finished in so short a time, he embraced Aladdin, and kissed his forehead. "My dear son," said he, "what a man are you, who can perform such wonders." Aladdin received the sultan's praises with great modesty, and replied to them in these terms:—"It is, sir, my greatest glory to observe the kindness and approbation of your majesty."

Aladdin had continued during several years to conduct himself in the same manner, when the African magician, who had unintentionally procured for him the means by which he was raised to so high a fortune, again remembered him, while residing in Africa, whither he had returned. Although he had persuaded himself that Aladdin had pined out a miserable existence in the subterraneous cavern, where he had left him, he nevertheless thought he might as well learn precisely what was his end. As he was perfectly skilled in geomancy, he took from a drawer a kind of square covered box, and seating himself on the sofa placed the square before him. He then uncovered it, and after levelling the sand which it contained, with the view of discovering whether Aladdin died in the subterraneous cave, he arranged the points, drew the figures, and formed the horoscope. On examining it, instead of finding Aladdin dead in the cave, he discovered that he had been liberated, that he lived in the greatest splendour, was immensely rich, had married a princess, and was highly honoured and respected. No sooner had the magician learned, by his art, that Aladdin was in the enjoyment of these honours, than the blood rushed into his face. "This miserable son of a tailor," exclaimed he, in a rage, "has discovered the secret and virtues of the lamp! I thought his death certain, while he enjoys the fruits of my long study and labour. I will either prevent his enjoyment of them, or perish." He did not long deliberate as to the method he should pursue. Early the next morning he mounted a horse, and began his journey. Travelling from city to city, and from province to province, without stopping anywhere longer than was necessary to rest his horse, he at last arrived in China, and very soon reached the capital of the sultan, whose daughter Aladdin had married. He alighted at a public khan, where he hired an apartment, and remained there the rest of the day and following night, to recover from the fatigue of his journey.

Next morning the African magician first inquired what was the general opinion formed of Aladdin, and how the people spoke of him. In walking about the city, he went into the most frequented, and best known place for people of distinction, where they assembled to drink a particular kind of warm liquor. He had no sooner taken his place, than they poured some into a cup, and presented it to him. As he took it, he heard, while listening to the conversation on each side, some persons speaking of Aladdin's palace. When he had finished his cup, he approached those who were talking on this subject, and inquired what there was in particular about the palace of which they spoke so highly. "Whence came you?" said the person to whom he addressed himself. "You must be but very lately arrived in this city, if you have not seen, or at least heard of, the palace of Prince Aladdin. I do not call it one of the wonders of the world, for it is the only wonder in the world: nothing was ever seen so grand, so rich, so magnificent. But see it, and you will then know if I have said anything beyond the truth." "Pardon my ignorance," replied the magician; "I arrived but yesterday; and, in fact, came from such a distance, that the fame of it had not reached that part when I left it. I shall not, however, fail to go and see it; my impatience is, indeed, so great, that I would this moment satisfy my curiosity, if you would do me the favour to show me the road."

The person to whom the African magician had addressed himself took a pleasure in describing the way he must go, to see Aladdin's palace; and the magician immediately arose, and set out. When he arrived, and had accurately examined the palace on all sides, he had not the smallest doubt that Aladdin had availed himself of the power of the lamp in building it. Stung to the soul by the happiness and greatness of Aladdin, he returned to the khan where he had taken up his abode. It was his object to ascertain where the lamp was kept, and this discovery he was unable to make by an operation in geomancy. He immediately took his square box and sand, and having completed the operation, he found that the lamp was in Aladdin's palace; at which his joy was so great, that he hardly could contain himself. "I shall have this lamp," he cried; "and I defy Aladdin to prevent my obtaining it, and reducing him to the original obscurity, whence he has taken so high a flight."

It happened most unfortunately for Aladdin, that he was absent upon a hunting expedition, which was to last eight days, and only three of them were yet elapsed. The African magician did not want to know more. He then went to the shop of a person who made and sold lamps. "Master," said he, "I want a dozen copper lamps; can you supply me with them?" The man replied that he had not so many finished, but that if he would wait till the next day, he would have them ready for him at any time he wished. The magician agreed to wait, desiring him to take care they were well polished; and having promised to give a good price for them, he returned to the khan.

The next morning, the African magician received the twelve lamps, put them into a basket, which he had provided, and went, with this on his arm, towards Aladdin's palace; and, as he approached it, he began to cry, "*Who will change old lamps for new?*" He repeated this cry so often, while he walked backwards and forwards on all sides of the palace, that at last the Princess Badroulbadour heard his voice; but as she could not distinguish what he said, on account of the shouting of the children who followed him, she sent one of her female slaves to learn the occasion of the noise. The slave soon returned, laughing so heartily, that the princess herself could not refrain from laughing also. "Well, simpleton," said the princess, "why do you not tell me what occasions your laughter?" "Princess," replied the slave, still laughing, "who could possibly avoid it, at seeing that fool with a basket on his arm, full of beautiful new lamps, which he does not wish to sell, but to exchange for old ones!" Hearing this, another of the female slaves said, "Now you speak of old lamps, I know not whether the princess has noticed one that lies upon the cornice. If the princess choose, she may have the pleasure of proving whether this fellow is fool enough to give a new lamp for an old one. The princess, who was ignorant of the worth of this lamp, and that Aladdin was so much interested in its preservation, ordered an eunuch to go and get it exchanged. The eunuch obeyed: he went down from the saloon, and no sooner passed through the palace gate, than he perceived the African magician; and calling him, he showed him the old lamp, saying, "Give me a new lamp for this." The magician did not doubt but that this was the lamp he was seeking; he therefore eagerly took it from the eunuch, and after having thrust it into his bosom, presented his basket, and bade him take his choice. The eunuch chose one; and leaving the magician, he carried the new lamp to the princess.

He suffered them to shout as much as they pleased; but, without staying any longer near Aladdin's palace, he insensibly proceeded to a distance, and no longer invited people to change old lamps for new. As soon as he was out of the square, he went along the most unfrequented streets; and as he had no further occasion either for the remainder of his lamps or his basket, he set them down in the middle of a street where he saw no person. He then turned down another street, and made all the haste he could to reach one of the gates of the city. As he continued his walk through the suburb, he bought some provisions, and advancing into the open country, turned down a bye-road, where there was not a probability of his being seen.

The magician remained in this place until the night was far advanced; he then drew the lamp out of his bosom, and rubbed it. The geni instantly obeyed the summons. "*What do you wish?*" cried he; "*I am ready to obey you, as your slave, and the slave of those who have the lamp in their hands, I and the other slaves of the lamp.*" "I command you," replied the African magician, "instantly to take the palace which you and the other slaves of the lamp have erected in this city, exactly as it is, with every living thing in it, and transport it, with me at the same time, into—such a part—of Africa." Without replying, the geni, assisted by the other slaves of the lamp, took the whole palace with him, and transported it in a short time to the very spot he had mentioned.

Let us now leave the African magician and the palace, with the Princess Badroulboudour, in Africa, and notice the surprise of the sultan. When he arose the next morning, he did not fail, as usual, to go to the cabinet, that he might have the pleasure of contemplating and admiring Aladdin's palace. He cast his eyes towards the side where he was accustomed to see it, but found only an open space. His astonishment was so great, that he remained motionless for some time, with his eyes turned to the spot where the palace had stood, but where it was no longer visible, reflecting on what he could not comprehend. "I cannot be deceived," said he to himself; "it was in that very place I beheld it; if it had fallen down, the materials at least would appear; and if the earth had swallowed it, there would be some marks seen." He at length retired; when, after looking once more behind him as he left the place, he returned to his apartment, and ordered his grand-vizier to be instantly called. The grand-vizier did not keep the sultan long waiting; he came in so great haste, that neither he nor his attendants observed, as they passed, that the palace of Aladdin was no longer in the same place. "Sir," said he, the moment he entered, "the haste in which your majesty has sent for me leads me to suppose that something very extraordinary has happened." "What has happened, is, indeed, extraordinary! Tell me, where is Aladdin's palace?" "The palace of Aladdin, sir!" replied the grand-vizier, with astonishment; "I have just now passed it; and it seemed to me to be on the same spot." "Go into my cabinet," said the sultan, "and come and tell me if you can see it." The grand-vizier went, as he was ordered; and the same thing happened to him as to the sultan. When he was quite certain that the palace of Aladdin no longer remained in the place where it was built, he returned to the sultan. "Well," demanded the latter, "have you seen Aladdin's palace?" "Sir," replied the grand-vizier, "your majesty may remember, I had the honour to tell you, that this palace was only the work of magic; but your majesty did not then think what I said deserving attention." The sultan was in the greater rage, because he was unable to disavow his own incredulity. "Where is this impostor—this wretch," he exclaimed, "that I may strike off his head?" "Sir," answered the grand-vizier, "it is some days since he came to take leave of your majesty; we should send to him, to inquire about his palace, of which he cannot be ignorant." "This would be treating him with too great indulgence," exclaimed the monarch. "Go, and order thirty of my horsemen to bring him before me in chains." The grand-vizier accordingly gave the orders; and instructed the officer how he might secure him. The troop set out, and met Aladdin about five or six leagues from the city. The officer, when he first accosted him, said the sultan was so impatient to see him again, that he had sent him to inform him of his solicitude.

Aladdin, who had not the least suspicion of the true cause that had brought the guard, continued hunting on his way home; but when he was within half a league of the city, the detachment surrounded him, and the officer said, "Prince Aladdin, it is with sincere regret that I inform you of the orders we have received from the sultan to arrest and conduct you before him, as a state-criminal. We entreat you not to take it ill that we do our duty, but to pardon us." As Aladdin saw that his attendants were much inferior to the detachment, he dismounted, saying, "Here I am, execute your order. I must, however, declare that I am guilty of no crime, either towards the person of the sultan, or the state." They immediately put a chain about his neck, which they then bound round his body, so as to confine his arms. When the officer had put himself at the head of the troop, one of the horsemen took hold of the end of the chain, and following the officer, he led Aladdin, who was obliged to proceed on foot; and in this state he was conducted towards the city.

Aladdin was conducted before the sultan, who, accompanied by the grand-vizier, waited for him in a balcony; and he no sooner saw him, than he commanded the executioner to strike off his head, without suffering him to utter a word, or requiring any explanation whatever. He drew his sabre, and prepared to give the fatal blow, only making the three usual flourishes in the air, and waiting for the sultan's signal, to separate Aladdin's head from his body. At this instant the grand-vizier perceived that the populace were scaling the walls of the palace in many places, and began to pull them down, in order to open a passage. The terror of the sultan, when he saw such eager and violent commotions, was so great, that he instantly ordered the executioner to put up his sabre, and set him at liberty. He also commanded proclamation to be made that he pardoned Aladdin, and that every person should retire.

When Aladdin found himself at liberty, he lifted up his head towards the balcony, and perceiving the sultan, he raised his voice, and addressed him: "Sir," said he, "I entreat your majesty to add a new favour to the pardon you have just granted me, by informing me of my crime." "Of your crime, perfidious wretch!" replied the sultan. "Come up here, and I will inform thee." Aladdin ascended; and when he presented himself, "Follow me," said the sultan, walking on before. He led the way to the cabinet; and when they reached the door, "Go in," said the sultan; "you ought to know where the palace was: look on all sides, and tell me." Aladdin looked, but saw no vestige of it: he perceived the space which his palace did occupy. This extraordinary and wonderful event so confused and astonished him, that he could not answer the sultan a single word "Tell me," said the latter, impatient at his silence, "where is your palace, and what is

become of my daughter ?" "Sir," replied Aladdin, "I confess that the palace is no longer in the place where it was, but I can assure your majesty that I have no concern whatever in this event." "The loss of your palace gives me no concern," returned the sultan; "my daughter I esteem a million times beyond it; and unless you return her to me again, no consideration shall prevent me taking off your head." "Sir," said Aladdin, "I entreat your majesty to grant me forty days, that I may make the most diligent inquiries." "I grant the time you desire," replied the sultan; "but do not think to abuse my favour, by endeavouring to escape my resentment."

Aladdin then passed through the courts of the palace with downcast eyes, and the principal officers of the court instead of approaching to console him, or offer a retreat in their houses, turned their backs. He remained three days in the city, walking through every part, eating only what was given him in charity, without being able to form any resolution. At length he departed towards the country. He quitted the high road, and, after traversing a considerable extent of ground, he arrived, at the close of day, on the borders of a river, when he gave himself up entirely to despair. "Whither shall I go to seek my palace?" he exclaimed to himself "In what country—in what part of the world—shall I find either that or my dear princess? It is much better, then, that I at once free myself from all my labours, which must be inutile, and all the cutting sensations that distract me." He was then going to precipitate himself into the river; but as a good Mussulman, he thought he ought first to say his prayer. To prepare himself for this ceremony, he advanced to the bank to wash his face and hands, according to the custom of his country; but as this place was rather steep, he slipped down, and would have fallen into the river, if he had not been stopped by a small rock that projected from the surface. Happily for him, he still wore the ring which the African magician had put upon his finger, when he made him go down into the subterraneous cavern to bring away the precious lamp. In holding against the rock, he rubbed the ring so strongly, that the same geni whom he had seen in the subterraneous cavern again appeared: "*What do you wish?*" cried the geni: "*I am ready to obey you as your slave, and the slave of him who has that ring on his finger, I and the other slaves of the ring.*" Aladdin was agreeably surprised by an apparition so little expected. "Save my life, geni, a second time, by informing me where the palace is, which I have built, or in procuring it to be instantly replaced where it was." "What you require of me," answered the geni, "is beyond my ability; I am only the slave of the ring; you must address yourself to the slave of the lamp." "If that be the case," rejoined Aladdin, "I command you, by the power of the ring, to transport me to the spot where my palace is, and place me under the window of the Princess Badroulboudour. Scarcely had he ended, before the geni transported him to Africa, where the palace stood, near a considerable city; and having set him down directly under the windows of the apartment of the princess he vanished. Notwithstanding the obscurity of the night, Aladdin readily recognised his palace and the apartment of the Princess Badroulboudour, but as the night was far advanced, and everything in the palace was quiet, he retired to a little distance, and seated himself at the foot of a tree.

The next morning he arose, approached the apartment of the princess, and walked for some time under the window, in hopes that she might observe him. While in this expectation, he considered within himself what could have been the cause of his misfortune; and after meditating on the affair, he no longer doubted but that it arose from his having left his lamp. His greatest embarrassment, however, was to determine, who could be so jealous of his happiness.

The Princess Badroulboudour arose this morning much earlier than she had been accustomed, since being transported into Africa. When she was dressed, one of her women perceived Aladdin, and instantly ran to inform her mistress. The princess, who could scarcely believe this news, immediately opened the lattice; the noise of which made Aladdin raise his head. He recognised and saluted her in a manner highly expressive of his joy. "Lose not a moment," cried the princess; "they are gone to open the door for you; enter, and come up."

It is impossible to express the joy they both felt in again meeting, after having concluded they were for ever separated. "Before we speak of anything else," said Aladdin, "tell me what is become of an old lamp, which I had placed upon the cornice of the saloon before I went on the hunting party?" The princess then related all that had passed, relative to the exchange of the old lamp for a new one, which she showed him; and how she found herself the next morning in Africa; a fact she learnt from the traitor who, by his magic art, had transported her there. "Princess," interrupted Aladdin, "by informing me that we are in Africa, you have at once discovered the traitor. But this is neither a proper time nor place to enter into a detail of his wickedness. I entreat you only to tell me what he has done with the lamp, and where he has put it." "He constantly," answered the princess, "carries it in his bosom. Of this I am certain, since he has taken it out in my presence, exhibiting it as a trophy." "Princess," said Aladdin, "I trust I have discovered the means of delivering you from our enemy. But, for this purpose, it is necessary I should go into the town. I will return about noon, and communicate to you the nature of my design. That you may be prepared, do not be astonished if you see me return in a different dress; and be sure to give orders that I may be admitted the instant I knock."

When Aladdin left the palace, he looked about on all sides, and at last perceived a peasant taking the road into the country. As this peasant was at some distance from the palace, Aladdin hastened after him; he proposed to change clothes, making him a present, to which the peasant readily agreed. The exchange was made behind a small bush. They then separated, and Aladdin proceeded towards the town. On entering, he went down a street which led from the gate, and reached that part where the different professions and trades occupy each a particular street. He went into that appropriated to druggists, and entering the shop which appeared the best supplied, he asked the merchant if he had a certain powder, which he named. The merchant, supposing he had not money enough to purchase it, replied, that he had it, but that it was dear. Aladdin immediately drew out his purse, and showing him the gold, desired to have half a drachm of the powder. The merchant weighed it, wrapped it up, and, presenting it, demanded one piece of gold for it. Aladdin paid him; and, without stopping any longer in the town, returned to the palace. He did not wait at the secret door. It was instantly opened, and he ascended to the apartment of the Princess Badroulboudour. "The detestation, my princess," said Aladdin to her, "which you have expressed for your ravisher, may probably occasion you some pain in following the counsel I am going to give you. But if you follow my advice, you will immediately adorn yourself in one of your most elegant dresses; and when the magician appears, make no difficulty in receiving him without constraint; yet still with some indication of grief. In your conversation with him, give him to understand that you are endeavouring to forget me. Invite him to sup with you, when you can say to him that you are desirous of tasting some of the best wine of his country. On which, he will not fail to leave you, in order to procure some. While he is absent, put into one of the drinking cups this powder. Set the cup apart, and tell one of your women to fill it, and bring it to you at a certain signal, which you must explain to her. When the magician has returned, after having eaten and drunk as much as you think proper, make them bring you the goblet containing the powder, and exchange it with the magician's. Scarcely will he have so done, when you will see him fall backwards." When Aladdin had finished, "I must confess," said the princess, "that I violently shock my own feelings in agreeing to make these advances to the magician. But what cannot one undertake against a cruel enemy! I will therefore act as you direct."

The magician did not fail to make his appearance at the usual hour. As soon as the princess saw him enter the saloon, she arose, in all the splendour of beauty and charms, and pointed with her hand to the most honourable seat. When he was in his place, the princess, regarding him in such a manner as to make him suppose he was no longer odious to her, thus addressed him:—"You are, doubtless, astonished at seeing me appear to-day so much altered; but you will no longer be surprised, when I tell you that I am naturally of a disposition so much the reverse of grief, that I endeavour, as soon as possible, to drive it from me by every means in my power. I have reflected on what you related concerning the destiny of Aladdin, and, from the disposition of the sultan, my father, I am persuaded that my husband could not possibly avoid the terrible effects of his rage. I have therefore concluded that, as my

tears would not revive him, if I were to weep all the remainder of my life, I ought, after having paid him, even in the tomb, every respect and duty which my affection demanded, to search for the means of consoling myself. I have ordered a supper to be prepared, but, as I have only some wine the produce of China, and am now in Africa, I should be very glad to taste what is made here."

Full of ideas of expected happiness, the African magician not merely ran to fetch the wine, he flew, and was back almost instantly. The princess, in his absence, threw the powder which Aladdin had given her into a goblet, and set it aside till she should call for it. When he had returned, and they had been a short time eating, she asked for wine, and, having drunk to the magician's health, "You are right," she cried, "in praising your wine; I never tasted any so delicious." "Charming princess," replied he, "my wine acquires a fresh flavour from the approbation you bestow on it." "Drink to my health," resumed the princess, "you find I understand it."

When they had continued eating some time longer, the princess gave the signal to the woman who served the wine, at the same time desiring her to bring her a goblet full, and also to fill the magician's, which they presented to him. "Drink," she cried; at the same time she carried the goblet she held to her mouth, but barely suffered it to touch her lips, while the African magician emptied his to the last drop. In hastening to finish the cup, he held his head back, and remained some time in that situation, till the princess observed that his eyes were turned up, when he fell senseless on his back. The princess had no occasion to give orders for opening the secret door to admit Aladdin. Her women gave the word one to the other from the saloon to the bottom of the staircase, so that the magician had no sooner fallen backwards than the door was opened.

Aladdin went up to the saloon, and, as soon as he saw the African extended on the sofa, he stopped Badroulboudour. "My princess," he cried, "there is no time for rejoicing; do me the favour to retire to your apartments." The princess, her women, and the eunuchs were no sooner out of the saloon than Aladdin shut the door, when, going up to the body of the African magician, he opened his vest, and took out the lamp. Having rubbed it, the geni instantly presented himself, with his usual speech. "Geni," said Aladdin, "I command you, in the name of this lamp, immediately to convey this palace to the same spot in China whence it was brought." The geni, after showing an inclination of the head that he would obey, vanished. In effect, the journey was made, and it was effected in a very little time.

The sun had not yet risen, when the sultan entered his cabinet, on the very morning that Aladdin's palace had been conveyed back. On entering, he was much absorbed in his own feelings, and so penetrated with sorrow, that he threw his eyes over the accustomed spot in the most melancholy manner. but finding this void filled up he conjectured, at first, that it was only a mist. He looked with greater attention, still he could no longer doubt its being the palace of Aladdin which he saw. He hastened back to his apartment, and ordered them instantly to saddle and bring him a horse; which was no sooner done than he mounted it, and set out, thinking he could not arrive soon enough at Aladdin's palace.

Aladdin, who anticipated the consequence, had arisen at day break; and as soon as he had dressed himself in one of his most magnificent robes, he went up to the saloon with twenty-four windows, from which he perceived the sultan's approach. He then descended, and was just in time to receive him at the bottom of the grand staircase. He conducted the sultan to the apartment of the Princess Badroulboudour, whom the prince had informed that she was no longer in Africa, but in China, and in the capital of her father. The sultan repeatedly embraced her, while the princess, on her part, showed every appearance of extreme pleasure at again beholding him. "My dear daughter," said the sultan at length, "I am persuaded it is the joy you feel at again seeing me, that makes you appear so little altered, but I am sure you must have suffered a great deal. Your sudden transportation, with the whole palace, must have occasioned you the greatest alarm and most dreadful feelings. Relate to me, I desire of you, all that has occurred, and do not conceal the least circumstance." "Sir," replied she, "if I appear so little changed, I beg your majesty to consider, that my recovery commenced yesterday morning, by the presence of my dear husband whom I have regarded and lamented as for ever lost to me; but the happiness I experienced in again embracing him nearly restored to me my former self. In regard to my removal, Aladdin had not the least concern in it; I alone was the cause, though innocently." To convince the sultan that she spoke the truth, she gave him a detailed account—how the African magician disguised himself as a seller of lamps, and offered to change new ones for old; of the joke with which she had amused herself in exchanging Aladdin's lamp, ignorant of its secret qualities; of the instant removal of the palace and herself, in consequence of this exchange, and their being transported into Africa. She then informed him of the persecution she had suffered until the arrival of Aladdin; how they had succeeded by her having the courage to dissemble her feelings, and to invite the magician to sup with her; with all that passed, till she presented the goblet to him containing the powder. Aladdin had but little to add. "When they opened the private door," said he, "I went up to the saloon, and saw the traitor lying dead on the sofa. As it was not proper for the princess to remain there any longer, I requested her to go to her apartment with her women and eunuchs. I have re-established the palace in its place, and have had the happiness of restoring the princess to your majesty." The sultan, after having commanded the drums, trumpets, tymbals, to announce a public rejoicing, had a festival proclaimed, of ten days' continuance, to welcome the return of the Princess Badroulboudour, of Aladdin, and his palace. In this manner, Aladdin, a second time, escaped an almost inevitable death.

The African magician had a younger brother, who was not less skilful than himself in the knowledge of magic. As they did not always live together, one sometimes being in the east, while the other travelled in the west, they did not fail once every year to inform themselves, by means of geomancy, in what part of the world the other was, how he was circumstanced, and whether either wanted the assistance of his brother. Some time after the African magician had failed in his attempt against Aladdin, his younger brother, who had not received any intelligence of him for a year wished to know where he was, whether he was well, and how he was engaged. Into whatever place he travelled, he constantly carried his square geomantic box. He took this, and having smoothened the sand, he cast the points, drew the figures, and formed the horoscope. On examination, he found that his brother was no longer alive, and that his death was sudden. Searching further, he learned that this event took place in a palace, then situated in a particular part of China; and that the person by whom he had been poisoned was a man of low birth, who had married a princess, daughter of the sultan. When the magician had thus ascertained the melancholy fate of his brother, he mounted his horse, and began his route towards China. He travelled over plains, rivers, mountains,

deserts, and after a long-continued journey he arrived at the capital, which his experiment in geomancy had pointed out. Certain of not being deceived, nor having mistaken one kingdom for another, he stopped in this capital, where he took up his abode.

The morning after his arrival, he introduced himself into the most frequented places, and was very attentive to the conversation that passed. At a place where people spent their time in playing at a variety of games, he heard them frequently mention, and highly extol, the virtues and piety of a female recluse, named Fatima, and even of the miracles she performed. As he thought that this woman might probably be useful in his undertaking, he drew one of the persons aside, and begged a more particular account of this holy female. "What!" exclaimed this man, "have you never seen or heard of her? Excepting Mondays and Fridays, she never leaves her hermitage. On those days she comes into the city, where she does infinite good." The magician did not want to know more on this subject. He only inquired of the same man in what quarter the hermitage was situated. Having obtained that information, he observed her whole conduct on the first day she appeared, and did not lose sight of her till she returned in the evening to her hermitage. When he had accurately remarked the spot, he returned to one of those places where a certain warm liquor is drank, and where persons, who choose it, may pass the night, particularly in hot weather, when the inhabitants of China prefer sleeping upon a mat. The magician, after paying the owner his demand, went out about midnight, and took the road to the hermitage of Fatima. He had no difficulty in opening the door, and having entered, he closed it again without noise; when, perceiving Fatima lying in the open air, upon a couch formed with a ragged mat, rather than a bed, he approached her, and, taking out a poniard, awoke her. "If you cry out," said he, "or make the least noise, I will kill you. Get up, and do what I desire." Fatima, who always slept in her clothes, arose, trembling. "Fear nothing," continued the magician, "I only want your habit; give it me, and take mine." When this exchange was made, he said to her, "Paint my face like yours, that I may resemble you, and so that the colour will not come off." Fatima then conducted him into her cell, lighted her lamp, and taking a certain liquid from a basin with a pencil, she rubbed it over his face, assuring him it would not change, and that there was no difference in colour between her countenance and his. She then put upon him her own head-dress, with a veil, and instructed him how she concealed her face with it, in walking though the city. In fine, after hanging a large necklace, or chaplet, round his neck, she put the stick with which she walked into his hand, and presented to him a mirror. "Look," said she. The magician found all as he wished; but he did not keep the promise he had made. That no blood might be discovered, he strangled her, and drew the body to the hermitage well, into which he threw it.

The magician, thus disguised like the holy woman, passed the remainder of the night in the hermitage. Very early on the morrow, though not the usual day for Fatima's appearance in the city, he did not hesitate to go out. When the people saw the holy woman, as everybody imagined him to be, the magician was soon surrounded by a great crowd. Some recommended themselves to his prayers, others kissed his hand, while others bent down before him, that he might lay his hands upon them, which he did, muttering a few words like a prayer. After stopping very often, to satisfy those sort of people, he at length arrived in the square before Aladdin's palace, where, as the crowd increased, the difficulty to get near him was also greater; and hence, several quarrels arose, the noise of which reached the ears of the Princess Badroulboudour. The princess inquired the occasion of the noise, and ordered an attendant to go and bring her an account. One of her woman looked through the lattice, and returned to inform her, that it arose from a crowd of people collected round the holy woman. The princess, who had long heard the holy woman extolled, felt a desire to see and converse with her. Having mentioned something to this effect, the chief of the eunuchs said, that if she wished, it would be easy to make her attend, and that she had only to command. The princess consented, and he immediately despatched four eunuchs to bring the pretended holy woman with them. As soon as the eunuchs had left the gate of Aladdin's palace, and were observed approaching towards the disguised magician, the crowd began to disperse; and, when he was thus more at liberty, he advanced to meet them, and with the greater joy, as he saw that his cunning scheme was likely to be successful. One of the eunuchs thus addressed him: "Holy woman, the princess wishes to see you. Come, follow us." "The princess highly honours me," replied the pretended Fatima; "I am ready to obey her commands," and he followed the eunuchs. When the magician was introduced to the saloon, and perceived the princess, he commenced a prayer, which contained a long catalogue of vows and wishes for her piety, and the accomplishment of everything she could desire.

When the false Fatima had finished her long harangue, "My good mother," returned the princess, "I have a request to make, which, I beg, you will not refuse me. It is, that you will reside here, that I may learn, from your good example, how I ought to serve God. I have several apartments unoccupied; you shall choose that you like best, and you shall have the power of attending to your devotions with the same liberty as if you were in your own hermitage." The magician did not make much difficulty in acceding to the offer of Badroulboudour. "Princess," he replied, "whatever resolution a poor and miserable woman, like myself, may have made to renounce the world, I dare not have the boldness to resist either the wish or the command of so pious and charitable a princess." On this answer, the princess herself got up, and said to the magician, "Rise, and come with me, that I may show you all the apartments I have unoccupied." He choose that which appeared to be the least elegant, hypocritically saying, at the same time, that it was much too good for him, and that he only took it to oblige her. The princess wished the impostor to dine with her; but as, in eating, it would have been necessary to uncover his face, he begged her earnestly to excuse him, declaring that he never eat anything but bread and dried fruits, and obtained permission to take his humble meal in his own apartment.

The princess then dined; and the false Fatima did not fail to return to her, as soon as informed, by an eunuch, that she had risen from table. "My good mother," said the princess, "I am delighted at enjoying the society of so holy a woman as you in my palace. And now I mention the palace—how do you like it?" At this inquiry, the pretended Fatima raised her eyes, and looked at the saloon, from one end to the other. "Indeed, princess," said she, "this saloon is truly beautiful, and worthy of admiration. But, so far as a recluse may judge, it appears to me

that one thing is wanting." "What is that, my good mother?" inquired Badroulboudour. "Pardon me," replied the disguised magician; "my opinion, if it can be of any consideration, is, that if the egg of a roc were suspended from the centre of the dome, this saloon would not have its equal in either of the four quarters of the globe." "My good mother," returned the princess, "what kind of bird is a roc, and where could the egg of it be found?" "Princess," answered the false Fatima, "the roc is a bird of prodigious size, which inhabits the summit of Mount Caucasus, and the builder of your palace can procure you one." After having thanked the pretended Fatima, the Princess Badroulboudour continued the conversation on various other subjects; but she did not forget the egg of the roc, of which she intended to inform Aladdin, when he returned from hunting. He had already been away six days; and the magician wished to take every advantage of his absence. Aladdin returned the same evening, at the time when the false Fatima had taken leave of the princess. As soon as he entered the palace, he went to the apartment of the princess, to which she had already retired; he saluted and embraced her, but thought she received him rather coolly. "I do not find you, my princess," said he, "in your usual good spirits." "It is a mere trifle," replied the princess, "but, since you have observed some alteration in me, I will not conceal the cause. I thought, with you, that our palace was the most superb, the most beautiful, and best ornamented, of any in the world. I will tell you, however, what has entered my head. Will you not agree with me, that if the egg of a roc were suspended from the centre of the dome, we should have nothing to desire?" "It is enough," replied Aladdin, "that you think the want of a roe's egg a defect. You shall see, by the diligence with which I repair it, that there is nothing my love for you will not induce me to perform."

Aladdin immediately went up to the saloon with twenty-four windows; when taking the lamp out of his bosom, he rubbed it; the geni instantly appeared before him. "Geni," said Aladdin, "it is necessary there should be the egg of a roc suspended from the centre of this dome, to render it perfect." Aladdin had scarcely pronounced these words, when the geni uttered so loud and dreadful a cry that the very room shook. "What, wretch!" he exclaimed, in a voice that would have terrified the most courageous man, "is it not enough that I and my companions have done everything that thou hast required, but that thou shouldst repay our services by unequalled ingratitude, and command me to bring thee my master, and hang him in the midst of this vaulted dome? But thou art fortunate in not having formed the desire, and that the command is not precisely your own. Learn who is the true author:—It is the brother of thy enemy, the African magician. He is in thy palace, disguised under the appearance of Fatima, the holy woman, whom he has murdered; and he suggested to thy wife the pernicious demand."

Aladdin lost not a syllable of the last words. He had before heard of the holy woman Fatima. Having returned to the apartment of the princess, without mentioning what had happened to him, he sat down, and complained of a violent pain that had suddenly seized his head. The princess immediately ordered the attendants to call the holy woman; and while they were gone, she accounted to Aladdin for her being in the palace. The pretended Fatima came; and, as soon as she entered, Aladdin said to her, "I am very glad, my good mother, to see you; it is for my benefit to have you here at this moment. I am tormented with a violent head ache, and I hope you will not refuse me that favour which you grant to all who are thus afflicted." At these words, he bent his head forward, and the disguised magician also advanced, putting his hand upon a poniard which was concealed in his girdle. Aladdin, who watched his actions, seized his hand before he could draw it, and piercing him to the heart with his own weapon, threw him dead upon the floor. "What have you done, my dear husband!" exclaimed the princess, "you have killed the holy woman!" "No, no, my princess," answered Aladdin, "I have not killed Fatima, but a villain who was going to assassinate me. This wretch, whom you behold," added he, showing his face, "has strangled Fatima, and disguised himself in her clothes, to murder me. Still further to convince you, know he is the brother of the African magician who carried you off." Aladdin then related to her how he had learned these particulars; after which, he ordered the body to be removed.

Thus Aladdin was delivered from the persecution of the two magicians. A few years afterwards, the sultan, having attained a great age, died; and, as he left no male issue, the Princess Badroulboudour, being his legitimate heir, succeeded to the throne, and of course transferred the supreme power to Aladdin.

THE ADVENTURES OF THE CALIPH HAROUN ALRASCHID.

SOMETIMES we experience such extraordinary transports of joy, that we immediately communicate this passion to all persons around us, or as readily partake of their mirth. Sometimes, again, we are so deeply affected with melancholy, that we become insupportable to ourselves.

The Caliph Haroun Alraschid was one day in this state of mind, when Giafar, his faithful grand-vizier, came into his presence. This minister found him alone, and as he perceived that he was in a gloomy mood, and did not even raise his eyes, he stopped till he should deign to regard him. At length the caliph looked up, and saw the vizier; but as quickly turned away, and again remained immoveable. As the grand-vizier perceived nothing which indicated displeasure towards himself, he thus addressed him:—"Commander of the faithful, will your majesty permit me to ask the cause of your dejection, and with which I have always thought you so little affected?" "It is true," answered the caliph, "I am little susceptible of that weakness; and but for you, I should not have been sensible of it now. If nothing new has happened to occasion your coming to me, you will give me pleasure in finding some means to dissipate it." "Commander of the faithful," replied the grand-vizier, "my duty alone has led me hither; and I take the liberty of bringing to your majesty's recollection, the obligation under which you have laid yourself, of witnessing in person that excellent system of police which you are desirous should be observed in your capital." "I had forgotten it," replied the caliph, "and you do well to remind me. Go, then, and change your dress, and I will do the same."

Having each of them assumed the habit of a foreign merchant they went, unattended, through a private door in the palace-garden, which opened into the country. They perambulated on the outside of the town, quite to the banks of the river Euphrates without noticing any irregularity. After passing the river in the first boat they found, they completed the circuit of the other part of the town, opposite to that which they had first visited. Having crossed a bridge, at the foot of it they met an old blind man, who was begging. The caliph turned round and dropped a

piece of gold into his hand; the blind man instantly seized his hand, and stopped him. "Charitable person," said he, "whoever you are, do not, I beseech you, refuse me a further favour, but give me a blow on the head—I deserve it, and even still greater punishment." The caliph, surprised at the conduct of the blind man, answered, "My good fellow, I cannot comply with your request; I shall certainly not destroy the value of my gift by the ill-treatment you require from me;" and saying this, he endeavoured to escape. The blind man made a still stronger attempt to detain him. "Sir," said he, "pardon my boldness and importunity; give me, I entreat you, the blow, or take back your alms which I can accept on no other condition." The caliph yielded to the blind man's importunity, and gave him a slight blow. The blind man immediately quitted his hold with thanks. The caliph went on with the grand-vizier, but, after a few steps, he said to him, "Surely the occasion of this man's behaving thus to those who bestow their alms upon him must be founded on some serious reason. I should like to be acquainted with it; therefore return; tell him who I am, and order him to come to the palace, at the time of afternoon prayer."

They re-entered the town; and passing through a square, found a great number of people, looking at a young well-dressed man, mounted on a mare, which he pushed at full speed round the square, so that it was covered with foam and blood. The caliph, astonished at the cruelty of the young man, stopped to inquire why he so ill-treated the animal, but nobody knew; he could only learn that he was every day, at the same hour, engaged in this inhuman exercise. They continued their walk; but the caliph desired the vizier to notice this square, and not to fail to cause the young man to come to him the next day, at the same hour on which the blind man was to attend.

Before the caliph reached the palace, he observed a new-built house, which seemed to be the residence of some great man belonging to the court. He asked the grand-vizier, if he knew to whom it belonged? the latter replied, he did not, but would go and make inquiry. He accordingly applied to a neighbour, who told him that the house belonged to Cogia Hassan, surnamed Alhabbal, from his trade of rope-making, and that, without knowing how he had been so favoured by fortune, he had acquired so much wealth, as to support, in a very splendid manner, the expense of the building. The grand-vizier then rejoined the caliph, and related what he had heard. "I would see this Cogia Hassan Alhabbal," said the caliph; "go, and desire him also to come to the palace at the same hour with the other two." The grand-vizier did not fail to execute the caliph's order.

Next day, when the afternoon prayers were ended, the caliph returned to his apartment, and the grand-vizier, immediately introduced the three persons, and presented them to him. They prostrated themselves before the throne; and when they had risen, the caliph asked the blind man his name. "I am called Baba Abdalla," answered he. "Baba Abdalla," resumed the caliph, "your mode of asking alms appeared yesterday so extraordinary, that I have ordered you here, to know what motive can have urged you to take so silly an oath as that you mentioned. Tell me, then, without disguise, whence this extravagant conceit arose; conceal nothing from me, for I will know the whole." Baba Abdalla prostrated himself a second time, and after rising, "Commander of the faithful," said he "I most humbly beg pardon for the boldness with which I have dared to demand of you a thing which in truth appears so very inconsistent. I confess my crime; but, as I did not then know your majesty, I implore your clemency, and hope you will consider my ignorance. As to your majesty's being pleased to treat what I did as extravagance, I confess it to be so, and my behaviour must appear such in the eyes of men; but, in the sight of God, it is but a slight penance for an enormous crime. Of this your majesty will yourself be a judge, when I have acquainted you with the nature of my heinous offence."

THE HISTORY OF BABA ABDALLA, THE BLIND MAN.

I WAS born at Bagdad, and possessed some inheritance from my father and mother, who both died within a few days of each other. Although I was but little advanced in life, I did not waste my fortune by extravagance and debauchery; on the contrary, I was always attentive to increase it by industry. At length I became so rich as to possess fourscore camels, which I let to the caravan merchants, and which produced me large sums every journey I made to different parts, whither I accompanied them. Thus fortunate, and with an earnest desire to become still richer, one day, as I was returning with my camels unladen, from Balsora, and had turned the beasts at liberty to feed in a spot where abundant pasture had induced me to halt, a dervise came up, and seated himself near me to take refreshment. I asked him whence he came, and whither he was going. He put the same questions to me; and after we had mutually satisfied each other's curiosity, we produced our provisions in common and ate together. During our repast the dervise told me that, in a place not far distant, he knew of a treasure of so immense value that if my fourscore camels were all laden with the gold and jewels, it would not seem as if anything had been removed. This intelligence at once surprised and delighted me—I was beside myself with joy. "My good dervise,' cried I, "I see plainly that you have little regard for the things of this world. Of what account to you, then, is the knowledge of this treasure? You are alone, and could carry off but a very small part of it—show me where it is, and I will load my fourscore camels, and present you with one of them, in return for the profit you have procured for me." My offer was trifling, no doubt, but it appeared to me considerable; and I considered the seventy-nine loads which would be mine as nothing in comparison with the one of which I should deprive myself, by giving it to him. The dervise, who perceived my covetousness, replied, without the least emotion, "Brother, what you offer me is in no proportion to the favour you request. I need not have said a word to you of the treasure; but what I have so frankly told you must convince you of the good intention I had, and still have, of obliging you, and of giving you cause to remember me for ever. I have, then, another proposal to make to you; it is for you to consider whether you will accept it. You said that you were in possession of fourscore camels; I am ready to conduct you to the treasure; we will together load them with as much gold and jewels as they can carry, but on condition that you give me one half of them with their burden, while you retain the other moiety for yourself; after which we can separate, and go where we please." I could not deny the fairness of the proposal; nevertheless, I regarded the giving up half my camels as a great loss, and particularly when I reflected that the dervise would be as rich as myself; but there was no room for hesitation—I must comply with the terms, or have to repent during my life losing the opportunity of obtaining a large fortune.

I instantly collected my camels, and we set out together. After travelling some time, we arrived in a spacious valley, the entrance to which was very narrow. When we were arrived within the pass of the mountains, "Let us go no farther," said the dervise. "Stop your camels, and make them lie down in the spot before you. I will go before you to the opening of the place where the treasure is." I acted as the dervise had advised, and immediately rejoined him. I found him, with a flint and steel in his hand, collecting a little dry wood for a fire. When he had kindled one, he threw upon it some perfume, uttering words which I could not understand, and instantly a thick smoke rose into the air. He divided this smoke; and in a moment, although the rock seemed not to have the least appearance of an opening, one was nevertheless made through the stone itself, like a passage. This opening exposed to our view, in a vast cavern sunk in the rock, a magnificent palace. I was not even struck with the infinite riches I saw on all sides; but, without stopping to notice the careful manner in which so much treasure had been arranged, I ran to the first heap of gold that presented, and put into a sack as much money as I thought I could carry. The sacks were large, and I would willingly have filled them all; but it was necessary to consider the strength of my camels. The dervise was likewise employed; but I perceived that he confined himself to the jewels. I followed his example, and we carried off a much greater proportion of precious stones than of gold. After we had filled our sacks, we had only to reclose the place and depart; but, before we left the treasure, the dervise went back again, and as there were many vases of gold, and other precious materials, I observed that he took from one of them a small box, which he put into his bosom, after he had shown me that it contained only a sort of ointment. The dervise repeated the same ceremony at closing up the treasure as he did on opening it; and the rock appeared with the same unbroken surface as before. We then passed through the same narrow path by which we entered the valley, and proceeded together till we came to the great road, where we were to separate: he, to pursue his journey to Balsora; and I, to return to Bagdad. We embraced each other with the highest satisfaction; and after having exchanged our adieus, we parted.

I had advanced but a few steps to overtake my camels, before the demon of ingratitude and envy got possession of my heart; I lamented the loss of my forty camels, and still more the wealth they carried. "The dervise has no occasion for these riches," said I, mentally; "he is master of the whole treasure, and can therefore help himself to as much as he pleases." I then ran after the dervise, calling to him as loud as I could, and made signs to him to stop and wait for me. When I had rejoined him, "Brother," said I, "no sooner had I quitted you, than a matter occurred to me which I never thought of before, and which, perhaps, you have never yet considered. Probably you are not aware of the trouble you have undertaken, in charging yourself with the care of so many camels. Believe me, you had better take away only thirty; I am certain you will have quite difficulty enough to manage them." "I believe you are right," replied the dervise, who found himself in no condition to dispute the matter with me; "and I confess I never once thought of it. Select, then, the ten most agreeable to you; and, with God's blessing, take them with you." I chose ten of them; and, after having turned them back, I put them in the road to follow mine. This increased my cupidity, and I flattered myself I should have little trouble in obtaining ten more. In effect, instead of thanking him for the rich present he had just made me, "Brother," said I again, "from the interest I take in your repose, I cannot determine to quit you, without beseeching you to consider once more, how difficult it is to conduct thirty laden camels; you would find it much better to repeat the favour you have just conferred upon me. What I recommend, you must perceive, is not so much for my own advantage, as for your ease and satisfaction." My discourse had all the effect I wished; and the dervise ceded to me the ten camels I demanded. After this, I think I ought to have been contented; but I felt additional anxiety to obtain the twenty which the dervise still possessed. I redoubled my solicitations to induce the dervise to give me up ten of those twenty. He readily consented. With regard to the remaining ten, I embraced him, I caressed him, with so much fervour, conjuring him not to refuse me these, that he surrendered them. "Make a proper use of them, brother," added he; "and remember that God, who bestows riches upon us, can also take them away, if we do not employ them to succour the poor."

My blindness was so great, that I was in no condition to reap advantage from this salutary advice. I was not satisfied with finding myself in possession again of my four score camels. It came into my mind, that the little box of ointment which the dervise had taken, might be something more precious than all the wealth for which I had yet been obliged to him. This determined me to endeavour to obtain it. I had just embraced him, and taking my leave; when approaching him again, "Apropos," said I, "what mean you to do with that little box of ointment? pray make me a present of it." Far from refusing me the box, the dervise immediately drew it from his bosom, and presenting it to me without the least displeasure, "There, brother," said he, "take it, you are welcome to this also. The use of it is surprising and marvellous. If you apply a little of this ointment round the left eye, and upon the eyelid, all the treasures concealed within the bosom of the earth will appear to your view; but if you make the same application to the right eye, you will become blind." "Take the box," said I, presenting it to him, "and apply this ointment to my left eye. I am impatient to make a trial of a thing which appears to me incredible." The dervise readily complied; he made me shut my left eye, and applied the ointment. When he had done so, I opened my eye, and found he had told me the truth. In fact, I saw an infinite number of places filled with riches, so prodigious and in such variety, that it would be impossible for me to particularise them. But as I was obliged to keep my right eye shut with my hand, which fatigued me, I begged the dervise to apply some ointment also round that eye. "I am ready to do so," replied the dervise; "but you must remember I told you, if you put any upon the right eye, you would instantly become blind." Far from being satisfied, I imagined that there was still some mystery which he wished to conceal from me. Under this strong prejudice, I fancied that, if this ointment had the power of enabling me to see all the treasures of the earth by applying it to my left eye, it might probably give me the disposal of them, if applied to my right. I persevered in entreating the dervise to apply it himself to my right eye. "After conferring on you, brother, so great a benefit," said he, "I cannot resolve to add so serious an injury." I carried my obstinacy to the extreme. "Brother," said I, with firmness, "you have hitherto generously consented to all I have required; would you wish me to part from you dissatisfied, on a point of so little consequence?" The dervise made every objection possible; but seeing it was my power to enforce compliance, "Since you are absolutely determined," said he, "I will satisfy you." He then took a little of this fatal ointment, and applied it on my right eye; but, alas! when I opened it, I could perceive nothing and I remained blind, as you now see me.

"Ah, ill-omened dervise!" cried I, "what you predicted is but too true! Fatal curiosity, insatiable desire of riches, into what an abyss of misery have you plunged me! but, my dear brother, so charitable and beneficent as you are, of the many wonderful secrets with which you are acquainted, is there not one 'by which my sight might be restored?" "Unhappy wretch!" returned the dervise, "hadst thou taken my advice, thou wouldst have avoided this misfortune: thou hast thy deserts." The dervise said no more to me, and I had nothing to reply; he left me alone, covered with confusion, and overwhelmed with an excess of grief; and, after having collected my fourscore camels, he led them away, and pursued his journey to Balsora. I entreated him not to leave me in this miserable condition, and to assist, at least, in conducting me to the next caravan; but he was deaf to my cries and prayers. Thus deprived of sight, and of everything I possessed in the world, I should have died of grief and hunger, if the next day, a caravan, returning from Balsora, had not had the charity to take me up.

I was compelled to solicit alms, and this has been my employment to the present hour; but, to expiate my crime I have imposed upon myself the punishment of a blow from every charitable person who may have compassion on my misery. In fine, commander of the faithful, if your majesty deign to judge of the penance I have imposed upon myself, I am persuaded you will think it too light, and much below my crime.

*   *   *   *   *

When the blind man had finished his history, the caliph said to him: "Baba Abdallah, your sin is great; you are sensible of its enormity, and have submitted to this public penance to the present time. It is enough; but you must, for the future, continue to ask pardon of God, and that you may not be interrupted by the necessity of begging for subsistence, I will give you a pension, during your life."

The Caliph Haroun Alraschid then spoke to the young man whom he had seen ill-treat his mare, and asked him his name, as he had the blind man; when the young man replied, he was called Sidi Nouman. "Sidi Nouman," said the caliph to him, "I have been in the habit of seeing horses exercised, but never did I see any urged in so cruel a manner as you pressed yours yesterday. I would know what the reason is, and have ordered you to come hither that you may may inform me of it. Be sure you tell me exactly the circumstance, and disguise nothing."

Sidi Nouman replied, "Commander of the faithful, I dare not say I am the most perfect of men; yet I am not wicked enough to have committed, nor even to form a wish to commit, any offence against the laws, so as to have occasion to dread their severity. I confess that the manner in which I have for some time treated my mare, as your majesty has witnessed, is strange, barbarous, and of very mischievous example; but I hope you will find my motive justifiable, and that you will think me more worthy of compassion than chastisement. This, then, is my story:—

THE HISTORY OF SIDI NOUMAN.

MY birth is not of sufficient importance to deserve the attention of your majesty. With regard to property, my ancestors left me as much as I could desire to live creditably, without ambition, and entirely independent. With these advantages, I could only want, to render my happiness complete, the society of an amiable wife, who, truly loving me, would be willing to share with me that happiness, but this God was not pleased to grant me. On the contrary, he gave me one who, the very day after our marriage, began to exercise my patience in a manner not to be conceived but by those who have been exposed to a similar trial. The first time I saw my wife without her veil, after she was brought to my house, I rejoiced to find I had not been deceived in the account which had been given to me of her beauty: she suited my taste, and I was pleased with her. The day succeeding our marriage, we had a dinner of several dishes. I entered the room where the table was set, and as I did not see my wife there, I desired she might be called. After having kept me waiting some time, she appeared, and we sat down together at the table. I began with some rice, which I took in the usual manner with a spoon. My wife, on the contrary, drew from a case a sort of ear-picker, with which she began to eat some rice, conveying it to her mouth by single grains. Surprised at this proceeding, "Amine," said I, "have you thus learned to eat rice in your family? Do you act in this manner, because you are a little eater? or are you desirous of counting the grains, that you may not eat more at one time than at another?" But, without uttering a single word, she continued eating in the same manner; and, in order to give me still greater uneasiness, she took these single grains of rice more deliberately. I supposed she might have been eating before; or, if not, that she reserved herself to eat alone, and at her ease. These considerations prevented my saying anything further which might intimidate her, or showing her any mark of my dissatisfacton.

The same proceeding was repeated at supper; the next day, and every time we were together, she behaved precisely in the same manner. I saw clearly that it was not possible a woman could live on the very little sustenance she took, and that there must be some mystery which I could not discover; this made me resolve to dissemble. One night, when Amine thought me fast asleep, she arose very softly, and I observed she dressed herself with extreme care, for fear she would awaken me. She finished dressing herself, and in a moment walked cautiously out of the room. The instant she was gone, I arose, and throwing my cloak across my shoulders, had just time to perceive, through a window, that she opened the street door, and went out. I ran immediately to the door, which she had not quite closed; and favoured by the moonlight, followed her, till I saw her enter a cemetery near our house. I then gained the end of a wall which terminated at the burying-place, and I perceived Amine with a female goule. Your majesty is not ignorant that goules, of both sexes, are demons, which wander about the fields. They commonly inhabit ruinous buildings, whence they issue suddenly and surprise passengers, whom they kill and devour. If they fail meeting with travellers, they go by night into burying-places, to dig up dead bodies, upon which they feed. They together dug up a dead body which had been buried that very day; and the goule several times cut off pieces of the flesh, which they both ate, as they sat upon the edge of the grave. When they had finished their horrid meal, they threw the remains of the carcase into the

grave, which they refilled with the earth they had taken from it. I precipitately returned to my house. On entering, I left the door partly open, as I had found it; and when I reached my chamber, I again lay down, and feigned to sleep.

In a short time, Amine followed me; she undressed herself, and returned to bed with great apparent satisfaction at having so well succeeded, without my perceiving what had passed. With my mind full of the idea of the savage and abominable action which I had just witnessed, a long time elapsed before I could again sleep. At length, however,

I did, but so slightly, that the first voice, which was the call to public prayers at day-break, awoke me. I dressed myself, and went to the mosque. When prayers were ended, I walked out of the town, and passed the morning sauntering in the gardens, considering what means I should take, to make my wife change her manner of living. In this train of thinking, I was insensibly led to my own house, which I entered just at the hour of dinner.

As soon as Amine saw me, she ordered dinner, and we sat down to table. Finding she still persisted in taking the rice grain by grain, "Amine," said I, in a manner perfectly composed, "you know how much cause I had to be surprised the day after our marriage, when I perceived you eating your rice only in such small quantities. My remonstrances have been, however, ineffectual; and to this day you have continually maintained the same conduct and given me the same uneasiness. Are not the dishes on our table better than the flesh of a dead person?" I had no sooner uttered the last words, than Amine gave way to the most inconceivable passion: her face was in a flame, her eyes seemed starting from her head, and she foamed with rage.

The frightful state in which I saw her terrified me. In the height of her fury, she took a glass of water, which was near her, and dipping her fingers into it, she muttered a few unintelligible words, and threw the water in my face, saying, in a furious tone, "*Wretch! receive the punishment of thy curiosity, and become a dog.*" Scarcely had Amine uttered these words, than I found myself changed into a dog. My surprise and astonishment at a transformation so sudden at first prevented my running away, which gave her an opportunity of taking a stick to beat me; and she used it with so much violence, that I scarcely know how I avoided death on the spot. I thought to escape by running into the court, but she pursued me with the same fury; and, nimble as I endeavoured to be, to avoid her blows, I could not shun them, and she inflicted them in great abundance. Tired, at length, and mortified at not having killed me, as she intended, she conceived a new means of effecting my destruction: she partly opened the door into the street, in order to crush me as I should pass to make my escape. I suspected her malicious design; and by observing her eyes and her motions, I took my opportunity so well, as to defeat her vigilance, with no further injury than having the end of my tail squeezed. The pain I felt made me cry and howl as I ran along the street. This occasioned other dogs to attack and worry me. To avoid their pursuit, I sought shelter in the shop of a man who sold sheeps' heads, tongues, and feet. He was one of those superstitious people, who consider dogs such unclean animals, that water and soap enough cannot be obtained to wash their clothes, if by accident a dog touch them in passing. After the dogs which had pursued me were driven away, he made many attempts to drive me out; but I hid myself, and baffled his endeavours. So I passed the night, in spite of him, within the shop.

The next day my host having gone out to make his purchases, returned loaded with sheeps' heads, tongues, and feet; and, while he was assorting his goods, I stole out of my corner, and was going away, when I saw a great many dogs drawn thither by the smell of the meat, assembled round the shop, waiting till he threw them something: these I joined, standing in the same suppliant posture. My host, considering that I had not eaten anything since I had taken refuge with him, distinguished me by throwing in my way larger pieces, and more frequently, than to the other dogs. When he had ended, I was desirous of re-entering his shop; but he was inflexible; he forbade my entrance with a stick in his hand, showing not the least compassion for me; so that I was forced to seek my destiny elsewhere.

After passing a few houses, I stopped at the shop of a baker, who seemed of a lively and merry disposition, as indeed he proved. He was then at breakfast, and threw me a piece of bread. I continued sitting near his shop, with my head turned towards it, to signify to him that at present I only wanted his protection. This he afforded me, and even took such notice of me, as to give me assurance that he would let me into his house. I was extremely well treated there, and he never breakfasted, dined, nor supped, without giving me a sufficiency; and, on my part, I felt for him all the attachment and fidelity he could expect from my gratitude.

I had been in this house some time, when one day a woman came there to purchase bread; in payment for which, she gave my host, with other good money, one bad piece. The baker who noticed the counterfeit, returned it to the woman. The woman refused to take it again, asserting it was good; my host maintained the contrary; and in the dispute, "The piece of money," said he to the woman, "is so visibly false, that I am sure my dog would know it. Come here," said he, calling me by my name. Hearing his voice, I immediately leaped upon the counter; and the baker, throwing the money before me, "See," added he, "if you can find out a piece of counterfeit money there." I examined all; and putting my foot on the false piece, separated it from the rest. The baker, who referred the matter to my judgment, merely to divert himself, was extremely surprised to see me immediately point it out. The woman, knowing it to be bad, had nothing to say, and was obliged to give another instead of it. The report of my ability in distinguishing false money was soon spread, not only in the neighbourhood, but through every part of the city. My reputation procured my master so much business, that he could with difficulty get through it. One day, a woman attracted by this novelty, came, as others had done, to buy bread, she threw down six pieces of money before me, one of which was bad. I separated it from the rest, and putting my foot upon it, I looked at her, as if to ask her if it were not so. "Yes," said the woman, looking at me, "that is the false coin, you are not mistaken." She paid for the bread she had just bought; and as she was going out of the shop, she made a sign for me to follow her. I had remarked the attention with which this woman examined me; and imagined she might possibly have some knowledge of my misfortune. I was not mistaken. I let her proceed, however, and contented myself with looking after her. She went but a few steps before she returned, and observing that I only looked at her, without quitting my place, she again made a sign for me to follow. Then, without longer deliberation I leaped from the counter, and followed the woman, who appeared to me to be much pleased at having carried her point. After going some distance, she arrived at her house, she opened the door, and when she entered, "Come in," she said: "you shall have no reason to repent having followed me," As soon as I was in the house, she shut the door, and led me to her apartment, where I saw a very beautiful young lady embroidering. "Daughter," said the mother, "I have brought you the baker's famous dog, that so well distinguishes false money from good. On the first report that was spread concerning him, you remember I told you my suspicion of his being a man." "You are not deceived, mother," replied the daughter; "as I will soon convince you." The young lady arose, took a vessel full of water, into which she dipped her hand, and throwing some of the water on me, she said, "*If you were born a dog remain a dog; but if you were born a man, resume the figure of a man by virtue of this water.*" Instantly the enchantment was broken; I lost the form of a dog, and saw myself once more a man.

Penetrated with gratitude for an obligation of such magnitude, I threw myself at the feet of the young lady; "My dear deliverer," I cried, "I feel so strongly the excess of your goodness, that I conjure you to tell me how I can express the extent of my gratitude; or, rather, dispose of me as a slave, to whom you have an unquestionable right; I belong to you. That you may know him who is at your disposal, I will give you my history in few words." Then, after having told her who I was, I gave an account of my marriage with Amine; of my compliance, and my patience in supporting her humour: of her extraordinary manners: of the indignity with which she had treated me through inconceivable maliciousness. "Sidi Nouman," said the daughter, "the consciousness of having served a worthy man, is a sufficient recompense. Let us talk of Amine, your wife: I knew her before her marriage; we

have even often met at the bath; but as we were of very different tempers, I took particular care to avoid every occasion that might lead to a connection with her. But, to return to your immediate concerns—what I have just done for you is not sufficient; I will finish what I have begun. It is not enough to have dissolved the enchantment; you must punish her for it, as she deserves, by re-entering your house, which I will enable you to do. Remain here, and converse with my mother; I shall soon return."

My deliverer went into a closet; and, while she remained there, I had time to express to the mother my sense of the obligation to her, as well as to her daughter. "My daughter," replied she, "as you find, is not less skilful in the magic art than Amine." The mother was beginning to relate some of the wonders she had witnessed, when her daughter returned with a little bottle in her hand; "Sidi Nouman," said she, "my books, which I have just been consulting, inform me, that Amine is not at this moment in your house, but will be there presently. From them I also learn, that the dissembler appeared before your servants to be very uneasy at your absence; and made them believe, that while at dinner, you recollected some business which obliged you to go out immediately; that, in going out, you left the door open, and a dog having run in, she had driven him out by beating him with a stick. Return, then, to your home, taking with you this little bottle. Having gained admittance, wait in your chamber till Amine returns. When she appears, go down into the court, and present yourself before her. Her surprise will be so great at seeing you again, that she will turn her back to fly from you; then throw upon her some of the water in this bottle, which you will hold ready for that purpose; and in throwing it, pronounce these words boldly, '*Receive the punishment of thy wickedness.*' I need not say any more; you will see the effect." After these words I took leave of her and her mother, with every expression of gratitude.

Everything passed precisely as foretold. Amine soon appeared; and as she advanced, I presented myself to her, with the water in my hand, ready to throw upon her. She uttered a loud shriek; I threw the water upon her, pronouncing the words the enchantress had taught me, when immediately she was changed into a mare, the same your majesty saw yesterday. I seized her by the mane; and, in spite of her resistance, led her to the stable. I put on her a halter; and, after having tied her up, reproaching her with her crimes and wickedness, I whipped her till fatigue obliged me to desist.

Commander of the faithful, I dare flatter myself your majesty will not disapprove of my conduct.

* * * * * *

When the caliph saw that Sidi Nouman had nothing more to relate, "Your history is singular," said he, "and the wickedness of your wife inexcusable; for which reason I do not absolutely condemn the chastisement you have hitherto inflicted on her. But I would have you consider how great her punishment is, to be reduced to the level of beasts, and I wish you would content yourself with letting her do penance in this state."

The caliph, after having declared his will to Sidi Nouman, addressed himself to the third person, whom the grand-vizier Giafar had introduced; "Cogia Hassan," said he, "in passing your house yesterday, it appeared so magnificent that I had the curiosity to inquire to whom it belonged. I was informed that you built it, after having followed a trade, the profits of which were barely sufficient to support you. I also learnt that you have not forgotten your humble origin, that you make a good use of the wealth, and that your neighbours speak highly in your favour. Speak to me then, with sincerity, that I may, from my own knowledge, have the pleasure of partaking of your happiness." On these assurances, Cogia Hassan prostrated himself before the throne, and after he had risen, "Commander of the faithful," said he, "any person who did not feel his conscience so pure and clear, would have been embarrassed at receiving an order to appear before your majesty; but as I have never entertained towards you any sentiments but those of respect and veneration, I was only troubled with the fear of not being able to support the splendour which surround you."

After remaining some moments silent to collect what he had to say, Cogia Hassan began in these terms:—

THE HISTORY OF COGIA HASSAN ALHABBAL.

THAT your majesty may clearly comprehend the means by which I attained the great happiness I now enjoy, I must begin by speaking of two intimate friends, citizens of Bagdad, still living, who can bear witness to the truth of what I relate. These two friends were called, the one Saadi, and the other Saad. Saadi, who is immensely rich, has always been of opinion that a man cannot be happy in this world without wealth sufficient to enable him to live entirely independent. Saad thinks differently, he allows that such a fortune as will procure the necessaries of life is requisite; but he maintains that virtue ought to constitute the happiness of men.

One day in a conversation on a similar matter, Saadi asserted that such persons only were poor as were born in poverty, or being born rich, had lost their fortunes by debauchery, or by some of those misfortunes which are not uncommon; "my opinion is," said he, "that the poor continue poor, solely because they cannot command a sum of money sufficiently large to draw them from their misery, and to employ their industry in improving it." Saad did not concur in the proposition. "The means you propose to render a poor man rich," said he, "do not appear to me to be so certain as you think them. Your ideas on this matter are very equivocal, and I could support my opinion against yours by many good arguments; a poor man may become rich by many other means as well as with a sum of money as you speak of, whatever good management and economy may be used to increase it by a well conducted business." "Saad," replied Saadi, "I perceive I shall not gain any advantage over you, by persisting to support my opinion against yours. I wish to make an experiment to convince you, by giving such a sum as I think necessary to one of those workmen who live by the labour of the day, and who die as poor as they were born. If we do not succeed, we will see if you can devise a more probable plan."

Some days after, it happened that the two friends passed through that part of the town where I was working at my business, as a rope-maker. My appearance and dress sufficiently bespoke my poverty. Saad, who remembered Saadi's plan, said to him, "there is a man whom I have long seen working at his trade as a rope-maker, and always in the same state of poverty. He is a subject worthy of your liberality, and the experiment of which we spoke the other day."

The two friends approached, and as I saw they wished to speak to me, I left off working. They both gave me

the common salutation—"Peace be with you," and Saadi asked me my name. I returned them the same salutation, and in answer to the question of Saadi, "Sir," said I, "my name is Hassan, and on account of my employment, I am commonly known by the name of Hassan Alhabbal." "Hassan," returned Saadi, "as every trade supports its master, I do not not doubt that yours maintains you; and I am astonished, that from the length of time you have been engaged in it, you have not acquired some property, and bought a good stock of hemp to increase your business, and to enable you to deal to a larger amount." "Sir," I replied, "you will cease to be surprised that I do not take the method, as you say, to become rich, when I tell you that, though I work hard from morning to night, it is with difficulty I can earn enough to procure bread and vegetables for me and my family. With a wife, I have five children, not one of whom is of an age to give me the least assistance. Although hemp is not an expensive article, one must nevertheless, have money to purchase it ; and the first I obtain by the sale of my goods, I lay by for that purpose, otherwise, I should not be able to maintain my family."

When I had given this account of myself to Saadi. "Hassan," he said, "my wonder has ceased; but if I was to present you a purse of two hundred pieces of gold, would you not make a good use of it? and do you not think that you would soon become as rich as the principal people in your business?" "Sir," I replied, "I am persuaded you do not mean to divert yourself at my expense, and that you are serious in the offer. I dare then affirm, that a much less sum would be sufficient, not only to make me rich, but even to enable me to acquire more wealth than all the rope-makers in this great city of Bagdad are worth." The generous Saadi immediately convinced me that he was serious in what he had said, he took the purse from his bosom, "Take it," said he, "there is the purse, and you will find in it, exactly two hundred pieces of gold. I pray God to bless you with it, and be assured, that my friend, Saad, here, as well as myself, will have the greatest satisfaction in learning that they have contributed to your happiness." When I had received the purse, I was so transported with joy, that I could not speak, and could only express my feelings to my benefactor by seizing the border of his robe, and kissing it, but he instantly withdrew it and continued his walk with his friend.

On returning to my work, the first thought that occurred to me, was, where I should put the purse for safety. In my poor little house I had neither box nor chest with a lock to it, nor any place where I could be sure it would not be discovered. In this perplexity, as I had been accustomed, like other poor people, to hide the trifle of money I had in the folds of my turban, I quitted my work, and went into my house, pretending to adjust my turban. I took my precautions so well, that, without my wife or my children's perceiving it, I drew ten pieces of gold from the purse, which I put aside for the most pressing wants. The principal expense of that day was in buying a good stock of hemp ; then, as we had not had meat for a long time in my house, I went to the market, and bought some for supper. As I returned home, I held the meat in my hand, when a half-starved kite darted upon it, and would have snatched it out of my hand, had I not held it firmly against him. But, alas! I had much better have let it go, than to lose my purse. The more resistance I made, the more determined the kite was to obtain the meat. He drew me from side to side, while he continued fluttering in the air, without quitting his hold ; but it happened, unfortunately, that in the efforts I made to resist him, my turban fell to the ground. Immediately the kite quitted his hold, and seizing my turban, flew away with it. I uttered such piercing cries, that all the people in the neighbourhood were alarmed, and joined their shouts with mine, to make the kite quit his hold ; but our cries did not frighten the kite, and he carried my turban quite out of sight.

I returned home very melancholy. I was compelled to buy another, which was a further diminution of the ten pieces of gold I had taken from the purse. I had already expended a part of it in buying hemp, and what remained was by no means sufficient to realise the fine hopes I had conceived. While the few pieces of gold I had remaining lasted, we felt the benefit of it ; but I soon returned to my former situation, and as totally unable to lessen its misery as before.

About six months after this misfortune, the two friends passed the place where I lived. The neighbourhood brought me to the recollection of Saad. "We are not far from the street in which Hassan Alhabbal lives, said he to Saadi. " Let us go there, and see if the two hundred pieces of gold, that you gave him, have contributed to place him in a better situation." "Willingly," replied Saadi; "I have for several days anticipated the great pleasure I shall feel in making you a witness to the success of my proposition." Saad saluted me as usual : "Well, Hassan," said he, "we do not ask you how your affairs have gone on, since we saw you ; the two hundred pieces of gold must have contributed to render them more prosperous." "Gentlemen," replied I, "I am much mortified at being obliged to inform you, that your wishes as well as mine, have not been attended with the success you had reason to expect, and I had promised myself." I then recounted to them all the circumstances that I have just mentioned. Saadi gave no credit to my story. "Hassan," he said, "you wish to deceive me : what you tell me is incredible : kites do not attack turbans. You have acted as people in your situation generally act. If they acquire extraordinary gain, or any good fortune unexpectedly happen to them, they abandon their work, living well as long as the money lasts, and when it is gone, they find themselves still in the same miserable situation, and with the same wants as before." "Sir," I replied, "I submit to all these reproaches, because I am conscious I do not deserve them. The circumstance is so well known in this quarter, that there is not a person who will not bear witness to it. I confess, I had never heard that kites would carry off turbans ; but the thing has happened to me." Saad took my part, and related so many histories of kites, not less surprising, some of which he had himself known, that Saadi again drew his purse from his bosom. He counted two hundred pieces of gold into my hand, which I put into my bosom, for want of a purse. When Saadi had finished telling out this sum, "Hassan," said he, "I once more make you a present of two hundred pieces of gold ; but take care to put them in a secure place."

After they had left me I went into my house. I laid aside ten pieces of gold, and wrapped the hundred and ninety in a cloth, which I tied up. It was necessary to hide the parcel in a safe place. After having considered for some time, I determined to put it at the bottom of a large earthen pot, full of bran, which stood in a corner. My wife returned soon afterwards ; and as I had but a little hemp left, without mentioning the two friends, I said I was going out to buy some. Whilst I was gone to make this purchase, a man, who sells fullers' earth, happened to pass through

the street crying it. My wife, who was in want of this earth, called to the man; and as she had not any money, she asked him if he would take her pot of bran in exchange. He desired to see it; my wife showed him him the jar, and the bargain was struck.

I returned laden with as much hemp as I could carry, followed by five porters, with the same merchandize, with which I filled a loft in my house. I satisfied the porters for their trouble; and, after they were gone, sat down to recover from my fatigue, when, casting my eyes towards the place where I had left the jar of bran, I observed it was not there. I hastily asked my wife what was become of it, and she told me of the bargain she had made, as a transaction by which she thought herself a great gainer. "Ah, miserable woman!" I cried, "you are ignorant of the mischief you have done to me. You thought you had only sold some bran, but with this bran you have enriched your seller of fullers' earth with a hundred and ninety pieces of gold." The despair of my wife, when she learnt the great fault she had through ignorance committed, was of no avail. "Wretch that I am!" cried she, "I am unworthy to live after having made so cruel a mistake. Ah, my husband, you have acted very wrong. Why did you keep an affair of this importance so secret from me? Had you placed some confidence in me, it would not have happened." "Wife," said I, "be composed; you are not aware that you will draw all the neighbours about us, by your cries and your tears; it is unnecessary they should be made acquainted with our distress. The most advisable conduct is to conceal our loss, and support it patiently, so that it may not be suspected, and to submit to the will of God." However just my arguments were, my wife was at first but little disposed to relish them. But time, which softens the greatest and most insupportable evils, at length soothed her distress.

The two friends were longer in paying me a visit, to inquire into my situation, than they had been before. Saad had often proposed it to Saadi, but he always wished to defer it. Saad had not the same opinion of the effect of his friend's liberality. "You think, then," replied he, "that your present will have been better employed this time than before. If the contrary should be the result?" "But," replied Saadi, "it does not happen every day that a kite carries away a turban. Hassan has been caught once; he will be very careful a second time." "I do not doubt it," returned Saad, "but some other accident, which neither you nor I can anticipate, may have occurred. I have a presentiment that you will not have succeeded, and that I shall be more fortunate in proving that a poor man can sooner become rich by any other means than with money."

At length one day when Saad was with Saadi, "It is too much," said Saadi; "I will this very day satisfy myself. Now is the time for walking; let us go and see which of us has gained the wager." The two friends accordingly set out, and I saw them at a distance. I was much disturbed, and was on the point of quitting my work, and hiding myself. Intent on my labour, I pretended not to see them, till they were so near, that they gave me the salutation of, "Peace be with you!" I immediately cast my eyes on the ground, and, in relating to them my last misfortune, I let them know the reason why they still found me as poor as when they first saw me. I ceased speaking, and Saadi thus replied. "Though I wish to persuade myself that all you have just related is true, I must nevertheless be cautious how I proceed, in continuing an experiment which might, in the end, ruin me. I do not regret the four hundred pieces of gold I have lost in endeavouring to draw you from your poverty. I have done it without expecting any other recompense than the pleasure of having served you." Then, turning towards his friend, "Saad," continued he, "you perceive by what I have just said, that I do not entirely give up the point to you. You are, however, at liberty to make the trial which you have so long maintained in opposition to me. Convince me that there are other means, besides pecuniary assistance, to establish the fortune of a poor man in the way I expect, and that you mean, and take Hassan for your subject." Saad held a piece of lead in his hand; while he showed it to Saadi, "You have seen me," said he, "pick up this bit of lead which lay at my feet. I am going to give it to Hassan, and you will see how valuable it will be to him." Saadi burst into a violent fit of laughter. "A piece of lead!" cried he; "what will he do with it?" Saad, in presenting the piece of lead, said to me, "Let Saadi laugh, and do not refuse to take it; you will one day tell us the good fortune it will have brought you." I thought that Saad could not be in earnest; however, I took the piece of lead, thanking him for it; and, to satisfy him, I put it carelessly into my vest. The two friends left me to finish their walk, and I continued my labour.

At night, when I undressed to go to bed, the piece of lead Saad had given me, and which I had not afterwards thought of, fell to the ground. I took it up, and put it into the first place that offered. That very night it happened that one of my neighbours, a fisherman, in preparing his nets, discovered that he wanted a piece of lead. He had not any to repair the loss of it, and at that hour could not buy any. He expressed his vexation to his wife, and sent her to ask his neighbours to supply his wants. The wife went from door to door, on both sides of the street, but could not get any lead. She carried back this answer to her husband, who asked her, naming many of his neighbours, if she had knocked at their doors? She said she had. "And at Hassan Alhabbal's?" The fisherman's wife went out grumbling, and came and knocked at my door. I had been some time asleep, but I awoke and asked what she wanted. "Hassan Alhabbal," said the woman, "my husband wants a little bit of lead to mend his nets." The lead which Saad had given me was so fresh in my memory, especially after what had happened to me in undressing, that I could not have forgotten it. I answered that I had some; and if she would wait a moment, my wife should bring it her. My wife rose, and feeling about, found the lead in the place where I told her it was. She half opened the door, and gave it. The fisherman's wife was delighted at not having come in vain. "Neighbour," said she, "the service you have done my husband and me is so great, that I promise you all the fish my husband may catch in the first throw of his nets."

The fisherman, charmed at finding, beyond his hopes, the lead he so much wanted, approved of the promise his wife had made us. Having mended his nets, he went to fish. In the first throw of his nets, he caught only one fish, but it was more than a foot long. He had afterwards many other draughts, which were all successful. But the fish were much smaller than the first he caught.

When the fisherman had finished his task, and returned home, his first care was to think of me; and I was extremely surprised, as I was at work, at seeing him come towards me. "Neighbour," said he, "my wife promised you last night all the fish that I caught in the first throw of my nets, I approved of her promise. God sent me only this one for you, which I beg you to accept." I carried the fish to my wife. "Take this fish," said I, "which the fisherman has just brought me, in return for the piece of lead he had last night. It is, I believe, all we are to hope for from the present Saad made me yesterday, though he promised it would bring me good luck." My wife

was on beholding at the sight of so large a fish: "What would you have me do with it?" said she: "our grid-iron is only fit to broil small fish."

In cleaning the fish, my wife drew out, with its entrails, a large diamond, which she supposed to be glass. She gave it to the youngest of our children as a plaything: and her brothers and sisters, who wished to see it, and handle it by turns, gave it to one another, to admire its beauty and its brilliancy. At night, our children perceived that it became brighter in proportion as my wife hid the light of the lamp, by carrying it about to prepare the supper. As trifles amuse children, and cause disputes among them, neither my wife nor I paid any attention to the subject of this noise, which almost stunned us.

After supper, the children again got together, and began to make the same noise as before. I then called the eldest to me, and asked him the cause of their dispute. "Father," said he, "it is a piece of glass, which shines brightest when we turn our backs to the lamp." I desired him to bring it to me, and tried the experiment my-self, which appeared to me very extraordinary, and induced me to ask my wife what it was. "I believe it to be a piece of glass," said she: "I took it out of the belly of the fish, in cleaning it." I imagined, as she did, that it was only a piece of glass: I nevertheless carried my experiment a little further: I told my wife to hide the lamp in the chimney: when the supposed piece of glass gave so great a light, that we could have seen to go to bed without the lamp. I made her put it out, and I placed the piece of glass at the side of the chimney, to give us light: "Here," said I, "is another advantage, that the piece of lead my friend Saad gave me procures us, in saving us the expense of oil." When my children saw that we had extinguished the lamp, and that the piece of glass supplied the place of it, they shouted so loud as to be heard throughout the neighbourhood. My wife and I augmented the noise, by endeavouring to silence them; and we could not entirely carry our point, till they were in bed and asleep, after entertaining themselves a considerable time, in their way, with the wonderful light of the piece of glass. My wife and I retired to bed soon after them; and early the next morning, as usual, I went to my work, without thinking any more of the piece of glass.

I must inform your majesty that my house and that of my nearest neighbour were only separated by a very slight partition of lath and plaster. This house belonged to a very rich Jew, a jeweller by trade, and the room in which he and his wife slept joined the partition. They were in bed, when my children made the noise, which awoke them, and a long time elapsed before they could get to sleep again. The next day the Jew's wife came to complain how much their sleep had been disturbed. "My good Rachael," (so the Jew's wife was called) said my wife, "I am very sorry for what has happened, and I hope you will excuse it. You know what children are; a trifle will make them laugh, and a trifle will make them cry. Come in, and I will show the cause of your complaint." The Jewess entered, and my wife took up the diamond. "See here," said she, "it was this piece of glass which oc-casioned all the noise you heard last night." Whilst the Jewess, who was acquainted with all sorts of stones, was examining this diamond, my wife told her how she had found it in the belly of a fish, and everything that had hap-pened respecting it. When my wife had done speaking, the Jewess said, in returning the diamond to her, "Aishach, I think, with you, that it is nothing but glass; but as it is better glass than common, I will buy it of you if you will sell it." My children, who heard the selling their plaything talked of, interrupted the conversation, by crying out and begging their mother to keep it; which, to pacify them, she was forced to promise. The Jewess went out: and before she left my wife, who accompanied her to the door, she begged her, in a low voice, if she intended selling the piece of glass, not to let anybody see it, without giving her notice.

The Jew had gone, early in the morning, to his shop, which was in that quarter of the town appropriated to jewellers. His wife went to him, and told him the discovery she had just made; she gave him an account of the size, of the probable weight, the beauty, the fine water, and the brightness of the diamond; and, above all, of the singular property which it possessed, of shining in the night. The Jew sent back his wife, ordering her to treat with mine for it; to offer at first such a trifling sum as she might judge proper, and to augment it in proportion to the difficulties she experienced; and, in short, to purchase the diamond, at whatever price. The Jewess, according to her husband's directions, spoke to my wife in private, without waiting to know whether she was determined to sell the diamond; and asked her whether she would take twenty pieces of gold for it. For a piece of glass, as she supposed it to be, my wife thought this a considerable sum. She would not, however, give her an answer; but only told the Jewess she could not listen to her proposal till she had first consulted me.

In the meantime, I left work and went home to dinner, while they were talking at the door. My wife stopped me, and asked if I would consent to sell the piece of glass she found in the belly of the fish, for twenty pieces of gold, which her neighbour had offered for it. I did not give an immediate answer. I reflected on the confidence with which Saad had promised me, in giving me the piece of lead, that it would make my fortune; and the Jewess, think-ing my silence arose from contempt at the sum she had offered, "Neighbour," said she, "I will give you fifty pieces for it. Will that satisfy you?" As I saw the Jewess so quickly raised her offer, from twenty to fifty pieces of gold, I kept firm, and told her she was far below the price for which I expected to sell it. "Neighbour," replied she, "take a hundred pieces of gold—it is a great sum of money; I do not even know whether my husband will approve of my offering so much." At this new rise, I told her I would have a hundred thousand pieces of gold for it; that I was certain the diamond was worth more, but to please her and her husband, I would be contented with this sum, and that, if they refused to take it at that price, other jewellers would give me more. The Jewess herself confirmed me in my determination, by the haste she showed to conclude the bargain, advancing as high as fifty thousand pieces of gold, which I refused. "I dare not," said she, "offer more, without my husband's leave; he will return to-night; but I shall take it as a favour if you will have patience to wait till he has spoken to you, and seen the diamond." This I promised.

At night, when the Jew returned home, he learned from his wife the little progress she had made; the offer she had tempted us with, of the fifty thousand pieces of gold, and the favour she had requested. The Jew observed the time I left work, and came into my house. "Neighbour Hassan," said he, on approaching me, "will you be kind enough to show me the diamond that your wife showed to mine?" I desired him to walk in, and showed it him. As it was nearly dark, and the lamp not yet lighted, he knew immediately, by the light the diamond gave, and by its great brightness in the palm of my hand, which was illumined by it, that his wife had given him a just account. He took it: and after having examined it with admiration a long time, "Well, neighbour," said he, "my wife tells me

she has offered you fifty thousand pieces of gold; but that you may be satisfied, I offer twenty thousand more." "Neighbour," returned I, "the price I have set upon it is a hundred thousand. You must give me that, or the diamond will continue mine." He argued a long time, but found me resolved; and fear lest I should show it to other jewellers determined him not to leave me till the bargain was concluded at my own price. He told me he had not a hundred thousand pieces of gold in his house; but that the next day, at the same hour, he would deposit the whole sum; and he brought me immediately two bags of a thousand pieces each, to secure the bargain. The next day he brought me the sum of a hundred thousand pieces of gold, and I delivered up the diamond.

I considered afterward the good use I ought to make of so considerable a sum of money. My wife wished me immediately to buy handsome clothes for herself and her children, to purchase a house, and furnish it elegantly. "Wife," said I, "it is not with these sort of expenses we ought to begin; trust to me, what you ask you shall have in time." I employed the whole of the day in visiting a number of persons of my own trade, and, giving them money in advance, I engaged them to work for me, in different kinds of rope-making. As this great number of workmen must produce work in proportion, I hired warehouses in different places; and in each I stationed a clerk, and very soon, by this management, my profits and revenue were considerable. Afterwards, to unite my warehouses, which were much dispersed, I bought a larger house. I pulled it down, and in its place built that which your majesty saw yesterday; but, whatever appearance it may have, it contains only the warehouses necessary.

Some time had elapsed, after I quitted my humble residence, to fix myself in my new house, when Saadi and Saad again remembered me. Having agreed to walk together, they entered the street in which they had formerly seen me, and were much astonished at not finding me employed as before, in my little trade of rope-making. Their wonder augmented, when informed that the person they mentioned was become a considerable merchant, and was no longer called simply Hassan, but Cogia Hassan Alhabbal; that is to say, *the merchant Hassan, the rope-maker*; and that he had built a house like a palace. The two friends were introduced, and I instantly recognised them; when rising, I invited them to be seated on a large sofa, at the same time pointing to a smaller one for four people, which was placed nearer my garden. I begged them to take the upper place; but they wished me to occupy it. "Gentlemen," said I to them, "I have not forgotten that I am Hassan Alhabbal; and were I any other person, and not under the obligations to you that I am, I know what is your due."

Saadi then began the conversation, and addressing me, "Cogia Hassan," said he, "I cannot express the pleasure I feel, in seeing you placed in the situation I wished, when I gave you the present—I do not speak with reproach—of the two hundred pieces of gold, which I twice gave you; but I am persuaded, that the four hundred pieces have made the wonderful change in your fortune. One thing only gives me concern, which is, that I cannot comprehend your reason for concealing the truth from me, in alleging you had met with losses, by accidents which then appeared and still appear to me incredible."

Saad listened to Saadi's discourse with great impatience. However, he suffered him to finish his speech, without opening his lips. When he had concluded, "Saadi," said he, "pardon me, if before Cogia Hassan reply, I first tell you, that I am surprised that you persist in not giving credit to the assurances he formerly made you. But let him speak; we shall learn from himself, which of us two has rendered him justice." After the two friends had spoken, I addressed them both: "Gentlemen," said I, "I will explain myself, in compliance with your desire; but first, I protest to you, it is with the same sincerity that I formerly made known to you what had happened to me." I then related the circumstances, but my protestations made not the least impression on the mind of Saadi. When I had ceased speaking, "Cogia Hassan," replied he, "the adventure of the fish, and of the diamond found in his belly, appears to be as little worthy of credit, as your turban being carried off by a kite, or as the jar of bran being exchanged for the fuller's earth. But, be that as it may, I am not less convinced that you are no longer poor but rich; and as my sole intention was, that you should become so by my means, I am most sincerely rejoiced at it."

As it grew late, they rose to take leave. "Gentlemen," said I, "permit me to request a favour of you, which I entreat you will not refuse; it is, that you will allow me the honour of giving you a frugal supper, and afterwards each a bed, that I may take you to-morrow, by water, to a small house which I have purchased in the country, to enjoy the air occasionally." "If Saad has not business to call him elsewhere," said Saadi, "I heartily consent to it." "I have not any," replied Saad. "We must, then, send to your house, and to mine, that our families may not expect us."

The next day, as I had agreed to set out early in the morning, that we might enjoy the fresh air, we were at the river's side before the sun rose. We embarked in a boat, spread with carpets, which was in readiness; and, by favour of six good rowers, and the current of the water, in about an hour and a half we arrived at my country house. On landing, the two friends stopped, less to contemplate the beauty of its exterior, than to admire its advantageous situation, in point of prospect, which was neither too much bounded nor too extensive, rendering it agreeable on every side. I led them through the apartments; pointing out the disposition of the rooms, with the offices and other conveniences; and they thought the whole very cheerful and pleasant. We went afterwards into the garden, where they were most pleased with a grove of every species of orange and citron trees, planted in walks at equal distances, and bearing fruits and flowers, which perfumed the air; water being conveyed from tree to tree, by a perpetual stream, directed from the river. The shade, the freshness, even during the sun's greatest heat, the gentle murmur of the water, the harmonious warbling of an infinite number of birds, and many other delightful things, engaged them so much, that they stopped at almost every step, sometimes to express their obligation to me for having brought them into so delicious a place, sometimes to congratulate me on the purchase I had made, and to pay me other obliging compliments. I led them to the end of the grove, which is very long and extensive, where I pointed out to them a wood of large trees, that terminated my garden. I then conducted them to a small room, open on all sides, but shaded by clumps of palm-trees which did not intercept the prospect. I invited them to enter, and repose themselves on a sofa covered with carpets and cushions.

Two of my sons, whom we had found in the house, and whom I had sent there with their preceptor, some time before, for the benefit of the air, quitted us on entering the grove, and as they were looking for birds' nests, they perceived a nest between the branches of a tree. They were at first tempted to climb it; but as they had neither strength nor skill for such an undertaking, they showed it to a slave, who always attended them, and desired him to obtain it. The slave climbed the tree; and when he reached the nest, he was much astonished to find it built in a turban. He brought away the nest, just as it was, descended from the tree, and showed the turban to my children;

but as he thought I should also like to see it, he told them so, and gave it to my eldest son to bring to me. I saw them at a distance running towards me, with an expression of pleasure, common in children who have found a nest; and presenting it to me, "Father," said the eldest, "see this nest in a turban!" Saadi and Saad were not less surprised than I was at the novelty; but my astonishment was greatly augmented on recognising the very turban the kite had carried away from me.

In the midst of my wonder, after I had examined it on all sides, "Gentlemen," said I," have you any recollection of the turban I wore on the day you first did me the honour to accost me?"

"I do not suppose," returned Saad, "that Saadi, any more than I, paid any attention to it; but neither of us can doubt, if the hundred and ninety pieces of gold are found there." "Sir," I replied, "you need not question its being the same turban: independent of my well knowing it again, I perceive also, by its weight, it is no other; and you will yourself be convinced, if you will give yourself the trouble to hold it." I presented it to him; he took it in his hands, and gave it to Saadi to feel the weight of it. "I am willing to believe it to be your turban," said Saadi: "I shall nevertheless be still more convinced, when I see the hundred and ninety pieces of gold in specie.' "At least, gentlemen," added I, when I had again taken the turban, "examine it well, I entreat you, before I undo it that you may observe it has not very lately been placed in the tree; and that the state in which you see both it and the nest—which is so neatly put together, evidently without the help of man—are certain proofs it has been there ever since the kite flew away with it, and that he let it drop, or placed it on the tree. Do not be offended that I make this observation, as I have so great an interest in removing every suspicion of deceit on my part." I took off the linen, which surrounded the bonnet, and I drew it from the purse, which Saadi knew to be the same he had given me. I emptied it on the carpet before them, saying, "Gentlemen, here are the pieces of gold: reckon them yourselves, and see if they are not right." Saad arranged them in tens, to the number of one hundred and ninety pieces, when Saadi, who could not reject so manifest a truth, thus addressed me: "Cogia Hassan," said he, "I allow that these hundred and ninety pieces of gold cannot have assisted in enriching you; but the other hundred and ninety, which you hid in the jar of bran, at least as you would make me believe, may have contributed to the purpose." "Sir," I replied, "I have told you the truth with respect to the last sum of money as well as to this. You would not have me retract, and tell you a falsehood?" Here the dispute ended; we arose and returned to the house, just as dinner was served, and sat down to table. After dinner, I left my guests at liberty to pass the heat of the day in reposing themselves, while I went to give orders to my steward and gardener. I rejoined them, and we then conversed on different subjects till the great heat was moderated, when we returned into the garden, where we remained in the cool till almost sunset. The two friends and I then mounted our horses, and, followed by a slave, we reached Bagdad, by moonlight, about two hours after dusk.

I know not by what negligence of my servants it happened that there was no corn for the horses on my return home. The granaries were shut, and they were too distant at that late hour. In searching about the neighbourhood, one of my slaves found a jar of bran in a shop; he bought the bran, and brought it in the jar, which he promised to carry back the next day. The slave emptied the bran into the manger, and in spreading it about, that the horses might have an equal share, he felt under his hand a piece of linen tied up, which was very heavy; he brought me the linen in the state he found it, and presenting it to me, said, perhaps it was the linen he had often heard me mention, in relating my history to my friends. Quite overjoyed, I said to my benefactors, "Gentlemen, it pleases God that we should not separate till you are fully convinced of the truth of what I have never ceased to declare. Here," continued I, addressing myself to Saadi, "are the hundred and ninety pieces of gold which I received from your hands; I am convinced by this linen rag." I untied the cloth, and counted the money before them. I ordered that the jar also should be brought to me; I knew it again, and sent it to my wife, to ask her, if she remembered it, desiring she might not be told what had just happened. She recognised it immediately, and sent me word, that it was the very jar she had exchanged full of bran for some fuller's earth. Saadi candidly acknowledged his error, and said to Saad, "I give up my opinion, and allow, with you, that money is not always a certain means to acquire money and become rich." When Saadi had finished speaking, "Sir," said I to him, "I dare not propose to you to take back the three hundred and eighty pieces of gold. I am sure you did not make the present with any expectation of having it returned; on my part, I do not wish to take advantage of it, contented as I am with what Heaven has bestowed on me; but I hope you will consent to my distributing the money to-morrow among the poor."

The two friends slept the second night at my house, and the next day, after having embraced me, they returned home well satisfied with the reception I had given them. I have not failed to go and pay my respects to each of them separately; and, since that time, I esteem myself highly honoured in being permitted to visit them, and to cultivate their friendship.

*   *   *   *   *   *   *   -

The Caliph Haroun Alraschid paid so much attention to Cogia Hassan, that he only perceived by his silence, that he had finished. He then said to him, "Cogia Hassan, it is long since I have heard anything which has given me so much pleasure. I have the satisfaction to inform you, that the diamond which has made your fortune is in my treasury; but, as it is possible there may still remain some doubts in the mind of Saadi, respecting the singularity of this diamond, I wish you to bring Saad and Saadi hither, that my treasurer may show it to the latter, as he may still be a little incredulous in believing that money is not always a certain means for a poor man to acquire great wealth in a short time. On concluding these words, as the caliph had indicated by an inclination of the head to Cogia Hassan, Sidi Nouman, and Baba Abdalla, that he was satisfied with them, they took their leave, prostrating themselves before his throne.

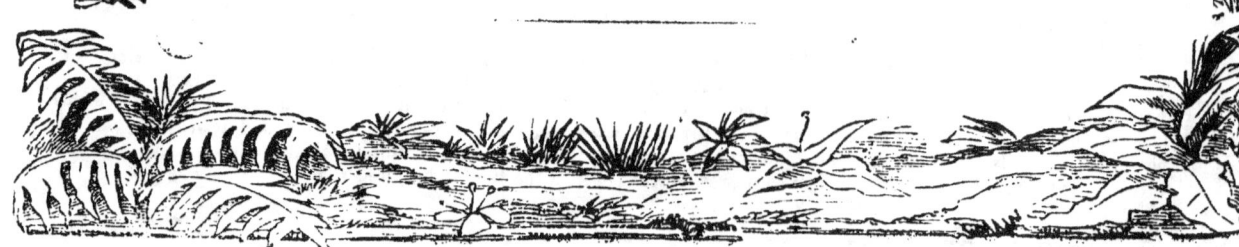

THE HISTORY OF ALI BABA, AND OF THE FORTY ROBBERS KILLED BY A SLAVE.

N a certain town of Persia, lived two brothers, one of whom was named Cassim, the other Ali Baba. As their father left them but little property, which they divided equally between them, it might have been expected, that their fortunes would be the same; chance ordered it otherwise. Cassim married a woman who became heiress to a well-furnished shop, a warehouse filled with good merchandise, and considerable property in land; he thus found himself quite at his ease, and became one of the richest merchants in the whole town. Ali Baba, who had taken a wife in circumstances not better than his own, lived in a very poor house, and had no other means of supporting his wife and children, than by going to cut wood in a neighbouring forest, and carrying it about the town to sell, on three asses, which were his whole wealth.

Ali Baba was one day in the forest, and had nearly cut as much wood as his asses could carry, when he perceived a thick cloud of dust rising in the air. He looked at it attentively, and was able to distinguish a numerous company of men on horseback, who were approaching at a quick pace. Although that part of the country was not known to be infested with robbers, Ali Baba nevertheless conjectured that these horsemen were of that denomination. He

No. 35.

accordingly climbed into a large tree, the branches of which, at a little height from the ground, were so close and thick as to be separated only in one small space ; he placed himself here, then, with the greatest assurance of security, as he could see without being seen. The tree itself also grew at the foot of an isolated rock. The men, who were stout, powerful, well-mounted, and armed, stopped near the rock, where they alighted ; and Ali Baba, who counted forty of them, had no doubt, from their appearance and equipment, that they were robbers. Nor was he deceived in his conjecture, for such, in fact, they were ; but they carried on their system of plunder at a considerable distance. Each unbridled his horse, and, having secured it, hung over its head a bag filled with barley, which he had brought with him. They then took off their travelling-bags, which appeared so heavy, that Ali Baba thought they were filled with gold and silver. The robber nearest to him advanced, with his bag on his shoulder, to the rock by the tree in which he had concealed himself. After the brigand had made his way through some bushes, he very audibly pronounced these words, *Open, sesame.* The captain of the band had no sooner uttered them than a door opened, and, after having made all his men enter before him, he followed, and the door closed.

The robbers continued a long time within the rock ; and Ali Baba was compelled to wait with patience for their departure. He was nevertheless strongly tempted to descend, seize two of their horses, mount one and lead the other by the bridle, and thus, driving his three asses before him, gain the town. At length the door opened, and the forty robbers came out ; the captain, who had been the last to enter, first appearing ; after he had seen all his troop pass out before him, Ali Baba heard him pronounce these words, *Shut, sesame.* Each man then returned to his horse, and remounted. When the captain saw they were all ready to proceed, he put himself at their head, and they departed.

Ali Baba, fearful they might return, did not quit the tree till a considerable time after he had lost sight of them. As he recollected the words which the captain of the robbers had used, to open and shut the door, curiosity induced him to try. He accordingly made his way through the bushes, went up to it, and calling out, *Open, sesame,* the door instantly flew wide open. Ali Baba expected to find only a dark and obscure cave ; and was much astonished at discovering a large, spacious, well-lighted room, dug out of the rock by the hands of men, and receiving its light from the top. He saw in it a large quantity of provisions, numerous bales of rich merchandise piled up, silks, stuffs, and brocades, and valuable carpets ; and, besides all this, great quantities of money, both silver and gold, lay in heaps, and part in large leather bags, placed one on another. Ali Babi did not hesitate long as to the plan he should pursue : he entered the cave, and the door shut ; but, knowing the secret by which to open it, this gave him no uneasiness. He paid no regard to the silver, but directed his attention to the gold coin. He took up at several times as much as the asses could carry. Having conducted them as near as he could to the rock, he loaded them ; and to conceal the sacks, entirely covered the whole over with wood. When he had finished, he went up to the door, and had no sooner pronounced the words, *Shut, sesame,* than it closed. This done, Ali Babi took the road to the town ; and when he arrived at his own house, he drove his asses into a small court, and carefully shut the gate. He threw down the small quantity of wood that covered the bags, which he carried into his house, where he laid them down before his wife. His wife examined the sacks, and when she found they were full of money, she suspected her husband had stolen them ; so that she could not help saying, "Ali Baba ! is it possible that you should ———." He immediately interrupted her. "Peace," exclaimed he ; "do not alarm yourself. You will change your bad opinion of me, when I have told you my good fortune." He emptied the sacks, the contents of which formed a great heap of gold, and when he had done so, he related his whole adventure, from beginning to end, conjuring her to keep it secret.

Recovering from her alarm, Ali Babi's wife began to rejoice with him on the fortunate circumstance which had befallen them, and was proceeding to count over the money that lay before her, piece by piece. "What are you about ?" said he ; "you are very foolish, wife ; you would never have done counting. I will immediately dig a pit to bury it in ; we have no time to lose." "It is proper, though," replied the wife, "that we should know nearly the quantity. I will borrow a small measure in the neighbourhood ; and while you are digging the pit, I will ascertain how much there is." To satisfy herself, the wife of Ali Baba set off, and went to her brother-in-law, Cassim, who lived at a short distance from her house. Cassim being from home, she addressed herself to his wife, whom she begged to lend her a measure for a few minutes. Her sister-in-law inquired, if she wanted a large or small measure ; and Ali Baba's wife having chosen the latter, she went to seek one ; but, acquainted with the poverty of Ali Baba, she was curious to learn what sort of grain his wife had, and therefore thought of concealing some tallow under the measure.

The wife of Ali Babi returned home, and placing the measure on the heap of gold, filled, and then emptied it at a little distance on the sofa, till she had measured the whole ; when her husband having dug the pit for its reception, she informed how many measures there were, with which they were both very well contented. While Ali Baba was burying the gold, his wife returned with the measure to her sister-in-law, but without observing that a piece of gold had stuck to the bottom of it. "Here, sister," said she, "you see I have not kept your measure long. I am much obliged to you for lending it to me." The wife of Ali Babi had scarcely turned her back, before Cassim's wife looked at the bottom of the measure, and was astonished at seeing a piece of gold attached to it. Envy instantly took possession of her heart. "What," said she to herself, "has Ali Baba measure his gold ! and where can that miserable wretch have obtained it ?" Cassim, her husband, was gone, as usual, to his shop, whence he would not return till evening ; the time of his absence appeared to her an age, in her impatience to acquaint him with a circumstance which she concluded would surprise him, not less than it had her. On his return home, "Cassim," said his wife, "you think you are rich, but you are deceived. Ali Baba is infinitely more wealthy ; he does not count his money as you do—he measures it." Cassim demanded an explanation of this enigma, and she unravelled it by acquainting him with the expedient she had adopted to make this discovery, and showing him the piece of money she had found adhering to the bottom of the measure ; a coin so ancient, that the name of the prince, which was engraven on it, was unknown to her. Far from feeling any satisfaction at the idea of his brother's being relieved from poverty, Cassim conceived an implacable jealousy on the occasion. He passed nearly the whole night without closing his eyes. The next morning, before sunrise, he went to his house. "Ali Baba," said he, "you

are very reserved in your affairs; you pretend to be poor and miserable, and yet you measure your gold!" "Brother," replied Ali Babi, "I do not understand you; pray explain yourself." "Do not pretend ignorance," resumed Cassim; and showing him the piece of gold his wife had given him, "How many pieces," added he, "have you like this, that my wife found sticking to the bottom of the measure which yours borrowed of her yesterday?" From this speech, Ali Baba was convinced that Cassim and his wife were acquainted with what he was so interested in concealing; but the fault was committed, and could not now be repaired. Without showing the least sign of surprise, he frankly owned the whole affair, and by what chance he had found the retreat of the thieves, and where it was situated; offering, if he would agree to keep it a secret, to share the treasure with him. "This I certainly expect," replied Cassim, in a haughty tone; "but," added he, "I desire to know also the precise spot where this treasure lies concealed; with the remarks and signs which may lead to it, and enable me to visit the place myself, should I feel inclined; otherwise I will go and inform the judge of the police of it." Ali Baba, actuated more by his natural goodness of heart than intimidated by his insolent menaces, gave the information he desired, and had even told him the words he must pronounce on entering the cave.

Cassim left him with the determination of superseding him in any further views he might have on the treasure. Full of the hope of possessing himself of the whole, he set off the next day before daybreak, with ten mules carrying large hampers, which he proposed to fill, indulging the idea of taking a much larger number in a second expedition, according to the sums he might find in the cave. He took the road which Ali Babi had described, and arrived at the rock and the tree, which he knew must be the same that had concealed his brother. He searched for the door, which he found, when pronouncing the words, *Open, sesame*, the door obeyed, he entered, and it immmediately closed upon him. Avaricious as he was, he could have passed the whole day in feasting his eyes with the sight of so much gold, if he had not reflected that his business was to load his ten mules with as much he could amass; he took up a number of sacks, and advancing to the door found that he had forgotten the necessary words, and instead of *sesame*, he said, *Open, barley*. He was struck with astonishment on perceiving that the door, instead of flying open, remained close. He named various kinds of grain, without mentioning the right, and therefore the door did not move. Cassim was not prepared for the result; in the imminent danger in which he beheld himself, fear took entire possession of his mind; and the more he endeavoured to remember the word *sesame*, the more was his memory confused. The robbers returned to their cave towards noon, and when they saw the mules belonging to Cassim, laden with hampers, standing about the rock, they were a good deal disturbed. While some were employed examining the exterior recesses of the rock, the captain and the others alighted, and, with their sabres in their hands, advanced to the door, pronouncing the words, when it instantly opened. Cassim, who, from the inside of the cave heard the sound of horses trampling, did not doubt that the robbers had arrived, and that his destruction was inevitable. Resolved, however, to attempt one effort to escape, and reach a place of safety, he stationed himself near the door, ready to run out as soon as it should open. The word *sesame*, which he had in vain endeavoured to recal to his remembrance, was scarcely pronounced, before it opened, and he rushed out with such violence, that he threw the captain on the ground. But he did not avoid the other thieves, who, having their sabres drawn, cut him to pieces on the spot.

The robbers' first care, after this execution, was to enter the cave. They found, near the door, the sacks which Cassim, after having filled them with gold, had removed there for the purpose of loading his mules; and they put them in their places again, without missing those which Ali Baba had previously carried away. Deliberating and consulting on this event, they could easily account for Cassim's not having been able to effect his escape, but they could not in any way imagine how he had entered the cave. They could not suppose he had entered by the door, unless he had been acquainted with the means which caused it to open; however, as their riches were no longer in security, they agreed to divide the body of Cassim into four quarters, and place them in the cave near the door, two quarters on one side, and two on the other. This determination formed, they put it into execution; and when they had nothing further to detain them, they left their place of retreat, mounted their horses, and set off to scour the country in such parts as were most frequented by caravans.

The wife of Cassim, in the meantime, was in the greatest uneasiness, when she observed night approach, and her husband did not return. Very much alarmed, she went to Ali Baba. "Brother," she said, "you, I believe, know that Cassim is gone to the forest, and for what purpose. He is not yet returned; I fear that some accident may have befallen him." Ali Baba replied that she need not yet feel any uneasiness concerning him, for that Cassim most probably thought it prudent not to return to the city until the night was considerably advanced. The wife returned to her house, and waited patiently till midnight; but after that hour her fears redoubled, and her grief was rendered still more distressing, as she could not proclaim it, nor even relieve it with cries. She then began to repent the silly curiosity which had induced her to pry into the private affairs of her brother and sister-in-law. She passed the night in weeping; and at daybreak ran to them, and announced the cause of her early visit, less by words than by her tears. Ali Baba did not wait for his sister's entreaties to go and seek for Cassim. He immediately set off with his three asses. Approaching the rock, he was much alarmed on observing that blood had been shed near the door. He reached the door, and, on pronouncing the words, it opened; when he was struck with the horrid spectacle of the body of Cassim cut into four quarters. He did not hesitate on the part he ought to take, in rendering the last duty to his brother. Having found the requisites in the cave to wrap up the body, he made two packets of the four quarters, and placed them on one of his asses, covering them with sticks, to conceal them. He quickly loaded the other two asses with sacks of gold, putting wood over them as before; and having commanded the door to close, he took the road to the city.

When he reached home, he left the two asses that carried the gold, desiring his wife to take care to unload them; and having, in a few words, acquainted her with what had happened to Cassim, led the other ass to the house of his sister-in-law. Ali Baba knocked at the door, which was opened to him by Morgiana. This Morgiana was a female slave; crafty, cunning, and fruitful in inventions to forward the success of the most difficult enterprise. When he had entered the court, he took off the wood and the two packages from the ass, and walking aside with the slave, "Morgiana," said he, "the first thing I have to require of you, is inviolable secrecy. These two packets contain the body of your master; and we must endeavour to bury him as if he had died a natural death; let me speak

to your mistress, and be attentive to what I shall say to her." Morgiana went to acquaint her mistress, and Ali Baba followed her. "Well, brother," said his sister-in-law, "what news do you bring of my husband?" "Sister," replied Ali Baba, "I cannot answer you, unless you promise to listen to me without interruption. In what has happened, it is not of less importance to you than to me, to preserve the strictest secrecy." "Ah," cried the sister, "this preamble convinces me that my husband is no more. I must do violence to my feelings; speak, I attend." Ali Baba then related to her what had occurred during his journey, until his arrival with the body of Cassim. "Sister," added he, "this is a subject of affliction for you. Although the evil is without remedy, if anything can afford you consolation, I offer to join the small property God has granted me to yours, by marrying you. I can assure you, my wife will not be jealous, and you will live comfortably together. If you agree to this proposal, we must contrive to make it believed that my brother died a natural death, and I will, on my part, contribute all in my power to assist you." The widow reflected that she could not do better than consent to this offer; she did not, therefore, refuse his proposal; on the contrary, she regarded it as a reasonable motive for consolation. She wiped away her tears, and suppressed those mournful cries which women usually utter on the death of their husbands, and thereby sufficiently testified to Ali Baba that she accepted his offer. Ali Baba left the widow of Cassim in this disposition; and having strongly recommended to Morgiana to acquit herself properly, he returned home.

Morgiana went out and repaired to the house of an apothecary who lived in the neighbourhood. Having knocked at the shop-door, she asked for a particular kind of lozenge, of great efficacy in dangerous disorders. The apothecary gave her the just quantity for the money she offered, asking who was ill in her master's family. "Ah!" exclaimed she, with a deep sigh, "it is my good master, Cassim himself. We cannot understand his complaint." Saying this, she went away with the lozenges, for which Cassim had no occasion. On the following day, Morgiana again went to the same apothecary, and, with tears in her eyes, demanded an essence which it was customary only to administer when the patient was reduced to the last extremity. "Alas!" cried she, "I fear this remedy will not be of more service than the lozenges! I shall lose a good master!" On the other hand, as Ali Baba and his wife were seen going dejectedly backward and forward to and from the house of Cassim in the course of the day, no one was surprised in the evening, on hearing the piercing cries of his widow and Morgiana, which announced the death of Cassim. At a very early hour the next morning, Morgiana, knowing that a cobbler lived near, went out in search of him. Having found him, she wished him a good day, and put a piece of gold into his hand.

Baba Mustapha was naturally of a gay disposition, and had always something laughable to say. Examining the piece of money, "A good hansel," said he; "what is to be done?" "Baba Mustapha," said Morgiana to him, "take what is necessary for sewing, and come directly with me; but on this condition, that you must put a bandage over your eyes." At these words, Baba Mustapha began to start difficulties. "Oh, oh!" said he, "you wish me to do something against my conscience, or my honour." Putting another piece of gold into his hand, "God forbid," said Morgiana, "come with me, and be under no apprehension." Baba Mustapha suffered himself to be led by the slave, who bound a handkerchief over his eyes, and conducted him to the house of her deceased master; nor did she remove the bandage until he was in the chamber where the body was deposited. Then removing it, "Baba Mustapha," she said, "I have brought you here, that you might sew these portions together; when you have done, I will give you another piece of gold." When Baba Mustapha had finished, and before he left the chamber, Morgiana again bandaged his eyes; and, after giving him the third piece of money, according to her promise, she conducted him back to the place where she had first put on the handkerchief; when, having again taken it off, she left him to return to his house, following him with her eyes until he was out of sight, lest he might have the curiosity to return and watch her movements.

Morgiana had heated some water, to wash the body of Cassim; and Ali Baba, who entered just as she returned, washed it, perfumed it with incense, and dressed it for interment, with the accustomed ceremonies. The undertaker also brought the coffin, which Ali Baba had taken care to order. To prevent observation, Morgiana took the coffin at the door, and, having paid the man and sent him away, she assisted Ali Baba to put the body into it. When he had nailed down the boards which covered it, she went to the mosque, to give notice that all was ready for the funeral. Morgiana had scarcely returned, before the iman and the other ministers of the mosque arrived. Four of the neighbours took the coffin on their shoulders, and preceded by the iman repeating prayers, carried it to the cemetery. As for the widow, she remained at home, lamenting and weeping with the women of the neighbourhood, who, according to the usual custom, repaired to her house during the funeral ceremony, and, joining their cries to hers, filled the air with sounds of woe. In this manner, the fatal end of Cassim was so well concealed, that no person in the city, so far from knowing the fact, entertained the least suspicion. Three or four days after the interment Ali Baba removed the few goods he had acquired, together with the money he had taken from the robbers' store, which he only conveyed by night, into the house of the widow of Cassim, to establish himself there, which proclaimed his recent marriage with his sister-in-law; as such marriages are common in our religion, no one showed any marks of surprise on the occasion. Ali Baba had a son who had served an apprenticeship with a merchant of considerable repute, and who had always commended his conduct. To this son he gave the shop of Cassim, with a further promise, that, if he continued to manage it with prudence, he would, ere long, marry him advantageously, according to his condition.

Let us now leave Ali Baba, and return to the forty thieves. They came back to their retreat in the forest at the time they had appointed; when they were greatly astonished to find the body of Cassim had been removed; but their consternation was indescribable on perceiving a visible diminution of their treasure. "We are discovered," said the captain, "and lost beyond hope, if we do not take immediate measures to remedy the evil. We shall insensibly lose all these riches, which our ancestors, as well as ourselves, have amassed with so much trouble and fatigue. All that we can at present judge of the loss we have sustained is that the thief, whom we fortunately surprised at the moment when he was making his escape, knew the secret of opening the door. But he was not the only one who possesses it; another must have the same knowledge; his body being removed, and our treasure diminished, are incontestible proofs of the fact. As it is not probable that more than two people are acquainted with the secret, having destroyed one, we must not suffer the other to escape. What say you, my brave comrades—are you not of my opinion?" This proposal was thought so reasonable, that they all approved of it, and agreed that it would be

advisable to relinquish every other enterprise, and occupy themselves solely with this, which they determined not to abandon until they had succeeded. "I expected this resolve, from your known courage and bravery," resumed the captain; "but it is first necessary that one of you should go to the city, without arms, and in the habit of a traveller, and employ all his art to discover if the treatment inflicted on the culprit is the topic of conversation, who he was, and where he lived. It is very important we should obtain this information, that we may not do anything of which we may have cause to repent, by making ourselves known in a country where we have been so long forgotten, and where our interest requires we should remain so?" Without waiting for the rest to give their opinions, one of the robbers said, "I willingly submit, and glory in exposing my life, by charging myself with the commission. If I should not succeed, you will at least remember, that I have not been deficient in either courage or good-will to serve the whole troop." This robber, after having received great commendation from the captain and his companions, disguised himself in such a manner that no person could have suspected his profession. He set off at night, and managed so well, that he entered the city as day was beginning to appear: when, proceeding towards the square, he saw only one shop open, which was that of Baba Mustapha.

Baba Mustapha was seated on his stool, with his awl in his hand, ready to begin his work. The thief went up to him, and wished him a good morning; and perceiving him to be advanced in years, "My good man," said he, "you begin your work betimes: it is not possible, so old as you are, that you can see clearly at this early hour; and even if it were broad day, I doubt whether your eyes are good enough to enable you to sew." "Whoever you are," replied Baba Mustapha, "you do not know me. Old as I am, I have excellent eyes; and so you would have said, had you known that, not long since, I sewed up a dead body, in a place where there was not more light than we have now." The robber was overjoyed at having addressed himself to a man who immediately gave him intelligence which, he had no doubt, related to his journey.

"A dead body!" exclaimed he, with astonishment, to induce the cobbler to proceed: "why sew up a dead body? —I suppose you mean, that you sewed the covering in which he was buried?" "No, no," replied Baba Mustapha, "I know what I say: you want me tell you more about it, but you shall not know another syllable." The thief needed no further information to be fully persuaded that he had discovered what he sought. He drew out a piece of gold, and putting it into Baba Mustapha's hand, "I have no desire to become acquainted with your secret," said he; "although, I can assure you, I should not divulge it, if you were to intrust me with it. The only thing I desire of you is to have the goodness to direct me, or to come with me, to the house where you sewed up the dead body." "Should I even feel myself inclined to grant your request," replied Baba Mustapha, "I assure you it is not in my power, and for this you may take my word. I will tell you the reason:—they took me to a certain place, and there they bandaged my eyes, whence I suffered myself to be led to the house; and after I had finished what I had to do I was conducted back to the same place, in the same manner. You see therefore, how impossible it is, that I should render you any service." "But, at least," resumed the robber, "you must remember nearly the way you went after your eyes were covered: pray come with me; I will put a bandage over them at that place, and we will walk together, in the same direction, and follow the same turnings which you will probably recollect to have taken before: and, as all trouble deserves a reward, here is another piece of gold:—come, grant me this favour:" saying this, he put another piece of money into his hand. The two pieces of gold tempted Baba Mustapha: he looked at them in his hand some time without speaking a word, considering how he should act. At length, he drew his purse from his bosom, and putting them in it, "I cannot be certain," said he, "that I remember exactly the way they took me; but since you will have it so, come along, I will endeavour to recollect it."

Baba Mustapha got up: and without shutting his shop, he conducted the robber to the spot where Morgiana had put the bandage over his eyes: "This is the place," said he, 'where my eyes were covered, and I was turned the way you see me.' The robber, who had his handkerchief ready, tied it over his eyes, and walked by his side, occasionally leading him. "I think," said Baba Mustapha, "I did not go further than here." The robber quickly made a mark on the door, with some chalk he had for the purpose; and then, taking the bandage from his eyes, asked him if he knew to whom the house belonged. Baba Mustapha replied, that he could not give him any information. As the robber found he could obtain no further intelligence, he thanked him for the trouble he had taken; and left him to return to his shop.

Shortly after, Morgiana had occasion to go out from Ali Baba's house on some errand: and when she returned, observing the mark which the robber had made on the door, she stopped to consider it: "What can this mark signify?" said she to herself: "Has any one a spite against my master. Be the notice what it may, it is advisable to be prepared for all events." She took some chalk, and, as two or three doors both above and below were the same, she marked them in a similar manner; and then re-entered the house.

The thief, in the mean time, continuing his road, arrived at the forest, and rejoined his companions. He immediately related the success of his journey, dwelling much on his good fortune in so soon discovering the very man who could give him the best information on the subject. He was listened to with great satisfaction; and the captain, thus addressed the party: "Comrades," said he, "we have no time to lose; let us arm ourselves, yet conceal our weapons, and depart; and when we have entered the city, let us assemble in the great square, while I will go and examine the house with our companion who has brought us this good news." The robbers all applauded their captain's proposal, and were very soon equipped for their departure. They went in small parties, of two or three together; and walking at a distance from each other, entered the city without creating any suspicion. The captain, and he who had been there in the morning, were the last to enter; and the latter conducted the captain to the street in which he had marked the house of Ali Baba. When they reached a house that had been marked by Morgiana, he pointed it out, saying that was it. But as they continued walking, the captain perceived that the next was marked in the same manner, and on the same part, which he noticed to his guide, inquiring whether this was the house, or that they had passed. His guide was quite confused, and knew not what to answer; and his embarassment increased, when he found that the four or five doors following had each the same mark. He assured the captain, with an oath, that he had marked but one:' and the captain, finding his design rendered abortive, returned to the great square, where he told the first of his people whom he met, to acquaint the rest, that they had lost their labor, and made a fruitless expedition. He set the example, and they all followed in the same order they came. When the troop had re-assembled in the forest, the captain explained to them his reason for ordering them to return. Immediately the conductor was by all declared deserving of death; he even joined in his own condemnation, by owning that he should have taken better precautions, and he presented his head with firmness to him who advanced to sever it from his body.

As it was absolutely necessary, for the safety of the band, that so great an injury should not pass unrevenged, another robber presented himself, and demanded the preference. It was granted him: he went to the city; and having, by the same artifice that the first had adopted, induced Baba Mustapha, with his eyes bandaged, to lead him to the house of Ali Baba, he marked it with red, in a place less discernible. But, shortly afterwards, Morgiana went out from the house, as on the day preceding and on her return, the red mark did not escape her piercing eye; she reasoned as before, and made a similar red mark in the same place on the neighbouring doors.

The robber, on rejoining his companions in the forest, boasted of the precaution he had taken, and the captain and the rest believed with him that it must succeed. They then repaired to the city, armed in the same way, ready to execute the blow they meditated; the captain and the robber went immediately to the street where Ali Baba resided; but the same difficulty occurred as on the former occasion. The captain was irritated, and the thief in as great a consternation as he who had preceded him. Thus was the captain obliged to return again on that day with his comrades. The thief, who was the author of the disappointment, suffered the punishment to which he had before voluntarily submitted himself.

The captain, seeing his troop diminished by two brave associates, was fearful it might still decrease, if he continued to trust to others the discovery of the house where Ali Baba resided. He therefore undertook the business himself; he went to the city, and with the assistance of Baba Mustapha, who rendered him the same service he had afforded to the two deputies from his troop, found the house of Ali Baba; when he made himself so thoroughly acquainted with it, not only by looking at it attentively, but by passing before it several times, that he was certain he could not mistake it, the captain then returned to the forest; and when he had reached the cave, "Comrades," said he, "nothing now can prevent our taking full revenge for the injury we have sustained. I know with certainty the house of the culprit. When I have explained to you the plan I have devised for this end, if any one can propose a better expedient, let him communicate it." He then told how he intended to proceed; and, as they all gave their approbation, he charged them to divide into small parties, to visit the neighbouring towns and villages, and buy nineteen mules, and thirty-eight large leathern oil-jars, one full, the others empty.

In the course of two or three days the thieves had completed their purchases. As the empty jars were rather too narrow at the mouth for the intended purpose, the captain had them enlarged; when, having made one of his men enter each jar, armed as he judged necessary, he closed them so as to appear full of oil, leaving, however, that part open which had been unsewed, to admit air; and, the better to deceive, he rubbed the outside of each jar with oil from that which was filled with oil: when the captain, as conductor, arrived about an hour after sunset, as he proposed, he went to the house of Ali Baba, intending to knock, and request admission for the night for himself and his mules. He was spared the trouble of knocking: he found Ali Baba at the door, enjoying the fresh air. He stopped his mules, and addressing himself to Ali Baba, "Sir," said he, "I have brought this oil which you see, from a great distance, to sell it to-morrow at the market, and at this late hour I do not know where to put up: you would confer a great obligation, by doing me the favour to take me in for the night." Although Ali Baba had seen, in the forest, the man who now spoke to him, and had heard his voice, yet he had no idea that this was the captain of the forty robbers. "You are welcome," said he, "come in;" and immediately made room for him and his mules to enter. At the same time, Ali Baba called to a slave, and ordered him, when the mules were unloaded not only to put them under cover in the stable, but also to give them some hay and corn; he did more; to show his guest all possible civility—after the captain of the robbers had unloaded his mules, and they were taken into the place he had commanded—observing that he was seeking for a place to pass the night in, went and begged him to come into the room. The brigand endeavoured to excuse himself under the pretence of not giving trouble; and it was not until Ali Baba had used the most earnest entreaties, that he complied. Ali Baba not only remained with his perfidious guest until Morgiana had served the supper, but he conversed with him on various subjects, which he thought might amuse him. He said, "Consider yourself at home: you have only to ask for whatever you want." The captain of the robbers rose with Ali Baba and accompanied him to the door; and while the latter went into the kitchen to speak to Morgiana he walked into the court. Ali Baba, having again enjoined Morgiana to be attentive to his guest, and to observe that he wanted nothing, added, "To-morrow, before day-break, I shall go to the bath. Take care that my bathing linen is ready, and give it to Abdalla;" (this was the name of his slave). After having given these orders, he retired to sleep. The captain of the robbers, in the meantime, on leaving the stable, went to give his people directions. Proceeding from the first jar to the last, he said, "When I throw some pebbles from the chamber where I am to be lodged to-night, rip open the jar from top to bottom with your knife, and come out: I shall immediately join you." This settled, he returned; and presenting himself at the kitchen door, Morgiana took a light, and conducted him to the chamber she had prepared for him.

Morgiana did not forget Ali Baba's orders; she prepared his linen for the bath; she then put the pot on the fire, to make broth, but while she was skimming it, the lamp went out. There was no more in the house, nor had she any candle. She had occasion for a light to see to skim the pot; and she mentioned her embarrassment to Abdalla, "Why are you so much disturbed at it?" said he; "go and take some oil out of one of the jars in the court."

Morgiana thanked Abdalla for the hint; she took the oil-can, and went into the court. As she approached the first jar that presented itself, the thief, who was concealed within, asked in a low voice, "Is it time?" Any other than Morgiana, in the moment of surprise, at finding a man in the jar, instead of oil, would have made a great uproar, which might have caused irremediable misfortunes. But Morgiana was superior to her fellows; she was instantly aware of the importance of secrecy, and also of the urgent necessity for devising a speedy remedy. Her quick imagination soon furnished her with the means; she collected herself, answering, "Not yet, but very soon." She approached the next jar, and the question was repeated; she went on to them all in succession, making the same answer to the same question, till she came to the last, which contained oil.

Morgiana, by this means, discovered that her master had afforded shelter to thirty-eight robbers. She quickly filled her oil-can from the last jar, and returned into the kitchen; and after having put some oil in her lamp, and lighted it, took a large kettle, and went again into the court to fill it with oil from the jar. She carried it back again, put it over the fire, and made a great blaze under it with a quantity of wood; for the sooner the oil boiled, the sooner her plan would be excuted. At length the oil boiled: she took the kettle, and poured into each jar, from the first to the last, sufficient boiling oil to scald the robbers, and deprive them of life, which she completely effected. This act being executed without noise, she returned to the kitchen with the empty kettle, and shut the door. She then blew out the lamp, and remained perfectly silent, determined not to sleep, until she had observed what might ensue. Morgiana had scarcely waited a quarter of an hour, when the captain of the robbers got up, and opening the window, looked out; as no light appeared, he gave the signal by throwing the pebbles, many of which fell on the jars. He listened; but heard nothing that could lead him to suppose his men obeyed the summons. He became uneasy at this delay, and threw some pebbles down a second and even a third time. They fell on the jars, yet nothing appeared to indicate that they were heard: alarmed, he descended into the court with as little noise as possible; and, approaching the first jar, was going to ask if the robber contained in it was asleep, when he smelt a strong scent of hot oil, issuing from the jar, from which he suspected his enterprise against Ali Baba had failed. He proceeded to the next jar, and to each in succession, and found that all his men had shared the same fate; mortified at having thus missed his aim, he jumped over the garden-gate and effected his escape. When Morgiana perceived that all was silent, and that the captain of the thieves did not return, she concluded he had decamped through the garden. Fully satisfied, and overjoyed in having so well succeeded in preserving the whole family, she at length retired to bed, and fell asleep.

Ali Baba went out before day-break, and repaired to the bath, followed by his slave, totally ignorant of the surprising event which had taken place in his house during his sleep. When he returned, the sun being risen, he was surprised to see the jars of oil still in their places, and that the merchant had not taken them to the market; he inquired the reason of Morgiana, who had left every thing in its original state, to convince him the more sensibly of the effort she had made for his preservation. "My good master," said Morgiana, in replying to Ali Baba, "you will be better informed of what you wish to know when you have seen what I am going to show you," Ali Baba followed Morgiana: and she led him to to the first jar: "Look in," said she. He did as she desired, when perceiving a man in the jar, he hastily drew back, uttering a cry of surprise. "Fear nothing," said she; "the man you see there will not do you any harm: he intended it, but he will never hurt either you or any one else again, for he is no longer living." "Morgiana!" exclaimed Ali Baba; "what is the meaning of all this? Pray explain it." "I will explain it," replied Morgiana; 'but moderate your astonishment, and do not awaken the curiosity of your neighbours, to learn what is of the utmost importance you should keep concealed. First look at all the other jars."

Ali Baba examined all the rest of the jars, one after another, till he came to the last, which contained the oil, and he remarked that its contents were considerably diminished. When he had finished, he remained motionless, sometimes looking at Morgiana, then at the jars, but without speaking a word, so great was his surprise. At length as if speech were suddenly restored to him, "And the merchant," said he, "what is become of him?" "The merchant!" replied Morgiana; "he is no more a merchant than I am. I can tell you who he is, and what has become of him." She then, in compliance with Ali Baba's command, recounted all the occurrences of the preceding night; and when she had finished her narrative, "this is the detail," she added, "you required of me; and I am convinced that it is the conclusion of a scheme, the beginning of which I observed two or three days ago, but of which I did not think it necessary to trouble you with an account.—One morning, as I returned from the city, at an early hour, I perceived the street-door was marked with white; and on the following day, with red, near the white mark: each time, without knowing the reason for these marks, I made the same kind of mark, and in the same part, on the doors of three or four of our neighbours, both above and below your house. If you connect that with what has happened, you will perceive that the whole is a machination contrived by the thieves of the forest, the troop of whom, I know not how, seems to be diminished by two. But, be that as it may, it is now certainly reduced to three at most. This proves, that they had determined on your death; and you will do right to be on your guard against them, so long as you know that one remains alive."

When Morgiana ceased speaking, Ali Baba, penetrated with the great obligation she had rendered him, replied, "I will recompense you as you deserve, before I die. I owe my life to you; and to afford you a proof of my gratitude, I from this moment, give you your liberty, and will soon reward you in a more ample manner.—We must now use the utmost despatch in burying the bodies, yet with so much secrecy, that nobody may entertain the least suspscion of their fate; and, for this purpose, I will instantly go to work with Abdalla." Ali Baba's garden was of considerable length, and terminated by large trees. He went immediately, with his slave, to dig a ditch, or grave under these trees, of sufficient extent to contain the bodies he had to inter. The ground was soft, and easy to remove, so that they were not long in completing their task. Having taken the bodies from the jars, and set apart the arms with which the robbers had furnished themselves, they carried the corses to the bottom of the garden, and placed them in the grave; and after having covered them with the earth, they spread about what remained, to make the surface of the ground appear level, as before. Ali Baba carefully concealed the oil-jars and the arms; and as for the mules, of which he was not then in want, he sent them to the market, at different times, where he disposed of them by means of his slave.

While Ali Baba was taking these precautions to prevent its being publicly known by what means he had become rich in so short a space of time, the captain of the forty thieves had returned to the cavern without forming any resolution how he should act respecting Ali Baba. The dismal solitude of this gloomy habitation appeared dreadful to him; "Brave associates!" cried he, "companions in my labours and my toils! where are ye! What can I accomplish without your assistance? Did I select and assemble you, only to see you perish all at the same moment, by a destiny so fatal, and so unworthy of your courage? When shall I be able to collect together another troop of intrepid men like you? and even should I wish to do so, how could I undertake it, without exposing so much specie, in gold and silver, and other riches, to the mercy of him who has already enriched himself with a part of this treasure? I cannot, I must not think of such an interprise, until I have put a period to his existence. What I have not been able to accomplish with such powerful aid, I will perform alone." Having formed this resolution, he felt no embarrassment as to the execution of it: and then, his mind filled with pleasing hopes, he fell asleep

and passed the rest of the night quietly. The next morning he awoke at an early hour, put on a dress suitable to the design he meditated, and repaired to the city, where he took a lodging in the khan. He was animated by a determination to neglect nothing that might hasten the destruction of Ali Baba, which he hoped to accomplish with safety and secrecy. For this purpose, he provided himself with a horse, which served him to convey to his lodgings several kinds of rich stuffs and fine linens, bringing them from the forest at various times, adopting all the necessary precautions for keeping the place whence he brought them still concealed. To dispose of this merchandise, when he had collected together as much as he thought proper, he sought for a shop. Having found one suitable, he furnished it with his goods, and established himself in it. The shop that was immediately opposite to his, was that which had belonged to Cassim, and had been a short time occupied by the son of Ali Baba.

The captain of the robbers, who had assumed tte name of Cogia Houssain, as a new resident, did not fail in proper civilities to the merchants his neighbours, according to the usual custom; but as the son of Ali Baba was young, and of a pleasing address, and the captain had more frequent occasion to converse with him than with the others, he very soon formed an intimacy with him. This he resolved to cultivate with greater assiduity and care, when, three or four days after he recognised Ali Baba, who came to visit his son, as was his constant habit, and he had learnt from his son, after his departure, that he was his father. He now increased his attentions to him; he made him several little presents, and also invited him to his table, where he regaled him handsomely. The son of Ali Baba was unwilling to receive so many obligations from Cogia Houssain without returning them; but he had no convenience for entertaining him as he wished. He mentioned his intention to his father, observing, that it was not proper he should delay any longer to return the favours he had received. Ali Baba very willingly charged himself with the entertainment: "My son," said he, "to-morrow will be Friday; and as that is a day on which the most considerable merchants, such as Cogia Houssain and yourself keep their shops shut, invite him to walk with you after dinner, and as you return, take my house in your way, and then beg him to come in. It will be better to act thus, than to give him a formal invitation. I will order Morgiana to prepare a supper, and have it in readiness."

On the Friday, the son of Ali Baba and Cougia Houssain met in the afternoon to take their walk. On their return, the son of Ali Baba led Cogia Houssain through the street in which his father lived; and when they were before the house, he stopped him, and knocked at the door. "This house," said he, "belongs to my father; in consequence of your friendship for me, he has desired me to procure him the honour of your acquaintance. I entreat you to add this pleasure to the many favours I have received from you." Although Cogia Houssain had now attained what he sought—which was, to gain admission into the house of Ali Baba, and thereby to destroy him, without hazarding his own life, or creating any suspicion—he nevertheless endeavoured to excuse himself, and pretended to take his leave; but as the slave of Ali Baba at that moment opened the door, his son took him by the hand, and entering first, I drew him forward, and as it were forced him to comply, apparently against his inclination. Ali Baba received Cogia Houssain in a friendly manner, and gave him a hearty welcome.

After a short conversation on indifferent subjects, Cogia Houssain offered to take leave; but Ali Baba stopped him: "Where are you going, sir?" said he: "I intreat you will do me the honour to stay and sup with me. The repast that I shall give you is little worthy of the honour you will confer on it; but, such as it is, I hope you will accept the intention with as much good-will as I offer it." "Sir," replied Cogia Houssain, "I am fully persuaded of your goodness; yet I intreat you to believe I do not refuse you from either incivility or contempt, but because I have a particular reason, of which I am sure you would not disapprove, were it known to you." "May I take the liberty, sir, of asking your reason?" returned Ali Baba. "I will confess it," replied Cogia Houssain: "I never eat of any dish that has salt in it." "If this be your only objection," said Ali Baba, "it need not deprive me of the honour of your company at supper, unless you have absolutely determined otherwise. In the first place, there is no salt in the bread which is eaten in my house; and as for the meat and ragouts, I promise you there shall be none in those which are served before you; I will immediately give orders to that effect: therefore, do me the favour to remain, and I will be with you in a moment." Ali Baba went into the kitchen, and desired Morgiana to prepare two or three additional ragouts without any salt. Morgiana, who was just going to serve the supper, could not avoid expressing some discontent at this order, and making inquiries of Ali Baba: "Who," said she, "is this difficult man, that cannot eat salt? Your supper will be spoiled, if I delay it any longer." "Do not be angry," replied Alia Baba; "he is a good man; act as I desire you."

Morgiana obeyed, though unwillingly, and she felt some curiosity to see this man who did eat salt. When she had finished, and Abdalla had prepared the table, she assisted him in carrying the dishes. On looking at Cogia Houssain, she instantly recognised him as the captain of the robbers, notwithstanding his disguise: and examining him with attention, she perceived that he had a dagger concealed under his dress. "I am no longer surprised," said she to herself, "that this miscreant will not eat salt with my master; he is his bitter enemy, and means to assassinate him; but I will prevent him from accomplishing his purpose." When Morgiana had finished assisting Abdalla to serve the dishes, she availed herself of the time while they were at supper, to make the necessary preparations for the execution of an enterprise of the boldest nature; and she had just completed them, when Abdalla came to acquaint her, that it was time to serve the fruit. Having placed a small table near Ali Baba, with the wine and three cups, she quitted the room with Abdalla, as if to go to supper together, and leave Ali Baba, according to custom, at liberty to enjoy himself with his guest, and to circulate the wine. Cogia Houssain, or rather the captain of the forty thieves, now thought that a favourable opportunity for revenging himself on Ali Baba was arrived: "I will make them both intoxicated," said he mentally: "and then the son, whom I do not wish to injure, will not hinder me from plunging my dagger into the heart of his father: I can escape through the garden, as I did before, while the cook and the slave are at their supper."

Morgiana, who had penetrated into the views of the pretended Cogia Houssain, did not allow him time to execute his intentions. Instead of supping, she dressed herself like a dancer, put on a head-dress suitable to the character, with a girdle round her waist of silver gilt, to which she fastened a dagger, made of the same metal; covering her face with a very handsome mask. When she had thus disguised herself, she said to Abdalla, "take your tabor, and let us go and entertain our master's guest, who is the friend of his son, as we sometimes do him." Abdalla took his tabor, and began to play as he walked before Morgiana, and entered the room. Morgiana following him, made a

low curtsey, with a deliberate air, to engage notice, as if to request permission to endeavour to amuse the company. "Come in, Morgiana," cried Ali Baba, "Cogia Houssain will judge of your skill, and tell us his opinion. Do not suppose, sir," continued he, addressing Cogia Houssain, "that I have been at any expense to procure you this entertainment. We have it all within ourselves; it is only my slave, and my cook, that you see. I hope you will find it not disagreeable." Cogia Houssain did not expect Ali Baba would add this entertainment to the supper he had given him; and it made him apprehensive he should not be able to avail himself of the opportunity he thought he had found. But, should that be the case, he still consoled himself with the hopes of success, by continuing his acquaintance with Ali Baba and his son. Therefore, although he would gladly have dispensed with this addition, he nevertheless pretended to feel an obligation, adding, that whatever gave Ali Baba pleasure could not but be agreeable to him. When Abdalla perceived that Ali Baba and Cogia Houssain had ceased speaking, he again began to play on his tabor, singing to it an air; and Morgiana, who ceded not to any professional dancer, performed her part so admirably, that every spectator, independent of the present company, of which perhaps Cogia Houssain was the least attentive, must have been delighted. After having performed several dances, she drew out the dagger, and, dancing with it in her hand, she surpassed all she had yet done by her light movements, and the wonderful efforts with which she accompanied them; sometimes presenting the dagger, as if to strike, and, at others, holding it to her own bosom, pretending to stab herself. At length, as if out of breath, she took the tabor from Abdalla with her left hand, and holding the dagger in her right, she presented the tabor with the hollow part upward to Ali Baba, in imitation of the dancers by profession, who thus solicit the liberality of the spectators. Ali Baba threw a piece of gold into the tabor; Morgiana then held it to his son, who followed his father's example. Cogia Houssain, who saw that she was advancing also toward him, had already taken his purse from his bosom, to contribute his present, and was putting his hand into it, when Morgiana, with equal courage and fortitude, plunged the dagger into his heart. Ali Baba and his son, terrified at this action, uttered a loud cry. "Wretch!" exclaimed Ali Baba, "what hast thou done? You have ruined me and my family for ever!" "What I have done," replied Morgiana, "is not for your ruin, but for your preservation." Then opening Cogia Houssain's robe, and showing Ali Baba the poniard which was concealed under it, "See," continued she, "the cruel enemy you were regaling! Examine his countenance attentively, and you will recognise the pretended oil-merchant and the captain of the forty robbers. Do you not recollect that he refused to eat salt with you? Can you require a stronger proof of his malicious designs? Before I had seen him, from the moment you told me of his objection to salt, I suspected his intention, and you are now convinced that my suspicions were not ill-founded."

Ali Baba embraced her. "Morgiana," said he, "I gave you your liberty, and at the same time promised you stronger proofs of my gratitude at a future period. The time is now arrived, and I make you my daughter-in-law." Then, addressing his son, "I believe you," said he, "to be so dutiful, that you will not be displeased at my bestowing Morgiana upon you, without previously consulting your inclination. We are under equal obligations to her. You plainly see, that Cogia Houssain only sought your acquaintance, the better to succeed in sacrificing me to his vengeance. You must further consider, that, in marrying Morgiana, you espouse the preserver of my family." His son willingly agreed to the marriage, not only in obedience to his father's desire, but also because his inclination strongly urged him to the union. They then prepared for the interment of the captain of the robbers; and this was so secretly performed, that the circumstance was not known till after the expiration of many years.

Ali Baba celebrated the nuptials of his son and Morgiana with great solemnity, and by a sumptuous feast, accompanied with dances, exhibitions, and other customary diversions. After the solemnisation of the marriage, Ali Baba, who had not revisited the cave since he brought away the body of his brother Cassim, still refrained from going even though he knew that thirty-seven of the robbers, with their captain, were destroyed, because he was ignorant of the fate of the other two. At the expiration of a year, however, as no attempt had been made to disturb his quiet, curiosity induced him to take a journey to the cave. He mounted his horse; and when he had nearly reached the cave, alighted, and went up to the door, and pronounced the words, Open, sesame. The door opened, and he entered. The state in which everything appeared in the cave, led him to conclude that no one had been in it from the time the pretended Cogia Houssain had opened his shop in the city; and that he was the only person acquainted with the secret of entering the cave, and consequently that the immense treasure it contained was entirely at his disposal. He had provided himself with a portmanteau, which he filled with as much gold as his horse could carry and then returned to the city.

Since that time, Ali Baba, his son—whom he took to the cave, and taught the secret to enter it—and after them their posterity, to whom the important secret descended, enjoying their riches with moderation, lived in great splendour, and were honoured with the first dignities of the city.

THE HISTORY OF ALI COGIA, A MERCHANT OF BAGDAD.

IN the reign of the Caliph Haroun Alraschid, there lived at Bagdad, a merchant named Ali Cogia; he was in moderate circumstances, and dwelt in his paternal house, without either wife or children. Free in his actions as in his will, he lived contented with what his business produced; but, during this period, he had for three successive nights a dream, in which an old man, with a venerable aspect, appeared to him, and reprimanded him for not having yet performed a pilgrimage to Mecca. This dream occasioned him great embarrassment. He was not ignorant of the obligation he was under to perform this pilgrimage; but as he was encumbered with a house and furniture, and a shop, he had always considered these as excuses sufficiently cogent, endeavouring to compensate for the neglect by charitable and other meritorious actions. But since he had this dream, he was so apprehensive of some misfortune, that he resolved no longer to defer acquitting himself of this act of duty. Ali Cogia began to sell his furniture; he then disposed of his shop; and he found a tenant for his house, to whom he let it on lease. The only matter to be done, was to find some secure place in which he could leave the sum of a thousand pieces of gold, and which would have encumbered him during the journey. Ali Cogia made choice of a jar of proper size; and having put the thousand pieces of gold into it, he filled it up with olives; when, closing it firmly, he took it to a merchant. "Brother," said he to him, "you are aware of my intention to set out on a pilgrimage to Mecca, I beg the favour of you to take charge of this jar of olives till my return." The merchant obligingly replied, "Here is the key of my warehouse; take the jar there yourself, and place it where you please."

The day for the departure of the caravan from Bagdad being arrived, Ali Cogia, with a camel loaded with the merchandise he had selected, joined it, and he arrived in perfect safety at Mecca. When he had acquitted himself

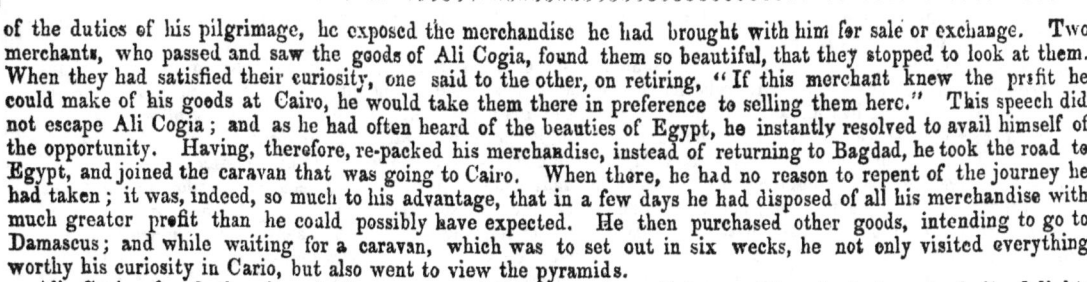

of the duties of his pilgrimage, he exposed the merchandise he had brought with him for sale or exchange. Two merchants, who passed and saw the goods of Ali Cogia, found them so beautiful, that they stopped to look at them. When they had satisfied their curiosity, one said to the other, on retiring, "If this merchant knew the profit he could make of his goods at Cairo, he would take them there in preference to selling them here." This speech did not escape Ali Cogia; and as he had often heard of the beauties of Egypt, he instantly resolved to avail himself of the opportunity. Having, therefore, re-packed his merchandise, instead of returning to Bagdad, he took the road to Egypt, and joined the caravan that was going to Cairo. When there, he had no reason to repent of the journey he had taken; it was, indeed, so much to his advantage, that in a few days he had disposed of all his merchandise with much greater profit than he could possibly have expected. He then purchased other goods, intending to go to Damascus; and while waiting for a caravan, which was to set out in six weeks, he not only visited everything worthy his curiosity in Cario, but also went to view the pyramids.

Ali Cogia found the city of Damascus so delicious a place, that everything he had read of its delights in the histories appeared to be very far below the truth, and he was tempted to remain there a considerable time. As, however, he did not forget Bagdad, he at length took his departure, and went to Aleppo, from thence, after having crossed the Euphrates, he took the road to Moussol, intending to shorten his journey by going down the Tigris.

By this delay, reckoning also the time he resided in each city, seven years had nearly elapsed since Ali Cogia quitted Bagdad, and he now determined to return. Till this period, the friend to whom he had intrusted the jar of olives, before he had left the city, had never more thought of either him or his jar. At the very time that Ali Cogia was on his return from Schiraz, one evening as his friend was at supper with his family, they happened to speak of olives, when his wife expressed a desire of eating some. "Now, you speak of olives," said the merchant, "you remind me that Ali Cogia, when he went to Mecca seven years since, left a jar of them, which he placed in my warehouse, to remain there till his return. But what is become of Ali Cogia, I know not. He must have died, as he has not been heard of during so many years; we may surely eat the olives, if they are still good. Give me a dish, and a light; I will go and get some, that we may taste them." "In the name of God," replied the wife, "do not, my dear husband, commit so disgraceful an action; you well knew that nothing is so sacred as a trust of this kind. Consider how infamous it would be for you and your family, if he were to appear, and you could not restore the jar into his hands in the same state as when he intrusted it to your custody. I declare that I neither wish for any of these olives, nor will I eat of them." The merchant turned a deaf ear, and proceeded to the warehouse, when, on opening the jar, he found the olives at top spoiled; but, to be convinced whether those underneath were equally so, he poured some into the dish, and shaking the jar, perceived that he had emptied nearly all the olives into the dish, and that what remained was gold. He put the olives again into the jar, and covering it, left the warehouse. He passed almost the whole night in devising a means to secure the money to himself, so that he might enjoy it in safety, should Ali Cogia ever return and claim the jar. Early the next morning he went out to buy some olives of that year's growth; he then threw away those which had been in Ali Cogia's jar, and taking out the gold, filled the jar with the fresh olives he had just bought, put on the same cover, and placed it in the same place where Ali Cogia had left it.

About a month after the merchant had committed this treacherous act, Ali Cogia arrived at Bagdad. As he had let his house before his departure, he alighted at a khan, where he took a lodging, until his tenant could procure himself another residence. The next day, Ali Cogia went to see his friend, the merchant, who received him with open arms, testifying the utmost joy at seeing him again, after an absence of so many years. After a mutual exchange of compliments, Ali Cogia begged the merchant to return him the jar of olives which he had left in his care. "My dear friend," replied the merchant, "here is the key of my warehouse, go and take it; you will find it where you put it yourself." Ali Cogia went and took out the jar; and having returned the key, went back to the khan where he lodged. He opened the jar, and thrusting in his hand, was extremely surprised at not feeling the thousand pieces of gold which he had concealed there. He remained motionless with astonishment; and raising his hands and eyes to Heaven, "Is it possible," cried he, "that a man whom I considered as my friend, could be capable of so flagrant a breach of trust?"

Ali Cogia, sensibly alarmed at the fear of having sustained so considerable a loss, returned to the merchant; "My good friend," said he, "be not surprised at my sudden re-appearance. I confess that I knew the jar of olives which I just now took from your warehouse to be mine; but, with the olives, I had put in it a thousand pieces of gold, and these I cannot find; perhaps you wanted them in your trade, and have made use of them. If that be the case, they are much at your service; I only beg of you to relieve my fears, and give me some acknowledgment for them; after this you may suit your convenience in returning them to me." The merchant, who expected to see Ali Cogia again, was prepared with an answer; "My friend," replied he, "when you brought me the jar of olives, did I touch it? did I not give you the key of my warehouse? did you not carry it there yourself? and did you not find it in the same place where you put it, exactly in the same state, and covered in the same manner? You told me it contained olives, and I believed you. This is all I know about the matter; you may believe me, if you please, but I assure you I have not touched it." Ali Cogia used the gentlest means to enable the merchant to justify himself. "I love peace," said he, "and should be sorry to proceed to extremities, which would not be very honourable to you in the eyes of the world, and to which I should not have recourse without extreme regret." "Ali Cogia," resumed the merchant, "you confess that you have deposited a jar of olives with me, that you took possession of it again, and that you carried it away; and now you come to demand of me a thousand pieces of gold!"

Some people had already stopped; and these last words of the merchant, pronounced in a tone of irritation, not only collected a larger number, but also brought the neighbouring merchants out of their shops, to inquire the reason of the dispute between him and Ali Cogia, and to endeavour to reconcile them. The merchant owned that he had kept the jar belonging to Ali Cogia in his warehouse, but he denied having touched it; and called upon them all to witness the insulting affront which had been offered to him in his own house. "You have drawn the affront on yourself," said Ali Cogia, taking him by the arm; "but, since you behave so wickedly, I cite you by the law of God. Let us see if you will have the effrontery to assert the same before the cadi." At this summons, which every true

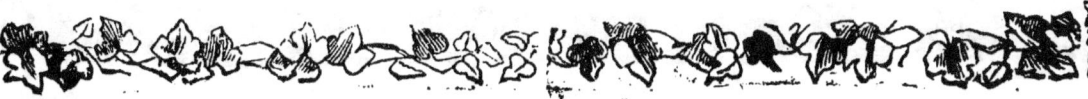

Mussulman must obey, the merchant had not the courage to resist : " Come," said he, " this is precisely what I wish, we shall then see which of us is wrong."

Ali Cogia conducted the merchant before the tribunal of the cadi, where he accused him of having stolen a thousand pieces of gold, deposited in his care, relating the fact as it took place. The merchant urged nothing more in his defence than what he had already said in the presence of his neighbours; and he concluded by offering to take his oath, after which he was dismissed as innocent. Ali Cogia protested against the judgment, and declared to the cadi, that he would lay his complaint before the Caliph Haroun Alraschid, who would do him justice.

While the merchant was triumphing in his success and indulging his joy at having secured the thousand pieces of gold, Ali Cogia drew up a petition; and the next day stationed himself in a street leading to the mosque, and, as the caliph passed, held out his hand with the petition. An officer who was walking before, left his place and took it, to present it to his master. As Ali Cogia knew that the Caliph Haroun Alraschid, when he returned to his palace, was accustomed to read all the petitions that were presented to him in this way, he followed the procession, and waited till the officer, who had taken the petition, should leave the apartment of the caliph. When the officer made his appearance, he told Ali Cogia, that the caliph had appointed the following day to give him an audience ; and having inquired the residence of the merchant, he sent him notice to attend at the same time.

On the evening of the same day, the caliph—with the grand vizier Giafar, and Mesrour the chief of the eunuchs, all three disguised in the same manner—went to make his usual excursion into the city, as was his frequent custom. In passing through a street, the caliph heard a noise ; he hastened his pace, and came to a door, which opened into a court, where ten or twelve children, who had not yet gone to rest, were playing by moonlight. The caliph curious to know how these children were amusing themselves, sat down on a stone bench, which was placed near the door ; and, as he was looking at them, heard one say to the others, " Let us play the cadi—I am the cadi : bring before me Ali Cogia, and the merchant who stole from him the thousand pieces of gold." No one disputed the part of the cadi with him who made choice of it ; and when he had taken his seat with all the pomp and gravity of a cadi, another personating the officer who attends the tribunal, presented two others to him, one of whom he called Ali Cogia, and the next the merchant against whom Ali Cogia preferred his complaint. The pretended cadi then addressed them, and gravely interrogating the feigned Ali Cogia, " Ali Cogia," said he, " what do you require of this merchant ?" The pretended Ali Cogia then made a profound obeisance, informed the cadi of every particular, and concluded by beseeching him to be pleased to interpose his authority, to prevent his sustaining so considerable a loss. The feigned cadi turned to the pretended merchant, and asked him why he did not return to Ali Cogia the sum demanded of him. The feigned merchant used the same arguments which the real one had alleged before the cadi of Bagdad ; and also offered to swear that what he had said was the truth. " Not so fast," replied the pretended cadi ; " before we take your oath, I should like to see your jar of olives—Ali Cogia," continued he, addressing the boy who acted this part, " have you brought the jar with you ?" As the latter replied that he had not, he desired him to go and fetch it. The feigned Ali Cogia disappeared for a few moments ; and then returning, pretended to bring a jar to the cadi, which he said was the same which had been deposited with the merchant, and was now returned to him. Not to omit any of the usual forms, the cadi asked the merchant if he owned it to be the same jar ; and as the merchant proved by his silence that he could not deny it, he ordered it to be opened. The feigned Ali Cogia then acted as if taking off the cover, and the cadi, as if looking into the jar : " These are fine olives," said he ; " let me taste them :" then pretending to take one to taste, he added, "They are are excellent ! But," continued he, " I think that olives which had been kept seven years, would not be so good. Order some olive-merchants to attend, and let me hear their opinion." Two children were then presented to him. " Are you olive merchants?" he asked ; and they having answered affirmatively, " Tell me, then," said he, " if you know how long olives can be preserved good to eat?" " Sir," replied the feigned merchants, " whatever care may be taken to preserve them, they are worth nothing after the third year ; they lose both their flavour and colour, and are no longer eatable." " If that be the case," returned the young cadi, " look at this jar, and tell me how long the olives that are in it have been kept." The pretended merchants then seemed to examine and taste the olives, and told the cadi that they were fresh and good. " You are mistaken," replied the cadi ; " here is Ali Cogia who says that he put them into the jar seven years ago." " Sir," said the merchants, " we can assure you that these olives are of this year's growth ; and we will maintain that there is not a single merchant in Bagdad who will not concur with us." The accused merchant was about to protest against this testimony of the others, but the cadi would not allow him time : " Silence !" said he ; " thou art a thief, and shalt be hanged." The children then joyfully clapped their hands, and finished their game by seizing the supposed criminal, and carrying him off to execution.

Next morning the grand-vizier went to the house where the caliph had witnessed the children's play, and demanded to speak with the master of it ; who being out, he was introduced to the mistress. He asked her, if she had any children ; she replied that she had three, whom she presented to him : " My children," said he to them, " which of you acted the cadi last night, as you were playing together ?" The eldest replied that it was he ; and, being ignorant of the reason for this question, he changed colour. " My child," said the grand-vizier, " come with me : the commander of the faithful wishes to see you." The mother was extremely alarmed when she saw that the vizier was going to take away her son, " Sir," said she, " is it to deprive me of my son entirely, that the commander of the faithful has sent for him ?" The grand-vizier quieted her fears, by promising her that her son should be sent back in less than an hour, and that when he returned she would learn the reason of his being sent for, which would give her pleasure. The grand-vizier conducted the boy to the caliph, and presented him at the time appointed for hearing Ali Cogia and the merchant. The caliph saw the child was rather terrified, and wished to prepare him for what he expected from him : " Come here, my boy," said he ; " draw near :—Was it not you who yesterday passed sentence on the case of Ali Cogia, and the merchant who stole his gold ? I both saw and heard you and am very well satisfied with you." The child began to gain confidence, and modestly answered in the affirmative.

" My child," resumed the caliph, " you shall to-day see the true Ali Cogia and the merchant ; come and sit down by me." The caliph then took the boy by the hand, and seating himself on his throne, placed him next to him, at the same time inquiring for the parties : they advanced, and the name of each was announced as he touched with his forehead the carpet that covered the throne. When they had risen, the caliph said to them, " Each of you plead your cause : this child will hear you, and administer justice : if anything be deficient, I will remedy it."

Ali Cogia and the merchant each spoke in turn, and when the merchant requested to be allowed to repeat the same oath he had taken on his first examination, the boy answered that it was not yet time, for it was first necessary to inspect the jar of olives. At these words Ali Cogia produced the jar, placed it at the feet of the caliph, and uncovered it. The caliph looked at the olives, and took one, which he tasted. The jar was then handed to some experienced merchants, who had been ordered to attend, and they reported that the olives were good, and of that year's growth. The boy told them that Ali Cogia assured him they had been in the jar seven years: to which the real merchants returned the same answer as the children had made. Although the accused merchant plainly saw that the two olive-merchants had thus pronounced his condemnation, he nevertheless attempted to plead in his justification: the boy, however, would not venture to pronounce sentence on him, and send him to execution: "Commander of the faithful," said he, "this is not a game; it is your majesty alone who can condemn to death seriously." The caliph, fully convinced of the treachery of the merchant, abandoned him to the ministers of justice, to have him hanged, and this sentence was executed. The monarch, after having advised the cadi who had passed the first sentence, and who was present, to learn from a child to be more exact in the performance of his duty, embraced the boy, and sent him home with a purse containing a hundred pieces of gold.

THE STORY OF THE ENCHANTED HORSE.

THE Nevrouz, or new day—which is the first of the year and of spring, is a festival so solemn and so ancient throughout the whole extent of Persia, that the holy religion of our prophet has been unable to abolish it; although, we must confess, it is a custom entirely Pagan, and the ceremonies observed are of the most superstitious nature.

During one of these festivals, after the most skilful and ingenious artists of the country, together with the foreigners who had repaired to Schiraz, had presented the king and his nobles with all the various spectacles intended for their entertainment; and the monarch had, as usual, distributed his gifts, according to the merit each had displayed, with an equality which satisfied all to the summit of their expectations; at the moment when he was preparing to retire, an Indian presented himself at the foot of the throne, leading a horse saddled, bridled, and richly caparisoned, and so skilfully represented, that at first sight every one supposed it to be real a horse. The Indian prostrated himself before the throne; and when he had risen, he showed the horse to the king. "Sir," said he, "although I am the last to present myself before your majesty, as a candida te for your favour, I can nevertheless assure you, you have not seen anything so marvellous as this horse, which I entreat you will condescend to notice." "I see nothing in this horse," replied the king, "but a strong resemblance to nature, which the workman, by art and industry, has given it." "Sir," returned the Indian, "it is not by its construction, nor by its exterior appearance, that I wish to attract your majesty's attention to my horse. It is only by the use I make of it, and for which every person besides myself can employ it, by means of a secret, which I am enabled to communicate. When I mount him, if I wish to transport myself through the air to any particular spot, I can accomplish it in a very short spare of time. In short, sir, "it is in this that the wonders of my horse consist: wonders of which nobody has ever hard speak, and of which I am ready to convince your majesty, if you choose to command me." The king of Persia, who was extremely curious in everything relating to the wonderful, and who had never met with nor heard of anything similar, told the Indian that he was ready to witness the truth of his assertion. The Indian instantly set his foot in the stirrup, and thew himself on the horse: when he had put the other foot in the opposite stirrup, and was seated firmly in his saddle, he asked the king of Persia, where he pleased to send him. "Do you see that mountain?" said the king; "it is there I wish you to go: the distance is not very great; but it is sufficient to judge of your diligence. And, as it is not possible for my sight to extend thus far, to prove your having been there, I desire that you should bring me a branch from a palm-tree which grows at the foot of the mountain." Scarcely had the king of Persia declared his will, when the Indian turned a small peg, which was placed on the horse's neck, at the same instant the horse rose from the ground, bearing the Indian though the air, as quick as lightning, to such an immense height that, in a few moments, even those who had the strongest and clearest sight could no longer discern him. Shouts of admiration were heard from all the spectators. A quarter of an hour had barely elapsed from the departure of the Indian, when they perceived him high in the air, returning with a palm-branch in his hand. He soon arrived over the square, and then descended immediately before the throne of the king, at the same spot whence he had set out. He alighted, and approaching the throne, prostrated himself, laying the palm-branch at the feet of the king.

The king of Persia, who had witnessed, with astonishment, the exploit which the Indian had just exhibited, immediately conceived a strong desire to possess the horse; and, as he was persuaded he should find no difficulty in treating with the Indian, being resolved to give him whatever sum he might demand for it, he already regarded it as his own. "Judging of your horse by its exterior appearance," said he to the Indian, "I did not suppose it could deserve the consideration which, as you have just shown me, it merits. I am obliged to you for having undeceived me; I am ready to purchase it, if it be for sale." "Sir," replied the Indian, "I had no doubt that your majesty would appreciate the value of my horse, when you were acquainted with its claims to your attention. I had also foreseen that you would immediately wish to have it in your own possession, as you have now informed me. For my part, sir, although I am perfectly aware of its value, and know that the possession of it is alone sufficient to render my name immortal, I am, nevertheless, willing to part with it, to gratify your majesty. But in making this declaration, I have a condition to propose, with which, perhaps, you may not be pleased. Your majesty will allow me to observe that I did not purchase the horse with money; I obtained it of the inventor

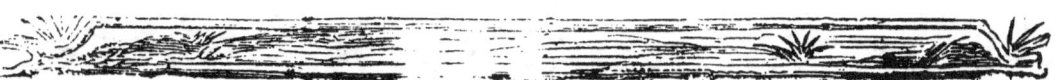

and maker, by giving him my only daughter in marriage, as a recompense, and he at the same time exacted from me a promise, that I would never sell it; and that, if I parted with it to another person, it should only be in exchange for what I might think proper." The Indian was proceeding, but the king interrupted him. "I am ready," said he, "to grant you anything in exchange that you will ask of me. I leave you to choose any city you please, to be yours in full sovereignty and power till the end of your days."

This exchange appeared to all the court of Persia an offer truly royal; but it was far below what the Indian had proposed to himself: his views extended to far higher prospects. He replied, "I am infinitely obliged to your majesty for the offer you have made me, and I cannot sufficiently thank you for your generosity. I entreat you, however, not to be displeased at my temerity, when I tell you, that I cannot deliver my horse into your possession, but on receiving the hand of the princess your daughter as my wife." The courtiers, who surrounded the king of Persia, could not avoid laughing at this extravagant demand of the Indian; but Prince Firouz Schah, the eldest son of the king, and heir to the crown, could not hear it without indignation. "Sir," said he, "your majesty will pardon me, if I take the liberty to ask you, if it be possible you can hesitate a moment on the refusal you ought to give to so insolent a request, or that you can allow him the slightest encouragement to flatter himself with the expectation of being allied to one of the greatest and most powerful monarchs of the earth." "My son," replied the king, "I receive your remonstrance in good part, and commend you for the zeal you evince in wishing to preserve the dignity of your birth in the same state as you received it; but you do not sufficiently consider the excellence of this horse; nor that the Indian, who proposes to me this method of obtaining it, may, if I refuse him, make the same proposition elsewhere, and have it accepted. But, before we conclude the bargain, I wish you to examine the horse, and make trial of him yourself, that I may have your opinion of him. I dare say he will have no objection to this proposal."

As it is natural to flatter ourselves with the hope of obtaining our wishes, the Indian thought he could perceive from this conversation, that the king of Persia was not averse to his alliance, and he thought that the prince, although he now appeared to oppose his views, might in time become favourable to them. Instead, therefore, of refusing the king's desire, he, on the contrary, seemed rejoiced at it, and approached the prince with the horse, to assist him in mounting, and afterward instruct him in the management of it. The prince mounted immediately without the assistance of the Indian: he secured each foot in the stirrups, and, without waiting for any further directions, turned the peg, as he had before observed the Indian do. The instant he had turned it, the horse rose with the swiftness of an arrow, and in a few moments the king, as well as all the numerous assemblage of people, lost sight of him.

Neither the horse nor the Prince Firouz Schah appeared again, and the king of Persia in vain strained his eyes to descry him in the air: when the Indian, alarmed at the consequences that might ensue, prostrated himself at the foot of the throne, and entreated the king to deign to hear him. "Your majesty," said he, "has seen that the prince, in his impatience, did not allow me time to give him the necessary instructions to govern my horse. He conceived any further advice needless, but he is ignorant of the means that are to be taken to turn the horse, and make it come back to the place whence it departed. Therefore, sir, the favour I have to request of your majesty is, that you will not consider me as responsible for what may befal his person." The Indian's speech gave the king infinite concern; he was aware of the inevitable danger his son must be in, if what the Indian said were true, that the secret for making the horse return was different from that which caused it to advance in the air. He asked him why he did not call him back. "Sir," replied the Indian, "your majesty observed the extreme swiftness with which the horse and the prince rose. But, sir," added he, "there is still some hope that the prince, in the embarrassment he must experience, may remark another peg, on turning which, the horse will cease to ascend, and will approach the earth, where he may alight in whatever spot he pleases." "Be that as it may," replied the king, "as I cannot rely on the assurances you make me, if, in three months, the prince do not return in safety, your head shall be the forfeit." He immediately ordered the Indian to be seized and closely confined, after which he returned to his palace in the greatest affliction.

Prince Firouz Schah, in the meantime, was elevated in the air, with the rapidity we have before seen; and in less than an hour he found himself at so immense an height, that he could no longer distinguish any object on earth. He then began to think of returning to the place whence he had departed; to accomplish this, he imagined, that if he turned the peg the contrary way, pulling the bridle at the same time, he should succeed; but his astonishment was inexpressible, when he perceived that the horse still rose with the same swiftness. He in vain turned it backward and forward; and he now felt the error he had been guilty of, in not procuring from the Indian all the instructions necessary for the management of the horse. Attentively examining the head and neck of the horse, he discovered another peg smaller than the first, near the right ear of the horse; he turned it, and instantly remarked that he was beginning to descend toward the earth, in a line similar to that by which he had ascended, but with less rapidity.

Night had veiled for more than half an hour the spot over which Prince Firouz Schah was at the time he turned the second peg; but, as the horse descended, the sun appeared to him to set with equal celerity, and he soon found himself enveloped in the gloom of night. Midnight had already passed, when the horse stopped, and Prince Firouz Schah dismounted, but greatly fatigued, and weakened from want of food. His first care was to endeavour to discover where he had alighted; and he found himself on the terraced roof of a magnificent palace, surrounded by a marble balustrade. Examining the terrace, he discovered the stair-case, leading to the interior of the palace, the door of which was half open; he opened it a little further, and descended cautiously, lest, by making a false step, he might awaken some of the inhabitants. He succeeded, and having reached a landing place on the stairs, found a door opening into a large room, where there was a light. He advanced a few steps, and, by the light of a lantern, perceived some black eunuchs, each lying with a drawn sabre by him; from which he concluded, that they were guarding the apartment of a queen or princess; of this he was soon convinced. The chamber where the princess slept, was next to the room containing the eunuchs, and was easily discernable by the great light which shone through a slight silk hanging that concealed the door. The prince advanced toward this hanging, and reached it without disturbing the eunuchs; he drew it aside, and entered the chamber, when his attention was wholly engrossed by observing several beds, only one of which was raised on a sofa, the others being below it. The princess' female attendants were lying on the lower ones, and the princess herself was in the bed that was elevated. Guided by this distinction, Prince Firouz Schah could not be mistaken in his choice whom to address. He approached the princess's bed, without disturbing either her or her women. When he was sufficiently near, his eyes beheld such surprising beauty that he was charmed, and instantly felt the flame of love; "Heavens!" exclaimed he to himself, "has my destiny led me hither, to deprive me of that liberty I have till now so perfectly maintained! Am I not to expect inevitable bondage, when those eyes are unclosed, which must add so much lustre and brilliancy to that assemblage of charms?" Occupied by such reflections, he placed himself on his knee, and taking hold of the princess's sleeve, which but partly concealed an arm of exquisite form and incomparable whiteness, he gently pulled it. The princess opened her eyes; and was in the greatest astonishment at beholding near her a man of handsome countenance, well formed, and elegantly dressed; but she did not betray any sign or fear of alarm. The prince seized this favourable moment; he bowed his head to the floor, and when he raised it, "Illustrious princess," said he, "in consequence of an adventure the most extraordinary and wonderful you can possibly conceive, you see at your feet a suppliant prince, the son of the king of Persia, who yesterday morning was assisting with his father at the celebration of a solemn festival, and who now finds himself in an unknown country, where he is in the most imminent danger of perishing, if you have not the goodness and generosity to bestow on him your succour and protection."

The princess was the eldest daughter of the king, who reigned over the kingdom of Bengal, and who had built this palace for her at a short distance from the capital, whither she frequently retired to enjoy the diversions of the country. After listening to the prince with the utmost complaisance, she replied to him with equal affability, "Prince," said she, "take courage; you are not in a country of barbarians; hospitality, humanity, and politeness, are not less observed in the kingdom of Bengal than in that of Persia. It is not I who grant you the protection you demand; you will experience it not only in my palace, but in every part of the kingdom." The prince of Persia was about to express his acknowledgments for the favour she had so obligingly granted him, and had already bowed his head very low to begin his compliment, but she prevented him. "I am very anxious" said she, "to be informed by what wonderful adventure you have travelled from the capital of Persia in so little time, and by what enchantment you penetrated into my apartment. But I will restrain my curiosity till to-morrow morning; and at present only give orders to my women to prepare a chamber, and provide everything necessary for your refreshment and repose." The princess's women had awakened in astonishment at the first words which Prince Firouz Schah addressed to their mistress; but they no sooner understood the princess's intentions, than they dressed themselves. They took one of the numerous lighted tapers which illuminated the princess's apartment; and when the prince respectfully took leave, they walked before him, and conducted him into a very beautiful chamber, where some of them prepared him a bed. The next morning the princess's first care was to perform the duties of the toilet. She had never before taken so much pains in adorning herself, and in consulting her mirror, as on that day; nor had her women ever been obliged to exercise so much patience, in doing and undoing the same thing several times, till she was contented. She ornamented her head with the largest and most brilliant diamonds, and wore a necklace, bracelets, and girdle, of the same precious materials.

The princess of Bengal was no sooner informed that the prince of Persia expected her, than she went to his apartment. After reciprocal compliments—the prince apologising for having awakened the princess out of her sleep, and she inquiring how he had passed the night, and if he now found himself recovered—the princess seated herself on the sofa, and the prince followed her example. The princess then began the conversation: "Prince," said she, "I feel the utmost impatience to become acquainted with the circumstances attending the extraordinary adventure which has procured me the happiness of seeing you; I entreat, therefore, you will oblige me with the detail of what I am so anxious to know."

Fully to satisfy the princess, Firouz Schah mentioned the enchanted horse, the description of which, with the marvellous feat performed on it by the Indian, convinced the princess that nothing could exceed it. The prince then spoke of his father's desire to purchase the horse; the Indian's presumptuous demand for it; and his own surprising adventure in making trial of its properties. "There is no occasion, princess," added he, "to describe what followed, with which you are already acquainted. Nothing remains but to thank you for your kindness and generosity. As, according to the rights of mankind, I am now your slave, and cannot therefore offer you my person, I can only tender my heart. But what do I say? This heart is no longer mine; you have ravished it from me by your charms. Permit me, therefore, to declare to you, that in you I acknowledge the mistress, not less of my heart, than of my will." She was not displeased with the sudden declaration; and the blushes which overspread her cheeks heightened her beauty, and rendered her still more interesting in his eyes.

Prince Firouz Schah was going to make the most solemn protestations to the princess of Bengal, that he had left Persia in full possession of his heart, when, at the instant, one of the princess's attendants came to acquaint them that dinner was served. This interruption relieved the necessity of an explanation, which would have been equally embarrassing to both. The princess remained in perfect conviction of the sincerity of the prince; and although she had not explained herself, he nevertheless judged, from the favourable manner in which she had listened to him, that he had every reason to be satisfied with his good fortune.

During two whole months, Prince Firouz Schah entirely devoted himself to the wishes of the princes. But when this period had elapsed, he took an opportunity of declaring seriously to her, that he had too long neglected his duty, and begged her to grant him permission to attend to the dictates of filial affection. "Princess," added he, "perhaps you are inclined to suspect my promises, from the request I have made, and already place me in the list of false lovers, who dismiss the object of their affection from their hearts as well as minds; but, as a certain proof of the strong and sincere love I feel for you, and which will render my life miserable when I am absent from so amiable a princess as yourself, I would ask the favour of conducting you with me, did I not fear that such a proposal might give offence." Prince Firouz Schah perceived the princess blush at his last words; he therefore continued: "Princess, if you doubt my father's consent to our union, allow me to dispel it. As for the king of Bengal, after all the proofs of affection, tenderness, and esteem he has always shown, he would be far different, or, rather, he would be the enemy of your happiness and peace, if he did not receive with kindness and good-will the embassy my father would send him, to obtain his approbation and consent to our marriage." The princess of Bengal made no reply; but her silence and downcast eyes convinced him, more than the most formal declaration, that she felt no repugnance to his proposal. The only difficulty which presented itself to her imagination was that the prince was not sufficiently acquainted with the management of his horse, and she was apprehensive of experiencing the same embarrassments which had happened to him when the made his first essay. But Prince Firouz Schah soon dissipated all her fears, by assuring her that she might safely trust to him. She now, therefore, thought only of taking proper measures for her departure, which she effected with so much secrecy, that no one in the palace had the slightest suspicion of her design.

Next morning, a little before daybreak, while all the inhabitants of the palace were enjoying profound repose, she repaired to the terrace with the prince: he turned the horse towards Persia, and placed it so, that the princess could easily seat herself behind. He mounted first, and when she had placed herself conveniently, she gave the signal for departure: he instantly turned the peg, and the horse rose with them into the air. The horse proceeded with his usual celerity; and Prince Firouz Schah managed it with so much skill, that in the course of two hours and a half he discovered the capital of Persia. He did not descend in the great square whence he had departed, but in a pleasure-house, at a little distance from the city. He led the princess into the most beautiful apartment, telling her that, to secure to her those honours which were due to her rank, he would go and acquaint his father of her arrival, and return immediately.

As he passed along, in his way to the palace, he was received with joy by the people, for they had despaired of ever seeing him again. The king was giving an audience, and was surrounded by his council, when he presented himself before them. His father embraced him with tears of joy and surprise, and immediately inquired, with visible anxiety, what was become of the Indian's horse. This question afforded the prince an opportunity of relating all the dangers and perils he had encountered. He told him how he had escaped, by alighting on the palace of the princess of Bengal, and the friendly reception he had met with from her; confessed the motive which had induced him to prolong his residence with her for a longer period than was proper, had he only consulted his duty; and enlarged on the desire she had shown, in every instance, to oblige him, so far as even to consent to accompany him into Persia. At these words, the prince was about to prostrate himself at the feet of his father, to solicit him to grant his request; but the king prevented him. "My son," said he, "I not only give my consent to your marrying the princess of Bengal, but I will go to her myself, to thank her in person for the obligations I owe her. The king, then, having given orders to prepare for the arrival of the princess of Bengal, commanded that the public rejoicings should immediately commence by a concert of various warlike instruments; after which, he desired the Indian to be released from prison, and conducted before him. His orders were instantly obeyed; and when the Indian was presented to him, "I had secured your person," said he, "that your life might have atoned for that of the prince my son. Return thanks to Heaven, for having restored him to me. Go, take your horse, and never again appear before my sight." When the Indian had left the presence of the king of Persia, having learned of those who had released him from prison that Prince Firouz Schah was returned with a princess, whom he had brought with him on the enchanted horse; as also, where he had alighted and left the princess, and that the sultan was preparing to visit her, to conduct her to his palace, he did not hesitate to take advantage of this intelligence, but immediately repaired to the country palace with so much diligence, that he reached it before the king and the prince of Persia: addressing himself to the steward of the palace, he told him that he had come, by order of the king and prince of Persia, to conduct the princess of Bengal on the enchanted horse through the air to the king, who, he said, was waiting to receive her in the great square before his palace, that his whole court and the people of Schiraz might witness the scene. The steward believed him without difficulty. He presented him to the princess; who was no sooner told that he came by order of the king of Persia, than she consented to do what she believed to be his wish. The Indian, delighted with the success of his wicked scheme, mounted the horse, took the princess behind him, and, having turned the peg, the horse instantly rose with him and the princess to an immense height in the air. At the instant the king of Persia, accompanied by the whole court, was leaving the palace, to repair to that in which the princess had been left—Prince Firouz preceding him, to prepare the princess for his reception—the Indian, to brave the anger of the king and the prince passed over the city with his prey. When the king perceived the ravisher, he stopped with astonishment at the sight, and his afflicting sensations were heightened by the reflection, that it would not be possible to make him repent of the flagrant affront he thus publicly offered to his dignity.

But what was the grief of Prince Firouz Schah, when he beheld the Indian tearing from him his adored princess, without whom he felt existence impossible. What course could he adopt? Should he return to the palace of his father, shut himself up in his apartment, and give loose to his affliction? His generosity, his courage, his love forbade it; and he directed his steps toward the country palace, where the princess had been left. On the appearance of the prince, the steward presented himself before him, with tears in his eyes, and throwing himself at his feet, confessed the crime he had committed, and condemned himself to death, which he expected from the prince's hand. "Rise," said the prince to him, "I do not impute the loss to you; I impute it solely to myself —to my own imprudence. Instantly procure me the dress of a dervise, and be careful not to discover that it is for me." At a little distance there was a convent of dervises, the scheik or superior of which was a friend of the steward's. Going to him, he pretended to entrust him with a profound secret, stating that an officer of distinction at court had incurred the displeasure of the king, and that he wished to afford him an opportunity of escaping his sovereign's revenge; by which story, the steward easily obtained what he required, and returned to the prince with the complete dress of a dervise. Firouz put it on, and, thus disguised, took with him a box of pearls and diamonds, to defray the expenses on the journey he was about to undertake, and left the country palace at the approach of night.

Let us now return to the Indian, who directed the course of the enchanted horse so successfully, that he arrived on the same day, at an early hour in a wood, near the capital of the kingdom of Cashmire. As he began to feel a want of food, he dismounted in this wood, on a lawn, where he left the princess, near a little stream of cool transparent water. During the absence of the Indian, the princess of Bengal thought of making her escape, and seeking some asylum from his power, but she found herself so weak, that she was obliged to relinquish her design; and had therefore no other resource than her fortitude, resolving to suffer death rather than be faithless to Prince Firouz Schah. She did not wait for a second invitation to partake of what the Indian placed before her; she ate, and soon recovered her strength sufficiently to be able to answer with courage and firmness the insolent speeches which he addressed to her. After several menaces, as she perceived the Indian was preparing to offer her violence, she rose to resist him, uttering at the same time loud cries. Her shrieks immediately drew to the spot a troop of horsemen, who surrounded both her and the Indian. These were the sultan of Cashmire and his attendants, who were returning from hunting, and, fortunately for the princess, passing that way, were attracted by the sounds they had heard. The sultan addressed himself to the Indian, demanded his name, and why he ill-treated the lady. The Indian boldly replied, that she was his wife, and no one had any right to interfere

between them. The princess, who was ignorant of the rank and quality of the person who so opportunely presented himself for her deliverance, contradicted the assertion. "Sir," said she, "whoever you are, have pity on a princess, and do not give credit to an impostor. He is an abominable magician, who has this day forcibly carried me away from the prince of Persia, to whom I was betrothed, and has brought me hither on his enchanted horse." She was going to proceed, but, instead of listening to her, the sultan, justly irritated by the insolence of the Indian, ordered his attendants to surround him, and immediately cut off his head. This order was executed with less difficulty, as the Indian was not possessed of any arms to defend himself. The princess, thus delivered from the

No. 37.

persecution of the Indian, was destined to undergo another, not less afflicting to her feelings. The sultan having ordered her a horse, conducted her to his palace, where he allotted for her use the most magnificent apartment. He himself led her to this apartment; and, without allowing her time to thank him for the obligation he had conferred on her, in the terms she had meditated, "Princess," said he, "I doubt not you must be in want of rest; I therefore leave you to repose, to-morrow you will be better able to relate to me the circumstances of the singular adventures that have befallen you."

The princess of Bengal felt inexpressible satisfaction at finding herself so soon delivered from the persecution of a man whom she could not regard but with horror; and she flattered herself that the sultan of Cashmire would complete his generosity by sending her back to the prince of Persia, after she had informed him in what manner she was affianced to him. But she was very far from experiencing the accomplishment of the hope she had conceived. In fact, the sultan of Cashmire had determined to espouse her on the morrow. When the sultan, who had desired to be informed as soon as she should be ready to receive his visit, had paid his compliments, inquired after her health, and acquainted her that the trumpets were flourishing in honour of their nuptials, which were to be solemnized, and to which he hoped she would not object, she was in such consternation, that she fainted away. The women, who were present, ran to her assistance, and the sultan also exerted himself to restore her to animation; but she remained a considerable time in this state. At length she began to recover; but, determined to perish rather than be faithless to Prince Firouz Schah, and affected to be insane. As he found she continued in the same state he left her with her attendants, whom he desired to pay her every attention, and take the greatest care of her.

Prince Firouz Schah, disguised in the habit of a dervise, vainly traversed several provinces, and visited all the principal cities in his route. Attending earnestly to the passing news of the day in each place he visited, he at length arrived at a large city of the Indies, where the general conversation seemed to turn on a princess of Bengal, who had lost her senses on the very day which the sultan of Cashmire had appointed for the celebration of his nuptials with her. At the name of the princess of Bengal, he determined to direct his route to the capital of Cashmire. On his arrival in this city, he took up his abode in a khan, where he immediately learnt the whole history of the princess, and of the tragical end of the Indian, who had brought her on the enchanted horse; a circumstance which fully convinced him that this was the princess he so anxiously endeavoured to find. The prince of Persia, having obtained all the necessary information, ordered a physician's dress to be made for him on the next day; and thus disguised, with the long beard he had suffered to grow during his journey, he was supposed to be of that profession as he passed through the streets. His impatience to see the princess would not allow him to defer his appearance at the palace of the sultan. He was conducted to the chief of the ushers, to whom, addressing himself, he said, that it might possibly be considered as great temerity in him to present himself, as a physician who wished to attempt the cure of the princess, after so many had failed; but that he flattered himself, by means of certain specific remedies, the efficacy of which he had experienced, to complete what had hitherto been attempted in vain.

Some time had elapsed since any physician had presented himself; and the sultan of Cashmire, with great grief, found himself deprived of all hopes of seeing the princess in the same state as when he first beheld her. When the officer, therefore, announced to him the arrival of another physician, he ordered him to be immediately introduced. The prince of Persia was presented under the disguise and appearance of a physician; and the sultan, without wasting time in superfluous conversation, acquainted him with the disorder of the princess of Bengal. He then conducted the prince into a little closet, which looked into her apartment, whence he could see through the lattice without being perceived. Prince Firouz Schah beheld his princess seated in a negligent posture, singing a song, in which she deplored her unhappy destiny, which had, perhaps, deprived her for ever of the object she so tenderly loved. The prince, moved with compassion at the unhappy situation in which he found his adored princess, wanted no other proof to convince him that her derangement was feigned. He descended from the closet, and after having told the sultan the nature of the princess's disorder, and that it was not incurable, he added, that to perform a cure, it would be necessary for him to converse with her entirely alone. The sultan ordered the door of the chamber to be opened, and Prince Firouz Schah entered it. No sooner had the princess perceived him, than supposing him to be a physician, she rose from her seat in a rage, using the most threatening language. This did not prevent him from approaching; and when he was advanced near enough to be heard, as he wished what he uttered to be for her ear alone, he said to her in a low tone of voice, and with a respectful air, "Princess, I am not a physician; recognise in me the prince of Persia, who is come to restore you to liberty. At the sound of his voice, the princess of Bengal began to grow calm, and immediately her countenance was brightened by the joy created by unlooked-for happiness. The agreeable surprise she experienced for some time deprived her of utterance, and allowed Firouz Schah an opportunity of relating to her his despair and proceedings subsequent to her loss, concluding by requesting her to inform him of all that had happened to her in the interval. The princess satisfied the prince in a few words. When Firouz Schah inquired if she knew what became of the enchanted horse after the death of the Indian. "I am ignorant," replied she, "of what orders the sultan may have given concerning it; but, after the wonders I related, it is not probable that he neglected to appropriate it to himself." As Prince Firouz Schah did not doubt that the sultan had carefully preserved the horse, he communicated to the princess his design of using it to convey her back to Persia.

The sultan of Cashmire expressed great pleasure when the prince related to him how far his first visit had operated towards her recovery; and when, on the succeeding day, the princess received him in a manner which convinced him that the cure was rapidly advancing, he considered him as the first physician in the universe; and after having exhorted her to attend implicitly to the directions of so able a physician, he retired, without waiting for any reply. The prince of Persia, who had accompanied the sultan to the princess's apartment, left it at the same time; and, as he passed, along with him, he asked him if he might inquire by what adventure a princess of Bengal happened to be in the kingdom of Cashmire. He hoped by this question, to lead the conversation to the subject of the enchanted horse and thereby learn, from the sultan's lips, what was become of it. The sultan repeated to him nearly the same account he had received from the princess of Bengal; adding, that he had ordered the enchanted horse to be conveyed into his treasury, as a rare curiosity. "Sir," replied the pretended physician, "the information which your majesty has now imparted to me, will furnish me with the means of completing the recovery of the princess. If your majesty choose to enjoy, and present to your court and inhabitants of your capital, a most surprising spectacle,

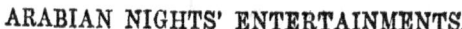

you have only to order the horse to be brought into the middle of the square before your palace, I promise to show you, and the whole assembly, in a few moments, the princess of Bengal in as perfect health as she ever enjoyed in her life. That this event may be effected with all the pomp such an event requires, it is advisable that the princess should be dressed as magnificently as possible, and decorated with all the most precious jewels in your majesty's possession." The sultan had no difficulty in complying with all the prince proposed. On the following day, the enchanted horse was, by his orders, placed in the great square of the palace. A report was soon circulated throughout the city, that preparations were making for some extraordinary exhibition, and a crowd of spectators assembled from all quarters. The sultan of Cashmire appeared; and when he had taken his place on a building erected for the purpose, surrounded by the principal nobles and officers of his court, the princess of Bengal approached the enchanted horse, which, with the assistance of her attendants, she mounted. When she was on the saddle, her feet in each stirrup, and the bridle in her hand, the pretended physician placed round the horse several small vessels full of fire, and going to each, he threw in a perfume composed of a variety of the most exquisite odours. After this, assuming a thoughtful air, he went three times round the horse, pretending to pronounce certain words; and, at the instant that the vessels all emitted a thick smoke, rendering the princess, as well as the horse, scarcely discernible. Firouz Schah availed himself of the opportunity, and lightly bounding on it, behind the princess, he turned the peg which was to cause the horse to rise; and, while ascending into the air, he pronounced these words. "*Sultan of Cashmire, when you wish to espouse princesses who implore your protection, learn first to obtain their consent.*"

By this stratagem the prince of Persia recovered the princess of Bengal, and conducted her, in a very short space of time, to the capital of Persia; but, instead of alighting at the pleasure-house, he dismounted in the middle of the city palace, opposite to the king's apartment. The king of Persia did not defer the solemnization of the nuptials longer than was requisite to make the necessary preparations for the ceremony to be performed with the utmost pomp and magnificence.

THE HISTORY OF PRINCE AHMED, AND THE FAIRY PARI-BANOU.

A SULTAN of India, who reigned in peace during many years, had the satisfaction of seeing in his old age, that the three princes his sons, and a princess his niece, were the ornament of his court. The eldest of the princes was named Houssain, the second Ali, the youngest Ahmed, and the princess his niece, Nourounnihar.

The princess Nourounnihar was the offspring of a junior brother of the sultan, he died, however, a few years after his marriage, and left his daughter very young. The sultan charged himself with his daughter's education, and had her conveyed to the palace, to be brought up with the three princes. To the possession of uncommon beauty, this princess added an excellent understanding, and her unsullied virtue distinguished her among all the princesses of her time. The sultan, her uncle, who designed to marry her to, and thus form an alliance with, some neighbouring prince, when she was of a proper age, was thinking seriously on the subject, when he found that all the three princes, his sons, were passionately in love with her. This discovery gave him great uneasiness. He talked to each in private; and after representing to them the troubles they would occasion by persisting in their attachment, he used every argument to persuade them, either to submit to the declaration which the princess herself should make in favour of one of the three, or altogether to relinquish their pretensions. But as in each of them he had met with an unconquerable obstinacy, he assembled them all three before him, and thus addressed them: "My children, since for your mutual tranquillity, I have not succeeded in persuading you to relinquish your thoughts of marrying the princess your cousin, and as I am not inclined to use my authority in giving her to one of you in preference to the other two, I think I have found out a means to satisfy you, and to preserve that union which ought to subsist between you. I think it, then, advisable, that you should separately go upon your travels, each on a different route, so that it may be impossible for you to meet; and, as you know I am very curious in everything rare or singular, I promise the princess my niece to him who shall bring me the most extraordinary rarity. To defray the expenses of travelling, and for the purchase of the rarity you are to procure, I will give each of you a sum suitable to your birth, but not enough to furnish a great equipage and a numerous retinue, which, by discovering your rank, would deprive you of the freedom which will be necessary to you, and enable you to derive the greatest possible advantage from your journey." As the three princes had always been obedient to the will of their father, and as each flattered himself that he should be the person whom fortune would most favour, they all testified their readiness to obey. The sultan immediately desired the sum he had promised to be paid them; and, on that very day, orders were given to make preparations for their journey; they even took leave of the sultan, that they might be prepared to depart very early the next morning. They went out at the same gate of the city, well mounted and equipped, dressed like merchants, each with one confidential attendant, disguised like a slave; and they continued together till they arrived at the first inn, where the road separated in three directions. At night, while regaling themselves with the supper they had ordered, they agreed to be absent a year, and to meet again at the same place, upon condition that those who arrived first should wait for the third; so that they might present themselves to the sultan at the same time, on their return. The next morning, at daybreak they mounted their horses, and each took one of the three roads, without the least difficulty in their choice.

Prince Houssain, the eldest of the three, who had heard of the grandeur and splendour of the kingdom of Bisnagar, took his route towards the Indian sea, and after a journey of three months arrived at Bisnagar, a city which gives its own name to the whole country of which it is the capital, and where its sovereigns have fixed their residence. He took lodgings in a khan, and, having learnt that there were four different divisions, where all the various merchants had shops for their goods, in the middle of which the palace of the king was situated, forming, as it were, the centre of the city, which had three enclosures at least two leagues in length from one gate to the other; he went on the next day to one of these quarters.

After walking through every street, meditating upon the immense riches which he saw, Prince Houssain felt him-

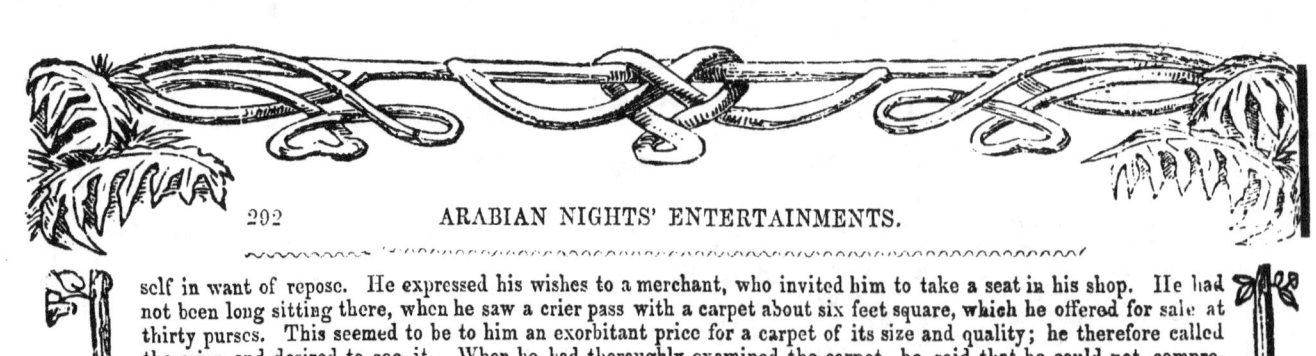

self in want of repose. He expressed his wishes to a merchant, who invited him to take a seat in his shop. He had not been long sitting there, when he saw a crier pass with a carpet about six feet square, which he offered for sale at thirty purses. This seemed to be to him an exorbitant price for a carpet of its size and quality; he therefore called the crier, and desired to see it. When he had thoroughly examined the carpet, he said that he could not comprehend why a floor-carpet, so small, and of such appearance, should be put up at so high a price. The crier, who took Prince Houssain for a merchant, replied, "If this sum, sir, appear to you excessive, you will be more astonished when I inform you that I am ordered not to let it go under forty purses." "There must, then," replied Prince Houssain, "be some secret quality that renders it so valuable." "You have guessed it, sir," resumed the crier, "and you will agree to it when you know that, only by sitting on this carpet, you will be immediately transported to whatever place you wish to go."

The prince, reflecting that the object of his journey was to procure some extraordinary rarity for his father, thought that he could not possibly meet with anything with which the sultan would be better pleased. "I will give you the forty purses you require," said he to the crier, "and also make you a handsome present." "Sir," replied the crier, "I assure you I have told the truth, and it will be very easy for you to be convinced of it; for, as soon as you have concluded the purchase, I will show you how to make the experiment. As you, probably, have not the forty purses here, and I must accompany you for payment to the khan, where you have taken up your abode, if the master of this shop will give us leave, we will retire to the back part of it, where I will spread out my carpet, and when we are both seated on it, and you have formed the wish to be transported into your apartment with me, if we are not instantly conveyed there it shall be no bargain." On the good faith of the crier the prince accepted the conditions. He concluded the bargain on the terms proposed, and then went to the back part of the shop. The crier spread out the carpet, and they both seated themselves, when the prince had no sooner formed the wish to be transported to his apartment in the khan than he found himself, with the crier, in the very place. As he required no further proof, he counted out the forty purses in gold, and added twenty pieces more as a present.

Prince Houssain's joy was extreme at having thus fortunately gained possession of a carpet so curious, that he had not the least doubt of obtaining the Princess Nourounnihar. In fact, he thought it impossible for either of his younger brothers to acquire anything in the course of their travels that could be compared with what he had been so fortunate as to meet with. By merely sitting down on the carpet, he might, without remaining any longer in Bisnagar, have instantly returned to the spot where they had agreed to meet; but, as he was desirous of seeing the king of Bisnagar and his court, and to inform himself of the laws, customs, religion, and condition, of the kingdom, he resolved to employ some months in satisfying his curiosity. The king was accustomed to give an audience once every week to foreign merchants, and under this character Prince Houssain, who did not wish to discover his real rank, saw him several times. As this prince, besides being handsome and well-featured, possessed a brilliant understanding, he was very much distinguished beyond the other merchants with whom he entered the king's presence. To him, therefore, the king addressed his conversation when he wished to make inquiries respecting the sultan of India and of his empire. On the other days the prince employed himself in viewing whatever was most remarkable either in the city or its environs.

Prince Houssain was also a spectator of a solemn feast, which is celebrated every year, to which the governors of provinces, the commanders of fortified places, the heads and judges of cities, with the Brahmins, so celebrated for their religion, are all obliged to repair. The assembly was held in a plain of vast extent, where they formed an astonishing spectacle. In the centre of this plain was a place of considerable size, bounded on one side by a superb building, forming nine floors or stories, like a scaffold, and supported upon forty columns; this was destined for the king and his court, and for those strangers whom he honoured with an audience once a week. The inside was handsomely ornamented and richly furnished; and the outside covered with paintings in landscape, in which were represented all sorts of animals, birds, insects, even flies and gnats, all naturally executed. The other three sides were likewise formed of buildings, four or five stories high, and painted in a similar manner. These buildings, or scaffolds, possessed this singularity, that they might be turned, and the decorations changed, from hour to hour. On each side of this place, and at a little distance from each other, were ranged a thousand elephants, sumptuously caparisoned, and upon the back of each was a square tower of gilt wood, containing musicians and buffoons. But what made Prince Houssain most admire the ingenuity of these Indians, was, to see one of the largest of the elephants balancing itself on the end of a post about two feet high, and tossing its trunk about in exact time with the instruments.

If Prince Houssain could have made a longer stay in the kingdom of Bisnagar, a variety of other curious things would have agreeably amused him, until the very last day of the year on which his brothers and himself had agreed to meet. But, fully satisfied with what he had seen, and continually occupied with the thoughts of the dear object of his affections; he fancied his mind would be more at ease, and that he should feel greater happiness, if he were at a less distance from her. After having, therefore, satisfied the master of the khan, and told him the hour when he might take the key, which would be left in the door, without giving any hint by what mode he meant to travel, he re-entered his room, spread out the carpet, and seated himself, with the attendant whom he had brought with him, upon it; and having wished to be conveyed to the place where he and his brothers had agreed to assemble, immediately perceived his arrival. He took up his residence there; and, without making himself known, waited their appearance.

Prince Ali, Houssain's next brother, who intended to travel to Persia, at length arrived at Schiraz, which at that time was the capital of the kingdom. As he had formed an intimacy during the journey with some of the merchants, he took up his abode at the same khan with them. While the merchants were the next day unpacking their bales of merchandise, Prince Ali proceeded to the quarter of the city, where jewels, gold and silver ornaments, brocades silk stuffs, fine linens, and other curious and valuable merchandise, were sold. Prince Ali examined it throughout, and reflected with admiration on the quantities of riches that were shut up, by the profusion of rich and costly merchandise, that was exposed for sale. Of the criers who went about exhibiting specimens of various articles for sale,

he was not a little surprised at seeing one holding an ivory tube in his hand, about a foot long, and rather more in thickness than a man's thumb, which he put up at thirty purses. He imagined the crier could not be in his senses; but, to be satisfied, he went up to a shop, and pointing the crier out to the merchant, said, " Pray, sir, am I deceived in believing that crier, who puts up the little ivory tube he has in his hand at, thirty purses to be insane ?" " Sir," replied the merchant, " if he be so, he has lost his senses since yesterday : for, I can assure you, he is the acutest of all our criers. He will pass again in a moment ; we will then call him, and you may obtain the satisfaction you desire : have the goodness in the meantime, to take a seat on my sofa, and rest yourself." Prince Ali accepted the obliging offer of the merchant ; and shortly afterwards the crier returned. The merchant called him by his name ; and, as he approached, " inform this gentleman," said he, " whether you are in your senses ; as, from your putting up that apparently insignificant ivory tube at thirty purses, he had some doubts on the subject." " Sir," replied the crier, addressing himself to Prince Ali, " you shall yourself judge, when I have explained its properties to you. In the first place, sir, you will please to observe that this tube is furnished with a glass at each end ; by looking through one of these two glasses, whatever you may desire to see will be instantly presented to your view." " I am ready to apologise," replied the prince, " if you will prove the truth of what you have advanced." As he held the tube in his hand, he examined the two glasses. " Show me the end through which I must look," said he. The crier complied, and the prince looked through, wishing to see his father, whom he beheld in perfect health, sitting on his throne in the midst of his council. Then, as nothing, after the sultan, was dearer to him than the princess Nourounnihar, he transferred his wish to her, and immediately saw her seated at her toilet, surrounded by her women.

Prince Ali was sufficiently convinced of this tube's being the most valuable thing in existence, and he thought that, if he neglected to purchase it, he should never again meet with so extraordinary a curiosity. He then said to the crier, " I freely retract the opinion I had formed of you ; and I believe you will be fully satisfied with the reparation I am ready to make, by purchasing your tube. As I should be sorry were any one else to obtain it, tell me the exact price the owner has fixed upon it, and you have only to accompany me, and I will count the sum out to you." The crier assured him that he was ordered not to let it go under forty purses, and if he doubted his veracity, he was ready to conduct him to the owner. The prince, however, took him with him, and counted out to the crier forty purses of gold. He now gave himself no further trouble, except in viewing whatever was most curious and worthy of observation in and about Schiraz, until the caravan was ready to return to India. Having quite satisfied his curiosity when the caravan was prepared to depart, the prince joined it, and began his journey. No accident retarded their progress ; and Prince Ali reached the rendezvous in safety, where his brother Houssain was already arrived. Here the two princes remained together, waiting the appearance of their brother.

Prince Ahmed had taken the route toward Samarcand, and, on the day after his arrival there, pursued the same plan adopted by his two brothers, and went to the bezestein. He had scarcely entered, before he saw a crier, carrying an artificial apple in his hand, which he put up at thirty-five purses. Prince Ahmed stopped the crier; " Let me see this apple," said he, " and tell me what virtue or extraordinary property it possesses." " Sir," replied he, " this apple, if you merely consider its external appearance, would seem of very little value, but if you reflect upon its virtues, you must confess it is inestimable. There is no disease, however dangerous, whether fever, pleurisy, plague, or other disorder, but it will cure, and restore the sufferer to as perfect health as if he had never been ill during his life. And this by the easiest means possible, simply by making the sick person smell to the apple." " If what you state be true," replied Prince Ahmed, " this apple indeed possesses a marvellous property, but how can I be convinced that there is neither disguise nor exaggeration in what you have related ?" " Sir," answered the crier, " the fact can be vouched for, by the whole city of Samarcand ; and you need only ask the merchants assembled here, when you will even find some that would not have been alive to-day, if they had not made use of this excellent remedy. But I must inform you, that it is the fruit of the study of a very celebrated philosopher in this city, who has, all his life, applied himself in investigating the virtues of plants and minerals, and who at length attained the knowledge of the composition you now see. An attack so sudden, that he had not time to use his sovereign remedy, caused his death a short time since ; and and his widow resolved to put it up for sale, that she and her family may live more at their ease." While the crier was informing Prince Ahmed of the virtues of the artificial apple, many people stopped, and the most part of them confirmed all he stated. One of them having said, that he had a friend whose life was despaired of, and that this would be a favourable opportunity for proving the virtue of the apple, Prince Ahmed told the crier, he would give him forty purses if the apple cured the sick person by only smelling at it. The crier, who was ordered to sell it at that price, replied, " Let us go, sir, to make the experiment, and the apple shall be yours." The experiment succeeded ; and the prince, having counted out the forty purses to the crier, who delivered the apple to him, waited with the greatest impatience for the departure of the first caravan, to return to India. He joined it, and, notwithstanding the unavoidable inconveniences of so long a journey, reached the place where his brothers Houssain and Ali were waiting for him.

When Prince Ahmed had rejoined the two princes his brothers, and they had mutually embraced and congratulated each on their happy meeting, Prince Houssain, as the eldest, thus spoke : " We shall have time enough hereafter to amuse each other with the particulars of our travels, let us now, therefore, only speak of what is of the most importance for us to know, we will no longer conceal from each other what we have obtained. To set you the example, I must inform you, that the rarity I have procured is the carpet upon which I am sitting. It appears common, and without attraction, as you may observe ; but when I have told you its virtues your astonishment will be the greater, as you can never have heard of any thing similar. The fact is, whoever sits upon this carpet as I now do, and wishes to be transported into any particular place, however distant, will instantly find himself there." Prince Houssain having finished what he had to say in praise of his carpet, Prince Ali next spoke in these terms :—" I own, brother, that your carpet is most wonderful, if it possess the property you have stated ; but you must acknowledge that there may be other things at least equally so with your carpet. To convince you, this ivory tube does not seem a rarity worthy of much attention ; I have, nevertheless, paid as much for it as you did for your carpet. In equity, you must acknowledge that I have not been deceived, when you are convinced that, by

looking through one end of this tube, you will behold whatever object you wish to see." Prince Houssain took the ivory tube, and putting it to his eye, with the intention of seeing the Princess Nourounnihar, Prince Ali and his brother Ahmed were extremely astonished at seeing him suddenly change countenance, as if he were not only very much surprised, but afflicted likewise. Houssain did not give them time to ask the cause: "Princes," he exclaimed, "we have in vain undertaken our painful journey, with the hope of being rewarded by the possession of the charming Nourounnihar; in a very few moments that amiable princess will be no more. I have seen her in her bed, surrounded by her women, who seem awaiting her dissolution. Here, look yourselves; behold her pitiable state, and join your tears to mine." Prince Ali looked through it, and having, with the most painful sensations, witnessed the same sight, he presented it to Prince Ahmed, that he might also see the melancholy and afflicting spectacle. When Ahmed had looked through it and seen the alarming condition of the princess, he thus addressed his brothers:— "The Princess Nourounnihar is truly in a state not far removed from death, but I am persuaded, if we lose no time, her life is still to be preserved." He then drew from his bosom the artificial apple. "This apple," added he, "cost not less than the carpet and ivory tube, which you have respectively brought home from your travels. The occasion that is now presented of making you witnesses to its wonderful virtues causes me to congratulate myself with the purchase. I must inform you that it possesses the virtue, by merely smelling it, of restoring a person to perfect health. I have been perfectly convinced of its efficacy, and you may now see the effect of it upon the Princess Nourounnihar." "If this be the fact," returned Prince Houssain, "we may be instantly transported to the chamber of the princess by means of my carpet. Let us, then, lose no time, but come and seat yourselves by my side."

Prince Ali and Prince Ahmed then seated themselves with their brother Houssain; and as they were all three equally interested, each instantly formed the same wish, of being transported into the apartment of Nourounnihar. Their desires were fulfilled; and with such celerity, that they seemed at the end of their journey almost before it had begun. Prince Houssain quitted the carpet, as did also the other princes, and advancing to the bed, he applied the wonderful apple to her nose. In a few moments the princess opened her eyes, turned her head from side to side, looking at those who stood near her; and raising herself in the bed, she desired to be dressed.

While Nourounnihar was dressing, the princes went to throw themselves at the feet of their father, and pay him their respects. When they came into his presence, they found that the principal eunuch had preceded them, and informed him of their unexpected arrival, and of the manner in which the princess had been, by their means, perfectly cured. After mutual congratulations the princes presented the rarities they had severally procured. Having each spoken in praise of his own acquisition, they delivered the three curiosities into the hands of the sultan, and entreated him to declare to which he gave the preference, and thus determine on whom he bestowed, according to his promise, the Princess Nourounnihar in marriage.

The sultan of India, after having listened to all the princes wished to say in behalf of their rarities, without giving them the least interruption, remained for some time silent, as if he were considering what to reply. He at length broke silence, and thus addressed them: "I would, my children, pronounce in favour of one of you with the greatest pleasure, if I could do so with justice. To you, Ahmed, the princess is certainly indebted for her recovery, by means of your artificial apple; but I ask—Could you have effected her cure, if the ivory tube of Prince Ali had not afforded you the opportunity of knowing the danger she was in, and the carpet of Houssain procured you the means of instantly coming to her assistance? You, Ali, by means of your ivory tube, discovered the irreparable loss yourself and brothers were likely to experience, in the death of the princess; and it must, therefore, be acknowledged that she is under a great obligation to you; but you must also allow, that this information would have been totally useless without the artificial apple and the carpet. Thus, as neither the carpet, the ivory tube, nor the artificial apple, possesses the least preference, I can bestow the princess only upon one of you; you must yourselves be aware, that the sole advantage you have derived from your travels, is the glory of having equally contributed to the re-establishment of her health. Such being the fact, it is necessary I should have recourse to some other means of determining me in my choice; and as we have a length of time before night, I wish this affair to be settled to-day. Let each of you, then, procure a bow and one arrow, and repair to the great plain without the walls. I will meet you there; and promise that I will give the princess to him who shall shoot his arrow to the greatest distance.

The three princes had nothing to reply to the decision which the sultan had pronounced. When they had left his presence, they furnished themselves each with a bow and arrow, and then repaired to the plain, followed by an innumerable crowd of people. The sultan did not keep them waiting; and as soon as he was arrived, Prince Houssain, as being the eldest, took his bow, and made the first shot. Prince Ali then drew his, and the arrow fell beyond that of Houssain. Prince Ahmed shot the last, but the arrow went out of sight. They ran and searched about; but notwithstanding all the diligence of the people, and of Prince Ahmed himself, the arrow could no where be discovered. Although it was probable his arrow had been shot to the greatest distance, and that he, in consequence, deserved the hand of the princess, yet the sultan determined in favour of Prince Ali. Preparations were accordingly made to celebrate the nuptials, which were solemnized in a few days with great magnificence.

Prince Houssain did not honour the festivities with his presence. His displeasure was, on the contrary, so sensible, that he abandoned the court, renounced his right to the throne, assumed the habit of a dervise, and put himself under the discipline of a very famous scheik, who enjoyed the highest reputation, on account of his exemplary life, and who had established his residence in an agreeable solitude. Prince Ahmed, actuated by the same motive, did not assist at the nuptials, but he did not, like him, renounce the world. As he could not comprehend how the arrow which he had shot, became as it were, invisible, he resolved to go and search for it so carefully, that he should at least have nothing to reproach himself with; he accordingly went to the spot where the arrows of Prince Houssain and Ali had been found; whence he walked straight forward, looking both to the right and left as he proceeded, till he had got to so great a distance without discovering what he sought, that he judged he was now giving himself only useless trouble. Led on, however, almost in spite of himself, he continued following the same direction, till some very elevated rocks presented themselves immediately before him. In approaching, the prince observed an arrow; he took it up, examined it, and, with the utmost astonishment, found it to be that he had shot. "It is the same," said he mentally; "but neither I nor any other mortal could possibly have strength to send it to such a distance." Meditating upon this subject, he entered into a hollow part of the rocks; and as he cast his eyes from one part to another, he observed an iron door, to which there was no appearance of a lock. He feared it might be other-

wise fastened; but, pushing against it, he found it opened inwardly, and saw a gentle declivity by which he descended. He expected to be in perfect darkness, but was soon surrounded by a light, totally different from that he had quitted. On entering a spacious opening, at the distance of fifty or sixty paces, he perceived a magnificent palace, and a lady of majestic air, and of incomparable beauty, adorned with valuable jewels, advanced, accompanied by a band of females, from whom she was easily distinguishable as their superior.

Prince Ahmed hastened forward to pay his respects to her; while the lady, on her part, who saw him advancing, prevented him, by addressing these words to him:—" Approach, Prince Ahmed, you are welcome." The prince was greatly surprised at hearing his own name, and was at a loss to comprehend how he could be known to a lady of whom he was entirely ignorant. "Madam," he replied, "I cannot but return you many thanks for the assurance you have given me that I am welcome. But may I be permitted to ask, how it has happened that I am not unknown to you, while I have not had, till this moment, the least knowledge of you, although you reside so near?" "Prince," replied the lady, "let us first go into the saloon; I can there answer your question more at our ease." She had no sooner said this than she led the way, and Ahmed followed her into the saloon. She went to the upper end, and seated herself on a sofa; and when Ahmed had taken his place by her side, at her request, "Prince," said she, "you express surprise at my knowing who you are, although you are unacquainted with me; but your wonder will cease, when I inform you who I am. You are doubtless not ignorant that the world is inhabited by genii as well as by mortals. I am the daughter of one of these genii, who is the most powerful and distinguished of his race; my name is Pari-Banou. You will, therefore, lay aside your astonishment at finding me acquainted with your name, as well as that of the Princess Nourounnihar. I am aware of your affection for her. I caused the artificial apple which you bought of Samarcand to be exposed for sale, as well as the carpet of Prince Houssain at Bisnagar, and the ivory tube of Prince Ali at Schiraz. This is sufficient to convince you that I am not ignorant of anything concerning you. I have only to add that you seem to me worthy of a better fate than in being united to the Princess Nourounnihar; and that, as I was present on that occasion when you shot the arrow you hold in your hand, and I saw that it would not go beyond even Prince Houssain's, I seized it in the air, and gave it sufficient velocity to strike it against the rocks. It will now depend only upon yourself, to take advantage of the opportunity which presents itself." As the fairy Pari-Banou pronounced these last words in a different tone of voice, and cast a tender look upon Prince Ahmed, blushed, and instantly fixed her eyes on the ground, the prince had no difficulty in comprehending the kind of opportunity she meant. He reflected that Nourounnihar could never be his, and that Pari-Banou infinitely surpassed her in beauty, in attractions, and in the qualities of her mind, as well as in immensity of riches; and he blessed the moment in which the idea of going to seek his arrow had struck him. "If I might, madam," he replied, "by becoming your slave have the power of admiring so many charms for the remainder of my life, I should be the happiest of mortals. Pardon my boldness in making such a request; and do not, in refusing it, disdain to admit in your court a prince who is entirely devoted to you."

"Prince," answered the fairy, "as I have long been mistress of my own actions, it is not as a slave that I wish to admit you into my court, but as the master; and in pledging your faith to me, everything I possess will belong to us conjointly." She presented her hand, which he kissed. "Prince Ahmed," said the fairy, while he held it, "will you not now pledge me your faith, as I do mine to you?" "Ah, madam!" cried he, "how could I obtain greater pleasure! Yes, my sultana, my queen, I give up my heart to you, without the least reserve." "Then," replied Pari-Banou, "you are my husband, and I am now yours. Marriages with us are contracted with no other ceremonies, yet they are more lasting and more indissoluble than among men, notwithstanding all the forms which they have adopted."

The nuptial rejoicings continued for several days, and Pari-Banou had no difficulty in diversifying the entertainments, with a variety of spectacles, all so uncommon, that Prince Ahmed would never have even thought of them, had his life lasted a thousand years. It was the intention of the fairy, not only to give the prince the strongest proofs of the sincerity and excess of her love, but she wished him also to believe that there was nothing at the court of his father, that could be compared with what she possessed. She completely succeeded; the affections of Prince Ahmed did not diminish, on the contrary, his love increased to that degree, that it was no longer in his own power to control it, even if he had been so resolved.

After the lapse of six months, Ahmed, who had always entertained a great regard for the sultan, felt a strong desire to gain some intelligence of him; and, as he could only satisfy his anxiety by going in person, he spoke to Pari-Banou on the subject, requesting her leave to that effect. This alarmed the fairy, who feared it might be only a pretence for abandoning her. "In what," said she to him, "have I given you cause for discontent? Is it possible that you have forgotten that you pledged your faith, and that you now no longer love me, who am still so passionately attached to you?" "I am, my queen," replied Prince Ahmed, "perfectly convinced of your affection, of which I should be unworthy, did I not show my gratitude. If you are offended at my request, I beg you will pardon me, and there is no reparation I am not willing to make."

Prince Ahmed so frequently, in his conversation with the fairy, spoke of his father, though without again mentioning the desire he felt to see him, that this very forbearance made her comprehend his solicitude. As she perceived, therefore, that he was restrained by the fear of displeasing her, and judging by her own feelings of her injustice in thus violently opposing the natural affection of a son for his father, she resolved to grant what she could not but observe he so ardently desired.

"The permission, prince," said she one day to him, "which you requested of me, to visit your father, gave me reason to fear, that it was only a pretext to abandon me; and I had no other motive in refusing your request; but as I am now as fully convinced that I may rely on your affection, I am willing to grant your request; but it must be upon this condition, that you pledge yourself not to be long absent." "My sultana," he exclaimed, "I know the value of the favour you have granted me; but I want expressions to thank you as I wish. Supply my inability, I conjure you; and whatever words you can use, be assured they will be inadequate to depict my feelings." "Go, prince," said she, "whenever you please; but do not take it ill, that I first give you some advice. I do not think it would be proper for you to mention your marriage to the sultan, nor my rank, nor the place in which you have resided; beg him to be satisfied with knowing that you are happy." She then gave him an escort of twenty horsemen, all well-mounted and equipped; and everything being prepared, Prince Ahmed took leave of Pari-Banou, embracing her, and renewing his promise to return as soon as possible.

As the distance to the capital of the sultan was not great, Prince Ahmed soon arrived there; and on entering the city, the people received him with acclamations; most of them, leaving their business, accompanied him, in crowds, to his father's apartment. The sultan received and embraced him with the greatest joy, complaining, nevertheless, of the affliction into which his long absence had thrown him. "And this absence," added he, " has caused me so much the more pain, as, after fate had determined, to your disadvantage, in favour of your brother Prince Ali, I was fearful you might commit some act of despair." "Sir," replied Prince Ahmed, "I will leave it to the consideration of your majesty, whether, after having lost the Princess Nourounnihar, I could resolve to be a witness to the happiness of Prince Ali. Your majesty may remember, that in drawing my bow, the most extraordinary occurrence happened to me that was ever known; it being impossible, in a plain so level, and so encumbered to find the arrow I had shot; in consequence of which I lost a cause, the justice of which was not less dear to my affection, than to that of the princes my brothers. I nevertheless pursued my search, continuing to proceed in the line I thought it was likely to fall. I had proceeded more than a league, when I began to reflect on the impossibility of my shooting an arrow to so great a distance, by doing which I should have excelled our most famous heroes. I was about to abandon my enterprize; when I felt myself led on, as it were, against my will; and after walking four leagues, and till the plain was terminated by some steep rocks, I perceived an arrow; I ran and took it, and knew it to be the very same I had shot. But this is a mystery, concerning which I entreat your majesty not to take it ill, if I remain silent. I am perfectly contented. In the midst of my happiness one thing only occasioned my uneasiness; which was, the distress I had no doubt you experienced from your ignorance of what had befallen me. I thought it, therefore, my duty to relieve you from your anxiety; and this was my sole motive for coming." "My son," replied the sultan, "I cannot refuse the permission you require; I should nevertheless, have been better pleased, had you determined to come and live near me. Tell me, at least, by what means I can gain intelligence of you." "Sir," replied Prince Ahmed, "I entreat you to suffer me to be silent on this point also. I will so frequently return to pay my respects, that I rather fear being thought importunate, than accused of negligence when my presence may be required."

The sultan of India did not press Ahmed any more on the subject; "My son," said he, "I do not wish to penetrate into your secret; I leave you sole master of it; but be assured, as your presence affords me the greatest pleasure you can now bestow, that you will be most welcome, whenever you can visit me."

Prince Ahmed remained only three days at the court of his father: he departed very early on the fourth morning, and Pari-Banou saw him return with great joy, and the haste he had made urged her to condemn herself for having entertained a suspicion of his fidelity to her, which he had so solemnly promised.

About a month after the return of Ahmed, and after the time when the prince had given her an account of his visit, and related his conversation with his father, in which he had obtained permission to pay his respects to him very often, the fairy took an opportunity of speaking on this subject: "Tell me, my prince," said she, "have you forgotten the sultan your father? Do you not remember the promise you made him, to visit him often? What you said to me on your return, has not escaped my memory; and I now remind you of it, that you may not delay any longer performing your promise." "Madam," replied Ahmed, "I do not feel myself culpable for the forgetfulness of which you accuse me, as I would rather suffer your reproach, than be exposed to the chance of a refusal, by expressing too much haste to obtain what it might occasion you pain to grant." "Prince," replied the fairy, "I do not wish you to show this deference to me; and, that the same thing may not again happen, visit him. Begin, then, to-morrow, and continue to visit him every month, I consent very willingly to this proceeding." Prince Ahmed accordingly set out the next day, with the same attendants, and was received by the sultan with the same joy and satisfaction as before. He regularly continued, for many months, thus to pay his respects, but always with a more magnificent equipage.

At length, some favourites of the sultan abused the liberty allowed them of speaking to him, by exciting in his breast anger against his son. They represented to him, that it was but prudent he should desire to know the prince's place of retreat, that it appeared he came to court only by way of boast, to show that he had no occasion for the sultan's liberality, to enable him to live like a prince; and that, in short, there was reason to fear he intended to excite a rebellion against his person, and dethrone him. The sultan replied, "You deceive yourselves: my son loves me; and I am the more convinced of his affection and fidelity, as I do not remember to have given him the least cause for dissatisfaction." One of the favourites then observed, "Although, sir, in the opinion of every sensible person, your majesty could not have adopted a more equitable plan than that which you followed in your disposal of the Princess Nourounnihar in marriage with one of your sons, who knows whether Prince Ahmed has submitted to his fate with the same resignation as Prince Houssain? May he not consider himself alone worthy of her. Your majesty is not ignorant, that, in so delicate an affair, it is necessary to be very circumspect: you should also consider that dissimulation on the part of the prince may amuse and deceive your majesty; and that the danger is the more to be dreaded, as Prince Ahmed seems to reside at no great distance. In fine, if your majesty had paid the same attention to circumstances as we have done, you might have observed, that every time the prince visits you, both he and his attendants are quite fresh, while their dress, and the ornaments of their persons and horses have the same lustre as if they had been that instant taken from the hands of the workmen. These are evident proofs that Prince Ahmed resides in the neighbourhood, and we thought we should be wanting in our duty, if we did not humbly represent them to your majesty, as well for your own preservation, as for the good of your state." When the favourite had concluded, the sultan put an end to the conversation, by saying, "However this may be, I do not believe that my son Ahmed can be so wicked. I am nevertheless, obliged to you for your advice." The sultan spoke in this manner to his favourites, that they might not perceive their discourse had made any impression on his mind; but he could not help being much alarmed, and he resolved to watch the conduct of Prince Ahmed. He sent for an enchantress, who was introduced by a private door of the palace, and conducted to his cabinet. "You told me the truth," said the sultan to her, "when you assured me that my son Ahmed was not dead, but you must now

do me a further service. Although I have since discovered him, and he now visits me every month, yet I have not been able to learn where he has fixed his residence; and I do not wish to put so great a restraint upon him, as to compel him to tell me against his will; I believe you to have sufficient skill to satisfy my curiosity; you know that he is here; and, as he is accustomed to depart without taking leave either of me or any other person, lose no time, but place yourself immediately on the road he takes, and observe him so well, that you may know to what place he retires."

Next morning, Prince Ahmed set off without taking leave of the sultan his father, or any of the courtiers, according to his custom; the enchantress saw him approaching, and followed him with her eyes, till she lost sight both of him and his attendants. As these rocks formed an insurmountable barrier to mortals, either on foot or horseback, the enchantress thought that the prince had retired into a cavern; accordingly, as soon as the prince and his attendants had disappeared, she quitted her concealment and went directly to the recess. Going in, she proceeded till the excavation ended in several turnings, when she looked about on all sides, but notwithstanding her diligence, she

could not perceive any entrance to the cavern, nor even the iron door, which had not escaped the eye of Prince Ahmed; in fact, this door was visible but to men, and only to such of those as the fairy Pari-Banou wished to see, and not at all to women. She therefore returned to give an account of her proceedings to the sultan; and having related the steps she had taken, she added, "Your majesty will readily believe, after what I have had the honour to inform you, that it will not be difficult for me to afford you all the satisfaction you desire respecting the conduct of Prince Ahmed. To enable me to accomplish what I have begun, I only request time and patience and permission to act at liberty, without being obliged to inform you of the measures to which I have recourse." The sultan was satisfied with the enchantress's proposal: "You are your own mistress," said he; "act as you judge proper."

As Prince Ahmed, since he had obtained permission to visit the court of his father, had never neglected to pay his respects there once a month, the enchantress waited till the lapse of that period. A day or two before its expiration, she did not fail to go to the rocks where she had lost sight of Ahmed and his attendants, for the purpose of executing the project she had formed. Early the next morning, when the prince came out at the iron door, with his usual attendants, he passed near the enchantress, but whom he did not know to be one; observing her lying down, and complaining like a person in great pain, compassion induced him to approach, to inquire if he could afford her any assistance. The enchantress replied, with apparent difficulty, that she had left her house in the city, and on the road was seized with a violent fever, so that she was obliged to stop, and remain in the state they then saw her—in a place very distant from any habitation. "Good woman," said Prince Ahmed, "you are not so far from assistance as you may suppose; you have only therefore to rise, and suffer one of my people to take you behind him." The enchantress made several pretended efforts to rise, complaining that her illness prevented her. Two of the attendants then dismounted, and placed her behind another of the prince's escort. While they were remounting their horses, Prince Ahmed turned back, and preceded them to the iron door, which was opened by one of the attendants. He entered, and when he had reached the court of Pari-Banou's palace, without dismounting, he sent one of the horsemen to say, that he wished to speak to her. The fairy made the greater haste, as she could not conceive the motive that had induced the prince to return so suddenly. Without giving her time to inquire the reason, "I entreat you, my princess," said Ahmed, pointing to the enchantress, " to have the same compassion on this poor woman that I have had. I found her in the state you see, and have promised her whatever assistance she may require." Pari-Banou, who had not removed her eyes from the pretended invalid, ordered two of her women to convey her into an apartment of the palace; and to attend her with as much care as they would her own person. During the time the two female attendants were executing the order, Pari-Banou approached Ahmed, and said, in a low voice, "I give you great praise, prince, for your compassion, and I experience pleasure in aiding your good intention: permit me, however, to tell you, that I am very much afraid this benevolent action will meet with a bad return. But do not let this afflict you; be assured that, whatever is intended, I will deliver you from all the snares which may be laid for you; go, therefore, and pursue your journey." He then took leave, and soon arrived, with his attendants, at the court of his father, who received him in his usual manner, endeavouring to hide the suspicions which the conversation of his favourites had excited in his breast.

In the meantime, the two females conducted the enchantress into a very beautiful apartment. When they had assisted her to bed, one of them left the room, and soon returned, with a basin of the finest porcelain in her hand, full of a certain liquor. She presented it to the enchantress, while the other female assisted her in sitting up. "Take this liquor," said the attendant; "it is water from the fountain of lions, and is a sovereign remedy for fevers of every kind." When she had again lain down, the two females covered her well over. "Remain as you are," said she who had brought this liquor, "and even sleep, if you feel disposed. We will now leave you, and hope to find you quite recovered when we return in about an hour."

They appeared at the time they had mentioned; when they found the enchantress risen, dressed, and sitting on a sofa, from which she got up, when she saw them enter: "Oh, admirable liquor!" she exclaimed; "it has produced its effect much sooner than you told me." The two females, who were of the fairy race, as well as their mistress, after having signified how much they rejoiced in her speedy cure, walked on before, and conducted her through many apartments, all more superb than that in which she had been, to the most magnificent and richly furnished saloon in the whole palace. Pari-Banou was in this saloon, seated on a throne of massive gold, enriched with diamonds of an extraordinary size. At the sight of so much magnificence, the enchantress was not only dazzled, but remained, after prostrating herself at the foot of the throne, motionless. Pari-Banou spared her the trouble of addressing her: "I am very happy, my good woman," said she, "in having been of service to you, and that I now find you in a condition to pursue your journey. I will not detain you, but, perhaps, you would have no objection to see my palace. Go with my women; they will accompany you, and show you everything worth your notice." The enchantress, still rapt in astonishment was conducted by the two fairies who before accompanied her. She saw, with astonishment, all the apartments, one after another, but what most surprised her, after having seen the whole palace, was the fairies' conversation respecting their mistress; that all this was but a small part of her grandeur and power; and that, in different parts of her dominions, she had other palaces, more than they could tell, all of different architecture, and not less superb and magnificent. They led her to the iron door, through which Prince Ahmed had brought her; they opened it, and having wished her a good journey, she thanked them, and took her leave.

After advancing a few steps, the enchantress turned round to observe the door, that she might again know it; but it was invisible to her. She now went back to the sultan, well satisfied, except as to this one circumstance, with the success of her plan. When she reached the city, she was introduced by the same secret door as before into the palace. The sultan ordered her into his presence; when, observing that her countenance was rather gloomy, he thought she had not succeeded, and immediately said, "I judge, from your looks, that your journey has not been successful; and that you can give me no information concerning the business intrusted to your care." "Sir," replied the enchantress, "the gloom on my countenance arises not from the want of success, for I trust your majesty will see reason to be well satisfied. I will now explain the cause, because my relation, if you have the patience to hear it, will sufficiently inform you." The enchantress then related to the sultan of India, how she had obtained admission into the fairy's palace, and concluded with describing the majesty and splendid appearance of Pari-Banou seated on a throne, thickly studded with precious stones, the value of which surpassed all the riches of the kingdom of India. Having finished this account of her success, she proceeded, " What does your majesty think of the fairy's unheard-of riches? Perhaps you will say that you rejoice at the high fortune to which Prince Ahmed is arrived, by thus partaking of them. With respect to myself, sir, I entreat your majesty to pardon me, if I presume to be of a different opinion; and to confess, that I am greatly alarmed, when I think of the misfortunes that you may in consequence experience. This was the cause of the uneasiness your majesty remarked in my countenance. I am persuaded that Prince Ahmed is, naturally, of too good a disposition to undertake anything hostile to your majesty's welfare; but who can be sure that the fairy will not, through the influence she has acquired over the mind of her husband, inspire him with the horrid wish of supplanting you, and seizing the crown." However satisfied the sultan of India was of the excellence of Prince Ahmed's disposition, he could not help being moved by the speech of the

enchantress. "I am obliged to you," he said, "for your salutary counsel. I am aware of its importance, and consider it necessary to advise with others on the subject." At the moment when the arrival of the enchantress was announced to the sultan, he was conversing with the same ministers who had already excited those suspicions in his breast against Prince Ahmed ; to them he now returned, taking the enchantress with him. After he had partly informed them of what he had learnt, and communicated to them his reason for fearing the fairy might alter the disposition of the prince, he asked them by what means they thought he could prevent so great an evil. One of the favourites then spoke in the name of the rest. "Sir," said he, "to counteract this evil, as your majesty knows the person who may become the author of it, and he is now in your court, you ought without any hesitation to arrest him, and closely imprison him for the rest of his life." The enchantress, who thought this counsel too violent, requested the sultan's permission to speak ; and when she had obtained it, "I am persuaded, sir," said she, "that a zealous interest in your majesty's welfare induces your ministers to propose to you the imprisonment of Prince Ahmed ; but I trust they will agree with me, in thinking it necessary, when they arrest the prince to arrest also all those who accompany him. But his attendants are all genii:—Do you think it will be an easy matter to surprise them, and will they not immediately inform the fairy of the insult you have offered to her husband ; for which she would take severe revenge. If your majesty has any confidence in my advice, you will induce Prince Ahmed, to procure you certain advantages, through the intervention of his fairy, under pretence of deriving considerable benefit from them. For instance, every time your majesty wishes to take the field, you are obliged to be at a prodigious expense, not only for pavilions and tents for yourself and your army, but even for camels, mules, and other beasts of burthen, to carry this apparatus ; now, could not you prevail on him, through the great influence he has over the fairy, to procure a pavilion for you, that might be carried in the hand, and yet sufficiently capacious to shelter your whole army ? If the prince should procure you this, there are many other requests of a similar nature, which you can make, till at length he must sink under either the difficulty or impossibility of satisfying them. By this means shame will prevent his appearing here any more, and he will be compelled to pass the remainder of his life with the fairy." When the enchantress had ceased speaking, the sultan asked the favourites, if they had anything better to propose ; observing that they remained silent, he determined to follow her advice, as it seemed to be the most rational.

The next day, when Prince Ahmed presented himself before the sultan, who was conversing with his favourites, and had seated himself by his side, at length, the sultan said, "When, my son, you first appeared and relieved me from the grief in which your long absence had plunged me, you made a mystery of the place you had chosen for your retreat ; I did not desire to penetrate into your secret, when I found that you did not wish it. I now know in what this happiness consists ; I rejoice in it with you and approve of the steps you have taken, in marrying a fairy so worthy of being beloved, so rich, and so potent, as I have been credibly informed. In the high rank to which you are elevated, I ask you, not merely to continue upon the good terms with me that you have hitherto preserved, but that you will employ your influence with the fairy, to obtain her assistance whenever I may have occasion for it ; and I shall immediately put your influence with her to the test. You are not ignorant of the vast inconvenience, to which my generals, and subaltern officers, as well as myself, are put, from being obliged every time we take the field during war, to provide pavilions and tents, as well as camels and other beast of burthen to carry them from place to place. If you consider the pleasure you can afford me, I am sure you will not object to request the fairy to give you a pavilion that may be held in the hand, and yet sufficiently large to cover my whole army. The difficulty of the thing will not occasion you a refusal, for all the world knows that fairies can perform wonders."

Prince Ahmed was totally unprepared for this request, which appeared to him very difficult, not to say impossible for, although he was not ignorant of the power of genii and fairies, he doubted, nevertheless, whether they were able to furnish such a pavilion as he demanded. He was, therefore, greatly embarrassed respecting the answer he should make. "Sir," replied he, "if I have made a mystery to your majesty of what has happened to me, it arose from my not supposing it a matter of sufficient importance for your notice. I am ignorant how this mystery has been revealed, but I cannot deny the fact, as you have represented it. I am the husband of the fairy you have mentioned, but of the influence which your majesty supposes I may have over her, I am entirely ignorant. Although so averse from my inclination, I will, notwithstanding, comply with your majesty's wishes, in making the demand to my wife ; but I cannot promise you that I shall obtain it." As soon as he arrived at home, the fairy, before whom he had always presented himself with an open countenance, inquired the cause of the change she observed, when, instead of answering her question, he asked after her health, and with an air that evidently showed he wished to evade it, she replied "I will satisfy your inquiries, when you have answered mine." The prince, for a long time endeavoured to convince her that nothing bad happened ; but the more he protested, the more she urged an explanation ; "I cannot," said she, "see you in this state, without desiring to know the cause of your anxiety." Prince Ahmed could no longer resist the fairy's solicitude : "Madam," he replied, "you well know the care I have taken, with your approbation, to conceal from my father my happiness in seeing and loving you, in deserving your good opinion and affection, and in the interchange of our mutual faith. He has, however, by what means I am ignorant, been informed of it." Pari-Banou interrupted the prince ; "I will tell you," said she. "Do you recollect what I said to you respecting the woman who excited your compassion ? she has informed the sultan of what you had concealed from him. I told you, she was no more ill than we were. In fact, after the two females, to whose care I recommended her, had persuaded her to take a draught of a certain water, which is infallible in every species of fever, though she had not the least occasion for it, she pretended that this water had cured her. But proceed, and let us see what the sultan has imposed on you." "You must have observed," resumed Prince Ahmed, "that I have till now been satisfied with your affection, and have never requested any other favour. I am not ignorant of your power ; but I considered it a duty to avoid putting it to the proof. Consider then, I entreat you, that it is not I, but the sultan my father, who makes a request which appears to me very indiscreet:—it is, that you would furnish him with a pavilion capable of sheltering from the weather, when he takes the field, himself, his court, and all his army, and which may nevertheless be held in the hand." "Prince," replied Pari-Banou, with a smile, "I am sorry that such a trifle should have caused you the uneasiness and embarrassment you have apparently suffered. Calm then, your mind ; be assured, that, so far from your being importunate, I shall always find the utmost pleasure in granting, through my affection for you, everything

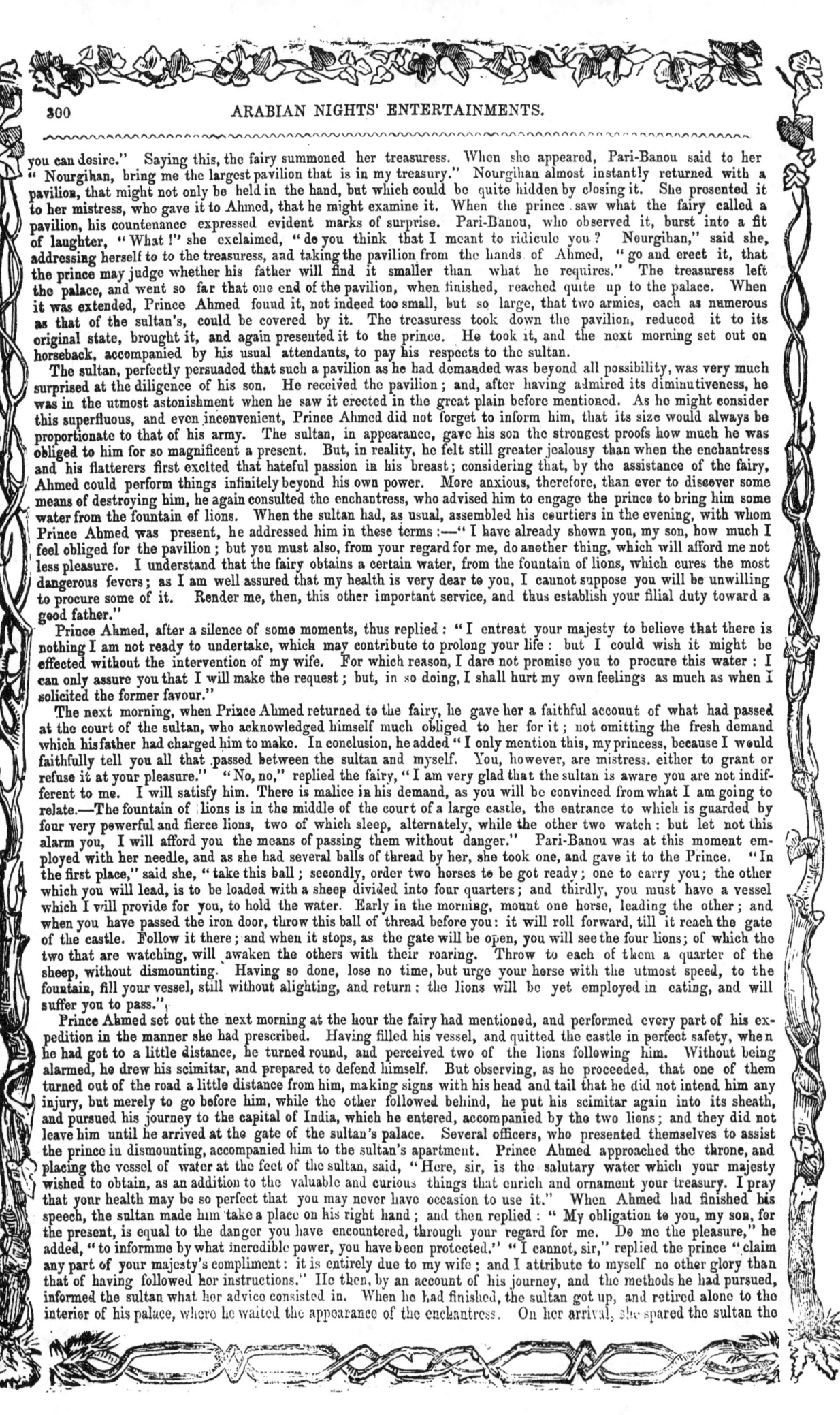

you can desire." Saying this, the fairy summoned her treasuress. When she appeared, Pari-Banou said to her " Nourgihan, bring me the largest pavilion that is in my treasury." Nourgihan almost instantly returned with a pavilion, that might not only be held in the hand, but which could be quite hidden by closing it. She presented it to her mistress, who gave it to Ahmed, that he might examine it. When the prince saw what the fairy called a pavilion, his countenance expressed evident marks of surprise. Pari-Banou, who observed it, burst into a fit of laughter, " What !" she exclaimed, " do you think that I meant to ridicule you ? Nourgihan," said she, addressing herself to to the treasuress, and taking the pavilion from the hands of Ahmed, " go and erect it, that the prince may judge whether his father will find it smaller than what he requires." The treasuress left the palace, and went so far that one end of the pavilion, when finished, reached quite up to the palace. When it was extended, Prince Ahmed found it, not indeed too small, but so large, that two armies, each as numerous as that of the sultan's, could be covered by it. The treasuress took down the pavilion, reduced it to its original state, brought it, and again presented it to the prince. He took it, and the next morning set out on horseback, accompanied by his usual attendants, to pay his respects to the sultan.

The sultan, perfectly persuaded that such a pavilion as he had demanded was beyond all possibility, was very much surprised at the diligence of his son. He received the pavilion ; and, after having admired its diminutiveness, he was in the utmost astonishment when he saw it erected in the great plain before mentioned. As he might consider this superfluous, and even inconvenient, Prince Ahmed did not forget to inform him, that its size would always be proportionate to that of his army. The sultan, in appearance, gave his son the strongest proofs how much he was obliged to him for so magnificent a present. But, in reality, he felt still greater jealousy than when the enchantress and his flatterers first excited that hateful passion in his breast ; considering that, by the assistance of the fairy, Ahmed could perform things infinitely beyond his own power. More anxious, therefore, than ever to discover some means of destroying him, he again consulted the enchantress, who advised him to engage the prince to bring him some water from the fountain of lions. When the sultan had, as usual, assembled his courtiers in the evening, with whom Prince Ahmed was present, he addressed him in these terms :—" I have already shown you, my son, how much I feel obliged for the pavilion ; but you must also, from your regard for me, do another thing, which will afford me not less pleasure. I understand that the fairy obtains a certain water, from the fountain of lions, which cures the most dangerous fevers ; as I am well assured that my health is very dear to you, I cannot suppose you will be unwilling to procure some of it. Render me, then, this other important service, and thus establish your filial duty toward a good father."

Prince Ahmed, after a silence of some moments, thus replied : " I entreat your majesty to believe that there is nothing I am not ready to undertake, which may contribute to prolong your life : but I could wish it might be effected without the intervention of my wife. For which reason, I dare not promise you to procure this water : I can only assure you that I will make the request ; but, in so doing, I shall hurt my own feelings as much as when I solicited the former favour."

The next morning, when Prince Ahmed returned to the fairy, he gave her a faithful account of what had passed at the court of the sultan, who acknowledged himself much obliged to her for it ; not omitting the fresh demand which his father had charged him to make. In conclusion, he added " I only mention this, my princess, because I would faithfully tell you all that passed between the sultan and myself. You, however, are mistress, either to grant or refuse it at your pleasure." " No, no," replied the fairy, " I am very glad that the sultan is aware you are not indifferent to me. I will satisfy him. There is malice in his demand, as you will be convinced from what I am going to relate.—The fountain of lions is in the middle of the court of a large castle, the entrance to which is guarded by four very powerful and fierce lions, two of which sleep, alternately, while the other two watch : but let not this alarm you, I will afford you the means of passing them without danger." Pari-Banou was at this moment employed with her needle, and as she had several balls of thread by her, she took one, and gave it to the Prince. " In the first place," said she, " take this ball ; secondly, order two horses to be got ready ; one to carry you ; the other which you will lead, is to be loaded with a sheep divided into four quarters ; and thirdly, you must have a vessel which I will provide for you, to hold the water. Early in the morning, mount one horse, leading the other ; and when you have passed the iron door, throw this ball of thread before you : it will roll forward, till it reach the gate of the castle. Follow it there ; and when it stops, as the gate will be open, you will see the four lions ; of which the two that are watching, will awaken the others with their roaring. Throw to each of them a quarter of the sheep, without dismounting. Having so done, lose no time, but urge your horse with the utmost speed, to the fountain, fill your vessel, still without alighting, and return : the lions will be yet employed in eating, and will suffer you to pass."

Prince Ahmed set out the next morning at the hour the fairy had mentioned, and performed every part of his expedition in the manner she had prescribed. Having filled his vessel, and quitted the castle in perfect safety, when he had got to a little distance, he turned round, and perceived two of the lions following him. Without being alarmed, he drew his scimitar, and prepared to defend himself. But observing, as he proceeded, that one of them turned out of the road a little distance from him, making signs with his head and tail that he did not intend him any injury, but merely to go before him, while the other followed behind, he put his scimitar again into its sheath, and pursued his journey to the capital of India, which he entered, accompanied by the two lions ; and they did not leave him until he arrived at the gate of the sultan's palace. Several officers, who presented themselves to assist the prince in dismounting, accompanied him to the sultan's apartment. Prince Ahmed approached the throne, and placing the vessel of water at the feet of the sultan, said, " Here, sir, is the salutary water which your majesty wished to obtain, as an addition to the valuable and curious things that enrich and ornament your treasury. I pray that your health may be so perfect that you may never have occasion to use it." When Ahmed had finished his speech, the sultan made him take a place on his right hand ; and then replied : " My obligation to you, my son, for the present, is equal to the danger you have encountered, through your regard for me. Do me the pleasure," he added, " to inform me by what incredible power, you have been protected." " I cannot, sir," replied the prince " claim any part of your majesty's compliment : it is entirely due to my wife ; and I attribute to myself no other glory than that of having followed her instructions." He then, by an account of his journey, and the methods he had pursued, informed the sultan what her advice consisted in. When he had finished, the sultan got up, and retired alone to the interior of his palace, where he waited the appearance of the enchantress. On her arrival, she spared the sultan the trouble of mentioning the prince, or the success of his expedition; for she was already informed, by the report circulated in the city; but she pretended she had discovered an infallible method of proceeding, of which she informed the sultan; and the next day in the assembly of his courtiers, the sultan declared it to Prince Ahmed, who was present, in these words: "I have now, my son, but one more petition to urge; after which, I will exact nothing further from your obedience; it is that you will procure for me a man, who is not more than a foot and a half high, with a beard thirty feet long, carrying a bar of iron on his shoulders that weighs five hundred pounds, which he uses as a quarter-staff, and who can speak." Prince Ahmed, who could not believe there existed such a man as his father demanded, was anxious to be excused; but the sultan persisted in his request, repeating that the fairy could perform the most incredible things.

The following day, when Prince Ahmed returned to Pari-Banou, and had acquainted her with the fresh demand of the sultan, which he regarded as an absolute impossibility, he added, "I cannot imagine in what part of the universe such a man is to be found. My father doubtless wishes to prove whether I have the simplicity to seek for a being of that description, or, if there be such a man in existence, it must be the sultan's intention to have me destroyed. For how can he suppose that I could seize so short a man, armed in the way he mentions?" "Do not, my prince, alarm yourself," replied the fairy, "there was danger in procuring the water from the fountain of lions, but there is none in finding the man he requires. Such a man, precisely, is my brother Schaibar, who is of so violent a disposition, that nothing can prevent him from giving sanguinary proofs of his resentment, whenever he is in the least displeased or offended. With this exception, he is always ready to oblige, in whatever may be required of him. He is exactly as the sultan has described, and he carries no other weapon than a bar of iron, that weighs five hundred pounds, without which he never stirs. I will bring him here, and you shall judge whether I have not spoken the truth. But, above all things, prepare yourself against being alarmed at his extraordinary figure, when he makes his appearance." "My queen," answered Ahmed, "do you not say that Schaibar is your brother?" The fairy then ordered a golden perfuming-pan, full of fire, to be brought under the vestibule of the palace, and also a box of the same metal, which was presented to her. She took out a perfume, and throwing it upon the fire, a thick smoke arose. A few moments after this ceremony, "My prince," said Pari-Banou, "there is my brother; do you not see him?" The prince looked, and perceived Schaibar, who was not more than a foot and a half high, and who gravely approached, with the iron bar of five hundred pounds weight upon his shoulder; his little pigs' eyes were buried in his head, which was of an enormous size, and covered with a pointed cap; added to all this, he had a projecting hump both before and behind. Schaibar, who, as he advanced, looked at Prince Ahmed with an eye that would have chilled his very soul, demanded of Pari-Banou who that man was. "Brother," she replied, "he is my husband; his name is Ahmed, and he is son to the sultan of India." At these words, Schaibar regarded Prince Ahmed with a gracious eye, which however, did not in the least lessen his fierce and haughty appearance. "Sister," said he, "is there any thing in which I can render him service? It is sufficient for me to know that he is your husband, to induce me to gratify him in anything he may wish." "The sultan his father," answered Pari-Banou, "is curious to see you; I beg you will have the goodness to let him be your conductor." "He has only to proceed," replied Schaibar. "I am ready." "It is too late, brother," returned Pari-Banou, "to undertake the journey to-day; defer it till to-morrow morning. In the mean time, as it is proper you should be informed of what has passed between the sultan of India and Prince Ahmed since our marriage, I will entertain you this evening with an account."

The next morning, Schaibar having been informed of what it was right he should not be ignorant, he commenced his journey early, accompanied by Prince Ahmed, who was to present him to the sultan. When they arrived, the porters fled on all sides, leaving the entrance quite free. The prince and Schaibar advanced without obstruction to the council hall, where the sultan was seated upon his throne, giving audience; and, the officers and attendants having abandoned their posts as soon as Schaibar made his appearance, they entered without the least hindrance. Schaibar, with his head erect, haughtily approached the throne, and thus addressed the sultan, "Thou hast demanded my presence, See, here I am!" The sultan, instead of answering, put his hand before his eyes, and turned away. Schaibar, enraged at this uncivil and offensive reception, after he had taken the trouble of coming, lifted up his bar of iron, exclaiming, "Wilt thou not speak then?" and letting it fall on his head, crushed him to the earth; and this he did before Prince Ahmed had the thought of soliciting his pardon. The prince had now the utmost difficulty to prevent him from destroying the grand vizier, who was near the sultan's right hand, and whose life he saved only by representing, that the counsel he had always given the sultan his father was equitable. "Where then are they," cried Schaibar, "who have given him such execrable advice?"—and saying this, he destroyed the other viziers who were on each side of the throne, all favourites and parasites of the sultan, and enemies of Prince Ahmed. Having completed this dreadful execution, Schaibar left the hall of audience; and when in the middle of the court, with the bar of iron on his shoulder, looking at the grand-vizier, who accompanied Prince Ahmed, "I know," said he, "there is a certain enchantress, a greater enemy to the prince, than those infamous favourites whom I have punished; let her be brought before me." The grand-vizier immediately had her conducted there; when Schaibar as he crushed her to atoms with his bar of iron, said, "Learn the consequence of giving pernicious advice, and pretending sickness.—This is not sufficient," added Schaibar: "I will destroy the whole city, if Prince Ahmed, my brother-in-law, is not instantly acknowledged as sultan of India." All who were present, and who heard the decree immediately made the air resound with—"*Long live the Sultan Ahmed!*" and in a short time the whole city echoed with the same acclamation.

THE STORY OF THE TWO SISTERS, WHO WERE JEALOUS OF THEIR YOUNGER SISTER.

HERE was a prince of Persia, named Khosrouschah, who found great pleasure in seeking adventures during the night; he often disguised himself, and accompanied by one of his attendants, perambulated the city, sometimes meeting with extraordinary occurrences.

A few days after the death of his father, who died at a very advanced age, leaving him sole heir of the kingdom of Persia, the new sultan Khosrouschah, as much from a motive of duty as from inclination, that he might personally inspect the transactions in his capital, left his palace one night, accompanied by his grand-vizier, disguised like himself. Passing through a street, where the common class of people only resided, he heard persons talking very loud; he approached the house whence the noise proceeded, and looking through a crevice of the door, perceived a light, and three sisters seated on a sofa, who were talking together after supper. By the discourse of the eldest, he soon learned that their wishes were the topic of conversation : "Since we are on the subject of wishes," said she, "mine is, that I may have the sultan's baker for a husband : I could then eat as much as I liked of that delicious bread, which is called the sultan's bread." "My wish," replied the second sister. "would be, to marry the head cook of the sultan's kitchen: I should then eat of excellent dishes ; and as I am well persuaded that the sultan's bread is commonly used in the palace, I should not want for that." The youngest sister, who was extremely handsome, spoke in her turn : "For my part," said she, "I do not confine my wishes to so low a standard; I take a higher flight; and, since we are about wishing, I should wish to be the wife of the sultan himself: I would give him a prince, whose hair should be gold on one side and silver on the other ; when he cried, the tears that fell from his eyes should be pearls; and when he smiled, his vermillion lips should appear like an opening rose-bud." The wishes of the three sisters and particularly the desire of the youngest, appeared to the sultan so singular, that he resolved to gratify them; and, without communicating his design, he charged the grand-vizier to take notice of the house, that he might fetch them on the following day, and conduct them before him.

The grand-vizer conducted them to the palace; and when he had presented them to the sultan, the latter said to them, "Tell me—Do you recollect the wishes you made yesterday evening. Attempt not to dissemble; I will know the truth." At these words of the sultan, the three sisters were in the utmost confusion; they cast down their eyes, and the blushes which overspread their checks added a lustre to their beauty, of the youngest in particular. As their modesty kept them silent, the sultan said, to encourage them, "Fear nothing; I will soon relieve you from your embarrassment. You," added he, "who wished to be my wife, shall be satisfied this very day, and you," addressing the eldest and the second sister, "shall also have your wishes gratified, by an union with my baker and with my head cook,." As soon as the sultan had declared his will, the youngest, setting her sisters the example, threw herself at the feet of the sultan. "Sir" said she, "my wish, since it is known to your majesty, was only spoken in mirth ; I am not worthy of the honour you intend me." The two elder sisters also wanted to excuse themselves; but the sultan interrupted them : "No, no," said he, "it must be so; the wish of each shall be accomplished." The nuptials were accordingly celebrated on the same day ; but with far different ceremonies.

The two elder sisters felt very forcibly the great disproportion that existed between their marriages and the elevation of their youngest sister. They had not yet had time to communicate to each other their sentiments of the preference which the sultan had given to their younger sister. But when they found an opportunity, some days after, of meeting at a public bath, "Well," said the eldest, "what think you of our younger sister?" "I confess," replied the other, "that I am astonished: I cannot conceive what attractions the sultan could see in her. Was it a sufficient reason for the sultan to prefer her to you, because she has rather a more youthful air than you have." "Sister," replied the eldest, "I should have nothing to say, if the sultan had selected you ; but that he should choose that dirty wench drives me to despair. I will, however, be revenged; and I entreat you to join with me, that we may act in concert, while I, on my part, promise to acquaint you with whatever my desire to humble her may suggest to me." After this malicious conspiracy, the two sisters saw each other often ; and, every time they met, their only conversation was on the measures they would adopt, to interrupt, and even destroy, the happiness of the sultana. They proposed several plans; but when deliberating on the execution of them, they found so great difficulties, that they dared not venture to attempt carrying them into effect. In the meantime, they occasionally visited her together and lavished on her every mark of friendship they could devise, to persuade her how delighted they were in having a sister raised to so high an elevation.

The period at length arrived, when the sultana was happily delivered of a prince, beautiful as the day ; but neither his beauty nor the delicacy of his form was capable of softening the obdurate hearts of the two sisters. They wrapped him up carelessly in some linen clothes, and putting him in a small basket, committed it to the current of a canal; they then produced a little dead dog, asserting that the sultana had been delivered of it. This unpleasant intelligence was announced to the sultan, who felt on the occasion a degree of indignation which might have proved fatal to the sultana, if his grand-vizier had not represented ro him, that he could not, without injustice, consider her as responsible for the caprices of Nature. The basket, in the meantime, in which the prince was exposed, was conveyed by the current beyond a wall that bounded the view from the apartment of the sultana. By chance the superintendant of the gardens of the sultan, was walking on the banks of the canal as he observed the basket floating, he called to a gardener, who was near, "Go quickly," said he, "and bring me that basket, that I may see what it contains." The gardener went immediately, and, with the spade he held in his hand, he dexterously drew the basket towards him, and took it out of the water. The superintendent was very much surprised at finding a child wrapped up in the basket, extremely beautiful. This officer had been married a considerable time ; but, though very desirous of progeny, Heaven had not yet granted his wishes. He discontinued his walk, desiring the gardener to follow him with the basket and child; and when he had reached his house, "My dear wife," said he, "we have no child, here is one that God sends us. Provide a nurse for him immediately, and take care of him as if he were my own son." His wife joyfully took the child, and felt great pleasure in the charge. The superintendent of the gardens did not choose to investigate whence the child came. "I plainly see," said he to himself, "that it is from the apartments of the sultana; but it is not my business to oppose what passes there."

The following year the sultana was delivered of another prince. Her unnatural sisters felt no more compassion for him than they had for his elder brother, but exposed him, in the same way, in a basket on the canal; and pretended that the sultana had produced a cat. Fortunately for the child, the superintendant of the gardens was near the canal at the time; he had him taken out and carried to his wife, charging her to attend to him with the same care as to the former. The sultan of Persia now felt still more indignant against the sultana than before; and his resentment would have burst forth, had not the remonstrances of the grand-vizier again appeased him.

The sultana at length lay-in a third time, not of a prince, but of a daughter; and the little innocent shared the same fate as the princes her brothers; for the two sisters had resolved not to desist till they had succeeded in their design, of reducing the sultana to the utmost humiliation. The princess was snatched from destruction by the compassionate superintendent, who had saved the princes her brothers, with whom she was nursed and educated. To this inhuman action, the two sisters, as before, added deceit and imposture: they showed a piece of wood, which they falsely affirmed to be a mole of which the sultana had been delivered. The sultan Khosrouschah could no longer contain himself, when he heard of this last extraordinary production "This vile woman," cried he, "will fill my palace with monsters. No, it must not be; she is a monster herself, and I will rid the world of her." He thus pronounced the decree for her death, and commanded the grand-vizier to see it executed. This minister, and the courtiers who were present, threw themselves at the feet of the sultan, to entreat him to revoke the sentence. "Sir," said he, "your majesty will allow me to represent to you, that the laws which condemn to death have been established only for the punishment of crimes. Your majesty may avoid seeing her, yet still suffer her to live. The affliction in which she will pass the remainder of her days, after having lost your favour, will be a sufficient atonement for the offence." "She shall live then," said he, "but I grant her life only on a condition, which will make her wish for death—let there be erected at the gate of the principal mosque, a wooden cage, with an open window. Let her be shut up in this prison, dressed in the coarsest habit; and command every Mussulman, who enters the mosque to say his prayer, to spit in her face as he passes. And that I may be obeyed, I command you, vizier, to appoint inspectors." It was accordingly executed, to the great satisfaction of the two jealous sisters. The cage being completed, the sultana was confined in it in the way the sultan had commanded, and ignominiously exposed to the derision of the populace.

The two princes and the princess were brought up with great affection, by the superintendant of the gardens and his wife, from the extreme beauty of the princess, who every day unfolded new charms; from their docility, and from their inclination, so much above the trivial pursuits of children in general. In order to distinguish the two princes according to their age, they named the first Bahman, and the second Perviz. When the princes were of a proper age, the superintendent of the gardens provided them with a master to teach them to read and write; and the princess showed so great a desire to learn also, that the superintendent gave her the same master. Her lively genius soon excited in her a desire to excel, and she shortly equalled her brothers. From that time they had the same preceptors in their studies, in which they made so rapid a progress, that their masters were astonished. During the hours of recreation, the princess learnt to sing, and play on different instruments. When the princes began to ride, she would not suffer them to have even this advantage over her; she practised with them, and thereby acquired the art of horsemanship, of archery, of throwing the javelin. The superintendent had been hitherto contented with his residence in the palace-garden; but he now purchased a house at a little distance from the city, which had much ground annexed, consisting of fields, meadows, and woods. As the building did not appear sufficiently handsome he had pulled it down, and spared no expense to render it the most magnificent in the neighbourhood. While it was furnishing, he had the garden laid out according to a plan of his own. He added to it a park of vast extent, which he had enclosed with substantial walls, and furnished with all kinds of animals for the chase. The superintendent then went to throw himself at the feet of the sultan; and after representing to him the length of time he had been in his service, and the infirmities of age he experienced, he entreated permission to resign his office and retire. The sultan granted him this favour, asking him what he could do to recompense him. "Sir," replied the superintendent, "I am so overwhelmed with the favours I have received from your majesty, that I can now only desire to preserve your good opinion." He then took leave, and removed to his country-house, with the princes Bahman and Perviz, and the Princess Parizade; his wife having been dead some years. He had not resided here longer than five or six months, when he was so suddenly surprised by death, that he had not time to say a word to them respecting their birth; which he had resolved to mention, as an inducement for them to maintain their rank, in conformity with the education he had given them, and the natural inclinations they evinced. The Princess Bahman and Perviz, and their sister Parizade, regretted him as a parent, and performed all the funeral duties which filial affection and gratitude demanded. Satisfied with the possessions he had bequeathed them, they continued to live together in the same union which they had hitherto preserved.

One day, while the two brothers were hunting, Parizade having remained at home, a very aged Mussulman devotee presented herself at the gate, and entreated admittance, to repeat her prayer. The princess gave permission, and she was ushered into the oratory. The devotee having repeated her prayer, was then introduced to the princess, who received her in a large saloon. "My good mother," said the princess, as she entered, "come here and sit by me; I am very happy in the opportunity chance afford me of profiting for some minutes by the good example and conversation of a person like you, who have wisely devoted yourself to God." Led on from one subject to another, the princess at length asked her opinion of the house. "Madam," replied the devotee, "I must have a very bad taste to find any fault in it: The situation is agreeable, and the garden most delightful. With your permission, however, I will take the liberty to tell you, that the house would be incomparable, if three things, which I consider wanting, where added to it." "My good woman," said Parizade, "what are they? I entreat you to inform me; I will procure them, if possible." "Madam," returned the devotee, "the first of these three things is the speaking bird, called Bulbulhezars. The second is the singing tree; the leaves of which are so many mouths, forming an harmonious concert of different voices, that never cease.

The third and last is the golden water, one drop of which let fall into the basin made for the purpose, in any part of a garden immediately fills it, and then rises in the middle as a kind of fountain, which never ceases springing-up and falling into the basin. "Ah, my good mother," cried the princess, "how much am I obliged to you for having told me of these curiosities! I had never heard that the world contained anything so admirable!" "I should be unworthy, madam, of the hospitality you have so bounteously shown me, if I refused to gratify your curiosity respecting what you are so desirous of being informed. Allow me, then, the honour to tell you, that the three things I have mentioned, are to be found, in the same place, on the confines of this kingdom, next India. The road leading to it passes by your house: whoever you send to procure them has only to follow this road for twenty days, and on the twentieth let him ask, where the speaking bird, the singing tree and the golden water are, and the first person he meets will satisfy him." As she concluded these words, she rose; and having made her obeisance, she went out, and continued her journey.

Parizade was absorbed in reflections, when her brothers returned from the chase: they entered the saloon, and instead of finding her cheerful as usual, they were surprised to see her meditating, without even arising her head. Prince first spoke: "Sister," said he, "where is the gaiety that has been hitherto your inseparable companion; has any Bahman misfortune be fallen you? has anything afflicted you?" After some time, the princess raised her head, and looking at her brothers, said it was nothing, and again cast down her eyes. "Sister," returned Prince Bahman, "you do not tell us the truth'. It is not possible that, in the short time we have been absent from you, so great a change can have happened without a cause. Do not, then, conceal from us what occasions this behaviour; unless you wish us to believe, that you renounce entirely the constant friendship which has, till now, subsisted between us." The princess, aroused at the idea of quarrelling with her brothers, would not let them remain in this opinion: "When I told you," said she, "that what gave me uneasiness was of no consideration, I meant only with respect to you, but since you so seriously urge me to explain it, I will tell you what it is. You thought, as I did, that this house was complete. I have, however, been informed to-day, that they are three things wanting, which would place it beyond comparison with every other country-house in the world: these are, the speaking bird, the singing tree, and the golden water." After, having stated to them what were their several excellences, the place where they were to be obtained, and the means, by which she had received her information, she added: "You may, perhaps, consider these things as of little consequence, and that our house will always be esteemed very handsome, notwithstanding this deficiency." "Nothing, sister," replied Prince Bahman, "that affects you, can be indifferent to us. It is sufficient that you are anxious to posses, the rarities you mention, to ensure our assistance. I will, then, take this charge: tell me only the road I am to go, and the place where they are to be found, and I will not defer my journey longer than tomorrow."

Early the next morning, Prince Bahman, having received full instructions from the princess, mounted his horse; and Prince Perviz and his sister embraced him and wished him a prosperous journey. At the instant of their saying farewell, the princess started an objection: "Until this moment, my brother," she exclaimed, "I did not recollect the various accidents to which people are exposed in their travels.—Who knows whether I shall ever see you again? Dismount, therefore, I conjure you, and do not undertake this journey." "Sister," replied Prince Bahman, "my resolution is taken. The accidents you mention, happen only to the unfortunate. It is true, I may be of the number; but I may also be a successful adventurer. As, however, events of this nature are uncertain, and I may fail in my enterprise, all that I can now do, is to give you this knife." Prince Bahman then produced a knife and tendered it, in its case, to the princess: "Take this," added he, "and occasionally give yourself the trouble to draw it out of the case: as you find it clean and bright, as it is now, rely on my being alive; but should you ever see drops of blood fall from it, you may be assured I am no longer living." This was the only concession the princess could obtain from Prince Bahman. He proceeded straight forward, without deviating either to the right or to the left, and, continuing to traverse the kingdom of Persia, on the twentieth day of his journey he perceived a most hideous old man: he was seated at the foot of a tree, at some distance from a cottage. His eye-brows were like snow—as also his hair, his moustaches, and his head. The nails of his hands and feet were of an excessive length, and he wore on his head a kind of flat hat, very large serving as an umbrella. The remainder of his dress was comprised in a single mat wrapped entirely round him. This old man was a dervise, who had long retired from the world, and had neglected his person to attach himself solely to the service of God.

Prince Bahman had been anxiously looking for some person who might be able to describe the place he sought, when, therefore, he came near the dervise, he dismounted, and advancing, while he held the horse by the bridle thus addressed him: "May God, my good father, prolong your days, and grant you the accomplishment of your wishes!" The dervise replied to the prince's salutation, but in a manner quite unintelligible. As the prince observed that the difficulty arose from the moustache of the dervise, and not wishing to proceed without obtaining the information he desired, he took a pair of scissors, with which he was provided, and after fastening his horse to a tree, said to him, "My good dervise, I have occasion for your advice, but your moustache prevent me from understanding what you say, I entreat you will suffer me to cut both these and your eyebrows, which disfigure you." The dervise made no opposition to the prince's design, but suffered him to act as he wished. As Bahman saw, when he had finished, that the dervise had a fresh and clear skin, and appeared less aged than he in reality was, he said to him, "If I had a mirror, my good dervise, I would let you see how much younger you appear: you are now a man; but no person could before distinguish what you were." "Whoever you are, sir," replied the dervise, with a smile, "I am obliged to you for the good office you have rendered me; and am ready to show my gratitude." "My good dervise," answered the prince, "I come from a good distance, and am in search of the speaking bird, the singing tree, and the golden water; I know they are somewhere in this neighbourhood, but am ignorant of the precise spot."

The dervise at last broke silence:—"Sir," said he, "the road you inquire for is well known to me; but the friendship I instantly conceived for you, makes me hesitate to grant the satisfaction you require." "What motive can hinder you?" asked the prince; "what difficulty can you have in giving it me?" "I will tell you," answered the dervise:—"the danger to which you will be exposed, is infinitely greater than you can imagine. Many other persons, besides you, and some who did not seem to possess less courage or perseverance, have applied to me for the

same information, but not one individual has returned. If, therefore you have the least regard for your life, and will follow my advice, you will not proceed a step further."

Prince Bahman, however, persisted in his resolution. "I am willing to believe," said he, "that your advice is sincere; and I feel myself obliged to you for this proof of your friendship: but however great the danger of which you speak, I am determined to proceed." "But those who will attack," replied the dervise "are not to be seen: How, then, can you defend yourself from invisible beings?" "All this is of no consequence," cried the prince; "whatever you may say to me, will not persuade me to act contrary to my duty. Since you know the road I am seeking, I once more entreat you to inform me of it." When the dervise found that he could make no impression on the mind of Prince Bahman, he put his hand into a bag that lay by the side of him, and taking out a bowl, which he presented to the prince, "Since you will not profit by my advice," said he, "take this bowl, and when you have remounted your horse, throw it before you, and follow till it lead you to the foot of a mountain. When there, dismount: and you may leave your horse with his bridle over his neck, as he will remain in that spot until you return. As you ascend the mountain, you will see, on each side of you, many large black stones; and will hear a confusion of voices abusing you, and saying a thousand things, to discourage you, and prevent your reaching the top: be careful not to be alarmed: and, above all things, be sure not to look behind you, for at that moment you would be changed into a black stone, such as those about you, and which are, in fact, so many men, who have failed in the enterprize. If you overcome this danger, and attain the top of the mountain, you will there find a cage, in which the speaking bird is confined; ask it where the singing tree and golden water are, and it will inform you." "The advice," replied Prince Bahman, after receiving the bowl, "I cannot follow: but I will endeavour to profit by your information; and I hope you will soon see me return, to thank you still more gratefully." The prince then mounted his horse, took leave of the dervise, by making a profound reverence with his head, and threw the bowl before him.

The bowl continued to roll on with the same celerity with which Prince Bahman first threw it forward: he followed it: and when it reached the foot of the mountain it stopped, and the prince dismounted, and left his horse unsecured. Having cast his eyes round the mountain, and observed the black stones, he began to ascend. He had not proceeded more than four or five steps, before he heard the voices which the dervise had mentioned. Some said, "What is the fool about? Where is he going? What does he want? Don't let him pass?" others cried, "Stop him! seize him! kill him!" while a third party, with voices like thunder, exclaimed, "O the thief! the assassin! the murderer!" Some, on the contrary, called out, in a tone of raillery, "No, no, do not hurt him; let the pretty fellow pass; he is the very person for whom the cage and bird are preserved." Notwithstanding these important exclamations, Prince Bahman continued to ascend with great fortitude and perseverance, encouraging himself to proceed: but the voices increased; and the noise became at length so great, and appeared so near, that he was very much alarmed: his feet and legs trembled, he felt himself faint; when, forgetting the advice of the dervise, he turned round, to save himself by retreating, and was instantly changed into a black stone. His horse also underwent a similar transformation.

Since Prince Bahman's departure, Parizade had constantly worn the knife at her girdle, to inform herself whether her brother was alive or dead; nor had she ever omitted to consult it several times during the day. She had thus the consolation of learning that he was in perfect health. At length, on the fatal day that Prince Bahman was changed into a black stone, as the prince and princess were, as usual, conversing about him in the evening, "Pray, sister," said Perviz, "let us consult the knife." She drew it out; and looking at its blade, they saw blood run from the point. Struck with horror, the princess threw down the knife: "Alas! my dearest brother," she exclaimed, "I have then destroyed you!—never shall I see you more!" Prince Perviz's affliction was not less; but without losing time in useless complaints, as he understood from his sister that she still ardently wished to obtain the speaking bird, singing tree, and golden water, he interrupted her: "All our sorrow is unavailing; neither our tears nor our affliction will bring Prince Bahman to life. Why should we now doubt the words of the devotee, after having hitherto supposed them just and true? We ought rather to suppose that the death of my brother arose from his own fault, or from some accident. Let not his death, therefore, prevent our pursuing the inquiry. I at first offered to undertake the journey: and as his example and fate have not in the least altered my opinion, I will set out to-morrow morning." The princess in vain did all she could to dissuade Perviz, lest she might have to lament the loss of two brothers. But, before he set out, that she might be informed of his safety, he gave her a chaplet consisting of a hundred pearls, saying, as he presented it to her, "Tell over this chaplet during my absence; and if it should happen that the pearls are fastened, as if glued together, it will be a sign that I have experienced the same fate as my brother."

On the twentieth day after Prince Perviz had commenced his journey, he met in the same spot the dervise whom Prince Bahman had encountered. Having received his advice he proceeded on the adventure, but was as unsuccessful as his brother, for both he and his horse were changed into black stones.

From the moment Prince Perviz had left her, Princess Parizade frequently consulted the chaplet. Every evening, when she retired to rest, she put it round her neck; and examined it when she first awoke in the morning. At length the fatal hour arrived, when Prince Perviz experienced the same fate as his brother Prince Bahman; at which time, as the princess began to count the pearls, she suddenly perceived that they no longer yielded to her efforts, but were stationary, and she then became too well assured of the death of her brother. As she had already formed her resolution, if this unfortunate event should happen, she did not waste time in external marks of sorrow; but the next morning, disguised in male attire, and well equipped, she set out, and pursued the same road as the two princes had taken. The princess, who had been much accustomed to ride, supported the fatigue of the journey very well; and, travelling exactly at the same rate as her brothers, she also met the dervise on the twentieth day of her journey. Approaching him, she alighted; and holding her horse by the bridle, seated herself by his side. The dervise endeavoured to deter her from the enterprise: but as he found she was resolutely fixed on the attempt, he took out a bowl, and presented it to her, with the same directions as he had given to her brothers.

Princess Parizide, having taken leave of the dervise, mounted her horse, and throwing the bowl before her, followed till it reached the foot of the mountain, where it stopped. The princess then alighted, and having stuffed her ears with cotton, she began to ascend with a steady pace and undaunted mind. She heard the voices, but found that the cotton was of considerable service to her. The farther she advanced, the more clamorous the voices became.

She heard many injurious expressions and satirical remarks, in allusion to her sex, with a contemptuous smile: "Neither your reproaches nor your rallery," said she to herself, "offend me: I shall only regard it with ridicule; nor will you prevent me from pursuing my way." At length she perceived the cage and the bird, which joined itself with the other voices in endeavouring to intimidate her, calling out, in a thundering tone, although so diminutive an animal, "Go back, fool." Still more animated by this sight, the princess doubled her speed: and when she had gained the top of the mountain, she ran directly to the cage, and laying her hand upon it, exclaimed, "I have you now, in spite of yourself, and you shall not escape me!" As the princess took the cotton from her ears. "Brave lady," said the bird, "do not suppose that I wish you any harm, from what I have done in conjunction with those who have made so many efforts to preserve my liberty. I know who you are, better than you do yourself: but the day will come, when I shall render you a service, for which, I trust, you will feel obliged to me. That I may give you some marks of my sincerity, tell me what you wish, and I will obey you." The princess, delighted with the acquisition she had made, replied: "I am highly pleased, bird, that you have anticipated my wishes. In the first place, I have understood that there is near here some yellow water, possessed of wonderful properties: inform me, therefore, where it is." The bird pointed out the spot, which was not far distant; there the princess went, and filled a large silver vessel. Returning to the bird, "This is not enough," said she; "I am in search also of the singing tree." "Turn round," replied the bird, "and you will see a wood, where you will find this tree." The wood was not far off; thither the princess went: when the harmonious concert led her directly to the tree she sought, but it was both large and lofty. She went back, and said to the bird, "I have discovered the singing tree, but I cannot take it up by the roots." "Neither is it necessary," answered the bird; "you need only break off the smallest branch, and carry it with you, to plant in your garden; where it will soon take root, and become, in a short time, as beautiful and fine a tree as that you have just seen." The princess having obtained the three things which the devotee had caused her so ardently to desire, again addressed herself to the bird: "All that you have yet done for me, bird, is insufficient. You have been the cause of the death of my two brothers, who are among the black stones which I observed as I ascended: I must take them back with me." The bird seemed very unwilling to gratify the princess on this point; "Bird," said the princess, "I wish you to remember that you are my slave, and that your life is at my disposal!" "I cannot deny it," answered the bird; "and, although what you require of me is a matter of the greatest difficulty, I will satisfy you. Cast your eyes round you, and look if you see a pitcher." "I do," said the princess. "Take it, then," resumed the bird, "and sprinkle, as you go down, a little of the water it contains upon each of the black stones; and by this means you will discover your two brothers." Princess Parizade took the pitcher with the acquisitions she had made, and began to descend, throwing a little water from the pitcher upon every stone she met with, each of which resumed its proper form. Recognizing Prince Bahman and his brother, as they also did her, "My dear brothers," cried she, "what have you been doing here?" When they replied, they had just awakened from a deep sleep—"Yes," she added, "but, without me, your sleep would perhaps have continued to the day of judgment. But let us not remain any longer in a place where we have nothing to detain us: let us remount our horses, and return to that part of the world whence we came." The princess then set the example, by taking her horse. Prince Bahman, who wished to assist her, requested her permission to carry the cage. "This bird, my brother," replied the princess, "is my slave, and I wish to carry it myself; but you may, if you please, take charge of the branch of the singing tree. You, brother, shall have the care of the vessel with the golden water in it, if it will not be troublesome to you." Prince Perviz took the care of it with great pleasure.

She immediately began to move forward; while her brothers, and all the rest, followed without distinction. As the company pursued their journey, every day produced a diminution in its numbers; for the individuals who composed it, having travelled from distant countries, continued to separate, on approaching the roads by which they had come; while Parizade and her brothers proceeded on their journey until they reached their own residence.

The princess having placed the cage in the garden, opposite the saloon, as soon as the bird began his song, the nightingales, larks, linnets, goldfinches, and a variety of other birds of the country, came to accompany it with their notes. With respect to the branch, she had it planted in her presence, at a little distance from the house: it immediately took root, and soon grew to a large tree, the leaves of which produced the same harmony and concert as the tree from which she had broken it. She had ordered a large basin of beautiful marble to be formed in the midst of the flower-garden; and, when it was finished, she poured into it all the golden water the vessel contained: instantly it began to increase and bubble up; and when it had filled the basin, it rose in the centre like a large fountain, twenty feet in height, and returned again into the basin without overflowing.

After a few days, Prince Bahman and Prince Perviz, having recovered from the fatigues of their journey, again began to pursue their former mode of life; and, as the chase was their usual diversion, they mounted their horses, and went to hunt at the distance of two or three leagues from the house. While they were engaged in their sport, the Sultan of Persia accidentally came to hunt in the same place they had chosen. As soon, therefore, as they perceived that he was about to arrive, they determined to retire, in order to avoid him. But they took the very route by which he approached; thus meeting him, and in a part of the road which was so narrow, they could neither turn out on one side, nor retreat without being seen. Their surprise was so sudden, that they had only time to dismount, and prostrate themselves to the earth, without even raising their heads to look at him. But the sultan, who saw that they were well mounted, stopped and ordered them to rise. The princes got up, and remained standing with an air unrestrained and easy, yet modest and respectful. The sultan earnestly observed them for some time, and, after admiring their open countenance and good manners, he inquired their names, and where they lived. "We are, sir," replied Prince Bahman, "the sons of the late superintendant of your majesty's gardens." The Sultan Khosrouschah entered into conversation with them, and was much pleased with their remarks, in short, he felt so strong a regard for the two princes, that he invited them to his palace. "Sir," replied Prince Bahman, "your majesty confers on us an honor of which we are undeserving." The sultan, who could not comprehend the motives of their refusal, asked them the reason. "Sir," answered Prince Bahman, "we have a sister, younger than ourselves, with whom we live in so close an union, that we cannot adopt any plan without first consulting her." "I highly commend your fraternal affection," said the sultan; "consult, then, your sister, and come to-morrow to hunt with me, and bring back your answer." The Princess Parizade was alarmed at this intelligence. "Your meeting with

the sultan," said she, "is fortunate for you, and may eventually be very advantageous—but to me it is truly melancholy and distressing. I see clearly that it is on my account you have withstood the wishes of the sultan. You would rather be guilty of an incivility toward the sultan, than act in opposition to the fraternal union we have sworn to preserve. But do you believe it will be easy to refuse the sultan in a point he seems so anxious to obtain? You see, then, my opinion; but, before we finally determine, let us consult the speaking bird." Princess Parizade ordered the cage to be brought, and after explaining to the bird their embarrassment, she asked what was most proper for them to do. "Your brothers," said the bird, "must comply with the wishes of the sultan; and even, in their turn, invite him." "But, bird," said the princes, "my brothers and I have an unequalled friendship for each other, and we are afraid our union will suffer from this mode of proceeding." "Not in the least," answered the bird: "it will even become stronger." "But in this case," added the princes, "will not the sultan see me?" "It is necessary he should see you," replied the bird; "and all will be the better.'

Next morning, Prince Bahman and Prince Perviz returned to the chase. The sultan continued his sport but a short time; for, as he conjectured that the princes possessed a not less cultivated mind than a daring and intrepid disposition, he was impatient to converse with them more at his ease. As they proceded towards the capital, he wished them to keep by his side;—an honour which excited the jealousy, not only of the principal courtiers who accompanied him, but even of the grand-vizier himself, who was extremely mortified at seeing them take precedence of him. The sultan's first proceeding, when he arrived at the palace, was to conduct the princes though the principal apartments. A very splendid repast was then served up, and the sultan made them sit at the same table with himself. He also condescended to promise a visit to their house the next day. Prince Bahman and Prince Perviz returned home the same evening, and related to their sister the kind reception the sultan had given them, at which she was much pleased.

The next morning, the princes were at the appointed place when the sultan arrived. He began the hunt, and continued it with great eagerness till the sun approached its highest elevation. Prince Perviz then put himself at the head of the company, to show the way. When they were within sight of the house, the Princess Parizade presented herself, and fell at his feet; her brothers, who were present, informed the sultan who she was, and requested him to accept the homage she rendered him. The sultan assisted the princess in rising, and after admiring her beauty, as well as the elegance of her form, and a certain gracefulness of manner, which did not at all bespeak a country life, "Here," he exclaimed, "are two brothers worthy of their sister, and a sister equally worthy of her brothers!"

The princess then conducted the sultan into the garden, where the first thing that attracted his eyes, was the fountain of yellow water, resembling gold. "Whence does this wonderful water come? Where is its source? and by what contrivance does it rise in this extraordinary manner?—I must examine it more nearly." As he said this, he went forward. The princess, continuing to conduct him, at length led him to the place where the singing tree was planted. As he approached it, the sultan, hearing a singular concert, stopped, and looked round for the musicians: "Where," he exclaimed, "are the performers I hear? With such charming voices, they would risk nothing by being seen." "They are not musicians, sir," replied the princess, "that form the concert which you hear · it is the tree which your majesty sees before you that produces it." The sultan went forward; and was so charmed with the sweet harmony of the concert, that he could not disengage his attention. At last, recollecting the golden water, he addressed Parizade in these words; "Tell me, I entreat you, how you obtained possession of this wonderful tree? by what name do you call it?" "Sir," replied the princess, "this tree is called the singing tree; but it is unknown in this country. It would occupy too long a time to relate the adventures by which it was placed here." The sultan then went into the saloon; and as the bird continued to sing, "My slave," said the princess, raising her voice, "there is the sultan—pay your compliments to him." The bird immediately ceased singing; "The sultan," said the bird, "is welcome, and may God cause him to prosper." As the repast was served on a sofa, near the window where the bird was, the sultan, on sitting down to the table, replied, "I thank you, bird, for your compliment, and am happy to see in you the sultan and king of birds." The sultan perceiving a dish of cucumbers, drew it towards him, and was astonished to see them dressed with pearls: "What novelty is this? why have a sauce of pearls?" The bird interrupted him; "Can your majesty express surprise at seeing cucumbers dressed with pearls, when you could so readily credit the account, that the sultana your consort was delivered of a dog, a cat, and a piece of wood?" "I believed it," replied the sultan, "because the attending women assured me of the case." "These women," answered the bird, "were the sultana's sisters, who were jealous of the honour and happiness you had bestowed upon her; and, to satisfy their animosity, they abused your majesty's good nature. The two brothers and the sister whom you behold, are your children, whom they exposed, but who were found by the superintendant of your gardens, and nursed and educated by his care." This speech of the bird immediately made the sultan comprehend the whole plan. "I have no difficulty, bird," he replied, "in giving full credit to what you have discovered to me. The inclination that attracted me towards them, the affection I already feel for them, both tell me they are my offspring. Come, then, my children, that I may embrace you all, and give you the first proof of my tender love as a father." He arose, and embraced them all, mingling his tears with theirs.

The sultan mounted his horse, and returned with the utmost diligence to the capital. He then, followed by all his attendants, went on foot to the gate of the grand mosque; and after having himself taken the sultana out of the narrow prison in which she had languished for so many years, "Madam," he cried, embracing her, "I am come to implore your pardon for the injustice I have done you; and to make you all the reparation that is justly your due."

Very early the next morning, the sultan and sultana, followed by all the court, set out for the house of their children. The sultan presented the sultana to Prince Bahman, Prince Perviz, and the Princess Parizade. "Behold, madam," said he, "your two sons and your daughter." Tears—but they were tears of joy—were shed in abundance by all, particularly the sultana, from the excess of her feelings, at embracing the innocent cause of her long and severe afflictions.

When nothing remained to detain the sultan any longer, he remounted his horse. Prince Bahman accompanied him on his right, and Prince Perviz on his left, while the sultana, with the princess on her left hand, followed the sultan. As they approached, the people met them in crowds; and they regarded the sultana, exulting at her happy change, after so long a penance, as much as they did the two princes and the princess, whom they accompanied with loud acclamations. Their attention was likewise attracted by the bird in its cage, which the princess carried before

her; they could not but admire its singing. In this manner Prince Bahman, Prince Perviz, and the Princess Parizade, were conducted to the palace; and in the evening brilliant illuminations, and the greatest rejoicings, took place, which continued for many days, not only in the palace, but throughout the city.

      *   *   *   *   *   *

The sultan of the Indies could not but admire the prodigious memory of the sultana, his consort.

A thousand and one nights had passed in this innocent amusement; his mind became softened, and he was convinced of the great merit and good sense of the Sultana Scheherazade. He well remembered the courage with which she had voluntarily exposed herself in becoming his queen. These considerations, added to the other excellent qualities which he knew she possessed, at last urged him to pardon her. "I see clearly," said he, " amiable Scheherazade, that it is impossible to exhaust your store of amusement. You have appeased my anger, and I freely renounce, in your behalf, the cruel law I had imposed upon myself. I receive you entirely into my favour, and wish you to be considered as the preserver of all the females, who would otherwise have been sacrificed to my just resentment." The sultana threw herself at his feet, embraced them tenderly, and gave every proof of the most perfect and lively gratitude.

The grand-vizier learnt this agreeable intelligence from the sultan himself. It was immediately circulated through the city and provinces, and drew down upon the heads of Sultan Schahriar and his amiable sultana, Scheherazade, the united praises and blessings of all the people of the empire of India.

THE END.